An Elm Creek Quilts Album

Three Novels in the Popular Series

❦

JENNIFER CHIAVERINI

SIMON & SCHUSTER
New York · London · Toronto · Sydney

SIMON & SCHUSTER
Rockefeller Center
1230 Avenue of the Americas
New York, NY 10020

This Simon & Schuster edition 2006

SIMON & SCHUSTER and colophon are registered trademarks
of Simon & Schuster, Inc.

DESIGNED BY LAUREN SIMONETTI

Manufactured in the United States of America

10   8   6   4   2   1   3   5   7   9

Library of Congress Cataloging-in-Publication Data
Chiaverini, Jennifer.
An Elm Creek quilts album : three novels in the popular series / Jennifer Chiaverini.
p. cm.
Contents: The runaway quilt — The quilter's legacy — The master quilter.
1. Female friendship—Fiction. 2. Quiltmakers—Fiction. 3. Quilting—Fiction. I. Title.
PS3553.H473E46 2006
813'.54—dc22   2006044398

ISBN-13: 978-0-7432-9656-4
ISBN-10:   0-7432-9656-7

For information regarding special discounts for bulk purchases,
please contact Simon & Schuster Special Sales
at 1-800-456-6798 or business@simonandschuster.com

These titles were previously published individually by Simon & Schuster, Inc.

Contents

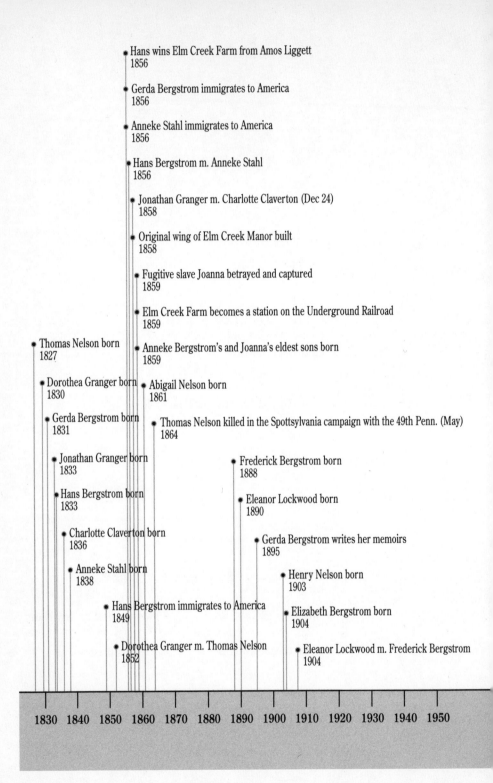

Hans wins Elm Creek Farm from Amos Liggett
1856

Gerda Bergstrom immigrates to America
1856

Anneke Stahl immigrates to America
1856

Hans Bergstrom m. Anneke Stahl
1856

Jonathan Granger m. Charlotte Claverton (Dec 24)
1858

Original wing of Elm Creek Manor built
1858

Fugitive slave Joanna betrayed and captured
1859

Elm Creek Farm becomes a station on the Underground Railroad
1859

Thomas Nelson born
1827

Anneke Bergstrom's and Joanna's eldest sons born
1859

Dorothea Granger born
1830

Abigail Nelson born
1861

Gerda Bergstrom born
1831

Thomas Nelson killed in the Spottsylvania campaign with the 49th Penn. (May)
1864

Jonathan Granger born
1833

Frederick Bergstrom born
1888

Hans Bergstrom born
1833

Eleanor Lockwood born
1890

Charlotte Claverton born
1836

Gerda Bergstrom writes her memoirs
1895

Anneke Stahl born
1838

Henry Nelson born
1903

Hans Bergstrom immigrates to America
1849

Elizabeth Bergstrom born
1904

Dorothea Granger m. Thomas Nelson
1852

Eleanor Lockwood m. Frederick Bergstrom
1904

1830 1840 1850 1860 1870 1880 1890 1900 1910 1920 1930 1940 1950

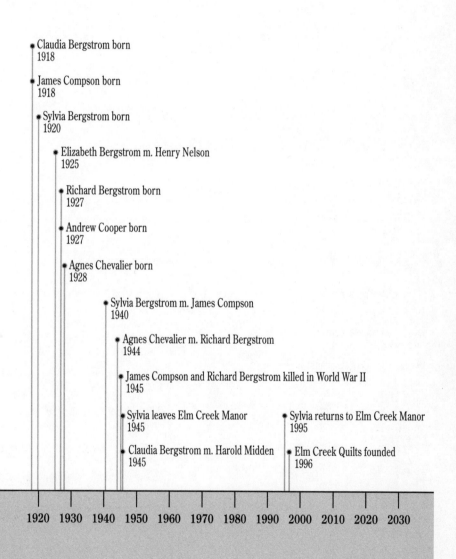

Claudia Bergstrom born
1918

James Compson born
1918

Sylvia Bergstrom born
1920

Elizabeth Bergstrom m. Henry Nelson
1925

Richard Bergstrom born
1927

Andrew Cooper born
1927

Agnes Chevalier born
1928

Sylvia Bergstrom m. James Compson
1940

Agnes Chevalier m. Richard Bergstrom
1944

James Compson and Richard Bergstrom killed in World War II
1945

Sylvia leaves Elm Creek Manor
1945

Sylvia returns to Elm Creek Manor
1995

Claudia Bergstrom m. Harold Midden
1945

Elm Creek Quilts founded
1996

1920 1930 1940 1950 1960 1970 1980 1990 2000 2010 2020 2030

THE
RUNAWAY
QUILT

Acknowledgments

This book would not have been possible without the expertise and guidance of Denise Roy, Maria Massie, Rebecca Davis, and Tara Parsons. Thank you for your wisdom and your friendship.

I am grateful to author Barbara Brackman for providing me with important historical information regarding Civil War–era quilts and the use of quilts as signals on the Underground Railroad.

Thank you, Christine Johnson, for reading the manuscript of *The Quilter's Apprentice* so many years ago and posing the question that became this novel.

I thank my friends and family, especially Geraldine Neidenbach, Heather Neidenbach, Nic Neidenbach, Virginia and Edward Riechman, Leonard and Marlene Chiaverini, Martin Lang, Rachel and Chip Sauer, Anne Spurgeon, Vanessa Alt, the Mad City Quilters, and the members of RCTQ, for your encouragement and support.

Most of all, I am grateful to my husband, Marty, and my son, Nicholas, who inspire me every day with their humor and their love.

To Marty and Nicholas,
with all my love.

Chapter One

When her sister, Claudia, died childless at the age of seventy-seven, Sylvia Bergstrom Compson became the last living descendant of Hans and Anneke Bergstrom and the sole heir to what remained of their fortune. Or so she had thought. She had certainly searched long and hard enough for someone else who could assume responsibility of Elm Creek Manor, for as difficult as it was to believe now, at the time she had thought the estate in rural central Pennsylvania too full of unhappy memories to become her home again. Her lawyer had told her she was the sole heir, an opinion corroborated by her private detective.

Now she wondered if they had overlooked something, a familial connection lost to memory but documented in a threadbare antique quilt.

She had never seen the quilt before; that much she knew to be true. She saw it for the first time after a speaking engagement for the Silver Lake Quilters' Guild in South Carolina. One woman had stayed behind to help Sylvia and her companion, Andrew Cooper, pack up Sylvia's lecture materials. As the three folded Sylvia's quilts and placed her slides carefully into boxes, the woman introduced herself as Margaret Alden and said that they had met before, for she was a former camper.

"Of course I remember you," Sylvia declared, but after a skeptical look from Andrew, she confessed otherwise. Margaret laughed and said she understood completely. So many quilters attended Elm Creek Quilt Camp each year that it was impossible to remember every one, although Sylvia felt that she ought to at least try. The campers were, after all, guests in her own home.

They chatted about quilt camp as they carried Sylvia's lecture materials to Andrew's motor home, but even after Sylvia thanked her for the help, Margaret lingered. "If you could spare me another few minutes," she said,

"I'd like to show you a quilt. It's been in my family for generations, but I think it might have some connection to Elm Creek Manor."

"I beg your pardon?" said Sylvia. "What sort of connection?"

"That's what I hoped you might know."

Andrew and Sylvia were eager to begin the first leg of their long drive back to central Pennsylvania, but Sylvia rarely passed up the opportunity to see a quilt, and certainly couldn't resist seeing one so intriguingly described. Margaret hurried to her car and returned carrying a bundle wrapped in a cotton bedsheet. With Sylvia's assistance, she unfolded it to reveal a quilt—or rather, what remained of one.

The pattern caught Sylvia's eye first: Birds in the Air blocks, each a square divided along the diagonal, a solid right triangle of medium or dark fabric on one side, three small right triangles surrounded by lighter background fabrics on the other. The blocks were arranged on point so that all the right angles of the triangles, large and small, pointed in the same direction. The fabrics themselves seemed to be primarily muslins and wools, so faded and worn that Sylvia could only guess their original colors. Water stains and deterioration suggested age as well as rough handling, as did the muted colors of the once bright dyes and the worn binding, through which the cotton batting was visible. Fine stipple quilting held the three layers together—where they *were* still held together. Elsewhere, the thread had been removed or torn out by accident, and the middle batting layer it should have held in place was long gone.

Only a reluctance to appear hypocritical prevented Sylvia from scolding Margaret for risking further damage to the quilt by bringing it to the quilt guild meeting, for Sylvia was very glad to see it. "It's lovely, dear." She bent closer and peered through her bifocals at the quilting stitches. There was something unusual about them, something she couldn't yet place.

"Lovely?" Margaret laughed. "Most people look at it and say, 'Hmm. Interesting.'"

"You can tell Sylvia's a true quilter," said Andrew. "She never fails to see through the wear and tear and find the beauty."

"True beauty stands the test of time," said Sylvia, straightening. "Although I must say it's a pity its previous owners didn't take better care of it."

"I know," said Margaret apologetically. "But my mother says it was just one of many quilts her grandmother had around the house. They didn't realize they were sleeping under a family heirloom."

"Of course not. I'm not faulting you or your ancestors. I'm not one of those who believes quilts should be showpieces kept safely away from anyone's bed." Sylvia returned her gaze to the quilt. "It's a simple pattern, pieced from scraps. It wasn't intended as the family's best quilt. I'd say by using it so well, your family followed within the quiltmaker's wishes."

Margaret smiled, pleased. Then Andrew caught Sylvia's eye, and she was suddenly aware of how her lecture had wearied her and how long they planned to drive before stopping for the night. She couldn't imagine what possible connection the quilt could have to Elm Creek Manor, unless Margaret hoped Sylvia would buy it and display it there. Briskly, she said, "Now, were you looking for an appraisal of the quilt or an estimate of its age? If so, I'm afraid I can't help you. I could place it in the mid- to late nineteenth century, but you'll need to consult a textiles expert for a more precise answer. As for what it's worth in terms of dollars and cents—"

"Oh, I could never sell it," said Margaret, shocked.

"I'm pleased to hear that." Sylvia wished all families would show such appreciation for the heirloom quilts their foremothers had so lovingly made. "Then tell me, what did you mean by a connection between this quilt and my home?"

Margaret turned the quilt so that only the solid muslin backing was visible. "When you look at the quilting stitches, what do you see?"

Pursing her lips, Sylvia carefully scrutinized the quilt. Without the distraction of color and pattern, the stitches were more clearly visible. "The stippling pattern isn't consistent," she said. "Some of the stitches are long, others quite small, and the small ones seem to be grouped together."

Margaret's nod told Sylvia she had responded just as the younger woman had hoped. "When I told my mother I had attended quilt camp at Elm Creek Manor, she told me that she had an old family quilt her grandmother had called the Elm Creek Quilt."

Sylvia looked up in surprise. "Did she, indeed?"

"At first I thought its name came from the quilting pattern used in the border. See the elm leaf motif, and how these wavy lines look like running water?"

"I suppose." Sylvia saw the leaves now that they had been pointed out, but in her opinion, the wavy lines resembled a common cable pattern more than a creek.

"It had another name, too. The Runaway Quilt."

"Runaway?" Andrew chuckled. "I've heard of quilters getting carried away with their work, but I didn't know a quilt could actually run away."

"Perhaps the quilt turned out much larger than its maker had intended," said Sylvia. "Perhaps she felt it ran on and on, with a life of its own."

"Maybe, but my mother says it was most often called the Elm Creek Quilt," said Margaret hastily.

Sylvia nodded and exchanged an amused glance with Andrew. Margaret seemed most eager to prove her point, but she had said nothing yet to persuade Sylvia.

"Now look at these designs." Margaret pointed out groups of stitches that she said resembled, in turn, a tobacco leaf, a star, a mountain pass, a group of horses—

"And these," said Margaret, watching Sylvia expectantly, "form a picture of Elm Creek Manor."

Sylvia could no longer nod politely at the woman's wild imaginings. "I'm sorry, dear. I just don't see it."

"Remember the quilter was working from the other side," said Andrew, more mindful of Margaret's feelings than Sylvia had been. "The designs would be in reverse."

Sylvia carefully unfurled the quilt before the motor home's full-length mirror and studied one small section near the top. To her amazement, the reflection revealed a perfect outline of a pass between several low mountains.

She stared at the quilt, speechless. "My goodness," she finally managed. "I must admit, that bears a striking resemblance to the pass into the Elm Creek Valley." She held up another section. "This could indeed be the west wing of Elm Creek Manor."

"You told us at camp that the west wing predates the rest of your home," said Margaret.

"It would have been the only part standing at the time this quilt was made." Sylvia traced the design with a fingertip. "The original entrance is in the proper place."

"So it's a side view now," said Andrew. "But back then—"

"This would have been the front view of the house." Sylvia shook her head, is if to clear it of nonsense. "I admit I'm tempted to believe there's some connection, but I'm afraid it's all a bit too fanciful for me. Many houses share a similar design, and elm trees and creeks are hardly exclusive to my family's estate . . ."

Her voice trailed off in disbelief.

Not far from the image of Elm Creek Manor appeared the outline of another building, one so unique and remarkable that there could be no mistaking it: a two-story barn, partially concealed by the slope of the hill into which it was built, exact in proportion and scale to the barn on the grounds of Sylvia's estate.

❧

Andrew photographed the quilt, front and back, with close-ups of the quilted images, while Sylvia recorded Margaret's memories. Margaret surmised, based upon family stories, that her grandmother's grandmother had sewn the quilt, but the five years Margaret had spent researching her family's genealogy had turned up little information from that era, since many important documents had been destroyed during the Civil War. Then Margaret added, almost as an aside, "If my grandmother's grandmother didn't make the quilt, I suppose one of her slaves could have."

"Her slaves?" echoed Sylvia. "Goodness. Your family owned slaves?"

"Yes," said Margaret, "but you don't have to look at me like that. I never owned any."

"My apologies, dear. I didn't mean to be rude." Sylvia composed herself. Of course, she had probably met the descendants of slave owners before, just as she had certainly met the descendants of slaves. It was just unexpected to hear someone admit to one's ancestors' moral failings with such nonchalance, especially since Sylvia's family had treated their forebears with respect bordering on reverence.

"It seems to me, the person who made this quilt must have seen Elm Creek Manor," said Margaret.

"Could be she was recording memories of a visit," said Andrew.

"I suppose there's no way to know for certain." Sylvia gazed at the sections of the quilt where the thread had been removed. What patterns would they have found within those stitches?

"Sylvia," asked Margaret. "Did any of your ancestors leave the family estate and move South?"

"Do you mean to say you think our families might be related?"

"I think it's possible. I had hoped your family records would be more complete than mine."

"I suppose it's not entirely unlikely. My cousin Elizabeth left Elm Creek

Manor when I was a young girl, but she and her husband went to California . . ."

"Anything else?" prompted Margaret. "Someone earlier?"

Sylvia searched her memory as best she could under the circumstances. Hans and Anneke Bergstrom had come to America in the middle of the nineteenth century, but Sylvia did not know the precise date. She knew they had had several children, but she could not recall how many had survived to adulthood. Surely some of them must have left to start families and households of their own, but if one of them was indeed Margaret's ancestor—

"I'm afraid I just don't know," said Sylvia, and lowered herself into a nearby seat.

Andrew must have seen how Margaret's questions had affected Sylvia, for he left her to her thoughts. He and Margaret exchanged addresses and phone numbers; then, with a promise to share whatever they discovered, Andrew showed her to the door. A few moments later, Sylvia heard him start the engine. Only then did she rouse herself and move to the front passenger seat beside him.

They drove in silence for nearly an hour before Sylvia spoke. "Do you suppose Margaret and I could have an ancestor in common?"

"It's possible." He kept his eyes on the road. "What do you think?"

"I think I was much more content before I learned I might have slave owners in the family."

"All families have members they're not so proud of."

"Yes, but slave owners?"

"Don't be too hard on them. They were people of their times."

"Plenty of other people of their times didn't own slaves. Hans and Anneke, for example. Elm Creek Manor was a station on the Underground Railroad, did you know that?"

He gave her a sidelong glance. "You might have mentioned it once or twice."

"If I've bragged, it's because I'm proud of them. I should be proud. That was brave and dangerous work. And now I'm supposed to accept that some of my relatives—well, I don't accept it." She folded her arms and glared out the windshield at the lights of other cars speeding down the freeway. Night had fallen, but the sky was overcast. She wondered where the North Star was. It ought to be directly overhead, or nearly so. So long ago, it had shown the way to freedom, and her family had offered sanctuary to many of those who had braved the hazards of the path it illuminated.

But Elm Creek Manor was so secluded, the North Star alone would not have been enough to guide a stranger to its door.

"Andrew," said Sylvia, "I don't believe the quilt preserved memories of Elm Creek Manor. I think it was meant to show the way."

She had heard of such things before, quilts with coded messages or even maps revealing safe pathways along the Underground Railroad. The very name of Margaret's quilt suggested it might be one of those legendary artifacts. But in all of Sylvia's decades as a quilter and lecturer, she had never seen one of these quilts, only heard lore of them around the quilt frame. Her friend Grace Daniels, a master quilter and museum curator, had once told her that not only had no one ever documented a map quilt from the era, no slave narrative or Abolitionist testimonial she had read mentioned one.

Sylvia respected Grace's expertise, and yet, in the stillness of her own heart, she yearned for the folklore to be true. Within her own family, a tale had been handed down through the generations about a quilt used to signal to fugitive slaves. Folklore carried a stronger ring of truth when one loved and trusted the person who spoke it.

But now, torn between her memories and the questions Margaret Alden's quilt raised, Sylvia would need more than folklore and family histories to discern the truth. She needed evidence only Elm Creek Manor could provide.

❧

Andrew and Sylvia preferred to drive at a leisurely pace, so it wasn't until several days after the encounter with Margaret Alden that they pulled off the freeway and headed down the two-lane road past picturesque farms and rolling, forested hills toward home. Sylvia sighed with happiness when they turned onto a gravel road that wound its way through a familiar leafy wood. Before long, Elm Creek came into view, marking the southern border of the estate.

When the road forked, Andrew stayed to the left, following the road that led to the parking lot at the rear entrance of the manor. The right fork would have taken them over a narrow bridge and across a vast lawn up to the front entrance—a more grand approach, especially for visitors, but impractical for Andrew's ocean liner on wheels. Before long the creek wound north and disappeared from sight, but the road continued west for a little way before turning north.

The wood gave way to a clearing. To the left was the orchard, where several women strolled among the apple trees. They waved as the motor home passed, and Sylvia waved merrily back. Ahead and to the right stood the two-story red barn built into the side of a hill. Sylvia's gaze locked on it.

"It's an accurate picture," said Andrew, meaning the pattern of stitches in Margaret's quilt. His words echoed Sylvia's own thoughts, but she merely nodded, unwilling to commit herself.

Just beyond the barn, the path crossed a low bridge over Elm Creek and widened into a driveway lined by tall elms. Then, at last, the manor itself came into view, its gray stone walls solid and welcoming. It was three stories tall—not counting the attic—and L-shaped, with black shutters and black woodwork along the eaves. Four stone stairs led to the back door, and as the motor home pulled into the parking lot, Sylvia watched as women bustled in and out.

"My goodness," said Sylvia. "It certainly is busy around here this morning. Isn't anyone in class?"

"You forget how many more campers you have these days," said Andrew.

"Only fifty each week."

"Yes, but your first year, you had only twelve. No wonder it looks like you have a crowd milling around."

No wonder, indeed. What would her sister think if she could see how their family estate had been transformed? More than fifty years before, grief and anger had driven Sylvia away from her family home and into estrangement from her elder sister. Only after Claudia's death had Sylvia returned, intending to prepare the manor for sale rather than live there haunted by reminders of departed loved ones. She never imagined that hiring Sarah McClure as her assistant would force her to face all those old resentments and painful truths about her own mistakes. Elm Creek Quilts had been Sarah's vision and Sylvia's lifeline, for turning the estate into a retreat for quilters had made the halls ring with laughter and happiness as they had not for decades. Now Sylvia knew that, except for her occasional jaunts with Andrew, she would live out her days on the estate her ancestors had founded. She knew this was exactly as it should be, and her heart was full of gratitude for the friends who had made this second chance possible.

Eager for the company of these friends, Sylvia kissed Andrew on the cheek and hurried inside while he remained behind to look over the motor home. Sarah met her at the back door and greeted her with a hug. Sarah launched into a description of the week's events, but Sylvia's news would not wait. "Sarah, dear," she interrupted, "I have a special favor to ask of you. Would you join me in the attic, please?"

❧

They began the search that afternoon.

Throughout the drive from South Carolina to Pennsylvania, Sylvia's thoughts had returned again and again to her great-aunt Lucinda's stories and the trunk she had described more than seventy years before. Somewhere among the dust and clutter of four generations there was a cherry hope chest with engraved brass fastenings, and in it—if Lucinda's stories were true—was a quilt Great-Grandmother Anneke had made.

Sylvia had always meant to find that quilt, but her long exile had made the search impossible, and upon her return, the improbability of finding it had been so daunting that she had put off the task. Even Grace Daniels's persistent requests to study the quilt had not been motivation enough. Now everything had changed. She did not know if Anneke's quilt could prove or disprove a connection between Margaret's quilt and Elm Creek Manor, but if it existed—and Sylvia refused to believe it did not—it might at least provide evidence that the manor had been a station on the Underground Railroad. Sylvia would be willing to acknowledge whatever other, more distant relations had done if she could first be certain her own direct ancestors had played a more noble role.

But after climbing the narrow, creaking staircase and surveying the attic, Sylvia knew that finding the trunk would be difficult, if not impossible, even with Sarah's help. The shorter, older west wing lay to her right, and the longer, newer south wing stretched out before her. Up here the seam joining old and new was more evident than below, the colors of the walls subtly different, the floor not quite even. Little visible evidence betrayed that fact, as the belongings of four generations of her family covered nearly every square foot of floor space.

"Four generations, and not one individual could be spared to tidy the attic," said Sylvia, her voice lost in the vast space. "Until me." Still, she was pleased her ancestors had left so much of themselves behind. She only hoped Great-Grandmother Anneke had not been the one exception to the family rule.

"We'll find it," said Sarah. She chose the nearest pile of stacked items and began. "But we'll save time if we leave tidying up for later."

Sylvia agreed and set herself to work. They could spare only a couple of hours before camp duties summoned them downstairs, but after the evening program, they resumed the search. Matt, Sarah's husband and the estate's caretaker, joined them, moving heavy loads Sylvia and Sarah had been unable to budge, but promising leads turned repeatedly into dead ends. By the time Sylvia went to bed that night, she had been begun to suspect that the search could take much longer than she had anticipated.

All week Sylvia and Sarah stole moments from their busy days to ransack cartons and uncover old furniture, all in vain. They found trunks, to be sure—dozens of them, full of historic mementos, or so a cursory examination hinted, but Anneke's hope chest eluded them. Sylvia had never been a particularly patient woman, but each day's frustrations only made her more determined to keep looking.

It didn't do her temper any good that Sarah squandered valuable time digging through trunks that didn't meet the description, marveling over an antique toy or portrait, uncovering the hidden treasures Sylvia, too, was tempted to study. Nor did the tenacious July heat, or the dust they stirred up as they worked, or Sarah's shrieks at the discovery of yet another spider.

On one particularly humid Friday afternoon, Sarah dared to voice the same question that had been nagging Sylvia. "Are you sure the trunk is even up here?"

Sylvia refused to hear her discouragement. "If you want to quit, go ahead."

"It's not that—"

"No, go on. I'm sure you have more important things to do than help me."

Without a word, Sarah left, rebuking Sylvia with her silence. Sylvia continued on alone, ashamed but too proud to go downstairs and apologize for her short temper.

Sensing progress in the increasing age of the artifacts she uncovered, for another hour she resisted thirst and fatigue until she was forced to admit that even her strong will was no match for the stifling conditions.

She decided to return after the campers' evening program, when nightfall would bring restful quiet and cool breezes to Elm Creek Manor.

She left the attic assuring herself she would find the trunk that night or some day soon thereafter, but darkness seemed to foster doubt. Perhaps her memory had failed her, or Great-Aunt Lucinda's had failed *her.* Or maybe Lucinda's tale had been nothing more than a fiction meant to amuse a young girl. Of all the possibilities, that was the one Sylvia dreaded most. She couldn't bear it if the stories of Elm Creek Manor that had sustained her throughout her long absence turned out to be false. At one time, they were all she had had to remind her of home and the family she had left behind.

She picked up the search where she had left off earlier that day and soon forgot her exhaustion and the late hour. Only a small portion of the attic remained to be searched, a far corner of the west wing where the ceiling sloped so low Sylvia could not stand upright. Her grandparents might have used the chair that now sat covered in dust before her; some unknown aunt or cousin might have sewn a wedding gown on the treadle sewing machine now rusted and missing its belt. Melancholy colored her thoughts, and she forced herself to admit that even if Lucinda's story was true, the chest with its contents might have been lost to the fire that had destroyed part of the manor in her father's youth, or sold off like so many other heirlooms when the family's fortunes waned. So many misfortunes could have befallen it—

But perhaps none had after all, she thought, as she glimpsed beneath a film of dust a trunk made from cherry and brass.

She braced herself for the resistance of weight, but the trunk was surprisingly light. Quickly she pulled it into the open and brushed off as much dust as she could, for if a quilt was inside, she would not wish to soil it. Then she seated herself on the floor and studied it, reaching into her pocket for the slender key Great-Aunt Lucinda had given her decades before. Sylvia had saved the key more in remembrance of her great-aunt than from any certain plan to find the lock it fit, but now she knew there was only one way to discover if Great-Aunt Lucinda's stories were true.

After a moment's hesitation, Sylvia fit the key into the lock.

It turned easily, but the lid was more reluctant to cooperate, and only after several minutes of wrangling did it open with a groan. Sylvia scarcely noticed the odors of stale air and aged cloth, for within the trunk she spied a folded bundle wrapped in a sheet of unbleached muslin. Carefully she picked it up, and knew at once from its texture and thickness that it was a quilt.

Her breath caught in her throat. The protective sheet bore signs of age and decay. She never should have neglected the trunk so long. If she had come sooner she could have stored the quilt properly. She could blame only herself for a good half-century of its deterioration.

Praying that the quilt itself was in better condition than the muslin cover, she gently unwrapped it and unfolded it upon her lap.

And there it was, the Log Cabin quilt she half-feared existed only in Lucinda's imagination.

The blocks looked to be about seven inches square, arranged in fourteen rows of ten blocks each. Sylvia's first glance took in shirting flannels and chintzes, calicoes and velvets—the scraps of worn clothing, no doubt. The scraps had been cut in rectangles of various sizes and pieced in an interlocking fashion around a central square, light fabrics placed on one side of a diagonal, dark fabrics on the other. The blocks were arranged in a Barn Raising setting so that the overall pattern was one of concentric diamonds, alternately light and dark, just as Lucinda's description had foretold. And to Sylvia's amazement and gratitude, the central squares of each Log Cabin block were black.

Sylvia stroked the quilt reverently, hardly daring to believe what she held in her arms. According to tradition, the central square in a Log Cabin quilt should be red, to symbolize the hearth, or yellow, to represent a light in the window. According to folklore, however, in the antebellum United States, a Log Cabin quilt with a black center square was a signal to slaves escaping north along the Underground Railroad, a sign indicating sanctuary. As a child Sylvia had listened eagerly to Lucinda's story of how Great-Grandmother Anneke Bergstrom's Log Cabin quilt with the black center squares had welcomed fugitive slaves into the safe haven of Elm Creek Manor. This quilt provided the evidence she needed to document this important part of her family history.

"Not quite," said Sylvia aloud, pursing her lips and scrutinizing the quilt. For all she knew, this quilt had been completed decades after the Civil War. Lucinda had always had an odd sense of humor. She could have pieced the quilt herself and left it in the attic for the young Sylvia to find, never imagining Sylvia wouldn't discover it until Lucinda was beyond explaining the joke. The fabrics resembled those Sylvia had seen in other quilts of that period, but until a knowledgeable appraiser inspected the quilt, she had no more proof than before she opened the trunk.

She folded the quilt with care and, setting it aside, was about to return the muslin sheet to the trunk when she saw that the Log Cabin quilt had concealed two other muslin-cloaked bundles, one considerably smaller than the Log Cabin quilt, the other approximately the same size.

Sylvia immediately took up the smaller bundle, hardly daring to hope that she would find more quilts sewn by her great-grandmother Anneke's hands. In a moment the muslin sheet was on the floor beside her, revealing the age-weathered back of a second quilt. "Such an embarrassment of riches," said Sylvia as she turned it over. Then, as the pattern appeared, she sat back against a stack of cartons, stunned.

"Birds in the Air," she murmured. It was impossible, but she couldn't deny the evidence she held in her own hands. The quilt that lay before her used the exact same block pattern as Margaret Alden's quilt. Only the arrangement of the individual blocks on the quilt top differed; whereas the blocks in Margaret's quilt were placed on the diagonal, this quilt used a straight setting, with the squares arranged in neat horizontal rows. This quilt was much smaller than Margaret's, too, and although it certainly looked antique, with the wear and tear of hard use and lye soap all too evident, it was in far better condition. Still, Sylvia could not dismiss the use of the Birds in the Air pattern as mere coincidence.

She studied the quilt for a long moment before carefully folding it and setting it on top of the Log Cabin. Then, with great deliberation, she reached into the trunk for the third bundle. Slowly, as if to prepare herself for yet another unsettling surprise, she unwrapped the muslin sheet, unfolded the quilt within—

—and stared in astonishment at what fell from the folds and tumbled to the attic floor.

"My goodness." It was a book, its unmarked brown leather cover cracked with age. Mystified, she carefully opened the slim volume, wary of worsening the damage, only to discover pages covered in graceful script.

Without her glasses, and in the dim light of the attic, she could not make out the words so elegantly written, but the shorter lines and numerals heading some of the pages suggested dates. A journal. It had to be. A journal, most likely Great-Grandmother Anneke's, hidden away within the folds of her most precious quilt. Sylvia clasped the book to her chest, forgetting her concerns about the Birds in the Air pattern in the growing awareness of her good fortune, and feared, for just a moment, that she was dreaming.

Quickly she gathered up the quilts and carried them down two flights of stairs to her bedroom suite on the second floor. She placed her treasures on the large chair beside her bed, put on her glasses, and took the journal into her sitting room, where she turned on the bright lamp beside her sewing machine and sat down. She caught her breath, then opened the journal to the first page.

✌ *October 2, 1895*

Autumn has come again to Elm Creek, and I, too, am in the autumn of my years.

My history has barely begun, and already my pride has bested me, for I know all too well that I have long since passed into winter. If I cannot be honest about such a small matter of vanity, how can I hope to be forthright about the harder truths, which few but I remain alive to remember? Yet I must be honest, not merely for the sake of my own soul, but to honor the memory of those whom I love—those whom I loved even as they betrayed me, and she I came to love as she deserved only after she was betrayed.

I do not know for whom I write these words. They cannot be for my own eyes, which are failing me, for the memories burn too strongly in my heart for me ever to forget them. They cannot be for my descendants, for I have none living. Even so, the Bergstrom family endures in America, and shall endure, both in name and in truth. Anneke has seen to that.

If she knew I spoke within these pages, she would beg me to be silent, to protect her children, and their children. She would say the future generations of Bergstroms will not thank me for my frankness, and if others discover the truths we have all pledged to conceal, they would surely destroy us. But I remain hopeful, despite all I have witnessed since coming to this land of freedom, this land of contradictions, and I hold fast to the belief that we owe a greater duty to Truth than to our own earthly comfort. They are not my children or grandchildren who will suffer, so perhaps it is true that I do not fully comprehend the burden my tale will place upon them. But who among us knows how our choices will affect generations yet unborn?

Reader, if you bear the name Bergstrom, know first that you came from strong, proud people, and that it is for you I write, for if we can bequeath you nothing else, we must make you the heir of our truths, for good or ill. Know this first, and read on.

❧

Sylvia read the passage again, slowly, underlining it with her finger. The graceful script had faltered near the end, as if written by a hand trembling with fear or anger. Or did she only imagine it so, shocked as she was by the words themselves?

Anneke could not have written those lines, that much was clear. But who, then, was the author? Surely not Hans; surely he would not have written such things about his beloved wife. The handwriting seemed feminine. Gerda, then? Was this the journal of Hans's sister? But it seemed more like a memoir than a journal, something written after the outcome of events was known rather than recorded day by day, as they were happening. The author had had time to reflect, to consider the effects of her words, and of her silence.

Then Sylvia had a disturbing thought: The family histories said little of Gerda after her arrival in America and the laying of the cornerstone of Elm Creek Manor. Was it possible that Gerda was the hypothetical ancestor who had left Elm Creek Manor to become the owner of slaves in the South? Was Margaret Alden's quilt her handiwork? How, then, did her journal come to be here, in the attic of Elm Creek Manor with Anneke's quilts, rather than in South Carolina?

Those whom I loved even as they betrayed me, Gerda had written. Whom did she mean? Not Hans and Anneke. It was incomprehensible that they would have betrayed her, and yet, if they had been on opposite sides of the Civil War . . .

Future generations of Bergstroms will not thank me for my frankness.

Sylvia closed the book and set it on her sewing machine. Her pleasure upon finding Anneke's trunk had transformed in a matter of moments into foreboding.

❧

Gerda's words haunted Sylvia as she tried to sleep. She woke at daybreak, restless and troubled, and her gaze fell upon the quilts she had left on the chair beside her bed. She had not even bothered to examine the third quilt, so captivated had she been by the journal.

She rose and made her bed, then spread the Birds in the Air quilt upon it. In the bright light of day, the deterioration seemed worse than she remembered. Some of the triangular pieces had entirely disintegrated, and the binding around the edges hung loose, where it remained at all. The quilting stitches were straight and even, pleasing though unremarkable in their layout, a simple crosshatch of diagonal lines in each block.

"I should look as good after a century and a half," remarked Sylvia, amused at her instinct to critique. This was obviously a utilitarian quilt, well used and no doubt well loved—and by a child, judging by the quilt's small dimensions. The faded colors had been vibrant once, the worn pieces whole and sound and strong. Sylvia found herself admiring the little quilt, and liking the long-ago quiltmaker whose matter-of-factness and pragmatism appeared in every frugal scrap and solid stitch.

Compared to the Birds in the Air Quilt, the Log Cabin seemed remarkably well preserved. A few small holes along several seams appeared to be the result of the quiltmaker's large stitches rather than the consequence of heavy usage, and the blurring of the fabric print seemed due to time rather than frequent washing. Frowning, Sylvia studied the quilt from different angles, wondering if it had ever even covered a bed. Families often set aside a special quilt to be used only infrequently by guests, but those quilts were typically the finest in the household. While this quilt had probably been quite comfortable in its day, it was simply not as elegant or as finely made as one would expect for a quilt reserved for company. Perhaps the quiltmaker had rarely used it because she had been disappointed with it—or perhaps she had used it often but had taken especially good care of it because it was her first effort, and thus had great sentimental value. Sylvia didn't suppose she would ever know for certain.

Her curiosity whetted, Sylvia carefully unfolded the third quilt and laid it beside the others. It was slightly larger than the Log Cabin quilt, and Sylvia soon found fabrics identical to those in the Birds in the Air quilt. That suggested the same hands had pieced both, but Sylvia wasn't convinced. The pattern, Four-Patches in a vertical strip set, seemed no more complex than the Birds in the Air or Log Cabin, but only at first glance. By alternating the background fabric in adjacent rows, the quilter had created dark and light stripes, as well as a more difficult project, one with more seams to match and bias edges that might have stretched out of place if she had not been careful. And while the three layers were held together by simple concentric curves, the stitches themselves were smaller and finer, often seeming to disappear into the surface, as if the quilt had been etched with a feather.

Perhaps the Log Cabin and Birds in the Air quilts had been made earlier, and the third years later, after the quiltmaker had improved her skills. There was no way to say for certain, unless Gerda had written about the quilts in her journal.

Behind her, a knock sounded on the door leading to the hallway. "Sylvia?"

"Just a moment." Sylvia couldn't resist a quick glance in the mirror as she pulled on her robe. Her hair needed combing, but Andrew knew what she looked like, and he seemed to like her anyway. She opened the door to find him dressed in neatly pressed slacks and a golf shirt. "Well, don't you look dapper this morning."

The compliment clearly pleased him. "And you look pretty, as always."

Sylvia laughed as he kissed her cheek. "You say that because you aren't wearing your glasses."

"I say it because it's true." He looked past her to the quilts on her bed. "What's that you have there?"

"Anneke's quilts." She beckoned him inside. "Or so I believe. I'll need Grace Daniels to examine them before I know for certain."

Andrew nodded, studying the quilts. "But she can't know for sure who made them, right? She'll only be able to tell you how old they are."

"Hmph." Sylvia gave him a sharp look, which she knew he noticed, although he pretended not to. "Spoilsport. If I know how old they are, then I'll know who made them. Why would Anneke keep someone else's quilts in her attic? Honestly, Andrew."

He merely shrugged and grinned, used to her moods and her sharp tongue. Sometimes she suspected he baited her for the enjoyment of watching her temper flare, but she liked him too much to stay indignant long. "I suppose you're right," admitted Sylvia. "But perhaps Anneke's sister-in-law will identify the quilter."

She returned to the sitting room for the journal, and as Andrew examined it, her eagerness to read the book rekindled. All her life she had wondered about Hans and Anneke Bergstrom, the first of her ancestors to come to the United States. Now part of their history—Gerda's thoughts in her own words—had been given to her. She told Andrew how she had found it, and was about to show him the troubling passage she had read the previous night when she noticed the time. She ushered Andrew from the room, promising to meet him downstairs for the Farewell Breakfast.

She readied herself quickly, unwilling to be late for one of her favorite parts of quilt camp. Since Sunday afternoon, the latest group of quilters had enjoyed classes, lectures, and fellowship with new friends and old, and it wouldn't do to simply send them packing when the week of camp concluded. Instead the campers and staff gathered on the cornerstone patio for one last meal together. After breakfast, they would sit in a circle, as they had seven days earlier for the Candlelight welcome ceremony. This time, each quilter would show off a project she had worked on that week and share a favorite memory of her stay at Elm Creek Manor. For Sylvia, their stories were one of the most gratifying rewards of the business. The campers' stories never failed to amuse or surprise her, and she was pleased to discover anew how much Elm Creek Quilt Camp meant to her guests.

Listening to their stories out on the gray stone patio made Sylvia treasure them even more. Surrounded by evergreens and perennials, the patio lay just outside what had once been the main entrance to Elm Creek Manor, back in the days of Hans and Anneke. Tree branches hid the cornerstone engraved "Bergstrom 1858" that had given the patio its name, but Sylvia thought of the marker each time she came there, and remembered how the patio had been her mother's favorite place on the estate.

By the time she arrived, the fifty campers and some of her teachers and other staff had already begun breakfast, laughing and chatting one last time together. *One of these years we're going to outgrow the patio,* reflected Sylvia as she returned the quilters' greetings. They might have to move to the north gardens or eat in shifts. The business had grown more rapidly than any of the Elm Creek Quilters had imagined, and what once had been a small camp operated by eight friends had become a thriving company with more than twice the employees and four times the campers of their inaugural year. Sylvia had retired from the day-to-day operations after her stroke nearly two years before, but she knew Sarah and her codirector, Summer Sullivan, valued her opinion and would continue to include her in the major decisions the company encountered.

Sylvia valued their opinions as well, which was why she couldn't explain her reluctance to tell them she had found Anneke's hope chest. Instead she joined in the Farewell Breakfast activities and later bid the campers good-bye as if her only concern was that they had enjoyed themselves, would tell all their friends about Elm Creek Quilt Camp, and would return next year.

When the manor was empty of all but its permanent residents, Sylvia returned to her room and studied the quilts. Then, abruptly, she decided to put them away, making the excuse that it was to minimize their exposure to light. She carefully refolded the quilts along different lines rather than return the stress to the seams and patches that had borne the burden for more than a century.

She then placed the quilts and the journal deep in the back of her closet and shut the door on them as if she could blot Gerda's words from her memory.

❧

That night, Sylvia had an unsettling dream about Lucinda. In it, she was a little girl again, sitting on the footstool beside her great-aunt's chair as Lucinda pieced a LeMoyne Star block.

"Your great-grandmother Anneke wanted the fugitives to know they would be safe here," said Lucinda as her needle darted in and out of the fabric, joining two diamond-shaped scraps. "They needed a signal, one that the escaping slaves would recognize but the slave catchers would ignore."

"So she made a quilt?" prompted Sylvia, who had heard the story many times.

Lucinda nodded. "A Log Cabin quilt with black squares where the red or yellow squares belonged. You see, slave catchers thought they knew what signals to look for, so they paid no attention to a quilt hanging out to dry. But the escaping slaves did. They would cross Elm Creek to throw the dogs off their scent, and hide in the woods until Great-Grandmother Anneke hung this special quilt on the clothesline. That told them it was safe to come inside."

Suddenly Lucinda set down her quilting and said, "I have something to show you." She took an object from her pocket and lifted Sylvia onto her lap. "Something secret, something you mustn't share with anyone, not even your sister or your cousins. Will you promise?"

Sylvia quickly did, and Lucinda placed a slender brass key in her hands. "Somewhere up in the attic," said Lucinda, "in the hope chest she brought over from Germany, Great-Grandmother Anneke hid her Log Cabin quilt. This key opens the trunk."

"Why would she hide her quilt?" asked Sylvia, turning the key over in her hands.

"To keep its secrets safe."

"From who? The slave catchers?"

"From whoever might use them to hurt the people she loved." Her great-aunt fell silent for a moment. "One day it will be safe to tell those secrets. Maybe you will be the one to tell. Or maybe your granddaughter. I don't think my mother wanted those secrets kept forever."

"Do you know what the secrets are?"

"If I did, I wouldn't tell you."

"Why not?"

But Lucinda merely smiled and busied herself with her sewing.

That was where the dream ended, the dream that was really a memory. But the memory had never unsettled Sylvia until she read the troubling words in Gerda's book. Sylvia had assumed the secrets were about the Underground Railroad, but now she suspected something more lay behind Gerda's decision to hide the quilts away and to record her secrets in a journal. Why had Lucinda trusted only Sylvia with the key to the trunk? And why had Gerda's journal not found its way into Lucinda's stories?

She woke several hours before dawn, brooding and unable to fall back asleep.

She dragged herself downstairs to breakfast in the kitchen, for on Sunday mornings, in the absence of the campers, they preferred the more intimate space to the banquet hall. She seated herself, bidding good morning to Sarah, Matt, and her own dear Andrew, who knew at a glance something troubled her. She patted his hand, a silent message that she was all right and would explain later, and fixed a smile to disguise her inner turmoil.

But she couldn't fool Sarah. "What's wrong?" asked the younger woman in an undertone as they left the kitchen after the meal. "You seem upset."

Sylvia regarded her fondly. In the years Sylvia had known her, Sarah had changed so much, but that core of compassion and frankness had always been present, and had grown with the passing of time. It was difficult now to remember that when they first met, Sylvia had found Sarah self-absorbed and unduly dissatisfied with her life. Elm Creek Quilts had been good for Sarah, allowing her to truly shine, to learn the great extent of her gifts. Ever since Sylvia's stroke, when Sarah had been forced to shoulder the greatest burden of day-to-day camp operations, she had transformed from an awkward, somewhat flighty girl into a confident, self-possessed woman.

Sylvia loved Sarah like a daughter. She owed her nothing less, as Sarah had befriended her after her long, self-imposed exile from her family home, and had saved Elm Creek Manor by proposing they create a quilters' retreat there. But she had come to love her fellow Elm Creek Quilter Summer Sullivan, too, and when Sylvia compared the two young women—which she knew she shouldn't do—she couldn't help thinking of herself and her elder sister. Claudia, the prettier and more pleasant of the two, had been admired and adored by all, unlike Sylvia, with her moods and tempers. Recalling her and Claudia's bitter sibling rivalry, Sylvia had feared jealousy might ruin the friendship between Sarah and Summer, especially when Summer had assumed a position nearly equal to Sarah's with Elm Creek Quilts. To her relief, Sarah and Summer proved themselves to be of stronger character than the two Bergstrom daughters. Sarah preferred to operate behind the scenes, working tirelessly on countless financial and managerial tasks, and never minded that Summer, with her more public role directing the teachers and activities, became the appealing face for the company. Neither envied the other her role or thought her own—or herself—superior.

"I'm not upset," answered Sylvia finally, regretting, as she had for most of her life, that she and her sister had not been friends. Gerda's cryptic remark in the journal hinted that Anneke had known her share of familial conflicts, too, although all the family tales of her and Hans portrayed them with virtues bordering on heroism. It would not be easy to relinquish those golden tales for the truth, but Sylvia wanted her real family, not idealized heroes.

The longer the ideal remained, the easier it would be to let it linger.

"What's bothering you, then?" asked Sarah.

"Come upstairs with me," said Sylvia. "I have something to show you."

Chapter Two

Once Sarah got over her surprise, she berated Sylvia for not telling her about the discovery immediately. Sylvia endured the complaints, figuring she had earned them, but as soon as Sarah paused to catch her breath, Sylvia said, "Are you going to scold me all day, or would you prefer to see the quilts?"

Immediately Sarah chose the latter, and after Sylvia retrieved them from the back of the closet, the two women carefully unfolded the quilts on Sylvia's bed.

Sarah exclaimed over the Log Cabin quilt, for Sylvia had shared Great-Aunt Lucinda's story with her, and she knew the significance of the black center square. She said nothing as she examined the Birds in the Air quilt, but stole quick glances at Sylvia as if attempting to judge her reaction to it. When Sarah turned her attention to the third quilt, she first noted the fabrics common to all three quilts, then asked, "Do any of these fabrics match those in Margaret Alden's quilt?"

Surprised, Sylvia said, "I honestly hadn't thought to look."

She brought out the photos Andrew had taken and gave them to Sarah, who scrutinized them carefully against the quilts on the bed. "Some of them look alike," said Sarah, "but the scale is so small, I can't be certain."

Sylvia retrieved a magnifying glass from her sewing kit and handed it to Sarah. "If you see something, don't think you're protecting me by pretending otherwise."

Sarah held the magnifying glass to the photos and studied them at length, but eventually she shook her head, still uncertain. Some of the fabrics looked similar, but as Sarah pointed out, that didn't necessarily mean Margaret Alden's quilt had any connection to the quilts in Anneke's trunk.

Quiltmakers of her time did not have the wide variety of prints modern quilters enjoyed, and the fading of the dyes could make even dissimilar fabrics seem alike in a photograph.

"Maybe we can find another connection," suggested Sarah.

"Isn't the choice of the Birds in the Air block a clear enough connection for you?"

Sarah dismissed that with a wave of her hand. "It was a common enough pattern. How many thousands of Birds in the Air quilts have been made throughout the years? I'm not going to assume anything based upon that, especially since the blocks don't even use the same setting."

Sylvia was glad to hear it, because she had been trying to convince herself that the same pattern choice was, at best, circumstantial evidence. "Very well, what *would* you base an assumption on?"

"Something that would be unique to a particular quilter's style. Piecing quirks, for example. You know, like how your sister used to chop off all the points of her triangles."

"Many quilters do that," said Sylvia. "Our own Diane is a master of the truncated tip. You've chopped off a point or two yourself."

"It's a shame we don't have Margaret's quilt here to compare to Anneke's quilts," said Sarah. "What about theme or symbolism? The Log Cabin block was supposed to represent the home, with the center square being the hearth or a light in the window, with the light and dark fabric representing the good and bad in life. Using the black center square gave it a special meaning on the Underground Railroad—"

"Except some say the Log Cabin block was designed to honor Abraham Lincoln," interrupted Sylvia. "If so, it couldn't have been used as a signal on the Underground Railroad."

"Why not?"

"Heavens. Didn't they teach you any American history at Penn State? The Underground Railroad operated much differently after the Civil War broke out, not long after Lincoln was elected. Quilts would have been useful as signals only before the war."

"You're the one who told me about Log Cabin quilts with black center squares," Sarah pointed out. "Are you saying you were wrong?"

"I'm saying there are alternative theories, and we can't have it both ways."

"I accept that, but my point is still valid. We might find some similarities in pattern choice to suggest that the same person made all four quilts."

Sylvia folded her arms. "I'm not even convinced that the same person made the three from the attic."

"Let's assume they were made by the same person, since they were together in the trunk," said Sarah. "Did Birds in the Air have any significance in the years leading up to the Civil War?"

"None that I know of." But then Sylvia reconsidered. "Well, birds migrate. Perhaps that pattern was a code telling slaves to follow the migrating birds as they flew north."

"Except birds only migrate north at a certain time of the year. In autumn—"

"Yes, I see. Escaped slaves would follow the birds farther south. That wouldn't do, would it?"

"If it's a code, it's not a very helpful one."

"Unless most escapes took place in springtime, to take advantage of fair weather."

Sarah nodded to the strippy quilt. "What pattern is this?"

"It's just a simple four-patch, as far as I know. I haven't seen it before."

"Maybe one of the other Elm Creek Quilters would recognize it."

"Grace Daniels certainly would." And if the unknown pattern or Birds in the Air carried any special significance, Grace would know that as well. Sylvia needed answers, but she doubted she could wait for Grace's visit in mid-August.

When Sarah left to return to her camp director's duties, Sylvia took up Gerda's memoir and carried it downstairs to her favorite room in the manor, a small sitting room off the kitchen. She settled into an armchair beside the window and, summoning her inner resolve, opened the book and read on.

Spring 1856 —
in which my adventure begins

The dowry that proved insufficient to impress the parents of my childhood sweetheart was more than enough to purchase second class passage aboard the *Anabelle Marie,* bound for New York from Germany. My heart was broken, and as I was already twenty-five and plain, my mother agreed that I was unlikely to find another suitor in the Old World, and might as well try the New. I wanted to journey not to become a wife, however, but to put an ocean between myself and the only man I thought I would ever love.

My brother, Hans, who had preceded me to America, agreed that I should come to him and help establish his claim out West. He sent me handbills about Kansas Territory, describing the fertile soil, the mild climate, and the industrious people who had already begun civilizing the wild frontier. Hans's letters glowed with the promise of the good fortune awaiting us, and since he never once suggested he planned to marry me off rather than allow me to participate fully in his ambitious plans to achieve prosperity, I was all too glad to go.

I will never forget my first experience of my new homeland after the long sea voyage—the disorienting humiliation of processing, interrogation by men full of their own importance, the babble of languages, the smells of unwashed bodies and unfamiliar foodstuffs. I spoke English passably well, and yet had to correct their spelling of my surname twice before they recorded it correctly. My heart went out to those who could not make themselves understood and waited in queues, fearful and uncertain. At least I could follow instructions, and knew that somewhere outside that vast room, my brother waited. I had thought myself adventurous, a woman traveling so far alone, and yet there were children in my queue far more daring than I.

Hans found me in the throng. "Gerda," a shout rang out, and before I knew it, I had been swept into the air by a man I was certain I had never seen before. Dumbstruck, I then recognized in this vigorous, laughing man the younger brother who had left the shelter of his family seven years before. Though my own height still exceeded his, Hans was at least three inches taller and forty pounds heavier than the boy I remembered, but his smile was the same, as were his eyes. His manner was cheerful and confident, as if all the treasures of the world lay before him.

I never wept, not even when E. had told me whom he would marry in my stead, and yet I nearly wept with joy then to see my brother so healthy and happy.

We collected my trunk—stuffed full of more books than clothes, which I assumed I could obtain in Kansas, once I knew better what a farm woman needed—and were making our way through the crowd to the exit when we discovered a beautiful young woman desperately arguing with a uniformed bureaucrat. She pleaded in German, he drowned her out in English, and around them gathered a crowd of men, enjoying the spectacle.

Hans, as I knew he would, halted and questioned some of the men. I started at first to hear Hans speaking so well; his accent was now better than mine, though he had spoken not a word of English when he departed our home. We learned that the beautiful young woman was supposed to have been met by her fiancé three days before. She had never met this man, and did not know how to reach him except by the address on the letters he had sent her father, but she was determined to wait for him until he arrived.

I suspected she would be waiting a very long time indeed, and was telling Hans so when another man added that the bureaucrat, having failed to convince the girl to move along, intended to hand her over to the police or, better yet, send her home to Germany.

Hans did not approve of either option. She had come so far to seek her fortune in America, as had they all. Why should she be punished for the failures of her betrothed? He gave me a sidelong look and said, "There's room in our wagon for one more."

I said, "Do you intend for her to accompany us all the way to Kansas Territory?"

"She can stay as long as it suits her."

I must say I was shocked. The very idea of an unmarried woman traveling with a strange man, even when that man was my dear brother, scandalized me. Then, suddenly, it occurred to me that my own mother had planned something very similar for myself, that Hans should marry me off to the first eligible man he could persuade to take me. At least in me, Hans and the young woman would have a chaperone.

And I will confess something else.

The beautiful young woman had brought with her a sewing machine, and I, who detested sewing, who thought working with needle and thread the most tedious and unendurable of a woman's domestic duties, saw in this young woman and her sewing machine the means of escaping the detestable chore indefinitely.

So I intimated that Hans was welcome to invite her to join us, which he did, in German, so the official would not comprehend. His arguments were charming, if unromantic; he pointed out that one man she had never met was as good as another, and that she was welcome to stay with us until she found her fiancé, or someone else, or decided she would be fine alone, or chose to return to Germany. He hoped, however, that she would decide to marry him.

She stood there speechless for a long while, and who could blame her for that, so unusual the offer and so enormous the consequences of her reply. But soon she agreed to depart with us, and I had the sense that she was conceding defeat in doing so. If Hans also suspected this, he gave no sign, but cheerfully escorted us outside, where his wagon awaited us.

That is how I made my acquaintance with Anneke, my brother's future wife.

❧

Sylvia clasped the book to her chest, exultant. Her suspicions that the memoir was Gerda's had been confirmed, and better yet, Gerda's account of how Hans and Anneke had met echoed the story she had heard as a young girl. Enough details matched perfectly to convince her of the authenticity of the memoir, and enough were dissimilar to further heighten her curiosity. She had never heard of Gerda's unrequited love, the mysterious E., or of plans to settle in Kansas. Had she forgotten those elements, or had they been culled from the history by the intervening generations of storytellers?

"Sylvia?" said Andrew from the doorway between the sitting room and the kitchen. "It's almost time for the new campers to arrive. The Elm Creek Quilters are waiting."

Sylvia stowed the book in the drawer of her writing desk and tucked her arm through Andrew's as he escorted her to the manor's grand foyer. "How's the *Queen Mary*?" asked Sylvia, referring to Andrew's motor home, still parked behind the manor where they had left it upon their return from South Carolina.

"She's ready to sail with the tide." He pulled out her chair at the registration table. "Are you?"

"Of course," said Sylvia, surprised. "You don't think I'd let you make this trip alone, do you?"

"I thought you might prefer to cancel the trip so you could bury your nose in that old book of yours. Or look at those old quilts a few hundred more times."

"I can read Gerda's memoir while you drive."

When Andrew merely shrugged, Sylvia was struck by the thought that—no, it couldn't be. Andrew, jealous? Of three quilts and a book? Guiltily she thought back upon her behavior ever since meeting Margaret Alden, and had to admit she had been distracted. Too distracted, perhaps, to pay as much attention to him as he liked. She would make it up to him, she promised herself. She would start by including him in the unfolding tale of her ancestors rather than hoarding Gerda's memories to herself.

After their newest guests arrived and Sylvia saw the week off to a good start, she asked Andrew to help her pack for their trip. As they did, she told him what she had learned from Gerda's memoir, and was pleased to see that by the time her suitcase was full, he was nearly as eager to learn the rest of the story as she was. Then, to show him she was as interested in his family as she wanted him to be in hers, she changed the subject. They chatted about their upcoming visit to Andrew's daughter, Amy, in Connecticut. Amy's husband planned to take Andrew fishing, and Sylvia had promised Amy her first quilting lesson.

❧

Once they were on the road, Sylvia found herself delighted to be traveling again. As much as she enjoyed passing the summer days at Elm Creek Manor, reminiscing about the summers of her girlhood and enjoying the lively activity of quilt camp, she was glad to spend time alone with Andrew. His quiet companionship was as comforting as a favorite quilt, and she grew fonder of him the more they shared memories of years they had spent apart. She liked to tease him that they got along so well because they never ran out of stories to share, and considering that they had more than fifty years' worth of catching up to do, they ought not to run out of conversation anytime soon.

Andrew had bought the motor home after his wife's death to make traveling between his daughter's house on the East Coast and his son's on the West more comfortable. "I don't mind having no permanent address," he had told Sylvia once. "It beats moving in with the kids." Sylvia agreed, but she noticed he took on a permanent address readily enough when she invited him to live with her in Elm Creek Manor.

After Sylvia began her partial retirement from Elm Creek Quilts, she had more time to join Andrew in his cross-country travels. His children had been startled to meet her. Apparently they never imagined Andrew would find a lady friend only three years after their mother's death, so devoted had he been to her throughout their more than fifty years together. But among her own friends Sylvia had seen that those who had known happy marriages were more likely to find love again than those who had been miserable. Granted, Sylvia had needed an interim of half a century, but she hadn't been looking.

Lately, unless they had merely learned to hide their feelings better, Andrew's children and their spouses had come to accept her, and it seemed that their father's newfound happiness pleased them. So Sylvia and Andrew passed much of the summer on the road, stopping by Elm Creek Manor for only a few weeks at a time, visiting the best fishing holes and quilt shops in the country and having a grand time.

At her insistence, Andrew had stopped fretting about appearances, and what other people thought of an unmarried couple traveling together. Sylvia thought his worries were nonsense. Most people were too busy managing their own lives and problems to give the private lives of a couple of senior citizens a second thought. Besides, since they both still wore the wedding bands of their first marriages, people probably assumed they were married to each other.

"If that's what people assume," Andrew would say, "then why not—"

"Don't even suggest it," Sylvia would reply firmly before he could finish the thought. Andrew would scowl grumpily for a while, but eventually his good humor would return. In recent months, he had learned to stop hinting at marriage, and thank goodness for that. Honestly. To become a bride again, at her age. The very idea made her laugh. What Andrew's children thought of their father remarrying, if they thought of it at all, Sylvia refused to conjecture.

The visit kept both of them so busy that Sylvia couldn't find a moment to take up Gerda's memoir, so as much as she enjoyed playing with Andrew's grandchildren and teaching Amy how to piece a Sawtooth Star block, she was glad to return home, unpack, catch up on all the camp news, and settle into her armchair with the book.

❧

For days we journeyed from New York City west across the state of New Jersey and into eastern Pennsylvania. At first, Anneke spoke little, perhaps intimidated by her unfortunate circumstances or ashamed that her fiancé had abandoned her. She had won my sympathies, however, as I understood something of what it felt like to be cast adrift by a man.

For his part, Hans conducted himself as a true gentleman, and before long he had charmed Anneke's story out of her. We learned that she was from Berlin, the third youngest of seven daughters. She had never met the man she was to marry, although she possessed a daguerreotype of him. I thought his physiognomy suggested a crafty, duplicitous nature, but Hans told me I was imagining things, influenced by what I knew of his behavior. Still, Hans looked none too pleased when Anneke carefully tucked the portrait away in her satchel instead of discarding it by the side of the road.

That small satchel contained a few dresses, some undergarments, two wool blankets, a Bible, and twenty dollars, all her worldly goods, save the sewing machine. Cumbersome though it was, she had brought the sewing machine with a singular purpose: to earn her keep, since she had no dowry, and did not wish to be a burden to her new husband. She had planned to purchase bolts of fabric in the East and take them out West to her husband's homestead in Missouri, where an enterprising woman could earn a modest fortune by sewing shirts for the unmarried men who populated the West. Anneke's thrift and practicality made me ashamed of the many books tucked in my hope chest among the coverlets my mother had made, as I disliked sewing too much to create anything useful myself. I was more embarrassed still that I, a spinster of twenty-five, had brought a hope chest in the first place, while Anneke, younger than I by at least six years and traveling to America to meet her husband, had not. In comparison I no doubt seemed vain and foolish, me with my plain face and unwomanly stature beside Anneke's dainty beauty.

We stayed at inns along the way, Anneke and I sharing the bed while Hans slept on the floor. Once, when there was no inn, Anneke and I slept by the hearth of a kindly farmer and his wife, while Hans slept in the barn near his horses.

And now I must tell you of these horses, for they play an important role in this history.

Castor and Pollux were the two most perfectly matched pair of stallions it had ever been my privilege to look upon. Coal black, each with a white spot on the forehead, they pulled the sawboard wagon with an air of patient dignity, as if they knew they were meant for greater things. They were not workhorses, and although the wagonload was light, I could not bear to think how they would endure hauling it all the way to Kansas Territory, and I told Hans so.

"They won't have to," said he. "We aren't going to Kansas."

I was so dumbfounded I could only echo, "We aren't going to Kansas?"

No, he told me, and then explained that the region was in turmoil, something his handbills had never mentioned. According to law, the settlers themselves would determine whether Kansas would be a Slave State or Free, and even as Abolitionists were helping opponents of slavery to settle there, others from neighboring Slave States, especially Missouri, were doing the same for people who would vote in their favor.

"All the more reason we should go" was my stubborn reply. "Even your one vote might make the difference."

But my brother shook his head gravely and said that people in Kansas had been injured and even killed in the violence as those on one side of the issue tried to drive out their rivals, and not even innocent women and children had been spared. Until matters of statehood and slavery were resolved there, Hans said, we would be better off in a region where the matter had already been settled, on the side of freedom.

I agreed this would be wise, but was compelled to inquire, "And where, precisely, is that?"

"Pennsylvania," came his reply, a farm on the outskirts of a town called Creek's Crossing. Now my brother became ebullient, and described in glowing terms the two-story stone house awaiting us, the fertile land nourished by the waters of Elm Creek, the corral, the paddock, and the stable full of horses just like the dazzling pair pulling our wagon.

Anneke, thinking of her plan to sew shirts for the bachelors of the West, perked up then and inundated my brother with questions about the town. No, he didn't know the population of Creek's Crossing; no, he wasn't sure how many churches it possessed; no, he wasn't aware if they had a lending library—each question made him squirm more than the last, and his answers became more evasive until I finally burst out, "Good heavens, Hans, have you seen this town or not?"

No, to be precise, he had not.

Anneke and I looked at each other, and then at him, and thus confronted by two bewildered and alarmed women, he was forced to reveal the truth. He had not seen Creek's Crossing, or Elm Creek Farm, or even a single leaf on a single tree in the region where these places were reputed to exist. All these many years, when I and my family back in Germany believed him to be a merchant's son turned gentleman farmer, working on his own thriving land, he had been wandering from pillar to post, working for one farmer and then another, living for a time in the city, earning a small fortune and losing it just as quickly in one business enterprise after another.

"Then how," asked I, as calmly as I could manage under the circumstances, "did you come to be master of Elm Creek Farm?"

By winning it, he confessed with more pride than I thought proper, in a horse race.

The previous owner, a horse breeder with a taste for whiskey, had come to New York to sell some of his prize horses. He was new to the business and trying to make a name for himself selling fine horses to the new generations of gentlemen sprouting up like weeds from the soil of their peasant forebears. He had overestimated the market and, his funds nearly exhausted, found himself with four horses and little to show for his journey. Naturally, as men do, he decided a drink would help him see a solution to his quandary, and as one drink turned into many, he took to wandering the streets, belligerently ordering passersby to examine his horses and admit they had never before seen their like.

Most ignored the man, but Hans humored him and said the horses were impressive to look at but were not, ultimately, a well-matched team. The man sputtered in rage and demanded that Hans explain himself. Hans indicated one horse, Castor, and said his gait was longer than the other three horses', so his superior speed would throw off the team.

"You're wrong, sir," said Mr. L., and to prove it, he would have Hans ride Castor while he himself rode one of the other three. If Hans lost the race or if the horses crossed the line at the same time, Hans must buy two of the horses; if Castor won, Mr. L. would give Hans all four horses free of charge.

Hans did not have the money to buy one, much less two, of the horses, but he knew that Mr. L. in his drunken state would not be able to sit a horse well enough to win the race. Sure enough, after witnesses were assembled and a course determined, Hans sailed across the finish line and found himself the proud owner of four horses.

Mr. L. promptly demanded that Hans allow him to win back his horses. At first Hans refused, but when Mr. L. called it a matter of honor and staked his farm in central Pennsylvania against Hans's newly acquired thoroughbreds, Hans consented. After another brisk run around the course, he found himself the owner of everything but what Mr. L. carried upon his person. Before Mr. L.'s pocket change and clothing should fall into his possession as well, Hans returned to him two of the horses and encouraged him to forgo additional gambling until a day when his luck was better.

Anneke, eyes shining, praised Hans for his cleverness and admired his generosity in giving Mr. L. two of the horses he had lost fair and square, but I was shocked—stunned and appalled that my brother would take such advantage of his fellow man. I reminded him what our father would have thought of his deportment, but Hans merely laughed at me and said, "Father's ways don't work in America, dear sister. That is why he remained at home, and I came here."

I did not like this, but lest the two of them think I, too, should have remained at home, I kept my arguments to myself and vowed to see that the Bergstrom family would not abandon all dignity and righteousness in this wild land.

"How far is this farm?" said I instead, thinking that though it was nearer than Kansas, our destination might yet be too far for the horses. Hans showed me on the map, and it seemed a more isolated place than I had ever imagined, although logically I realized it could not have been any worse than Kansas Territory, far to the west, and likely it would be better. There, Hans declared, he would raise crops to support us and the livestock, but he would make his fortune in horse breeding.

"Make your fortune as Mr. L. made his?" inquired Anneke, thinking, as I did, of how Mr. L. had been unable to sell the four horses he had brought to New York.

"I hope you did not intend to breed Castor and Pollux," said I, "since they are both males."

"And gelded," added Anneke.

We dissolved into laughter at Hans's scowl, and soon he joined in, reminding us of the other horses awaiting us at Elm Creek Farm. "A stable full," said he, including the very horses that had sired and foaled the regal animals before us.

Our laughter faded, and I could see in my companions' faces that mirth had been replaced with anticipation and eagerness. As for myself, I thought of the unfortunate man who had lost those beautiful horses, along with his farm and his entire livelihood. I imagined him returning to Creek's Crossing in defeat to break the news to his family, if he had one, and to his workers, who perhaps even now were caring for the horses and wondering if they, too, would be driven from their homes or if the new owner wanted for stablehands.

However, my pity for Mr. L. was short-lived.

When at last we reached Creek's Crossing, we were pleased to discover a quaint, pleasant village built along the banks of Elm Creek, which, in my estimation, should have been named a river. We had driven our wagon beside it for many miles, and only here did runoff into lakes and marshland north of the town cause the creek to narrow and slow enough for ferries to provide not entirely hazardous passage across the waters.

We traversed the town and discovered several churches, and saloons enough to equal their number, as well as various thriving businesses, including a general store. Here Hans stopped to obtain basic provisions, planning to purchase more once we learned what, if anything, Mr. L. had left behind.

In the meantime, Anneke and I made an errand of our own, to a tailor's shop across the street, where I pretended to inquire about prices but in truth was helping Anneke study the competition. We exited the shop armed with the knowledge that another tailor as well as a dressmaker were already well established in town, but Anneke was untroubled, confident that her plans would yet succeed.

Hans was waiting in the wagon, frowning in a bemused fashion. When we inquired what was the matter, he said, "Maybe nothing." Then he paused and added, "The men inside have never heard of Elm Creek Farm."

Anneke and I looked at each other but said nothing. We could not bring ourselves to tease him, as we had about the horses. His manner was too pensive to elicit our laughter.

But the deed to Elm Creek Farm awaited us at the bank as Mr. L. had promised, and once it was in Hans's possession and the transfer of ownership was in order, our concerns faded. We headed out of town, following the road and the directions Mr. L. had provided. The creek accompanied us for a time as we passed other, well-established farms, then wound away from us and disappeared into a thick wood. Soon afterward, at a path through the trees barely wide enough to accommodate our wagon, the road and Mr. L.'s directions diverged.

On any other occasion I might have enjoyed the sublime beauty of the forest and delighted in the sunbeams as they broke through the leafy boughs, but that day I felt only trepidation. Then Elm Creek emerged again, which brought us some measure of relief, as Mr. L. had said the water crossed his property.

But although he spoke truthfully in this regard, nearly every other detail proved false.

Even now, knowing how we prospered in the end, it pains me to recall the sorry sight that greeted us. Of the forty acres Hans now owned, just four were cleared. The two-story stone house was nothing more than a cabin a stone's throw from the creek, barely twelve feet by twelve, with two oilcloth windows, a dirt floor, and sunlight streaming though the logs where the chinking had fallen out. The stable of horses was empty, which perhaps was just as well, since it was but a ramshackle lean-to, with just enough room for Castor and Pollux.

When we had surveyed our domain, Hans seemed furious and humiliated but resigned. Anneke looked as if she might weep; when Hans held out a hand to comfort her, she stormed away and climbed aboard the wagon to sit beside her sewing machine. She looked as if she heartily regretted her decision to leave New York in our company, and I cannot say I blamed her. When she thought herself unobserved, she brought out the portrait of her intended and regarded it with a strange look in her eye. Perhaps she wondered if she had not waited long enough for him in New York, and if she should seek him out. With the awareness of all that befell us since, I cannot help contemplating how different my life and Hans's would have been if at that moment she had summoned up the courage to leave us and make her way on her own.

The sun was beginning to disappear behind the trees, we were tired and hungry, and all our happy prospects seemed to lie in ruins. This, I told myself, is what comes of such ill-gotten gains. But I lacked the cruelty to say so aloud, so instead I said, "We have less than what we thought we had, but we still have the land, and two horses, and our own fortitude. That is far more than we had upon our arrival in New York. So Mr. L. did not do the work of clearing the land and planting the crops and building us a fine house. Very well. We shall do it ourselves."

My brother still looked discouraged, so I added, "Did we not intend to work in Kansas? Was someone to have done everything for us there?"

Anneke sighed and rested her head in her hands. Hans idly brushed straw from the horses' coats. They were moments away from giving up and turning back, and we had only just arrived!

I was no less disappointed than they, but suddenly I grew angry. "It's just as well we didn't go any farther west," I declared, snatching up a parcel Hans had purchased at the general store and marching over to the cabin with it. Alone I unloaded the wagon of all but my trunk and the sewing machine, which were too heavy for me to lift. Then I built a fire in a circle of stones that Mr. L. had arranged not far from the entrance to the cabin, filled a cook pot at the creek, and soon had potatoes on the boil. As the sun set and my companions' appetites grew, they left their isolated places and joined me at the fireside. Wordlessly I handed them their tin plates and cups and served them potatoes and dried beef as I had on the road. We ate in silence, with only the noises of the forest to welcome us home.

Then, suddenly, my brother spoke. "Tomorrow I'll find the borders of our property. There must be neighboring farms. They will tell us where our acres end, or I'll find a surveyor in town." He poked the fire with a stick. "There might be some crops in, somewhere. He's been feeding his horses something."

"I'll ready the cabin," said Anneke in a soft voice. "When I have enough daylight to see by."

"I'll help you," said I, and that was how we decided to stay at Elm Creek Farm.

❧

"A horse race," said Sylvia, shaking her head.

Andrew looked dubious. "It could have been worse."

"I suppose. Hans could have held the man at gunpoint and robbed him that way."

"It wasn't robbery," said Sarah. "It was gambling."

"A horse race with a drunken man who was certain to lose is no gamble." Sylvia rose and carried her empty coffee cup into the kitchen, but instead of returning to the sitting room and her friends, she exited the manor through the back door. She crossed the empty parking lot and followed the back road to the bridge over Elm Creek, where she sat down on a bench and gazed at the water.

She wondered where that old cabin had stood. Gerda described a four-acre clearing a stone's throw from the creek, which narrowly ruled out the location of the manor. Any area cleared in Gerda's time could have become overgrown since, so Sylvia doubted she'd ever find the right place, if in fact any trace of it remained to be found. A cabin so decrepit in 1856 most likely would not have lasted into the next century.

Sylvia knew she should sympathize with her ancestors' predicament, but instead she found herself more than a little pleased that no two-story stone house had awaited the three travelers at the end of their journey. A run-down cabin was more than Hans deserved after swindling a man out of his home and livelihood. All her life she had admired Hans and Anneke for building the Bergstrom estate out of nothing—which, admittedly, they apparently had done, but not without trying to take the easy way out first.

She brooded until Andrew joined her. "Are you all right?"

She moved over to make room for him on the bench. "I'm fine. Merely . . . disappointed."

"Why so?"

"Why so? Why not? All my life, Hans and Anneke have been held up to me—to all of their descendants—as the epitome of the courageous immigrant fulfilling the American dream. And now I find out—"

"That your heroes are merely human?"

Sylvia knew any word she uttered would sound petulant, so she said nothing.

"You have a choice, you know," said Andrew. "You don't have to keep reading."

"Of course I do. I have to see how everything turned out."

"You already know." With his thumb, Andrew pointed over his shoulder at the manor.

Sylvia's gaze followed the gesture, and as she studied the gray stone walls that only weeks before had seemed so strong, so secure, she wondered if she knew anything at all about how things had turned out.

Chapter Three

S ummer and her mother had lived in Waterford since Summer was nearly eleven, but neither had ever heard Waterford referred to as Creek's Crossing. The details Sylvia had shared about Gerda Bergstrom's journal had piqued Summer's curiosity, so she arranged to have Sarah cover for her at Elm Creek Quilt Camp so she could investigate.

She crossed the street to the campus of Waterford College and walked up the hill to the library, where the Waterford Historical Society kept its archives. After scrutinizing her alumni association card, a library assistant led her to a remote room, indicated the location of various books, databases, and maps, and allowed her to search undisturbed. If not for one dark-haired man sequestered in a corner carrel, she would have been completely alone.

Just a few minutes with the map cabinet made Summer realize that she should have allotted more time. It took her nearly half an hour to locate the proper drawer, only to discover that the maps weren't sorted according to any logical order she could discern. *Sylvia's ancestors must have designed this filing system,* she thought ruefully, thinking of the manor's attic. With a sigh, she pulled open the first drawer and began paging through the maps.

Fortunately, by the time she had to leave, she had found two maps of the county that merited more scrutiny. One, dated 1847, showed only a town called Creek's Crossing, much smaller than present-day Waterford but at the very bend of the creek where the oldest district of the downtown now existed. The second, dated 1880, depicted the entire state, but Waterford was clearly labeled in its appropriate location. Sometime between 1847 and 1880, the name of the town had been changed.

Remembering the reportorial technique she had learned in her journalism seminar at Waterford College, Summer identified the town's name change as the "what"—now she needed to learn when and why. The "who," of course, were the Bergstroms.

Whether the family had played any role in the transformation of Creek's Crossing into Waterford, she could only guess, but her instincts—and her knowledge of how Sylvia's family had influenced the town's fortunes in later years—told her she was not pursuing a false lead.

Summer through winter 1856— in which we become farmers, and I am unwittingly courted

So passed our first evening at Elm Creek Farm. By morning's light, my companions had gained more resolve, while I felt my own weakening, as I began to realize how very far I was from home and everything familiar. But, I reminded myself, that was precisely what I had wanted, and since I could not bear to return to Germany in defeat even if I could afford the passage, I had to make the best of it.

By the end of the day, we discovered that our circumstances were not quite as dire as we had imagined. Mr. L. had put in a kitchen garden, so we would soon have fresh vegetables. We learned that an acre of corn had been planted, and this news cheered us immensely. Since much of our land had not been improved, our woods were full of game, and thus we celebrated our second night at Elm Creek Farm with a feast of venison and seed potatoes, eaten by the fireside under the stars.

As the weeks passed, we set the cabin to rights as best we could; Anneke and I filled the spaces between the logs while Hans repaired the roof enough to keep out the rain. Each day I marveled anew at the changes in my brother. He had left my father's house seven years before knowing a great deal about the textiles trade in Baden-Baden but little of horses and nothing of farming. Now he put in late crops and drove the team as if he were born to it.

Castor and Pollux did not pull the plow, of course. One of Hans's first acts as master of Elm Creek Farm was to trade them with the owner of a livery stable for a team of till horses, a pig, and a flock of chickens. We were all downcast to part with the elegant creatures, especially Anneke, who grew teary-eyed whenever she saw them prancing before a carriage in town. Hans promised her that one day, when his business was established, he would give her far superior horses, born and bred on our own land. Anneke didn't quite seem to believe him, but the promise pleased her just the same.

When our immediate needs were seen to, Anneke asked Hans to turn his attention to improving our little cabin. He had made us each a bed by stringing rope between oak posts, upon which Anneke placed straw ticks she had sewn, but only a curtain separated our beds from his, and we had no fireplace, which would surely be a problem come winter. I added my voice to Anneke's, but Hans instead set himself to work on the barn.

He had met a neighbor, a Mr. Thomas Nelson, whose land abutted ours to the north. His wife, Dorothea, befriended me, and in later years became my dearest friend and confidante—closer to me in many ways than Anneke ever was. Anneke thought Dorothea too solemn and bookish, but I admired her keen mind and sensible temperament. After the day's work was finished, we enjoyed many evenings discussing literature and politics, and I learned a great deal about our new country from her. Often we gathered at the Nelsons' home, which despite its simplicity seemed a palace compared to our cabin, but I had too much pride not to reciprocate their kind invitations, and we entertained our neighbors nearly as frequently as they did us.

We spoke English with the Nelsons, since they did not speak German. Anneke would have preferred to sit silently with her sewing rather than have Hans or me translate the conversation, as her inability to speak English shamed her, but Hans said, "You will never learn if you don't try, and you need English in America." He was right, of course, and though Anneke's attempts at conversation were at first reluctant, she gradually acquired a rudimentary knowledge of English. But in those first years, she spoke rarely to strangers, a behavior that some of the women in town misinterpreted, considering her aloof and unfriendly. Later these same women were to decide that they had been mistaken: Anneke was the friendly and charming one, while I was arrogant and full of strange notions. Their opinions might have troubled me if I had not made other friends through Dorothea, but since I had, I cared not what Anneke's acquaintances thought of me. Perhaps I was a bit arrogant after all.

Hans and Thomas often exchanged work, and after Hans helped Thomas bring in his harvest, Thomas helped Hans lay the foundation for the barn, about twenty paces east of our front door, between ourselves and the creek.

I did not think this a wise location, for although the winds typically blew from the southwest, placing the cabin upwind of the animals' odor, I did not relish the thought of passing the barn several times a day to fetch water. I did not mention this, of course, as I knew this to be a ridiculous complaint from someone who fancied herself a settler. It was not until the men began to raise the walls that I understood my brother's thinking and realized what a marvel of architecture he had designed. He ingeniously built the barn into the hillside with one entrance at the foot of the hill and a second at the crest, so that one could drive the team into either story with equal ease.

The occasion of our barn raising drew the aid of other neighbors: the Grangers, the Watsons, the Shropshires, the Engles, and the Craigmiles. How warmly I regarded them as I saw their carriages and wagons emerging from the forest onto Elm Creek Farm. Some I still hold in high esteem, but to others, my heart has turned to cold stone.

But, of course, I did not know then how I would come to feel later. Neither, I daresay, could they have imagined what scandal we Bergstroms would bring into their midst. If they had suspected, some of them would have brought down that barn upon our heads. It amazes me now, gazing back into the past, that nothing distinguished future friend from foe, and that I never would have imagined who would later shun us and who would prove true.

I race ahead in my eagerness to unburden myself, but I must not allow my urgency to muddle this history.

After the barn, Hans put in a corral, intending, to my surprise, to pursue horse breeding after all. I had thought he had abandoned this idea with the loss of Castor and Pollux, but if anything, his interest had grown. "Mr. L. did not make such a good go of it," ventured I, when I saw that Hans was determined.

Hans merely grinned at me and said, "Sister, I think I've shown you I'm much more clever than Mr. L."

So I said nothing more to dissuade him, although to this day I do not believe Hans gained Elm Creek Farm through cleverness.

As for Anneke and me, in addition to assisting Hans with the crops as needed, we divided our women's work in shares that suited us both. Anneke, with her gift for needle and thread, took care of all the mending and sewing. Relieved to be rid of those detested chores, I was glad to care for the kitchen garden. In those days I was happiest working outside, the bright sun on my cheek, the fresh soil between my fingers. Anneke washed and tidied the cabin, while I cooked our meals. We took turns caring for the chickens and, after Dorothea instructed us, milking the cow.

Daily we improved Elm Creek Farm, and daily, too, did Anneke and Hans grow more fond of each other. Theirs was a peculiar courtship, indeed, conducted while they lived in the same small house, with only an elder sister as chaperone. I had always imagined true love to be as mine was for E., evolving slowly over time as friendship transformed from the sweetness of childhood affection into steadfast and respectful devotion. But Hans and Anneke seemed to admire each other from the start, with only a token reluctance on Anneke's part to abandon thoughts of her first intended. They married six months after their meeting in New York, before the first snow fell.

As a wedding gift for his bride, Hans added to our cabin a fireplace, a root cellar, and a second room. Not long after her own marriage, perhaps because she wished me to know a happiness like that she had found with my brother, or perhaps because she sought greater privacy than my presence would allow, Anneke began entertaining thoughts of finding a husband for me.

Among those who had come to help us those early days was Mrs. Violet Pearson Engle, the twice-widowed dressmaker, and her grown son from her first marriage, Cyrus Pearson. Mrs. Engle was a stout woman, domineering and loud-voiced, whose main contribution to the barn raising had been to bark orders at us women laboring over our outdoor cooking fires to prepare enough food for all those men. As for Mr. Pearson, upon our first meeting I found him polite, if somewhat disdainful, with a quick grin that some might have called a smirk. But that impression might have been merely my own prejudice, as I never fully liked or trusted handsome men, perhaps because they rarely expressed interest in plain girls such as myself. Still, since he seemed pleasant enough, I thought nothing of it when Anneke suggested we invite him for supper.

On the appointed evening, Mr. Pearson arrived, bearing an apple tart his mother had baked for us, and a bouquet of wildflowers which he presented to me—in error, I thought, assuming he had meant them for the lady of the house. I promptly handed the flowers to Anneke and took his coat, while Hans offered him a chair by the fire. Since the fireplace was also my cookstove, I necessarily passed between it and the table several times as the men talked about their horses and crops. Before long, I noticed that every time I approached the table, Mr. Pearson bounded out of his chair. At first I thought it charming, but when he persisted in the ridiculous formality, I entreated him to remain seated for fear he would be bouncing in and out of his chair all evening like a jumping jack. He agreed with a smile that did not completely conceal his displeasure, but he no longer rose when I did, although he tensed in his chair as if it took all his strength to remain seated.

"I did not notice it before," I murmured to Anneke in passing, "but Mr. Pearson has a haughty temperament, don't you agree?"

"He's a perfect gentleman," hissed Anneke, glancing at him to be sure he had not overheard. "And he's a guest, so mind your manners."

"I have no intention of doing otherwise," I protested in a whisper, but Anneke merely glared at me.

The meal itself was an even more baffling affair, with Hans the only one of us perfectly at ease. Anneke interrogated Mr. Pearson about his education and prospects with a directness that would have seemed rude if not for her charming manner and lack of fluency in English, but Mr. Pearson did not seem to mind. In fact, he seemed to relish the opportunity to talk about himself, but instead of responding to Anneke, he directed his replies to me. I was embarrassed for him, that he should slight Anneke and Hans so, when suddenly it occurred to me that he was behaving exactly as eager suitors did in novels.

This realization so astounded me that I could not reply when Mr. Pearson remarked for at least the seventeenth time how wondrously sublime my cooking was. Perhaps I should have perceived Mr. Pearson's intentions sooner, but E. had been my first and only love, and we had known each other since childhood. Our courtship had possessed none of the silly rituals with which adult men and women torment each other. I was not accustomed to the language of romance, nor did I ever expect it to be directed toward me. Nor, I knew with great certainty, did I wish to hear any more of it from Mr. Pearson. I looked from Anneke to Hans and back again, pleading silently for their aid, but Hans appeared oblivious to my distress, and Anneke seemed to enjoy it.

"You're so accomplished, Mr. Pearson," said Anneke then, disarmingly, "that I must wonder why there is no Mrs. Pearson."

"I have not yet found a woman deserving of that title."

"Oh, you must keep looking," said I, thinking, *But not at Elm Creek Farm.* "I'm sure you'll find her."

Some of the brightness faded from his smile, and he looked to Anneke for an explanation. Before she could speak, Hans said, "Tell me, when you find your Mrs. Pearson, will you give her a home of her own or bring her into your mother's house?"

"My mother's home will be her home, as it is mine."

"Come now," persisted Hans. "You know how women are. Asking two to share a kitchen is like throwing two wet cats into a sack and tying it shut. Asking them to share a home is asking for trouble, unless it is clear from the start who will be mistress of the household."

Anneke gave her husband a slight rebuke, but Mr. Pearson chuckled. "Mother will not be dictated to in her own home."

"So your Mrs. Pearson will have to know her place?"

"Indeed."

"You couldn't have her speaking her mind or acting contrary to Mrs. Engle's judgment."

"Of course not, but I do not anticipate any conflict. The only woman I could love would be of such purity of heart and generosity of spirit that she would love my mother as if she were her own. She would tend to my mother's needs with the same tender, unselfish eagerness as she would to mine."

Anneke twisted her pretty features into a frown. "You sound as if you are looking for a nurse or a housekeeper, not a wife."

"It would only be for a little while," said Mr. Pearson, with a hasty glance at me. "Once Mother passes on, my wife will be the mistress of the household, but until then—"

"Until then she is to be a servant in her own home?" said I, indignant on behalf of this unfortunate bride, forgetting, for the moment, that Mr. Pearson hoped I would be she. "My goodness, but you require a great deal of patience and forbearance in a wife. I do not think half the women of my acquaintance could manage it."

"It would not be as bleak as I have made it seem," said Mr. Pearson.

"I should hope not," said I. "If I were to marry into such circumstances, I might be tempted to hasten your mother's demise."

"I hope your future bride lacks my sister's temper," said Hans to Mr. Pearson in a confidential tone. "If not, you'd better find someone else to do the cooking."

Mr. Pearson glanced down at his plate in alarm as if expecting to find some deadly poison amid the mashed turnips. As Hans and I laughed merrily, he grew red-faced and said, "Yes, I'll be sure to do that."

"Your bride will be a lovely woman," said Anneke soothingly, glaring at Hans and me in turn. "Do not let their silly jokes trouble you."

Mr. Pearson let out a thin laugh as if to show us he understood our joke. Anneke steered the conversation to other matters, but for the remainder of the meal, Mr. Pearson spared no opportunity to avoid looking in my direction. Afterward, he thanked Anneke for her kind hospitality, shook Hans's hand, gave me a curt nod, then made some excuse about needing to tend to a sick horse.

As soon as the door shut behind him, Hans and I burst into laughter again.

"I fail to see what is so amusing," said Anneke.

I tried to speak. "The thought of that man—"

"—and my feisty, opinionated sister," finished Hans. "Married!"

Anneke folded her arms and pursed her lips, but eventually she, too, allowed a small smile. "Perhaps they would not be such a good match after all."

"Perhaps not, my love," said Hans, smiling tenderly. "But I can't blame you for trying."

"I can," said I. "I cannot imagine why you thought we were well suited for each other."

"You're both unmarried."

"True enough, but I would hope to base my future happiness on something more substantial than that."

"I agree," said Hans. "But I thought it would be easier for Mr. Pearson, and for our friendship with his family, if he realized on his own that you would not make him a good wife rather than hearing it in your refusal."

Only then did I understand that my brother had deliberately prodded Mr. Pearson into revealing his weaknesses as a husband for me so that I might better reveal my inadequacies as a wife for him. All the while I had thought Hans oblivious to the drama of manners playing out before him, he had been directing the action from behind the scenes. I studied him with new respect. Hans Bergstrom of Baden-Baden was not known for subtle calculation, but this man was Hans Bergstrom of America. I resolved not to underestimate him again.

"Mr. Pearson might not make Gerda a proper husband," declared Anneke, "but someone will."

Thus I learned, to my dismay, that Anneke was not easily daunted, and that despite the evening's failure, she was resolved to see me happily wed.

ℒℯ

"The more things change," said Sylvia, "the more they remain the same."

Andrew looked up from his newspaper. "What's that?"

"Gerda's sister-in-law wants to marry her off." Sylvia slipped off her glasses and stretched her neck, which had an painful kink in it, so intently had she been reading. "Honestly. It is a truth universally acknowledged that a woman without a husband is eager to find one, no matter what she says to the contrary, and that all her married friends and acquaintances are obligated to help her nab some poor fellow before he knows what hit him."

Andrew peered at her over his bifocals. "You know, not everyone is as opposed to marriage as you are."

"I'm not opposed to marriage in principle. I was very happily married myself once, I'll remind you. Marriage is fine for youngsters with their whole lives ahead of them, who want to build a future with the one they love. I have no objection to that, if that's what they want."

Andrew returned his gaze to the newspaper and said, "If you ask me, people ought to build their futures with the ones they love no matter how old they are, even if that won't add up to as many years as the young folks get."

Sylvia was about to concur, but she thought better of it and said nothing. If she agreed with his principles, one of these days she might find herself accidentally agreeing to a proposal.

ℒℯ *Winter 1856 into summer 1857 —*
in which we complete our first year at
Elm Creek Farm and begin a second

I had not told Anneke about E., and although Hans might have told her I had been disappointed in love, I was certain he had not explained the intensity of my sorrow. He could not have, since I do not believe he thought his sensible elder sister capable of such depth of feeling. How could either of them, entranced as they were with each other upon first sight, know what it was to have a love slowly blossom over time, only to have it crushed beneath the heel of parents who cared more for class distinctions than for the happiness of their son?

In those years, I wanted to believe E. the cruel victim of his parents' contempt for my family's lack of rank. Now I realize that if he had truly wanted to be my husband, he would have followed me to America. That would have meant abandoning the wealth and social position that had prevented us from marrying, and apparently he had no wish to do so, or the thought never occurred to him. Either way, his inaction proved that either our love was not true, or it was, but he was unworthy of it.

Time, hard work, and the newness of my life in America eased the pain of my grief, and I reconciled myself to being no more—and no less—than Hans Bergstrom's spinster sister. As our first autumn passed in a frenzy to make Elm Creek Farm livable for the coming winter, I realized I did not mind the role as much as a properly brought up girl ought to have done. Anneke and Dorothea were fortunate in their choice of husbands, but other women of my acquaintance were not, and I soon learned that an unmarried woman can do and say things a wife cannot. In any event, I envisioned a future doing my part to make Elm Creek Farm prosper, looking after Hans and Anneke and their children yet to be born, being a part of their family, and never desiring one of my own.

Winter snows had cut us off from contact with all but our closest neighbors, but the coming of spring brought a renewed liveliness to the town. Our dependence upon the kindness and generosity of others had impressed upon Anneke the importance of friends, and she became determined to establish the Bergstroms in Creek's Crossing. Being well regarded in society would help Hans's business, she said, and she prodded me to do my share to socialize with the wives and daughters of important men who might be in a position to help Hans later. At first I shuddered at the very notion of society, remembering how it had cost me my dearest love, but society in Creek's Crossing bore little resemblance to that of my homeland. As one would expect, however, it remained the province of the oldest and wealthiest families, but in a land where anyone willing to work hard could prosper, no obstacle remained to prevent the meanest immigrant from elevating his status.

"Unless the immigrant is colored," observed Dorothea, when I remarked upon this.

I could not refute the obvious truth in her words, and her reflection soured the appeal of the town for me. While Pennsylvania was a Free State, and most of us took pride in our righteousness and disdained the Southern slaveholder, freedmen were not, it must be said, any more welcome here than elsewhere, except among themselves and, perhaps, the Abolitionists. As for myself, although I was a staunch opponent of the institution of slavery, I had never actually befriended a colored person, former slave or free-born.

This troubled me, but when I repeated Dorothea's comment to Anneke, she merely laughed and said, "Only Dorothea would say such a thing."

"What do you mean?"

"Well, of course the coloreds can't rise in society. I don't condone slavery," she added with great haste, because she knew my views, "but we want to keep to ourselves just as they want to keep to themselves. Only Dorothea would look upon this as a crime."

I did not think Dorothea was thinking of parties and balls when she talked of elevating one's status, but rather of bettering oneself through hard work and education. The latter interested her far more than the former, as she attended few society gatherings, instead dedicating her spare hours to charity and the women's suffrage movement.

I must admit, the issue of women's suffrage sparked a passion within me as well, and as time passed, and I read more of the books and newspapers Dorothea shared, I became her equal in desire for the right to vote. I even endured sewing to learn more about the movement, because as the weather improved, Dorothea welcomed to her home numerous prominent speakers of the women's rights movement, acquaintances from back East. Invariably, since they could not drum up enough interest in our little village to fill a meeting hall, these women would speak at Dorothea's quilting circle.

One would suppose, perhaps, that a woman from a family of textile traders would have known of the art and craft of quilting, but I had never heard of it until emigrating to America. Dorothea and the other women of Creek's Crossing discussed their needlework with great interest and exchanged new patterns with delight. I could not muster up such enthusiasm, but even I could see the appeal in the cunning designs Dorothea and her fellow quilters created in patchwork, and I respected the frugality of not wasting a single hard-earned scrap of fabric. I will admit, however, that I gritted my teeth as Dorothea taught me to make my first quilt, and I accomplished little when I was meant to be piecing a Shoo-Fly block, but instead hung on every word of the speakers' passionate lectures on the Rights of Women.

Anneke did not attend the quilting bees, for as I said, she was not so fond of Dorothea as I, was embarrassed by her poor English, and thought politics unwomanly. Hans found Dorothea's ideas amusing and her visiting friends harmless—a view which, I must confess, annoyed me a great deal, though I suppose it was preferable to that of some of the townsmen, who forbade their wives to join Dorothea's sewing circle. However, I suspected some in Creek's Crossing objected not so much to Dorothea's position on women's suffrage as to the Nelsons' firm and unabashed Abolitionist views. While there were those in Creek's Crossing who silently agreed with them, far more felt that on the issue of colored people, objecting politely to slavery sufficed, but one needn't make such a fuss about it.

Every other week I attended Dorothea's sewing circle, where I forced myself to take up needle and thread so I could engage in enlightening discourse. I returned home glowing with visions of a future justice, but Anneke saw only the patchwork block in my hand, inattentively and reluctantly pieced. On one such evening, she took the Shoo-Fly block, smoothed it on her lap, and studied it, back and front. "Your hands were not meant to sew," said she mournfully, as if I would be grieved by the pronouncement. Then, to my astonishment, she asked if she might join me at the next meeting.

So Anneke and I began to attend the sewing circle together, I for the edification of my social conscience, Anneke for the lessons in patchwork. A gifted needlewoman, she took to the craft immediately and became Dorothea's most eager apprentice. Within weeks she had mastered setting in corners, sewing curved seams, and appliqué, and completed an entire sampler in the time it took me to finish a few haphazard Shoo-Fly blocks.

But I did not care. My days were full of hard work and the satisfaction of seeing Elm Creek Farm flourish with our labors; my evenings full of borrowed books and lectures and interesting people. Dorothea's guests included many whose activities would later make them famous—or infamous, some would say: Mrs. Sarah Grimké, Miss Susan B. Anthony, Mrs. Elizabeth Cady Stanton. Not all of our speakers were women—nor were their interests limited to suffrage. Frederick Douglass spent the night on his way from one speaking engagement in Philadelphia to another in Ohio, and other prominent figures such as William Lloyd Garrison, editor of the Boston Abolitionist newspaper *Liberator,* also graced the Nelson household. Nor were all of those in attendance women. The men did not deign to join us for sewing, of course, but they often appeared after our meetings and drew our guests aside for brandy or cider, the Nelsons being teetotalers.

A most frequent visitor was Jonathan Granger, Dorothea's younger brother, whose farm lay to the northeast of Creek's Crossing. He often found occasion to visit Dorothea and occasionally accompanied her to Elm Creek Farm. His somber, direct manner reminded me of his sister. Like Thomas, he did not believe woman's intellect inferior to man's, but spoke to me as if he expected an intelligent reply. Hans, for all his fine qualities, was not infallible in this regard, and I admit I found Jonathan's company refreshing.

At first, however, I had mistaken him for the postman.

From overheard conversations, I learned he traveled around the county quite a bit, and when he attended the gatherings at his sister's, he occasionally distributed letters to her guests. I wondered that someone with his keen mind had chosen to become a postman instead of attending university, but shrugged off my puzzlement, choosing instead to admire him for delivering the post as well as managing his father's small farm. Only after he was called away from a lecture on the troubles in Kansas to deliver Mrs. Craigmile's third child did I discover that he was the town's physician, and carried letters as a favor to his neighbors, who did not travel as much as he. I grew very red in the face, for thankfully I had been spared much embarrassment, as I had in my pocket a letter that I had planned to ask him to carry to Philadelphia. I suspect he might have done it and thought nothing of the request, as he was a generous, unassuming sort.

We spoke often, discussing philosophy or the politics of the day; Jonathan recommended books to me, and I to him. Through my discussions with him, as well as with Dorothea, I began to see how inextricably intertwined were the Rights of Women and the Rights of the Slave, simultaneous battles in the same war.

I write so much of our evenings one would think I was a woman of leisure and did nothing all day but read and anticipate conversations with engaging companions. That would be far from the truth, for never had I worked so hard as I did in those first few years in America. And not only for my brother's happiness was I glad for Anneke's presence, for I cannot imagine how we would have managed without her. Our work began before dawn, and although we never allowed ourselves an idle moment except on Sundays, we fell into bed at night having completed only the most necessary of our chores. Sometimes, I admit, exhaustion and the relentless flood of duties needing my attention threatened to overwhelm me, but something spurred me onward. Perhaps it was the knowledge that our neighbors had managed, proving that it could be done. Perhaps it was the fear of disappointing Hans and Anneke. All I know is that I persisted, undaunted, sustained by Hans's vision for Elm Creek Farm and those precious times with Dorothea and Jonathan.

By the end of our second summer in Pennsylvania, Hans had purchased two thoroughbreds, a mare and a stallion, thus fulfilling part of his promise to Anneke, that she would once again have horses as lovely as Castor and Pollux.

❧

"Those must have been the first Bergstrom Thoroughbreds," said Sarah. She had read the passage aloud as Sylvia worked on her latest project, an English paper pieced Tumbling Blocks quilt in homespun plaids. It was Sunday morning, in the last peaceful time they would enjoy together that week, the interval between breakfast and the arrival of the new group of quilt campers.

"I suppose so." Sylvia wondered that she did not feel more intrigued at the thought. Bergstrom Thoroughbreds, the business founded by Hans and Anneke—and Gerda, she added, amending the family history—had made the family's fortune. Later generations had sustained and expanded the business, but it had all been lost in Sylvia's time, when her sister, Claudia, and Claudia's husband had sold off the horses and parcels of land to pay the debts of their lavish lifestyle. Sylvia did not blame them alone. If she had not abandoned her family home, she would have continued to run Bergstrom Thoroughbreds. If the war had not claimed her husband and brother—and indirectly, her father and unborn daughter—she never would have left, and perhaps she would have passed the business to the next generation. But instead she had left it to her sister, knowing full well Claudia could not manage on her own, but too proud to return home and seek reconciliation, even to preserve Hans's and Anneke's legacy.

And Gerda's, she added silently, for based upon what Sarah had read, Sylvia could not believe that Gerda had left Elm Creek Manor to become a slave owner in the South. Perhaps she had left to marry Jonathan, but it sounded as if his farm was relatively near, certainly near enough that Gerda's strong will and temperament would have continued to influence the family. Sylvia had become certain that Gerda had been as instrumental as Hans and Anneke in shaping the Bergstroms' history.

"Gerda has never been given enough credit for what she contributed to this place," said Sylvia.

"Neither have you."

"You must be joking. Our campers would have you believe I laid each stone of Elm Creek Manor with my bare hands."

"Our campers give you plenty of credit, but you don't. You shoulder all the blame for the demise of Bergstrom Thoroughbreds, but you don't take enough credit for Elm Creek Quilts." Sarah gestured, indicating not only the sitting room but the entire manor. "Take a good look at this place. Think of what we've accomplished here."

"Our success has been your doing. Yours and Summer's and the other Elm Creek Quilters."

"You're the heart and soul of Elm Creek Quilts, and you know it," declared Sarah. "Or you ought to."

But I'm merely paying back a debt, Sylvia almost said. Her ancestors had created something great, and she had allowed it to be destroyed. She was merely trying to earn back what she had squandered. The burden had weighed heavily upon her heart for the more than fifty years she had been estranged from her sister, but although the success of Elm Creek Quilts had alleviated it a great deal, when she read in Gerda's own words how they had struggled to establish Elm Creek Farm, she felt her failures to her family anew.

Suddenly Sarah took her hand. "Come on."

"Where are we going?" asked Sylvia, as Sarah helped her to her feet and led her from the room.

Sarah guided her through the kitchen and out the back door. "We're going to find the cabin."

Sylvia laughed. "If the cabin were still around, I think I would have noticed it."

"There might be something left." Sarah tugged her arm to get her moving again. "Gerda said Hans built the barn twenty paces east of the cabin. So let's go to the barn and pace."

Despite her doubts, Sylvia felt a stirring of anticipation. The barn still stood, so perhaps something of the cabin remained after all. Of course, Hans, a far more able carpenter than the hapless Mr. L., had built the barn, and the structure had been carefully maintained. And yet . . .

She quickened her steps as she and Sarah crossed the bridge over Elm Creek.

Sylvia watched from the shade of the barn as Sarah measured off twenty paces west and carefully searched the ground. Since her steps had taken her to the edge of the well-worn dirt road, Sylvia was not surprised when, after a moment, Sarah rose and shook her head. She returned to the barn and tried again, heading off at a slightly different angle. Again she searched the ground, and once more she found nothing.

"Gerda describes herself as tall," said Sylvia. "Maybe you should lengthen your strides."

Intent on her task, Sarah nodded and tried again, stepping in exaggerated, long paces through the grass, leaving the barn from different places and varying her angles slightly, but always heading west. One attempt finally took her to a small rise at the edge of the orchard, and this time, when she stooped over to search the ground, she suddenly grew very still. "I think I've found something. It's wood."

"Likely it's just a tree root."

"No, I don't think so." Sarah scuffed the ground with her shoe, then looked up with wide eyes. "There's a log here, embedded in the ground."

"Trees look remarkably like logs," scoffed Sylvia, but she felt a tremor of excitement as she went to look for herself. Kneeling on the ground, Sarah pulled up clumps of dead grass and brushed aside dirt around what appeared to be a faint depression in the ground. At first Sylvia thought it was nothing more than darker soil, but as she drew closer, she perceived the fibrous splinters of what could only be wood and that the portion Sarah had uncovered lay in a nearly perfect straight line.

"My word," breathed Sylvia. She kneeled on the ground and gingerly began brushing aside decades' worth of accumulated soil. Sarah ran off to find some tools and returned with Matt and Andrew, carrying whisk brooms and trowels. Sylvia extrapolated a straight line extending in both directions from the exposed part of the log and directed her friends to positions along it. Quietly and quickly they worked, their eagerness to uncover the find tempered by wariness that they might damage whatever lay beneath.

"Look here," called out Andrew from his place at the end of the line. "I think I've reached a corner."

The others hurried over. Andrew had indeed reached a place where the first wood line ended and another commenced at a slightly obtuse angle. As Matt helped Andrew dig around the bend, Sylvia saw to her amazement that there the direction of the wood grains varied, first tending horizontal, then vertical.

"The pieces dovetail," said Matt, and then Sylvia could envision perfectly the corner of a cabin, perpendicular logs interlocking.

They had found it. The cabin where Hans, Anneke, and Gerda had first lived, the place where they had dreamed and planned and built their legacy, lay within arm's reach. She could touch the very walls that had first sheltered them.

Chapter Four

S ylvia grudgingly acquiesced when Matt suggested they break off their excavation until they could consult a specialist who would help them preserve their find. If not for the concern that she might ruin what remained of the cabin, she almost thought she could dig it up with her fingernails, so exhilarated was she by their discovery. Somehow the cabin made Gerda's story real in a way her words had not. It was proof, something tangible, that made the memoir ring true.

In their excitement, they had lost track of the time. The morning had waned, and the sun shone almost directly overhead. Sarah raced off to shower and change before the new quilt campers arrived while Matt gathered their tools. Sylvia was perspiring and out of breath from excitement and labor, but she tried to hide her fatigue as she and Andrew returned to the manor, knowing Andrew would worry if he thought she had overexerted herself.

By the time she had tidied herself, the other Elm Creek Quilters had arrived and were preparing for registration. Summer and her mother, Gwen, a stout woman with hair the exact shade of auburn as her daughter's, were placing chairs behind a long table to one side of the manor's elegant foyer. Gwen was a professor at Waterford College, as was Judy, who was arranging forms on the table with the help of Bonnie, the owner of Grandma's Attic. Diane, a strikingly pretty blonde who, along with Summer, occasionally assisted Bonnie at the quilt shop, had just entered with Agnes on her arm. As much as she delighted in all her friends, Sylvia's heart warmed most at the sight of Agnes, the closest thing to an actual relative Sylvia supposed she had. Long ago, Agnes had married Sylvia's younger brother, and long ago both women had been made war widows on the same day. Friendly fire, the officials called it, the senseless accident that had taken their husbands' lives on a remote Pacific island. The euphemism, meant to protect them, hurt worse than the truth, for it mocked their grief.

How Sylvia regretted that she and Agnes had not come together in their mourning and made the burdens of their grief lighter by sharing their losses. Instead Sylvia had fled Elm Creek Manor, unable to live there haunted by memories. She had returned home only after the death of her estranged sister, Claudia, but at least she and Agnes had forgiven each other—more than that, they had become friends. Still, as much as this consoled Sylvia, whenever she thought of Claudia, she tasted the bitterness of reconciliation sought too late.

With a sigh, Sylvia pushed aside her regrets. She could not change the past. She could only make her future as happy and worthwhile as possible. That was how to best honor those she loved and had lost.

She honored them a great deal, she thought, on Sundays when quilt camp was in session, when she and the other Elm Creek Quilters opened the manor to their guests. Sarah rushed downstairs, her hair still slightly damp, just as the first campers arrived. Soon the foyer was so full of activity that Sylvia hardly had a moment to catch her breath, much less share the discovery of the cabin with her friends. She and Diane shared the task of distributing the class schedules, a job that always involved last-minute adjustments as campers decided their interests had changed or requested a switch so they could be with people they already knew. Sylvia was reluctant to make changes for the latter reason, for one of the most important points of camp was to make new friends, and how could they if they went around in little cliques? Honestly. But since she wanted her guests to be happy, and being comfortable accomplished that for most of them, she adjusted their schedules. The evening programs would get them mixing properly.

The flood of new arrivals eventually slowed to a trickle, then ceased. It was time to clear away the registration tables and prepare for the welcome banquet. As Sarah went off to supervise the kitchen and banquet hall, Sylvia was finally able to share the news. Her friends' surprise and delight rekindled her eagerness to excavate the cabin, but she remembered Matt's warning and promised herself she would get the job done in due time with the proper supervision.

Gwen offered to contact a professor of archaeology she knew at Penn State, explaining that she knew of no one at Waterford College with the expertise they needed. Sylvia thanked her and wished she and Andrew weren't leaving first thing in the morning. But Andrew was itching to get on the road again, and she could not ask him to withdraw from the trout fishing competition he had entered, not when he was the defending champion in his age group. Besides, she had scheduled two speaking engagements for the return trip.

Sylvia could hardly swallow a bite of the delicious meal served at the welcome banquet, so distracted was she by thoughts of the cabin. When she glanced out the window and fretted aloud about the likelihood of rain, Matt assured her he had covered up the logs with a tarp, adding, "That should do until we hear from Gwen's expert."

"The cabin's lasted this long," said Sarah to Sylvia, with a teasing smile. "It will last through the night."

"It's the next night and the next that concern me," retorted Sylvia. "I won't be here to keep an eye on it."

"We'll be here," said Matt.

"Yes, but who's going to keep an eye on you?"

Matt clasped a hand to his chest and winced as if she had wounded him. "I'm the caretaker," he said with an exaggerated woe that provoked laughter from the others at the table. "I'll take care of it."

"But it's my responsibility. I can't let anything happen to it."

Sarah remarked, "You say that as if you wish we hadn't found it."

Sylvia found herself speechless. "Don't be ridiculous," she managed at last, and was glad when Andrew quickly changed the subject. How close were Sarah's words to the truth? Sylvia was pleased they had found the cabin; the thrill of its discovery nearly had her racing outside just to be sure she had not imagined it. Still, she worried and wondered if they should have left the log alone as soon as Sarah uncovered the first portion. She couldn't bear destroying yet another part of the Bergstrom legacy, not when so much had fallen into ruin on her watch.

After the banquet, she returned to her room to pack, but she was so accustomed to filling her suitcase that she quickly finished. As twilight fell, she knew she ought to go to bed—Andrew wanted to get an early start the next day—but she decided to attend the welcome ceremony instead. It seemed appropriate to visit the cornerstone patio on the same day she had discovered an even earlier foundation of the Bergstrom family at Elm Creek.

The quilt campers had already finished their dessert and had gathered in a circle on the gray stone patio when Sylvia arrived, but they eagerly made room for one more chair. The murmur of excited voices hushed as Sarah rose and lit a candle in a crystal holder.

"At Elm Creek Quilt Camp, we always conclude the first evening with a ceremony we call Candlelight," said Sarah, meeting the eyes of each camper from her place in the center of the circle.

Sylvia smiled, remembering how nervous Sarah had been the first time she took a turn leading the Candlelight. Now Sarah spoke with serene confidence, her voice somehow both comforting and inspiring.

"Elm Creek Manor is full of memories," continued Sarah, with a look that told Sylvia the younger woman intended a special meaning for her. "Some we know well, but others, like the memories you will make here this week, have yet to be discovered. The Elm Creek Quilters are enriched by your experiences here, and we thank you for sharing your stories with us."

As Sarah explained the ceremony, Sylvia sensed the quilters' conflicted emotions. The campers would pass the candle around the circle, and one by one, each woman would hold the candle and explain why she had come to Elm Creek Quilt Camp and what she hoped to gain from the experience. They had been asked to bare their hearts to people they hardly knew. Some of the women around the circle, Sylvia knew, would not be entirely honest; some would choose to keep their secrets, as was their right. But those who shared the truth, those who were *ready* to share the truth, would find themselves accepted and affirmed more than they could have imagined possible. This was what Sylvia had learned after so many Candlelight ceremonies, that the truth, however painful, though sometimes hard to say and difficult to hear, had to come out.

Suddenly she was struck by the realization that this, surely, was how Gerda had felt, bearing the weight of the family history alone, determined to see that the heirs to the Bergstrom legacy should know more than just a partial truth about themselves and their origins. No matter how difficult those truths were for Sylvia to learn, she owed it to Gerda to read with an open heart, as accepting and nonjudgmental as the women who now sat around the circle, their faces illuminated by a single candle.

And, finally, as the women around her shared their secrets, she admitted to herself what she was too proud to say aloud: She feared herself inadequate to the responsibilities Gerda demanded of her. She who had always prided herself on her strength now doubted the one quality that had always sustained her. But Great-Aunt Lucinda had trusted her, even though Sylvia had been only a small child when Lucinda gave her the key to the hope chest. In her way, too, Gerda had trusted her, by having faith that a future descendant to whom she could confide her secrets would one day find the memoir. If Lucinda and Gerda both had found Sylvia a worthwhile heir, Sylvia would not fail them.

Besides, she had no choice. There was no one else. For good or ill, these heirlooms belonged to the Bergstroms, and she was the last remaining.

✒ Autumn 1857—in which we have unexpected visitors

Our first harvest season arrived, and though we would reap but a modest bounty, we were exceedingly proud of our first efforts in farming. The corn had done well, and by Hans's estimation we would have plenty of hay and oats to see our stable of horses through the winter. My garden had thrived, and I worked long days putting up stores and selling what I could in town. I had an agreement with the owner of the general store Hans had first visited upon our arrival in Creek's Crossing: He would display my wares in exchange for a share of the profits. He sometimes chose to take my wild raspberry jam instead of money, but that suited me fine.

Anneke had not forgotten her original scheme to open a seamstress shop, and I believe she envied me my mercantile success, modest though it was. When we were in town together, I spied her gazing wistfully at the rows of storefronts; once she remarked in an offhand manner that extra income would permit Hans to obtain more horses without hurting our efforts to economize. Silently I agreed that any money Anneke might earn would not go to waste in our household, but I did not see how she could afford to bring in outside sewing when we had so much work to do already. As for opening a shop, Hans had neither the capital nor, I fear, the inclination to help his wife find employment outside the home. He never said so aloud, but I suspect he wanted every cent of his dream to be funded by his own efforts. My earnings were acceptable, since I was a spinster sister and ought to contribute to my keep. It was another matter entirely to send his own wife out to work.

Jonathan and I discussed this, and he agreed that I would not be interfering too much if I tried, discreetly, to encourage my brother to put Anneke's wishes ahead of his pride. Sometimes I would bring to Hans's attention the other women of Creek's Crossing who helped support their households:

"Mrs. Barrows runs the inn on First Street," said I.

"Only because Mr. Barrows is a shiftless lout."

And another day: "I hear Miss Thatcher and Miss Bauer run the school exceptionally well."

"As soon as they get married, they'll have their own children to look after."

And yet another occasion: "Mrs. Engle may expand her dressmaking shop, or so I hear."

Too late I realized Mrs. Engle was the worst possible example I could have mentioned. Not only did Hans remark that it was a shame that Mr. Engle had died without leaving her better off, because a widow with three young children and a grown son should not have to work so hard, but he also pointed out that a town the size of Creek's Crossing hardly needed yet another seamstress, now, did it, and wasn't it fortunate that Anneke would not feel obligated to provide that service to the community?

How fortunate, indeed.

"Anneke should just tell Hans she wants to open her shop," Jonathan told me.

But that was not Anneke's way. She demonstrated exceptional talent in subtle remarks and sidelong glances that conveyed deeper meaning than the words themselves contained, tools she used to bring Hans around to her way of thinking more successfully in other matters. I, as ungraceful in speech as I was in dancing and sewing and all other pursuits feminine (save cookery, in which I excelled), was the one for straightforward, blunt statements. But as I told Jonathan, Hans was as stubborn as his sister, and if he did not wish his wife to work in town, she would not.

They had been married not even a year, and already this pattern, which was to last throughout their married life, was well established. Watching them, I wondered what sort of husband E. would have been to me. Would he have expected me to submit to him in everything, obey him in everything? I could not have borne that yoke, not even for love. This was what I told myself when I remembered E., and when I saw how happy Anneke and Hans were together, and Dorothea and Thomas.

In the middle of harvesttime, an unfamiliar wagon came to Elm Creek Farm. I recognized the driver, a slight, sour-faced man with greasy blond hair and tobacco-stained teeth who worked odd jobs on the waterfront. Hans was in the fields, and the mistress of the house, embarrassed by her poor English, hid inside as always, so I greeted him.

He looked me over suspiciously before speaking. "This the Bergstrom farm?"

I assured him it was. "Do you have a delivery for us?"

"I'm supposed to give this to the Bergstroms at Elm Creek Farm."

"I am Gerda Bergstrom, and this is Elm Creek Farm," said I, with some impatience, because the large wooden crate in the wagon behind him had captured my interest.

"That's what I don't understand." He studied me with sullen belligerence. "I thought this here's the L. place."

I had not heard the name of Mr. L. in so long that the remark caught me off guard. "Indeed, Elm Creek Farm did once belong to Mr. L.," stammered I, "but it has since passed to my family."

"Passed how?"

I was suddenly conscious of Hans's absence. "Quite legally, I assure you. My brother has the deed, if you require proof."

"I'm only askin' because . . ." He shrugged. "L. still has friends in these parts. They might not like it if they thought you 'uns took his farm out from under him."

"Certainly not," said I primly. "Though I must say, they must not be especially good friends if they have not missed Mr. L. before now. If there's nothing else—" I made as if to retrieve the large crate myself.

"I'll get it," grumbled he, setting the reins aside and climbing down from his seat. With great effort, he lifted the crate from the wagon, but rather than carry it into the cabin, he left it on the ground beside the front door. I paid him and gave him my thanks, but without another word, he drove away, casting one sullen backward glance over his shoulder before disappearing into the forest.

Anneke immediately joined me outside. "What did he want?"

"Only to deliver this," said I lightly, not wishing to worry her, and then excitement drove the surly man from my thoughts, for upon examining the crate, I discovered it had been sent from Baden-Baden. Anneke ran off to tell Hans, and they quickly returned, Hans bearing his tools. He brought the crate indoors and pried off the lid, and Anneke cried out with delight, for inside, tightly packed, were bolts of fabric—velvets and wools, even silks—as fine as anything I had ever seen in Father's warehouse.

There were letters, too, for all of us. Mother's to Anneke welcomed her into the family and informed her the fabrics were a wedding gift. Father's to Hans congratulated him on taking a bride and expressed hopes that Hans would be able to obtain a good price for the fabrics. Father's letter to me cautioned me to be sure my younger brother invested the profits into Elm Creek Farm rather than squandering them unwisely. Mother's to me was full of news of home; she provided the latest gossip on all of my acquaintances, except, of course, for E., who became the more conspicuous for his absence.

Our siblings had written as well, and as I hungrily read their letters, Anneke knelt on the floor and withdrew the fabrics from the crate, delighting anew with each bolt. Suddenly she looked up at me, stricken. "Oh, my dear Gerda. I'm so sorry."

"Whatever for?"

"Your parents sent me all these nice things, but they sent you nothing."

I indicated the pages in my hands. "They sent me letters."

"Yes, of course, but . . ." She hesitated. "Don't you feel slighted?"

Until that moment, I had not. "Of course not," said I, thinking a crate so large surely could have accommodated a small book or two.

Anneke forced a smile. "Likely when you marry, they will send an even finer gift."

Hans guffawed. "Likely they will, once they recover from their shock."

I poked Hans in the ribs as if we were children again and laughed with him, but Anneke merely shook her head at us, astounded and scandalized that we would treat my spinsterhood with such an inappropriate lack of shame.

"This is really a gift to us all," added Hans, in a nod to Anneke's concern for my feelings. "With what we can earn from the fabric, I can buy another two horses, and next spring, I can build us a real house."

Anneke rewarded him with a smile, but she ran her hand lovingly over each bolt as she returned it to the crate, and I could not help thinking that she would prefer to keep the fabric for herself, to create clothing for the townsfolk of Creek's Crossing in a shop of her own and piece quilts from the scraps.

But I soon forgot Anneke's thwarted ambitions as the most arduous labor of the harvest set in. By sharing work with Thomas, Jonathan, and other neighbors, Hans soon had our crops in, and they theirs. Elm Creek Farm had provided only enough to see us through the winter, and not a surplus to sell in town, as Hans had hoped, but at least we would not have to rely on the generosity of friends as we had the previous year.

Creek's Crossing was an industrious community, so our more experienced neighbors had fared even better than we neophytes on Elm Creek Farm. Everyone seemed content and satisfied, eagerly anticipating the Harvest Dance in mid-November, where, Dorothea said with a gentle smile, the women would wear their finest dresses and bring their tastiest recipes, which they would disparage until one would think they had worn rags and served slop, while the men would exaggerate the yield of their crops and the quality of their livestock until one was convinced the farmers of Creek's Crossing alone could provide for the entire Commonwealth of Pennsylvania. I, too, looked forward to the Harvest Dance, for Jonathan had danced with me at the previous year's celebration, and I was hopeful he would be my partner in even more dances this year.

Anneke, who was interested in finding me a more lasting partner, offered to make me a dress, in which, she said, I would dazzle the eye of all who saw me.

Scoffed I, "And after the dance, I'll wear it to dazzle the eye of the cow and the chickens?"

"You'll set it aside for special occasions." Her gaze went to the crate of fabrics, tucked away in a corner of the cabin until Hans could determine how to best sell them. "There's a lovely blue silk that will be very becoming to your eyes."

I laughed at the thought of scattering chicken feed clad in silk, but when she insisted, I said that if she must make me a dress, let it be a sturdy calico I could wear new to the Harvest Dance, and later as I did my chores. She grew impatient and pointed out that she knew much more about sewing than I did, and if I didn't want her lecturing me on politics or on the proper pronunciation of English words, I should not attempt to instruct her in dressmaking. Then her eyes took on a steely glint I had never before seen there, and have seen only rarely since. "Let me show you how to best dispose of your parents' gifts," said she. "Let me show you what I can do when permitted to follow my own judgment."

I knew it was not I she intended to impress. "What will Hans think of you cutting up a bolt of fabric? Won't he see it as the loss of at least the mane of a horse, or a wall of the new house?"

"Didn't your mother's letter say the fabric was a gift to me?"

So dumbfounded was I by her unexpected determination that I had no choice but to submit, especially as I suspected she had an underlying purpose. I will also admit that although I knew what obstacles my plainness presented to even the finest seamstress, I found Anneke's promises that she would make me look handsome dubious but perhaps not entirely outside the realm of possibility, because she was, after all, exceptionally talented with a needle.

One morning, a week before the dance, we rose early and raced through our morning chores so we could get to work on the dress as soon as Hans left to care for the horses. Thus I was standing in my corset as Anneke fit the bodice when a knock sounded on the cabin door.

"L.?" a gruff voice called from outside. "You there?"

Wide-eyed, Anneke scurried off to the other room, leaving me in my corset to welcome our visitor. I snatched up my calico work dress and threw it on over the pinned silk bodice, wincing as a pin found flesh. "Good morning," said I, pulling open the door, breathless.

Two men with rifles stood before me, one regarding me with his mouth in a grim line, the other taking in the exterior of our altered cabin with bemusement. Two weary horses nibbled at the thin shoots of grass behind them.

"I'm looking for L.," said the first man.

"He no longer lives here," said I. "I'm afraid I don't know where he is."

The second man gave me a hard look. "We hear tell you 'uns stole his farm."

I drew myself up, hoping he would not detect my nervousness. "You heard incorrectly."

At the sound of my accent, the second man nudged the first. "Dutch," spat he, in a most disparaging tone.

"We don't mind you Dutch," said the first man, addressing me, but speaking as if to remind his companion. "Not as much as some. Your man around?"

"My brother is in the barn." *Without his rifle,* I thought, feeling a pang of fear.

"We'll go talk to him there." The first man tugged at the brim of his slouch hat. His companion merely scratched his dark beard and glowered. As they turned to go, I saw over their shoulders that Hans was hurrying toward us from the barn. To my relief, Jonathan was at his side. He must have arrived only moments before the two men, as he had not yet come to the cabin to greet me.

"What brings you gentlemen to Elm Creek Farm?" Hans called out, with an easy smile.

The two men exchanged a look, then the first one said, "We're looking for a n——."

Someone else would have said "Negro" or "colored man." I have seen the injury caused by the word he did use, and I will not repeat it here.

"A runaway n——," added the second man.

Jonathan winced slightly at the word, but Hans's expression did not change. He merely shrugged and said, "Everyone at Elm Creek Farm stands before you, except my wife."

"He might be hiding in your barn." The second man took one step toward it before Hans put out an arm to stop him.

"I just came from there," said he, with that same easy smile. "There's no one hiding in my barn."

The first man said, "We might do well to check for ourselves."

"You might, if I were not a man of my word." Hans looked up at them steadily. "Is that your meaning?"

The second man swore impatiently, but the first man held Hans's gaze. "You're new to this country, and maybe you don't know the law. This may be a Free State, but anyone helping a n—— escape is breaking the law."

"We know the law," said Jonathan.

I prayed he would not choose this moment to distinguish for our visitors, as he had many a time at Dorothea's sewing circle, the difference between a just law, which ought to be obeyed, and an unjust law, which by a just man must be broken.

The second man squinted at Jonathan. "Ain't I seen you at the Nelson place?"

"Very likely you have, as Mrs. Nelson is my sister."

The second man spat on the ground and muttered to his companion, "G—— Abolitionists."

Jonathan stiffened, but restrained himself without need of the hand Hans placed on his shoulder. "That's no way to talk about a man's family," Hans said, and he held the second man in a gaze so firm that the man eventually looked away and muttered something resembling an apology.

The first man turned around in a slow circle, scanning the clearing surrounding our cabin. Suddenly he asked, "What happened to L.?"

"L. sold me Elm Creek Farm more than a year ago."

"We haven't been through these parts in some time," said the first man. He broke off scanning the horizon and, after an inscrutable glance at Jonathan, smiled at Hans in a friendly manner. "L. might have been a Yankee, but he was not unsympathetic to our employers. We could always count on him for a hot meal and a bed on the floor near the fire."

I felt myself balling my dress in my fists, and I forced myself to remain calm. Perhaps Elm Creek Farm had once extended its hospitality to slave catchers, but no more!

I was just about to declare the same when Hans said, "I'll have my wife fix you some eggs."

"Hans," I exclaimed, and Jonathan shot him a look of stunned amazement.

"Sister," said Hans in a level voice, "tell Anneke to fix these gentlemen some breakfast while they feed and water their horses."

I opened my mouth to protest, but when Jonathan gave his head the barest of shakes, I swallowed back my words and went inside. My thoughts were in turmoil as I delivered Hans's instructions. Anneke nodded wordlessly and obeyed, while I went to the window and watched as the slave catchers headed to the creek while Hans and Jonathan returned to the barn. I could not bear to witness the hay and oats we had harvested for our own horses going to feed those of slave catchers, so, fuming, I took off my dress and unpinned the blue silk bodice of my dancing gown, and flung the pieces onto Anneke's sewing machine.

"Don't be angry with me," Anneke said from the fireplace as I dressed. "Be thankful he didn't ask *you* to cook for them."

That was the first I realized he had not, which was unusual, since I did almost all the cooking for the family. But if Hans thought it would be enough for me that my own hands were unsullied, he was mistaken.

None too soon the men finished their meal and left, shaking Hans's hand and tugging their hats at me and Anneke. As soon as they were gone, I burst out, "Hans, how could you?"

"I could hardly feed their horses but not them, now could I?"

"Yes, you surely could have. Slave catchers are the lowest of men, and you have given them sustenance necessary to continue their pursuit. Better to send them away hungry, too weak and distracted to find this unfortunate slave."

"If they did not eat here, they would eat at another farm. Best not to make enemies of them."

Jonathan made a noise of disagreement, and I, disbelieving Hans could mean what he said, asked, "Do you want them to believe you're a friend to their cause?"

"I couldn't send those horses away before giving them a rest." Hans dropped onto a bench beside the fireplace. "They've been running them too hard. If they keep up that pace, I don't see how they'll survive the return journey. That's a long way to travel on horseback."

"That's a long way to travel on foot," said Jonathan, referring to their quarry. "Especially in this season. The nights are cold, colder still for a man hunted in a strange land."

"Likely he's found shelter along the way."

"More likely than not, he hasn't."

"If he's made it this far, he must be made of sterner stuff than you and I," said Hans, mustering up a grin. "I must say, his owner must sorely miss him to pursue him so far."

"Never underestimate the extent or the strength of a man's greed, especially when his pride is insulted."

Now Hans laughed. "You sound more like the minister every day."

"But Hans—"

Hans's smile vanished. "I will not be drawn into an argument."

"Into this argument," said Jonathan, "willing or not, we will all eventually be drawn."

As the entire nation would soon discover, he was correct.

❧

Whenever she could spare time from Elm Creek Quilts and Grandma's Attic, Summer returned to the Waterford Historical Society's archives to pore over the maps and page through bound volumes of city resolutions and legal affairs.

One particularly fruitful visit had turned up two intriguing maps of the county. The first, dated 1858, identified the town as Creek's Crossing, but unlike the Creek's Crossing map from 1847 that Summer had found during her first library search, labels identified Elm Creek Farm as well as the farms of other families. A map from 1864, however, called the town Water's Ford, but it was clearly the same region as the one depicted on the first map, with the additional development not unexpected after a six-year interval. Although a dashed line still indicated the town boundaries, Elm Creek Farm was shaded to suggest that it lay outside the border proper. Furthermore, while other farms were labeled by name as before, Elm Creek Farm was not.

It looked to Summer as if someone wanted to pretend Elm Creek Farm did not exist.

On a later visit, with the date of the name change more narrowly defined, Summer had turned to the town government records. In the volume from 1860, she finally found an official proclamation renaming the town, but although the document cited the need to "restore dignity to the village and its people," it provided no specific reasons.

The town's name appeared as Water's Ford in every source from the decade that followed, but gradually Waterford came into greater use. Since Summer found no official proclamation noting the change, she surmised that Waterford was a corruption of Water's Ford. The archives became somewhat muddled after Waterford was used exclusively, since another town in Pennsylvania shared the name and some of the documents from it had been filed among those of the former Creek's Crossing.

After Sylvia told her friends about the Bergstrom's encounter with the slave catchers, Summer decided to extend her search to local newspapers published in Gerda's time. Even though the town proclamation had not provided any details, surely a scandal shameful enough to make them change the name of the town would have appeared in the Creek's Crossing newspaper.

After hours of studying microfiche, Summer remained convinced that some long-ago reporter would have broken the scandal in the paper, but to her dismay, she could not say for certain.

The archives of the *Creek's Crossing Informer* ended in mid-1859. When they resumed in 1861, the paper was called the *Water's Ford Register*.

Summer was no cynic, but she found it difficult to believe the paper wasn't published during the exact period something significant had occurred in the city.

She would have bet her entire fabric stash that either the Waterford Historical Society wasn't interested in preserving the newspapers from those years or someone had made sure no copies would remain to be preserved.

❧❧

"How delightful," said Sylvia dryly when Summer told her what she had learned. As if it weren't bad enough that Hans had obtained the farm through less than honorable means, now it appeared that the Bergstroms had done something so scandalous that the town had had to change its name to divert the shame of it. "My family certainly made their mark on this town, didn't they?"

"We don't know for a fact that your ancestors were involved," said Summer. "It might just be coincidence."

Sylvia took off her glasses and rubbed her eyes. "Nonsense. On the map of Creek's Crossing, Elm Creek Farm appears, but on the map of Water's Ford, it's been all but expunged. Gerda herself writes of a scandal, and you call it coincidence?"

"Well . . ." Summer hesitated. "Until we have more proof . . ."

The poor girl looked as if she wished she had not told Sylvia what she had uncovered. "Now, dear." Sylvia patted her hand. "You mustn't worry about sparing my feelings. I have already come to terms with the fact that my ancestors were not the sterling characters I thought them to be."

"Maybe, but aren't they much more interesting this way?"

"Yes, I suppose they are." They were much more real, too, more like people Sylvia would enjoy chatting with than the remote figures from the family stories.

Still, the more she pondered Gerda's cryptic asides, the more she suspected there might be parts of her family history she would not wish to divulge, not even to her closest friends.

Chapter Five

❦ *November 1857 — the Harvest Dance*

I never learned whether the two slave catchers found the man they pursued, but they did not return to Elm Creek Farm. I prayed often for this unknown, unfortunate man, and was encouraged by Jonathan's assurances that the longer he remained free, the greater his chances of escaping to Canada.

When I first came to Pennsylvania, I assumed that it and all Free States were havens for the escaped bondsman, and that once a runaway crossed the border into the North, he could not be compelled to return to his former masters. That was, sadly, not true. In 1850, as part of a compromise meant to placate Southern states angered by measures to check the spread of slavery elsewhere in the growing nation, Congress passed the Fugitive Slave Law. It proclaimed that runaways, even those who managed to reach Free States, must be returned to their owners, and that federal and state officials and even private citizens must assist in their recapture. Moreover, anyone—freeman or fugitive—suspected of being a runaway slave could be arrested without a warrant and, once apprehended, could neither request a jury trial nor testify on his own behalf.

This Jonathan told me, indignantly adding, "I cannot and will not submit to any law that compels me to act against the dictates of my conscience and my God."

I admired him for his convictions, for his sentiments were the same as my own. In comparison, Hans's reluctance to risk offending the two slave catchers troubled me. If the fugitive had been hiding in our barn that day, would

Hans have delivered him into the hands of his pursuers? I did not wish to believe this of my brother, and I disliked that my admiration and faith in him had been so shaken.

Anneke, of course, believed that Hans had acted appropriately. They were a good match, I suppose, as neither would believe any evil of the other. She refused to discuss the matter with me, both out of loyalty to her husband and from her exasperation that I did not understand that citizens, especially immigrants, must obey the laws of the land—all laws, not merely those that suited one's own tastes. I, in turn, could not abide her blindness to one's moral obligation to disobey unjust laws. Anneke responded, "You would not say such a thing except to please Jonathan."

This flustered me a great deal, so much that I refused to speak to Anneke for the rest of the day, which suited her fine as she was not interested in conversing with someone who would criticize her husband. But by the next morning we were speaking again, more from necessity than choice, as it was impossible to avoid each other in our two-room house. It was Anneke who broke our silence, by offering to finish the task the two slave catchers had interrupted. I accepted her offer gratefully, and by noontime, she had finished the bodice of my new dress. The entire gown was complete the morning of the dance.

"You look enchanting," declared Anneke, and I heartily wished I could believe her.

Saturday dawned cool and crisp, and we completed our chores with glad hearts, looking forward to the evening's festivities. I baked two pies, one of apples Dorothea had shared with us from their trees, one of wild blueberries I had discovered growing near the creek, and I also made potato pancakes with soured cream. I did not know what our neighbors would think of the latter, but since numerous other families of German descent inhabited the town, I suspected few would remain on the platter, if only accounting for Hans's appetite.

We rode into town on the wagon pulled by two of Hans's horses— "Bergstrom Thoroughbreds," he liked to call them—to find the streets of Creek's Crossing full of other families, laughing and calling greetings to one another. We met Dorothea and Thomas at the grassy square in front of the City Hall, where already the picnic had begun. Four tables had been arranged in a long row to one side of the square, and the women of the town had covered them with all manner of mouthwatering dishes, to which I added my contributions. We filled our plates and set out quilts to sit upon. I was careful not to muss my blue silk dress, in which, I admit, I felt rather fair for a plain girl, and as we ate, I searched the crowd for Jonathan, disappointed that he did not join us. After Anneke's remark about how I sought to please him, however, I could not bring myself to ask Dorothea where he was, not within Anneke's hearing.

The dancing was well under way when Jonathan finally appeared. He told me I looked lovely, which, to my embarrassment, made me blush. I quickly replied, "It is the dress. Anneke has skill with a needle I will never know."

Too late, Anneke shot me a look of warning. Hans's eyebrows rose, and Anneke quickly took his arm. "Come, Hans. Dance with me."

He accompanied her without argument, but I knew from his expression that he had deduced where the fabric for my dress had come from. As Dorothea admired Anneke's handiwork, I watched my brother and his wife as they joined the line for the next dance, and was relieved to see that Hans did not seem angry.

Dorothea was not the only one to admire my dress, and I took every opportunity to sing my sister-in-law's praises, but never more so than when Mrs. Violet Pearson Engle, the dressmaker, passed by our quilt on the way for another serving of cake. She asked me to rise so she might better examine the drape of the skirt. "Fine silk," she announced as she had me turn around before her. "And the handiwork is finer still."

I knew Anneke would delight in the compliment, and wished that Jonathan would escort me to the dance so I might whisper it to her in passing, but as one song ended and the musicians called for another, Jonathan extended his hand to his sister instead. At the conclusion of that dance, Hans and Anneke returned to our quilt breathless and laughing, and since I would no longer be left there alone, Thomas left to claim his wife's hand from her brother. Jonathan did not return as I expected, and as the music resumed, I spied him whirling about with a bright-eyed, dark-haired young woman I had never met. Once more he danced with her, to my growing consternation—and then, to my astonishment, Cyrus Pearson approached and asked me to be his partner.

I did not wish to dance with him, but I could not refuse without good reason, so I gave him my hand and allowed him to escort me to the dance. He was a fine dancer, much better than I, but his lead was strong and confident enough that I managed to avoid treading on his feet. Rather than strike up a

conversation with me, he directed his attention to his friends, who exchanged greetings and jokes in passing. I had no objection to this, for it was
a complicated dance that required my full attention, and moreover I could
not think of any particular subject I wished to discuss with him. He seemed
satisfied that I smiled at his silly jokes.

I thought I was faring rather well, until he said, "You are accomplished in
so many things. I had expected dancing to be one of them."

"I'm sorry to disappoint you," said I shortly. I had at that moment spotted
Jonathan partnered for yet another dance with the pretty dark-haired girl.

"I would not call it disappointment, merely surprise," said he. "Perhaps in
your youth you should have been practicing your dancing instead of sharp-
ening your wit."

I halted at once and released his hand. "Perhaps you should have been
practicing your manners." I meant to leave him there in the middle of the
dance, but my grand gesture was spoiled by the musicians, who chose that
moment to end their song.

I marched back to our quilt, fuming and wishing I had stayed home,
when suddenly Jonathan appeared before me. "Are you free for this dance?"

"Oh, she's free," drawled Mr. Pearson, behind me. "Good luck, Doctor."

Jonathan watched him as he brushed by us, and then looked question-
ingly at me. Embarrassed, I took his arm and urged him toward the dance
floor before he could ask me to explain.

In Baden-Baden I had learned to be amusing on the dance floor since I
could not be graceful, and what I lacked in comeliness, I believe I more than
made up for in wit. Jonathan seemed to enjoy himself well enough in my
company; he smiled much more with me than with his previous partner, and
I made him laugh out loud where the dark-haired girl had only made him
smile. And yet, after two dances with me, he escorted me back to the quilt
and requested a dance with Anneke, followed by one with his sister, and
then the dark-haired girl was on his arm again.

"Her name is Charlotte Claverton," murmured Anneke as I watched them
dance.

I had thought my observation discreet, and so Anneke's awareness of my
interest bothered me. "Is it," said I, feigning indifference, but glad that Anneke had, in my absence, apparently asked the questions I could not.

"Her family's farm lies adjacent to the farm of Jonathan's and Dorothea's
parents. He has known Charlotte all her life."

"We must endeavor to make her acquaintance, then," said I. "I would surely like any friend of Dorothea's."

"I did not tell you this so that you might become her friend," said Anneke. "I told you so you would not worry. If he has known her all his life, surely if he meant to marry her, he would have asked her by now."

My hopes, which until that day I had been unwilling to admit even to myself, rose. I nodded, unable to find words in my relief. Anneke smiled reassuringly, and just then, I caught Dorothea's eye. She smiled her serene smile and resumed conversing with Thomas, but I wondered how much she had overheard.

As afternoon turned into evening, I danced again with Jonathan, and with my brother, but I was happiest with Jonathan. Other men invited me to dance, too, but it was not until later that I realized I had been quite a popular partner that night. I would have enjoyed myself enormously if I had noticed, and if I had not been acutely aware that Jonathan seemed to be at Charlotte's side at least as often as mine.

The hour grew late, and one by one, the families from the most distant farms began to depart. At last Charlotte rode off in a wagon with her father and mother, and only then did Jonathan remain with me. He was an attentive and courteous escort, and so I repeated Anneke's reassurances to myself and tried to forget young Charlotte with her shining dark hair and graceful figure.

Not long after Charlotte's departure, the Nelsons bid us good night. Jonathan walked with Hans, Anneke, and me to our wagon before heading for his own home. Anneke gave me a look that implied this was of great significance, but I had to wonder if he would have helped me into our wagon if Charlotte had remained, or if he would have assisted her instead.

On the drive home, Anneke deliberately avoided Hans's eye and said to me, "I overheard many compliments of your dress."

I was ashamed that in my distraction with Jonathan I had forgotten my sister-in-law's problem. "I have you and your skill with the needle to thank," replied I.

"And our parents," remarked Hans. "Don't forget, they provided the fabric for that fine dress. Fabric I intended to sell in town to pay for our new house."

There was only a mild rebuke in his words, so I quickly added, "Mrs. Engle, especially, admired your sewing."

"I spoke with her myself," said Anneke. "She said she would have work for me in her dressmaker's shop, if I am so inclined."

"Did she," said Hans. "What about your work at home?"

"Whatever work she cannot do, I can, as well as my own," said I.

Anneke gave me a grateful look, and said to Hans, "We will get a much better price for your parents' fabric if I sew it into clothing first."

Hans looked thoughtful, and for a long while we rode in silence, Anneke and I watching him anxiously. By the time we reached home, he had decided that Anneke would be permitted to assist Mrs. Engle one day each week in her dressmaker's shop, and that she could dispose of the fabric however she saw fit. "I'm pleased you had the good sense to ignore me when I said to leave those bolts be," said he, smiling affectionately at his wife.

I was delighted for Anneke, and pleased that Hans had not let pride get the better of his pragmatism, but in my wistful heart, I wished that someone would smile so affectionately at me, too, and that that someone would be Jonathan.

❧

On the following Sunday afternoon, Sylvia greeted the new campers on the veranda, guiding them inside while impatiently eyeing the circular driveway for the shuttle bus that would bring Grace Daniels back to Elm Creek Manor.

Sylvia and Grace had been friends for more than fifteen years, united by their love for quilting. In addition to her work as a curator for the De Young Museum in San Francisco, Grace was a master quilter who had once specialized in story quilts, folk-art-style appliqué works that interpreted historical stories or themes, often with African-American subjects. Her passion for history had not diminished when multiple sclerosis forced her down a new creative path, and she had long wished to see the quilts from the manor's past. Grace attended Elm Creek Quilt Camp the same week every year, to reunite with friends she had made on her first visit as well as to see Sylvia. This time, at long last, Sylvia intended to fulfill her promise to show Anneke's quilts to Grace.

Another airport shuttle bus arrived, and finally Sylvia saw Grace emerge, supporting herself on two metal crutches. Matt spotted her, too, and bounded down one of the semicircular staircases to assist with her luggage. When Sylvia called to her and waved, Grace looked up and called, "When do I get to see the quilts?"

"As soon as you like," Sylvia promised, delighted to see her friend looking so well and in such good spirits. Grace rarely spoke about her illness over the phone, leaving Sylvia to wonder how much it had progressed between their visits.

After Grace completed her camp registration, Sylvia instructed Matt to deliver Grace's bags to her room. Then, before Grace's friends could whisk her off for their annual reunion, Sylvia invited her to the west sitting room off the kitchen, where she had laid out the quilts in anticipation of Grace's visit.

"What a find, Sylvia," exclaimed Grace when she saw the quilts. She studied them without speaking, occasionally lifting a corner up to the light or bending close to inspect a particular scrap of fabric. Every so often she jotted notes on a pad, then returned her attention to the quilts.

"Well?" prompted Sylvia.

"I don't suppose you'd consider donating these to the museum?"

"Absolutely not," declared Sylvia, then conceded, "Not yet, at least. I might consider leaving them to you in my will, since I know you'll take good care of them."

"In that case, I'm willing to wait a long time." With effort, Grace sat down on the sofa beside the Log Cabin quilt and turned it over, searching the muslin backing for an appliquéd tag or embroidery, just as Sylvia had done weeks earlier. She shook her head when she found neither. "I wish the quilter had documented her work."

"There might be a record of their history, even so." Sylvia retrieved the slim leather book from her writing desk and handed it to Grace. "My father's great-aunt Gerda's memoir. I believe my great-grandmother Anneke Bergstrom made the quilts, and I hope Gerda wrote about them."

Grace glanced at the first page. "That would definitely help determine their dates of origin."

"Can't you do that by inspection?"

Grace shook her head and returned the memoir to Sylvia. "Only to some extent. The pattern choices tell us something, and I can place the fabrics, but I can't determine when the quilts were pieced from them. Think about how long you've had some of the fabric in your stash. The material might be from 1987, but your quilt will be completed in the twenty-first century."

"Of course." Sylvia thought of the Tumbling Block quilt she had begun earlier that summer with hundreds of diamonds trimmed from scraps used over several decades of quilt making. Fortunately, she always embroidered her name and date in the border of her quilts, so no one would mistake who had made them, or when.

"There are some fabulous examples of the dye and discharge process in here," said Grace, touching several of the logs gently. Her finger lighted on a yellow fabric with a small, close print. "This was called a butterscotch print. They were popular in Pennsylvania from around 1840 through 1860."

Sylvia nodded, pleased that the dates corresponded so well to Gerda's time.

"Prussian blue," continued Grace, indicating several scraps in turn. "Here's a turkey red, and here's another. Oh, I've seen this purple print before, or one very like it. It's probably imported."

Sylvia frowned at the brown fabric. "That doesn't look very purple to me."

"The dye was fugitive. All of these"—Grace pointed to several different brown pieces, some dark prints on light backgrounds, others medium in value and embellished with small, white floral designs—"were purples once."

An awful feeling struck Sylvia. "Is it possible that the black center squares were not originally black?"

"No," said Grace, studying the quilt thoughtfully, "I don't believe so."

Relieved, Sylvia inhaled deeply to settle her nerves and asked, "What about the other quilts? I've spotted some of the same fabric in all three."

"Yes, I noticed that, too." Grace looked from the Log Cabin quilt to the four-patch and then to the Birds in the Air, examining the quilting stitches closely. "They seem to be the same age, but I don't believe the same quilter made all three. Even accounting for a quilter's improvement with practice, the quilting stitches in the Log Cabin and the Birds in the Air aren't as accomplished as those in the four-patch. And, of course, the Log Cabin and Birds in the Air are machine-pieced. I'm surprised you didn't mention that."

"I didn't realize it."

Grace must have detected her dismay, for she smiled. "Don't worry. That doesn't mean they weren't completed in your great-grandmother's time. Quilters have been piecing by machine for as long as there have been sewing machines."

"One of my Elm Creek Quilters won't be happy to learn that," said Sylvia dryly, thinking of Diane, who insisted that only quilts made entirely by hand could be considered "true quilts."

"She's not the only one. Many people become uncomfortable when they discover their traditions are founded on shaky ground."

"My great-grandmother did own a sewing machine, but if different quilters made the three quilts, I suspect Anneke made the four-patch and Gerda made the Log Cabin." Family lore attributed the Log Cabin quilt to Anneke, but it seemed the most logical explanation. "I'm not sure about the Birds in the Air."

"The piecing quality is inconsistent," noted Grace, "as is the quilting. Maybe they worked on this one together."

"Of the two, Anneke was the better seamstress. Gerda—Hans's sister— quilted only because she had to. She despised sewing."

"She must not have despised it too much. Whoever made the Log Cabin put a great deal of care into it."

"I should think so." Sylvia gave Grace a pointed look over the top of her glasses. "I've told you my great-aunt Lucinda's story about this quilt."

"And I've given my professional opinion about that story," replied Grace. "It's highly unlikely that Log Cabin quilts with black center squares were used as signals on the Underground Railroad. The block didn't even come into widespread use until the 1860s, years after the Underground Railroad functioned as it did in the time leading up to the Civil War. I've looked, and the earliest published description of the Log Cabin block I could find was in 1869."

"That hardly matters," scoffed Sylvia. "Patterns were transmitted from quilter to quilter long before they were printed up in magazines and newspapers. Have you ever been to the Carnegie Natural History Museum in Pittsburgh?"

The apparent change in subject clearly baffled Grace. "What?"

"The Carnegie Natural History Museum in Pittsburgh. The Egyptian exhibit, to be precise. I saw the mummy of a cat there once, and its wrappings were made up of tiny folded Log Cabin quilt blocks."

"I don't deny that the design itself might have existed, but I'll guarantee you the Egyptians didn't call it a Log Cabin block."

Grace's painstaking distinctions made Sylvia impatient. "But why, then, do so many stories—not merely my great-aunt's—describe Log Cabin quilts with black center squares used on the Underground Railroad?"

"Unfortunately, most of these stories are based upon misdated quilts." Grace sighed. "Look. I'm a quilter, I'm an African-American, and I'm someone who loves a good story, but I'm also a historian, and I have to go by the evidence in the historical record. Until now, there haven't been any surviving quilts of that era meeting that description."

"Until now?"

Grace hesitated. "Well—"

"I distinctly heard you say, 'Until now.'"

"I admit I'm puzzled. The pattern suggests that the Log Cabin quilt is Civil War era or later, but the fabric predates the war."

"Which suggests the quilt was made before the war."

"Or that the quilter saved her scraps for later use," Grace reminded her. "Still, the quilting pattern also displays characteristics of the antebellum period. And when I consider the Four-Patch quilt . . ."

"Yes?" prompted Sylvia.

"Well, the picture becomes even less clear." Grace frowned and fingered the edge of the four-patch. "I believe Anneke would have called this the Underground Railroad pattern."

"That couldn't be. I would have recognized it. The Underground Railroad pattern was merely the Jacob's Ladder by another name, was it not?"

"Again, we have to go back to the historical record. The earliest quilts containing the modern Jacob's Ladder pattern date back to the end of the 1900s, no earlier. If the Jacob's Ladder block we know today was renamed Underground Railroad, it happened long after the events that inspired the name."

"Dear me." Sylvia sat down, hard, on the ottoman of her armchair. "I've been perpetuating a myth."

"At least one, maybe more."

"Thank you, Grace," said Sylvia dryly. "You don't need to make me feel worse. Why did you say you think Anneke's quilt was called Underground Railroad, then?"

"These strippy quilts were very popular in Anneke's time." Grace placed her hands on the quilt, isolating five of the four-patches and the setting triangles surrounding them. "Imagine these as one nine-patch block. Do you see how it resembles our Jacob's Ladder pattern?"

Sylvia studied the pieces for a moment before she could see the similarity. "Goodness, yes. Do you mean to say that a quilt such as this was called Underground Railroad, but a later quilter saw the secondary pattern within the arrangement and determined that the block's name had been changed?"

"It's possible. I'm afraid it's another theory."

"You and your theories."

"I wish I could give you definitive answers, but I can't. I don't even know for certain if this quilt was called Underground Railroad. I'm surmising that since it was found with the Log Cabin." Grace frowned and returned her gaze to it. "Which, I'll admit, does puzzle me."

Sylvia hated to let go of the folklore that had enchanted her for so many years. "Allow me to play devil's advocate, if you please."

"Certainly."

"Based on all the other evidence, but excluding Anneke's choice of the Log Cabin pattern, when would you have dated these quilts?"

"I can't ignore the pattern. It's one of the most important clues."

"Indulge an old woman's fancy, would you, please? Just this once?"

Grace smiled wryly and conceded, "I'd say somewhere between 1840 to 1860."

"Now, just because no one has ever found a Log Cabin quilt predating the Civil War, that doesn't mean they never existed, correct?"

Grace hesitated. "Well, no, but lack of evidence to the contrary isn't reliable evidence."

"But it is possible, however improbable, that Anneke's quilt does predate the Civil War, and that it could have been used as a signal on the Underground Railroad? Here, at Elm Creek Manor, if nowhere else?"

"I suppose it's possible, but—"

"Thank you," said Sylvia, triumphant. "You can stop there."

Grace laughed and shook her head. "Okay. You win. Your quilts pose an interesting puzzle, and I'll need more time to figure it out."

"More time and more evidence," said Sylvia. "I do wish you could have seen Margaret Alden's quilt in person. All I have are photos."

"I can look at those, at least."

Sylvia went to fetch them, unable to keep the smile off her face. Grace had done all she could to caution her, and Sylvia knew she ought to reserve judgment until they had more evidence, but she couldn't help feeling elated. Despite all the qualifiers and contradictions, Grace had admitted that Sylvia might have stumbled upon the one remaining Log Cabin quilt that had served as a signal on the Underground Railroad.

Surely Gerda's memoir would prove the folklore true.

*✷ December 1857 through January 1858 — in
which I encounter hints of future unhappiness
and signs of ill times to come, and ignore them all*

Within a month of the Harvest Dance, Anneke began working for Mrs. Engle at her dress shop in Creek's Crossing. Once a week I drove her into town, delivered my preserves and bread to the general store and collected my earnings, and completed whatever errands the farm required before rewarding myself with a visit to friends from Dorothea's sewing circle. The mornings flew by as we exchanged books and gossip, and all too soon I would have to hurry away to fetch Anneke home again, her newest sewing projects in a neat bundle on her lap, in time for me to make Hans his dinner. He did not mind his wife's enterprising spirit as long as it did not postpone his mealtimes.

The first snow of the season fell around that time, but the worst harshness of winter held off, and so we enjoyed cold but sunny days until the end of December. Our Christmas was an especially joyous one; Hans's business had begun to grow, Elm Creek Farm was flourishing from our attentive labors, and all around us were signs of our imminent prosperity. We Bergstroms were well liked by our neighbors, and we never suffered from loneliness, despite the relative isolation of our home.

The Nelsons remained our closest friends, and to this day I thank the Lord for blessing us with such generous neighbors. Dorothea was such a practical, capable woman, and in countless ways she helped Anneke and me better manage our household. Although Creek's Crossing was not the Kansas wilderness I had planned for, it was frontier enough for women of Anneke's and my inexperience. Without Dorothea's gentle guidance, we would not have fared nearly half so well.

Anneke made other acquaintances, too, by virtue of her days spent at Engle's Draper and Fine Tailoring. The young ladies of the finest families in town frequented the establishment, and while some snubbed Anneke as an "illiterate immigrant," their more practical friends, who recognized the wisdom of an alliance with such a gifted seamstress, befriended her. Mrs. Engle grew quite fond of her and introduced her to her circle of friends, the matrons of the town, and before long each had exacted a promise from her husband that he would consider purchasing one of Hans's Bergstrom Thoroughbred foals come spring.

I was so pleased that Mrs. Engle had given Anneke employment that I felt guilty when I could not bring myself to like her more. I did try to like her, at least at first: I ignored the small jokes she made about immigrants and clenched my teeth when she spoke of the necessity of slave labor to the economy of the South, especially cotton, the cultivation of which directly affected her business; I told myself that if Anneke could bear the tone of self-important condescension with which Mrs. Engle addressed her, surely I could as well. But I lost my temper when she published a letter in the *Creek's Crossing Informer* denouncing the vote for women and beseeching men to guide their daughters with a firm hand lest they, too, succumb to corrupting influences. "Women's suffrage and the desire for the right to vote render our young ladies argumentative, unfeminine, and unsuitable for marriage," wrote she. "We doom our precious daughters to embittered spinsterhood if we do not teach them humility and obedience."

"She was not speaking of you," said Anneke when I grumbled over this. "She knows you tried to marry."

"And how would she know that?" asked I, too astounded to say that whether Mrs. Engle referred to me personally was irrelevant.

"I told her how you came to be unlucky in love."

Thus I had embarrassment to compound my outrage.

Mrs. Engle's letter concluded on a note that would have been ominous if it had not been so prim and ridiculous: "Certain Factions, especially those which bring in outsiders to inflame our minds and hearts, ought not to imagine they speak for all the Ladies of Creek's Crossing, or they may find themselves without Friends."

Her letter set the sewing circle all abuzz with indignant calls for us to compose a rebuttal for immediate publication in the *Informer,* and we all clamored for Dorothea, the obvious target of Mrs. Engle's last rebuke, to author it. "I will write to explain my position and the righteousness of our cause," replied Dorothea, "but I will not engage in petty argument simply for the sake of defending my injured pride."

"We cannot allow her insults to go unanswered," protested one of our circle. "She should not have been allowed to write such things."

We others chimed in our agreement, but Dorothea merely smiled and said, "Remember, we also fight so that Mrs. Engle may vote."

That sobered us. We had assumed that all women, once secured the right, would naturally vote as we would have them do, and that together we would bring about a new renaissance of justice and peace in our country. But when we could not forge solidarity even among ourselves, how could we hope to transform the entire nation?

A few of our sewing circle vowed never again to patronize Mrs. Engle's shop, a decision that pained me for Anneke's sake until I discovered this would account for the loss of only two dresses a year. Still, I was relieved that Anneke had not joined us that evening, and my heart was troubled when I thought of how she would react to news of the resolution. But some of my good humor was restored by our second declaration, which was unanimous: We would henceforth call our little group the Certain Sewing and Suffrage Faction of Creek's Crossing, Pennsylvania.

After that, I could not bring myself to enter the dressmaker's shop out of fear I would tell Mrs. Engle exactly what I thought of her and cost my sister-in-law her employment, but left and collected Anneke at the door without stepping inside even to warm myself for the drive home. "Without Friends," indeed. Dorothea and I had friends enough among the Certain Faction, and would scarcely notice the absence of Mrs. Engle and her cronies.

Only then did I realize how rarely the two circles mixed. I, who prided myself on my powers of observation and inference, had not noticed until prompted by Mrs. Engle's letter the schism that divided the women of the town. Anneke alone seemed capable of traveling freely in both circles, earning the respect of one with her perseverance and determination to learn, charming the other with her beauty, skill, and eagerness to please.

When I remarked on the divide to Hans and Anneke, Anneke claimed, rather sharply, that it was nothing a little pleasantness and restraint on Dorothea's part wouldn't mend.

Said Hans, more soberly, "It's worse among the men."

The following week, Dorothea's reply appeared in the *Informer;* Anneke reported that it was not well regarded in the dressmaker's shop, nor was Dorothea. But with the coming of Christmas, the women of Creek's Crossing set aside acrimony in the spirit of the season, and the tensions between us settled once again beneath the surface, unspoken and unnoticed.

As they had the previous year, the Nelsons invited us to spend Christmas Day with them, and what a joyous holiday it was indeed. Jonathan came, as I had hoped he would; he brought his and Dorothea's parents in the senior Mr. Granger's sleigh, which pulled up to the house soon after ours with a jingling of merry bells. Mrs. Granger treated me with such kind affection that

I allowed myself to hope that her opinion of me had been formed as much by Jonathan's reports as by Dorothea's.

After a delicious meal, Dorothea and her father entertained us with the music of organ and fiddle, respectively, and we sang Christmas carols. I recollect that evening as the most joyful I had yet spent in America, and it was to remain one of my happiest memories. We laughed and joked and shared stories of Christmases past in lands far away. No one regretted the evening's end more than I, but Mr. and Mrs. Granger needed to return to their farm, so Jonathan and Hans went to the barn to hitch up their horses.

They observed storm clouds gathered in the southwestern sky, so urged us not to delay our departure. As Anneke and I rose to don our winter cloaks and scarves, Jonathan murmured in my ear that he should like to speak with me alone for a moment.

My heart seemed to tremble, but I nodded, and we slipped into the kitchen while the others said their farewells. I was too nervous to speak, so I stood in silence and waited.

Jonathan did not meet my eyes as he fumbled in his pocket and said, "I had hoped for a better moment to give you this." He withdrew a small paper-wrapped parcel and placed it in my hands.

Speechless, I looked from the parcel to Jonathan.

"Please open it," said he, glancing over his shoulder.

Mindful that our time alone might be brief, I quickly unwrapped the gift and discovered a beautiful hair comb embellished with mother-of-pearl. "It's lovely, Jonathan. Thank you." He smiled to see me so pleased with his gift, as I truly was. I did not have many fine features, but my hair was thick and dark, and fell below my waist when unbraided, and I admit to being a trifle vain of it. I thanked him for the gift, and warmly wished him a merry Christmas.

He wished me the same, and I thought he might say more, but behind us, someone cleared her throat. Dorothea stood in the doorway, watching us. "I thought I might send you home with some of my dried apples, Gerda, if you think you might use them?"

"Of course I would," said I. "Thank you."

She nodded and passed between us on her way to the root cellar, glancing at her brother as she went, but Jonathan did not look at her, and instead excused himself to help his parents prepare for the trip home.

By the time Dorothea returned, I had composed myself and had hidden

Jonathan's gift in my pocket. We both remarked on how delightful the evening had been, but then Dorothea fell silent, her expression troubled. "Gerda," said she at last, "I do not wish to speak out of turn, but . . ."

"But?" prompted I, when she hesitated.

"I hope you are not setting your cap for my brother."

The colloquialism puzzled me. "Setting my cap?"

"She means, do you think to marry him," said Anneke, who had entered the room in time to hear the exchange.

"I don't mean any offense," said Dorothea.

"Of course not," said I. "I assure you, I don't plan to set my hat for anyone."

"You needn't worry about my sister-in-law," said Anneke, grinning naughtily. "She's often said she will never trade her freedom for the bondage of matrimony. She does not wish to become old married women like us, and subject to the whims of a man."

Dorothea's eyebrows rose.

"I did not say it in quite that manner," said I with haste, embarrassed. "Anneke misrepresents me."

"Your words, perhaps, but not the sentiment," said Anneke.

"Sometimes the yoke is not so difficult to bear," said Dorothea with a small laugh. "It depends upon the husband."

I wondered, did Dorothea think Jonathan would make a poor husband? Or did she think I would make him a poor wife? I was so conflicted by her unexpected remarks and Anneke's teasing that I could not bring myself to give voice to my questions. Dorothea and I were friends. If I had indeed set my cap for Jonathan, why would Dorothea find this objectionable?

Suddenly I was relieved that we were leaving. The mother-of-pearl comb felt heavy and conspicuous in my pocket, even when concealed beneath my outer wraps. I couldn't meet Jonathan's eye as Hans, Anneke, and I bid our friends good-bye and climbed into our wagon. I buried my chin in my scarf to ward off the cold and said not a word as Hans drove the horses back to Elm Creek Farm, and when we reached home, I hid the comb in my hope chest before Anneke could see it.

When at last I showed it to her, a few days later, she squealed with delight and commanded me to tell her every word Jonathan and I had exchanged. This I accomplished soon enough, as we had had little time alone. Dorothea's interruption had been so troubling that I had forgotten the pleasure Jonathan's gift had first brought me, but Anneke's enthusiasm soon rekindled it. That he had given me any gift was a promising sign, she insisted, but such a beautiful ornament surely indicated he wished to increase our intimacy.

As always, I feigned disinterest. "Jonathan is my friend's brother, and so naturally he is my friend as well, but you mustn't imagine he is anything more."

"Hans and I are his friends, too, but he didn't give us Christmas presents."

This I could not deny, but I did my best to assure her I had no interest in Jonathan beyond friendship.

You may wonder why I insisted on this deception, which was in all likelihood becoming transparent, or perhaps you will have guessed the reason to be my disappointment with E. I was determined not to become an object of pity in my new country as I had in my homeland. If my heart were to be broken a second time, my one consolation would be that no one save myself would know it. True, I cherished our conversations, looked forward to our meetings, and noted with pleasure the signs of Jonathan's increasing affection for me, but until he made some declaration of his intentions, I must assume he had none.

The New Year came, followed by a series of January snowstorms that for several days kept us confined to Elm Creek Farm. Hans had his endless chores and Anneke her sewing for Mrs. Engle, but I longed for the companionship of the Certain Faction. When Anneke complained at my stalking about the cabin, I took up my sewing basket and worked on my Shoo-Fly quilt to appease her. To my surprise, the hours passed quite pleasantly as Anneke and I sewed side by side in the firelight. She told me stories of her childhood in Berlin, and I told her about my family's life in Baden-Baden. By the time the storms broke, I had nearly finished enough blocks for a quilt top, and Anneke and I had deepened our understanding of each other. I reflected then that I had known my younger sisters all my life, and I missed and loved them dearly, but Anneke and I had shared hardship and hope in a strange land, and that bound us closer than any ties of blood or affection ever could.

In later years, only by recollecting the closeness we shared in those days was I able to set aside my hatred and remember that once I had loved Anneke. If not for my resolution to try to love her again, I might have left my family forever rather than share a home with her.

But I must remember to record this history in the order in which it transpired, or it will make no sense at all to my reader, even if by your day, these events are well known to every Bergstrom.

Our first visitor after the weather cleared was Jonathan. He met Hans in the barn, to discuss a horse he intended to buy, but then he came to the cabin. I was pleased to see him, and glad that I had worn the hair comb; though I had intended to save it for special occasions, seeing the sun again had made the day special enough. He accepted the tea I offered him and joined me and Anneke by the fire, but his attempts at conversation were uncharacteristically awkward.

Eventually Anneke made some excuse and left us, and soon we heard her sewing machine whirring as she worked the treadle with her foot. "I'm glad you ventured out to see us," said I. "I wished to return the book you lent me. It was quite good. Thank you."

He nodded and took it absently. "Gerda, I must speak with you on a difficult subject."

In the other room, the treadle ceased abruptly. "Not until I give you your Christmas gift," said I, quickly. My heart pounding, anticipating his words, I retrieved and presented his gift. "It's belated, but I think you will like it all the same."

Slowly he unwrapped the book and read the title. "Franklin's *Autobiography*."

"You've often said you admired him, and you enjoyed the French version," said I, wondering why he did not smile. "This is the English version his grandson published later, with additions to the manuscript."

"Thank you," said he. "I'm sure I will enjoy it." Only then did he look up and meet my eye, but just as quickly his gaze alighted on the ornament in my hair. "You're wearing the comb." Involuntarily I touched it, my cheeks growing warm, and I nodded. "It suits you."

"It suits my hair," said I, attempting a laugh. "It keeps it out of my eyes, which is a great benefit when one is trying to sew, I assure you."

"Or to dance." His voice grew distant. "At the Harvest Dance, that lock above your ear kept slipping out of place and tumbling across your cheek."

"I did not think you had noticed," said I, nervous, and trying once again to tease him out of his serious mood. "As I recall it, we saw little of each other that night. You danced with your sister and with Charlotte Claverton as much as with me."

"Yes." He looked up at me gravely. "I suppose I did." Then he took a deep breath and stood. "Gerda, there are things I must tell you, but perhaps you have guessed them already."

I shook my head.

At that moment, someone pounded on the door. "Dr. Granger," a young voice shouted. "Dr. Granger, are you there?"

Alarmed, I flew to the door and opened it. In tumbled a boy of about thirteen, gasping for breath, his face red and frightened.

"Daniel?" said Jonathan.

"Mrs. Granger said you would be here," said the boy, panting so hard I could barely make out his words. "It's my pa. He's been shot."

Jonathan was already throwing on his coat. "Where is he?"

"Home. Susanna's looking after him."

Susanna, I was to learn later, was the boy's ten-year-old sister. Daniel's mother had died two years before while giving birth to his youngest brother.

"When did this happen?" asked Jonathan, as he followed the boy out the door.

"Same day the storms hit. He was out in the barn—" Daniel swallowed hard. "They hit him in the stomach. He was bleeding real bad, but I couldn't get to your place any sooner. The snow—"

"It's all right, son. We'll get back to your place in no time." Suddenly Jonathan looked at me. "There's no time to stop for Dorothea—"

"I'll come." Quickly I threw on my wraps, my mind racing. The same day the storms hit, Daniel had said, which meant his father had been suffering for four days.

Anneke, who had returned to the room at the pounding upon the door, fled to the barn, where Hans saddled a horse for me and one for Daniel, whose mare was spent from the long run first to the Granger farm and then to ours. In minutes we were on our way.

As we rode, Daniel gasped out the story. When the storm worsened, his father had gone to the barn to check on the livestock, and discovered two men engaged in stealing his horses. Unarmed, Daniel's father attempted to flee, but before he could escape, one of the pair fired upon him.

"Did your father recognize the men?" asked Jonathan.

"He said he didn't, but I know who they were," said the boy, his voice full of hate and exhaustion. "Only one kind of people shoot a man for his horses then run off without the horses."

But the road and our pace prevented him from saying more.

We raced on, north through the woods to the Wilbur farm, which lay to the northwest of Creek's Crossing. At last we arrived, expecting the worst, only to find a familiar wagon in the yard. Jonathan's parents had come.

His mother met us at the door, relieved to see her son but still anxious. Her husband, she reported as Jonathan hurried inside, was upstairs, distracting the other children. Nodding, Jonathan requested soap and two basins of water, which his mother quickly made ready. "Wash your hands," he instructed me, and did so himself before racing to his patient's side.

I obeyed, then quickly joined him in the other room. Mr. Wilbur lay on a bed, eyes closed and pale, a blood-soaked dressing covering his abdomen. He moaned in pain as Jonathan lifted the bandage to inspect the wound. I glimpsed raw, seeping flesh and felt my head grow light, but Mrs. Granger held me steady and whispered that I should not think of what I saw, but must steel myself and provide what assistance Jonathan required of me.

I gulped air, nodded, and followed Mrs. Granger to the bedside, where we helped Jonathan as he fought to preserve Mr. Wilbur's life. My memory is a blur of blood and flesh, but I know I followed Jonathan's instructions automatically, rapidly and without thinking, numb and frightened. I had cared for ailing relatives, I had assisted in childbirth, but never had I witnessed a struggle to repair so great a wrong done to the human body, and my mind was numb with disbelief that any man could knowingly inflict such agony on another.

It seemed hours until Jonathan stepped away from the bed, exhausted, and said that he had done all he could. He withdrew to wash himself and rest, while his mother and I tried to make Mr. Wilbur more comfortable by changing his soiled bed linens. Mr. Wilbur little noticed our efforts, as he had long ago fallen unconscious from the pain.

Mrs. Granger offered to watch by his bedside. I thought then of the children whom I had not yet seen, and since I could do nothing else, I went to the kitchen to prepare them something to eat.

Jonathan was in the kitchen, slumped in a chair, his head in his hands.

"You saved his life," said I, quietly, as I scrubbed my hands clean.

"I did nothing of the sort." His voice was oddly emotionless. "I came too late."

"He's alive. We'll care for him until he recovers."

"No. He's lost too much blood. The bullet remained in him too long. The wound was not tended properly, and nothing I can do can help him. He will not live out the week."

I could not bear to think of those children left without their only remaining parent. "He has survived four days already. He may make it."

Jonathan did not reply. I knew he disbelieved me but was either too tired or too kind to contradict.

When the meal was ready, Mr. Granger brought the children downstairs to eat. They wanted to see their father, but Jonathan told them he was sleeping, and they must be good little children and let him rest. They ate somberly, even the youngest, still just a baby. Jonathan beckoned to his father, and quietly they slipped outside to the barn, where I imagined them looking over the scene of the terrible act.

Later, I put the three youngest children to bed and returned downstairs to find Jonathan gently asking Daniel to tell them all he remembered about the two men. Daniel repeated the story, adding little to what he had told us earlier, but I listened intently to each detail, certain he would confirm what I had already decided: The two men must have been the two slave catchers who had visited Elm Creek Farm the previous autumn. The greatest evil I had ever heard of and the greatest evil I had ever seen had become intermingled in my mind, so that I could not picture the crime without seeing those two slave catchers in the place of the horse thieves.

I waited for Daniel to provide the details that would prove my convictions true, but once more he said although he had run outside at the sound of the gunshot, he had glimpsed only the men's backs as they rode off, heading west, away from Creek's Crossing.

"Did your father have any enemies?" asked Mr. Granger.

"Yes," said Daniel venomously. "Those g—— Abolitionists."

Shocked, I looked to Jonathan, who gave me the barest shake of his head to warn me to be silent. "Why would Abolitionists wish to kill your father?" asked Jonathan.

"Because they know what Pa thinks of them, and they came to quiet him, just as Pa always said they would. They always want to kill a man who thinks different than them." Suddenly he exploded with anger. "I know why they wanted our horses, too. So those g—— Abolitionists could ride 'em to Kansas. My pa says all the g—— Abolitionists should go the h—— to Kansas if they want and leave us alone, and I wish they would, I wish they would!"

The words choked out of him as he struggled not to cry. I wept inside to see so much hatred and pain in such a young boy, but I stood frozen, helpless, unable to comfort him and afraid that he would learn Abolitionists were in his house that moment, and that his father's life was in their hands.

But Jonathan knew exactly what to do. He clasped the boy's shoulder and said, "We don't know who committed this terrible act, but you were very brave to try to help. You tended your father well during the storms, and you came for me as soon as you were able. I'm sure your father is very proud of you, and he'll tell you so himself, when he wakes up."

He said this, I knew, believing Daniel's father would never wake.

Mr. Granger had to return home to care for his livestock, but Jonathan, Mrs. Granger, and I remained, tending to Mr. Wilbur through the night and watching over the children. By the next morning, Mr. Wilbur had been taken with a fever. He lived two days more, but then, as Jonathan had foretold, he perished.

Mr. Granger and other men from town saw to the burial. Jonathan saw me back to Elm Creek Farm. It seemed as if months had passed since last I had been there.

We did not speak as we rode along. I do not know what thoughts occupied Jonathan, but I worried about the young Wilbur children, now orphaned, and wondered what would become of them. And although I tried to tell myself the two men were surely long gone, my heart quaked with fear knowing that two murderers had come among us and might yet lurk nearby.

"Why did Daniel believe them to be Abolitionists?" I heard myself ask.

Jonathan was silent for a long moment before he spoke. "It is no secret that Wilbur supports the Southern cause. I know he earned at least one bounty by informing upon a family that helped escaping slaves." He paused again. "L., the man who owned Elm Creek Farm before your brother—he and Wilbur were friends, and of like minds in this."

I nodded to show that I understood, but I felt bile rise into my mouth, picturing our barn the scene of the recent crime, and Hans bearing Mr. Wilbur's fatal wound. "Do you think Daniel was right?" asked I. "Could Abolitionists have done this?"

"I do not and cannot believe that," said Jonathan. "Likely the men were common horse thieves. What troubles me is that young Daniel is firmly convinced otherwise. His father taught him hatred well, and I do not know if such a deeply planted belief can ever be uprooted."

"You knew Mr. Wilbur hated Abolitionists, and yet you helped him."

He looked at me, surprised. "Of course."

I said nothing more, and yet I marveled at him. Creek's Crossing and all the country had begun to whisper of a conflagration to come, in which Free Staters and slaveholders would fight in every corner of the nation as they were now fighting in Kansas Territory and Missouri. And yet Jonathan had struggled to save the life of this man who was already his enemy, and who might one day desire to kill him. He had fought with all his strength and skill, persisting even when he knew all hope was lost. He had tried to save the man even when he knew he would fail, because it was right, because it was necessary, because to Jonathan even the life of an enemy was precious.

Mrs. Engle, who had known Mrs. Wilbur well, wrote to her family informing them of Mr. Wilbur's passing. Mrs. Wilbur's sister replied, requesting that the farm be sold and the proceeds used to send the children to her and her husband. Within weeks the matter was settled and the children were on their way to Missouri.

I do not know what became of them after that.

Chapter Six

Grace examined the photos of Margaret Alden's quilt under a magnifying glass, but although she did not find any fabrics that definitely matched the three at Elm Creek Manor, she could not rule out the possibility. One cotton print in particular, an overdyed green print of leaves scattered on a black background, seemed to appear in all four quilts, but without actually seeing Margaret Alden's quilt, Grace could not say for certain.

Sylvia was so confounded by the newly revealed contradictions between folklore and historical fact that she did not know how to react to Grace's conclusions. She felt that she had come to know Gerda quite well, and she was certain Gerda could not have left Elm Creek Farm to become a slave owner—and Margaret Alden's ancestor—in South Carolina. Still, although the responses of her quilt campers proved that Elm Creek Manor could make a strong impression on its residents, she could not believe a mere casual visitor would have stitched such a tribute to it. If not for the quilted picture of Hans's unique barn and the overdyed green cloth possibly linking the four quilts, Sylvia could convince herself the so-called Elm Creek Quilt had nothing to do with the Bergstrom estate, despite the nickname Margaret's grandmother had applied to it. One thing was certain, however: Whatever location the quilt immortalized, the quilter had more than a passing acquaintance with it. The unknown quiltmaker's desire to remember that place forever was evident in every stitch.

Before her week of camp concluded, Grace photographed Sylvia's quilts and promised to further investigate the fabrics and patterns. "In the meantime, keep reading that memoir," said Grace, as she bid her friend goodbye Saturday after the Farewell Breakfast.

"I most certainly will," Sylvia assured her, but that was not all she had planned. She would write to Margaret that very day and ask her for more information about her family history, including any other family quilts possibly sewn by the same quilter. And a week hence she would welcome a professor from Penn State to Elm Creek Manor. She had invited him to study the half-buried log that might be what remained of the Bergstrom's cabin, and was pleased by his enthusiastic acceptance.

As the weekend passed, Sylvia frequently took up the memoir with the intention of reading on, but instead she found herself returning to the passage in which Gerda described how she and Anneke had passed the bitter January storms by sharing stories of their lives back in Germany. Sylvia wished with all her heart that Gerda had recorded those stories. She ached to know what Gerda and Anneke had learned about each other in those four days. Instead her ancestor teased her with glimpses into the past—Anneke's childhood, the daily life of Hans's immediate family—and left her with a thirst for knowledge she doubted even Gerda's memoir could fully quench.

But on Monday, before the evening program, Summer provided her with a small but satisfying taste.

Surmising that Mr. Wilbur's murder would have shaken the town, Summer had returned to the Waterford Historical Society's archives and searched the *Creek's Crossing Informer* microfiche. Sure enough, news of the murder occupied a prominent position in the January 15, 1858, edition, but Summer also found several smaller articles in subsequent issues, which she printed out and proudly delivered to Sylvia.

"'Local Man Murdered in Cold Blood,'" said Sylvia, reading the headline aloud. "Dear me."

"The story mentions Jonathan," said Summer, and Sylvia needed no further inducement to read on:

LOCAL MAN MURDERED IN COLD BLOOD!
FOUR CHILDREN ORPHANED

Mr. Charles Wilbur, a longtime resident of Creek's Crossing, was shot in his barn by persons unknown six days ago. He was said to have interrupted two men as they were engaged in stealing his horses, and though he was unarmed, they fired upon him as he made to depart. Mr. Wilbur's eldest son responded to the sound of gunfire in a brave attempt to defend his father, but arrived too late to see who committed this cowardly and heinous act. The youth sustained his father's life for four days with only his younger siblings to assist him, their mother being dead, but he could not summon help, for like many of us his family was snow-bound during the most recent spate of storms. Dr. Jonathan Granger arrived to find the victim yet drawing breath, but despite prodigious skill, the doctor was unable to preserve his life.

It is said that the two murderers and would-be horse thieves left the Wilbur farm heading west and that they will probably not return, but all citizens should keep a sharp eye out for suspicious strangers entering the town and take care to lock up their horses at night.

Mr. Wilbur will be laid to rest on Sunday at the First Lutheran Church with a sermon by Reverend Lawrence Schroeder. The Ladies' Aid Society is seeking contributions for the unfortunate children orphaned by this outrageous crime.

Another article, dated January 20, announced a "Covered-Dish Supper" at the First Lutheran Church to raise money for the four Wilbur children, and a second, published a few days later, reported that the event had raised thirty-two dollars and praised the residents of Creek's Crossing for their generosity. The last of Summer's articles, dated February 2, stated that the culprits had not been caught, although a trail of horse thefts and attempted murders suggested that the two men had headed west and south, on a meandering course "to escape justice in the lawless West."

Sylvia read the articles again more carefully, not surprised that neither Hans nor Anneke appeared in any of the stories, but disappointed that Gerda, who might have been mentioned for her role in caring for Mr. Wilbur before his death, was not named either.

As far as the *Creek's Crossing Informer* was concerned, Gerda might have spent those harrowing days secure within her own home—which only strengthened Sylvia's reluctance to rely on the official historical record alone.

❧ Spring and autumn 1858 — in which we build our new home

The murder of Mr. Wilbur transformed our town, making even the bravest wary of strangers. It also widened the ideological divide between the Abolitionists and those sympathetic to the slaveholder. The Abolitionists were convinced the two would-be horse thieves had been slave catchers, seeking fresh mounts upon which they would pursue their unfortunate prey. Most anti-Abolitionists, among them Mrs. Engle, insisted the murderers were Abolitionists, stealing horses for escaped slaves to ride to Canada. Others believed as her son did; Cyrus Pearson wrote an editorial in the paper declaring that the two men wanted to steal the horses for Abolitionists planning to settle in Kansas Territory, where they would skew the electorate and make Kansas a Free State. He called for "all just Men of our Virtuous City" to donate money and arms to send to "our Brethren whose blood has watered the fair fields of Missouri."

"If the Engles care for Missouri so much, they would do well to move there," I grumbled, "and spare the just people of our virtuous city any further diatribes."

"If you don't like what they write in the newspaper, don't read it," snapped Anneke.

"How will I know whether I like what is in the newspaper," said I, "unless I first read it?"

I should not have baited her, but each time she defended the Engles, I grew more irritated. I understood that Mrs. Engle was her friend and employer, but Anneke owed them no loyalty in matters of politics and virtue. In my opinion, which I would have given if asked, Anneke should have left Mrs. Engle to start her own shop, or obtained a position with the tailor, whose wife was one of the Certain Faction and whose dislike of slavery was well known. Anneke would have done so immediately if Hans had asked, but he did not, and I knew he would not. Hans would neither condemn the Engles and their ilk nor support them, preferring to deal equitably with all. This was not merely a businessman's pragmatics on his part; he had told me once that the argument over slavery was not his fight, and that he had no desire to make it so. I believed that his silence lent his tacit support to the Southern cause, but I could not persuade him of this and eventually gave up trying.

Hans did have one decided opinion: Abolitionists or slave catchers, the men were clearly dangerous, and having killed once, they might kill again. Thus did my brother, who had since our arrival at Elm Creek Farm sheltered his horses better than his family, become determined to build us a house with firm stone walls. With the help of Thomas and Jonathan, he broke ground as soon as the soil thawed enough to give way to a pickax.

As other farmers prepared for the spring planting, Hans helped them clear away stones from their fields, exchanging his labor for the stones. He hauled some from riverbanks and creek beds, many from our own land, and others from the countryside for miles around. One large limestone boulder he delivered to a stonecutter, and when it was returned to us, it had been squared off and engraved with the words "Bergstrom 1858." Hans, Anneke, and I each placed our hands upon it and together laid it in place at the northeast corner of the foundation.

Upon this cornerstone, we built our home.

It was a magnificent house by the standards to which we had become accustomed. Two stories and attic, four rooms downstairs and five above, with a kitchen and a fireplace and all the comforts we had longed for throughout those cold winter months in Mr. L.'s cabin. Anneke had saved all her earnings since going to work for Mrs. Engle, and now she poured them into the house, ordering glass windows and a cunning new cookstove, as well as other furnishings. By day I helped Hans in the fields so that he could have more time to work on the house; by night I took on Anneke's share of the housework so that she might accept more work from Mrs. Engle. My brother and sister-in-law devoted themselves to this grand project knowing they would live out their days within those walls; I worked with no less fervor, but with an increasing hope that I might yet have a home of my own someday, and not be dependent upon their kindness forever.

Still, with a superstitious fear that yet embarrasses me, I furnished my own room with special care, as if anticipating my departure would delay it forever. To the bed Hans had made me I added a desk with a comfortable chair, a bookcase, and a table for my washbasin and lamp. Anneke taught me to braid a rag rug for the floor, and sewed curtains for me rather than allow me to waste precious fabric attempting to make them myself. My hope chest I placed at the foot of my bed, and the bed itself I covered with my Shoo-Fly quilt, at last completed.

I had hastened to finish that quilt so that I might sleep under it our first night in the house. That is the only excuse I will make for the glaring error I discovered in it once it was fully spread out upon the bed. In one block, rather than sew the four corner triangles with the vertices touching the central square, I had arranged them pointing out. Naturally, I had not placed this errant block on an edge where it might have been easily hidden, nor in the exact center, where I could pretend I had intentionally contrived a variation on the design, but off to one side near the top, as conspic-uous as could be.

At first, I thought I must promptly fix the mistake, but then I recalled all the hours I had spent cutting and piecing and quilting, and I could not bear to undo any of that labor, even to fix an obvious mistake. At last, exasperated with myself, I decided that no one would see the quilt but myself, and since I would rather have the quilt finished than perfect, I decided to leave it as it was. If I did happen to invite a friend into my room, the artful placement of a pillow would disguise the flaw.

But for Dorothea's first visit I did not hide my error but left it in plain sight, knowing she would enjoy a good laugh with me about it. To my amazement, however, Dorothea did not notice the mistake until I prompted her to search for it! Once alerted, her experienced eye found it immediately, and she consoled me with assurances that the quilt was nonetheless lovely. I retorted that it was warm, and it was done, and that was all that truly mat-tered to me, although it would have been nice to show off my handiwork at the next meeting of the Certain Faction as was customary whenever a mem-ber completed a project. Now I considered my quilt unworthy of such a dis-play.

Dorothea told me I must bring it anyway, mistakes and all. "No one needs to know you did not intend to alter the pattern," added she with a gentle smile. "Tell them it is a humility block."

I had never heard of such a thing, and so Dorothea explained that some would consider it a sin of pride if one attempted to create something without flaw, for only God can create perfection. Therefore, a quilter might deliber-ately place an error in her quilt as a sign of her modesty and humbleness.

I found this quite amusing and promised Dorothea that my quilt would be in no danger of achieving perfection even if I had not sewn that particular block incorrectly. In fact, it seemed to me an even greater sin of pride to as-sume that one needed to add intentional flaws to one's handiwork lest it ap-proach the perfection of the Divine. I told Dorothea so, and she laughed and agreed that perhaps the humility block was invented by a quilter less able to admit her own mistakes than I, and was used more frequently to explain un-intentional mistakes than for its ostensible purpose.

Still, even with the glaring error in my quilt, I was pleased with the sim-ple comforts of my room, but it seemed Spartan in comparison to the room Anneke and Hans shared, with its frilly bed curtains, dainty pillows, and double-ruffled draperies. I choked on silent laughter, imagining my brother surrounded by such pretty things so unsuited for him, but he did not mind, or if he did, he did not complain. Of course, he usually collapsed into bed at night thoroughly exhausted and rose before dawn, so perhaps he never saw the furnishings by the light of day.

But it would be unfair to make light of Anneke's handiwork without giving her credit for assuring our comfort as she increased her sewing skills. The designs she practiced on her own home later appeared in items she created for her customers. There was nothing created by thread and cloth that Anneke could not duplicate, simply by viewing it, without benefit of a pattern or instruction. She could make an elaborate gown after glancing at a drawing in a magazine, or piece a quilt block from memory, having seen the original hanging out to dry as she rode through town.

As much as I then admired my sister-in-law's talent, I cannot now think back on it without a curious mixture of pride and remorse. If not for her gift, we would have been spared the trials that awaited us—and yet, remembering the good we did, I cannot wish she had never picked up a needle. I would not have changed what Anneke's talent and fate conspired to bring our way; I would banish only the fear that led to our undoing.

At the time, of course, I knew only the comfort Anneke's gift brought to our home. She transformed simple calicoes into curtains and tablecloths; with the scraps from her dressmaking she pieced quilts enough to warm every bed in the house several times over. I saw her piecing smaller quilts, too, from the most delicate cottons and softest wools, but since she made no announcement and I saw no change in her manner, I concluded that she and Hans had not yet been blessed with a recipient for these tiny quilts.

I was stumbling along on my second quilt, a Variable Star, when Anneke began piecing what must have been her twentieth, or so it seemed to one as clumsy with a needle as I. Unlike her previous quilts comprised of individual blocks, this one was fashioned of squares and triangles arranged in vertical stripes. "What do you call this pattern?" asked I, curious.

She looked up from her work, startled, and only then did I realize she had thought me lost in a book and herself unobserved. "I do not know the name."

"It's quite pretty. Is it a design of your own invention?"

"No. I saw the block in one of Dorothea's quilts. She did not say it was an original design, so I saw nothing wrong in duplicating it."

"I'm not accusing you of stealing her patterns," said I, surprised by her defensive tone. "Beside, even if it were an original design, I'm sure Dorothea wouldn't mind your using it. She would probably be flattered."

"I suppose so," said she, more conciliatory. "But she behaved so oddly when I asked her about the quilt. When I remarked that the pattern was different from the styles she usually prefers, she simply smiled at me, and when I asked her the name of the pattern, she pretended not to hear me and began a conversation with someone else."

This sounded very unlike Dorothea. "Perhaps she truly did not hear you. Or perhaps you misunderstood her."

Anneke regarded me skeptically. "My English is not *that* bad."

I said nothing more on the subject, uncomfortable hearing criticism of my friend. In all likelihood Anneke had misunderstood Dorothea, but even if she had not, I could think of many reasons why Dorothea would not divulge details about her quilt. Perhaps it was in fact an original design she did not wish to share, or perhaps the quilt was intended as a surprise gift for Thomas, and Dorothea feared Anneke would carelessly give away the secret.

As time passed, and I saw no further evidence of discord between my sister-in-law and my friend, the conversation slipped into the back of my mind. By the time Anneke's quilt was complete, I had forgotten about the exchange entirely, until later events promptly evoked the memory. There were so many other things to think about: the unrelenting work around the farm, the Certain Faction, Jonathan, and our new home, which was taking shape stone by stone.

In hindsight I do not know how we managed it, but by autumn both abundant crops and a new house had risen from the soil of Elm Creek Farm. The first Bergstrom Thoroughbred foals had sold for better prices than even Hans had expected. Anneke's reputation as a seamstress had spread beyond Creek's Crossing, so that Mrs. Engle raised her wages rather than risk having her become a competitor. We rejoiced in the fruits of our labor and assured ourselves that only prosperity and happiness awaited us, just over the horizon.

We did not hear the distant thunder.

❧

"This can't be right," murmured Sylvia.

Andrew looked up from the fly he was tying in preparation for his next fishing trip. "What can't be right?"

"Gerda's memoir." Sylvia hardly knew what to make of it. "She writes that they built the original house in 1858, which I knew, since that's the date engraved on the cornerstone. However, my grandfather was supposed to have been present when they placed the cornerstone, but Gerda expressly states that Anneke and Hans had not yet had any children."

"Are you sure Gerda is the one who has it wrong?"

"I'm not sure of anything anymore," said Sylvia. "Gerda's is most likely the correct version." She wondered why the incongruity troubled her so much. It was hardly the first or even the most drastic she had encountered in the memoir.

"It's probably only a matter of a few years," said Andrew. "It's no surprise a few details got garbled over time."

"That's precisely the problem. I can't help wondering what else has been garbled." Sylvia could feel the first stirrings of a headache, and she rubbed absently at her temples. "It's bad enough to discover that Hans was indifferent to the Abolitionist movement, and Anneke—well, she was far worse, wasn't she? If I didn't know better, I wouldn't be surprised to discover she is the ancestor Margaret Alden and I have in common."

"Don't forget, you're only getting Gerda's side of the story," said Andrew. "The memoir's from her point of view. If you read Hans's memoir, or Anneke's, things might look a lot different."

Sylvia knew Andrew was trying to help, but his observation made her feel worse. The only factual evidence she had was what Anneke had stitched into her quilts and what Gerda had recorded in her memoir, but Grace had made her doubt the authenticity of Anneke's handiwork and now Andrew wanted her to question Gerda's. "If only I had some other record, something to fill in the gaps as well as corroborate what Gerda wrote."

"Summer could search the historical society's archives again."

"But only if I knew what to tell her to look for." She sighed, frustrated. "Why *didn't* Hans and Anneke cooperate by leaving journals of their own? I'd settle for a page or two from Great-Aunt Lucinda, as fanciful as her stories were."

"Was Lucinda your grandfather's elder sister or younger?"

"Younger, although by how much, I don't recall." Suddenly inspiration struck. "Oh, my word. Why didn't I think of it before?"

"Think of what?"

"My mother's Bible," Sylvia called over her shoulder as she hurried out of the sitting room and through the kitchen, startling the cook and his assistant as she passed. By the time Andrew caught up with her, she was halfway down the hall. "It's the family Bible," she explained as they crossed the grand foyer on their way to the carved oak staircase. "Claudia and I were allowed to look at it, but only as my mother held it open for us as we sat on her lap. It was her grandmother's, an heirloom from her side of the family, and she forbade us to touch it without permission. After she died—well, I suppose it sounds foolish, but even as a grown woman I never felt comfortable handling my mother's Bible." Not since that day soon after their mother's death, when Claudia had found her reading it in her refuge, a large, smooth stone beneath a willow tree on the bank of Elm Creek. Claudia had snatched the Bible away and scolded her for taking Mother's treasured possession outside. Sylvia had not touched the Bible since then, but she knew where it would be, if Claudia had not sold it as she had so many of the family's other prized possessions.

Andrew followed Sylvia upstairs to the second floor and down the hallway to the library, where, always the gentleman, he quickened his pace so he could open one of the double doors for her. "So this Bible kept a record of the Bergstrom family milestones—births and deaths and what have you?"

"Births and deaths, marriages and baptisms, all the usual things," said Sylvia. "But as it was my mother's family Bible, the records preceding her marriage to my father are for her family, the Lockwoods."

"Then how will it help?"

"It might not," admitted Sylvia. "But my mother was a conscientious woman, and she would have wanted us to know about our father's ancestors as well as her own. I trust she would have left some record of them."

Sylvia went to the center of the room, which spanned the width of the far end of the south wing. Bright morning sunlight streamed in through the tall windows on the south and east walls, while those on the west wall still had curtains drawn over them. Between the windows stood oak bookcases, their shelves lined with books. Not long after Sylvia's return to Elm Creek Manor, she had hired Sarah to help her prepare the estate for auction. Sarah's first assignment—aside from sweeping the veranda, which didn't really count—was to clean this very room. Sylvia had told her to save what looked worthwhile and toss the rest, dismissing Sarah's hesitant suggestion that Sylvia ought to decide that for herself rather than risk her discarding something important out of ignorance. Surely Sarah would have known to save a Bible, a fine, leather-bound Bible. But there had been so many books, and the library had been so cluttered then, and Sylvia so hard-hearted and uncaring about anything to do with the estate . . .

She went to the first bookcase. "It had a black leather cover," she told Andrew, who had gone to a bookcase on the opposite wall. "Old, but not worn."

"We'll find it," said Andrew reassuringly, as if he sensed her apprehensions. Which, of course, he almost certainly did. Sylvia paused to watch him fondly as he studied the spines of the books before him, head tilted slightly, brow furrowed in concentration.

Then she set herself to work.

Minutes passed in silence as they scanned the shelves, occasionally removing a thick volume with no markings on the cover in order to examine the pages. When one bookcase was finished, they moved on to the next, working down their opposite walls toward the fireplace at the far end of the room. When only one bookcase remained on her side, Sylvia heard Andrew say, "I think I've found it."

She quickly joined him. "Where?"

He nodded to the top shelf. "Up there."

Sylvia followed the line of his gaze to find a black leather book embellished with two thin gold lines above and below the words "Holy Bible." The sight called forth a distant memory, and she suspected they had found it, although it looked much smaller than she remembered.

"I believe that's the one," she said. "Would you get it down for me, please?"

Andrew reached for the book, then hesitated and let his arm fall to his side. "No."

Sylvia stared at him. "No?"

"Not unless you say you'll marry me."

"Andrew, please. I'm in no mood for games."

"This is no game. I mean it."

Sylvia scowled at him and strained to reach the book, but her fingertips only brushed the leather cover. "Stop teasing me and get the Bible down. Please," she remembered to add.

But Andrew merely folded his arms. "You can stretch all you want, but we both know you're not tall enough."

"I'm plenty tall," she retorted, straining for the top shelf once more, hating to admit Andrew was right. "Well, Matthew is taller than you. I'll get him to help me, if you're going to be difficult."

She began to march out of the library, but Andrew called after her, "Don't bother. When Matt gets up here, I'll talk him out of it."

"And what makes you think he'll listen to you instead of me?"

Andrew shrugged. "I think most folks around here would like to see us get married."

"Well, *I* think most folks would agree you've finally lost your marbles."

Andrew allowed a smile. "Maybe I have. Or maybe I'm just taking a lesson from Hans. When he wanted something, he took charge, didn't he? Look how he got Anneke to marry him."

Sylvia cast her gaze to heaven. "Oh, certainly, he's a fine example to follow."

"I love you at least as much as he loved Anneke, and we've known each other much longer than they did." He reached for her hands, and grudgingly, she allowed him to take them. "Come on, Sylvia, say yes."

"I can get the book down myself, you know. All I need to do is fetch a chair."

"I know. But I hope you won't."

"You wouldn't really want me to accept under these circumstances, would you? Knowing you had to blackmail me into marrying you?"

"At this point, I'll take what I can get."

"Andrew . . ." She studied him, dismayed to see that he was in earnest. "What if I promise that I won't marry anyone but you?"

He was silent for a long moment, but then he asked, "Is that the best you can do?"

"I'm afraid so."

"Then I guess I'll have to settle for that." Abruptly he released her hands, then reached up for the Bible. Without meeting her gaze, he handed it to her and strode quickly from the room.

Sylvia watched him go. He ought to know better; he *did* know better. Why would he ask her again, when he had agreed not to, when he knew she would refuse? Had he been dishonest with her when he had made that promise, and had he been hoping all along that she would change her mind, or had he simply found his promise impossible to keep?

What would she do if he decided he could no longer continue as they had been? If the alternative was to lose him, something she did not think she could bear . . .

"I would manage," she said, determined. She had managed alone for decades, and now, with Elm Creek Quilts and her friends, she would not be alone even if Andrew drove away in his motor home and never returned. She would not marry him out of fear or guilt. If he was willing to take her on those terms, then he was no man she wanted as a husband, or even as a friend.

Resolute, she seated herself at the large oak desk on the east side of the room and examined the cover of the book Andrew had handed her. Yes, it was certainly her mother's Bible, and it looked almost exactly the way she remembered it, little changed despite the passage of time. She turned to the first page, to the records of births and deaths and marriages written in several different hands. The last entries were her mother's.

Sylvia's heart welled up with sadness as she gently ran a finger over the lines her mother had written so many years before. The last entry recorded the birth of Sylvia's brother, Richard; no one had thought to record her mother's own death a few years later. If she had lived seventeen more years, she would have written of her son's passing, and that of her husband, her son-in-law, and her only grandchild, born too early to survive.

Sylvia sighed and closed her eyes. Too many of her memories were of people she loved dying too soon. Perhaps that was why she cultivated so many friendships among the young; she was hedging her bets that she'd be the one mourned rather than the mourner for a change.

It was a morbid thought, but she couldn't help a wry chuckle. She opened her eyes and turned the page, promising herself she would return to study her mother's side of the family more carefully another time. Neglecting the Lockwoods' history in favor of the Bergstroms' had been an inevitable consequence of growing up at Elm Creek Manor, but Sylvia could and would remedy that situation.

Today, however, she had another mission. She turned several pages of blank lines where her mother had expected her descendants to continue the family record, until she came to the last space. The facing page would have been blank, except for a few words written in her mother's careful script at the bottom. Between the two pages was a folded sheet of paper.

Sylvia slipped on her reading and quilting glasses, which hung by a fine chain around her neck, and scanned the page. The first words were her parents' names and birthdates; beneath them and connected to the line above by a vertical line were Sylvia's own name and birthdate and her sister's.

A family tree, Sylvia realized, except her mother had never completed it.

She carefully unfolded the piece of paper inserted between the book's pages. Again her mother's handwriting caught her eye, but this time the script seemed less precise, as if the words had been hastily written:

My Freddy (the eldest), his younger brothers Richard, Louis, (both killed in Great War) and William, sister Clara (died age thirteen in influenza epidemic).

Their parents: David Bergstrom, Elizabeth Reece (Reese?) Bergstrom

David's siblings: Stephen, Albert, Lydia, George, Lucinda (definitely youngest), David the eldest or 2nd? Was Stephen or Albert his twin?

Their parents: Hans Bergstrom and Anneke (maiden name?) Bergstrom

Anneke's family?

Hans Bergstrom's siblings: Gerda Bergstrom (married name?) Others? Freddy unsure—ask Lucinda.

"Didn't you ask?" exclaimed Sylvia in dismay, turning over the page in case the list continued on the other side. It was blank, leaving Sylvia with a brief list of names that failed to provide her with the information she had sought, and also posed new questions. How was it that the names of David's five brothers and sisters were known, but not their birth order? Did the parenthetical remark after Gerda's name indicate she had eventually married—and had she married Jonathan? And what was this about David—Sylvia's grandfather—having a twin?

No wonder her mother had not completed the Bergstrom family tree, when so little was known of its branches. Sylvia leafed through the rest of the Bible, hoping in vain to find another page of notes or some other clue, but she found nothing more. Sighing, she closed the Bible and was about to return it to the shelf, but she couldn't resist one more look at her mother's handwriting.

My Freddy (the eldest), her mother had written, and later, *Freddy unsure.*

Tears filled her eyes, but Sylvia smiled. She did not remember ever hearing anyone call her father Freddy instead of the more dignified Frederick. It warmed her heart to think of her mother using the endearment, and for a moment she could imagine her parents a young couple in love, celebrating the intertwining of their two family histories in the births of their children. How her mother must have delighted in each detail of her Freddy's heritage, hungering, as young people in love have always done, to know the child her beloved had been, and wishing that they had met as children, so that their love, which she hoped would extend many years into the future, could also be extended into the past, and thus enjoy an even greater duration.

For a lifetime with the man you loved was never long enough—and a mere few years without him, interminable.

Sylvia slowly closed the Bible upon her mother's notes again and returned the book to its shelf.

Chapter Seven

After the Farewell Breakfast the following Saturday, Gwen Sullivan brought her friend from Penn State's archaeology department to Elm Creek Manor to investigate the half-buried log that Sylvia and her friends hoped had been a part of the Bergstrom cabin. Dr. Frank DiCarlo and the two graduate students who had accompanied him examined the site and, to Sylvia's relief, did not criticize them for uncovering it. Instead, the students photographed the log from several angles while DiCarlo quizzed Sylvia about the cabin. She told him the little she knew, pleased to see his interest pique when she mentioned Gerda's memoir.

The students had brought enough tools for themselves and several helpers, so Matt and Sarah offered their services as work began to unearth the rest of the log. Before long Gwen joined in, and when Andrew took a break from working on the motor home's engine and wandered over to check on their progress, he, too, took up a short-handled brush and began sweeping away at the base of the log. Sylvia doubted her back and knees were up to all that crawling around on the ground, so she contented herself with supervising and keeping the archaeology team supplied with water and lemonade, and seeing to it that they took breaks for meals.

As the hours passed under the hot sun, DiCarlo and his assistants gradually uncovered the rest of the first log and another that met at the corner Andrew had discovered the first day. Then, as the light was beginning to fade, one of the graduate students announced that she had found another log directly beneath the first one.

DiCarlo decided it would be best to end for the day on a high note, so after they secured the site, Sylvia invited everyone inside for supper. Gwen alone begged off. "I'm going home to bed," she said with a groan. "I'm too tired even to lift a fork to my mouth."

"I've never seen you that tired," teased Sylvia, but Gwen bid them all good night and walked—slowly and stiffly—back to her car. The others followed Sylvia inside, then upstairs to the rooms she had prepared for them to shower and change. By the time they returned downstairs and joined her in the banquet hall, she and the cook had set a table with a delicious fried chicken dinner with all the trimmings, pitchers of lemonade and iced tea, and a steaming pot of coffee made from fancy beans Sarah had purchased at a café downtown. It seemed too hot for coffee to Sylvia, but Sarah had insisted that graduate students drank pots and pots of the stuff at all hours of the day, in any weather, so Sylvia permitted it.

As they ate, relaxing and enjoying the satisfaction of a day's work well done, DiCarlo entertained them with stories of other archaeological digs they had undertaken. His projects had taken him to so many exotic locales, investigating sites of such historical importance that Sylvia was taken aback, embarrassed that such important research had been set aside for Mr. L.'s humble shack. She tried to apologize, but DiCarlo assured her he was glad to assist. "This is good training for my students," he said, then grinned and added, "Besides, I owe Gwen a favor."

"Well, I feel I owe you a favor," said Sylvia, nodding to his students to indicate she included them, too. "And to think you're doing all this work for what might be nothing more than a pile of old firewood."

The others laughed, and DiCarlo added, "But that's the mystery that makes this job so exciting. You never know what you're going to turn up. Maybe treasure—"

"Maybe trash," interrupted Sylvia.

The two students exchanged a quick look. "Don't get him started," the one seated beside Matt begged, too late, as DiCarlo launched into an earnest description of what could be learned about a culture by studying its long-buried garbage dumps. Some of the details Sylvia would have preferred to hear another time, preferably when she was not eating, but she was fascinated nonetheless.

"If we could find where your ancestors disposed of their trash," DiCarlo concluded, "you'd learn more about them than you ever dreamed possible."

Sylvia winced. "I don't know if I want to know them *that* well."

The others laughed, and Sylvia joined in, pleased to have such enthusiastic new friends to help her uncover the Bergstroms' past—and equally glad that the next morning they would return to unearthing the cabin, not a landfill.

Unfortunately, by noon Sylvia began to suspect that the archaeology team had exhausted all their good luck the previous day. No amount of searching revealed any adjacent logs that might have formed the third and fourth walls of the cabin, nor did there appear to be anything beneath the logs they had already uncovered. DiCarlo thought he found evidence of a fire, but could not say for certain if it was the cabin itself, some object it contained, or merely logs in a fireplace that had burned. One of the graduate students found a tin spoon and what appeared to be a shard from a teacup, which Sylvia cradled in her hands, wondering who had last used them. Aside from those small treasures, the day ended with nothing new to show for their efforts.

"I almost wish we could find the Bergstroms' garbage heap after all," said Sylvia to Sarah as they helped stow DiCarlo's tools in the back of his truck. "But I couldn't imagine where to look for it."

Sarah shrugged and brushed dirt from her hands. "If Matt had been with them, they would have made a compost pile near the garden."

"The garden," gasped Sylvia. "Sarah, you're a genius." Quickly she returned to the dig, where DiCarlo and his students were securing the remains of the cabin. "Professor, it seems I have another archaeological find to show you."

Mindful of the fading light, she led the excavation team back across Elm Creek, past the manor, and into a thick grove of trees to the north. If Sarah had not prompted her memory, Sylvia would have forgotten entirely to show the professor Hans's gazebo.

The story of the gazebo in the north gardens was one of the first she had shared with Sarah about the history of Elm Creek Manor, as they were taking their first tentative steps toward friendship. The octagonal gazebo with the gingerbread molding had been in near ruins then, but the Log Cabin blocks fashioned from wood veneers fitted into its seats were still visible. One of those seats had a block with a black center square, and if pushed in just the right way, the wooden slats folded into a hidden recess beneath the bench like a rolltop desk, revealing a hiding place beneath the gazebo. According to family lore, fugitive slaves would conceal themselves in the hiding place until nightfall, when one of the Bergstroms would escort them into the safety of the manor.

Sylvia repeated the tale to her companions as they walked, but when the gazebo came into view, DiCarlo's expression shifted from intrigue to polite interest. She showed him the Log Cabin blocks and enlisted Matthew's help in pushing back the top to the secret bench, hoping to whet his eagerness again, but before long DiCarlo shook his head.

"I don't know anything about quilt blocks," said DiCarlo. "But I can tell you this gazebo couldn't have been built in your great-grandfather's day. It's far more recent."

"How recent?" asked Sylvia.

Carefully, as if reluctant to disappoint her, he indicated several features that helped him date the structure, including everything from the good condition of the wood to the type of concrete in the foundation to the bolts holding the benches together. "In my estimation, the gazebo doesn't predate the twentieth century."

"It's been refurbished," said Sylvia, unwilling to believe him. "Matthew, tell the professor how you repaired it so he can focus on the original structure."

Matthew complied, but as he listed his alterations, Sylvia realized that DiCarlo had detected the recent work and had accounted for it in his evaluation.

"I don't understand," said Sarah. "If the story about the gazebo isn't true, then—" She broke off at a warning look from Matthew.

"No, go on. You might as well finish the thought." Sylvia sank heavily onto the nearest bench. "If that story isn't true, how can we believe anything my great-aunt Lucinda told me?"

"She described the trunk accurately and gave you the key," said Andrew.

"There is that. Pity. Now I can't simply dismiss her as a pathological liar," said Sylvia dryly. "Then at least I would know everything she told me was false. Now she forces me to sift through her stories, hoping the lies slip through my fingers and the truth remains in my hands."

"I can't believe she would be so malicious as to deliberately deceive you," said Sarah. "Maybe she thought the story about the gazebo was true."

"I suppose." Sylvia sighed and rose. "But that means someone lied to her."

"Or they told her the truth, but she misunderstood," said Andrew.

Despite her disappointment, Sylvia had to laugh. She reached up and patted Andrew's cheek, then smiled at her friends. "You all do try to keep my spirits up, don't you? I appreciate your loyalty to my ancestors, but you don't need to defend them so ardently." She caught Andrew's eye. "I've accepted that the Bergstroms were mere mortals after all."

And one of them had built the gazebo with a hiding place indicated by a Log Cabin block with a black center square—but who, and more puzzling still, since it could not have been done to conceal fugitive slaves, why?

After supper—a more subdued affair than the previous night's meal—DiCarlo and his students vacated their rooms and loaded their belongings into DiCarlo's truck. Before they left, DiCarlo told Sylvia how to properly preserve the site. "You might want to continue the excavation on your own," he suggested. "You might find something we missed."

"Such as a garbage heap?" said Sylvia. "Thank you, Professor, but if you and your students couldn't find anything, I doubt we amateurs will have any better success."

"I know you're disappointed we didn't find more, but don't forget, you did find a cabin exactly where that journal of yours said it would be."

As DiCarlo and his companions drove away, her pride in their discovery rekindled. The professor was right. It did not matter how much of the cabin they had found, only that they now knew with confidence that they *had* found it, and not some mere woodpile or fallen tree. It was enough to know she had found Gerda's first home in America, the first home on Bergstrom land.

❧ *Late autumn through December 1858 — in which I reap a bitter harvest*

The first crisp evenings of autumn meant that harvesttime would soon be upon us, and Elm Creek Farm bustled with activity as we prepared for the coming winter. Anneke offered to make me another dress for the annual Harvest Dance, and this year I promptly accepted, determined to look as lovely as a plain woman could. Jonathan and I had known each other for more than two years, and there was no mistaking his growing affection for me, nor mine for him, although we never spoke of it. I thought any day he might ask me to become his wife, and when he did, I planned to accept with all my heart. The days when I ached for the loss of E. seemed dim and far away.

Anneke sewed me a gown of beautiful lavender silk brocade, and when I tried it on, even Anneke was amazed by my transformation. I felt myself blushing like a young girl as I envisioned the pleasure in Jonathan's eyes when he first beheld me, and when I drifted off to sleep at night, I imagined his hand at the small of my back as he pulled me close to him in a dance. It would not be long, I knew, I hoped, until I would call him husband.

But a week before the Harvest Dance, when I met Anneke at the door of Mrs. Engle's dressmaker's shop, my sister-in-law seemed troubled. "Gerda," said she as she climbed onto the wagon seat beside me. "I have dreadful news."

"Mrs. Engle and Mr. Pearson are finally moving South?"

"This is not a joking matter."

Only then did I see how pale she had become, and how reluctant she was to speak. "Tell me," said I. "Whatever it is, it cannot be that bad."

Anneke took two deep breaths and placed a hand to her stomach before speaking. "Charlotte Claverton came to be fitted for a dress today."

"Did she, indeed?" I had not forgotten the beautiful, dark-haired girl who had been Jonathan's dance partner far too often for my taste the previous autumn, but Jonathan and I had become such intimate friends that I no longer feared her as a rival. "I suppose she wants to cut a fine figure at the Harvest Dance, like the rest of us." Perhaps a tiny spark of jealousy remained. "I don't suppose you'd be willing to sew a few crooked seams just this once?"

"Gerda. It wasn't a dress for the dance. It was her wedding gown."

"She's getting married? How delightful for her."

"She's marrying Jonathan."

Through the ringing in my ears I heard the steady clop, clop, clop of the horse's hooves on the road. I heard wind rustling in the trees as we passed, and the splash of water in Elm Creek.

"Gerda, did you hear me?"

"You must be mistaken." My voice sounded high and thin in my ears, falsely nonchalant. "She can't be marrying Jonathan. Not . . ." *Not my Jonathan,* I almost said.

"She is. I heard her tell Mrs. Engle. They will have a Christmas wedding."

"You must have heard wrong." It took every bit of my strength to get the words out. "Jonathan would have told me himself. He, or Dorothea."

"Gerda—"

"It cannot be true." I shook the reins and urged the horses onward at a faster pace, overcome by the need for home. "I refuse to listen to such nonsense."

Anneke said nothing more, but I could sense her fighting back tears. My mind was a blur of confusion and worry. Anneke believed what she told me; that was certain. She could have been mistaken—but that seemed unlikely. What was there to misinterpret about a woman being fitted for her wedding gown?

At home I began to prepare our supper without a word for Anneke or my brother. She must have told Hans the news when I was outside in the kitchen garden, for all evening he spoke to me with gentle kindness rather than the brotherly teasing to which I was accustomed. I retired early, but I was too sick at heart to sleep. Never in all my conversations with Jonathan had he even hinted that he planned to marry Charlotte Claverton. However, I was forced to admit that neither had he said he wished to marry me.

As the night passed and my apprehensions grew, I subjected my memories to unflinching scrutiny. Had I read too much into Jonathan's attentions? Had I perceived love where there was only friendship? But as I reviewed the past two years once, and again, and again, I could not believe that he did not care for me as much as I cared for him. His words, his actions, the smiles that lit up his face when we greeted each other—no, I concluded, I had not deluded myself. It was improbable that Anneke had misunderstood Charlotte Claverton, but equally so was the idea that Jonathan was in love with someone other than myself.

I held fast to that dim hope and somehow managed to drift off to sleep. I woke a few hours later, the pain in my heart having faded to a dull ache, and remembered it was a Saturday. Jonathan would arrive by midmorning, and we would stroll along Elm Creek together until lunchtime, as we had done every Saturday morning for months. Usually we discussed books or politics or matters of faith, but today I would have no choice but to speak plainly to him regarding ourselves.

But the morning passed, and then midday, and still he had not arrived. With each hour that crawled by, the sickening knot of dread in my stomach tightened. Each moment of his absence made Anneke's rumor seem more credible. I completed my chores for the day, and yet he still had not appeared. Finally I took up my Churn Dash quilt and tried to forget my distress in the rhythm of the stitches, telling myself he would surely arrive before I finished piecing a single block.

Two completed blocks had joined the others in my sewing basket when I finally heard a horse approaching, and then the sound of Jonathan calling out a greeting to my brother as he rode past the barn. I waited for his knock on the door before I set my sewing aside and rose to meet him.

I opened the door, and when I saw Jonathan's expression, all my hopes were destroyed.

"I'm sorry I'm late," said he, his face white and remorseful. "The Watson boy fell from his horse and broke his arm."

"Will he be all right?"

"Yes . . . yes, he'll be fine." He hesitated. "Gerda, may I come in?"

I nodded, not trusting myself to speak. My legs felt so weak that I quickly returned to my chair. I picked up my sewing again, hoping to disguise my grief by feigning normalcy, but my hands trembled so badly that I simply held the pieces in my lap, my eyes fixed upon them. I did not know what to do. I knew that the moment Jonathan spoke, my illusions that I would ever become his wife would vanish for good.

"I understand . . ." He tried again. "I am told you visited Mrs. Engle's dress shop yesterday."

"In a manner of speaking. I waited for Anneke in the wagon. I did not go in."

He nodded and looked around distractedly. "But Anneke—she told you who was inside?"

I could not bear his careful maneuvering as he tried to determine how much I knew. "She did mention one customer. Charlotte Claverton. I believe you are acquainted."

"Gerda, you must let me explain."

"Tell me first if it is true."

"Gerda—" He paced to the fireplace and back. "Yes. It is true. Charlotte Claverton and I will be married in six weeks."

It seemed an eternity until I could speak. "I see."

In a moment he was on his knees beside my chair, his hands grasping mine. "Gerda, I never meant for you to find out this way. I wanted to tell you myself. I tried to tell you so many times, but—"

"But?"

"I found I could not."

I strangled out a laugh. "In the course of all our conversations, you could not find one appropriate moment to mention you were going to be married?"

"I could not—" His voice broke off, and he seemed to struggle to find the words. "I did not, because I knew it would mean the end of our friendship, and I could not bear that."

"You were no true friend to me," said I, coldly.

"I know." He rose and raked a hand through his hair. "I regret that more than you will ever know. But Gerda, you must understand. Charlotte and I have known each other since we were children. Our parents' farms are adjacent properties. We were promised to each other before we knew what that meant. It was always understood that we would marry one day."

I could not believe what I was hearing. "You will marry because your parents arranged it? You, with all your modern ideas, would agree to such a marriage?"

"It is not that simple. When I came of age, I asked for her hand and made my parents' promise my own. It was expected of me, and I did not know . . ."

"What?"

"That one day I would meet you."

I held his gaze long enough to read the remorse and frustration tearing him apart. "Break off the engagement," I heard myself say.

"It is too late for that."

"No." I shook my head and flew from my chair to his side, where I grasped his hands. "You have not yet exchanged marriage vows, so it is not too late. She has an unfinished gown and a promise made long ago. There will be a small embarrassment, but it will be forgotten soon."

"She thinks she loves me."

"She is a young woman. She will find someone else. If she cares for you, she will not begrudge you your happiness."

"Gerda, I will marry Charlotte." He caressed my cheek with the back of his hand. "I made her a promise. I gave her my word, and I am a man of my word."

I choked back tears. "Your honor is more important than our happiness?"

"I thought you knew me," said he, his voice a quiet rebuke. "Breaking my word would result in the injury of an innocent young woman. You could not expect me to do that merely to satisfy my own desires."

And what of my desires? I wanted to shout, but I knew this would not move him. "Tell me you do not love me and that you do love Charlotte. Tell me this and I will say nothing more on the subject."

He regarded me for a long, silent moment. "I cannot say that."

"Why not?"

"Because it would be a lie. You know I love you."

My heart swelled with grief. At last he had told me what I had so longed to hear, but the words meant nothing now. "Then you do Charlotte no favor by marrying her. She deserves a husband who loves her. If she knew the truth, she would release you from your promise."

He shook his head. "She suspects my affection for you, and yet she still wishes to marry me. As long as she holds me to my promise, I will honor it. And as long as I live, I will be a good husband to her. If I do not in time come to love her as a husband should, she will never know it."

I shook my head vehemently, unable to believe what I was hearing. I wanted to tell him that they were both fools, but I was afraid that if I spoke, I would burst into sobs. And I had too much pride to show him the depth of my grief.

"Gerda, I would not have you despise me for the world. Tell me I have your blessing."

The pleading ache in his voice dissolved my remaining composure. "I wish you and Charlotte every happiness," I choked out, and fled to my room.

I did not hear Jonathan leave, but before long, Anneke came and tried to comfort me. I would not be consoled. I grieved not only for the loss of Jonathan but also in anger and shame, that I should again be humiliated by a man who claimed to love me. I had fled my home in Germany to escape that embarrassment, but this time I could not leave my grief behind. I would remain in Creek's Crossing until the end of my days, where the sight of Jonathan and Charlotte together would again and again tear open the scar over my wounded heart.

Later that evening, Hans took me aside and asked me somberly if Jonathan had ever made any promises of marriage to me. I shook my head, and Hans nodded in relief. "If I thought he had misled you," said he, "I would not allow him to set foot on my farm again."

"It is I who misled myself." At that moment I vowed I never would again.

Naturally, after that, Jonathan refrained from visiting Elm Creek Farm, and I could not bear to call on the Nelsons. I missed the Certain Faction and longed for Dorothea's company, and yet I could not help but bear a smoldering anger for her, my dearest friend. She must have known about her brother's engagement, and yet she had said nothing, despite witnessing the growing affection between Jonathan and me. I could not understand her silence, and I resented her for it.

A week passed, and the day of the Harvest Dance arrived. I had no intention of going, but Anneke entreated me. "You must not let anyone see that you have been hurt," said she. "You will wear the lavender silk brocade and look lovely in it, and you will hold your head high. Don't cower at home as if you are the one who acted shamefully."

Her bitterness surprised me, and only then did I realize she had not mentioned Jonathan's name the entire week. "He never lied to me," said I, unwilling to hear him criticized.

"No, but he knowingly deceived you, and that is just as bad."

I was unused to Anneke's anger, so I agreed to attend the dance rather than argue. And as difficult as it was, I obeyed her instructions. I danced with other men as if I did not long for Jonathan's embrace. I expressed delight when the news of the engagement spread through the gathering, and wondered aloud with everyone else how they had managed to keep it a secret so long. When Anneke and I crossed paths with Jonathan and Charlotte as they left the dance floor, I gave them my best wishes for a long and happy marriage, conscious of the watchful eyes upon me.

Only with Dorothea could I not disguise my true feelings. I knew this as soon as I saw her arrive on Thomas's arm. She called out to me, but I pretended not to hear, and for the rest of the evening, I avoided her.

I would have happily avoided Cyrus Pearson as well, but to my chagrin, he sought me out. Three times I managed to snatch another partner before he could ask me for a dance, but the fourth time, he shouldered some other fellow aside and grabbed my hand. "Well, if it isn't the lovely Miss Bergstrom," said he. "At last I have the honor to escort you to the dance floor."

"The honor is mine, Mr. Pearson," said I. Anyone listening would have thought it a cordial exchange, but we knew differently.

"Did you hear the good news?" asked he as we began to dance.

"What news is that?"

"Dr. Granger and Miss Claverton are going to be married." He assumed a look of mock sorrow. "Oh, I suppose you wouldn't consider that good news at all, would you?"

"Of course I would. I'm delighted for them."

"Some people say you aspired above your station and sought to become the doctor's wife."

"Aspired above my station?" I regarded him with feigned astonishment. "My goodness, is this not America, where all are created equal? Did I return to Europe without realizing it?"

His mouth twitched in a scowl, but he persisted. "My mother told me Anneke was quite disturbed when she learned of the engagement. And since you and Dr. Granger's sister are such intimate friends, one naturally assumes—"

Scornfully, I said, "Between your assumptions and my sister-in-law's matchmaking, I should have been married a long time ago."

"Indeed, Miss Bergstrom," said he. "With your great beauty and charming manner, it is a miracle you remain a spinster."

He had guided us to the edge of the dance floor as he spoke, and with those last words, he bowed, released my hand, and left me there. My face flaming, I spun around and returned to the quilt where Anneke and Hans were resting between dances. In a low voice, I begged them to allow us to leave, but Anneke was resolute that I should remain and continue to behave as if all was well. When Hans echoed her, I reluctantly acquiesced, but only after they promised to keep Cyrus Pearson away from me. Anneke frowned, as she always did when reminded how poorly I got along with her employer's eldest son, but they agreed. As it turned out, there was no need; his mission to wound me accomplished, Mr. Pearson spared me no more than a passing glance the rest of the evening.

For the next two weeks, neither Anneke nor I attended the meetings of the Certain Faction. Apparently she did not feel I needed to maintain my facade of indifference before Dorothea, whom she held partially responsible for my disappointment. I assumed I would have to learn to live without Dorothea's friendship as well as Jonathan's love, but Dorothea was unwilling to sacrifice our friendship to her brother's foolishness.

In those days, as a part of their training for married life, young ladies would learn to sew by piecing quilts. It was the custom among some families in our region that a young woman of merit would have completed twelve quilt tops by the time she reached marriageable age. The thirteenth quilt was to be her masterpiece, a sign that she had learned all the womanly arts of needlework she would need as a wife and mother, and these quilts were often elaborate works of appliqué, embroidery, and stuffed work called trapunto. When the young woman became engaged, all the bride-to-be's female friends and relations would gather for a quilting bee, where the thirteen pieced and appliquéd tops would be quilted. These were festive occasions, full of merriment and congratulations for the future bride, and I had attended several since arriving in Creek's Crossing. As the sister of the groom, Dorothea appropriately offered to host Charlotte Claverton's bee, and since the Clavertons were well regarded in society, and Jonathan well respected as the town's only physician, it was seen as the most important social event of the year for the women of the town, even more important than the Harvest Dance.

When Anneke and I received two of those sought-after invitations, my instinct was to throw them on the fire, but Anneke stayed my hand. "If we do not attend, it will confirm the rumors that you resent Charlotte and want her betrothed for yourself."

I did resent Charlotte, and of course I wanted Jonathan, but since I could not have him, I could not bear for the entire town to know it.

Hans considered that reason enough for me to avoid the gathering. "As many people will be watching you as the bride," said he. "You have never been one to conceal your emotions. Your true feelings will be plain for all to see."

It seemed no matter what I did, the people of Creek's Crossing were likely to see a scandal simply because they wished to. Since I could not win, I took Hans's caution as a challenge and decided to attend the quilting bee.

Anneke, whose imperfect English remained a source of embarrassment for her, asked me to respond to the invitation, and so I did, feeling a curious mixture of eagerness and dread with each stroke of my pen. I missed my friends, even Dorothea, who had betrayed me with her silence, and longed for the warmth of their company. I grew weary when I imagined maintaining a pretense of contentment all day under the scrutiny of gossips, but I convinced myself that once that day had ended, the whole sad business would be in the past. And, although many women in my situation would have wished to avoid their rival in her moment of triumph, I hungered to see Charlotte Claverton. We had never spoken except for our brief exchange at the Harvest Dance, and I wanted to take my measure of her. I was convinced that everything I learned about her would confirm that she was a selfish child and a poor match for Jonathan, and that he would have been infinitely happier with me. I needed to confirm this—and I wanted Charlotte Claverton to know me, so that she would reach the same conclusion.

At last the day of the quilting bee arrived, so Anneke and I rolled up our thimbles, needles, and spools of thread in clean aprons and rode to the Nelson farm. I wondered how Dorothea would address me—if she would act as if nothing ill had passed between us, if she would pretend as I was forced to pretend that her brother meant nothing to me. Thomas greeted us when we arrived and took care of the horses while we went inside to join the ladies. I did not realize until that moment how much I had hoped to find Dorothea so eager to apologize that she had waited on the front porch or, better yet, had come halfway down the road to meet me.

Inside, Anneke and I were greeted by joyful embraces of the Certain Faction and friendly welcomes from what seemed to be all the womenfolk living within twenty miles of Creek's Crossing. How like Dorothea, I thought, to invite so many that the house seemed full to bursting, rather than hurt anyone's feelings by excluding them. And not long after, I discovered how inclusive Dorothea's invitation had been: Not only was Mrs. Engle present, but so, too, was Mrs. Constance Wright, a colored woman whose family owned a farm about a mile southwest of ours, as well as a number of other colored women I did not know. I forgot my own turmoil for a moment in looking forward to making their acquaintance—but I will confess, instead of contemplating how I could make these women feel welcome when some present would surely scorn them, I instead looked forward to enjoying Mrs. Engle's discomfort at their presence. Fortunately, Dorothea treated them with more than enough friendly intimacy to compensate for my defects of character.

The two front rooms of the Nelson home had been given over to the party, and in each a large quilting frame had been set up and chairs arranged alongside. "We seem to have far more willing hands than necessary," I murmured to Anneke, secretly pleased that I might be spared the insufferable chore of helping Charlotte Claverton complete her wedding quilts.

"We will take turns," retorted Anneke, knowing my thoughts, "and you will do your fair share."

I frowned and scanned the crowd in vain for Dorothea or Charlotte. Over the din I heard laughter coming from the kitchen, and I knew at once that I would find Dorothea within. Just then I saw Mrs. Engle approaching, full of smiles for my sister-in-law. Given the choice between confronting Dorothea or forcing polite conversation with the mother of Cyrus Pearson, I decided to brave the kitchen.

Dorothea spotted me as soon as I entered; she immediately broke off a conversation, dusted her hands on her apron, and approached me. "I'm so sorry, Gerda," said she in a murmur so that we would not be overheard.

"You could have told me," said I, shortly, for I still resented her. "You would have spared me a world of pain."

"It was not my secret to tell." She placed a hand on my arm, and her eyes were full of tears. "Gerda, so many times I urged him to tell you the truth. So many times I tried to convince him to reconsider his engagement. He is a fool to marry Charlotte when his heart belongs to you. I told him so, but he would not listen."

Her words—and the heartfelt sorrow with which she spoke them—melted my anger. I had lost Jonathan, but I would not allow my dearest friendship to perish because of it.

Somehow I endured the day. Despite the many eager workers, there was a great deal of quilting to be done, and although the more experienced quilters set a pace far more brisk than I was accustomed to, I was determined to keep up. I meant to show with every stitch I put into those quilts that I did not covet Charlotte Claverton's husband-to-be.

And although my bitterness had eased with Dorothea's apology, as we finished all thirteen of Charlotte's beautiful quilts, I could not help appraising Charlotte's every word and action. She was obviously my superior in beauty; I provided not the least competition in that regard. She was charming and seemed kind, and everyone from Dorothea to Mrs. Engle was fond of her, although of course Mrs. Engle's esteem hardly held much merit with me. She was, thankfully, an Abolitionist in spirit, although her behavior more closely mirrored Hans's isolationist stance than Dorothea's activism. However, she was unlearned, and reluctant to express an opinion differing from whomever she happened to be speaking with at the moment. With Jonathan's help she could learn, if she was willing, and if she applied herself, but her unwillingness to speak her mind would be more difficult to overcome. I thought of all the conversations—heated debates they were, sometimes—Jonathan and I had shared, and when I pictured him attempting to draw out the same intellectual passion from Charlotte, my heart grew troubled. By the end of the evening, I concluded that indeed Jonathan and I were of like minds and would have made a far more excellent match. But this realization, which I had thought would bring me satisfaction if not peace, instead made me sadder yet.

In the interim between the quilting bee and the wedding, I prayed that the engagement would be called off, that Jonathan would sacrifice his honor to my happiness, or that Charlotte Claverton would release him from his ill-made promise. I wished no harm to befall either one of them, but I sometimes prayed to die before they exchanged wedding vows, for witnessing that, I was certain, would kill me.

It did not, of course. Such ill strokes occur only in romances or in song.

Jonathan and Charlotte married on Christmas Eve, before all their happy friends and one plain woman from Germany who closed her heart around her grief and tried to wish her beloved happiness with the fate he had chosen. Instead, she hoped—I hoped—that he would come to regret his decision, and that he would be as desperately unhappy in marriage as he had made me in my spinsterhood. Today I am ashamed of my bitter thoughts, but on his wedding day, which should have been ours, I could not feel otherwise.

Jonathan took his bride into his parents' home, and when the couple's parents passed on, Dr. and Mrs. Jonathan Granger's inheritances combined to form the largest farm in the county, just as their parents had wished. They fared well, and had four children, and many grandchildren as well, although I do not remember exactly how many. There is no reason why I should remember, since it had nothing to do with me.

Perhaps you wonder, Reader, why I bothered to record these events here. Since I did not marry Jonathan and he did not join the Bergstrom family, it would seem his life had little bearing on the Bergstrom legacy. I assure you, I do not relive those painful days for my own amusement, but because it is important that you know what sort of man he was. Anneke made the choice that condemned us, but with Jonathan's help, she brought about what I hope will be our redemption.

❧

Sylvia sat lost in thought, the memoir resting open on her lap. She longed for some magic that would allow her to reach back into the past and comfort Gerda, whose pain she understood all too well. Their circumstances differed, of course, but both she and Gerda had been forever separated from the men they loved: Sylvia by death, Gerda by marriage.

Memories of her own husband suddenly sparked Sylvia's indignation. Gerda wished the Bergstrom descendants to know what sort of man

Jonathan Granger had been—and Sylvia knew, all right. He was a spineless, selfish fool. Even in her anger Gerda seemed to want to excuse his behavior, but Sylvia wasn't buying. He should have told Gerda about the engagement the moment he sensed the growing attraction between them. And what utter nonsense, to marry because one's parents wanted to join two farms together! Gerda was better off without such in-laws, and certainly better off alone than linked for life to a dishonest rascal. Sylvia couldn't imagine why Gerda thought it would be important for future Bergstroms to know about Jonathan, except to warn the young ladies of the family about deceitful young men.

She glanced down at the last page she had read, and frowned when she read the final sentence in the entry. More cryptic allusions that Anneke had done something dreadful. Wondering what on earth her great-grandmother had done to provoke Gerda's harsh judgment was enough to drive Sylvia to distraction.

"Then why don't you just flip through the book until you find the section where she explains?" asked Sarah later that week. The Elm Creek Quilters had gathered in the formal parlor for their weekly business meeting after the Wednesday evening camp activities, and as usual, after these matters had been discussed, they caught up on their personal news.

"She doesn't want to spoil the suspense," said Gwen.

"It would be like peeking at her presents before Christmas morning," added Agnes with a smile.

"That's not it," said Sylvia. "I'm also looking for information about the quilts, something Gerda might have mentioned in passing or something that can only be deduced based upon the context. If I don't read carefully, I might miss the one piece of evidence I need."

"You can always read it more thoroughly later," said Sarah. "Won't you at least skim through it until you find out how Gerda and Jonathan ended up together?"

"Yes, do it," urged Diane. "I mean, was the ceremony invalid for some reason? Did Charlotte die, or what?"

Sylvia studied them. "What makes you think Gerda and Jonathan eventually married?"

They exchanged a look. "I don't know," said Sarah. "I just assumed they did."

"Well, I think it's quite evident they did not." Abruptly Sylvia rose. "Honestly, Sarah. These were real people living real lives, not characters in a storybook. Don't expect a happy ending."

Without another word, she left the room, leaving her friends gaping in astonishment. Halfway to her bedroom, Sylvia regretted letting her temper get the better of her. She considered returning to apologize, but she was in a foul mood, and whatever she said was likely to come out wrong and make matters worse. Fortunately, the Elm Creek Quilters weren't ones to hold grudges. After all, they'd forgiven her for far worse.

Sure enough, the next morning at breakfast, Sarah acted as if nothing had happened. Sylvia was glad her young friend didn't ask her to explain her outburst, because Sylvia wasn't sure what had made her temper flare. She was angry at Jonathan and frustrated that she could do nothing to help Gerda—and she felt foolish for allowing events of the far distant past to affect her so.

Later that afternoon, she returned to her sitting room determined to read on as objectively as she imagined Professor DiCarlo approached an archaeological dig. She had just picked up the memoir and had settled into her favorite armchair when Summer knocked tentatively on the door frame. "Is it safe to come in?"

"Of course, dear. I've vowed not to act like an ogre today."

Summer grinned. "That's a relief. I left my ogre repellent at home." She sat down on the footstool and placed her backpack on the floor between her feet. "I stopped by the library today."

"And what did you discover?"

In reply, Summer removed a manila folder from her backpack and handed it to Sylvia. Inside was a document, a certificate of some sort, reproduced from microfiche. Quickly Sylvia slipped on her glasses and scanned the page. "Oh, my word."

"It's their marriage certificate, isn't it?" asked Summer, eager. "It has to be them."

"I don't see how it could be anyone else." Sylvia ran a finger along each line as she read aloud. "Dr. Jonathan Granger, Miss Charlotte Claverton—the date is correct, too. December twenty-fourth." Sylvia set down the folder and beamed at Summer. "My dear, you are a wonder."

"You say that, and you didn't even see what else is in the folder."

Quickly Sylvia looked under the first sheet and found a second. "Mr. Hans Bergstrom, Miss Anneke Stahl—" She gasped. "You found my great-grandparents' marriage record!"

"It wasn't difficult, once I found Jonathan's and figured out the filing system." Summer grinned. "But you can go ahead and call me a wonder again, if you like."

"You are certainly that, and many other delightful things as well." Sylvia gazed at the paper and suddenly gasped again. "Anneke Stahl—my goodness, I know her maiden name now. Even my mother didn't know that."

"Now you can add it to your family Bible."

Sylvia nodded as if she had intended to do so all along, but Summer's suggestion caught her by surprise. It had not occurred to her to finish the record her mother had begun, and she could not explain why. Was it a sense of prohibition lingering from childhood, or did she wish to preserve the Bible exactly as her mother had left it? Sylvia had no descendants who would chastise her for failing to fill in the gaps in the family history, and yet leaving the record incomplete didn't feel right.

"I think my mother would have wanted that," said Sylvia slowly. Yes, she was sure of it.

"Sylvia . . ." Summer hesitated. "Because of what Sarah and Diane said, I looked for a marriage record for Gerda and Jonathan. I didn't find one."

"Of course not, dear. I would have been astonished if you had."

"But just because I didn't find the record, that doesn't mean they didn't marry eventually," added Summer hastily. "They could have married after the years I searched, or they could have married somewhere other than Creek's Crossing, or maybe the record was lost—"

"Now, now, Summer. You don't need to keep my hopes alive." Sylvia closed the folder and set it on the table beside her armchair. "Jonathan married Charlotte and that's that. Gerda said quite explicitly that she did not marry Jonathan and he did not join the Bergstrom family. I don't know why Sarah and Diane assumed otherwise."

"Maybe because they wanted it to be true. I know I did." Again Summer paused. "I thought you should know, I also looked for a marriage record for Gerda and Cyrus."

"What?" Sylvia stared at her. "Why on earth for? They despised each other."

"They did in 1858, anyway."

"What do you mean? What did you find?"

"Nothing," said Summer quickly. "I didn't find a record for them."

"Well, my heavens." Sylvia tried to compose herself. "Goodness. You could have said so at the beginning."

"I only meant that their feelings could have changed with time," said Summer, looking as if she was choosing her words carefully in order to avoid alarming Sylvia again. "Would it really be that extraordinary if they fell in love? He did try to court her once. Now Jonathan has abandoned her, she's lonely, and you have to admit, she and Cyrus do have rather intense feelings for each other."

"Yes, intensely negative. Don't you remember what Mr. Pearson wrote in the Creek's Crossing newspaper? How could an Abolitionist like Gerda marry someone like that?"

Summer shrugged, uncomfortable. "Remember that Jonathan and Dorothea were the ones who first introduced Gerda to the Abolitionist movement. They betrayed Gerda. Maybe in anger she turned against everything they believed in."

"I don't accept that." Sylvia frowned and shook her head. "Remember, she was writing in 1895, so she knows how things turned out, even if we don't. There would have been some sign of it in her memoir."

"You're right. It was just a thought. Anyway, it turned out not to mean anything, because I couldn't find a record for them."

"And thank goodness for that," declared Sylvia, as if that put an end to the matter.

But in her heart she knew the question was far from settled. Sylvia's mother had written a comment in the Bible that could mean that she was uncertain of Gerda's married name, unsure whether she had married at all, or both. Cyrus Pearson and his mother had apparently expressed interest in moving to the South. If they had done so, and Gerda had left Elm Creek Farm to marry Cyrus, she might have made a quilt in memory of the home and family she had left behind . . .

No. Quickly Sylvia closed her mind to such thoughts. Even in her disappointment, Gerda would not have turned her back on her principles. Sylvia would not believe it, despite the many inconsistencies and questions a marriage between Gerda and Cyrus would explain.

Sylvia closed the book and shut it firmly away in her desk drawer. If Gerda had married Cyrus, Sylvia would rather not know.

Chapter Eight

I f Sylvia's friends noticed she left the memoir untouched the rest of the day, they said nothing about it. Only Andrew mentioned the book, when he reminded Sylvia to pack it for an extended weekend trip to Door County, Wisconsin. They were well into Ohio before Andrew suggested she read aloud from it as he drove, and when Sylvia told him she had left it at home, he merely nodded and turned on the radio instead. Sylvia didn't tell him she had left it behind on purpose, but she suspected he knew.

They spent two days in Sturgeon Bay, where they enjoyed a traditional fish boil and boating on Lake Michigan as the guests of one of Andrew's army buddies and his wife. Then they drove north and west to a campsite overlooking Green Bay, not far from the quaint shops and charming restaurants of Egg Harbor and Fish Creek. Andrew persuaded Sylvia to join him on a tandem bicycle for a jaunt through Peninsula State Park. Sylvia half feared she was in for a teeth-chattering ramble over rocky hiking trails, but Andrew knew all the paved routes from previous visits and only occasionally made her shriek with alarm by steering too close to a tree.

They woke Tuesday morning to the sound of rain pattering on the motor home's roof, but they did not mind the change in the weather, since they had planned to head back that day anyway. Only as they crossed the Illinois border did Sylvia feel melancholy creeping into her thoughts. Although every bit of the heat and humidity felt like summer, the northern Wisconsin forest they had left behind had already begun changing into autumnal hues. She didn't like the reminder that within weeks summer would soon end, and Elm Creek Quilt Camp would conclude for the season. Although Sylvia wasn't as involved with the day-to-day operations as she had once been, she would miss the campers' presence, and the way they filled her home with their laughter and energy.

Andrew spread the drive home to Waterford over three days, giving them plenty of time for sight-seeing along the way. They pulled into the parking lot behind the manor just in time for supper on Thursday evening. In honor of their return, all the Elm Creek Quilters stayed for the meal. It was almost like old times again, back when their business was new, when each day of camp presented unexpected challenges and they were never quite sure if they would survive until the campers left after breakfast on Saturday. Back then they had assured one another that eventually they would fall into a smooth, well-functioning routine, but now that they had, Sylvia occasionally felt nostalgic for the odd calamity that forced them to create solutions out of little more than inspiration and hope.

After supper, she agreed to act as master of ceremonies for the campers' talent show. Of all the evening entertainment programs, this was Sylvia's favorite, for it allowed her guests to express their interests beyond quilting. The shows never failed to be highly entertaining, with musical acts, skits, and other performances that defied classification, delivered with widely varying degrees of talent and polish. New campers put together their acts on the spot, while veterans of previous years often prepared ahead of time. Four members of a quilting guild from Des Moines dramatized a scene from *Little Women,* while three veteran campers, who had discovered a shared interest in the accordion at last year's camp, brought their instruments and performed a medley of Bach cantatas. Best of all, however, was a new camper whose gift for mimicry rendered them helpless with laughter at her impersonations of some of the camp's more vivid personalities. The evening was the best welcome-home present Sylvia could have imagined.

But the talent show was not all that had awaited her.

When she finally bid her friends good night, kissed Andrew, and retired to her room, she found her mail stacked neatly on her bedside dresser. She crawled into bed, snuggled beneath her blue and gold LeMoyne Star quilt, and thumbed through the envelopes. A return address from South Carolina caught her eye, and she realized it was a letter from Margaret Alden.

Apprehensive, Sylvia set the other letters aside and opened the envelope.

August 13, 2001

Dear Sylvia,

I hope this letter finds you and your friend Andrew well. Your program for the Silver Lake Quilters' Guild received rave reviews. We all hope you'll consider returning someday to share more of your quilts with us.

Since we spoke that evening, I've increased my efforts to learn more about the Elm Creek Quilt. While I still haven't conclusively determined who made it, I have learned a few details about its history that I thought might interest you.

My aunt Mary, my mother's younger sister, says she believes the quilt was completed shortly before the War of Secession began. This would follow what my mother told me, that during the war itself, the women of the family rarely made any new quilts, but made do with what they had. They could no longer obtain fabric from the Northern mills, and since Southern cotton gins and textile mills were frequently attacked as military targets, thread sometimes became scarce. Eventually they resorted to spinning their own thread on a spinning wheel and conserving it for the most necessary sewing projects, such as blankets, bandages, and other items for the soldiers.

According to my aunt, it's something of a miracle the quilt survived the war at all. The plantation was frequently overrun by troops from both sides, depending upon who controlled the territory at the time, and the soldiers scavenged food and supplies from people whose resources were already scarce. Sometimes the troops offered receipts for what they took, but more often they did not, though there was little likelihood of redeeming the receipts, anyway.

In order to protect their valuables, my grandmother's grandmother hid the family silver and other heirlooms under her daughter's mattress. When the family heard soldiers arriving, her daughter would dash upstairs, climb into bed, and pull the Birds in the Air quilt over herself. Then she would groan and toss about as if suffering from some terrible illness, while her mother pretended to care for her. When the soldiers entered the house and were told that the daughter was afflicted with typhus, they would not enter the room. My grandmother's grandmother made sure to leave items of lesser value elsewhere in the house, so the soldiers would not suspect they had a hidden cache, and grow angry and destructive at the prospect of leaving empty-handed.

This scheme preserved their property for nearly the entire duration of the war, but when their region was finally overwhelmed by Federal troops, the family was forced to flee. They took what they could carry and bundled the rest in the Birds of the Air quilt, which they buried on their property. Previous attempts to hide their valuables had taught them that scavenging soldiers knew to look for recently overturned soil, so again my grandmother's grandmother devised a deception. She placed the quilt at the bottom of a deep hole, covered it up with several feet of dirt, then on top laid the remains of her beloved dog, which had been shot only days earlier by a scavenger. After filling in the hole, she remarked that her faithful friend was a loyal guardian for the family even in death.

When they finally were able to return to the plantation months later, they found most of the house an utter ruin. The soil over the hiding place had been disturbed, but their valuables were still there at the bottom of the hole. Whoever had searched the site in their absence must have struck the dog's bones and decided they had found only a grave, and gone no further.

I think this at least partially accounts for the quilt's dilapidated condition, wouldn't you agree? It certainly explains the water stains in the middle of the top row.

When I told my aunt it was a shame they buried the quilt, though, she told me that was the only reason the quilt remained within the family at all. When they fled their home, they took the fancier quilts with them, including a broderie perse wedding quilt and a whole-cloth trapunto coverlet they used only for company. At some point during their flight, they were robbed on the road, and the thieves took the quilts along with everything else. So only because the Elm Creek Quilt had been considered utilitarian rather than fine did it survive the war—and if you ask me, those fancy silk quilts wouldn't have survived burial as well as the Birds in the Air quilt did, with its sturdy linsey-woolsey and muslin. I wonder, though, if those two stolen quilts became some other family's heirlooms. More likely they were used as horse blankets or cut up to patch worn shoes. It's unlikely a thief would appreciate all the time, effort, and affection that went into those quilts.

I hope this new information will shed more light on the history of the Elm Creek Quilt, although we must keep in mind that it's only as accurate as my aunt Mary's memory of old family stories. Why didn't more women document their quilts with a tag or at least their signature? I suppose they never imagined the frustrations they were creating for their descendants.

Please keep me posted about your own research. I'm eager to hear from you, whether you have good news or bad, or no news at all.

Sincerely,
Margaret Alden

Sylvia read the letter a second time, then folded it carefully and returned it to its envelope. Why, indeed, didn't women document each and every quilt they made? As the Alden family story proved, sometimes the everyday quilts rather than the painstakingly stitched masterpieces were the ones to endure for future generations.

But of course, quilters didn't often think their creations deserved documentation. In Sylvia's opinion, they valued themselves—and the work of their hands—too lightly. If a quilt was worthy of the thread that held it together, it was surely worthy of a simple appliquéd tag identifying the quilter, her geographic location, and the date of completion. More details would be even better, but Sylvia would settle for those.

She placed Margaret's letter on top of the others and returned the stack to the top of her dresser, then switched off the light and settled into bed. She closed her eyes and tried to still her thoughts, but images from the Birds in the Air quilt's perilous journey through the years played in her mind.

Suddenly a phrase from the letter jolted her memory. Quickly Sylvia groped for the lamp switch and snatched up the letter and her glasses. She scanned the lines until she reached the third to the last paragraph, where she spotted the familiar words. Linsey-woolsey. Grace had mentioned that type of fabric years ago in one of her lectures. Sylvia could not remember the exact context, but she knew it was significant.

She glanced at the clock and had a moment of dismay before remembering the three-hour time difference between Pennsylvania and California.

She threw back the quilt, pulled on her dressing gown and slippers, and within moments was hurrying down the hallway, Margaret's letter in hand. Too many telemarketers had spoiled perfectly good naps for her to consider keeping a phone in her room, and the nearest was in the library.

Grace answered on the second ring. Sylvia barely gave her friend a chance to say hello before she launched into a summary of Margaret's tale. "Linsey-woolsey," Sylvia repeated when she finished. "When I saw the quilt, I assumed it was wool and muslin. I didn't think to inquire if it was something else."

"It would be easy to mistake them if you didn't know what to look for," said Grace. "Linsey-woolsey was woven using a cotton warp and a wool weft. It was a rough and uncomfortable cloth, but cheap and durable."

"That's what I thought," said Sylvia, triumphant. "There's our proof that this so-called Elm Creek Quilt has nothing to do with the quilts I found in my attic. Not a scrap of linsey-woolsey appears in any of them. They were pieced from silks, cottons, chintzes—just about everything but linsey-woolsey. Anneke used scraps from her dressmaking, remember? And much of that fabric was the fine imported material Hans's parents sent as a wedding gift."

"Sylvia," said Grace, "the presence of identical fabric in all three quilts could have proven a connection, but the absence of identical material doesn't disprove one. Do all of your quilts contain one common fabric?"

"What a silly question." But Sylvia hesitated and admitted, "No. Of course not."

"The quiltmaker could have resorted to linsey-woolsey when her better fabric scraps ran out. During the Civil War, many Southern families resorted to homespun when other fabric became too difficult to obtain. On the other hand . . ."

"Yes?" prompted Sylvia.

"Homespun was a common fabric used for slaves' clothing."

Sylvia could not speak.

"I'm sorry, Sylvia. I knew you wouldn't like to hear that. But since Margaret Alden believes the quilt was finished before the Civil War began . . ."

"Someone must have been wearing that homespun, and it probably wasn't the mistress of a plantation." Sylvia took a deep breath. "So. You believe my ancestors were slave owners."

"Not necessarily *your* ancestors. Margaret Alden's, and we knew that about her already. We don't know that one of your ancestors pieced Margaret Alden's quilt. We still don't know that the Bergstroms have any connection to the Aldens. The presence of homespun in the quilt changes nothing."

"I simply cannot imagine Gerda the mistress of a plantation, wearing fine silks and ordering people about." And then, with a sudden flash of insight, Sylvia nearly laughed aloud from relief. "And that's not all she wouldn't do."

"Meaning?"

"Gerda hated to quilt. She hated anything to do with sewing, but she did understand fine fabric. She wouldn't have spent all that time and energy quilting elaborate images from Elm Creek Farm into a top pieced from homespun."

"It does seem rather incongruent, for any quilter," mused Grace. "Any quilter who had access to better fabric, anyway."

Sylvia hardly heard her, so pleased was she with her new realization. "Thank you, Grace. You've put my mind at ease."

Grace laughed. "You're quite welcome, although I don't think I really did all that much."

Sylvia laughed, too, her heart light. Gerda could not have made Margaret Alden's quilt. Anneke surely had not, either, because family stories after the Civil War placed her right where she should have been, at Elm Creek Farm. And Hans, too, could be ruled out, for that same reason, and because he probably never lifted a needle in his life.

Whoever made the Alden family's heirloom, the unknown quilter could not have been a Bergstrom.

❧

When Sylvia returned to the memoir the next morning, it was with renewed confidence that her ancestors' reputation for courage and goodness would yet be proven true.

❧ *January 1859 —*
what the New Year brought

By the first days of January, Anneke could no longer hide what I had suspected: She and Hans were expecting a child.

I embraced Anneke with great joy when my persistent questioning at last compelled her to reveal the truth. I was nearly overcome with delight to know that a tiny baby boy or girl would be joining our family, although I admit I pitied Anneke the pains of childbirth she would experience, and considered myself fortunate to be spared them. If Jonathan had married me, however, I am sure I would have felt differently.

As the winter snows fell outside the windows of our happy home, Hans fashioned a cradle from trees felled on our own land, and Anneke pieced tiny baby quilts from the soft fabrics my father had sent from Germany. Perhaps I need not explain how Anneke's glad news brought me comfort from my own grief. The promise of new life brought me hope, and I knew I would find solace in the hard work that would be required of me as Anneke's confinement approached and my niece or nephew entered the world.

It seemed that nothing would diminish the pleasure of our anticipation, but troubled times awaited us.

For one, Anneke was loath to give up her position at Mrs. Engle's dress shop, which brought her not only wages but also work she enjoyed and friends. She was certain Mrs. Engle would dismiss her when her condition became too obvious. She put off telling Mrs. Engle the news as long as she could, and when she finally summoned up enough courage, she begged me to accompany her.

Only for Anneke's sake, and that of my niece or nephew, would I agree to voluntarily subject myself to that woman's company. I even promised to be cordial. But we had not even entered the shop when I realized I would not be able to keep my vow.

For nailed to a post just outside the door was a handbill, which I preserved, since naturally I tore it down, and have enclosed here.

❧

Sylvia turned the page, and in the fold of the book she discovered a brittle, yellowed piece of paper. It was torn along one edge, and it seemed so fragile that Sylvia almost didn't dare to unfold it, but she couldn't resist. As carefully as she could, she laid it on top of her desk and gingerly peeled back the corners.

$20 REWARD!

For the capture and return of a Negro woman, runaway or stolen
from me two days after Christmas. She is of medium height and
build; she may attempt to pass as White or Free but you will know

her by the fresh mark of a flatiron, which I made on her right cheek. She is an expert with the needle and may have in her possession a silver thimble and needle case, which belonged to my late Mother and which the Negress has stolen. The above reward of twenty dollars will be given upon return of the said Negress to me or my agents, and an additional ten dollars will be provided for the restoration of my stolen goods. Josiah Chester, Wentworth County, Virginia, December 29, 1858.

A shiver ran down Sylvia's spine. She set the handbill aside and quickly returned to the memoir.

❧

As I gazed upon the deplorable announcement, my indignation quickly turned to white-hot outrage. The nerve of Mrs. Engle, to permit such a posting on her property!

"My goodness." Beside me, Anneke was staring at the handbill with shocked intrigue. "The mark of a flatiron upon her cheek. Can you imagine it?"

I could imagine it all too well. "If I burned a woman's face with a flatiron, I would not be so quick to boast of it." And with that, I snatched the handbill right off the nail and crumpled it into my pocket.

Anneke looked around, fearful someone had seen. "You can't do that."

"I most certainly can, and I believe I just did," said I. "Twenty dollars for a woman. Ten for a thimble and a needle case."

"They're silver," explained my sister-in-law.

I was too angry to reply, so I returned to my seat on the wagon, determined to wait for Anneke outside despite the cold. After a moment Anneke entered the shop, and after a frigid half hour passed, she returned outside carrying a bundle of sewing.

"She said I may continue to work for her as long as my condition is not apparent to the customers," said Anneke in a subdued voice as we rode off. "After the child is born, if I wish to, I may resume my work."

I merely nodded. The anger that had reduced to a simmer now resumed a steady boil. How could Anneke even think of prolonging her association with Mrs. Engle now? I had faith that the decent people of Creek's Crossing would assist a fugitive slave if the opportunity arose, but there were others in our town of weaker character who would be tempted by the promised reward into betraying that unfortunate woman. If she were delivered to her owner because of that handbill, the shame and the sin would be Mrs. Engle's.

I yearned to discuss the matter with Jonathan, for I knew he would understand my outrage. Instead I confided in Dorothea, whose compassion for all sorts, even her enemies, left me unsatisfied. Rather than joining me in my denunciation of Mrs. Engle, she urged me to leave the matter to God, to pray that Mrs. Engle would see the light one day, and to ask the Lord to protect the fugitive woman, wherever she was.

I could do the latter, but regarding Mrs. Engle, I was unforgiving and unrepentant. "I simply cannot abide such handbills littering our main streets."

"Nor can I," said Dorothea, "but I fear we will soon grow accustomed to it."

"What do you mean?"

"Many routes north through Pennsylvania are obstructed by the Appalachians. The slave catchers know there are only so many passes through the mountains, and they watch them carefully. Gaps to the east and west of us are so well known to the slave catchers that the slaves have been forced to discover other, more hazardous mountain passes. One that still remains little known lies directly south of Creek's Crossing."

This knowledge gave me a thrill of apprehension. "This pass is becoming better known, I think, if slave owners know to post handbills here."

"I fear you are correct." Dorothea set down her sewing and gazed out the window. "This woman has avoided capture for several weeks. It is possible she may reach Canada soon, if she is not there already. We must pray for fair weather."

But I had followed her gaze out the window, and saw as she did that a dark cloud loomed in the southwest, which meant we would have snow before nightfall.

I hurried home, arriving only minutes before the first flakes fell. As the blizzard raged for two days and nights, my thoughts went often to the Negress of the handbill, and I wondered what would have compelled her to flee captivity in winter that could not be endured until spring. Then I recalled the horrors I had read of in Jonathan's books and heard of from Dorothea's speakers, and I believed I understood, as well as anyone who had never been a slave could.

At last the storms ended, and suddenly the weather grew as temperate as spring; the January Thaw was upon us. It was a peculiar quirk of the climate in the region that for a few days each January, we enjoyed a brief respite from cold temperatures and snow until winter resumed in full force. Energized by the precious sunshine, Anneke and I flung open the windows and decided to accomplish what spring cleaning we could in the time available. While Anneke scrubbed the floors and beat our few rugs, I washed our quilts and hung them out to dry as Anneke had taught me: colors in the shade, and whites in the sunlight.

Since the days were not any longer despite this prelude to spring, twilight had descended by suppertime. Hans, Anneke, and I made merry over our supper, our spirits greatly elevated by the day's fair weather. We laughed and talked so loudly that when the knock came at our door, we could not be certain our unexpected guest had not been trying to get our attention for some time.

Anneke excused herself to answer the door, and when she returned, she looked pale and strange. "It's a woman," said she. "I don't know what she wants. I did not understand her English."

"Why did she stay outside?" ask Hans.

Anneke glanced over her shoulder and wrung her hands. "I believe . . . I think she may be a Negress."

Wondering which of our neighbors she had left standing on the doorstep, I said, a trifle sharply, "Why didn't you invite her in?"

Distractedly, Anneke brushed her right cheek with the back of her fingers. "She has a burn, like a flatiron."

Hans and I had time to exchange a quick glance before we bolted to our feet and hurried to the door. Just outside, where shadows yet hid her, stood a woman. In the poor light I might have thought her a white woman if not for her clothing, which was fashioned of coarse and soiled cloth, and the haunted look in her eye, which, when our gaze met, struck me with nearly physical force. Her shoulders slumped from exhaustion, and although she stood warily as if prepared to run, there was a determined set to her jaw that convinced me she could just as readily hold her ground if she must.

And upon her cheek blazed the mark of a flatiron, red and blistered and sore. It sickened me to look upon it.

Somehow I knew the woman had expected a much different reception from us. Just as she shifted her weight to hurry away, I called out, "Wait. Come in. You're safe here."

She seemed to weigh my words for a moment before she nodded and entered.

I closed the door firmly behind her, my heart pounding. "Draw the curtains," said I, but Hans had already begun to do so. I directed the woman to a chair beside the fire and hurried off to fetch a dressing for her injured cheek.

Anneke trailed after me. "We should send her on her way."

"We will. As soon as she is rested and fed, and I have tended to her burn, we will help her determine the best route north."

Anneke seized my arm. "I mean we must send her on her way now."

"Hungry and tired, and with no proper guidance north?" I brushed off Anneke's hands and snatched up clean linen for bandages. "What if she wandered to the Engles' farm and sought help there?"

"They would turn her over to the authorities."

"Precisely. What do you think would become of her then?"

Anneke looked as if the thought sickened her, but then she shook her head. "I don't like it, but it's the law. If we don't send her away, we could be discovered and prosecuted."

"No one saw her arrive."

"Are you sure?"

I was not, but I would not admit it. "Of course. No one can see the house from the main road because of the forest, and if a pursuer had followed her onto our property, he surely would have come to the door by now."

My voice sounded glib, but my knees were shaking with fright as I hurried back to the fireside. I heated water and tended to the woman's burn rapidly, without speaking, hardly aware of the movements my hands made. The burn was badly infected, and her skin radiated fever. Anneke brought her something to eat, and the woman wolfed down bread and cheese and meat without pausing to speak or barely to breathe.

Before she finished, Hans left the house, rifle in hand, to see if anyone had followed her. None of us women spoke; with my brother gone, the house felt cloaked in a fearful silence. I heated more water so the woman could wash and fetched her some of my own clothing to wear, the sturdiest I had, and the warmest. She was considerably shorter than I, but still a good deal taller than Anneke, so my things would have to do.

She thanked me as I offered her my things and set her empty plate aside. I averted my gaze as she tended to her toilet, but not quickly enough to avoid seeing the whiplash scars crisscrossing her back. I swallowed hard and could not look upon them again, but Anneke stared in horrified fascination.

"You're the slave," she accused. "The one who escaped from Josiah Chester in Virginia."

The woman gave her a hard look. "This here's Pennsylvania," said she, pulling my dress over her head, slowly, as if her every muscle ached. "I ain't nobody's slave now."

"This is Pennsylvania, but you're not safe here," said I. "You need to continue north to Canada."

"I know." She said it matter-of-factly, but something in her words conveyed an exhaustion so complete I could have wept for her, thinking how much farther she would have to travel.

I said, "You don't need to leave until you're rested."

"I go tomorrow, at nightfall," said she, thanking me with a nod. "But where I go from here? Where the next station?"

I stared at her, uncomprehending. "Station?"

She stared back at me, and gradually I saw something in her eyes transform from relief to confusion to fear. She glanced at Anneke, then back to me. "Lord help me," she whispered. She struggled to her feet and tried to run, but she collapsed halfway to the door.

In a moment I was kneeling by her side, attempting to succor her, but she fought me off. "Calm yourself," said I, bewildered and frightened by her sudden desperation. "We want to help."

If she heard me, she gave no sign. "But I saw it," said she, over and over, nearly delirious. "I saw it."

I tried to soothe her, to assure her she was safe, but her outburst had drained the last of her strength, and she slipped into unconsciousness.

"We must get her to bed," said I, and Anneke rushed to assist me, without a word of protest.

The infection within her burned cheek had leached its poison into the woman's blood, and none of us thought she would survive until morning. I thought of Mr. Wilbur, slowly dying as Jonathan fought to preserve his life. I longed for Jonathan's skill, I longed for his presence, but we could not send for him, lest we force him to shoulder our own defiance of the law.

For two nights and a day the woman lay more asleep than awake in the bed we made up for her in Anneke's sewing room, murmuring and sometimes crying out, tormented by fever. I remained at the bedside, doing the little I could to see her through each hour, terrified that she would die before my eyes. Anneke's earlier objections were forgotten as she changed the woman's bed linens, soaked with perspiration, and tended to me as well, helping me keep up my strength. And although Hans had found no sign of pursuers, we expected the slave catchers to arrive at any moment.

Then, at last, on the second day, the woman's fever broke. She roused herself enough to drink a cup of broth, then slipped into restful sleep.

With the immediate threat of her illness now diminishing, other worries began to plague me. We would have to find some means of concealing the woman until she could continue her journey north. She had seemed to expect us to know where she could next find respite along the way, so we must find such a place. How, I did not know. And how Anneke, who wore her emotions plain upon her face, would avoid raising Mrs. Engle's suspicions in the days to come, I could not imagine.

I sat at the woman's bedside as she slept, brooding, wishing that she had approached some other farm, and despising myself for such thoughts. I had learned something about myself in the short span of time since her arrival, something I did not like: I was a staunch enough Abolitionist when slaves were mere abstractions, far removed from my own hearth and home, but weak-willed indeed when a runaway had become a threat to my own safety and freedom and comfort.

I knew well that this threat would grow with every day she remained under our roof, and those days would number longer than I had anticipated when I had offered her shelter for the night. I had not yet told Hans or Anneke, but in the course of caring for her, I had discovered that she was afflicted with more than exhaustion and fever.

Although my dress hung loose upon her shoulders and limbs, it fit snugly around the midsection. The fugitive slave was with child and, as best I could estimate, was nearly as far along as Anneke.

She would not be fit to travel for months, and knowing that, I could not bring myself to send her away—

☙

The line ended abruptly, followed by one crossed out so heavily that whatever Gerda had originally written was almost completely obscured. Sylvia strained her eyes, trying to make out the words, but all she could perceive

were a few letters, and these were a scrawl compared to the elegant preci-
sion she had come to expect from Gerda's writing.

It was the only cross-out in the book, which made Sylvia all the more
determined to know what it said.

She hurried to her bedroom for her magnifying glass, but when it failed
to help her, she went in search of Sarah. She found her at the library computer, working on the business's accounts. After Sylvia explained the problem, Sarah offered to examine the line herself.

"I can't bear not knowing what she wrote," said Sylvia as Sarah held the
book up to the bright lamp on the desk. "When I think of the other things
she did not cross out—some of them not very pleasant—I can't imagine
what could have been so terrible that she had to obliterate it. No, I *can*
imagine, and that's worse. What if she said, 'I could not bring myself to
send her away, but I did anyway'? or, 'So Hans did it for me'?"

Sarah smiled, her eyes fixed on the book. "I doubt that's what it says."

"Well, we don't know, do we?" said Sylvia grumpily. "Can you make out
anything?"

"I'm not sure."

"Try this." Sylvia handed her the magnifying glass. "I think perhaps this
last bit refers to Gerda's mixed feelings. Could that say, 'heart was torn'?
Do you think that means she's going to send the woman away?" She could
not bear it if it was true.

"Where do you see 'torn'?"

"Here." Sylvia pointed.

"That looks too wide to be a 't.' I thought it was a capital letter."

"Isn't that the end of the previous word?"

"It could be . . ." Sarah turned the page and held it up to the light, looking at the obscured line from the back. "No, there's a space before the letter, not after. You can see the ink is lighter there, as if she didn't have to
mark out anything." She returned to the previous page. "And I think this
says 'born,' not 'torn.' You know the context; would that make sense?"

"Both Anneke and the slave woman were expecting."

"Maybe the line says, 'until her child was born.'"

Sylvia took the memoir and studied the line. She perceived no more than
she had before, but Sarah's interpretation did seem to match the peaks and
dips of the pen, if not perfectly. "Or perhaps instead of 'her child,' she
wrote the child's name."

"That would make sense."

"Except for one small matter: Why would Gerda feel compelled to blot out such an innocent remark?"

Sarah frowned, uncertain. "Maybe because at that time, she didn't know what the baby's name was going to be. She knew when she wrote the line, of course, in 1895, but not at that point in the memoir, months before the baby was born. Maybe she crossed it out to avoid confusing the chronological order."

Sylvia shook her head. "That doesn't follow. In other parts of the memoir she leaps forward in time. We already know Jonathan and Charlotte are going to have four children, for example. If divulging future information doesn't bother Gerda elsewhere, why should it here?"

She could tell from Sarah's expression that her young friend could not think of a logical explanation, either.

Chapter Nine

February through March 1859 — in which Elm Creek Farm becomes a station

By the time our guest had recovered enough to sit up in bed and talk, the January Thaw had passed, usurped by the brooding skies and bitter cold of February.

"How long I been here?" was her first question to me, as her eyes darted around the room, unnaturally darkened by the storm outside.

"Six days."

She pushed back the bedclothes. "I best be going."

"You can't leave now." I drew the quilt over her again. "You're not strong enough, and there's a storm."

"Slave catchers come after me if I don't keep on."

"The storm will slow them. But if anyone does come, we're arranging a hiding place. You'll be safer there than outside."

To my relief, she accepted this and sank back into bed again. I offered her a glass of water, which she drank thirstily, her dark eyes fixed on the window. "The last storm was worse than this one," said she. "I got lost in it, couldn't find the path. Don't know what I would've done if I hadn't seen the signal."

I nodded as if I understood, wary of alarming her as I had that first night. "Was it easy to find?"

" 'Course. Right there on the clothesline like they told me at the last place. Lady there drew the Underground Railroad picture in the dirt, showed me how the pieces go. I make quilts on the plantation, but never seen that pattern before. Missus likes fancy work." She glanced at the quilt covering her—my own humble first attempt at quilt making—and I could see she was trying not to smile. "This quilt here, now, this called Shoo-Fly. It plenty warm, but missus think herself too good for it."

"No one would ever mistake any of my quilts for fancywork," said I, dryly. "It keeps off the chill, and that's about all."

"That's plenty. Even missus be mighty grateful for it if she ever be cold as I was."

It was the highest compliment anyone but Dorothea had ever given my handiwork, and despite my distaste for needlework, including my own, especially this quilt with its humility block, I was pleased. "My name is Gerda," I told her. "Gerda Bergstrom."

Her name was Joanna, and as I tended to her that day, I pieced together how chance and misunderstanding had brought her to our door. After leaving her last place of refuge, she had become lost in the snowstorm that had struck the day after I discovered the handbill on Mrs. Engle's store. When the January Thaw brought fair weather, she had tried in vain to resume her previous course and, in her wanderings, encountered Elm Creek. She followed it, knowing she could cross the waters if need be to throw pursuing dogs off her scent, until it led her to an abandoned cabin near a barn. Too fatigued to go on, she slept the rest of the night and all the next day. When she rose at sunset, determined to continue her journey despite her increasing sickness, she spied a house on the other side of the creek. Near it was a clothesline, upon which hung several quilts, including one pieced in the Underground Railroad pattern—the signal her previous benefactors had told her would indicate the next station on her journey north.

I hid my astonishment as best I could and quickly deduced the rest: The signal Joanna referred to was the quilt Anneke had made of squares and triangles arranged in vertical stripes. In copying Dorothea's design, Anneke had inadvertently created an echo of the message. Now I understood why Dorothea had not responded when Anneke had asked her the name of the pattern—and I also discovered Joanna's intended destination.

The Nelson farm was a station on the Underground Railroad. Knowing the depth of their feeling for the Abolitionist cause, I was not surprised by this revelation, but I was astounded that Dorothea had managed to conceal the truth so well, and, I will admit, somewhat hurt that she had not confided in me. Upon further reflection, however, I realized that because of the inherent danger to both runaway and stationmaster, she could not have entrusted the truth to even the closest friend. The less others knew, the less they could reveal through accident or under duress. Even Mr. Frederick Douglass himself had faulted some stationmasters for concealing their activities so poorly that they allowed slave owners and slave catchers to discover their methods, thus helping to perpetuate the very institution they sought to undermine. Dorothea and Thomas would never allow themselves to be included in their number.

One deduction quickly led to another: Dorothea would know the next destination in Joanna's flight north. By the time Joanna was prepared to continue her journey, I intended to tease that information from my friend without revealing why I sought it, for I needed to maintain secrecy just as the Nelsons did.

Days passed, and as Joanna recovered from her illness, our expectation that the slave catchers would arrive at any moment began to ebb. Or so it was with Hans and me; Anneke seemed never to forget her anxieties. She took little consolation in knowing Hans had devised an ingenious hiding place in her sewing room, nor in his repeated assurances that no ill would befall our family.

"Hans does not wish to alarm us, but I know the truth," confided Anneke to me when we were alone. "Mr. Pearson says anyone assisting fugitive slaves will be prosecuted under the law. We may be fined, or even sent to prison."

"We will face no punishment," said I, "because we will not be detected."

Anneke looked doubtful, and my own heart was full of misgivings when I wondered how that particular subject had come up in a conversation with Mr. Pearson.

Joanna's care fell almost entirely to me, as Anneke was burdened by her duties for Mrs. Engle as well as the fatigue of her condition. Even when she did assist me, however, she shied away from Joanna, avoiding her gaze and speaking to her through me, if at all. I can only guess why Joanna made Anneke so uncomfortable: perhaps because she knew few colored people, perhaps because of the danger her presence put us all in, perhaps because her dialect, which I have but poorly reproduced in these pages, was difficult for Anneke to comprehend.

"She want me gone," said Joanna to me, unexpectedly, after Anneke stopped by the room on some errand and left as quickly as it was completed, with scarcely a word for either of us.

"She wants you safe in the North" was all I would concede. "As do we all."
And then, as a way of making her seem more sympathetic, to show that the
women shared a common experience, I added, "She, too, is in a condition.
You know what it is to worry for the fate of your child."

"I don't know nothing about that."

"Of course you must," said I, confused. "Or am I mistaken? Are you
not . . . expecting?"

From the shock and emotion that came into her eyes then, I first thought
she had not surmised her condition, and then I knew she had indeed suspected it but had not allowed herself to believe it.

"You must be well into your fifth month, at least," said I, gently.

Her voice was dull. "Sixth, more likely."

I nodded, mute, for although Anneke was only a few weeks further along,
her condition was significantly more apparent, for she had never lacked sufficient nourishment. "Your child will be born in a Free State, and you will raise
him in freedom." I expected that to cheer her, but it did not, and I thought I
understood the reason why. "His father, I assume, is still in the South?"

She snorted. "That where he likely be, all right."

I placed my hand upon hers, and said consolingly, "Do not despair. Perhaps someday your husband will follow you North to freedom."

She jerked her hand away. "I ain't got no husband."

"Well . . ." I hesitated. "Your man, then."

"No man of mine gave me this baby." Her voice stung with contempt. She
rolled over on her side on the bed, putting her back to me. "I don't care if it
live or die, so long as I get my freedom."

Shocked, at first I could only gape at her. "Be that as it may," said I, when
I found my voice. "You should remain with us until after your time, when
you and the baby are strong enough to travel again. For your sake, if not for
your child's."

She said nothing, and with nothing more to say myself, I left her alone.

❧

As Joanna gradually regained strength, she began to grow restless. She was
still too weak to take any exercise but for slow walks the length of my room,
but she could sit up in bed well enough. When she told me of her desire for
something to occupy her time and distract her from her worries, in my
thoughtless way, I offered her one of my books.

"I can't read," said Joanna. "Massa don't allow it."

My cheeks flamed, and I busied myself with the sock I was darning. "Oh. Of course."

"Don't matter none."

It matters a great deal, I almost replied, but instead said, "Perhaps I could read to you."

She shrugged, dubious, but said, "That be nice."

I set my mending aside, went to my room, and scanned the titles on the bookcase Jonathan had made for me. When my gaze lit on a certain volume, I pulled it from the shelf. "Here's one," said I, returning to my chair by Joanna's bed. "It was written by a man who was once himself a slave, but acquired his freedom, and has fought to win the same right for others."

At that, her interest was piqued, and thus I commenced reading the *Narrative of the Life of Frederick Douglass, an American Slave.*

I had almost finished William Lloyd Garrison's preface when Anneke entered, made curious by the sound of my voice. Not quickly enough, I set the book aside and snatched up the sock and needle, for I had promised Anneke to help with the darning and had long put off the task. When Anneke said, in a teasing manner, that she could always count on me to shirk my household duties, Joanna spoke up: "I can do the darning."

Anneke and I exchanged a stricken glance. "Anneke is only teasing me," said I. "You are our guest. We don't expect you to work for us."

"It ain't for you, it for me," said Joanna. "I go out of my head sitting here in bed all day and all night, nothing to do but listen for the slave catchers' dogs. You read, and I'll darn."

She insisted, so reluctantly I agreed, but I was greatly disturbed that this woman, so recently near death, and so recently forced to work for white people, now found herself darning white people's socks. I cannot commit to paper why this troubled me so; it simply felt wrong. But unable to articulate an objection, I wordlessly handed her the pile of stockings.

Joanna asked for her bundle, and Anneke, who was nearest, retrieved it from the corner, not quite able to conceal her distaste. Joanna untied the coarse blanket of homespun, upon which every mile of her hazardous journey had apparently left its mark in sweat and grime, and withdrew two shining objects. Anneke gasped, and I nearly did, too, so markedly did the elegant silver needle case and thimble contrast with the bundle that had carried them.

"You *are* the woman from the handbill," exclaimed Anneke. "You stole those things from Josiah Chester."

A dangerous glint appeared in Joanna's eye. "I didn't take nothing that wasn't owed me."

"Be reasonable, Anneke," said I, hurriedly. "The trifles are a poor recompense for the lifetime of suffering she endured at his hands."

"I didn't mean to steal nothing," said Joanna to me. "I was in the sewing room—I was a house slave. The missus have me do all her laundry and sewing and quilting. Massa Chester come after me when I alone there. He always come after me, but this time—that time I just couldn't. I hold the scissors, cutting silk for a dress, and when he grab at me, I point those scissors at him and tell him to leave me be, or I tell the missus he be coming to my cabin when he tell her he going riding. He bring his fist down on my hand, and I drop the scissors, and then he grab me and put his hand over my mouth and push me against the wall. I try to get free, and my hand touch something—I don't know what, but it hard, so I grab it and hit him with it. It scratch his face, his scalp, and draw blood. The blood run all down his face, down into his mouth, and he stand there screaming at me, the blood and spit flying. I try to crawl away, but he take the flatiron off the fire, and then he do this."

Her hand went to her scarred cheek.

"I be too hurt to fight him no more. I don't remember when he finish and go. My mind just went out my body, and when it came back, he was gone, and I still be on the floor. I didn't think about it, I didn't plan nothing, I just got up and left. Middle of the day yet, and me with no idea where I going. I just up and left. I pass other slaves working in the fields, I even walk right by Missy Lizabeth, the massa's daughter, on the road, but no one stop me. They all think I do an errand for the missus. She always have me going here and there, sewing for her friends.

"I walk all day. Only when night come and it get too dark to see do I stop. That when I realize what I done, run off, and how it too late to go back, unless I want a beating that like to kill me. So I hide in a haystack."

She looked down at the gleaming silver objects in her hand. "Before I fall asleep, I open my fist and find Mrs. Chester's needle case, with a little bit of blood on the corner. That what I grab without looking, that what I hit Massa Chester with." She looked at Anneke, unflinching. "So you see, I didn't mean to steal nothing. It just happen."

Anneke, white as a sheet, made no reply. Joanna calmly slipped the thimble onto her finger and began darning one of Hans's socks. Anneke watched her for a moment, then turned on her heel and left the room.

I wanted desperately to apologize for my sister-in-law, or to at least explain her way of thinking, but her condemnation of Joanna's thievery shamed me, especially when I compared it to her tolerance for Mrs. Engle's posting of the handbill. So instead I cleared my throat and resumed reading Douglass's *Narrative*.

••

Whether out of anger with me, or fear that she might reveal our secret, Anneke chose not to attend the next meeting of the Certain Faction. We met irregularly during wintertime, as the weather would permit, and thus I had spent two impatient, anxious weeks since Joanna's arrival longing to speak with Dorothea.

I was the first to reach the Nelson home, for I knew once the others arrived, I would have little opportunity to speak with Dorothea alone. As we set up her quilting frame, she shared the latest news from her household, and I bided my time until I could casually remind her of the handbill. She smiled and said, "Dear Gerda, are you still plotting some dire revenge against Mrs. Engle?"

"I cannot forgive her as easily as you, but no, I am not," said I. "I was merely wondering about the unfortunate runaway. She might have been driven from her intended path by the storms, or was forced to change direction when the slave catchers passed through town. They must have, don't you agree?"

"I suppose they must have," said Dorothea, "if only to deliver their handbills. We can only pray she was able to elude them."

I learned more from my friend's expression and the mournful note in her voice than she had intended to tell me: After seeing the handbill, Dorothea had anticipated the runaway would soon appear at her door, and when she had not, Dorothea had given her up for lost. Perhaps she thought Joanna had wandered the Pennsylvania countryside until she had frozen to death, or had been recaptured, or had suffered another equally dire fate, and perhaps Dorothea wrongly blamed herself.

My heart went out to her as I imagined her anguish. "I'm certain she did elude them," said I, ignoring, for the moment, the need for secrecy. "But perhaps circumstances forced her to seek an alternate refuge."

Dorothea's eyes darted to mine. "I suppose that might have been necessary."

I busied myself with smoothing the back layer of a new quilt in the frame, and said in a careless manner, "I do hope that isn't the case, however."

"Why not?"

"Her new protectors would hardly know where to send her next, would they? They could point north and say, 'Head in that direction and mind you don't stumble over any slave catchers on the way,' but that's not very helpful, is it?"

Dorothea gave me a long, searching glance and, after a long moment, finally said, "You're right. They would not know about others who would help the fugitive. There are many others, but more are always needed."

And then, in elliptical language that suggested more than it explicitly stated, Dorothea told me how Joanna would know the next safe house on her journey north. Our conversation was oddly restrained for two close confidantes, but necessarily so, for neither knew what one might someday be required to say under oath about the other.

Reader, you will forgive me, I hope, if I do not record those identifying details in these pages. That family's role in the Underground Railroad is their story, not mine, to share with their own descendants or not, as they see fit.

I told neither Hans nor Anneke what Dorothea had revealed to me, only that I knew where Joanna should go when she departed Elm Creek Farm. They did not press me for details, Hans because he was aware that as few people should know the route as possible, Anneke because she was relieved to be spared the burden of yet another secret.

Her relief was to be short-lived, I knew, for Dorothea's words lingered in my thoughts: *There are many others,* she had said, *but more are always needed.* One fugitive had found shelter within our home. If others happened to pass our way, I would not deny them our hospitality.

Naturally I could not proceed without Hans's consent, for although I was the elder sibling, he was master of Elm Creek Farm. It took some impassioned pleading on my part, and heartfelt appeals to the best parts of his nature, but eventually he agreed. He did not agree because knowing Joanna had influenced his opinion of the dispute between Slave State and Free; he persisted in the belief that what did not directly affect him did not concern him. What he did acknowledge was that as beneficiaries of America's promise of freedom and opportunity for all, we Bergstroms would be remiss if we did not assist others who braved unimaginable dangers and risked their very lives in the struggle to achieve what we now took for granted.

When he made up his mind, he told Anneke his decision. She shot me one accusing look, then returned her gaze to her husband and gave him a wordless nod of acceptance. I wished he had asked her for her consent rather than merely telling her how things would be, but it could not be undone, and I allowed myself to believe the result would have been the same regardless.

From that day forward, whenever we did not anticipate visitors, whenever the winter weather was such that a clothesline strung outdoors would not raise suspicions, we hung Anneke's Underground Railroad quilt and waited for a knock on the door in the night.

❧

Joanna had been with us a month when the knock finally came.

It was shortly before dawn. I started at the sound, instantly awake with a pounding heart, and leapt from my bed. I threw on my dressing gown and hurried downstairs, pausing only to rap upon Joanna's door and warn her to hasten to the hiding place. Hans was not a second behind me as I opened the outside door to discover two figures shivering in the cold.

We beckoned them inside, and as I stoked the fire and prepared a meal for them, Hans took his rifle and went to search for pursuers. By the time he returned, Anneke had come downstairs to help me to tend to the newcomers, and Joanna, assured by the lack of uproar that it was safe to leave her hiding place, had joined us—but rather than take a place by the fire with the other guests, she began to help me with the cooking, without a word and as naturally as if she had been doing so for years.

The arrivals were two men, escaped from the same tobacco plantation in South Carolina. After they were warmed and fed, they told us something of their lives in captivity, and though I think they spared us the most gruesome details, their brief accounts were horrific enough to convince me that no risk was too great to help them toward freedom. Anneke's bleak silence, and the courteous manner in which she addressed the fugitives, so different from the skittishness she had first displayed toward Joanna, told me she agreed.

But something else also occupied Anneke's thoughts. "They think she's white," murmured Anneke when the others could not overhear, nodding toward the two men, and to Joanna, who wore my dress and worked alongside us as one of the family.

Taken aback, I studied the men surreptitiously and soon concurred with Anneke's observation. Perhaps because her skin was indeed quite light, or perhaps because the ugly scar on her face drew attention away from her features, the two newcomers did not see a fellow runaway in Joanna. Perhaps they did not look upon her long enough to discern her true heritage; upon her first appearance, each man had glanced at her scar, then quickly diverted his gaze as if he did not wish to appear rude. Once Joanna's dialect exposed her, however, there was a subtle shift in the men's address—mild surprise, which they well concealed, was followed by a new warmth, a familiarity, that did not enter into their voices when they spoke to Anneke or me.

Throughout that day, as the men slept in the beds we made up for them in the nursery, I pondered Joanna's inadvertent duplicity and wondered if we might not somehow use it to help her elude capture when she resumed her journey north.

The men left shortly after dusk, clad in some of Hans's stout winter clothing and carrying bread and cheese enough to sustain them until the next station. Joanna watched them go, her longing to accompany them plain upon her face. Then her hand absently went to her gently swelling abdomen, and she turned away from the window.

❧

Not a week later, another knock woke us in the night; two days after that fugitive's departure, another arrived to take his place. With each escaped slave who found shelter beneath our roof, our confidence grew, and the Underground Railroad quilt appeared more frequently on our clothesline.

We grew confident—perhaps overconfident. Thus one late night when a man and a boy of about eight years pounded frantically on the door, we were rudely restored to our senses. As we beckoned them inside, the man told us through labored breathing that the slave catchers were not far behind.

I stood stock-still for a moment, and so it was Anneke who sprung into action. "This way," said she briskly, guiding them upstairs. I quickly looked over the first floor for any sign of Joanna or the new arrivals, and followed the others upstairs. Anneke and I helped the fugitives into the hiding place, then returned to our bedrooms, to feign sleep.

Perhaps a half hour passed before the baying of dogs and a second pounding interrupted the quiet night. I prayed God would make me a good liar as I followed Hans and Anneke downstairs. My brother pulled open the door, and to my dismay and astonishment, we found ourselves facing the same two slave catchers who had disturbed us during our first autumn at Elm Creek Farm. This time, each held a yelping bloodhound by the collar.

Without waiting for us to ask their purpose, the first man demanded entry to our home. "We're in pursuit of two runaway n——s, a man and a boy," said he. "We know they came this way."

Annoyed, Hans said, "That's why you woke my family in the middle of the night? I thought the devil himself was after you."

"Let us in, g—— d—— it," snarled the other. The dogs barked and panted, and would have leapt past Hans and inside if they had not been restrained.

"Did you check the barn?" inquired Anneke, her eyes wide and innocent. "Last time, you said sometimes runaways hide in the barn." She turned to Hans, stroking her abdomen as if comforting the child within her womb. "These runaways won't hurt us, will they?"

Hans put his arm around her protectively. "Don't you worry, dearest." Then he glared at the men as if to shame them for frightening a poor defenseless woman.

But they were not deceived. "Yes, we surely did check your barn, and we checked L.'s cabin, too," said the first man. "And that is where we discovered this."

He held out a worn shawl of linsey-woolsey, filthy and torn.

"That's mine," said I, and took the slave cloth from him. "My goodness, when I think of how long and hard I searched for this—"

"We found footprints, too," interrupted the second.

"Of course you did," said Hans, with perfect bemusement. "We used to live there."

"Likely we left many other things behind, besides," said I.

The first man addressed Hans. "If you don't allow us to search your house, I'll come back with the law, and we'll force our way in."

"Not with those filthy curs, you will not," I declared. "I will not have them tracking mud all over my clean floors."

"Surely they wouldn't bring the dogs inside, would they?" Anneke shrank back, putting Hans between herself and the door. "Hans, please say they won't."

"As you can see, my wife is as terrified of dogs as my sister is of a dirty floor," remarked Hans dryly. "I suppose I could let you in if it will get rid of you, but the dogs stay outside."

The second man fumed. "See there?" said he to his companion. "They're afraid. They know what the dogs will find."

"Oh, come now," said I. "Be reasonable. Would your own wives allow those muddy paws in their homes? Surely our house isn't large enough to conceal someone from two experienced slave catchers, dogs or no dogs."

I do not know if my caustic remark injured their pride or if they thought of their own wives and decided my obsession with a clean floor was quite typical for my sex, but, muttering complaints and curses just loud enough to be heard, they tied the hounds' leashes to a post. Hans opened the door and waved the men in, and they wasted no time searching through the first level as we Bergstroms sat in the front room and pretended we feared nothing more than the loss of a few hours' sleep. "Don't track dirt into the baby's room," called Anneke after the two men as they trooped upstairs. Then we all fell silent.

We listened to their boots on the floorboards as they moved from room to room above us. We knew the precise moment they entered the sewing room. I could scarcely breathe, silently willing the fugitives to be as still as stone, waiting for a triumphant shout of discovery that would announce our undoing.

But the shout did not come.

The footfalls moved from room to room a second time, and then, after what seemed an eternity, we heard them coming slowly, reluctantly, down the stairs. Hans shrugged at the men as if to say he had tried to prevent them from wasting their time, but the two men were unmollified. So great was the first man's fury that he could scarcely strangle out a vow that he would be watching us, and that one day he would catch us helping runaways and see us hanged for it.

"Threaten my family again and I'll kill you," said Hans.

He said it as easily as if he had made killing men his life's work. The two slave catchers frowned, but they did not look as if Hans's threat troubled them. Still, they left our home in great haste, and soon even the sound of their horses' hooves on the road faded into the distance.

"Fools," said Hans. "They don't hang a man for helping slaves."

Anneke gave me a look that suggested she found little consolation in that fact, and she set herself down heavily in the nearest chair.

"Joanna," said I, remembering with a jolt her own condition, and how three fugitives were sharing a refuge meant for one.

I raced upstairs to the sewing room to find it in a shambles, as if two slave catchers had spitefully strewn fabric and quilts about when their search turned up nothing amiss. Picking my way through the mess, I went to Anneke's sewing machine and pulled it away from the wall, revealing a minuscule crack in the new plaster behind it. I slipped my fingernails into the crack and tugged, and away came the makeshift door. "They're gone," said I. "It's safe to come out."

Joanna was the first to emerge, looking faint. I helped her back to bed as the man exited, but upon my return, I found him sitting beside the hole in the false wall, earnestly appealing to the young boy to come out. The boy refused, and I cannot say I blamed him. In the end, we agreed to allow him to remain inside as long as he wished; we left the wood-and-plaster covering off, but nearby, where it could quickly be replaced if need be.

"I apologize for the cramped accommodations," said I as I made up a bed for the man on the floor beside the opening, where he wished to remain, to comfort the boy. "That space was once a closet, but even then it was little more than a nook. Hans plastered over the door remarkably well, but he had no way to enlarge the space."

"We hide out in worse places than that," said he. "Once we hide in a pigsty, another time an outhouse. Slave catchers be low types, but even they don't like that stink."

"Imagine that," said I, dryly. "I would have thought them perfectly suited for such a stench. Their souls reek of the filth of their occupation."

He chuckled grimly in agreement, and I felt my fear lifting, replaced by a relief so complete I felt light-headed. Our secret alcove had passed its first test, and I was greatly reassured that the fugitives who sought shelter with us would be safe within our walls.

But as I drifted off to sleep, I thought of the young boy who feared capture too much to quit the hiding place. If not for an inexplicable quirk of fate or the unfathomable caprice of God, he could have been born in the North and free. He could have been Anneke's child, and Anneke's child could have been born into slavery.

When I read over these lines they seem no more than ramblings, although at the time I felt I had touched on something profound. I cannot trace the path my thoughts traveled that night, but in my fatigue and my fear, I saw quite plainly a sameness linking all of us entangled in this great conflict, so that I felt at once both guardian and fugitive, both slave and free-born. Slavery made slaves of us all, it seemed to me, imprisoning those with dark skin in the iron shackles of injustice, those who owned slaves in chains of sin, and those of us complacent in our freedom with the heavy yoke of obligation to help our enslaved brethren.

❧

But while the events of that night brought me increased confidence and insight, they brought Anneke greater fear.

I did not know how she felt until later. If I detected anything unusual in her demeanor, any reluctance to help the fugitives or desire to forgo displaying the Underground Railroad quilt on the clothesline, I must have ascribed it to her condition. If she seemed fearful of our safety, I must have assumed hers was the ordinary preoccupation of a new mother nearing her time. Our days and nights were such a whirlwind of activity that I do not recall what I thought, or if, in fact, Anneke gave any noticeable sign of her increasing apprehension.

A certain occasion I do remember clearly: One afternoon, when I retrieved Anneke from Mrs. Engle's shop, she greeted me in a distracted fashion and responded with little more than monosyllables and shrugs to my attempts at conversation. I attributed her mood to disappointment, as Mrs. Engle had recently begun urging Anneke to rest at home rather than come in for more sewing work, but suddenly Anneke said, "Does it not trouble you that we are breaking the law?"

"It is wrong to obey an unjust law," said I. "Sometimes submitting to God's law means we must disobey those created by man."

"Yes, of course, but . . ." She hesitated. "Is it not possible that slavery is also the will of God?"

"Anneke," said I, astounded.

"I know what you and Dorothea say, but tell me, is it not possible? Slavery surfaces so often in the Bible—"

"So does sin, so does evil, but we are not meant to perpetuate them."

"But there are directives given for how one is to treat a slave. Why would such things appear in holy scripture if there were not some divine purpose for them? Mr. Pearson says that the African races are the descendants of Ham, condemned by Noah to live in bondage to his brothers. If this is true—"

"It is not true. It is utter nonsense." I hardly knew what to say, so bewildered was I by Anneke's questioning of obvious truths. "I do not think it is wise for you to discuss such issues with Mr. Pearson. You know his views. He is a rigid, blind rule follower with neither the sense nor the judiciousness to decide matters for himself. He would turn his own mother in to the authorities if he thought her in violation of some law."

"He might," countered Anneke, "if he thought it was for her own good. In any event, you needn't worry about me conversing with Mr. Pearson in the near future, for today Mrs. Engle told me quite firmly not to return until after my confinement."

And thus, I thought, the true reason for her contrariness was revealed. I abandoned our argument in lieu of consoling her, reassuring her that she would return to her sewing work in no time, and mocking Mrs. Engle for her silly notions that a pregnant belly was an abominable sight best kept locked indoors where it could not cause offense. Ordinarily Anneke sprang to her employer's defense, but that day, she was understandably receptive to my criticism, and to my great pleasure, she even joined in with a few pointed barbs of her own.

❧

If Anneke conversed as often as I did with Joanna, she would not have entertained even for a moment the ludicrous idea that God intended any of His children to own another. The horrors Joanna described were beyond anything I could have imagined, and I marveled that she, that anyone, had been able to endure it. I yearned to ask Mr. Pearson if he had considered such brutality when concluding that slavery had been ordained by God.

As our intimacy grew, Joanna made it plain that, as I had surmised, her master was the father of her unborn child. Little wonder, I thought, that she displayed such indifference to it. Joanna had been taken by force more times than she could remember, the first when she was but a young girl. Her circumstances so differed from Anneke's, who carried a child conceived in love and awaited with eager joy, that I could not fault her for her feelings.

And yet, over time, I began to notice a subtle shift in her temperament. She began to respond to Anneke's tentative overtures to discuss the condition they shared; she asked for scraps to piece a baby quilt, which I gladly gave her. And as she sewed, if I had completed my chores or desired a respite from them, I would read to her.

I knew something had changed in her sentiments toward her child when she asked me to read again a passage from Douglass's *Narrative,* which we had completed several weeks before, wherein Mr. Douglass describes how he was separated from his mother in infancy, and saw her but a handful of times before her death, and how slave owners conspired to destroy the natural affection a mother feels for her child and the child for his mother.

She sat in silence after I finished, her silver needle darting swiftly through the fabric scraps in her hands. "If I didn't run off, they likely take my baby away," said she. "Sell him off farther South, maybe. The missus don't like seeing her husband's babies from other women."

"It's hardly the fault of the women," said I, indignant.

Joanna regarded me with amusement. "Don't you hear nothing I tell you about that place? You think it matter that we don't want him? It easy to blame us. She can't get rid of her husband, so she sell us farther South and get rid of the problem. Until the massa take a liking to another."

"This will not happen to you," said I. "You have escaped that fate. Your child will know you and love you, and your affection will make him thrive."

"Freedom make him thrive," corrected Joanna, but she allowed a smile.

Then she asked me to read a later, lengthier excerpt, the story of how Mr. Douglass learned to read and write. As I read his words aloud, I stole glances at Joanna. First she stopped sewing, then a faraway look came into her eye. When I concluded, she briskly took up the quilt pieces again. "This Frederick Douglass a clever man."

"Ingenious," said I. "There is perhaps no more powerful voice championing the Abolitionist cause than Mr. Douglass."

"Maybe it's true what he said, that learning to read spoil a slave, because it make him discontent and unhappy," said she, "but I plenty discontent and unhappy already, and I can't read."

"You could learn. I could teach you."

"Maybe a house slave don't need to read, but a free woman in Canada probably do." She placed a hand on her abdomen. "I'll want to read to my baby, read him the Bible and Mr. Douglass's book, so he know where he came from, and where he can go."

My heart swelled with admiration and affection, and we began our lessons that very day.

So Elm Creek Farm passed from winter into spring, with furtive activity in the night, growing anticipation for the two children who would soon be born, and danger always present, always lingering on the frontiers of our thoughts.

Only later did I realize our greatest threat lay much nearer, that it had crossed our threshold and lay curled up by the hearth, watching us unnoticed, and biding its time.

Chapter Ten

Sylvia's sense of vindication that Elm Creek Manor had been a haven for slaves was tempered by the knowledge that her family had only unwittingly become stationmasters.

"But they did," said Sarah. "That's what matters. When Joanna knocked on the door, they sheltered her. They just as easily could have sent her away."

"I suppose so," admitted Sylvia. And even if they had felt they had no choice but to assist Joanna once she stumbled upon them, they had actively sought to help the later runaways. Sylvia ought to be glad for that, and that this newest revelation did not contradict any of the family stories passed down through the generations. The stories said only that the Bergstroms had run a station on the Underground Railroad, not how they had begun it.

"They continued even after that scare with the slave catchers," said Sarah.

"Yes, indeed. They certainly could think on their feet, couldn't they? Even Anneke. I must say that pleased me. From the way Gerda described her, I feared she would fall apart and blurt out the secret the moment those two slave catchers arrived."

Sarah laughed but added, "In her defense, remember we're only seeing Gerda's interpretation of Anneke, not the real person."

Sylvia cast her gaze to heaven. "Our friend Gwen, the college professor, already gave me the lecture on 'reliable narrators.' Well, I for one believe Gerda is reliable, and I'm confident her portrayal of Anneke is accurate." She paused. "At least, accurate within a modest margin of error."

"I wonder," mused Sarah. "Where was this hiding place she wrote about?"

"I have no idea." Sylvia wasn't sure which room had been Anneke's sewing room. For that matter, Gerda had not even specified which room had been her own.

"Maybe she assumed her reader would be a more recent descendant, someone who would know whose rooms were whose."

Sylvia shrugged. "Perhaps." But if Gerda's preface was any indication, she had intended her words to be read long after the principal participants in her memoir had passed on.

Sarah gave Sylvia her hand. "Come on. Let's go find it."

"Now?" Sylvia allowed herself to be pulled to her feet. "Don't you think our campers will mind having their privacy invaded?"

"Are you kidding? They'll probably be delighted to be in on the mystery."

Sylvia conceded the point, and so she accompanied Sarah upstairs to the second floor, trying not to allow her hopes to rise too high. The manor had undergone so many changes since Gerda's time, from the addition of the south wing to the extensive remodeling after the fire that occurred in her father's day to the modernizations her sister, Claudia, had added a generation later. Not only might Anneke's sewing room be unrecognizable, it might be gone entirely, its place usurped by the hallway linking the original wing with the new.

They began with the unoccupied rooms, and since it was late August, there were more of these than there would have been earlier in the summer. But while the closets in the first four rooms were not very big, especially by modern standards, they were substantially larger than a "nook" or an "alcove," the two words Gerda had used to describe the hiding place.

"The closets could have been enlarged in the renovations," said Sarah.

Sylvia had no choice but to agree, and felt their chances of identifying the correct room dwindling.

She hesitated before entering the last vacant room. She allowed this suite to go unoccupied during all but their busiest weeks, and even then she had to resist the urge to ask campers to double up rather than assign someone to it. The pink, white, and yellow Grape Basket quilt remained on the wall where Sylvia had discovered it upon her return to Elm Creek Manor, but she and Sarah had long ago substituted a strip-pieced Trip Around the World quilt for the pink-and-white Flying Geese quilt that had once adorned the queen-size bed. Whether because of their estrangement or in spite of it, Sylvia could not bear the thought of someone else, even a friendly quilter, sleeping beneath the quilt her sister Claudia had used as her own.

Sylvia pursed her lips and opened the door. "This closet is certainly large enough," she said briskly, to disguise the hesitation she always felt upon entering her late sister's room. "Claudia wouldn't have settled for anything else. I'm surprised she chose rooms in the west wing, since the south-wing suites are larger and more comfortable."

Sarah led the way into the adjoining room. "I'm surprised there are any suites in the west wing at all."

"There weren't, originally. My father had doorways cut in some of the walls to turn adjacent rooms into suites." She looked around the room. "Well, there's no closet here, large or small. I suppose we'll have to disturb our campers after all."

"Wait." Sarah placed a hand on her arm to prevent Sylvia from leaving. "What about the loveseat?"

Sylvia eyed the floral tapestry cushions. "What of it?"

"It's set into a nook. Don't you see?" Sarah crossed the room and measured the depth with her hand. "I'd say it's about a foot and a half deep."

"That's not a closet," scoffed Sylvia. "In the room on the other side of the wall, there are two closets, there and there." She pointed to the corners on either end of the concavity in turn. "They encroach on this room's space."

"All the more reason to believe there was once a closet on this side, too. This wall was a part of Hans's original design, right?"

"I can't say for certain . . ." Sylvia hesitated. "I suppose it must have been. My father had a predilection for enlarging spaces, not for making them more intimate."

"Gerda did say the hiding place was shallow, even for a closet."

"True." Sylvia joined Sarah and inspected the wall. Sarah's measurement was conservative, but even so, the alcove could not have been more than two feet deep and five feet long, and Hans's false wall would have taken up some of that space. It was difficult to imagine anyone hiding there for long, in stifling darkness, listening to the bewildering noise of the search, with nothing but a thin wall of plaster separating the fugitive from the pursuer. "I suppose its very narrowness makes it a better hiding place."

"And harder to detect by someone searching in the other room. If it had been any larger, the missing space would have attracted attention."

Sylvia ran her fingertips along the wall, then flipped back the braided rag rug on the floor, but if Hans's false wall had once occupied the space, no sign of it remained. "I'll reserve judgment until I see the other rooms."

They collected an eager group of assistants as they went from one camper's room to the next, explaining their errand and searching for an alcove resembling Gerda's description. Upon completing the last room, however, they concluded that Claudia's room was the most likely candidate.

"That doesn't mean it's definitely the one," cautioned Sarah, when she and Sylvia were alone again. "Gerda doesn't say that Anneke's sewing room was the only one in the house with a nook instead of a proper closet. There might have been others."

"Yes, either lost when the addition was put on or renovated beyond recognition." Sylvia shook her head, exasperated. "Why is it that every time I think we've obtained some evidence, something tangible to prove Gerda's story true, we end up with so many cautions and qualifiers that we're no better off than when we started?"

"It seems that way, doesn't it?" Sarah laughed. "Then you're really not going to like my next question."

Sylvia sighed wearily. "Pose it anyway."

"According to your family stories, the Log Cabin quilt with the black center square was the signal, but it turns out the Underground Railroad quilt was," said Sarah. "So how does the Log Cabin quilt you found in Gerda's hope chest figure into all this?"

❧ April 1859 — in which our waiting ends

Come springtime, talk around Creek's Crossing turned to the rising tensions between North and South as often as it did to planting and the weather. Kansas, where we had once planned to settle, had become soaked in the blood of courageous Free-Staters and hostile Missouri raiders, but although I am loath to admit it, the Abolitionists committed their share of atrocities as well. More than once I thanked God for delivering us to Elm Creek Farm three years before, thus sparing us from the violence we otherwise would have faced. I saw the good we did in helping fugitive slaves as but a small show of gratitude for His Providence.

With the return of fair weather came an increase in the number of fugitives who sought shelter with us, but it also increased the number of slave catchers poking about. Far too often I was forced to keep the Underground Railroad quilt inside because earlier that day a patrol had trespassed upon our property or had been bold enough to knock upon our door and inquire if we had seen any suspicious Negroes wandering about, who might be slaves passing as free. I would respond with a curt negative and send them on their way. But their questions did make me reflect upon the situation of the free coloreds around our town. It seemed to me they had been keeping to themselves even more than usual, and I cannot blame them for their wariness. Dorothea had spoken of treacherous slave catchers who, when unable to find their actual prey, would seize upon some poor freedman and pass him off as the runaway. Once spirited off to a Slave State, he could expect no one to believe his accusations against his deceitful white captors, and would be sold into slavery, leaving his family and friends ignorant of his fate and unable to rescue him even if they did know.

Sometimes the slave catchers mentioned Mr. L. and assumed we were on friendly terms with him, since he had sold us his farm (as they believed); they assumed, too, we would offer them the same hospitality he had. Hans provided as little as he could, as cordially as he could. He wished to avoid making enemies or raising suspicions, but he did not want to encourage future visits, lest our secret activities be discovered.

Then one night, I was roused not by a knock on the door but by a groan of pain from down the hall. My first thought was that Joanna's time had come, but then Hans appeared in my doorway, carrying a light and beckoning me to help. It was Anneke's cries I had heard, though her baby was not supposed to come for another month.

I thought, at first, that it was a false labor, and that it would fade within an hour. I had seen that happen before, especially with a woman's first child. But as the birth pangs grew more painful and more frequent, we all realized that the infant's arrival was imminent.

Hans raced from the house to fetch Jonathan, for I was not so confident in my own abilities that I did not welcome his guidance, especially considering that none of us had expected this child quite so soon. I had assisted my mother as she cared for women in labor, but never had I been alone at the bedside, nor even in charge with helpers of my own. I did what I could to ease Anneke's sufferings, bathing her brow, speaking of the joys she would soon feel upon holding her child, but nothing I did could comfort her for long. She cried from pain and from fear, repeating again and again that it was too soon, that it had to stop, and that I must help her. My longing to do so brought tears to my eyes, but I was powerless.

Roused by Anneke's cries, Joanna soon joined us. When Anneke screamed from the shooting pains in her lower back, Joanna immediately had her go upon her hands and knees on the bed. To my astonishment, this did seem to relieve much of the pain, but when I complimented Joanna on her cure, she only shook her head, grim-faced. "That mean the baby's head the wrong way," said she in an undertone. "Gonna be hard to push him out, so hard."

My alarm growing, I prayed Hans and Jonathan would return soon. When they did, it was so sudden that there was no time for Joanna to conceal herself within the secret alcove. Instead, with a speed that belied her cumbersome belly, she crawled beneath Anneke's bed. I threw a quilt over her as the two men ran up the stairs.

Joanna lay there as still as stone throughout the night and into the day, when the first light of dawn pinked the sky, and Anneke's cries had grown faint and hoarse. It was as Joanna had said; the baby's head was turned directly opposite the way it should have been, which made for long, exhausting hours of pushing. But, thanks be to God, by the time sunlight shone in through the windows, Anneke had delivered a beautiful son.

Jonathan examined the baby and declared him apparently healthy in every way, despite his early arrival. I wept with joy when Jonathan handed him to me to bathe and wrap in a blanket. Afterward I kissed the babe's head and placed him in Anneke's arms, which were trembling from fatigue so that she could not clasp them about her son. Hans embraced her so that his arms supported hers around their precious bundle.

When Jonathan spoke to me next, to ask my assistance in tending to Anneke, I felt his words like a jolt. As foolish as it might sound, until that moment I had thought of him only as the doctor, not as Jonathan, who had once been *my* Jonathan. I tried not to meet his gaze as we cared for the new mother and her child, but my every nerve was raw and conscious of his presence. When our eyes accidentally met, I knew at once that he was thinking, as I was, that we would never together know the joy Hans and Anneke now felt.

But then my heart chilled against him. All that had prevented our mutual happiness was his stubbornness and a misguided sense of duty. He would very likely know the delights of fatherhood with Charlotte, while I would likely never know the joys of motherhood. Jonathan could have married me, if he had been courageous enough, if he had truly wished to. In that respect he was no different than, and no better than, E.

Jonathan remained with Anneke for a little while, but as soon as he departed, I hastened to assist Joanna from her hiding place beneath the bed. She seemed weary, and little wonder, but when I asked her how she felt, she assured me she was fine. Only after I had helped her back into her own bed did she confide that she had never witnessed a birth as difficult as Anneke's. "I hope mine go easier," said she, faintly. "Don't know if I could have done all she just done."

"You have endured more than I would have thought possible for any woman, or any man, for that matter," said I, stroking her head. "You are stronger than you know. You will do just fine."

My words seemed to reassure her, and as she drifted off to sleep, I marveled that a woman who bore such scars upon her back and heart could doubt her ability to endure childbirth.

❧

Summer tilted her head to the side, scanning the titles on the spines of the books. If she had known the Waterford College Library had so many books on block patterns and quilt history, she would have visited this wing a long time ago. Not that she had lacked quilt information—in addition to those she bought from Grandma's Attic with her employee discount, the Elm Creek Quilters routinely exchanged books from their personal libraries, and Sylvia was virtually a walking encyclopedia on the subject of all things quilt-related.

But her friends' resources weren't exhaustive, or she wouldn't be scanning the library shelves looking for more. Unfortunately, while she found many books about quilts from the Civil War era, books focusing on the years before the war were more scarce. Even those three that she had found did not mention signal quilts or the Underground Railroad in their indexes, but Summer planned to check them out anyway, in hopes that a closer examination might turn up, if not the specific information she sought, other references worth pursuing.

She finished looking over the bottom shelf and moved on to the top shelf of the next case where the books on textile history continued. Most of the books were older titles, with enough dust to suggest they were rarely used. Her gaze lit upon a promising-looking volume, and as she rose on her tiptoes to reach for it, a man's voice said, "Here. Let me get that for you."

"I'm fine—" Summer started to say, but the man reached past her and snatched the book so quickly that her fingertips brushed the back of his hand. "Thanks." *I guess,* she added silently, since she had not needed his help.

"Anytime." The man grinned at her in such a cheerful manner that she found herself no longer minding his unnecessary assistance. He was about her age, with dark, tousled hair and wire-rimmed glasses, and he carried a stack of books under one arm. In the other hand, he still held Summer's book.

Summer suppressed a smile and held out her hand. "Did you want to read it first, or . . . ?"

"Oh." Quickly he handed her the book. "Sorry."

"That's okay." She turned back to the bookshelf and opened the book to the table of contents.

"Is this for your local history project or are you starting something new?"

Summer looked up, surprised. "How did you know about that?"

She might have been mistaken, but for a moment, she thought he looked disappointed. "I've seen you in the historical society's archives at least twice a week all summer."

Then Summer recognized him. "Oh, right. You're the guy who helped me find the court files. You're usually hunched over your books in the carrel by the window, oblivious to the world."

He grinned but said, "Not *that* oblivious." He craned his neck to read the title of the book in Summer's hands. "*Quilts and Their Makers in Antebellum Pennsylvania.* Sounds interesting."

Summer gave him an appraising look, wondering if he meant it. "It is," she said when she decided he was sincere. "It's related to my historical society research project."

"Can you talk about it, or"—he glanced over his shoulder as if to make sure no one could overhear—"are you afraid someone might steal your topic and publish the results before you do?"

Summer couldn't help laughing. "It's not like that." She explained the mystery that had brought her so frequently to the library archives. At first she provided only a sketchy narrative, but when she saw he was truly interested, she warmed to her subject and filled in more details. She concluded by telling him the focus of this particular library search: to find, if it existed, some mention of quilts used as signals on the Underground Railroad.

"I haven't found much," admitted Summer, "and what I have found mentions signal quilts only in passing, as if it's common knowledge that certain patterns were used to designate stations or to transmit directions. Not one book or article has provided a photo of one of these quilts or gives any other kind of concrete documentation that such quilts existed. It's as if the author heard of them from one person, who heard about it from another person, and so on."

"That must be frustrating."

"That's one of the milder words I've used."

He laughed, but then grew thoughtful. "You know, it's the nature of secret signals that they aren't published or even spoken about, or they lose their efficacy. There might not be any published records out there to be found."

"I realize that, but I thought by now diaries or other family records might have been published, since revealing the secrets so many years after the Civil War, wouldn't do any harm."

He shrugged. "More than fifty years ago, my grandfather and his parents fled from Nazi Germany to Switzerland with the help of the underground movement. He told me that even after they came to America, even when the war had been over for decades, his parents said very little about the secret signals and communications they used during their escape."

"Why?"

"They said they couldn't risk it, since one never knew if those signals would be needed again someday."

☙ April into May 1859 — in which we raise and attempt to dispel suspicions

Anneke and Hans's good news spread rapidly through town, and Elm Creek Farm was soon besieged with well-meaning well-wishers, bearing covered dishes and baby quilts, all eager for a peek at the beautiful little boy. Anneke delighted in the attention paid to her son, and I was grateful for the food, since I was so busy playing nurse I could scarcely find a moment to catch my breath, much less put together a meal for the new parents, Joanna, and myself. Hans and I had agreed we could not display the Underground Railroad quilt under such circumstances, and I was plagued by thoughts of fugitives spending the night in the woods within sight of our house, unable to receive food or clothing or the comfort of a reassuring word.

Joanna helped me as she could, but with visitors arriving unannounced at all hours of the day, she found herself scrambling for the hiding place so often she finally decided it would be most prudent for her to remain there throughout the day. Thinking of her shut up in that confined place drove me to distraction, and I yearned for the flood of neighbors to slow to a trickle.

Our most frequent visitor was someone who would have been chagrined to learn her presence kept Joanna shut up within the secret alcove: my dear friend Dorothea, who came over nearly every evening after her own chores were finished to assist me with mine. Would that every woman could be blessed with a friend possessing such a willing heart and generous spirit! Frequently during those weary days, when I was tempted to fall asleep on my feet or crawl under the bedclothes and stuff my quilt into my ears rather than help Anneke soothe her howling infant, Dorothea's unwavering serenity and quiet confidence cheered me, and helped me marshal my strength so that I could be the kind of aunt my family needed.

Two of the last guests were, in my view, the two least welcome. A fortnight after my nephew was born, Mr. Pearson and Mrs. Engle paid their respects to the new mother. They arrived at dinnertime, just as Hans returned hungry from the fields, so I was obliged to entertain them better than I otherwise would have done. While Anneke and Mrs. Engle sat in the front room, with Mrs. Engle holding the baby and cooing to him while Anneke looked on, radiant, I set out some of the dishes the neighbors had brought and hoped Mr. Pearson would not feel the need to assist me. He did not, apparently, for when he entered the dining room, he merely stood there smirking, as if I should be grateful he chose to keep me company.

"Anneke looks well," he remarked, leaning against the door frame and watching me set the table.

I made a noise of agreement but otherwise ignored him.

He followed me in a leisurely fashion as I went back and forth, carrying dishes from the kitchen to the table. "How fortunate is she to know the bliss of motherhood," said he. "It is truly the highest state to which women can aspire, don't you agree?"

All manner of retorts rose to my sharp tongue, but I withheld them. If he hoped to provoke within me even a spark of jealousy toward my sister-in-law, he was wasting his own time as well as mine. "Anneke has been richly blessed, and I am truly overjoyed for her," said I, and I meant it with all my heart.

He seemed disappointed by the lack of venom in my response, and his gaze turned away from me—and alighted on the Underground Railroad quilt, folded and forgotten on the sideboard. "What's this?" asked he, unfolding it.

"A quilt."

"Yes, of course, I see that," he snapped, but then he frowned. "I do believe I've seen this pattern elsewhere."

"Perhaps your mother has made a similar quilt."

"No, that's not it."

He studied the quilt with such intensity that I grew agitated. "Oh, indeed, Mr. Pearson, are you such a connoisseur of patchwork that you know every quilt block your mother has made?"

He looked up from the quilt, his eyebrows raised in mild surprise. "She would like it better if I did, but I confess I only pretend to listen when she chatters about her needlework." He folded the quilt and returned it to the sideboard. "If you'll excuse me, Miss Bergstrom." With his usual smirk in place, he returned to the front room.

I chided myself for my shaky nerves and resolved to conceal my emotions so well that I would be thought as serene as Dorothea. Knowing that Mr. Pearson could not possibly understand the quilt's significance steeled my confidence, and since he dared not bait me too much in front of the others, dinner passed without a mishap.

With so many other distractions to occupy my thoughts, I put the incident out of my mind. When another week passed, and it seemed safe again, I draped the Underground Railroad quilt over the clothesline and made ready for new arrivals.

There was, indeed, much to prepare, so much we did not know about when Joanna first knocked upon our door. Food and rest were the most pressing needs, but after that, the fugitives often needed new clothing, especially shoes, for the men, and gloves and bonnets for the women, the better to pass themselves off as free if they were seen. They also needed papers declaring them free citizens, although I sometimes wondered what good these would do if they were apprehended by slave catchers. Still, if the documents spared only one runaway from the clutches of slavery, they were worth far more than the paper and ink and the work I put into them. I must say I became quite an accomplished forger. Once Hans said, in jest, that he knew people from his vagabond days who could help me turn a nice profit with my skills, but Anneke was decidedly not amused by the suggestion. She said we broke enough laws on Elm Creek Farm not to joke about violating more for mere lucrative gain. For someone who went about day and night beaming over her beautiful son, motherhood had rendered Anneke rather humorless.

In addition to clothing and forged papers, the fugitives needed food for their journey. I learned to bake hardtack and sent them off with that as well as dried apples and hard cheese that would not spoil quickly. They needed directions to stations farther north; Hans determined the most prudent courses based upon rumored slave-catcher activities. Most of all, our guests needed hope, and so we provided encouragement in abundance.

Sometimes our visitors shared news from the places they had abandoned, and their accounts confirmed what we had begun to read in the papers: that Southern animosity for the North was increasing as Northern condemnation of Southern slaveholding became louder and more insistent. Even Southerners who did not own slaves resented Northerners for their self-righteous attempts to interfere in Southern matters, which, they feared, could destroy the economy of the entire South. "Abolitionist" was a word spoken with venom by Southern whites, and slaves knew better than to utter it, even to ask in all innocence what it meant.

But most runaways who passed through our station were too exhausted and wary to converse much about the institution of slavery. Their strength they reserved for the difficult flight to Canada; their thoughts they saved for the family and friends they had left behind, and would almost certainly never see again.

Four weeks passed between the birth of Anneke's son and the restoration of the signal quilt to the clothesline; another five days passed with no knock on the door in the night. Then one morning shortly after dawn, when Hans was already in the fields and I was tending to my household chores, two quick raps sounded.

I opened the door and discovered a colored man dressed in farmer's clothes, the brim of his hat pulled down low over his eyes—and our Underground Railroad quilt folded over his arm. A flash of panic shot through me—did he not realize how he endangered himself and us, approaching the house so boldly in daylight, the signal quilt in hand?—so that I did not at first recognize him as Mr. Abel Wright, the owner of a farm lying roughly a mile south and west of ours outside the boundaries of Creek's Crossing, whose wife I had met at Charlotte Claverton's quilting bee.

I stammered out a greeting and invited him inside, but he refused, saying that he had to return to his fields. Then he held out the quilt to me and said, "I just wanted to tell you not to use this quilt no more." When I told him I did not understand, he looked away, paused, and added, "Too many people know about it. Someone talked. Someone down the line, or someone captured—I can't rightly say who. But you ought not to use this anymore." Then he looked directly into my eyes and said, "Do you get my meaning?"

I did indeed, but I also found myself wondering why it had not occurred to me before that free Negroes in the North might also be stationmasters. Even now it shames me to admit this, but until that moment, I had assumed the Underground Railroad was operated solely by benevolent whites. Though I had prided myself on being an enlightened sort, I had never suspected that Negroes might be perfectly able and willing to help one another, without the benefit of some white person's direction. What this said about me, with all my high ideals and rhetoric, it troubled me to ponder.

I thanked Mr. Wright and hurried off to find Anneke. She was in the baby's room, rocking and nursing contentedly, but when I repeated the warning to her, her eyes grew large with fright, as if she could already hear the pounding hooves of slave catchers' horses storming up the road toward us. Indeed, I had to struggle to maintain my own composure, for although I could not discern the connection, I knew our neighbor's warning was somehow linked to Mr. Pearson's odd musings about the Underground Railroad pattern. That despicable man would bring us trouble. He had not done so yet, and so I had no explanation for the intensity of my feelings, but I was certain he meant us harm.

"We shall have to contrive another signal," said I.

Anneke declared she knew exactly the thing: a quilt pattern common enough that it would not attract unwanted attention, and yet simple enough that even I could fashion it well. It was called Birds in the Air, and as it was fashioned of many triangles, we could, by the placement of the quilt upon the line, indicate in which direction the fugitives could find a safe haven.

At first I was dubious; I suggested a pattern of logs in the woodpile or an arrangement of buckets by the well, anything as long as it bore no resemblance whatsoever to the signal that had become a danger. But Anneke noted that slave catchers, being men, were likely to ignore clotheslines, and even if a slave catcher did take note of it, he would ignore other quilts in his search for the one pattern he knew Abolitionists favored. "They would not suspect we would substitute one quilt pattern as a signal for another," said Anneke. "That is why it is the perfect choice."

Thus she persuaded me, and thus we began our second signal quilt.

Since nearly every moment of Anneke's days and nights was given over to the care of her son, the task of completing the quilt fell to me, the least able quilter in the county. Anneke suggested that I make a crib-size quilt, both to hasten its completion and to contribute to our ruse: No one would think it odd to spot the same baby's blanket so frequently upon the clothesline, for as I had recently learned, infants rarely kept garments or bedding clean for long. Moreover, I finally consented to learn to use Anneke's sewing machine, something she had been pestering me to do since our arrival at Elm Creek Farm. Pumping the treadle and guiding the fabric through the machine was hardly work at all in comparison to the tedious drudgery of hand sewing. I worked swiftly, feverishly, whenever my other chores would permit, and as the days passed, one Birds in the Air block after another joined the rising pile beside the sewing machine. Now that Joanna did not need to hide continuously in the secret alcove, she, too, learned to use the sewing machine, and she completed as many blocks as I.

Working side by side, Joanna and I joined the blocks into rows, sewed the rows together, then layered the pieced top, cotton batting, and a muslin lining in Anneke's frame. We devoted one long stretch from dusk until dawn quilting, and in the morning when Anneke came downstairs with the baby in her arms, she found us putting the last stitches into the binding.

The three of us inspected the quilt. "It'll do," said Joanna matter-of-factly.

I nodded, too tired to do anything more, but Anneke took the quilt and wrapped it around her son. "It's beautiful." She cradled her son in her arms and kissed his brow.

My heart swelled with pride. Anyone else would have laughed in surprise to hear this quilt, sturdily though hastily made, pieced of scraps and quilted in simple lines, given such praise. But I understood my sister-in-law's meaning. The quilt was beautiful not for itself but for what it represented, and what it would accomplish.

It was the finest thing my hands ever made, then or since.

We sent word to stations south of us—as before, I shall not explain the particulars of how—so that fugitives would know to look for our new signal. Within days of the completion of the quilt, it had beckoned a runaway from Virginia into our home. The Elm Creek Farm station of the Underground Railroad was open once again.

Chapter Eleven

The second time the librarian passed by to remind Summer that the Waterford Historical Society's archives closed early on Fridays, Summer nodded absently and glanced at her watch. She had five more minutes to search the database before the librarian would kick her out and lock the door, but with the pitiful luck she'd had so far that day, five minutes more or less probably wouldn't make much difference.

She sighed and shut down the computer, admitting to herself that she might be wasting her time. Lately she had turned up nothing related to the Bergstroms or Elm Creek Farm, so she had not even told Sylvia about her searches. She would rather have Sylvia believe she was too busy to investigate rather than dash her hopes that something remained out there, waiting to be found.

"That was one heavy sigh. You're supposed to be quiet in the library."

Summer looked over her shoulder to find the same dark-haired man who had tried to help her in the stacks smiling at her from his usual carrel. "Sorry," said Summer. "Does this mean you have to confiscate my library card?"

"I don't think that happens on the first offense." He rose and crossed the aisle, and nodded to the computer. "Are you having trouble finding something?"

"Are you kidding? I've been here for two hours and all I've found is frustration." Summer laughed ruefully. "I wouldn't mind if at least one of my possibilities would have led somewhere."

"Maybe I can help. What are you looking for?"

"Birth records, death records, documents relating to a family that immigrated here before the Civil War. I looked through the hard copies of the city government files already, but when I couldn't find what I wanted, I tried the database. Unfortunately, it's even less complete than the books."

"Did you look in the old local newspapers? The historical society has microfiche of issues going as far back as the 1800s."

"I looked, but the years I wanted are missing."

"Did you ask at the newspaper office?"

Summer nodded. "They said they might have the issues but they couldn't be sure, and they couldn't spare the personnel to help me look."

"That's rude of them. I think I'll cancel my subscription in protest."

"Don't do it on my account. It's not their fault." Summer checked her watch and, seeing that the archives were about to close, began gathering her notebooks and photocopies. "All I can give them is a last name and a time period. If I could be more specific about what I was looking for, they could probably be more helpful."

The man picked up his stack of books and followed her to the door, where the librarian waited, key in hand. "Have you checked the phone book?"

Summer raised her eyebrows at him. "They didn't have phones back then, so they didn't have much need for phone books."

"No, I mean our phone book. The family you're researching lived in this area, right? Maybe there are some living descendants who would be willing to talk to you. Even if they don't have the specific details you need, they might be able to point you in the right direction. They could give you additional names to research, like other branches of the family."

"Oh, I know there are living descendants," said Summer. One living descendant, anyway, but if Sylvia had that information, Summer wouldn't be searching for it. And as far as additional names were concerned—

"That's it," exclaimed Summer. She had to get home and get her hands on a phone book. "Thank you so much, um—"

"Jeremy. And you're?"

"Summer. Thanks, Jeremy. You've given me a great idea." She left the archive room and headed briskly for the stairs, Jeremy close behind. "I should have asked you for help before. I'm so glad I happened to be here during your shift."

"My shift?"

She glanced at him. "You don't work for the library?"

"Nope. And not for the historical society, either."

Summer stopped short and regarded him with a skeptical grin. "But you offered to help me search the archives."

He shrugged. "I'm just a good citizen." When Summer laughed, he added sheepishly, "I'm a grad student in history. I study in the Waterford Historical Society's room because it's quiet. Usually no one comes in there except for you. Not that I'm keeping track or anything."

He looked so embarrassed Summer couldn't resist teasing him. "Well, if I need any more research assistance, I'll be sure to ask."

He grinned, pleased. "You know where to find me."

❧ May 1859—in which we enter our darkest hours

Our new signal quilt proved so successful that I allowed myself to believe we had eluded the dangers Mr. Pearson's apparent recognition of the Underground Railroad pattern had hinted at and our neighbor's warnings had confirmed. How foolish I was. I should have been more vigilant, but even in hindsight I do not know how I could have predicted from which direction the most dangerous winds would blow.

Fair weather brought a steady stream of runaways; they followed the creek north to our home, with slave catchers never far behind. Elm Creek Farm, which as recently as winter had seemed so remote, now was assured of a visitor at least every second day—and for every three friends we ushered inside to safety, we encountered one unfriendly stranger, full of suspicions and questions. And once again, the same two slave catchers who had searched our home in March came to contend with us.

They arrived amid a fierce thunderstorm, the sudden, violent sort we had learned to expect in that region each spring, but which awed us anew each season. Our first warning of the men's approach came in a respite between thunderclaps: the high, shrill whinny of a horse, so close and sudden we started. Barely a heartbeat later there was an urgent pounding upon the door.

Needless to say, our usual night visitors did not arrive on horseback. Joanna hurried as fast as she could from the fireside upstairs to the secret alcove, and as I assisted her inside, my heart raced with alarm. I wondered who was outside, and if they had glimpsed Joanna through the windows.

When I returned downstairs and found the two familiar and unwelcome figures dripping water in our foyer, I felt a lump in the pit of my stomach, which did not fade until I realized they must not have seen Joanna, for if they had, they would even now be dragging her from the hiding place. I longed to order them from the house, but we could not send them back out into the storm without raising their suspicions. Instead Hans took them to the barn where they could leave their dogs and tend to their horses, and I began to prepare them something to eat.

Suddenly Anneke clutched my arm, stricken. "Gerda," said she, and nodded out the window toward the clothesline.

I raced outside to snatch the Birds in the Air quilt from the line. I returned inside, thoroughly drenched, and hurried upstairs, where I wrung out the quilt in my washbasin and hid it beneath my bed. I had barely enough time to change into dry clothes and return to the kitchen before the men returned.

My own stomach was in knots, so that I hardly dared speak to them as I served their supper, lest they detect my turmoil. Anneke busied herself with the baby, as if too distracted by him to notice the men. To my relief, they conversed with Hans as if they did not notice anything out of the ordinary; or perhaps they noticed but had grown accustomed to odd behavior from the Bergstrom family, as we were never at ease when they were around. I prayed they would soon depart, but as the hour grew late with no abating of the storm, we had no choice but to invite them to spend the night.

They bedded down beside the fireplace, and as I climbed the stairs, I thought of Joanna crouching in darkness almost directly above her enemies. Upstairs, I paused outside the hidden alcove long enough to murmur a warning to Joanna, then crept off to my own room, where I lay in bed, too tense to sleep. If Joanna should cry out as she slumbered—if slumber was possible in such close quarters—or if she did not hold perfectly still and silent, the men below might hear her. We might be able to convince them that Anneke or I had made the sound, but what if—and this was my greatest fear—what if Joanna's child should decide to enter the world that very night?

Eventually snores drifted up the stairs, telling me the slave catchers were resting peacefully, but they were the only ones in the household to do so. Even the baby, who woke twice to nurse, did not rouse them with his cries. I heard Hans and Anneke whispering, but from the sewing room, there was not even the smallest noise. For my part, I held perfectly still in bed, clenching my quilt in my fists, praying that we would somehow manage to avoid detection a second time.

When finally the morning sun began to pink the sky, I dressed and went downstairs to the kitchen to prepare breakfast, making no attempt to work quietly and allow our unwelcome guests to sleep any longer than absolutely necessary. I heard them stirring in the other room, speaking in low voices, then one or both left the house briefly and returned. By the time I summoned everyone to the breakfast table, I had regained my confidence. The men had not demanded to search the house, and perhaps our hospitality would once and for all convince them we had nothing to hide.

We Bergstroms all but wolfed down our food in our eagerness to bring a swift end to the meal, and we could barely contain our relief when the first of the two remarked that they would need to set off immediately, to make up for time lost. Then he looked directly at me and said, "Miss Bergstrom, I don't wish to trouble you none, but if you could spare some of that bread, we'd be mighty grateful for it on the road." He smiled. "We never know when we'll come across a home as welcoming as this one."

"Of course." I hastened to the kitchen and packed a bundle as quickly as I could, and spinning around to return to the dining room, I ran right into the slave catcher. I gasped, startled, and stepped back. "Excuse me," said I, and tried to laugh. "I did not realized you followed me."

He stepped toward me. "Why so nervous, Miss Bergstrom?"

"I'm not nervous, not at all." I thrust the bundle at his chest, shoving him backward. "Here. Enjoy the bread."

He caught my arm. "Yesterday, when we arrived, you wore a blue dress," said he, stroking the fabric of my sleeve with his other hand. "When we returned from the barn, you were dressed in brown."

"You are mistaken," said I, and pulled myself free. "You have confused me and Anneke. I was dressed in brown. She wore blue."

"Miss Bergstrom, are you accustomed to hanging your laundry out to dry in the middle of a rainstorm?" He fixed his gaze on mine. "Or is that how you Dutch wash your bedclothes?"

I feigned embarrassment. "Oh, I fear you have discovered me. And I had so hoped no one had noticed. Please don't tell Anneke I forgot the baby's quilt outside. She'll be so upset."

He scowled, but before he could speak again, Hans entered and offered to help the two men with their horses. The slave catcher nodded, his gaze still upon me, but suddenly he turned and addressed my brother. "What are your plans for L.'s cabin?"

Hans shrugged. "I haven't yet made any plans for it."

"Seems strange to leave it unused, a good, solid building like that," said he. "Or maybe it doesn't go unused. Maybe you don't care if passersby sleep there, so long as they don't bother you up at the big house."

"That cabin is on my land. Anyone entering it is trespassing, whether they're sleeping or looking for someone who is."

"That's good to know. You don't want to encourage vagrants." The slave catcher slung the bundle over his shoulder. "Of course, it could be people stay there without your knowing about it."

"I'd know." Hans's voice was like ice. "Now it's time you were on your way."

The man had little choice but to challenge Hans or obey, so at last he and his companion departed, leaving me shaken and afraid. The more I tried to alleviate the slave catchers' suspicions, the more I gave them reason to scrutinize us. They would not cease to observe us, I knew, whenever their searches took them near Creek's Crossing.

As soon as their horses disappeared into the forest, I hurried upstairs to free Joanna from the secret alcove. Faint and hungry, she asked me in a strained voice to help her to bed. I brought her water, which she drank thirstily, and something to eat, which she picked at but seemed unable to stomach. She kept touching her abdomen and wincing in pain, but when I asked her if she thought the baby was coming, she shook her head and told me the pains had been coming for days now, but they always faded when she rested.

I assured her that now that the slave catchers had departed, she would most likely not need to stir from bed for a while. She nodded wearily, and I prayed that my assurances would not be proven false.

Fortunately, as it happened, we had no visitors, friendly or otherwise, for three days and two nights. But on the third night, my slumber was interrupted as it had been a month before: not by a knock on the door, but by a woman's cry of pain.

Anneke heard it, too; she reached Joanna's room at the same moment I did. We entered to find Joanna on her feet and drenched with perspiration, one hand at the small of her back, the other on the bureau, supporting her weight. "The baby be here soon," gasped Joanna. "This been going on all night."

"You should have woken us earlier," I scolded, and tried to assist her back into bed, but Joanna brushed me off and said she felt better on her feet. With Anneke on one side and myself on the other, we helped her walk about the room, pausing when Joanna wished, which was when the pain was greatest.

She paused more and more frequently as one hour passed, and then two, but by then her legs trembled with fatigue so that she could scarcely stand.

We helped her into bed and made ready to deliver the baby, and I said a silent prayer that my experience assisting Jonathan was fresh enough in my mind that Anneke and I would be able to manage without him. At first Joanna's labor progressed as we had expected based upon Anneke's experience, but just as Anneke assured Joanna she was nearly through the worst of it, Joanna screamed in pain. "It's coming," she gasped. "It's coming now."

I glimpsed Anneke's surprised expression, a mirror image of my own, before I examined Joanna. I discovered, to my horror, not the baby's crown but a tiny foot, already entering the world.

Again Joanna screamed, and Anneke, coming to see what I saw, drew a sharp breath. "Don't push," said I to Joanna. It was all I could think to say. We needed more time, time for me to figure out what to do.

"We need Dr. Granger," said Anneke in a low voice.

"We can't summon him." Joanna's freedom, our own security, and the safety of future runaways seeking shelter with us depended upon our secrecy.

"We must. And quickly." Anneke left me to take Joanna's hand and mop her brow.

Joanna looked from her to me, and I knew she had detected our alarm. "What's wrong?" she asked, then sucked in a breath and screamed in pain.

I needed no further inducement. I ran for my brother, and within minutes he was on his way to summon Jonathan. "How will I explain Joanna?" asked Hans before he left. "What should I tell him?"

"Tell him only that a woman is in labor and that she and the child are in distress," said I. That was all Jonathan needed to know to help her. I would worry about the consequences of divulging our secret after she was safe.

The wait seemed endless, but no more than an hour passed before Jonathan arrived. He attended at once to his patient, speaking to me and Anneke only to ask our assistance.

Once before I had witnessed Jonathan save a life, but on that night I believe I watched him save two. The child entered the world feet first, entangled in the cord that had sustained him in the womb, and when he made no sound upon feeling the cold air upon his skin, I thought for certain he was dead. But Jonathan worked upon him and rested him upon his mother's bosom, and as Joanna placed her arms around her son, I saw the little limbs move, the chest rise and fall. When at last he uttered an angry, indignant cry, tears of relief filled my eyes, and I whispered a prayer of thanksgiving.

Jonathan glanced up at me from caring for Joanna. "Anneke can assist me with the rest," said he quietly. "Hans might need you outside."

"Why? What's wrong?"

"The cabin is burning."

Only then did I detect the faint odor of woodsmoke upon Jonathan's clothing. I stared at him, my mind in a whirl, then bolted downstairs and outside.

The odor hit me full force the moment I left the house. Ashes drifted like snowflakes on the air, and through the trees on the other side of Elm Creek, something glowed a fierce red. I ran toward it, and before I even reached the bridge I saw the churning clouds of smoke and heard the roaring as the flames consumed our former home. My brother was silhouetted against the flickering light, motionless.

I did not realize I was screaming as I ran until Hans spun around and seized me about the waist. "Gerda, stop. Stay back."

"Why don't you fight it?" I shouted, but my voice was nearly lost in the din.

"I tried." His voice was low in my ear. "It was too far gone. All I can do is let it burn, and be sure it doesn't spread to the barn or the house."

I watched as his gaze followed sparks rising from the fire, carried aloft to the treetops, brighter than the stars against the night sky. The fire cracked and popped, and a bright shower of sparks shot out, igniting a patch of grass several yards away. Immediately Hans was upon it, beating out the fresh flames with a gunny sack drenched in water.

Then I noticed the buckets scattered on the ground, only one among them still upright and full of water, and the smoldering sacks among them. Without another word I took a sack in hand and joined Hans in his vigil. We kept watch all night and into the day, sometimes one on guard alone as the other ran to fill the water buckets in the creek, sometimes both of us racing from one place to the next as several fires erupted at once. By midmorning our former home was nothing more than a smoking ruin, but the barn and the new house were undamaged.

Hans studied the ground encircling what remained of the cabin. A horse, perhaps two, had left deep impressions in the mud leading up to and surrounding the smoking timbers. "The slave catchers?" I asked him, examining the hoofprints.

"Could be, but they didn't make these prints the night they stayed with us. I watched them leave, and they didn't pass this way. If they were up here before coming to the house, the prints would have been washed away in the storm."

He walked amid the ruins, kicking rubble aside with his heavy boots. Suddenly he bent down and examined a half-buried object. "Sister, would you know if we forgot a can of kerosene up here when we moved to the new house?"

"I know very well that we did not."

"Someone else must have brought this one I see here, then."

Despite the heat radiating from the ruins, I shivered. "Who?"

"I don't know."

"I doubt any of the runaways left it."

"I'd bet my best horse they didn't." Hans stood and regarded me gravely. "You should know, the cabin wasn't burning when I left to fetch Jonathan."

I nodded, absorbing the full meaning of his words. Not only had someone set fire to our cabin, but whoever had done so had arrived when Joanna was in the worst of her travail. At that distance, he—or they—might very well have heard her screams of pain. The slave catchers, Mr. Pearson and his cronies—anyone who might have wanted to frighten us because of our Abolitionist sympathies would have known Anneke had already had her baby, and that I was not with child.

Soberly, we returned to the house. Anneke was in the kitchen, carrying her son in one arm and setting out breakfast with the other. Hans took the baby from her and stayed to explain what had happened with the fire, while I continued upstairs. I peered in the doorway of Joanna's room to find Jonathan packing his instruments and Joanna reclining in bed, nursing her child, who was swaddled in the quilt she had made.

Jonathan looked up and saw me but quickly looked away. "She has a fine, healthy son," he told me.

"And Joanna?"

"She needs rest, and something to eat." He returned to the bedside and spoke briefly with her before picking up his bag and joining me in the hall. "She should not travel for at least a week. I would have her wait a month for the baby's sake, if she can. If it is safe for her to do so."

"I understand."

"I'll return tomorrow to check in on them, but be sure to summon me immediately if either encounters any difficulties." Still he would not look at me. "You should have called for me earlier."

The rebuke, mild though it was, stung, perhaps because I had been chiding myself for the same lapse in judgment. "You know why I could not."

"Yes, I do."

We descended the stairs in silence, and I led him to the door. There I turned and regarded him defiantly. "Aren't you going to ask me who she is and what she is doing here?"

At last he met my gaze. "I have many questions. Someday, when it is not so unwise for you to answer, I will ask them."

We stood in the doorway, nearly touching, and for one frantic moment I thought he might kiss me, but then he tore his eyes from mine and bolted out the door. I shut it behind him, hard, and turned my back to it.

Hans entered and lowered himself into a chair beside the hearth, exhausted. Anneke followed close behind; she handed her son to me and went to her husband to remove his boots and wipe the soot from his face with a wet cloth. I was conscious then of my own fatigue, and my disheveled appearance. I cannot explain it, but despite all the terrible events of the previous night, at that moment I could think of nothing but how I must have looked to Jonathan compared to the graceful loveliness of Mrs. Charlotte Claverton Granger, and I felt coarse and ashamed.

But those thoughts lasted only a moment, for Anneke looked up at me, her mouth in a tight, angry line. "This time it was the cabin," said she. "Next time it might be the house."

I tried to retort but coughed instead. My eyes stung from smoke; my lungs felt thick and rough, my throat raw. "No one would dare."

"How can you know that?" demanded Anneke. "Are these such compassionate, scrupulous men that they will merely terrorize us and not murder us as we sleep?"

Wearily, Hans held up a hand. "Anneke, you are in no danger."

"Don't speak to me as if I am a child." Anneke rose, strode across the room, and snatched the sleeping baby from my arms. "I will not have it, from either of you. I will not be treated like a fool."

I was dumbstruck, but Hans said, "Very well. You're right, Anneke. We are all in danger, every one of us, even the baby. Every day Joanna and her child remain beneath our roof we risk discovery and prosecution. Every day we hang that quilt upon the line we risk our freedom and our lives. Is that what you want to hear?"

Anneke began to weep. "I cannot bear this anymore. I cannot endure this constant fear, this endless worrying. We have done our part to help. Now we have our son to think of."

"If we stop now," said I, "how many fugitives will we condemn to death or recapture?"

"If we do not stop, to what will we condemn my child?"

"How can you think only of your own child, when Joanna is upstairs with a child of her own? Would you like to see her back in chains? Would you like to see that helpless infant torn from her, sold off like a pig or a horse to the highest bidder? How would you feel if you could never see your son again?"

"Better her than us," shrilled Anneke.

My words choked in my throat, and I gaped at her, shocked into silence.

Anneke glared at me, defiant. "If we are captured, we will be thrown into prison, and my son will be taken from me just as Joanna's would have been taken from her had she remained a slave."

I found my voice. "You cannot truly believe that."

"Mr. Pearson assured me that is the law."

"Mr. Pearson," said I, scornful. "What does he know of the law?"

"Better yet," said Hans, "what does he know of our activities?"

His voice was hard, and Anneke blinked at him. "Nothing."

Hans regarded her, his gaze piercing. "You're certain."

"As certain as I can be," stammered Anneke. "Do you—do you think I would tell him we're part of the Underground Railroad?"

"Have you told him?"

"Of course not." Anneke's face was scarlet. "How could you accuse me of betraying you? Have I ever lied to you? Have I ever deceived you?"

"Anneke, my love." Within an effort, Hans rose from his chair and put his arms around his wife. "I did not mean to suggest you would intentionally tell him, but perhaps in a moment of fear, you might have accidentally—"

Anneke tore herself away from him. "I am neither that stupid nor that careless."

I knew Hans would not care for her disrespectful tone, but it was too late to warn her.

"Be that as it may," said my brother sternly, "we cannot take that risk. I forbid you to speak to Mr. Pearson as long as Elm Creek Farm is a station on the Underground Railroad."

Anneke stared at him. "You cannot mean that."

"I do." Hans returned to his chair, his back to us.

"And how am I to avoid speaking to him when I resume working for Mrs. Engle? He is her son, you recall, and he does upon occasion visit his mother at her shop."

"Then you will not resume working for her," said Hans tiredly. "You have too much to do as it is, with the baby."

Anneke stood motionless, the baby in her arms. Her mouth opened and shut without a sound, as if she longed to argue but was too astounded by his demands to muster up a retort.

Hans was oblivious to her fury. "When we no longer harbor runaways, our lives will return to normal. Then, if you still wish to, you may resume working for Mrs. Engle without fear."

"How long will that be?"

"I do not know. Until the crisis passes. Until we are no longer needed."

Without a word, Anneke left us, the baby in her arms. I heard her steps light on the stairs and on the floor above as she went to the room she and Hans shared. "You have angered her more than you realize," said I. "Do you think forbidding her to work was necessary?"

"I thought you would have been the first to support my decision," said Hans, surprised. "Do you truly think allowing her near Mr. Pearson and Mrs. Engle is wise?"

Of course I did not, and I could not deny I was relieved Anneke would be protected from their influence. Still, the way Hans had ordered Anneke to accept his decision made me uneasy. He did not treat her as an equal, but as an inferior subject to his will. I did not doubt he loved her, and that he was a good man with a good heart—and yet he wielded his authority as the man of the household in a way that made me wonder what he would do or say if I or Anneke challenged him. Unlike Anneke, I would not be able to defer to him if his choices went against my conscience or good judgment.

Troubled, I excused myself, and after washing and changing into clean clothes, I went to see Joanna. She was sleeping when I entered, her tiny son nestled beside her beneath the Shoo-Fly quilt I had made, still swaddled in his own quilt. Joanna had told me the pattern was called Feathered Star, and that she had chosen it because often she had used the North Star as her guide out of the land of slavery. "When he old enough to understand," said she, "I show him this quilt and tell him how his mama brought him North to freedom."

Remembering the pride and love that had shone in Joanna's eyes as she had spoken of the babe within her womb, I stroked his head and marveled at the perfection of his features; I touched his little hand and felt my heart swell with delight as he seized my fingertip in a strong grip. This beautiful boy was a precious child of God, but if Josiah Chester of Wentworth County, Virginia, could see him, he would think only of his worth on the auction block. If he were to feel the baby's grip, he would think with smug satisfaction of how strong a field hand he would one day become.

Joanna stirred in her sleep, and I placed my free hand upon her brow, stroking her hair to soothe her, watching her as she slumbered. The scar from the burn of the flatiron would forever mar her face, but nothing could diminish the beauty of her spirit. She had shown more courage than any of her protectors, not only in fleeing her captors but also in finding the strength to endure sickness, fear, and unimaginable danger to win the freedom that should have been her right; and in finding the strength to love the child she had not wanted, the child who had come from herself but also from her greatest enemy.

Joanna slept peacefully now, sheltered at Elm Creek Farm, knowing no one could tear her child from her arms, confident that she would soon resume her journey north to Canada and freedom. As I looked upon them, I knew I could never consent to abandoning the good work we had begun by responding to Joanna's knock upon our door. Not only for Joanna and her child, but for every woman who had been raped by a man who dared call himself her owner, for every mother who had ever wept as her child was sold away from her, for every son who had been powerless to defend his mothers and sisters and friends who cried out in pain and grief—for them we must continue, despite the risks. What were our risks compared to those of the people who sought shelter with us? Let slave catchers suspect and challenge us. Let cowards burn our cabin in the night. They would not deter me from doing my small part to forward the cause of freedom and equality for all in this new land.

I had left the stratified society of the Old World behind only to find it, steadily and surely, being reproduced in the New. This was not the America I had envisioned as I crossed the sea; this was not the America I had learned to love as we Bergstroms tilled the soil and laid the cornerstone of our home. That America had not been waiting for us, so we must build it with the sweat of our brow and the work of our hearts, as surely as we had built Elm Creek Farm.

❧

"Why can't you tell me where we're going?" asked Sylvia, clutching her purse in her lap and hoping she wasn't overdressed in her beige striped suit.

Summer kept her eyes on the road. "It's a surprise."

"Hmph. It will be a fine surprise indeed for our friends if we aren't back in time for our business meeting."

She glimpsed the smile Summer tried to hide, and couldn't help allowing some of her grouchiness to ease—but only some. A cloud of foreboding had hung over her thoughts ever since she had put down Gerda's memoir the previous day, and the agenda for the Elm Creek Quilters' upcoming business meeting only worsened her gloom. Granted, she didn't like to dwell on the bittersweet conclusion of the camp season, but she usually enjoyed helping plan the annual end-of-the-season party, where the faculty, staff, and their families would celebrate another successful year. This year, though, her mood was so melancholy she almost wished she could miss the whole affair rather than risk ruining everyone else's fun, but she was supposed to be the hostess, so she couldn't very well dodge her responsibilities.

She eyed Summer suspiciously. Maybe her friends suspected her misgivings and had contrived this little jaunt with Summer to keep tabs on her. "I have no intention of avoiding the meeting," she told Summer firmly, just in case. But Summer merely laughed and assured her she wouldn't miss it either, and she'd be sure to have them back in plenty of time.

The car turned onto a residential street near the downtown, into a neighborhood populated by the families of Waterford College faculty and administrators. "Are we going to Diane's house?" asked Sylvia, admiring, despite her mood, the changing colors of the maples and oaks lining the streets.

"No." Just then Summer pulled into the driveway of a neat white colonial house with black shutters. She shut down the engine and turned to her passenger. "We're here."

"Where's here?" demanded Sylvia, but Summer merely bounded out of the car and came around to open Sylvia's door. Sylvia grumbled under her breath as they walked up the stone path to the front door, but Summer's mystifying behavior had piqued her curiosity, and as her young friend rang the doorbell, she waited eagerly to see who would answer.

A woman in her middle years opened the door. "Yes?"

"Kathleen Barrett?" said Summer. "I'm Summer Sullivan, and this is my friend Sylvia Compson."

Kathleen smiled. "Oh yes. You wanted to see Mother." She opened the door wider and beckoned them inside. "She's been looking forward to your visit ever since you phoned. She doesn't get many callers. She's a little tired today, but when I asked her if I should postpone your meeting, she absolutely forbade it."

"We won't keep her long," promised Summer.

Kathleen nodded and led them into the living room, where a woman who looked to be in her late eighties sat in an armchair, an antique Dove in the Window quilt pieced from indigoes and turkey-red cottons draped over her lap. Her daughter introduced the visitors to her mother, Rosemary Cullen, then disappeared into an adjoining room.

"What a lovely quilt," exclaimed Sylvia, taking a seat beside Rosemary. "May I have a closer look?"

Rosemary beamed and held out the quilt to her. As Sylvia and Summer admired it, Kathleen returned with a tray of tea and cookies. After the women had served themselves, Summer at last revealed the purpose behind their visit. "Sylvia," said Summer, "Rosemary is the great-granddaughter of Dorothea Nelson."

Sylvia gasped. "I don't believe it." She looked from Summer to Rosemary to Kathleen and was delighted to find them all smiling and nodding. Sylvia clasped Rosemary's hand. "My word, dear. I feel like we're old friends."

"We ought to be," said Rosemary. "If what your young friend here says is true, my great-grandmother and your great-grandfather's sister were very close."

"They were the best of friends," declared Sylvia. "Gerda wrote of Dorothea quite often in her journal. Dorothea taught Gerda how to quilt— although Gerda was a reluctant student." Suddenly she gasped and clasped her hands together. "My goodness—I suppose this means Dorothea and Thomas had children. They had none at the time of the memoir."

"My grandmother was born shortly after the Civil War began," said Rosemary. She gestured to a sepia-toned portrait hanging above the fireplace. "She's the baby, there, sitting on her mother's lap. The man is my great-grandfather."

Returning the quilt to Rosemary, Sylvia rose and drew closer to the portrait. "This is Dorothea?" The woman looked kind but ordinary. From Gerda's description, she had expected Dorothea to be beautiful, her serenity and benevolence evident in every line of her features. Suddenly it occurred to her that she had no basis for that assumption. Gerda had never described Dorothea's appearance, only her spirit.

Sylvia's gaze shifted to the man, a slight, scholarly fellow who nonetheless had an air of steadiness and strength. "Now Thomas, on the other hand, looks exactly as I imagined him."

"We're fortunate to have any picture of them together," said Kathleen. "Not only because of their era, but also because Thomas died a few years after this picture was taken."

"He fought with the Forty-ninth Pennsylvania in the Civil War," said her mother. "He was killed in the Spotsylvania campaign, in May 1864."

"Oh, dear." Sylvia felt a pang, as if she had just heard of the recent passing of a dear friend. "I know it happened so long ago, but my heart goes out to Dorothea. From what Gerda writes, she and Thomas seemed devoted to each other."

"They were," agreed Rosemary. She stroked the fragile quilt on her lap gently but lovingly, and her gaze grew distant. "This was one of the quilts Dorothea pieced as a young wife. She sent it off with her husband when he went to war. After he died, the quilt was not among the possessions returned to the family. Dorothea assumed it had been lost."

"But it wasn't?" prompted Summer when the older woman's voice trailed off.

Rosemary roused herself. "No, indeed. It was stolen. Perhaps 'found' is a better word. Thomas lost it somehow—in the chaos as they retreated from the enemy, or it was taken from him after he died—we'll never know. But somehow it ended up in the hands of a Confederate soldier." She shrugged. "I can't blame him for keeping it once he had it. It is a lovely quilt, and it must have seemed a godsend to a weary soldier on a cold night.

"The soldier's conscience must have plagued him, though, for several years after the war ended, he sent the quilt back to Dorothea with a letter. He wrote that his wife was a quilter, and knowing how much love she put into every stitch of her creations, he couldn't rest until this quilt was returned to its proper owners."

"I think his wife must have made him write that," said Kathleen.

Rosemary smiled. "Be that as it may, Dorothea had her husband's quilt restored to her, and it has remained in our family ever since."

Summer looked intrigued. "How in the world did he know where to send it?"

"Well, I'll show you." Carefully Rosemary turned the quilt over to reveal a small section of embroidery. "Dorothea put her name right here."

"'Made by Dorothea Granger Nelson for her beloved husband, Thomas Nelson, in our sixth year of marriage, 1858. Two Bears Farm, Creek's Crossing, Pennsylvania.'" Sylvia sat back in her chair, pleased. "At last, someone who knew how to properly label her quilts."

"Too bad she didn't pass that lesson along to Gerda and Anneke when she taught them to quilt," said Summer.

Sylvia was about to agree when she saw that Rosemary's eyes had taken on a faraway look again. "My great-grandparents were true sweethearts. He wrote to her often from the front lines, very affectionate letters, and she saved them all." She shook her head. "The poor man. He was not meant to be a soldier. He was too gentle and good to ever become accustomed to killing his fellow man. But he believed completely in the Union cause, and he was determined to fight for what he believed in. That much is evident from his letters."

"I would like very much to read them," said Sylvia, without thinking, and hastily added, "That is, unless you wish to keep them within the family."

Rosemary looked uncertain. "Well, I hate to let them out of the house. They're so fragile, you see. But I think I might be willing to share them with you in exchange for a peek at that memoir of your great-great-aunt's."

Sylvia hesitated, unwilling to promise to divulge Gerda's secrets before she knew what they were. Before their hostesses could have detected her discomfort, Summer quickly spoke up to cover for her. "What about Dorothea's brother, Jonathan Granger?" she asked. "Do you know what became of him?"

"Oh yes, Jonathan." Rosemary pursed her lips and thought. "I'm not certain whether he survived the war. He and Thomas weren't in the same unit, so Thomas had no news to pass along about him. Thomas mentioned Jonathan only to ask Dorothea if she had heard from him, and to say he was keeping Jonathan in his prayers."

"Jonathan became a soldier?" asked Summer in disbelief.

"He joined the army as a doctor, not to fight," explained Kathleen. "From what Thomas says, Jonathan was as passionate about the Union cause as he was, but it was his devotion to medicine that inspired him to enlist. Doctors were needed desperately, and so he went."

"I understand Jonathan and his wife had children," said Sylvia.

"Oh my, yes," said Rosemary. "Four or five, I believe. Anytime I hear the last name Granger, I always wonder if we're related somehow."

Sylvia nodded, because it would have been rude to scold her hostess for not maintaining better ties with her distant relations. Besides, Sylvia could hardly criticize Rosemary for losing track of a third cousin twice removed when Sylvia herself had allowed fifty years to pass without speaking to her own sister.

Instead Sylvia took a deep breath. "Did Thomas ever mention the Bergstrom family in his letters?" She prepared herself for a disappointing reply.

"I don't recall offhand," said Rosemary apologetically. "I'd have to go back and read them again. He did mention neighbors and friends occasionally, but since the names were unfamiliar, I always skimmed right past them."

"Dorothea would be the one to have news about the Bergstroms," said Summer to Sylvia. "What we really need are Dorothea's letters to Thomas."

Kathleen shook her head, regretful. "I'm afraid we don't have any of those. I'm sure Dorothea wrote to her husband at least as often as he wrote to her, but his letters were the ones to survive, since they were mailed to Dorothea at home. Dorothea's letters could easily have been lost or destroyed on the battlefield."

Sylvia nodded glumly, thinking of the precious information lost forever. "I suppose we ought to be grateful we have any of these fragile paper records to remember our ancestors by. My memoir and your letters aren't nearly as durable as most monuments to the past. It's quite a responsibility now that they belong to us, isn't it, to make sure they endure so that we can pass them on to future generations?"

Rosemary and Kathleen exchanged a look. "Did you hear that, Kathleen?" inquired Rosemary.

"I heard it," said Kathleen, with a laugh. To her guests she added, "You've stumbled upon a little family disagreement."

"In my will, I've left the letters and the Dove in the Window quilt to Kathleen. She's my eldest." Rosemary patted Kathleen's hand. "It's just as you said, Sylvia: I want to pass these treasures on to future generations, and I know Kathleen will be a faithful steward until it comes her time to pass them on." She leaned forward and confided, "Kathleen thinks I should leave them to a museum. Can you believe it? The very idea. Giving our family heirlooms to strangers."

"A museum would know how to properly care for them," said Kathleen. "Part of good stewardship is ensuring that something lasts so that it may be passed down. Those papers are getting more fragile every day, Mother, and the quilt is, too."

Sylvia decided it would be prudent to stay out of the argument, but Summer said, "I'll bet Waterford College would love to have them."

"That's exactly what I suggested." Kathleen turned to her mother. "Think of what the students could learn from Thomas's letters. And think of your great-grandparents' contribution to history and to the cause of freedom. Shouldn't some part of their memory be preserved, and in a way that would teach others about all they did?"

"You just want to brag about your family," admonished Rosemary. "Well, I think Dorothea and Thomas would be the last people to brag about themselves."

"I don't want to brag, but I am proud of them." To Sylvia and Summer, Kathleen explained, "They ran a station on the Underground Railroad."

"Yes, I know," said Sylvia, delighted to have another detail of Gerda's journal confirmed. "Gerda and my great-grandparents operated one, too, on Elm Creek Farm. The Nelsons and the Bergstroms each knew about the other family's station, but they didn't speak about it openly."

Rosemary looked puzzled. "Why not? I gathered that everyone knew about my great-grandparents' activities."

"Well . . ." Sylvia hesitated. "I don't believe that was so. Gerda only stumbled upon the truth about your great-grandparents by chance, and she mentioned several times that both stations were run with the utmost secrecy."

"But then . . ." Rosemary looked to her daughter for help. "How did everyone know about it?"

Kathleen shrugged. "Maybe the truth came out after the war started."

"No, no." Rosemary shook her head firmly. "That's not it. This was before the war, when they stopped running their station. I know it was before the war."

Surprised, Sylvia and Summer exchanged a look. "The Emancipation Proclamation and the war changed the way the Underground Railroad operated, but it was still needed until then," said Summer. "Your great-grandparents were devoted Abolitionists. Why would they stop running their station early?"

"Well—well, I must say I don't know." Rosemary gave her daughter a pleading look. "Do you remember, dear?"

"Did they close their station because they were discovered?" asked Sylvia.

"I—I suppose that could be how it happened," said Rosemary, distressed. "I'm not sure. I know I heard something about it somewhere, maybe in those letters. Or maybe my grandmother told me. I'm afraid I don't remember."

Sylvia could see that Rosemary had become troubled and anxious, so she was relieved when Kathleen rose, signaling an end to the interview. "It's all right, Mother. Maybe it will come to you later, but if not, that's fine."

"What really counts is that we were able to meet you," said Summer, rising. She reached over and took the older woman's hand. "I really enjoyed hearing your stories. Thanks for sharing them with us."

"It was my pleasure, dear," said Rosemary, but she seemed fatigued.

Sylvia thanked her as well, and she and Summer left. They drove back to Elm Creek Manor in silence, both mulling over Rosemary's words. Sylvia puzzled over the new details about the Nelson family as well as Rosemary's strange insistence that their Underground Railroad station had ceased operation while it was very likely still needed, wondering what it all meant.

Suddenly Sylvia's thoughts returned to another part of Rosemary's story. "Summer, do you suppose Margaret Alden's Elm Creek Quilt could have a history similar to Rosemary's Dove in the Window?"

"How do you mean?"

"Perhaps Anneke made the Elm Creek Quilt for Hans to take into battle—I don't know if he fought in the Civil War, but let's say for the sake of argument that he did. Maybe she quilted those scenes of Elm Creek Farm into the cloth, to remind him of his home. Perhaps he lost the quilt, or traded it for a pair of boots or some other necessity, and eventually it fell into the hands of Margaret Alden's ancestor."

Summer was silent for a long moment. "It's as logical as any other explanation we've thought of."

"Hmph," said Sylvia. Summer meant well, but Sylvia recognized faint praise when she heard it.

Chapter Twelve

𝕰 *June 1859 — in which we are undone*

A chill descended upon our household, but since I was certain it would eventually lift, I paid it less attention than I should have. To be sure, with two young babies in the house, we adults had no time to idly ponder one another's moods and tempers. Sometimes I felt as if I spent all day on the run, racing from one chore to the next, from wiping one infant's face to changing the other's diaper, from singing to one while Anneke rested to rocking the other so Joanna could sleep. It occurred to me once, when I was feeling overtired and self-pitying, that I had inherited all of the drudgery of motherhood but none of the joys.

I knew Anneke resented Hans's decision to forbid her from working for Mrs. Engle so long as we remained stationmasters. I could see it in the set of her jaw, in the abruptness of her conversation, in the way she brooded in her chair after her son had fallen asleep in her arms. The warmth that had entered her behavior toward Joanna cooled again, surprising me, for I had expected their shared experiences to draw them together.

I also knew Anneke was angry, but I did not know how angry until the storm that had been gathering on the horizon finally crashed down upon us, like a cloudburst from a clear blue sky.

I remember that it was a Friday, for the next day I had planned to attend a quilting bee at Dorothea's. Though I looked forward to the event with pleasure, all that week my heart had been filled with wistful anticipation, for Joanna and I had been planning her continuing journey north. She insisted she felt well enough to go, and her baby certainly seemed healthy and strong; in fact, though nearly a month younger than Anneke's son, he was nearly as big and at least as alert.

We planned her route carefully, knowing she would be carrying a precious burden, and would need certain shelter whereas other runaways could endure a night or two sleeping under the stars. For that reason—and because she had become so dear to us, and because her particular appearance encouraged us to believe our scheme could succeed—we devised an unusual means for her to journey on.

Anneke gave her two dresses, a hat, and a pair of gloves. I gave her forged documents identifying her as Caroline Smith, a widow from Michigan. Hans gave her the best present of all: a one-horse carriage and a Bergstrom Thoroughbred to pull it. Joanna and her son would travel in fine style indeed, and seeing her, not only would people assume she was a lady, but they would also take for granted that she and her child were white.

Joanna was the only one who doubted she could pull it off. "Soon as I talk, they know what I be."

"Then pretend you have an affliction of the throat," said I. "Pretend that the same accident that scarred your face robbed you of your voice, and that you must communicate through writing. You can do that."

"Yes, I can," said she. "Thanks to you."

I was so moved by her plainspoken gratitude that I embraced her. As thrilled as I was that Joanna would soon make a new life for herself and her son in freedom, I would miss her, for we had grown close over our lessons and chores. She promised to send word once she was settled, but I feared that I would never hear from her again, and would forever wonder what had become of her.

Those worries had settled into the back of my mind that Friday morning as Joanna and I took stock of her son's layette and made plans to sew more clothes for him before they set off on their journey. I was holding the baby, and we were laughing over something I can no longer recall when I heard the door burst open downstairs. "There's trouble coming," shouted Hans.

There was a terrible note in his voice that filled me with dread. Without a moment to lose, Joanna scrambled into the hidden alcove, and I replaced the false door and the sewing machine behind her. Then, just as I spun around and discovered to my horror the baby still on the bed where I had left him while assisting his mother, I heard the baying of dogs, the pounding of horses' hooves, then boots on our front porch and fists on the door.

"Bergstrom, open up," shouted a man, and then came a crash as the door burst open beneath the weight of many arms.

Without thinking, I snatched up the baby and fled to my room. He looked up at me, solemn and uncomprehending, as I wrapped him in a quilt and set him on the floor of my closet, praying he would not cry out for his mother. I pulled dresses down from their hooks and flung them upon him, then tore back the quilt from my bed. In the moments it took to make my room seem carelessly untidy so no one would think to poke through quilts on the floor of my closet, I heard an exchange of angry voices from below, and Anneke's scream. My heart quaked with panic as I shut the closet door and fled from the room to help her and Hans.

I made it only as far as the top of the stairs; from there I spied Hans sprawled unconscious on the floor, and Anneke kneeling by his side, weeping. Led by their dogs, the two slave catchers who had plagued us in the past were running up the stairs toward me, followed closely by two men from town I recognized but did not know by name.

I tried to block their way, but they easily shoved me aside and ran past me, down the hall and into the sewing room. I heard the sewing machine moved aside, then the cracking of plaster, and then the shout of triumph: "We've got ourselves a n——, boys!"

White-hot fury burned away my fear. I did not think; I ran into the sewing room and found those hateful men with their hands upon Joanna, and I lashed out at them with all the strength in my body. I do not know how I managed it, but somehow I freed her. "Run, Joanna," I screamed, but then a fist swung out and struck me hard in the face, and I collapsed.

Groggy, I watched as the men dragged Joanna from the room. Even now, when I close my eyes against my tears, I hear her low moan of despair, and my heart is rent once more, always in the same place, so no scar will ever form.

I gasped in pain as a boot connected with my side. "Got any more n——s here?" demanded the second slave catcher. I said nothing and rolled over to get away from him. "You answer me when I ask you a question, b——!" He kicked me again, harder, and I heard a rib crack.

I watched as he hastily searched the room, then stormed out. I heard him enter the vacant room next door and ransack it; by the time I stumbled into the hallway, he had moved on to the room Anneke and Hans shared. My instinct was to snatch Joanna's baby from his hiding place and flee into the woods, but I knew I would never make it. Instead, gasping from pain, I descended the staircase, praying that the little boy would be as still and silent as stone. My only hope came from knowing that the slave catchers' dogs could not have been given the baby's scent.

Behind me, the slave catcher entered my room with his dog at the ready, but I refused to watch, lest he become suspicious and search it more thoroughly. I forced myself to continue taking each stair one painful step at a time, until I reached the first floor. Dazed, I watched Anneke cradling Hans's head in her lap. Through the front door, I saw the other slave catcher bind Joanna's wrists and lash the other end of the rope to the pommel of his saddle.

He dug his heels into the horse's side, and as he pulled Joanna into a stumbling run, her head flung back and her eyes met mine. A desperate, silent plea passed between us, and then she was gone, yanked out of sight by the trotting horse.

Hans groaned and sat up, and the two men from town immediately dragged him to his feet. At that moment, the second slave catcher came downstairs, muttering curses. "That's the only one here now, but I swear they had others," he told his companions.

"One is enough to break the law," said one of the townsmen. With that, he declared that my brother was under arrest. As he took Hans's arm to lead him away, the other man placed his hands upon me.

Anneke followed us outside as my brother and I were taken into custody. "You were only supposed to take the runaway," said she, weeping. "Mr. Pearson promised me they would not be punished."

My captor made some retort about how Anneke ought to be grateful she was allowed to remain free, and if not for their kind hearts and her infant son, they might have acted otherwise. But I hardly heard him for the ringing in my ears.

Anneke had betrayed us.

Hans stared bleakly at her as we were forced onto the men's wagon and taken away.

They took us to the city courthouse, where, to my amazement, Dorothea and Thomas Nelson were already imprisoned. Dorothea's face was ashen, and Thomas was bruised and bleeding. A second posse of slave catchers and local lawmen had descended upon them at the same time we were assaulted; two runaways, a husband and wife, had been discovered hiding in their cellar. Not long after our arrival, another wagon brought Mr. Abel Wright—the colored farmer who had warned us about the Underground Railroad quilt pattern—his wife, Constance, and their two sons. The younger clutched his arm to his side, gritting his teeth from the pain. Later we learned it had been broken in two places.

They left us in a cell for hours with no food or water, and not a word about the charges against us. Perhaps they thought our crime so evident that the normal rules of law need not be followed. We spoke in hushed voices about what we ought to do when they finally did address us; Dorothea led us in prayer. And still we waited.

We slept as best we could on the cold stone floor and were awakened before dawn by a constable offering us water and bread. Later that morning, the chief of police arrived in an indignant fury, having heard of our arrests only upon his arrival. He had us brought a decent meal and separated Dorothea, Constance, and me from the men, thinking this nod to our modesty another act of kindness, though we would have preferred to remain with the others.

As afternoon turned into evening, Dorothea urged us to take courage. Her friends in the Abolitionist movement would see to it that we had the best lawyers to plead our case, and surely no jury would punish us harshly for disobeying the Fugitive Slave Law so reviled in the Northern states. "The worst they can do to us is break our spirits," said she. "And we will not allow that."

I nodded, but at that moment I believed my spirit had already been shattered. In my mind's eye I saw Joanna, her hands bound, being pulled behind the slave catcher's horse. I thought I heard her baby's muffled cries as he lay hidden in my closet beneath the quilt and my scattered dresses. Surely Anneke would have searched for him, knowing that he had not departed with his mother—but what would she have done upon finding him? Anneke, who would betray her own husband—what would she do with Joanna's child?

What, I wondered, would become of Joanna now?

My heart was filled with despair, despite Dorothea's attempts to comfort me.

In the evening, Jonathan was finally permitted to see us. Never had I seen him so angry, though outwardly he remained calm and promised us that everything possible was being done to arrange our release. It was through Jonathan we learned that Mr. Pearson had arranged the raids on all our homes, having enlisted the aid of powerful friends in the local government sympathetic to the Southern cause. But they were in the minority, Jonathan assured us; our allies included most of Creek's Crossing, including the chief of police and the judge who would most likely preside over our arraignment, should one occur. Even now the Nelsons' solicitor, a friend of Jonathan's from university, was demanding we be charged or released immediately, and he promised to bring to justice all who had violated our rights.

Dorothea seemed greatly reassured, and she asked about the men. Jonathan hesitated before responding. Thomas was fine, though angry and worried about his wife. Jonathan had set the youngest Wright son's broken arm and had persuaded the chief to release him into Jonathan's custody so that he might recuperate in better surroundings, but he might yet be compelled to return to prison. Jonathan paused and gave his sister a look that she immediately understood, for she put an arm around Constance to lend her friend strength.

Only then did Jonathan tell us worse news than we could have imagined: One of the slave catchers had declared that the Wright men were runaway slaves recently escaped from his employer's plantation.

"But Abel has been free all his life," cried Constance. "Both of my sons were born right here in Pennsylvania."

We knew, of course, that the Fugitive Slave Law rendered the truth irrelevant. The slave catcher's sworn testimony alone was sufficient to detain the Wright men, and once his employer corroborated the lie, the Wright men would be condemned to slavery.

"We cannot allow Abel and his sons to be put in chains," said Dorothea. "We cannot."

"We won't," said Jonathan. "They aren't allowed to testify for themselves, but there are people enough in this town who will speak up for them."

"People enough?" echoed Constance bitterly. "What people? My people? Since when does the law listen to my people? Or do you mean white people? Which white people do you mean? Which white people in this town are going to risk themselves for my family?"

Dorothea and Jonathan exchanged a glance, and Dorothea said, "You do have friends, Constance. White as well as colored."

"You will also have documented evidence even Cyrus Pearson cannot refute," said Jonathan. "I will have certified birth records at hand before the week is out, as well as an affidavit from the doctor who delivered your sons.

Do not fear, Constance. They can threaten you all they want, but their lie will not persist."

Constance seemed little reassured by their words, perhaps because history had taught her to put more faith in actions, but there was a glint of resolve in her eye that told me the slave catchers would not take the Wright family without a fight.

We comforted Constance as best we could, then I remembered my brother and asked Jonathan how he fared. Hans had asked about me and about Anneke, Jonathan said, but otherwise he sat apart from the others, brooding in silence, his disbelief and shock impossible to conceal.

"I promised to send him word about you," said Jonathan to me. "What should I tell him?"

"Tell him I am fine." I was not about to give Hans reason to worry about me; he had enough to occupy his thoughts with Anneke.

"Gerda would not complain, but she is injured," said Dorothea.

I demurred, but Jonathan insisted upon examining my injuries through the bars separating us, whereupon he discovered my broken rib. If I had thought him angry when he arrived, he was truly furious now. He stormed off down the hallway from whence he had come, and I do not know what he said to the chief of police, but in a few minutes Jonathan returned with a constable, who meekly unlocked the cell and told me I was free to go.

I hardly knew what to think, but when Jonathan put his arm about me, protecting my injured side, I allowed him to lead me away. The constable swung the door shut again with a loud clanging of metal—and Dorothea and Constance still trapped inside. I stopped short. "What about my friends?"

"It's all right," said Constance firmly. "We'll be fine."

"Let's go before they change their minds," murmured Jonathan.

"No." I reached through the bars and extended my hands to Dorothea and Constance. "I will not leave you here alone."

"I only got orders to let you go," said the constable. "The others stay."

"Then I stay, too." I pulled away from Jonathan. "Unlock this cell, or give me the key and let me do it myself."

"Gerda, this is not necessary," said Dorothea.

"I said, I'm staying." I was nearly in tears. Dorothea, Constance, and Jonathan pleaded with me, but I was resolute. Joanna had just been dragged off to face her fate alone. I could not similarly abandon Dorothea and Constance.

Before he left, Jonathan treated my injury as best he could, but I still feel it, even to this day. If I had gone with him as he had entreated me to do, the bone might have knitted properly. For years afterward, whenever I complained of the stiffness, Dorothea would smile gently and remind me that it was my own fault.

The next two days were a blur, fear alternating with boredom, numb disbelief with despair. Sometimes we heard voices shouting outside, too faint for us to make out their words. Jonathan visited us daily, and the Nelsons' lawyer came once, accompanied by a newspaperman. With grim determination he took down our every word and assured us that once people read his story, there would be such an outcry against our imprisonment that our captors would be wise to change their names and move out West.

On the morning of the third day, Jonathan arrived with mixed news: We women were free to go, but the men must remain in custody. "The people of Creek's Crossing are outraged that women should be held for so long without any charges brought against them," said Jonathan.

"They ought to be outraged, not because we are women, but because we are citizens with the right to due process," said Dorothea. "A right that has been shamefully denied us."

I marveled at her composure and strength. The same ordeal that had cowed me had invigorated her, and while I wanted nothing more than to flee to the seclusion of Elm Creek Farm, Dorothea seemed ready to challenge any accuser. Her courage warmed me, and I grew determined to fear no more. Whatever became of us, I was not ashamed of our so-called crime, and I would face the consequences with head held high.

As the constable escorted us from the cell to the common area, the chorus of voices that had been barely audible grew louder. The room where we were discharged had windows facing the main street of Creek's Crossing, and through them, we beheld a large crowd, men and women alike, milling about and shouting, some with signs bearing slogans. The officer who processed us warned that despite our release, we would in all likelihood be brought to trial, and that we must not attempt to flee the county. As he spoke, he seemed harried by the noise outside and declared that if it were up to him, he would set free the lot of us if it would quiet that crowd.

Dorothea and I exchanged a look, and that was the first moment I realized the commotion was about us.

When we went outside, the deafening cheer of the crowd hit me with such force I might have stumbled if not for Jonathan's strong arm supporting me. There seemed to be more people in the street than in the whole of Creek's Crossing.

"They've been gathering for days as word spreads," said Jonathan. "People have come from several counties around."

Dorothea gasped and touched my shoulder. "Do you see that?" said she, nodding to a banner in the midst of the crowd.

I could not miss it. In foot-high letters, it demanded: RELEASE THE CREEK'S CROSSING EIGHT!

"Dear me." I felt faint.

"It appears the battle is joined," said Jonathan to his sister, wryly.

"Then we will fight," declared Dorothea, and she waved to the crowd, both arms stretched high above her head. They responded with a roar of approval.

"Do not be misled by this," warned Jonathan. "Pearson's cronies work in the shadows, but they are numerous, and they have powerful allies. We will have a fight on our hands, and you did break the law."

"I would break it again in a heartbeat," I heard myself say, thinking of Joanna. Dorothea squeezed my hand, eyes shining with pride and sympathy; Constance nodded solemnly but glanced back at the courthouse with misgivings, as if she could not bear to leave her husband and eldest son behind.

Jonathan had arrived that morning on horseback, not knowing we would be released, and so he had sent to the livery stable for a horse and carriage. None too soon for my liking, it carried us away from the throng, following the road out of town toward Elm Creek Farm.

Dorothea offered to stay with me until Hans came home or my injury ceased to pain me, but I told her there was no need. *Anneke will be there,* I almost said, and then my heart trembled. I could not bear to see her again. I thought of how she might greet me, with tears of remorse, with defiance, justifying her treachery, and I wished with all my remaining strength that I would return home to find her gone, the children placed in a neighbor's safekeeping.

Three years we had lived together, and I had come to love her as a sister, and yet I must not have known her at all. I could not comprehend her betrayal. Was it as simple as spite? I had forced her into sheltering runaways by hanging that quilt upon the line week after week; Hans had forbidden her to continue work that she loved. Was that why she had confessed to Mr. Pearson, to have her revenge upon us?

Beside me, Dorothea, Jonathan, and Constance talked of strategy for our defense, but I pondered the mystery that was Anneke. She had betrayed us, and yet it could be said that we Bergstroms had betrayed her time and time again, ever since our fateful meeting in New York. Hans had lied to her about what awaited us in Pennsylvania; I had shared her house instead of allowing her peace and privacy with her husband; we both had dismissed her fears that our clandestine activities would be discovered. And so they were at last, but only through her agency.

My heart swelled with anger, and silently I cursed the moment we rescued her from the bureaucrats in Immigration. How much better it would have been for all of us if we had left her there, alone. How well she had repaid us for our good intentions!

"Gerda?"

Dorothea's gentle voice interrupted my thoughts, and I realized the carriage had stopped at the front door of my home. My companions regarded me inquisitively, and Dorothea asked again if I would like her to stay. Once again I refused. Unless Anneke had indeed fled in shame, I would have to confront her eventually, and postponing the encounter would not make it easier.

But I was in no hurry. I remained outside and watched as the carriage drove off. Only when it had reached the bridge over Elm Creek did I realize why the livery horse had seemed so familiar. He was Castor, or perhaps Pollox—I never could tell them apart. He was older now, and less vigorous than he had been when Hans won him from Mr. L., but as proud and elegant a creature as he had ever been. As for me, I felt myself to be an entirely different woman from the one he had brought here three years before. How little that woman had known of what awaited her in this place.

Behind me, the door burst open. "Gerda!"

I stood frozen in place, eyes closed against my tears; I could not even turn around. Suddenly Anneke was on the ground at my feet, clutching my skirt and weeping. "I am so sorry," said she through her sobs. "It was never meant to happen this way."

My voice was cold; I could not even look at her. "Where are the children?"

"Inside."

I entered the house. Anneke had moved the cradle to the front room, beside her chair; in it, David and Stephen slept side by side. I cannot describe my relief upon seeing them safe and sound. As much as I had wanted to avoid seeing Anneke and wished her away, I had feared she would have taken the children with her or, worse yet, taken her own son and abandoned Joanna's.

Anneke had followed me inside. "Where is Hans?" Her voice was muffled as she fought to control her tears.

I told her, abruptly. She asked me if Hans would soon be freed, and I told her I did not know. Then Stephen woke and began crying; I reached for him, but Anneke darted in front of me and picked him up. I watched her as she comforted him. Her face was bleak. "Please, Gerda, let me explain."

I wanted to shut my ears to her voice, but my profound bewilderment at her betrayal needed an answer, so I listened. She told me how Mr. Pearson had frightened her with tales of the terrible punishments lawbreakers received in the American judicial system; he filled her with stories of the suffering of Abolitionists in Kansas. All the while she worked at Mrs. Engle's shop he worried her thus, playing the role of a concerned friend, aware of the Abolitionists among her friends and family. After the baby was born, he doubled his efforts; she did not tell him about our secret activities, yet he suspected nonetheless. Since Anneke rarely went into town, he came to Elm Creek Farm when he knew Hans and I were away, insisting that unlawful behavior of one member of the family would condemn the entire household. For her own safety, and for the safety of her son, Anneke needed to come forward with the truth. The burning of the cabin ought to be sign enough that we were under suspicion, and we would want the law on our side if angry neighbors continued to show their disapproval in such a frightening fashion. If Anneke confessed, she would avoid punishment and would ensure better treatment for Hans and me, much better than if we were discovered, which Mr. Pearson made seem a certainty.

So at last she told him. She had not meant to mention the Nelsons or the Wrights, but once she let the secret out, Pearson pounced on it and forced the rest from her. His manner changed entirely, and whereas she had only moments before thought him her benefactor, she now feared him. She begged him to tell no one and to forget everything she had confessed, but he insisted he could not, lest he be drawn into our guilty conspiracy. All he would promise was that although any runaways found on our land must be taken, we Bergstroms would be permitted to remain free.

As Anneke spoke, my heart, which had been filled with icy contempt for her, began to soften. Guileless Anneke cared for her family more than anything in the world, and knowing this, Mr. Pearson had deliberately preyed upon her feelings. Anyone subjected to that constant barrage of fear and threats might have succumbed in time; I might have myself, if I did not so despise Mr. Pearson and suspect his every word.

But just as I was about to tell her so, Anneke added, "You and Hans were never supposed to suffer. I would need a lifetime to tell you how sorry I am. Will you ever forgive me?"

I chose my words carefully, to be sure I understood her. "You regret betraying us?"

"With all my heart."

"Because Hans and I were imprisoned."

"Yes," said Anneke passionately, taking my arm. "Only Joanna was meant to be taken."

My heart became like cold stone toward her again. "I cannot forgive you for what you did to Joanna. I cannot forgive you for what you have done to her son." I tore my arm away from her. "As for what you have done to us, if Hans can bring himself to forgive you, so will I. But only then."

And thus, I thought, I would never need to forgive her.

The next morning I went to Dorothea's to consult with her about freeing the men from prison. My injured side pained me with every step the horse took and my mind was a tempest of anger and grief. By the time I reached the Nelson farm, a plan had coalesced: I would contact Josiah Chester and find Joanna. If he had sold her farther south, as she had always feared he would, I would make him tell me who had bought her. Then I would buy her freedom. If it took every cent I had, if it took Elm Creek Farm itself, I would not rest until I saw her free again, free and reunited with her son.

When I arrived at the Nelson farm, Dorothea, her parents, and their lawyer were engaged in an urgent discussion of our legal entanglements. Breathlessly I announced my plan to Dorothea; she kindly did not warn me of the difficulty of the task, but allowed me to believe I could accomplish it presently—after our immediate concerns were resolved. I agreed and sat down as the discussion resumed, but as the others debated and planned, I was feverish with eagerness to begin my search for Joanna. I composed a letter to Mr. Chester in my head, determined to send it off that day.

But by the time I returned home, my side throbbed and ached so that I had to grit my teeth to keep from moaning. I cared for the horse and stumbled into the house, where Anneke immediately perceived something afflicted me. I confessed my broken rib, and although in my pride I wanted to disdain her help, when she hastened to assist me, I hurt too much to refuse.

I hardly stirred from my bed the next day; Anneke brought the babies in to keep me company, and I was so glad to see them I clung to them, sleeping and waking, barely allowing Anneke enough time to see they were kept with full bellies and clean diapers. Gradually my coldness toward Anneke thawed; she had become a sister to me, and I was too heartsore to hate her as passionately as I once thought I could.

The next morning I moved downstairs to the front room, where I wrote to Mr. Chester and exacted a promise from Anneke that she would post my letter that very day. My mind somewhat more at ease, I played with the boys while Anneke worked in the kitchen garden. Then, suddenly, I heard a horse upon the road, and Anneke cry out. I hurried to the window and, to my glad astonishment, discovered the rider was Hans.

Anneke had run out to meet him; they exchanged words I could not discern, but Anneke's impassioned plea for forgiveness was unmistakable. My brother replied tersely, stoic and unmoved by Anneke's tears. On and on they went, Hans proud and angry high atop his horse, Anneke remorseful and ashamed, clinging to his leg and to the bridle as if she feared he might ride off. The boys began to grow restless and hungry, but I stood frozen at the window, my heart in my throat, wondering how it would end, if this would be the end of our family.

Then Hans slid down from his horse and embraced his wife.

I drew back from the window and hugged both babies to my chest, not knowing whether I was glad or disappointed. I loved Anneke, but whenever I thought of Joanna, my heart hardened and I knew a lifetime of apologies would never compensate for how Anneke had ruined her.

Together Hans and Anneke entered the house. They said nothing of what words or promises they had exchanged, but I knew eventually the chasm between them would close.

We entreated Hans to tell us how his release had been accomplished, for as recently as yesterday, the Nelsons' lawyer had said we were in for a long, difficult struggle.

For months tempers around town and across the county had been growing hard and brittle like dry grass in a drought, and the news of our arrests had been the spark to set off the conflagration. Neighbors who had lived together peaceably enough despite their disagreements on the slavery question now argued outright, and everyone had been forced to account for his position. As word of the conflict spread, the city officials who had endorsed the raids on our homes had been denounced in one Northern newspaper and public forum after another. One man's home had been burned to the ground; a second man had been badly injured when an argument turned into a brawl. One violent act sparked another, and as the ugliness grew and spread, one matter became clear: The faction approving of the arrests of the Creek's Crossing Eight found themselves increasingly on the defensive, forced to justify their support of the Fugitive Slave Law, which every decent Pennsylvanian abhorred.

"Creek's Crossing has earned the reputation of being populated with Southern sympathizers," said Hans. "Pearson and his ilk are nervous and getting more so."

My brother seemed righteously satisfied by this turn of events, but his face was gray with exhaustion and strain, and his voice was hoarse. Anneke insisted he go to bed immediately, and when he protested that he had to see to the farm, I added my voice to hers, and Hans had no choice but to comply.

By the next day he seemed nearly recovered from his physical ordeal, though an air of polite formality lingered between him and Anneke. Still, it was apparent he had forgiven her, but if Anneke remembered what I had said about extending my own forgiveness, she said nothing of it. Truly I wanted to forgive her, but Joanna's face haunted me, and every time I held her son I thought of how his mother could not. I grew more fierce in my determination to find her, and, impatient for a reply, I sent off another letter to Josiah Chester.

Two days after Hans's return, two men came riding up to the house while my brother worked in the fields. I needed only a moment to recognize them as the two men who had arrested us. If they were disturbed by the conflict Hans had spoken of, which seemed to me so distant from the peace of Elm Creek Farm that it was difficult to believe it was real, they gave no sign of it as they demanded entry to the house to search for evidence against us.

I knew nothing of whether I should or must let them enter, but saw no reason to hide in shame. They had found a runaway in our midst; if that was not evidence enough to convict us, nothing else they found would be.

I followed them as they poked about the front room, the kitchen, the dining room, and down into the cellar, making no effort to disguise my impatience. They ignored me and addressed only each other, carelessly handling our possessions and making rude remarks about "n—— lovers." I thought of what Hans had said, about theirs being a minority point of view, and held my temper in check. I would not do anything to worsen our position, not that I supposed it could have become much worse.

Their search took them upstairs, to Hans's room, then to mine; they spent a scant few moments in the spare room and lingered longest in the sewing room, where they scrutinized the hidden alcove inside and out and exchanged pointed and gleeful remarks about how damning that evidence would be at the trial. As if they knew what I was thinking, they warned me sternly against destroying it, assuring me that would do me no good whatsoever, since they were both witness to it.

Then they headed for the nursery, and with a stab of fright I realized Anneke was inside with the children.

Before I could think of how to prevent them, the two men had entered the room. Beyond them I saw Anneke turn in surprise. David was in her arms, while Stephen lay in the cradle where she had just placed him. Anneke's eyes darted to mine, and I saw them widen in shock, but her voice was calm when she said, coldly, "I cannot possibly imagine what more you two would want with us." She turned her back on the men and picked up Stephen again, cradling a baby in either arm protectively.

The two men studied her and exchanged a bewildered look. The first one said, "I don't remember there being two babies last time."

Anneke laughed sharply and regarded the men with scorn. "As I recall, you were occupied with other matters."

"How fitting that Creek's Crossing would send its most observant citizens to investigate us," I added, contemptuous. My heart pounded with fear, and I fought the urge, as I had before, to seize Joanna's son and flee to safety. "Were you searching for babies, too? Is it now against the law to shelter one's children?"

The second man's eyes narrowed, and he drew closer to Anneke. "Whose children are these?"

Her grasp about them tightened. "They are mine, of course."

"Both of them?"

"Yes."

"They look to be nearly the same age."

"They're twins," said Anneke, as if it were the most obvious thing in the world.

The second man looked dubious. "I only saw one baby last time." He pointed at Joanna's son. "This here one. You were holding him, and he was crying."

Anneke's eyes were fierce. "Crying because you terrified him. You should be ashamed of yourself. It took hours to calm him."

"His brother was in his cradle," said I. "I know one of you must have seen him, because you snatched his quilt off him and threw it on the floor. It was torn in two places."

Anneke's voice was acid. "Did you think he was hiding a runaway beneath his quilt?"

"Let it be," the first man advised the second. "Anyone can see this child is white."

"And anyone can see he wants his mother," sniffed Anneke, handing her own son to me. "Gerda, would you help, please?"

Dumbfounded, I could only nod as Anneke took to her rocking chair and, full of contempt for the men watching her, began to nurse Joanna's son.

Embarrassed by the sight, the two men hastened to leave the room. I returned my nephew to his cradle and followed them as they quickly searched the last room, then departed our house with unwelcome assurances that they would be back if they thought it necessary.

Slowly I returned upstairs to the nursery. I watched from the doorway as Anneke finished feeding Joanna's son, then returned him to the cradle, picked up her own baby, and began to nurse him. "Anneke—" My voice faltered. I wanted to tell her she had certainly saved the little boy, but my heart was too full for words.

Anneke looked up at me. "How many people know I had only one baby?"

"All our friends," said I. "Anyone else they might have told."

"A great deal, then." Her gaze was far away, brooding. "We will have to get Joanna's son to safety before someone reveals the truth."

"I will take him to the next station," said I. "They will have to take him to the next, and so on, until he can be placed with a free Negro family in Canada."

Anneke gazed at the innocent child, drifting off to sleep in the cradle. "It will be a hazardous journey, and he is all alone in the world."

I felt tears spring into my eyes. *I will take him to Canada myself,* I nearly declared, but then thought of Joanna, and decided we should keep him with us as long as possible. Perhaps I could find Joanna and purchase her freedom before the truth about her son came out.

I thought I would have weeks, perhaps longer, but the first inquiry came in a matter of days.

The sight of Mr. Pearson coming up the road to the house so astonished us that at first Anneke and I could only stare at him from the nursery window, and I almost convinced myself I was mistaken as to the identity of the horse and rider. Anneke was the first to turn away. "I will not speak to him," said she, her voice bitter. I was even more reluctant to greet him, but my amazement at his gall and curiosity as to his purpose compelled me downstairs.

I opened the door to his knock but neither addressed him nor invited him inside.

"Good day, Miss Bergstrom," said he.

"What do you want?" said I bluntly, all pretense to politeness long past.

He promptly dropped his facade. "I understand Mrs. Bergstrom is suddenly the mother to two children."

I arched my eyebrows at him. "'Suddenly'? There was nothing sudden about it. The twins are nearly two months old. The pregnancy was of the usual length, and the labor longer than most."

"Your sister-in-law did not give birth to twins," said Mr. Pearson sharply.

"She most certainly did."

"You forget, my mother and I visited you shortly after the child was born. Anneke had only one son then."

"Mr. Pearson, I fear your memory has failed you," said I, feigning puzzlement. "Perhaps you should consult Dr. Granger."

"Don't make me out to be a fool, Miss Bergstrom," snapped he. "If I consult Dr. Granger, it will be to confirm what I already know is true. He was present at the birth, and he knows how many children he delivered that night. Despite his Abolitionist beliefs, Dr. Granger is a man of integrity. He abhors a lie, and he will not depart from his principles merely to protect you. He would not falsify birth records, and he would certainly not sacrifice his own security and that of his family to abet you in your deceit."

Just as a thrill of fear rose in my heart, I realized Mr. Pearson was utterly, entirely wrong. Indeed, Jonathan was a man of integrity and principle, but that did not preclude a well-placed lie or omission of the whole truth if he believed some greater good would be served—even if he knew he would eventually be discovered. If the fiasco with Charlotte Claverton had taught me nothing else, it had taught me that.

So I looked Mr. Pearson squarely in the eye and said, "Ask him anything you wish. I do not fear his response."

"He is not the only one who will testify as to the truth."

"On the contrary, I think you will discover a great many people will remember that Anneke had twins."

His mouth narrowed, and his eyes were bright with hatred. "I do not know whose child that is, but it is not Anneke's."

"If indeed he is not," said I, defiant, "would he be the only child to call his aunt mother?"

My words brought his threats to an abrupt and decisive conclusion.

A change came over his features as rage transformed into understanding. "Why, Miss Bergstrom," said he, the familiar smirk returning. "I knew you were no lady, but I had no idea you were a whore."

I said nothing.

Mr. Pearson laughed, and the sound was full of vengeful merriment. "I wonder if Dr. Granger is aware of this. Well, I suppose he must be. Unless there is another?" He peered at me inquisitively, but I regarded him stoically, my expression revealing nothing. "Of course not. I must say that entirely changes my opinion of the veracity of his record-keeping."

"I suppose asking you to say nothing of this would be a wasted effort."

"Indeed it would, Miss Bergstrom."

I have never seen a man so pleased with himself as Mr. Pearson was as he rode off, believing himself to be the diviner of great, scandalous truths, when in fact all he took away from his interrogation was a lie devised to conceal another lie.

Chapter Thirteen

❧June 1859 and after—in which
we perfect the art of lying by omission,
or, how it ended

With Dorothea's help, I sent word to Jonathan before Mr. Pearson could speak with him, so when Mr. Pearson inquired whether Anneke had indeed given birth to twins, Jonathan replied in the affirmative. More than that, he showed Mr. Pearson the official paperwork confirming that fact, and naming Hans Bergstrom as the boys' father.

Mr. Pearson knew this to be false but was entirely mistaken as to the truth. My falsehood provided him such gleeful triumph that he had no need to seek another explanation. He wasted no time spreading the tale of my ostensible shame throughout town, which, as his mother was one of the leading gossips of her era, assured that the entire county knew of the scandal within a fortnight. Mrs. Engle was careful to add that she had suspected my whorish nature long before a child was born of it, for I had often attempted to seduce her son. For Charlotte Claverton Granger, the betrayed wife, and Anneke, the virtuous woman who took in my bastard child without complaint, she had only praise, though it was tempered by disappointment that these two women had unfortunate connections to Abolitionists. In their defense, she added, they were linked to the Creek's Crossing Eight only by ties of marriage; they had not brought shame to our fair town through their own fault.

But the Creek's Crossing Eight never did come to trial, and circumstances eventually encouraged Mrs. Engle to cease her criticism of the group. The Nelsons' journalist friend was true to his word, and within weeks, our arrest and Joanna's recapture had been denounced in every Northern newspaper I had ever heard of, and several others I had not. Creek's Crossing became the butt of jokes, with the worst foibles of the worst portion of its populace exaggerated and distorted, until the town's name became synonymous with ignorance and mob rule. So embarrassed were our town leaders that they swiftly dismissed all charges against us, including the dangerous threats to the Wrights' freedom, and tried as best they could to put the terrible events in the past, but the memory of the public was long, and the reputation of Creek's Crossing never recovered. In the years to come, businessmen eschewed Creek's Crossing and brought prosperity to other towns; major roads linked nobler villages and bypassed ours, as did the commerce that traveled along them; surveyors who could make train tracks cling to the ridges of the Appalachians somehow found the route into the Elm Creek valley inaccessible. Eventually the town leaders tired of this and ruled to change the town's name to Water's Ford, retaining the original sense of Creek's Crossing while setting aside the taint it had acquired. It remains to be seen whether their efforts will be rewarded.

My reward, I admit, was seeing Mr. Pearson and Mrs. Engle surprised and eventually undone by the consequences of their actions. I am sure I have my friends to thank for the emergence of new rumors telling how Mr. Pearson had manipulated the innocent Anneke into confessing to the authorities. If not for that, the whispered accusations told, our village never would have experienced its greatest shame. The vitriol mother and son had published in the *Creek's Crossing Informer* over the years soon came to mind, and nothing more was needed to make them the county's least popular citizens. Within a year of the arrests, Mr. Pearson and Mrs. Engle moved away; some say to Virginia, others as far away as Florida. Neither I nor any of my friends ever heard from them again, which, as you can imagine, bothers me not at all.

Before he departed, improving our town with his absence, Mr. Pearson saw to it that my own reputation was ruined entirely. The Certain Faction fought to preserve it, and each and every one of them would have sworn before the highest court in the land that she had seen Anneke cuddling twin boys within hours of their birth. But people inevitably prefer to believe the scandalous over the mundane, and so it was with me. Accordingly, the likelihood of my finding a husband, which my plainness and age had made small enough already, diminished entirely. Fortunately for me, I suppose, I never found anyone else I liked so well as Jonathan, so it did not matter.

But Mr. Pearson, Mrs. Engle, and their associates were not the only ones to receive the condemnation of the town. Although publicly we Bergstroms were exonerated and defended, privately we were lumped in with our enemies and forced to shoulder the blame for tarnishing the town's reputation. We were never quite as welcome in society as before, and over time, we accepted that the frost in our fellow citizens' address would never thaw, and we gradually withdrew into the company of our ever growing family and the warmth of the circle of our most intimate friends, which included the Nelsons, the Wrights, and the Certain Faction. We stopped attending town events, such as the Harvest Dance, and I once even overheard one gentleman respond to a visitor's questions about the "rumored scandal of years ago" with the assertion that Elm Creek Farm lay outside the city proper, so its residents were not truly citizens of Water's Ford. But although our neighbors politely shunned us, the reputation of Hans's Bergstrom Thoroughbreds had spread far beyond our little valley, and so our fortunes soared. Our prosperity might have impressed the townsfolk and increased their desire for our company if not for the Creek's Crossing Eight scandal and my ruined reputation, but instead it merely strengthened their enmity.

Jonathan's reputation, I should add, suffered little from the scandal, and within the span of a year he once again enjoyed the high esteem of his fellow citizens, while I was whispered about until I was gray-haired and stooped with age. One might say Jonathan was forgiven and I was not because he was the town's highly respected physician while I was merely a spinster of unremarkable social position, but I know it was because he was a man and I was a woman. The woman is always left to carry the burden of shame, while the man is free to go his own way. But I do not begrudge him his reprieve, for although I did not consult him before allowing Mr. Pearson to believe him my lover, Jonathan never publicly denied it, allowing the true heritage of Joanna's son to remain secret all his life.

For I am sure by now you understand what I have needed this entire history to confess: Joanna's son never went to Canada, nor did he rejoin his mother elsewhere. Instead he lived as a Bergstrom from the time Anneke first claimed him as her own.

We never intended this to happen. After Joanna's capture, finding her became my obsession, and when Josiah Chester failed to reply to the scores of letters I sent him, I decided to travel to Wentworth County, Virginia, to speak to him in person. Then war broke out, as we had all feared and expected it would, and my plans lay in ruins. The conflict forced me to set aside my search and tend to matters closer to home. Hans and Anneke had added to their family, so I had the children to think of, and the obligations and consequences of war to endure. So much I could write of that dark, unforgiving time, but I cannot divert from this history to recount it now, not when I am so near the end. Perhaps I will chronicle those events someday, if I can bring myself to do it, if I live long enough.

After the war, I immediately resumed my search, but my efforts were repeatedly thwarted by one obstacle or another. Despite my frustrations, I clung stubbornly to hope, and often played in my mind's eye a glorious and triumphant scene of Joanna's return to Elm Creek Manor and her reunion with her son. So feverishly did I believe this event would take place that I began piecing a quilt, a gift for Joanna, in anticipation of her arrival. I chose a pattern that would be easy to sew, as I had allowed my quilting skills to languish during the war, but one that had special significance: the Log Cabin, named for the interlocking design of its rectangular pieces. The design was invented, or so Dorothea once said, to honor Mr. Abraham Lincoln, and since he had granted Joanna her freedom, I thought it an appropriate choice for her quilt. The square in the center of the block was supposed to be yellow, to signify a light in the cabin window, or red, to signify the hearth, but I cut my central squares from black fabric, to symbolize that an escaped slave had once found sanctuary within our own log cabin.

Time passed, and as my Log Cabin quilt neared completion, the black center squares took on another meaning. Black was also the color of mourning, and as my relentless searches proved fruitless over and over again, I began to mourn my lost friend, who I feared would never see the quilt I had made for her.

My letters finally reached a daughter of Josiah Chester's, but she claimed to know nothing of what had happened to Joanna after she ran away. She did note that her father usually brought recaptured slaves to the home plantation for a few days of brutal punishment before selling them to family or acquaintances in Georgia or the Carolinas, to show other slaves what fate awaited them should they run off. She did not remember this happening to Joanna, but she did not know Joanna well and might not have recognized her, or so she claimed.

I might have believed her, had Joanna not told me she was a house slave and did all the sewing for the family. At the very least, Josiah Chester's daughter would have seen Joanna every time she was fitted for a new dress, and likely more often than that.

The years went by. Joanna's son grew tall and strong never knowing his real mother, and my hopes, which I had clung to fiercely throughout the war, gradually slipped from my grasp. I did not give up because I loved Joanna any less; on the contrary, I loved her more, seeing the fine young man my nephew had become, and knowing how Joanna's courage and sacrifice had brought him into our lives. No, I finally stopped searching because I believed Joanna dead. Surely if she had lived, she would have returned to Elm Creek Manor for her child. She had found her way here once as a hunted fugitive; as a free woman, she could have done so again, and certainly would have, knowing her son awaited her return. Only death could have prevented her sending word to us. I am certain of it.

But if you are a Bergstrom, Reader, you already know her son was not awaiting her return.

You may wonder why we never told him the truth about his heritage. You may question our judgment; I know I have many times over the years, ever more so as I feel my own death lurking just beyond my sight, and I know it will not be long before I must account for my life before my Creator.

At first we did not tell him because he was too young and would not understand. Then we did not tell him because we feared he might reveal the secret to strangers in an innocent remark, as children sometimes do. Later we said nothing because Joanna's return seemed increasingly unlikely, and Anneke had forbidden us to tell him. She would not see his heart broken in mourning a mother he had never known, and she did not want him to feel loved any less than his brothers and sisters. Even when he became a man, fully capable of bearing and accepting the truth, still we did not tell him, for we had discovered that granting a people freedom did not bring them equality, and we were reminded daily of the brutality of ignorant folk who would love our precious boy today but despise him tomorrow if they knew the truth. Right or wrong, we could not do this to him.

When he was still a child, Anneke pleaded with me to swear never to tell her son—for that is how she thought of him, no less her child than if she had truly borne him—about Joanna, about himself. I complied, but not without misgivings. Indeed, all my life I have wondered if in protecting my nephew from prejudice and malice we did not inadvertently perpetuate those very evils. Perhaps we should have announced the truth from the rooftops and dared anyone to treat him differently than any other Bergstrom—but we loved him, and may God forgive us if it was wrong, but we put his safety before our principles. In our defense, if we had not done so, it would not have brought Joanna back to us.

But since I did so swear, I never told my nephew the truth, nor will I ever tell him. Since I cannot tell him, I instead tell you, not only because this is part of your legacy, your rightful inheritance, but also because I could not bear to have Joanna forgotten.

Anneke has been gone these past fifteen years, and yet I think I hear her reproach me for divulging our family secrets so long and so carefully hidden. Perhaps she is correct, and whoever reads these words will despise me for what I have done. That is a risk I shall willingly take, for I do not believe, as Anneke did, that this truth will destroy us. It is the missing chapter of our family history that must be restored if we are to be whole, and if we are to truly know ourselves. Guard this, your legacy, closely, and treasure it in the quiet of your own heart.

I offer these words in memory of Joanna, whom I loved, and whom I pray found in the Kingdom of Heaven the peace, freedom, and joy she was denied in this world.

Elm Creek Manor, Pennsylvania
November 28, 1895

Sylvia closed the book and brushed the tears from her eyes.

Andrew had held her left hand in both of his as she read the last pages of the memoir aloud. Now he squeezed it and brought it to his lips. The compassion in his eyes threatened to bring forth more tears.

Sylvia cleared her throat and straightened in her chair, composing herself. "Well, I don't know quite what to think." And then her voice failed her, because her emotions refused to be translated into words. Her heart ached for Joanna, who had lost both her child and her dream of freedom. She was sickened and shamed that Anneke had betrayed her own family, and in so doing had ruined the lives and happiness of those dearest to her. But most of all, she was stunned. She felt as if the foundation of her universe had caved in upon itself.

"My family," said Sylvia, slowly, "was not what I believed it to be."

This time she did not mean merely that reality had failed to live up to the family legends.

"You see . . ." She sat lost in thought for a long moment. "I know David was my grandfather. And my mother's Bible indicates he had a twin brother."

Andrew nodded, waiting for her to continue.

"But Gerda does not say whether Anneke bore David or Stephen."

Andrew's voice was quiet. "I noticed."

"In fact, she quite deliberately avoids saying whose child was whose." Suddenly Sylvia remembered that odd crossed-out line earlier in the memoir, the one she and Sarah had tried in vain to decipher. They had supposed that Gerda had written the name of Joanna's child there, and now she understood why Gerda might have wished to blot it out. It was not an error, but a purposeful obscuring of the truth.

Sylvia's mind reeled. She felt as if she were swirling down a drain, faster and faster, moments away from tumbling from her safe, certain world into an ocean of unfathomable uncertainty. "Why?" she said, her voice shaking. "Why confess so much, yet hold back that last detail?"

"Maybe she was trying to protect you—you, or whoever found her book."

"Protect me?"

"She didn't know you. She didn't know how strong you are. It's quite a blow, finding out you've been lied to all your life."

"You don't need to tell me that." Sylvia felt the first faint stirrings of anger. "Then why write at all? Merely to unburden herself?"

Andrew shrugged, silent.

"She did not trust me," said Sylvia, bitter. "She did not trust me with the whole truth, so she gave me only enough to make me doubt everything I ever believed about myself, only enough to throw my entire identity into question." Even as she spoke, she felt rents appearing in the fabric of her history.

Andrew's hand was warm and strong around hers. "Your family isn't your entire identity. You're still Sylvia Bergstrom—a strong, capable woman. A quilter, a teacher, a friend, and the woman I love. What you learned from that book doesn't change any of that."

"But it changes nearly everything else." All her life Sylvia had prided herself on being descended from Hans and Anneke Bergstrom—courageous pioneers, valiant Abolitionists, founders of a family and a fortune. She had long since come to terms with Gerda's revelations that her ancestors were not the heroes she had believed them to be, but now her ancestors might not even be her ancestors.

Sylvia corrected herself. Her parents were still her parents; their parents were still her grandparents. It was the link to Hans and Anneke that was in question, nothing more. But that was so much.

"Would it be so bad to be Joanna's great-granddaughter?" asked Andrew gently.

"No." Sylvia had responded automatically, but then she forced herself to consider the question more thoroughly. Gradually, within the dizzying mix of emotions flooding her, she recognized wonder, intrigue, and awe. "I would be proud to be that brave woman's descendant." Then, in a painful flash of insight, she realized who else she would be related to, if Joanna were her great-grandmother.

"I had not wanted to believe we had slave owners in the family." She paused, her throat constricted with emotion. "And now I discover I might be the great-granddaughter of a monster who not only owned slaves but raped and tortured them as well."

"Don't think about him," urged Andrew. "Joanna didn't when she held her son. She only thought of how much she loved him."

"I would like very much to forget Josiah Chester, but if I am going to accept part of my heritage, I must accept all of it."

"Let's not forget, you don't know for certain whether it *is* your heritage. We're jumping to conclusions a bit, don't you think? Anneke could have been David's mother, just as you've always believed."

Sylvia was about to retort that Gerda would have had little need to expose the family secret in that case, but then she reconsidered. There were other branches of the family besides her own; perhaps they were the ones Gerda had sought to protect. And there was Gerda's desire to make known Joanna's story, since the vow Anneke had exacted had nearly banished her from memory. It was entirely possible—in fact, even likely—that Sylvia's heritage was exactly what she had always believed it to be.

She didn't suppose she would ever know for certain.

❧

Sylvia spent two days contemplating how much she would reveal about Gerda's revelations and to whom. Her friends knew only that she had finished the memoir and that something she had read there troubled her, but thankfully, rather than pester her with questions, they allowed her time alone to think.

She tried to explain to Andrew that her mixed feelings came not from rejecting her new ancestry, if in fact it was hers. It was the uncertainty that tore at her, as well as the enormous shift in her sense of self Gerda was forcing her to make. "If I had discovered the memoir decades ago, I might feel entirely different," said Sylvia. "I might have been able to embrace this change. But to have to come to an entirely new understanding of myself at my age . . . I don't think I can do it."

"You don't have to," said Andrew. "You are the same wonderful woman you have always been, and whether all those things I love about you came from Anneke and Hans or Joanna and Josiah Chester, your soul is still your own. You're not just your parents, you know. You're the sum of everything you've ever done, every wish you've ever made, every person you've ever loved, and everyone who has loved you. No one can take that from you, not Gerda, not anyone. I don't care how many darn memoirs they write."

He broke off, embarrassed, and Sylvia stared at him, amazed by his uncharacteristic speech making. His unshakable faith in her warmed her more than he could have imagined possible, but she was too fond of him to embarrass him further by telling him so.

"Perhaps I just need more time," she said instead, and Andrew agreed.

A week had passed when Sylvia realized she had come to accept the mystery Gerda had bequeathed her. She could only guess why the same woman who felt she was obligated to make the Bergstrom descendants "the heir of our truths, for good or ill," would stop short of revealing the most important secret the family had ever kept, so she decided to stop trying.

She also decided to stop second-guessing every other sentence in the memoir, trying to discern which of the two women had borne her grandfather. If a certain inflection in one sentence suggested Anneke, two paragraphs later she was sure to find a description that indicated Joanna. In attempting to puzzle it out, Sylvia had read and reread the memoir so many times she thought she might be able to transcribe it from memory, backward. When she found herself speculating that perhaps Gerda and Jonathan were her great-grandparents after all and the entire memoir was Gerda's attempt to protect her descendants from the shame of illegitimacy, she knew she had gone too far. Instead of untangling the threads of her history, she was tugging them into an ever tightening knot.

And so she gave up. Or rather, as she told herself, she acquiesced. Gerda had meant for her to know only a small measure of her history, not the whole. Since that was more than Sylvia had possessed before reading the memoir, she would accept the gift and not question the motives of the giver.

Her heart might have rested easy, if not for the image that had once haunted Gerda and now stole into her own dreams: Joanna's face as the slave catcher led her away, her silent and desperate plea. It jolted Sylvia awake at night, and before she could fall asleep again, a voice whispered in her thoughts: *My great-grandmother might have died far from here, alone, enslaved, despairing.*

She shared all her thoughts, agonizing though some of them were, with Andrew. She cried in his arms more than once, mourning her lost surety, fuming at Gerda for leaving her so many questions. Even as a child Sylvia had been proud of herself, of her family—some might say too proud. Now she did not even feel like a Bergstrom anymore. She no longer knew what it meant to be a Bergstrom.

She accepted Gerda's right to leave her an imperfect, incomplete family history, but that did not mean she had to like it. Nor did it mean that she would uphold the family traditions of silence and secrecy.

First, she told Sarah. As the heir to Elm Creek Manor and someone Sylvia thought of as a daughter, Sarah had the right to know. Even as Sylvia recounted Gerda's bombshell, she felt the burden of her worries ease as her young friend shouldered some of the anxieties weighing down her spirit.

As to the question of whether Sylvia was a Bergstrom, Sarah's firm response both surprised and comforted her. "Don't be ridiculous," said Sarah, her expression making it clear that she would not accept any self-pity or brooding from her friend—so clear, in fact, that for a moment Sylvia suspected Sarah was mimicking her.

"I didn't think I was being ridiculous."

"Well, you are," retorted Sarah. "Even if Joanna was your great-grandmother, Anneke and Hans raised her son as their own. Are adopted children any less a part of the family than one's biological offspring?"

"Of course not."

"I'm glad to hear you say that, because otherwise some of our friends wouldn't be very happy with you. Diane's adopted, did you know that? And Judy's stepfather adopted her after marrying her mother. Are you going to tell them they aren't really their parents' children?"

"I wouldn't dream of it."

"Then you shouldn't do the same to Joanna's son," declared Sarah. "Of course you're a Bergstrom. What a question."

Sylvia allowed a smile. "I suppose I am."

But what that meant, she still wasn't sure.

❧

With a sense of recklessness, as if to spite Gerda for providing only partial truths, Sylvia set about telling her closest confidantes what the memoir had revealed. Guard these secrets in the quiet of her own heart, indeed. It was Sylvia's history, and she was free to do with it as she saw fit.

After speaking with Sarah, Sylvia next phoned Grace Daniels. To her astonishment, when she finished recounting Gerda's last cryptic pages, Grace laughed and said, "Well, let me be the first to welcome you into the family."

"I'm glad this amuses you," said Sylvia dryly.

"I've always wondered why we get along so well, and now I know."

"Why, Grace, I'm hurt. You mean to tell me we've been friends for more than fifteen years, and all this time—"

"I'm just teasing you."

"Same here," retorted Sylvia. "Although I admit I'm surprised to find myself joking about this. Gerda's memoir has my mind so twisted up in knots I hardly know what to think."

"You shouldn't blame Anneke and Gerda for keeping their secrets," said Grace. "I'm not saying our day and age is perfect—far from it—but it was radically different then. Anneke probably thought she was rescuing Joanna's son from an incredibly difficult and dangerous life."

"Was she?"

Grace hesitated. "That's not an easy question to answer."

"Please, Grace," urged Sylvia. "The whole truth. That's been too scarce around here lately."

"Well . . ." Grace sighed. "I'm torn between applauding them for adopting Joanna's son and raising him as a member of the family, and condemning them for robbing him of his true heritage. On the other hand, I don't know if it's fair for me to judge them, all safe and smug in my twenty-first-century life. The most immediate consequence of his heritage would have been slavery, and I can't wish that on anyone just to satisfy my pride. Besides, if they had sent him away with those slave catchers, he and Joanna would have been separated soon anyway, and she never would have known where to look for him."

"They might have killed him, even, rather than be troubled with a baby on the road."

"I doubt that," said Grace, with an edge to her voice. "He was valuable property, remember? Josiah Chester might have made the slave catchers pay for him."

"True enough." Sylvia sighed. "So the Bergstroms kept him safe, thinking to reunite him with his mother, although it never happened. Still, after he grew up, they could have told him the truth."

"They could have. Maybe they should have. But since he could pass, they probably thought it better to let him."

"I don't like that word, 'pass,'" said Sylvia. "It sounds like there was some sort of test, and one either passed or one failed."

"There was a test," said Grace. "And even now, in the twenty-first century, when history has provided us with innumerable lessons why it's wrong, for some people and in some places, there still is a test. To those ignorant enough to think they can judge me, I fail it every day. The ignorance of Gerda's day not only lives on, it thrives."

Sylvia did not know what to say.

Grace continued, gently. "You said you no longer know what it means to be a Bergstrom. Do you still think you know what it means to be black or white?"

❧

Two days later, after the Elm Creek Quilters' weekly business meeting, Sylvia told them how Gerda had concluded her memoir with a mystery. Her friends took in the news with intrigued amazement—except for Diane, who claimed to have guessed it the minute she heard both Anneke and Joanna were pregnant.

"You did not," retorted Gwen, nudging Diane so hard she nearly fell out of her chair.

Diane shoved back. "I did so. I read a lot of mystery novels. Gerda's memoir wasn't nearly as complicated."

"In that case," said Sylvia, "perhaps you could put your deductive powers to work on the question of who my great-grandmother is."

Gwen grinned at Diane. "Get to work, Sherlock."

"Goodness," said Sylvia, shaking her head. "They way you two get along, I wonder why you sit beside each other every week. Maybe we should assign you chairs on opposite sides of the room."

Gwen and Diane looked at each other, and then at Sylvia, in surprise. "Are you kidding?" said Diane. "I look forward to needling her all week."

Gwen smirked. "The way you sew, you might mean that literally."

The Elm Creek Quilters laughed, and Sylvia felt their mirth lifting her own subdued spirits. She could almost forget for a moment the loss she felt, thinking that if only Gerda had trusted her a little more, the question of her ancestry could have been answered conclusively. The more time that passed, the more Sylvia realized that the truth, whatever it was, was preferable to this empty space in her history.

Then Agnes's quiet voice broke into the laughter. "I for one hope that Joanna was your great-grandmother."

All eyes went to her. Sylvia regarded her sister-in-law, her baby brother's widow, with surprise. "Why is that?"

"She sounds like a remarkable woman. Strong, courageous, proud." Agnes smiled affectionately across the circle of friends at Sylvia. "Whether she is your great-grandmother or not, I do believe I see her in you."

❧

The next day, Summer returned to the Waterford College library and the historical society's archives, not quite sure what she was looking for. All summer she had scoured the records until she suspected she had handled nearly every scrap of paper in every file and on every shelf, and she knew the information Sylvia most wanted could not be found there. But the urgency to keep looking was too compelling to ignore. At the business meeting, Sylvia had spoken in her usual straightforward way, but Summer sensed the very real pain lingering behind her brave front. She wanted to help—all the Elm Creek Quilters did, and out of Sylvia's hearing they had all agreed to do what they could—but she did not know where to begin.

Leaving her backpack at her usual carrel, she studied the shelves and hoped her gaze would fall upon a record she had not yet examined, but all the titles were familiar.

Suddenly someone reached past her and pulled a book down from the shelf. "If you're looking for something compelling, I highly recommend this one."

Summer glanced over her shoulder to find Jeremy smiling at her. She grinned back and glanced at the title of the book he had chosen. "*A History of the Elm Creek Valley Watershed.* Sounds like a real page-turner. Does it have a happy ending?"

"The main character is really a ghost."

Summer made an exasperated face. "Now you've spoiled it for me, so I don't need to read it." She took the book from him and returned it to the shelf.

"Let me make it up to you," said Jeremy. "Last time we spoke, you said you wanted a look at the old local newspapers, the issues missing from the Waterford Historical Society's collection. Are you still interested?"

"Of course. Are they here somewhere? How did I overlook them?"

"Not here. In the *Waterford Register*'s archives."

"But they told me they couldn't spare a staff member to help me search."

"One of my students is an intern there, and he agreed to take you around after one of his shifts."

"That's wonderful," exclaimed Summer. "When can I start?"

"This afternoon, if you're free." Jeremy hesitated. "There's a catch, though."

"What sort of catch?"

"Nothing major. I have to promise him extra credit on a homework assignment. But there's something else."

"That would be two catches."

"True. But this is the most important one."

Summer regarded him with amusement. "Go on."

"You have to have dinner with me."

"I see." She hid a smile. "Do you usually have to bribe women to have dinner with you?"

"Only very rarely."

Summer pretended to ponder the matter. "I guess if that's the only way I'll get into those archives . . ." She shrugged. "Okay. But only because this friend is very important to me."

❧

That evening, unaware of Summer's plans, her heart still warmed by Agnes's words and the comforting assurances of her friends, Sylvia retired for the night hopeful that one day soon she would be able to think of

Gerda's memoir without regretting all that her ancestor had left unsaid. But first she went to the library and took pen and paper from the top drawer of the great oak desk that had belonged to her father. She wrote one letter to Rosemary, Dorothea Nelson's great-granddaughter, to inform her that her great-grandparents had indeed closed their Underground Railroad station before the Civil War began, and why they had been forced to do so. She then wrote a second, longer letter to Margaret Alden to tell her how Gerda's memoir had concluded, and to invite her and her mother to Elm Creek Manor to see the quilts Sylvia had found in the attic.

Perhaps together they could figure out how—or even if—the Bergstrom quilts were linked to Margaret's.

Chapter Fourteen

On a mid-September afternoon, Sylvia Compson stood in the library looking out the window over the front entrance to her home. On the other side of the sweeping green front lawn, the trees along Elm Creek lifted scarlet, yellow, and orange leaves to the clear autumn sky, but Sylvia scarcely noticed them. Her gaze was fixed on the road, for soon a car would emerge from the forest and bring Margaret Alden and her mother, Evelyn, to Elm Creek Manor.

Sylvia ordered herself to stop pacing around like an agitated cat. Margaret had visited before, as a camper, and her mother was likely to be a pleasant enough woman. Still, in her response to Sylvia's invitation, Margaret had expressed disappointment that the Bergstrom and Alden families did not appear to be related after all, but had not mentioned Joanna. Sylvia figured Gerda's last revelation was astonishing enough to merit some sort of response, and she didn't know what to make of Margaret's silence.

"Sylvia, do you have a moment?"

Sylvia turned to find Sarah lingering in the doorway, with Summer just behind her, carrying a large manila envelope. "For you two, I'll make time," said Sylvia with a smile. The two young women had been trying to lift her out of her melancholy ever since she had finished reading the memoir. Their jokes and diversions did not cheer her as much as the knowledge that they cared enough about her to try.

Sylvia let the curtain fall back in place as Sarah and Summer joined her at the window. "We know how disappointed you've been feeling lately," said Sarah. "We wish we could find the answers you want, but since we can't, we thought we'd at least try to find as much information about Gerda as possible."

"All that time in the library paid off again." Summer handed her the envelope. "I met someone there who managed to get me into the *Waterford Register*'s archives. They don't have all the missing back issues, but they do have many."

Sylvia was already opening the envelope. "Oh, how wonderful, dear." She removed a handful of microfiche printouts and glanced at the first few headlines. "'Underground Railroad Unearthed! Eight Citizens Arrested.' Goodness. 'Justice and Mercy Triumph! Creek's Crossing Eight Released from Prison.' 'Creek's Crossing a Haven for Southern Sympathizers? A Righteous Nation Wonders.' My, they certainly had a gift for hyperbole, didn't they?"

"It's all there," said Summer. "The whole story, just as Gerda recorded it."

"There's even a letter to the editor from Mr. Pearson," said Sarah. "I guess the editors felt they had to show an opposing view."

"Hmph. I look forward to reading it," said Sylvia. "What does he say?"

"Exactly what you'd expect from him."

"Best of all," added Summer, "the intern who helped me at the paper said I was welcome to come back anytime, so if you ever want to look up your father or grandmother—"

"Or your great-aunt Lucinda," Sarah interrupted, "or Claudia, to find out about those years you were away—"

"Just say the word, and I'll investigate."

"I might just do that one of these days," said Sylvia. "Thank you. Thank you both." As she returned the clippings to the envelope to read more thoroughly later, she noticed Summer and Sarah exchanging mischievous glances. "All right. I know that look. I'm expecting visitors, so whatever you two are plotting, it will have to wait."

"Actually, it can't wait," said Summer. "Because . . . some of your guests are kind of already here."

"Nonsense. I've been watching the front drive." *For the past hour,* she almost added, but decided against it. No need to let them see how anxious she was. Then she understood. "Oh, I see. This is your surprise. You invited someone else to join us, and you sneaked them in the back way. Well, who are they and where are they hiding?"

"Rosemary Cullen and Kathleen Barrett," said Sarah. "And they aren't hiding. They're having coffee in the parlor."

"Why didn't you tell me earlier?" exclaimed Sylvia. She left the library with such haste that Sarah and Summer didn't catch up until she reached the door. "Honestly, you two," she grumbled as they hurried after her down the stairs. "Haven't I taught you any manners? You don't abandon guests so you can come upstairs and have a private chat."

"Andrew is with them," said Sarah.

"That's something, at least," said Sylvia, but she gave her two young friends an exasperated shake of the head as they crossed the marble foyer and hurried down the west wing to the parlor. There she found the two women chatting with Andrew. "Rosemary and Kathleen. What a delight to see you again."

"The pleasure is ours," said Rosemary. She clasped the hand Sylvia extended to her, and to Sylvia's relief, she seemed to feel not at all neglected. "I must say, your letter has me more excited than I've been in years. It's wonderful to have so many details about my great-grandparents' lives verified. I feel like I'm getting to know them so much better, thanks to Gerda and her memoir."

"I know the feeling," said Sylvia, smiling. Of course, in her own case, as many details about her grandparents had been proven false as had been confirmed.

"After your visit, I went back and reread Thomas's letters to Dorothea," said Kathleen. "He mentions your family in at least a dozen letters."

"Does he, indeed? You're certain he meant my family?"

"Absolutely." Rosemary patted the sofa to encourage Sylvia to sit between her and Andrew. "He mentions them by name, and some of their children, too."

Sylvia's heart seemed to skip a beat, and she sat down more suddenly than she had intended. She wondered which children, and what Thomas had said about them. Surely he had been in on the secret. Even if the Bergstroms had not told him, the Nelsons had known Anneke bore only one child, and they had visited Gerda often enough to be aware that she had not been pregnant. They also knew the Bergstroms had sheltered runaways, and Dorothea's own brother had delivered Joanna's child.

"I would very much like to see those letters," said Sylvia to Rosemary.

"Usually Mother doesn't like to take them out of the house," said Kathleen, but she reached for her purse. "From what you've shared about Gerda's memoir, we knew this letter would be of particular interest to you, so Mother decided to make an exception."

With that, Kathleen placed a fragile sheet of paper in Sylvia's hand.

"Why . . ." Sylvia's voice trailed off, and with her other hand, she slipped on her glasses, which hung about her neck on a fine silver chain. She glanced at Summer and Sarah to steel her confidence, and began to read.

November 7, 1863

My Beloved Dorothea,

Dusk approaches, and finding myself with a few idle moments to spare, I improve them in writing to you. Forgive the shaking of my hand. We fought hard today, against as cunning and dangerous an enemy as I ever thought to face in my lifetime. They have entrenched themselves for the night, to wait and rest in expectation of our charge at dawn, but if I am to believe the rumors flying about our camp, we march at dusk. Since I do not know if I will live to see the sun rise, I must imagine the bright warmth of day, which always seems to surround me when I remember your smile and the fondness in your eyes.

I miss you and Abigail with all my heart. Kiss her for me, and tell her Daddy will be home soon. I tell myself the war will surely end by Christmas, but then doubt steals over me, and I fear I will never see you again in this world. But as you have often said, my dearest, I must not dwell on such thoughts, but rather pray for a swift, just conclusion to this conflict.

So, instead I will imagine you are here with me, or rather, that I am there with you, for though I know you to be a woman of remarkable fortitude, I would not wish you to look upon the scene that lies before me.

When I close my eyes and think of home, it is springtime, with the smell of freshly tilled soil in the air. It is evening, our day's work is done, and I am pushing you and little Abby on the swing your brother hung for us from the oak tree near the pasture. The sun is setting, and the baby shrieks with delight, and you look over your shoulder at me and smile, and I know that I am still alive.

I pause in my reverie to tell you I have, at last, received word from Jonathan. When he discovered one of his patients would join us here after his recovery, he bade him carry a letter to me, which I very gladly received. He wrote little about his activities, saying, in summary, that battlefield medicine is like nothing he learned at university. When I reflect on the broken bodies we send him, I cannot imagine any education that could have prepared him sufficiently.

Jonathan said he had heard from you, and that your letters gladden his heart. He also mentioned receiving word from our friend Gerda Bergstrom. Apparently Gerda has taken to your knitting lessons, for she sent him three pairs of thick wool socks, which, he said, he was quite glad to receive. She also sent him a book of poetry, which he confessed he has not yet opened, for at the end of the day, he is too exhausted from his labors to do anything more than remove his boots and drop off to sleep.

He did not mention hearing from Charlotte. I hope this was an oversight on his part and not an indication that Charlotte's condition is afflicting her too greatly to write, for as I recall, her confinements with the two eldest were difficult. I suspect, dear wife, that your brother had indeed heard from her, but his thoughts were so full of Gerda that Charlotte was crowded out of his letter.

When I reflect upon our friends, I cannot help but pity Jonathan and pray for his heart to find peace. I know what it is like to find one's great love, and having been married to her for so many delightful years, I cannot imagine living without her, or being married to another. I know Jonathan respects and admires Charlotte, and I am certain he is a dutiful husband to her, but it is a pity he cannot spend his life with the one to whom he has given his heart.

I need not tell you to say nothing to your brother or to Gerda of my opinions. These are simply the ramblings of a weary mind, but I know you will indulge me and not chasten me for dallying in idle gossip. Indeed, any talk of those I hold dear, however trivial it may seem, carries great significance in each and every word when I am far from the warmth of their affection.

Now I am told I must douse my light, so I must end my letter in haste. I know you will forgive me for not sending Jonathan's letter on to you. He wrote that he sent you a letter of your own, and the cheerful tidings of loved ones are a comfort to me in this wretched place, and I would like to keep Jonathan's to read again at my leisure.

I miss you, my sweet wife, and once more I vow that when I return to the shelter of our little farm in the valley, I will never leave it again.

Kiss Abby again for me, and know that I remain,

Your Loving Husband,

Thomas

Sylvia removed her glasses and cleared her throat, blinking back a tear. "Well." She carefully refolded the letter and handed it to Kathleen. "I'm glad that Gerda and Jonathan remained friends, although it would have pleased me more to learn they had found some happy ending together." Her heart ached for them. They could have enjoyed a love as devoted and enduring as that Thomas and Dorothea shared, if only the fates had cooperated.

"But what of Hans and Anneke's children?" asked Sarah. "Kathleen said some of Thomas's letters mentioned them."

"They do," said Kathleen. "But mostly in passing, I'm afraid. He refers to gatherings at one family's farm or the other's, and recalls games the children played together."

Sylvia nodded. She longed to read any letter that mentioned the Bergstroms, regardless of how few details they provided, but twice she had asked to read them and had been rebuffed. She did not feel she should ask again.

"I do so hate to let those letters out of my sight," said Rosemary. "I'm sure you feel the same way about the memoir, Sylvia."

Sylvia forced a smile, trying to hide her disappointment. "Of course."

"So I think we ought to arrange to read together. You could bring your memoir to my house, or I could bring my letters here, and we can trade. What do you think?"

"I think it's a wonderful idea."

"Are you sure it wouldn't be an imposition? You must be a very busy woman, with your own business to run. You might not have time to sit and read on a schedule."

Sylvia glimpsed Kathleen's slight frown of worry and realized that both mother and daughter were as eager for the social aspect of their arrangement as for the information contained in the memoir. Fortunately for everyone, Sylvia had every intention of accepting their proposal. "I have plenty of time, and I couldn't think of a better way to spend it."

Rosemary smiled, delighted, and she and Sylvia soon agreed to meet every Wednesday at noon for lunch followed by an hour of reading, one week at Rosemary's home, and the next at Elm Creek Manor.

Kathleen looked pleased by the arrangements, but added, "I'm looking forward to seeing more of Elm Creek Manor myself. I might even sign up for a class or two."

Rosemary regarded her with amazement. "Did I hear you correctly? After all these years, my daughter finally wants to learn to quilt?"

Kathleen looked so embarrassed that Sylvia half expected to see her squirm like a little girl caught in some mischief. "I thought I might."

Rosemary laughed and said to the others, "You have no idea how long I tried to get that one to pick up a needle. She told me she'd die of boredom stitching together old scraps all day long."

Everyone chuckled except Kathleen, but even she managed a sheepish grin. "I've had second thoughts," she explained. "Reading Thomas's letters again helps me appreciate the Dove in the Window quilt Dorothea made for him. I thought I'd like to make one for myself, in remembrance of them."

"What a lovely idea." Sylvia recalled all the quilts Gerda had mentioned, especially those most important in her memoir—the Log Cabin, the Birds in the Air, and the Underground Railroad, of course, but also the Shoo-Fly Gerda had so reluctantly made, and the Feathered Star Joanna had pieced for her unborn child. And Sylvia could not forget Margaret Alden's quilt, which, as far as Sylvia could discern, Gerda had never seen. Yet it was perhaps the most important of all, because although its origin remained a mystery, it had compelled Sylvia to the attic, where she had found the journal.

"Our next camp session starts Sunday," Sarah told Kathleen. "We could sign you up for Beginning Piecing, if you like."

"Camp will conclude for the season soon," said Sylvia, "but afterward, I'd be happy to continue your lessons myself."

"Say yes," advised Sarah. "Sylvia's a wonderful teacher."

"Say yes," echoed Rosemary, and to Sylvia, added, "We've got to get her hooked while we have the chance."

"I heard that," said Kathleen, laughing, but within minutes she and Sylvia had made the arrangements, and Sylvia had added another weekly get-together to her schedule. Perhaps the coming winter without the campers wouldn't be so lonely after all.

After Kathleen and Rosemary left, Sylvia fell silent, Thomas's words haunting her. Andrew put an arm around her shoulders and absently stroked her hair as lines from Thomas's letter played in her thoughts. Thomas knew what it meant to find one's great love, he had written, and he could not imagine living without her or being married to another. He had pitied Jonathan for the obstinacy that had led him to marry Charlotte when his heart belonged to Gerda. Jonathan meant to do what was honorable no matter how much it pained him, but he had wounded Gerda at least as much as himself, and he had no right to do that.

Sylvia didn't know if Andrew was her great love or if she was his, and there was certainly no question of her marrying anyone else, but she had learned from her ancestors' history and had no intention of repeating it.

She rose and took Andrew's hand. "Come with me."

"Where?"

She tried to pull him to his feet, impatient. "We're going for a walk."

His eyebrows rose. "Now?"

"Yes, now. Get up."

"What about Margaret and Evelyn?" asked Sarah as Andrew shrugged and stood.

"If we aren't back in time, you and Summer can amuse them until we return." She ignored the puzzled look Sarah and Summer exchanged, took Andrew's arm, and steered him from the room.

"What's all this about?" asked Andrew as they left the manor by way of the cornerstone patio.

"I just wanted a moment alone with you, that's all."

"I gathered that, but why?"

"You'll find out in a minute. Honestly. I'm not taking you to the far side of the moon. Have some patience."

He almost managed to stifle his laugh, so Sylvia pretended she had not heard it. She quickened her step, eager to get to the north gardens and say her piece before she changed her mind.

They sat side by side in the gazebo as they had so many times before. Sylvia took his hands in hers, closed her eyes, and took a deep breath. When she open her eyes, she found Andrew staring at her curiously. "Sylvia, are you all right?"

"Yes, I'm fine." Or perhaps she was completely out of her mind. "Andrew, dear, do you remember a particular question you asked me here, last summer in this exact spot, a very important question?"

Andrew studied her, his face expressionless. Then he nodded.

"Well, if you wouldn't mind—" She cleared her throat. "I would like very much if you would ask me again."

"Are you sure?"

"Yes, I'm absolutely sure."

He considered. "Well, okay then." He paused. "Sylvia . . ."

"Yes, Andrew?"

"What do you want for lunch?"

"Not that question," she spluttered, but her embarrassment turned to indignation in the moment it took her to realize he was laughing at her. "Andrew Cooper, you rascal, you know very well which question I meant."

"You can't blame me for teasing you after all the times I've asked and you've refused." He grinned. "Maybe I should wait for you to ask me."

Sylvia was prepared to do just that, but only as a last resort.

"We're going to do this properly or not at all," she said, her voice as stern as she could make it considering how warmly Andrew was smiling at her. "So unless you're no longer interested—"

"I'm interested."

He took her hands again, and in words as simple and straightforward as they were affectionate, he told her again how much he loved her, and how he had loved her since he was a boy. He told her that he would love her the rest of his life and that he would prove that to her every day they were together. He promised to do everything in his power to make her as happy as she made him, and that he would be the luckiest and proudest man alive if she would consent to be his wife.

This time, Sylvia told him she would.

❧

Andrew was dancing Sylvia about the gazebo in celebration when Sarah arrived to warn them that a car was coming up the drive. She had to call out over the sound of their laughter, and after she delivered the message, she regarded them curiously. "What are you two so happy about?"

"We'll tell you later," said Sylvia before Andrew could speak. She wanted to enjoy their promise in privacy a little while longer before announcing the news to their friends.

Sylvia and Andrew met Margaret and her mother at the front door. As soon as they entered, their smiles and cheerful greetings seemed to bring the crisp freshness of the bright autumn day in with them, banishing the few lingering worries Andrew's proposal had not quite driven from Sylvia's mind. By the time introductions were made, Sarah's husband, Matt, had arrived to take the visitors' bags to their rooms—except for one tote Evelyn wished to keep with her—and Sarah announced that lunch was ready.

Sylvia and Andrew led Margaret and Evelyn to the banquet hall, where they found Summer making one last adjustment to the centerpiece. Sylvia thanked her with a smile. Her young friends realized how important this meeting was to her, and they had not overlooked even the smallest detail. Sylvia only hoped that if they had any more surprises in store for her, they would wait until Margaret and Evelyn retired for the night. She took more than a little pleasure in knowing that none of their surprises could beat the one she had for them.

Matt and Sarah joined them, completing their party of seven. The cook himself served the meal, and he presented every dish in as elegant a fashion as Sylvia could have desired.

As everyone got acquainted, Sylvia used the opportunity to take her guests' measure. Evelyn reminded her of Rosemary Cullen in age and appearance, and she seemed somewhat shy and reserved, quite the opposite of her outgoing daughter. Sylvia had to hide a smile watching Margaret, for the former camper seemed so delighted to be at Elm Creek Manor again that Sylvia figured the cook could have served cold hamburgers from a local take-out joint and she might not have noticed. As they enjoyed the meal, Margaret described her camp experiences to her mother and reminisced with Sarah and Summer about the highlights of the week. She still kept in touch with all of the students in her Heirloom Machine Quilting class, and they had recently completed a row round-robin through the mail.

"We're planning a reunion here next summer," said Margaret. "We're just waiting for our registration forms."

"I'm glad you'll be back," said Sylvia, and she turned to Evelyn. "Will you be joining us, too?"

Evelyn shrugged shyly. "Oh, I don't know about that. I don't travel much anymore. I'm more comfortable in my own place."

"We'd do our best to make you comfortable here, too," said Summer, with the smile that never failed to charm the object of her attention.

"Think about it, Mom," urged Margaret.

"If you wouldn't think it an intrusion on your friends, I'd consider it, except—" Evelyn looked around the table. "I hate to admit it in such company, but I don't know how to quilt."

"What better reason to attend quilt camp than to learn?" said Sarah, and Sylvia chimed in her agreement. After assuring Evelyn she would not be the only new quilter—or "Newbie," as Summer called them—Evelyn brightened and said she would plan to come.

Andrew leaned over to murmur in Sylvia's ear. "First Kathleen and now Evelyn. Two converts in one day. Not bad."

Sylvia pursed her lips at him as if to scold him for being saucy, but she knew he saw the merriment in her eyes.

After dessert—a heavenly confection of fudge cake and white chocolate mousse that Sylvia decided ought to be added to their regular menu—the conversation turned to the memoir. Margaret and Evelyn peppered her with so many eager questions that Sylvia marveled they had been able to hold them in so long. She sent Sarah to fetch the memoir, and she read aloud from it when they asked her to elaborate on certain events she had mentioned in her letters. Evelyn and Margaret listened most intently when Sylvia read the passages in which Gerda described her unsuccessful attempts to find Joanna. Perhaps the stresses of the day had finally caught up with her, or perhaps it was sharing the journal with the woman whose startling inquires had been the impetus for all Sylvia had learned about her family, but Sylvia found herself so overcome with emotion that she frequently stumbled over the simplest phrases, until she was so embarrassed by her unusual lack of composure that she passed the book to her guests so they could read it for themselves. But no one at the table would permit it. Instead they gently urged her to read on, for they wanted to hear Gerda's words in Sylvia's voice.

Heartened, Sylvia took a deep breath and continued until the final page of the memoir. Then she closed the book softly and rested it on her lap. She imagined Gerda sitting in her room in the west wing of Elm Creek Manor, pen in hand, pouring her grief and longing into the slender, leather-bound book, never knowing who would one day read her words or how they would be received. Or perhaps she had written in the peace of the north gardens, seated in the gazebo, which Hans might have designed not to conceal runaway slaves but to preserve the memory of one, the woman who had given him his beloved adopted son. She imagined Gerda wrapping the completed record in the Underground Railroad quilt and locking it safely away in her hope chest along with the Birds in the Air quilt and the unique Log Cabin quilt, which she had been unable to give to Joanna. Then, or perhaps years later, or perhaps not until her last will and testament, she had given the slender key to Lucinda, who eventually bestowed it upon Sylvia.

After a long moment, Evelyn broke the silence. "Margaret—" She paused to clear her throat, and she removed her glasses to dab at her eyes with a handkerchief. "Margaret, dear, would you hand me my bag, please?"

Margaret nodded, and after a quick, inscrutable glance at Sylvia, she retrieved the large tote from beneath the table and placed it on her mother's lap, allowing most of the weight to fall upon her own hands. Evelyn unfastened the straps, pulled back the zipper, and withdrew a folded bundle wrapped in a cotton sheet. Sylvia immediately recognized it as a quilt, and judging by the reverence with which Evelyn cradled it, there could be no mistaking which quilt it was.

Sylvia stifled a gasp of delight as Evelyn and Margaret unfolded their own Birds in the Air quilt and held it up so all could see. What a joy it was to behold the mysterious quilt again in all its tattered, water-stained glory!

Sarah and Summer cried out in surprise, for Sylvia had told them how fragile the antique quilt was, and they had never expected to see it except in photographs. Sylvia watched fondly as her two young friends pointed out the features of the quilt to each other—the fabric held in place with careful, painstaking stitches; the worn batting with the cotton hulls still visible through the muslin lining; the delicate, cryptic quilting patterns that Sylvia had once dared think might depict scenes from Elm Creek Manor.

"Thank you so much for bringing the quilt with you," said Sylvia as all admired it. "I only wish my friend Grace Daniels were here. She would have been thrilled to see it."

"Oh, I imagine she'll get her chance," said Margaret.

"I'm afraid she's several hours away by airplane, or I'd be on the phone inviting her over at this very moment."

"Then she can see it the next time she's in town," said Evelyn.

Puzzled, Sylvia glanced at Andrew before replying. "What do you mean?"

Evelyn gazed at the quilt as if memorizing it, then sighed and passed it to Sylvia. "Just promise me you'll take good care of it."

"What—" Sylvia took the quilt, but her eyes were fixed on her guest. "You can't mean you're giving this to me."

"I am."

"But . . . but it's priceless. It's a family heirloom."

"It *is* a family heirloom," agreed Evelyn. "But not my family's."

"Evelyn—" As much as Sylvia longed to keep the quilt, she could not do it, knowing her only claim to it was the name Evelyn's mother had given it and a few odd quilting designs that could be interpreted many different and contradictory ways. "As much as I would love to, I simply can't accept this. We have no proof that your quilt has any connection to me or to Elm Creek Manor. Just because it was once called the Elm Creek Quilt—"

"We have more proof than that," said Margaret. "You're forgetting the quilt had another name. It was also called the Runaway Quilt."

Sylvia felt her reply catch in her throat.

Gently, Evelyn said, "In her memoir, Gerda wrote that she learned Josiah Chester would sell off his captured runaways to family or acquaintances in Georgia or the Carolinas."

Sylvia could only nod. She took Andrew's hand and held it tightly.

"My grandfather had a brother," said Evelyn. "That brother had a tobacco plantation in Virginia, and his name was Josiah Chester."

❧

That evening, long after her guests and her friends had retired for the night, Sylvia lay awake in bed, her mind so full of wonder that she could not rest. Moonlight spilled in through her window, enticing her out from beneath her quilts. She dressed warmly and, with great care, took up the Runaway Quilt from the quilt rack in the corner.

Outside the air was cool and still. She crossed the bridge over Elm Creek and made her way to the remains of the cabin Gerda, Hans, and Anneke had once called home. In the moonlight the half-buried logs looked straighter and sturdier than they seemed by day, and yet at the same time they more closely resembled the tree roots Sylvia had first thought them. The night had enchanted the ruin, making it both a more solid foundation and a living thing rooted in the earth, ever growing, ever changing.

Sylvia tucked her hands into the fold of the quilt to warm them, marveling at chance and fate, and wondering if those long-ago events had not instead been shaped by a merciful providence. If Joanna had not lost her way in the storm, if she had not stumbled across the abandoned cabin and found shelter there, the lives of the Bergstrom family would have taken an entirely different, forever unknowable course. Sylvia might never have existed.

Yet she very well might have. She would never know whether Joanna was truly her great-grandmother. She had reminded Margaret and Evelyn of this, repeatedly, warning them that they might be giving their precious family heirloom to someone with even less certain ties to the quiltmaker than their own. But they insisted Sylvia keep it, saying they were acting on faith rather than proven fact.

So Sylvia accepted the quilt with a grateful heart.

She allowed her gaze to travel from the ruins of the cabin to the sky. She found the North Star, as bright and as constant as when Joanna had followed it to freedom, but a freedom that was not destined to endure. For Joanna's son, the dream had come true, although he was never to know the sacrifice his mother had made in allowing only herself to be taken away, though she must have longed to bring him with her, even into slavery, if only to hold him one last time.

A wind stirred, rustling the boughs of the elm trees lining the road to the back of Elm Creek Manor. Sylvia snuggled her hands deeper into the quilt and turned back toward home.

She passed the red barn Hans Bergstrom had built into the side of the hill, twenty paces east of what had once been the cabin's front door. She crossed the bridge over Elm Creek, and from there she spotted a light in a window. Andrew's room. He likely had heard her rise and depart, and even now waited for her safe return. She wondered if Joanna had seen a light in the window of the Bergstrom home upon her arrival so long ago, and if she had found comfort in its warm glow.

Sylvia gazed to the heavens and said a prayer for Joanna, hoping, as Gerda had, that she had at last found the peace and comfort denied her in life. For Sylvia knew by faith if not by fact that Joanna had planned to return to Elm Creek Manor for her son. That much was evident in every stitch of the Runaway Quilt, which Joanna must have pieced by night after her day's work was done, quilting patterns to help her remember where she had traveled, how she had made her journey, so that one day she could find her way back again. In stolen moments she had labored on her masterpiece, recalling the signal she had helped Gerda make, biding her time until she could once again take flight like the Birds in the Air she created from the castoff fabric of the household, piecing a symbolic map from the discarded clothing of her owners, who must have mocked "that runaway's quilt" and the inscrutable effort of the woman who made it. Somehow Joanna had been prevented from following the patchwork cues north to Elm Creek Manor, and the descendants of those who had enslaved her had claimed her quilt as their own. Joanna would never know that generations later, her quilt would complete the journey she herself had been unable to undertake.

Sylvia climbed the stairs and crossed the veranda. She was home. This was her home, and this was her family, as it had always been and would ever be. Whoever her real grandparents were, she was the descendant of Joanna and Anneke and Gerda. The women who had shaped her origins had shaped her, and she would cherish them all as her ancestors, and accept their mystery as she had all else they had bequeathed her.

Author's Note

The Runaway Quilt is a work of fiction. The debate about the role of quilts as signals on the Underground Railroad is ongoing, with the oral tradition often at odds with documented historical fact. In this novel, I have tried to remain faithful to the historical record while also presenting a plausible explanation for the evolution of the legend. For more information about quilts during the era of the Underground Railroad and the Civil War, please see Barbara Brackman's excellent resources, *Clues in the Calico, Quilts from the Civil War,* and *Civil War Women.*

The Quilter's Legacy

Acknowledgments

I owe a deep debt of gratitude to Denise Roy, Maria Massie, and Rebecca Davis for their ongoing support of my work. Thank you for doing what you do so well.

Thank you to Janet Finley and the staff and volunteers of the Rocky Mountain Quilt Museum for generously sharing information about their museum and city.

Many thanks to Anne Spurgeon for her research assistance, but most of all, for her friendship.

I am grateful for the unwavering encouragement, faith, and tolerance of my friends and family, especially Geraldine Neidenbach, Heather Neidenbach, Nic Neidenbach, Virginia and Edward Riechman, Leonard and Marlene Chiaverini, Martin Lang, and Rachel and Chip Sauer. Thank you, Vanessa Alt, for playing with Nicholas while I wrote this book.

My husband, Marty, and my children, Nicholas and Michael, have enriched my life with their love and laughter. I could not do it without you.

To my mother, Geraldine Neidenbach

Chapter One

S ylvia supposed all brides-to-be considered eloping at some point during the engagement, but she had never expected to feel that way herself, and certainly not a mere few weeks after agreeing to become Andrew's wife. She shook her head as she flipped through the magazines someone had left on the desk—*Bride's, American Bride, Country Bride*—and dumped the whole stack into the trash can. Unless they came out with an edition of *Octogenarian Bride*, she would leave the pleading overtures of the bridal industry to the younger girls. Surely she could fend for herself when all she and Andrew wanted was a small, private ceremony in the garden.

The door to the library swung open, and in walked her young friend and business partner, Sarah McClure, neatly dressed in jeans and a button-down shirt, the glasses she wore only reluctantly tucked into the breast pocket. She carried a small white box in one hand. "Do you have a moment?"

"Yes. I was just doing some light housekeeping." Sylvia gestured to the trash can. "Are you responsible for this?"

"Are you kidding? After you scolded me for offering to take you shopping for your wedding gown?"

"I'm glad you learned your lesson." Sylvia frowned. Who could it have been, then? All of the Elm Creek Quilters had free run of the office. Summer spent more time there than anyone other than Sarah, but she was not the bridal magazine type. "Diane," she declared. "Just yesterday I overheard her say that this will be her only chance to plan a wedding because both of her children are boys. Do you suppose she forgot the magazines or left them deliberately, hoping I would be caught up in the wedding planning frenzy that seems to have captivated everyone else around here?"

"Ask her yourself," said Sarah, smiling. "She and Agnes are coming over to discuss new courses for next season."

"Already? Elm Creek Quilt Camp won't open until spring."

"Would you rather have them work ahead on next year's classes or plan your wedding?"

"I suppose you're right."

"You can't blame us for being excited. After you turned down Andrew the third time, most of us gave up hope that you two would ever get married."

"If you were disappointed, it was your own fault for treating our relationship like a spectator sport."

Sarah laughed. "I wasn't disappointed. I always knew it would happen eventually. In fact, I've been saving something for you for months with this occasion in mind."

She set the box on the table.

"What is it?" asked Sylvia, wary. "I distinctly said we did not want any engagement gifts."

"This doesn't really count."

"How could it not count? It's in a wrapped box; it's quite obviously a gift." But Sylvia smiled and unwrapped it. Inside was nestled a pair of silverplated scissors fashioned in the shape of a heron. "My goodness." She slipped on her glasses and studied the scissors, astonished. "My mother had a pair exactly like these. Where on earth did you find this?"

"In your attic, earlier this summer when we were looking for your greatgrandmother's quilts," said Sarah. "You ordered me back to work every time I got sidetracked, so when I found them, I set them aside to show you later. When you found the quilts, I forgot about the scissors in all the excitement."

"In the attic. Then—" The weight and shape of the scissors felt so familiar in her hands that, even with her eyes closed, she could have described the pattern of nicks on the blades. "Then these must be my mother's. I should have known them immediately. Did you know these were given to her by the woman who taught her to quilt? An aunt, or someone. My mother was just a girl when she used these scissors in making her first quilt."

"I thought you might like to use them when you make your bridal quilt."

Sylvia nodded, scarcely hearing. She could picture her mother slicing through fabric with a sure and steady hand, cutting pieces for a dress or a quilt. She remembered sitting beneath the quilt frame as her mother and aunts quilted a pieced top, eavesdropping on their conversation, watching as they worked their needles through the layers of fabric and batting. The weight of her mother's scissors as they rested on the quilt top made the layers bow at her mother's right hand, the depression vanishing and reappearing, accompanied by a brisk snip as her mother trimmed a thread. Those were the same scissors Sylvia and her elder sister, Claudia, had fought over as they raced through their first quilt project, each determined to complete the most Nine-Patch blocks and thereby earn the right to sleep beneath the quilt first. It was a wonder the scissors had not been damaged beyond repair that wintry afternoon, the way Claudia had flung them across the room in frustration when she tried to pick out a poorly sewn seam and jabbed a hole through her patches instead.

"What pattern are you going to use?"

Sylvia looked up. "Hmm?"

"What pattern are you going to use for your wedding quilt?" Sarah regarded her, curious. "You are planning to make one, aren't you?"

"I honestly hadn't thought about it," said Sylvia. "Do you think Andrew expects a wedding quilt?"

"'Expects'? No, I don't think he expects one, but don't you want one? You'll need something for your new bed anyway, unless you're planning to squeeze both of you into your bed or Andrew's."

"Oh, of course," Sylvia said. "You're right. We'll need something."

Sarah's eyebrows rose. "Did you forget about that part? Most married people, you know, cohabit. Unless you were planning on twin beds a discreet distance apart?"

"Our sleeping arrangements are none of your business." Then Sylvia paused. "Actually, I suppose this sounds foolish, but I forgot we would be sharing a room."

Sarah put an arm around her. "I know it's probably been a while, but there's nothing to be nervous about. Especially with Andrew. I'm sure he'll be—"

"No, you don't understand," said Sylvia. "I'm not talking about what you think I'm— You're going to force me to say it, aren't you? Very well, then. Sex. I'm not talking about sex. I said share a room, not share a bed."

"I think you should be prepared to do both," said Sarah carefully. "Andrew might be disappointed if you don't want—"

"I said I'm not talking about sex," exclaimed Sylvia so forcefully Sarah jumped back in surprise. "Andrew and I will be fine in that department, and that's the last I'll say on the subject. My concern is with my room. I haven't shared a bedroom since—well, since James passed. Before then, even. Since he went overseas."

"I see. You're used to having a room of your own. Your own space."

"Precisely." If her bedroom didn't reflect Andrew's tastes and interests as well as her own, he would feel more like a visitor than an occupant. Hardly anyone but herself ever entered the adjoining sitting room, one of her favorite places to read or sew when she wanted solitude. Would she have to shove her fabric stash aside to make room for Andrew's fishing gear? "I don't think there's enough space in my suite for two people."

"Didn't you manage to make room for James when you married him?"

"That was different. I was younger. I didn't have so many things, and neither did James." When Sarah looked skeptical, Sylvia added, "Besides, when James came to live at Elm Creek Manor, I left my old bedroom and we moved into the suite together. That made it our room, not merely mine."

"Why don't you and Andrew do the same? You could move into the master suite on the third floor."

"I couldn't. That was my parents' room."

"But it's just sitting there empty and it's the largest suite in the manor."

"I suppose," said Sylvia, reluctant. But that would not solve the problem. She was content with her room as it was. It was private and it was hers. She did not want to change it or move somewhere else, but what was the point of getting married if they meant to leave things exactly as they were?

Sylvia stroked the heron scissors with a fingertip and carefully returned them to the box. She would just have to get used to the idea. If she told Andrew how she felt, he might think she was having second thoughts about marrying him.

Whatever they decided about the room, they would still need a quilt. Sylvia could no longer sew as swiftly as she had before her stroke, and she did not want a half-finished quilt covering their bed on their first night as husband and wife. She could ask the Elm Creek Quilters for help, or—

"I know just the thing." Sylvia rose from her chair, tucking her mother's scissors into her pocket. "Thank you, Sarah. Your gift has inspired me."

"Where are you going?"

"Up to the attic, to look for my mother's bridal quilt."

ℒℯ

Sylvia stifled a laugh, amused by Sarah's baffled expression. It was nice to know that, in spite of their closeness, Sylvia could still surprise her young friend.

Sylvia went upstairs to the third floor, then climbed the narrow, creaking stairs to the attic. Rain drummed on the roof as she fumbled for the light switch Sarah's husband, Matt, had only recently installed. The overhead light illuminated the attic much better than the single, bare bulb it had replaced, but even now the sloped ceiling and the stacks of trunks, cartons, and the accumulated possessions of four generations cast deep shadows in the corners of the room.

Directly in front of her stretched the south wing of the manor, added when her father was a boy; to her right lay the older west wing, the original home of the Bergstrom family, built in the middle of the nineteenth century by her great-grandparents and her great-grandfather's sister. Only a few months before, Sylvia had searched the attic for the hope chest her great-aunt Lucinda had described, the one containing her great-grandmother's quilts. One of those quilts, the family stories told, had acted as a signal to runaway slaves in the years leading up to the Civil War, beckoning fugitives to the sanctuary of a station on the Underground Railroad. Sylvia had found the hope chest and much more, for it had contained three quilts made by her ancestors and a journal, a memoir written by Gerda Bergstrom, her great-grandfather's sister. Within its pages Gerda confirmed that Elm Creek Manor had indeed been a station on the Underground Railroad, but the particular circumstances differed greatly from the idealized tales handed down through the generations.

Despite these new uncertainties, Sylvia still knew much more about her father's side of the family than her mother's. Until that summer she had excused her ignorance as a consequence of growing up on the Bergstrom family estate; naturally her father's family tended to talk about their own. Her mother died when Sylvia was only ten years old, and the few stories her mother had shared about her youth were almost certainly edited for a young girl's ears. Her mother spoke of strict, wealthy parents who raised her to be a proper young lady, and since this was the very sort of well-behaved child Sylvia invariably failed to emulate, her mother's stories seemed like dull morality tales. Sylvia eventually decided that the Bergstrom family was far more interesting than the Lockwoods and paid little attention when that distant look came into her mother's eyes as she remembered events long ago and far away.

The events of the past summer had pricked Sylvia's conscience, and for the first time in her life, she regretted neglecting an entire half of her heritage. Sarah's gift—the silverplated scissors Sylvia had so often seen in her mother's hand—had flooded her mind with images and conversations long forgotten and a warmth of remembered love. Mother had tried to pass on more than quilting skills as she taught Sylvia how to work a needle. If only she had paid more attention to her mother's reminiscences, she might feel as if she had truly known her, and known her family. Now all Sylvia had were her memories and the incomplete list of names, birthdates, baptisms, marriages, and deaths recorded in the Lockwood family Bible.

She surveyed the attic. Somewhere in one of those trunks or cartons were her mother's quilts. Claudia must have stored them up here, for upon Sylvia's return to the manor after Claudia's death, only a few of Mother's most worn utility quilts had been spread on beds in the rooms below, awaiting guests who never came. Her mother's bridal quilt was sure to be among those that had been put away for safekeeping.

"Now, where to begin?" mused Sylvia. The search earlier that summer had focused on a specific hope chest, so she had ignored those that did not fit the description. Still, she had opened enough, just in case, to detect a pattern within the clutter. The newest items were closest to the stairs, as if Claudia or her husband had merely stood on the top step and shoved the boxes inside. Moving deeper into the attic was like stepping back in time, with an occasional object from another era juxtaposing the past and present: an electric lamp missing its shade rested on top of a treadle sewing machine; a pile of Sylvia's schoolbooks sat on the floor beside a carton of clothing from the seventies. For the most part, however, the pattern held true, and since Sylvia had found Gerda Bergstrom's journal in the deepest part of the west wing, possessions from her mother's era ought to be somewhere in the middle of the south wing.

She chose a trunk at random, tugged it into the open, and had just lifted the lid when she heard the stairs creaking. She turned to find Agnes emerging from the opening in the floor. "Oh, hello, dear," Sylvia greeted her. "Did you finish your business with Sarah and Diane?"

"We didn't even get started," said Agnes, touching her curly white hair distractedly. "Once Sarah told me what you were up to, I came right upstairs."

"If you came to help, you're a brave soul. It took me weeks to find Gerda's hope chest."

"Sylvia." Agnes hesitated, removed her pink-tinted glasses, and replaced them. "About your mother's quilt—"

"Oh yes, of course," exclaimed Sylvia, suddenly remembering. "You've seen it—the burgundy, green, black, and white New York Beauty quilt. It was on the bed of your guest room when you visited us that first time." She chuckled at the memory. "We used it for only our most important visitors, but you apparently had no idea how we had honored you. The next morning, when you complained about how cold you had been all night, I wanted to snatch it off your bed and give you a few scratchy wool blankets instead. I would have, except my brother would have been furious."

"I don't remember complaining . . ." Agnes shook her head and began again. "Sylvia, dear, I hope you don't have your heart set on using your mother's bridal quilt."

"I don't plan to, not every day. Just on our wedding night." She sensed Agnes's dismay and amended her words. "I wouldn't damage an antique quilt just to indulge a whim. If it seems too fragile, I'll just display it at the reception instead."

"I'm afraid that won't be possible, Sylvia." Agnes took a deep breath. "The quilts aren't here."

"Of course they are. They must be."

"I don't mean they aren't in the attic. They aren't in the manor. Claudia sold them."

"What?"

"She sold them. All of them, except for the utility quilts."

"I don't believe it." Sylvia steadied herself with one hand on the trunk, then slowly closed the lid and sank to a seat upon it. "Not even Claudia could have done such a thing. Not even Claudia."

"I'm so sorry." Agnes worked her way through the clutter and sat down beside her. "After the family business failed, the money ran out. Claudia and Harold sold off the horses, acres of land, furniture, anything to raise cash. I—I did, too, of course, but mostly to keep them from selling off the rest of the land and the manor with it."

"She sold Mother's bridal quilt?" Sylvia repeated.

"And the others, her other fine quilts." Agnes took Sylvia's hands. "I would have prevented it if I could have. I wish you knew how hard I tried."

"I'm sure you did." Sylvia gave Agnes's hand a clumsy pat and pulled away. She rarely allowed herself to imagine what life in Elm Creek Manor had been like after her angry and abrupt departure, but for Agnes, it must have been a nightmare. Sylvia suspected she owed the survival of what remained of the estate to her sister-in-law. Agnes never spoke of those days, which Sylvia considered a kindness. What she imagined pained her enough.

She never should have run away.

"When Claudia made up her mind, there was no reasoning with her," said Sylvia. "The quilts were hers to do with as she wished, since I abandoned them. It's not your fault she sold them."

"But—"

"It's not your fault." Suddenly the attic seemed dark and confining. "It's mine."

❧

Sylvia left the attic without another word, without looking back. She retreated to the sanctuary of the sitting room adjoining her bedroom. Ordinarily she preferred to quilt in the bright cheerfulness of the west sitting room on the first floor where friends came and went as they pleased, but she was too distressed now to welcome company. She brooded as she worked on her Tumbling Blocks quilt, piecing the diamond-shaped scraps together and thinking about her sister.

The fading light reminded her she had spent too much time alone with her thoughts. Tonight was supposed to have been her turn to prepare supper for herself, Andrew, Sarah, and Matt, but Agnes's revelation had driven all thoughts of eating from her mind. Finally, she set her quilting aside and hurried down the grand oak staircase, across the marble floor of the foyer, and down the west wing toward the kitchen. When camp was in session, they served breakfast in the banquet hall off the foyer, but in the off-season, they preferred the intimacy of the kitchen.

Andrew and Matt were setting the long wooden table for four when she entered. "Glad you could join us," said Sarah as she took a steaming casserole dish from the oven.

Andrew took her hand and kissed her on the cheek. "Are you feeling any better?" he asked in an undertone.

"Who said I was feeling poorly?"

"You shut yourself in your room all day," said Andrew. "That's usually a pretty accurate sign."

"It's nothing," she said, giving his hand a pat and forcing a smile. "I'll explain later."

But Sarah's curiosity would not wait. They were barely seated when she gave Sylvia a searching look and said, "Did you and Agnes have an argument? She came down from the attic upset about something, but when I asked what was wrong, she just shook her head and asked Diane to drive her home."

"We didn't argue," said Sylvia, and told them what she had learned about the fate of her mother's quilts.

"Oh, Sylvia," said Andrew, his brow furrowed in concern. "That's a real shame."

"It can't be helped," she said briskly when Sarah and Matt nodded in sympathy. "What's done is done, and I have only myself to blame. If I hadn't run away—"

"Don't blame yourself," said Sarah.

"Oh, don't worry, dear. I've set aside plenty of blame for my sister, too. I don't understand how she could have parted with our mother's quilts." She waved her hand, impatient. "I've sulked about this enough for one day. May we please change the subject? I'd rather talk about anything else, even the wedding."

"That's good," said Sarah, "because Diane wants Andrew to find out how many of his grandchildren are coming in case we need to set up a special playroom for them during the reception."

"She's moving right along, isn't she?" said Sylvia. "I suspect she'll have my dress picked out soon."

Andrew looked dubious. "I think my grandkids are too old to be interested in a playroom unless it has video games, but I'll ask."

"I suppose we ought to set a date before Diane does," said Sylvia. "Did you find out when the grandkids will be out of school for the summer?"

Andrew shrugged. "I forgot to check."

Sylvia gave Sarah and Matt a knowing look. "What he means is that he still hasn't summoned up the courage to tell his children we're engaged."

"That's not the kind of news you spring on someone over the phone," protested Andrew.

Sarah's eyebrows rose. "You say that as if you don't expect them to be happy for you."

"They will be," said Andrew, "once they get used to the idea."

Sylvia patted his arm. "I love you, dear, and I promise I'll marry you with or without your children's blessing, but I think we should tell them soon, before they hear about it from someone else."

"I want to tell them in person."

"Do you really think that's necessary?"

Andrew nodded.

"Very well. Shall we break the news together?"

"I'd like you to travel with me, but I'll tell them myself, alone. Bob first, and then Amy. Bob knows how to keep a secret, but Amy would be on the phone to her brother within five minutes."

Clearly he had given the matter a great deal of thought. "I'm sure we'll have a lovely visit and they'll be delighted for us," said Sylvia. She smiled encouragingly and squeezed his hand, wishing she felt as certain as she sounded.

❦

The next day, Sylvia attended to her household chores and made mental notes about what she should pack for the upcoming trip. Bob lived in Southern California, which at this time of year meant warm, sunny days and cool evenings. If they left tomorrow, as Andrew wished, and took time to see the sights along the way, they would arrive the following Friday.

After calling his son to arrange their visit, Andrew spent the day working on the motor home, checking the engine and purchasing supplies. He and Sylvia kept so busy that, except at lunch, they barely had time to exchange a word. Sylvia found herself uncomfortably relieved by their separation. She knew she shouldn't take Andrew's concerns personally, but she couldn't help it. If Amy and Bob were going to be unhappy, how would telling them in person change anything? They had no business giving Andrew anything less than their wholehearted support of his decision to remarry.

Just when she had worked up enough irritation to tell him so, Andrew appeared at the door of the laundry room and said, "Sylvia, may I speak with you a moment?"

"You certainly may, but I want to speak first." She closed the lid to the washing machine and was just about to give him a piece of her mind when she saw that Summer Sullivan, Sarah's codirector of Elm Creek Quilts, had followed him into the room. "Oh, hello, dear. I didn't know you were working today."

"I'm not," said Summer, smiling. The youngest of the Elm Creek Quilters, the auburn-haired beauty was also their Internet guru and most popular instructor. "I came over to help you look for your mother's quilts."

"Look for them?" Sylvia barked out a laugh and punched the buttons on the washing machine. "Didn't anyone tell you? They aren't here. They've been gone for more than forty years. Nearly fifty. We'll never find them."

Andrew placed a hand on her shoulder. "You ought to hear what the young lady has to say."

Sylvia frowned at him, but he and Summer looked so hopeful that she gazed heavenward and sighed. "Oh, all right. If you make it quick. I have work to do."

"I'll help you with the laundry after," said Summer, taking Sylvia's hand. With Andrew bringing up the rear, she led Sylvia to the library, where the computer was already connected to the Internet. Summer pulled out the high-backed leather chair and motioned Sylvia into it. "There's this awesome Web site—"

Sylvia raised a hand. "You know I don't do e-mail. I appreciate what the Internet has contributed to our business, but I will not drive another nail into the coffin of the fine art of letter writing."

"No one will force you to send e-mail." Summer guided her into the chair. "This is a Web site. It's different."

"Go on," urged Andrew. "It's important."

Sylvia sat down, slipped on her glasses, and peered at the computer. The title at the top of the screen read, "The Missing Quilts Home Page." Down the left side ran a list of phrases: "Home Page," "Help Find Missing Quilts," "Report Your Missing Quilt," and "Reunions! Quilts Found." Other quilt-related topics followed, including articles about protecting quilts from theft and how to properly document quilts—which had long been one of Sylvia's pet causes.

"Perhaps this is worth a look," she admitted.

Summer slid the mouse into Sylvia's hand. "Use this to move the pointer over the links, and if you want to read the article, click the mouse."

"I have used a computer before, dear," said Sylvia dryly, but she did as instructed. First she read the page about documenting quilts and was pleasantly surprised to discover the author provided a clear and thorough description of the appropriate steps. Next she clicked on the "Help Find Missing Quilts" link. On the screen appeared the names of at least fifty quilts, accompanied by pictures too small to be seen clearly even with her glasses.

"Click on the thumbnail." Summer took the mouse and clicked on the first tiny picture. That took them to a new page, which included a larger photo of the quilt, a list of the quilt's dimensions, colors, pattern, and fabric, and a brief narrative describing how it had disappeared from the quiltmaker's car after an accident. The quilter had been taken from the scene in an ambulance, and by the time she could arrange to have her possessions secured, the quilt was gone.

"How terrible," exclaimed Sylvia. "What kind of person would steal a quilt, especially from someone in such circumstances? It's outrageous."

"Keep reading," said Summer, and used the mouse to direct Sylvia to the previous page.

From there, Sylvia linked to each of the missing quilts in turn and read about quilts taken from summer cottages, vanished from the beds of residents of nursing homes, fallen from baby strollers or left behind at schools, stolen from quilt shows or lost in the mail en route to and from quilt shows, and, perhaps most troubling of all, more than two hundred children's quilts made by a Michigan church group for an orphanage in Bosnia, taken in the theft of the truck hired to transport them to the airport.

"It's tragic," muttered Sylvia, shaking her head. All those precious quilts so lovingly and painstakingly made, separated from their proper owners, perhaps forever. "Please tell me there's some good news."

"Try that Reunions link," said Andrew.

Sylvia clicked on "Reunions! Quilts Found," which linked to a photo gallery of quilts that had eventually found their way home. The stories of their discoveries were comforting, but few.

"They don't find many, do they?" said Sylvia, pushing back her chair and removing her glasses.

"But they do find some," said Andrew. "That red-and-white one was missing for thirty years, and it was finally found."

"My mother's quilts have been missing longer than that."

Summer sat on the edge of the desk. "You'll never find them if you don't look."

"Chances are I won't find them this way, either."

Summer frowned. "You know, you sound exactly the way you used to, before Elm Creek Quilts, back when you first returned to Waterford. Contrary and negative and pessimistic about everything."

"I most certainly do not. Not now and not then. I'm just being realistic." Indignant, she added, "How would you know anything about my temperament back then? We didn't become friends until months later."

"True, but I worked at the quilt shop, remember? When you came to Grandma's Attic to buy supplies and to sell your quilts on consignment, I would overhear you talking to Bonnie. 'I don't know why I bothered to bring this quilt downtown. No one will want it.' 'I have no business buying so much fabric. I won't live long enough to use it up.'"

"Sylvia," protested Andrew.

"I never said any such thing," declared Sylvia, but she remembered, vaguely, entertaining similar thoughts, and it was possible she had given voice to them. "Even if I did, I have changed considerably since then."

"That's a relief," said Andrew.

"Then don't be such a cynic," said Summer. "If you really want to find your mother's quilts, let's look for them."

Sylvia pursed her lips, unconvinced, but wavering. "They were never photographed that I can recall."

"We don't need photos." Summer pulled up a chair beside Sylvia's and took over the computer. "I'll use my drawing software to create illustrations based on your descriptions. You write down everything you remember about your mother's quilts—colors, sizes, any unique identifying marks—"

Suddenly, with a flash of insight, Sylvia remembered: "My mother always embroidered her initials and the year on the backs of her quilts. She wrote with a pen, then backstitched over the writing with contrasting thread."

"Perfect," said Summer, typing rapidly. "That's a start."

"This might take a while." Sylvia glanced at Andrew. Now that she had decided to proceed, she didn't want to delay the search until they returned from California. "I still have to pack if we're going to leave tomorrow."

Andrew smiled and patted her shoulder. "I think this is important enough to delay our trip a day or two."

Sylvia placed her hand over his and thanked him with a smile.

❧

At first Sylvia wanted to concentrate on her mother's wedding quilt, but Summer soon persuaded her that by broadening their search, they increased their chances of finding at least one. While Summer produced an illustration of the burgundy, green, black, and white New York Beauty quilt from notes she jotted as Sylvia described it, Sylvia carried a pad of paper and a pen to a chair beside the fireplace and tried to coax memories of the quilts to the forefront of her mind. Eventually the clattering of Summer's fingers on the keyboard became a distraction, so Sylvia went outside to the cornerstone patio where she could be alone.

She was glad for her sweater. The day was sunny but cool, and the leaves on the trees surrounding the gray stone patio had already begun to turn. The cornerstone patio had been her mother's favorite place on the estate, but Sylvia's memories almost always placed her there in spring, when the lilacs were in bloom. The door leading to the patio had once been the main entrance, back in the day of Sylvia's great-grandparents. The patio's name came from the cornerstone Hans, Anneke, and Gerda had laid in 1858, when the west wing of the manor was built. Sylvia's grandfather added the south wing when her father was just a boy, after the hard work of their immigrant forebears had paid off and the family prospered. Now evergreens and perennials hid the cornerstone from view, but every time Sylvia visited the patio, she recalled the passage from Gerda's memoir that described how her ancestors had built their home upon it.

Sylvia seated herself on a teak armchair, pen in hand, and let her mind wander. Her mother had made so many quilts over the years, most of them simple utility quilts pieced from scraps. Some she had given away to charities sponsored by her church; others had kept Sylvia and her siblings warm throughout the cold Pennsylvania winters. Her mother's skill truly shone, however, in her five "fancy quilts," as Sylvia had always called them. Mother devoted years to their making, and often purchased fabric especially for them rather than selecting from her scrap bag.

The first, the oldest of the five, was a Crazy Quilt of silks, wools, brocades, and velvets, heavily embroidered and appliquéd. Mother had displayed it draped over a small table beside her bed, but since Sylvia was only rarely permitted to enter her parents' bedroom, she remembered little except its dark, formal colors and its heaviness. She closed her eyes and concentrated, willing the vague impressions to clarify.

She wrote down all she remembered: the diamond-shaped blocks covered with crazy patchwork; the appliquéd horseshoe, chess piece, and the silhouette of a woman; the embroidered spiderweb and initials; the one block cut from a single piece of fabric, a linen handkerchief monogrammed with the monogram ALC. The L surely stood for Lockwood, but Sylvia had no idea what the A and C represented, since she had found no A. C. Lockwood listed in the family Bible. Although she could not recall her mother telling her so, she knew, somehow, that while the Crazy Quilt appeared to be the work of an accomplished, experienced quilter, it was one of the first her mother had completed. Her grandmother had disapproved of it.

Sylvia sat stock-still. The idea had sprung into her head from heaven knew where, but Sylvia was certain it was true, albeit mystifying. Why would Grandmother Lockwood have disapproved of such a beautiful piece? It was impossible to believe she had found fault with her daughter's handiwork. Crazy Quilts by their nature were more for show than for warmth or comfort; had Grandmother Lockwood thought her daughter's efforts would be better spent on a more practical project?

Sylvia frowned and tapped the pen on the arm of her chair, wishing she knew.

Eventually Sylvia decided to set that puzzle aside for another time. She turned to a fresh page on the pad, and, although she had already told Summer most of what she knew, she jotted a few additional notes about her mother's wedding quilt. Given the complexity of the pattern and the length of time Mother typically devoted to her showpiece quilts, she had probably begun the New York Beauty by 1904 in order to have it finished for her wedding in 1907. But had she even known her future husband then? She would have been only fourteen. Sylvia wished she knew for certain. She wondered if her mother had dreamed about her wedding day as she hand-pieced the hundreds of narrow fabric triangles into arcs. As she set the quarter-circles into the arcs, she might have imagined embracing her husband beneath the finished quilt. Perhaps she hoped the quilt would grace their wedding bed throughout the years, as she and her husband grew old together.

"Sentimental nonsense," scoffed Sylvia, ignoring a twinge of guilt that perhaps she had wronged Andrew by not indulging in such romantic daydreaming. She reassured herself by noting that her mother probably hadn't, either. Most likely, the New York Beauty was already in progress before Father proposed. Knowing she would not have enough time to start a new quilt from scratch, Mother had simply decided to make the New York

Beauty her wedding quilt. It was an option Sylvia would do well to consider.

Sylvia's notes on the New York Beauty filled only half a page, but Summer's computer illustration would supplement them. Summer would need better drawing skills than Sylvia possessed to create a picture that would do justice to Mother's third quilt, a white whole cloth quilt. A masterpiece of intricate quilting, it was so much smaller than the others that Sylvia might have assumed it was a crib quilt except that no infant had ever slept beneath it. Sylvia's memory and the quilt's pristine condition concurred on that point. It could have been intended for a fourth child wished for but never conceived, or even a grandchild, but Mother had completed it several years before Claudia had been born. Sylvia had always wondered why Mother had not given that beautiful quilt to her eldest child, and why she had not embroidered her initials and date on the back, the last, finishing touch she had added to all her other quilts. Perhaps it was not a crib quilt at all, but a stitch sampler where Mother had practiced her hand-quilting and auditioned new patterns. If that were true, Mother might have thought a practice quilt too humble to commemorate the birth of her first child, despite its beauty. Claudia certainly would have been offended if she had learned of it, so perhaps Mother made the right choice.

At the top of a fresh page, Sylvia started to write "Sick Quilt" before she caught herself and wrote "Ocean Waves." Better to call it by its traditional title, since no one else would be able to identify her mother's blue-and-white quilt with the nickname Sylvia and Claudia had given it. Sylvia was not sure how the family custom developed, but whenever children in the family fell ill, Mother would take the Ocean Waves quilt from her cedar chest and allow them to use it on their beds until they felt better. In hindsight, Sylvia assumed the privilege of using the special quilt was supposed to boost the sick child's spirits and thereby hasten recovery, but she recalled that when she was particularly queasy, the arrangement of blue and white triangles resembled an ocean's undulating surface enough to make her feel worse rather than better. She would kick off the quilt rather than look at it, but Grandmother Bergstrom, her father's mother, would replace it while Sylvia slept. Grandmother Bergstrom never admitted it aloud, but she seemed to believe the quilt had miraculous curative powers. Sylvia once asked her mother if this were true. Mother said that Grandmother's ideas were merely harmless superstitions, and Sylvia shouldn't let them trouble her. Then her eyes had taken on a faraway look, and she said that she had prayed for the safety of her family every moment she worked on that quilt, and perhaps an answer to her prayers lingered in the cloth.

Sylvia turned to a new sheet and sketched the Elms and Lilacs quilt, smiling as she worked. The Elms and Lilacs quilt was Sylvia's favorite of all her mother's quilts; indeed, it was quite possibly her favorite out of all the quilts she had ever seen. A masterpiece of appliqué and intricate, feathery quilting, the Elms and Lilacs quilt displayed her mother's skills at their finest. The circular wreath of appliquéd elm leaves, lilacs, and vines in the center gave the quilt its name; a graceful, curving double line of pink and lavender framed it. The outermost border carried on the floral theme with elm leaves tumbling amid lilacs and other foliage, and intertwining pink and lavender ribbons finished the scalloped edge. The medallion style allowed for open areas, which Mother had quilted in elaborate feathered plumes over a delicate background crosshatch. Then an image flashed in Sylvia's thoughts: her mother quilting the Elms and Lilacs quilt in the nursery while Sylvia, Claudia, and baby Richard played nearby.

Sylvia laughed, remembering how her father and Uncle William had struggled to disassemble the quilt frame and carry it up the stairs. The Elms and Lilacs quilt had been a gift for Father on her parents' twentieth anniversary, and Mother had brought it to the nursery so she could work on it unobserved. It was a wonder she finished it in time with Sylvia at her elbow begging to be allowed to contribute a stitch or two. Sylvia hesitated, her pen frozen in mid-stroke. She vaguely remembered that Mother had, in fact, allowed her to work on the quilt, and Claudia, as well, but something had brought their work to an abrupt halt. Perhaps it was an argument; many a quilting lesson had ended prematurely thanks to the sisters' rivalry. Or perhaps their mother had been too ill to continue for a time. Mother's slow decline had already begun by then, and she had been forced to set aside many of her favorite pastimes. Quilting had been among the last she relinquished. She had quilted until the very end, when she could do little more than sit outside on the cornerstone patio and admire the garden Father had made for her.

Sylvia finished her notes on the Elms and Lilacs quilt with a description of its colors and fabrics and an estimate of its size. She wrote down all she remembered. She had her doubts about Summer's Internet, but the tiniest detail might prove to be the key to locating the quilts and determining their identity. And if, through some fortunate turn of events, the quilts could be restored to her, Sylvia might learn more about the woman who had made them.

Chapter Two

E leanor stole down the hallway past her sister's room, where Abigail and Mother struggled to open Abigail's trunk. Eleanor heard Mother wonder aloud how the latch had acquired that peculiar dent, but she did not hear what excuse her sister invented. She doubted Abigail would admit she had kicked the trunk when she could not close the latch. Eleanor had been standing on the trunk at the time, helping her sister compress her clothing enough to squeeze in one more dress, more than willing to postpone her own packing and delay their return home.

She raced down the stairs to the front door and darted outside, picking up speed as she ran down the length of the porch. She scrambled over the railing and leapt the short distance to the lawn. The grass was damp on her stocking feet; it must have rained that morning. At the summer house, the morning had dawned clear and breezy, with no hint of autumn.

Eleanor felt a pang that had nothing to do with her bad heart. She missed the summer house already, and it was only their first day back in the city. Mother permitted things in summer she allowed at no other time—dancing, brief games of badminton or croquet, long strolls outdoors. The previous three months would have been perfect if Eleanor had been allowed to learn to ride horseback. Abigail had learned when she was two years younger than Eleanor was now, and Eleanor had hoped and prayed that this would be the year Mother and Father would relent. Every Friday evening when Father joined them at the summer house, Miss Langley had tried to persuade him, but he returned to the city each Sunday without overruling Mother's decision.

A cramp pinched her side. Eleanor dropped into a walk, gasping for air, sweat trickling down her back. Her stockings itched; her long-sleeved sailor dress felt as if it had been woven from lead. Mother dressed her daughters by the calendar, not the weather—"Or common sense," Miss Langley had murmured as she tied the navy blue bow at the small of Eleanor's back— and September meant wool. Her short sprint had left her faint; she blamed the sultry air and her heavy, uncomfortable clothing. She refused to blame her heart.

Everyone knew Eleanor had a bad heart. They called her delicate and fragile and, when they thought she wasn't listening, spoke of her uncertain future in hushed, tragic voices. Eleanor did not remember the rheumatic fever she had suffered as a baby and did not understand how her heart differed from any other. It seemed to beat steadily enough, even when she woke up in the night fighting for breath. If it pounded too fiercely when she ran, it was only because she was unaccustomed to exerting herself. Sometimes she placed her head on Miss Langley's chest and listened, wondering how her own flawed heart would compare to her nanny's. Her imagination superimposed the wheezing of steam pipes and the clanging of gears.

It was Miss Langley's responsibility to make sure Eleanor did not run, or climb stairs too quickly, or overexcite herself, or take a fright. Miss Langley was English, and before coming to America to raise the Lockwood children, she had traveled to France, Spain, Italy, and the Holy Land. Eleanor thought New York must seem desperately dull after such exotic locals, but Miss Langley said every land had its beauties. If Eleanor learned to find and appreciate them, she would be happy wherever life took her.

Eleanor agreed with her in principle, but everyone knew she would never be strong enough to go anywhere, except to the summer house for three months every year. It was a fact, just as her bad heart was a fact.

If Miss Langley had not been occupied unpacking her own belongings, Eleanor could not have slipped away. She regretted deceiving her nanny, since Miss Langley was her only ally in a household that expected her to collapse at any moment. If not for her, Eleanor's life would have been even more limited, since Mother had not even wanted her to attend school. Mother had feared exposing Eleanor to the elements and the jostling of her more robust classmates, even when Miss Langley reminded her that Eleanor's fellow pupils would be from the same respectable families as the young ladies in Abigail's class, well-bred girls unlikely to jostle anyone. When Mother would not budge, Miss Langley ignored the sanctity of Father's study and emerged twenty minutes later with his promise that

Eleanor would be permitted to attend school. Eleanor doubted Mother ever learned about that clandestine visit; if she had known Miss Langley had persuaded Father, Mother would have yanked Eleanor from school just to spite her.

The cramp in Eleanor's side eased as she walked. She had fled the house not caring where she went as long as it was away from Mother and Abigail, and now she did not know where to go. They had chattered about the upcoming social season all the way home from the summer house, and Eleanor couldn't endure another word. She was not jealous, not exactly, but she was tired of pretending to be happy for her sister.

She saw the gardener and quickly veered away before he spotted her. Ahead, the stable seemed deserted; by now the horses would have been curried, watered, and fed, and the stable hands would have left for their dinner. No one would think to look for her there, since she could not ride and was not even allowed to touch the horses' glossy coats. Only when no one else could see did Miss Langley let her brush Wildrose, the bay mare Father had given her for Christmas. Mother had called the gift an extravagance unbefitting Miss Langley's position, but her friend Mrs. Newcombe had said Mother could not get rid of the horse without raising uncomfortable questions.

Eleanor slipped inside the stable, took two apples from the barrel near the door, and tucked one into her pocket. "Hello, Wildrose," she called softly, polishing the second apple on her sleeve. She heard an answering whinny from a nearby stall—but no stern questions from a lingering stable hand, no alarmed shouts for her mother. Emboldened, Eleanor approached the mare, who poked her head over the stall door, sniffing the air. Eleanor held out the apple, and when Wildrose bent her neck to take a bite, Eleanor stroked the horse's mane. "I'm sorry we had to come back to the city. You and I like the summer house better, don't we?"

Wildrose snorted, and Eleanor blinked to fight off tears. She would not cry. She might be fragile, as everyone said, but she wasn't a baby, crying over rumors. "Father would never sell the summer house," she said, feeding Wildrose the rest of the apple. "We'll go back every year until we're old, old ladies. You'll see."

Wildrose whickered as if she agreed—and suddenly Eleanor felt a prickling on the back of her neck. She glanced over her shoulder to find Jupiter watching her.

She quickly looked away, then slowly turned again to find the stallion's deep, black eyes still upon her. No one but Father rode Jupiter, and only the most trusted stable hand was allowed to groom him. "That's what the Lord can create when He's had a good night's sleep," Father had proclaimed last spring as he admired his latest purchase. Only Eleanor saw the disapproving frown Mother gave him. She disliked blasphemy.

Father said Jupiter had gained a taste for blood in the Spanish–American War and would rather trample a little child beneath his hooves than take a sugar cube from Eleanor's palm. She fingered the apple in her pocket—and jumped when Jupiter tossed his head and whinnied. She caught her breath and took one soft step toward him. She drew closer, then stretched out her hand and held the apple beneath Jupiter's muzzle.

He lowered his head, his nostrils flaring, his breath hot on her skin. Then he took the apple from her hand and backed away, disappearing into his stall.

Delighted, Eleanor lifted the latch to the stall door to follow—and then felt herself yanked back so hard she nearly fell to the ground. "What are you doing?" cried Miss Langley. She quickly closed the stall and snapped the latch shut. "You know you're not allowed near your father's horse. You could have been killed."

"I only wanted to feed him," said Eleanor, shaken. "He kept looking at me, and I felt sorry for him, since none of us ever play with him—"

"Jupiter does not play, not with you children or anyone else."

"Please don't tell," begged Eleanor. "I won't do it again. I know I should stay away from the horses. I'm delicate."

"Jupiter is a proud creature, and very strong. He is not safe for children. I would have given Abigail the same advice though she is four years older."

"You wouldn't have needed to. Abigail's afraid of him."

"Don't be saucy." But Miss Langley almost smiled as she said it, and she brushed a few stray pieces of straw from Eleanor's dress. "Your father is a formidable man. Don't cross him until you're old enough to accept the consequences."

It had never occurred to Eleanor that anyone might intentionally cross Father. "How old is that?"

"I suppose you'll know, if the occasion ever arises."

Miss Langley took Eleanor by the hand and led her outside.

As they returned to the house, Eleanor looked up at Miss Langley and asked, "Do you really think Father will sell the summer house?"

"I know he does not want to." Miss Langley absently touched her straight, blond hair, as always, pulled back into a neat bun at the nape of her neck. "However, it would be more frugal to maintain only one household."

Eleanor had hoped for something more encouraging, but Miss Langley never lied, and Eleanor knew her father was concerned about debt. She had overheard him say that the family business had never completely recovered from the Panic six years earlier. It would surely not survive another unless he took on a partner.

"If he has to sell a house, I wish he'd sell this one," said Eleanor.

"You might find the summer house rather cold in winter."

"Mother would bundle me in so much wool I'd never notice the cold," said Eleanor, glum, then stopped short at the sight of her mother, holding up her skirts with one hand and approaching them at a near run.

"Miss Langley," Mother gasped. "What on earth are you doing?"

Abruptly, Miss Langley released Eleanor's hand. "Walking with Eleanor."

"I can see that." Mother knelt before Eleanor, held her daughter's face in her hands, and peered into her eyes. "Why would you bring her outside after such a hard day of travel, and without a word to anyone? My goodness, where are her shoes? Have you given no thought to this poor child's health?"

Miss Langley drew herself up. "Mrs. Lockwood, if I may, moderate exercise has remarkable curative effects—"

"Curative? Look at her. Her face is flushed. She looks positively ill."

"She does now. She did not before you arrived."

"Your impertinence might pass for the voice of experience if you had children of your own." Mother took Eleanor's hand. "Use better judgment in the future or you shall convince Mr. Lockwood that our trust in you has been misplaced."

Mother led her daughter away without giving Miss Langley a chance to reply. When they reached the house, Mother told Eleanor to go to her room, finish unpacking, and rest until supper.

Eleanor did as she was told, listening through the closed door for Miss Langley. She had to pass Eleanor's room to get to her own, the smallest bedroom on the second floor and the farthest from the stairs. Although only a wall separated her room from Eleanor's, Miss Langley moved about so soundlessly that Eleanor rarely heard her. Miss Langley must have been able to hear Eleanor, though, for if Eleanor was ill or had bad dreams, Miss Langley was at her side almost before Eleanor cried out. Still, it sometimes seemed as if the nanny simply disappeared once she closed her door on the rest of the house.

Eleanor had been invited into Miss Langley's room only a handful of times. The furnishings appeared neat but not fussy like Mother's parlor. A few framed portraits, which Miss Langley had identified as her parents and a younger brother, sat on a bureau; leafy green plants and violets thrived in pots on both windowsills. Displayed to their best advantage were two embroidered pillows on the divan, a quilt draped artfully over an armchair, and a patchwork comforter spread over the bed. The room was very like Miss Langley herself: no-nonsense yet graceful and elegant.

Eleanor waited and listened, but Miss Langley did not come. Heavy-hearted, she put away the last of her dresses and climbed onto the bed, wishing she had not run off. She lay on her back and studied the patterns the fading daylight made on the ceiling, wondering if she should risk upsetting Mother a second time in the same day by leaving her room to find Miss Langley.

She must have drifted off to sleep, because suddenly Abigail was at her side, her long blond curls swept back from her face by a broad pink ribbon. "Why is Mother angry?" asked Abigail. "What did you do?"

Eleanor wasn't sure if it was more wrong to lie to her sister or to expose Miss Langley's deception, so she said, "Nothing."

"You must have done something, because I know I didn't."

Eleanor sat up and made room for her sister on the bed. "I went outside without asking Mother."

"Is that all? You must have done something else to make her this mad. Come on, tell me the truth."

Eleanor shrugged. Mother didn't know about the horses, so that didn't count.

"You should have just finished unpacking, as Mother told us to." Abigail climbed onto the bed and sat cross-legged beside her sister. "If you would just obey her, you wouldn't get in trouble so often."

"I can't help it. I forget."

"You don't forget. You just don't think you'll get caught." Abigail smiled, showing her dimple. "Maybe I should go downstairs and break some dishes or kick Harriet in the shin. If Mother's mad at me, she might forget what you did."

Eleanor was tempted, especially by the image of Mother's maid howling and clutching her leg, but she shook her head. "It wouldn't work."

"I suppose not."

"I wish we had stayed at the summer house."

"Not me. I hate that place. The bugs, the wind messing my hair—and I hate seeing Father only on weekends."

They saw him so little on weekdays that Eleanor saw no difference between the summer house and home in that respect, but she knew better than to seem to criticize Father in front of Abigail. Eleanor hesitated to say anything negative about him at all, as if her very words would make him appear.

"I bet the walk was your idea," said Abigail airily. "Miss Langley wouldn't dare defy Mother except for you. You have her wrapped around your little finger. She treats you much nicer than she treated me when I was your age."

"She does not."

"It's true. She lets you do exactly as you please because you're the baby and you're . . ."

"What?" Eleanor fixed a piercing gaze on her sister. "Go on, say it. I'm going to die. Right? That's what you were about to say."

"You're not going to die."

"You and Miss Langley are the only ones who think so." But Eleanor knew Abigail didn't really mean it.

Timidly, Abigail said, "You won't tell Mother I told you?"

Eleanor sighed and sat up. "No."

"If it makes you feel any better, I think Mother's more angry with Miss Langley than you."

That was nothing new; Mother became displeased with Miss Langley over the littlest things, while Harriet could oversleep or lose Mother's best gloves and Mother would forgive her. Once Eleanor overheard the cook say she thought it a wonder that Miss Langley had not resigned long ago, but Miss Langley did not seem to mind Mother's tempers as much as Eleanor did.

Eleanor remembered her warning and asked, "Do you think Mother will send Miss Langley away?"

Abigail shrugged. "She might. You're too old for a nanny, anyway."

"Maybe they want her to stay in the family in case they have another baby."

Abigail giggled. "I don't think that's very likely."

"Why not?"

"If you can't figure it out, you're not old enough to know." Then a puzzled frown replaced her grin. "I wonder why Mother said Miss Langley had no children of her own."

"Because she doesn't."

"That's not what I heard."

"What?"

"Promise you won't say anything."

"I promise."

"I heard Mother tell Mrs. Newcombe that Miss Langley had a baby. It was ages ago, when she was just a few years older than I am."

"But she's not married."

"That's why she had to leave England. Mrs. Newcombe said that Mother was a model of Christian charity but that she herself would not trust her menfolk with a fallen woman in the house, however humbled and redemptive the woman might be."

Eleanor did not want to believe it, but Abigail had mimicked the haughty Mrs. Newcombe perfectly. "If that's true, where's the baby?"

"It died when it was only a few hours old." Abigail regarded her thoughtfully. "Maybe that's why Miss Langley is so fond of you. Maybe you remind her of her baby, because you're so frail."

"She would have told me." Miss Langley did not lie, but as far as Eleanor could recall, Miss Langley had never explicitly denied having children. Eleanor had never thought to ask. "Why didn't she tell me?"

"You're just a little girl, and she can't tell anyone. Can you imagine what a scandal it would be if everyone knew the character of the woman who practically raised us? No one would ever want to marry me then." Abigail flung herself back against the pillows. "Sometimes I think you're the lucky one. You don't have to worry about learning to dance and sing and act like a lady. You don't have to worry about your beauty or your reputation or marrying into the best family. You never have to leave home or Father, not ever. Sometimes I think it would be so much easier if I could die young, too."

Eleanor nodded, but her mind was far away, imagining Miss Langley cradling the cooling body of a brown-haired infant daughter. The woman Eleanor imagined did not cry. She had never seen Miss Langley cry.

☙

When Mother's maid, Harriet, came upstairs to tell them to dress for supper, Abigail bounded off to her own room. Eleanor dressed more slowly, wondering at Abigail's enthusiasm. Father expected children to be silent at the supper table and absent shortly thereafter. He might give Abigail an indulgent smile and a pat on the head when she asked to be excused, but nothing more than that. Only when he was in a particularly leisurely mood would he linger at the dinner table to enjoy his cigar and brandy in their company instead of retiring to his study. On those occasions he would reminisce about his childhood or tell them stories about the company.

Father's two passions were his business and his horses. Mother had once remarked that she was fortunate her husband did not decide to combine his two passions, or she might find herself married to a groom or a jockey, or worse yet, a gambler. Father had chuckled and said, "I am content to befriend grooms and jockeys, and yes, even gamblers, since I cannot become one myself."

Mother had sniffed. She disdained "horse people," as she called them, and her mouth set in a hard line whenever her husband announced one would be their guest. "I cannot bear to entertain another one of his pets," she had complained to Mrs. Newcombe when Father invited Mr. Bergstrom to spend a weekend at their home. The horse farmer had brought his son with him, a boy named Fred, only two years older than Eleanor, and he had stayed inside to play with Eleanor when Mother insisted it was too cold for her to go out. Eleanor never had friends visit, and she was grateful to Fred, for she knew how much he had wanted to see Father's horses.

Mrs. Newcombe had consoled Mother with reassurances that no one would think less of her for these strange guests; the Bergstroms had traveled all the way from Pennsylvania, after all, and they must stay somewhere, and besides, everyone knew the invitation had been another one of Father's whims. "No man can completely forget where he came from," she said, patting Mother's hand.

Mother's mouth turned sour, and she declared that it was beneath the Lockwood family to have people who were little better than common laborers sit around the same table where the Astors, the Rockefellers, the Carnegies, and William McKinley himself had dined. It was bad enough that Miss Langley dined with the family rather than in the kitchen with the rest of the help, but the children were fond of her and Father appreciated her international perspective on politics, which he said was remarkably keen, for a woman.

"I am sure it is her international perspective he appreciates," said Mrs. Newcombe dryly, then she and Mother remembered Eleanor, reading in a nearby armchair, and changed the subject.

Eleanor had heard Father recount his self-made success so often that she thought she could have repeated the tale from memory, but she never tired of hearing it. Even before marrying Mother he had contrived to start his own business, a respected department store specializing in women's fashions. When Grandfather died, Father invested Mother's inheritance into buying out several of his smaller competitors and opening a dazzling, modern Lockwood's on Fifth Avenue. True, the Panic had hit them hard, but they would come back, Father said, and had been saying for as long as Eleanor could remember.

She wished she could make her own way as Father had done, but when she told her sister so, Abigail tossed her head and said, "Business isn't for women. Did you ever hear Mother talk about sales or fuss over an inventory? All we have to worry about is marrying a prosperous man and hoping that he is also handsome and kindly. Have you seen Father's friends? They're odious, except Mr. Drury, and Father says he's a fool."

For once, Eleanor pitied her sister. "They're old, too."

"I won't marry one of the old ones," snapped Abigail. "Honestly, Eleanor. Maybe you can't help being jealous, but you don't have to be spiteful."

Father would not have been pleased to hear his eldest daughter speak favorably of Mr. Drury, his chief competitor and bitter enemy. Mr. Drury had been Father's rival for more than twenty years, ever since Mr. Drury had rejected Father's offer to purchase his company. Even worse, Mr. Drury had responded by snapping up several smaller stores Father wanted for himself. Three times Mr. Drury outbid Father and convinced the seller to sign a contract before Father could make a counteroffer. If Father did not exactly blame Mr. Drury for his current financial problems, he did see him as an obstacle to getting clear of them.

As much as Father loved horses and horse people, Eleanor knew he would never leave his store and become a groom or jockey. He had spoken too often of his struggles to build his company, and he surely loved his work, too, because he often left for the office before the children rose for breakfast and did not return home until supper, after which he retreated to his study until long after Eleanor had been sent to bed. Sometimes he worked so late he fell asleep there. Eleanor knew this because several times she had passed his door at midmorning to find the maids gathering up rumpled sheets from the leather sofa.

On their first night home from the summer house, no guests, "horse people" or otherwise, would join them for supper. When Miss Langley at last rapped on her door, Eleanor accompanied her to the dining room and seated herself only moments before Father entered. "Confounded radicals," he grumbled as he strode into the room. He paused to kiss Mother's cheek before taking his seat at the head of the table. "How was your trip home?"

Mother beckoned for the meal to be served. "We are not confounded radicals, but our trip was uneventful, thank you."

"I was not addressing you, and you're quite right to point out my rudeness. Darling, girls, Miss Langley, welcome home."

"It's good to be back, Daddy," said Abigail.

"I do hope you'll cheer up before eight," remarked Mother. "We have a party at the Newcombes' this evening."

"Good. I need to talk to Hammond about these blasted union organizers."

Mother's smile tightened. "Why can't a party be merely a party? Must you conduct business everywhere?"

"If you want me to keep a roof over these children's heads, I must."

"Are the union organizers the confounded radicals you spoke of?" Miss Langley broke in.

Father dabbed at his mouth with his napkin and held up his other hand to forestall her lecture. "Let's not spoil your first night home with another argument. The men on my loading docks aren't paid any worse than those at my competitors."

"Yes, but they aren't paid any better, either. Your workers built your business. They created your wealth, and they're entitled to share in it."

Mother's laugh tinkled. "My husband is better qualified than you to decide what his workers should earn."

"They do share in it," said Father to Miss Langley. "You seem to think their share should be as great as mine."

"Or greater," said Mother.

"I founded this company. I managed fine without unions, and so shall my successor." He smiled at Abigail. "Whoever the lucky fellow to marry my beauty shall be."

Miss Langley asked, "What will you do if the workers strike?"

"They wouldn't dare," declared Mother, but when Father said nothing, she added, "Surely they aren't talking of a strike."

"Merely rumors," said Father.

"If your informants have heard talk of a strike," said Miss Langley, "it's likely the planning is well under way."

"I won't cave in to threats. First they'll want higher wages, then fewer hours, and eventually they'll demand enough to drive the company into bankruptcy."

"Not if they have a share in the company's good fortune. If their success is tied to yours, not through obligation and fear but ambition and loyalty, your employees will work harder and better than your competitors'. You will attract the best workers, and they will be more productive because they have a stake in the outcome of their labors. The evils of capitalism are great, but not insurmountable. Is it more important that you make enormous profits, or that you treat your workers like human beings?"

Mother's voice was ice. "You have been told repeatedly not to air your radical ideas in front of the children."

"I have to stand firm," said Father to Miss Langley. "I pay fair and honest wages. I don't hire children. I provide for any worker who is injured in the service of my company and I don't fire them if they fall ill. You see how they thank me—they take those agitators' handbills and listen to their speeches. The business owners of my acquaintance already accuse me of weakness on these facts alone. I will not give them more reason."

"If you lead, others will follow," said Miss Langley. "We are moving into a new century. You can either ride the crest of the wave or be swept away by it."

"Stuff and nonsense," said Mother. "Darling, what would Mr. Corville think if he heard you were considering allowing a union to organize at Lockwood's?"

"I am not considering it."

Miss Langley sighed so softly that Eleanor doubted anyone else noticed. She did not understand why Miss Langley provoked Father so, and why he permitted it.

"Finish your supper, girls," said Mother.

Eleanor picked up her fork, her appetite spoiled. She wished they had never left the summer house.

Later that evening, Eleanor and Abigail watched from their hiding place on the upstairs balcony as Father escorted Mother, clad in a new Lock-wood's gown and wrap, outside to the waiting carriage. "If all you do is talk business, we're coming home early," they heard Mother say before the door closed behind them.

"If she doesn't want to go, I will," Abigail said. "Father is a fine dancer. I wouldn't care if he conducted business as long as he danced with me now and then."

Eleanor thought that if Mother refused to go, Father would be wiser to take Miss Langley in her place. Miss Langley knew how to talk with important people, and Abigail giggled too much. Mother loved society gatherings as much as Father loved horses, however, so Eleanor couldn't imagine Father could conduct so much business that Mother would refuse to go.

"You'll be allowed to go when you're sixteen," she told her sister.

"That's three years away. I want to go now. Why should I take dancing lessons if I'm only to stay home?"

"To improve yourself?" suggested Eleanor, wearily. It was a response Miss Langley often used with her. At the moment, it seemed especially good advice, and Abigail the least likely person to accept it.

"You're just envious because you want to go, too, and you know Father would choose me instead." Abruptly, Abigail rose. "I never get to go anywhere. I might as well be a nanny like Miss Langley or an invalid like you."

Watching her storm off to her room, Eleanor was struck by a sudden thought: If she lived, and if she were not an invalid, she could become a nanny. Perhaps Miss Langley had been preparing Eleanor for that all along. Eleanor could think of no better explanation for her vigilance in seeing that Eleanor received an education. At last she understood how her defiance of Father would one day come about: He would surely object if one of his children, even his strange youngest daughter, went into service in another household. He would rather Eleanor remain an invalid forever.

❧

Although Abigail insisted she was too old for a nanny, she did not mind Miss Langley's company when the alternative was another etiquette lesson from Mother. As the week between their return to the city and the first day of school passed, Abigail joined them more often in the nursery, and Eleanor was surprised by how quickly she agreed to read aloud to them while she and Miss Langley sewed.

Among the accomplishments Miss Langley had passed on to the Lockwood daughters was needlework. Abigail had no patience for it and her first project, an embroidered sampler, was also her last. When Miss Langley had suggested she attempt a small embroidered pillow next, Abigail had declared that when she married she would hire a woman to do her sewing, as Mother did. Therefore, she had no need to learn any new stitches and no desire to practice those she already knew. Miss Langley merely smiled and said, "Very well. You may practice piano instead."

Abigail disliked playing the piano only slightly less than sewing; the saving grace of music was that people watched and admired her as she performed. Still, she had no choice but to pick up a needle or turn on the metronome, so she left without another word, and before long the sounds of scales and arpeggios came faintly up the stairs to the nursery.

It was Eleanor who had completed an embroidered pillow for Abigail's hope chest, and then a second, and then she started a patchwork quilt for her doll. Mother frowned when she discovered Eleanor piecing together squares of flowered calico and asked Miss Langley if the nanny might not find a better use for Eleanor's time.

"Sewing requires less physical exertion than playing the piano, which Eleanor has shown us she can endure," said Miss Langley. "A small doll's quilt will consume little of her time. Quilting will teach her patience and thrift, and to see a task through to its end."

Mother relented with the condition that in the future Miss Langley limit her lessons to embroidery and the finer needlecrafts. Patchwork was vulgar, the province of the lower classes, who pieced quilts from necessity. For all her frailties, Eleanor was a well-bred young woman. It would not do to have her practice the skills of a common housemaid.

"I suppose a well-bred young woman should never be useful if she can be merely decorative," said Miss Langley after Mother left, but Eleanor wasn't sure if her nanny mocked Mother's opinion of patchwork or her own indulgence in the craft. Heedless of Mother's scorn, Miss Langley enjoyed relaxing in the evening with a needle in her hand and a basket of fabric scraps on the floor beside her chair, piecing quilt blocks as Eleanor read aloud. Miss Langley completed several quilts a year and donated them to a foundling hospital. In a brave moment, Eleanor had told Mother that by making patchwork quilts from scraps, Miss Langley both prevented wastefulness and performed acts of charity, but although Mother admired those traits at other times and in other people, they did not elevate quilting in her esteem.

After Eleanor sewed the last stitch on the binding of her doll's quilt, Miss Langley obeyed Mother's orders and taught Eleanor new embroidery stitches. Eleanor balked and pretended to be unable to learn, but she could not bear to be dishonest with Miss Langley, especially when it made her look clumsy and stupid. She had so longed to make a patchwork quilt to brighten her own room. The patterns with their charming names—Royal Cross, Storm at Sea, Dutch Rose—evoked romantic times and far-off places, and Eleanor longed to learn them all.

She could not agree, either, that patchwork was vulgar, for Abigail had seen a quilt in Mrs. Newcombe's parlor, and Mrs. Newcombe never permitted anything in her home that did not adhere to the most current trends in fashion and good taste. Abigail could not describe the quilt very well, but even the few details she remembered were enough to convince Eleanor it must be a Crazy Quilt, the same type of quilt Miss Langley kept on her armchair. The Crazy Quilt was the one sign of chaos in Miss Langley's ordered world, the one nod to ornamentation for the sheer pleasure of it in a room dedicated to usefulness and practicality. When Eleanor was ill or downcast, Miss Langley would let her curl up beneath the quilt in the window seat in the conservatory, warmed by the privilege rather than the quilt itself, which, in the style of Crazy Quilts, was pieced of more delicate fabrics than traditional quilts and had no inner layer of batting.

Eleanor admired the wild and haphazard mosaic of fabric, so carefree, reckless, and robust. In contrast to the undisciplined pattern were the luxurious fabrics and formal colors—silks, velvets, brocades, and taffetas in black, burgundy, navy blue, and brown. Embroidered borders, initials, and figures embellished the few solid cotton or wool pieces. Eleanor's favorite was the spiderweb in one of the corners. Miss Langley had told her that an embroidered spiderweb was supposed to bring the quilt's owner good fortune, but she had included the design in her quilt because the story amused her, not because she believed the superstition.

Another embroidered outline had often caught Eleanor's eye: two tiny footprints, outlined in white. Eleanor had assumed the little feet had sprung from Miss Langley's imagination, like the spiderweb, but Abigail's tale of Miss Langley's shocking secret made her wonder. She longed to ask Miss Langley whose tiny footprints had been immortalized on the black velveteen, but she feared Miss Langley would deny their existence and forbid Eleanor to see the quilt ever again.

Fortunately, Miss Langley apparently did not take Mother's prohibition against quilting lessons to mean that Eleanor was not allowed to watch her quilt, nor did she refuse to answer Eleanor's questions. But that was in their companionable solitude in the summer house. With Abigail present, Eleanor did not dare show too much interest in her nanny's quilts. Instead, as Abigail read to them from Dickens or one of the Miss Brontës, Eleanor worked on a needlepoint sampler and counted the hours until school began.

❦

On the last Wednesday of the summer recess, Mother and Abigail attended a luncheon at Mrs. Corville's. As soon as Father left for work, Mother announced that Eleanor must play in the nursery by herself while Miss Langley helped Abigail prepare. Stung that she should be sent away like a child, Eleanor hovered in the background while Miss Langley and Harriet bathed Abigail, brushed her golden curls until they shone, and dressed her in a light blue dress with white lace at the collar and matching gloves.

As Mother supervised and fussed, Eleanor learned why this particular occasion was so important: the Corvilles had a fifteen-year-old son. Mr. Corville owned a store a few blocks from Father's, and while it was smaller than his, it was so prosperous that Mr. Corville had opened branches in Boston and New Rochelle. Father had once said that he could never buy out Mr. Corville, but he would not object to becoming the man's partner. Unfortunately, there were rumors Mr. Drury had the same idea, and he also had a daughter Abigail's age, though not as pretty.

"If Abigail marries Mr. Corville's son, Mr. Corville couldn't become Mr. Drury's partner instead of Father's," said Eleanor to Miss Langley after Mother and Abigail hurried out the door.

"He could, but he wouldn't."

Eleanor felt a surge of sympathy for her sister. Abigail did not want to leave home, but she would obey to make Father happy. "I hope she likes Edwin Corville," said Eleanor, dubious. That might not influence the decision, but it would make the inevitable easier to bear.

Miss Langley sighed. "So do I, for her sake."

They went inside to the nursery, where Miss Langley said, "Since our presence is not required at their silly luncheon, how would you like to spend the rest of the morning?"

Eleanor almost asked for a trip into the city, but something held back the words. Something in Miss Langley's expression told her that the offer was meant to compensate for more than the missed luncheon. She looked Miss Langley straight in the eye, steeled herself, and said, "I want to ride Wildrose."

Miss Langley's smile faded.

"Or Princess," said Eleanor quickly. "Abigail will never know. You could ride Wildrose and we could ride together."

"Eleanor—"

"Don't say no. I know I'm not allowed, but I'm not allowed to do anything. Please, Miss Langley. I'll be careful. Don't say it's too dangerous, because if it's not too dangerous for Abigail—"

"Eleanor." Miss Langley's voice was quiet but firm. "You cannot ride Wildrose or any of the family's horses. We could not go riding without at least a half-dozen people witnessing it. We cannot count on them to keep silent."

Eleanor knew Miss Langley was right. She took a deep breath, nodded, and tried to think of something else.

"I know," said Miss Langley. "You've admired my Crazy Quilt for years. I'll teach you to make your own."

"I don't want to make a Crazy Quilt," said Eleanor. Not today, not when the forbidden lessons had been offered only because what she truly wanted was impossible. "Abigail was younger than I am when she rode for the first time. I'm tired of being treated like I'm sick when I'm not. I don't have a weak heart. I don't."

"I know you don't," Miss Langley said. "You have the strongest heart of anyone I know."

She extended a hand, and when Eleanor took it, Miss Langley pulled her onto her lap. Eleanor clung to her and fought off tears. She would not cry and prove that everyone was right about her, that she was fragile and a baby.

Miss Langley stroked her hair and kissed the top of her head. "Eleanor, darling, don't judge your parents too harshly. They're doing the best they know how."

Eleanor made a scoffing noise and scrubbed her face with the back of her hand.

"Good heavens, Eleanor, please use a handkerchief." She handed Eleanor her own. "From the time you were a baby, your parents were told you would surely die. Try to imagine what that must have been like for them. Some families might have responded by spoiling you, by giving you your heart's desire every day of your life to make up for all the days you would not have. Other families distance themselves from their child so that when that terrible day comes they will be able to bear it. It wounds them a little every day to do so, but they tell themselves that they can survive these wounds. They think only of the size and not their number."

Eleanor sat silently, absorbing her words, but a merciless voice whispered that Miss Langley was only trying to be kind. The simple truth was that her parents didn't love her. How could they, when her poor health made her such a disappointment?

Miss Langley was watching her with such compassion that Eleanor couldn't bring herself to say what she really felt. Instead she said, "I wish my parents had been the kind who gave their child her heart's desire."

"I for one am glad they are not. You would have been insufferable."

Eleanor smiled, and when Miss Langley offered the quilting lesson a second time, she accepted.

To avoid Harriet's prying eyes, they carried Miss Langley's sewing basket outside and spread a blanket in the shade of the apple trees on the far side of the garden. Eleanor hugged her knees to her chest as Miss Langley unpacked needles and thread, her favorite pair of shears, and several small bundles of muslin, velvet, satin, and silk, which Eleanor recognized as scraps Mother's dressmaker had discarded.

Miss Langley had also brought along two diamond-shaped "blocks" for a new Crazy Quilt she had begun. "Most Crazy Quilts use squares as the base unit shape," she said, "but I chose diamonds."

"Then I'll use diamonds, too."

With Miss Langley's guidance, Eleanor carefully cut a diamond foundation and appliquéd a velvet scrap to the center. She then selected a triangular piece of dark green silk and held it up to the foundation, trying it in one position and then another, until she liked the angles and shapes it created. She stitched it in place, sewing over one edge of the velvet in the center. In this fashion she added more fabric scraps, working from the center outward, varying the angles and sizes of the added pieces to create the characteristic random appearance. When the entire surface of the foundation was covered, she trimmed off the pieces that extended past the edges until she had a Crazy Quilt diamond like Miss Langley's, if not quite so perfectly made.

"Shall I begin another?" asked Eleanor, reaching for the muslin to cut a new foundation.

Miss Langley shook her head. "You haven't finished this one yet. Has it been so long since you've seen my quilt that you've forgotten about the embroidery?"

"But I already know how to embroider. I want to learn more quilting."

"You've embroidered on solid fabric," said Miss Langley. "Embroidering a Crazy Quilt is quite another matter. Your stitches will follow the edges of the patches, so you will have to sew through seams, which you have never tried. You also need to learn how to choose the perfect stitch for each piece. A skilled quilter uses a variety of stitches to achieve the desired effect."

"What's the desired effect?"

"That's entirely up to you. Sometimes your embroidery will frame the fabric piece, defining it, highlighting it, but other times the fabric recedes to the background and becomes a canvas for the embroidery."

"Such as when you embroider a picture?" asked Eleanor. "Like the spiderweb in your quilt—or the little baby footprints?"

"Precisely." Miss Langley held out her hand for the muslin.

Eleanor had watched Miss Langley's face carefully, but not a flicker of emotion altered her expression at the mention of the baby footprints. If Eleanor had seen the slightest hint of pain at the reminder of a secret tragedy, she could have asked Miss Langley what troubled her, but Miss Langley gave away nothing.

Reluctantly, Eleanor handed her the muslin. "Why couldn't we do the embroidery later, all at once, after the diamonds are sewn together?"

"We could, and I suppose some quilters probably do. As for me, I find it easier to embroider something small enough to hold in one hand."

Miss Langley traded Eleanor's sewing sharp for a longer, sturdier embroidery needle. Eleanor took it, but couldn't resist adding, "We could embroider this right in front of Mother and she wouldn't even get mad."

"If I didn't know better, I might think you only want to quilt in order to anger her. Or perhaps you're simply pouting. Very well. If embroidery has become too routine for you, I'll teach you a few new stitches."

She did teach Eleanor new stitches—the Portuguese stem stitch, the Vandyke stitch, and the Maidenhair. They were more difficult than any she had previously mastered, and attempting them required all her concentration.

The morning passed. Eleanor would have gladly spent the whole day sewing in the shade of the apple trees with Miss Langley, but as noon approached, her nanny began to glance more frequently toward the house. Then she announced that the lesson was over.

"But Mother isn't home yet."

"Not yet." Miss Langley began packing up her sewing basket. "But she will be soon, and I would like your Crazy Quilt block safely out of sight before then. And you do recall it is Wednesday?"

Eleanor's heart sank. She had forgotten it was Miss Langley's afternoon off. "Do you have to go?"

"I'm afraid so." Miss Langley rose and held out her hand. "Harriet will look after you until your mother and sister return."

Harriet. Eleanor pretended not to see Miss Langley's hand and climbed to her feet without any help. Without a word, she picked up her things and headed for the house.

Miss Langley fell in step beside her. "Now, Eleanor, don't sulk. I'll be back in time to tuck you in."

Eleanor did not care. Harriet would scold Eleanor if she tried to read or play the piano and would probably have her polishing silver within minutes of Miss Langley's departure. Worse yet, Miss Langley surely knew that, but she was leaving anyway.

She stomped upstairs to the nursery and slammed the door, something she never would have dared to do if Mother were home. She sat in the window seat with a book on her lap, listlessly looking out the window. When she heard the heavy front door swing shut, she pressed her face against the window and saw Miss Langley striding toward the carriage house. She had changed into a brown dress and hat with a ribbon, and a well-worn satchel swung from one hand.

Eleanor jumped to her feet, then hurried downstairs and outside. She stole into the carriage house just as the driver finished hitching up the horses, chatting with Miss Langley as he worked. Her heart pounding, Eleanor held her breath and climbed onto the back of the carriage as she had seen the grocer's boy do. With a lurch, the carriage began to move.

Dizzy and fearful, Eleanor tore her eyes away from the ground passing beneath the carriage wheels and fixed them on the house, waiting for Harriet to burst through the front doors and run shouting after her. But the iron gates closed, and the carriage pulled onto the street. She pressed herself against the carriage, both to make herself smaller and less visible to others, but also out of fear that she would tumble from her insecure perch. The short drive to the train station had never seemed longer, but eventually the carriage came to a halt. Eleanor knew she should leap to the ground and hide before Miss Langley descended, but she could not move. She squeezed her eyes shut and took a deep, steadying breath. She would not be afraid. She would not.

The carriage door closed; Miss Langley's shoes sounded on the pavement. Eleanor heard the driver chirrup to the horses, and with a gasp, she jumped down from her seat a scant moment before the carriage drove away.

At once a crowd of passersby swept her up and carried her down the sidewalk. She managed to weave her way through the crowd to the station house, where she looked about frantically for Miss Langley. She was not waiting in the queue at the ticket window, nor was she seated in any of the chairs. Eleanor went outside to the platform, where a train waited. She did not know if this was Miss Langley's train, and it would do no good to ask about its destination, for she had no idea where her nanny went on her afternoons off. Even if she had known, she had no money for the fare.

"Miss Langley," she whispered, and then shouted, "Miss Langley! Miss Langley!"

She called out again and again, until suddenly a hand clamped down on her shoulder and whirled her about. "Eleanor." Miss Langley regarded her, incredulous. "How on earth—" She glanced at her watch and shook her head. "I cannot send you back alone, and there isn't time to take you back myself." She gave Eleanor a searching look. "I suppose if I had allowed you to ride Wildrose as you asked, you would not have been so determined to accompany me. Well, there's nothing to be done now but make the best of it. Stay close, and say nothing of this to your parents."

Eleanor shook her head. Of course she would tell them nothing; she fervently hoped they would never know she had left the nursery. She mumbled an apology as Miss Langley marched her back into the station and bought her a ticket. Miserable, Eleanor wondered what portion of a day's wages Miss Langley had spent on her charge's fare.

Miss Langley took her hand and led her aboard the train. "Sit," she instructed when she found two unoccupied seats across from each other.

Then she directed her gaze out the window as if she had forgotten Eleanor was there. Eleanor stared out the window as well, hoping to lose herself in the passing scenes of the city, but she couldn't bear the punishment of Miss Langley's silence.

"Where are we going?" she finally asked, less from curiosity than from the need to have Miss Langley acknowledge her.

"The garment district."

Eleanor nodded, although this told her nothing. She knew little of New York except for the streets right around her father's store.

They rode on in silence, and gradually Eleanor forgot her guilt in her anticipation of the outing. Where would Miss Langley take her? To meet her family? A beau? The former seemed unlikely, as the only relatives Miss Langley had ever mentioned were far away in England, but the latter was impossible. She could not picture her nanny linking her arm through a man's and laughing up at him as Mother did to Father when they were not fighting. Not even Abigail's tale about the baby could change her mind about that.

After a time, the train slowed and they disembarked. As Miss Langley led her from the platform to the street, Eleanor looked about, wide-eyed. This station seemed older than the one closer to home, older and dirtier. The street was even more so. Not one tree or bit of greenery interrupted the brick and stone and steel of the factories; the very air was heavy with bustle and noise. She slipped her hand into Miss Langley's and stayed close.

They walked for blocks. Miss Langley asked her if she needed to ride, but Eleanor shook her head, thinking of the money Miss Langley had already spent. The noises of the factories lessened, but did not completely fade away until Miss Langley turned down a narrow, littered alley and rapped upon a weather-beaten wooden door. On the other side, someone moved a black drape aside from a small, square window. Then the door swung open, and a stooped, gray-haired woman ushered them inside without a word.

"The others are upstairs," she told Miss Langley, sparing a curious glance for Eleanor.

Miss Langley noticed. "You can see the reason for my delay."

The older woman tilted her head at Eleanor. "Shall I keep her in the kitchen?"

"No. I think it will be all right."

The older woman clucked disapprovingly, but she led the way down a dark, musty hall and up a narrow staircase that creaked as they ascended. They stopped at a door through which Eleanor heard a murmur of voices. The older woman knocked twice before admitting Miss Langley. Eleanor followed on her heels, but stopped just inside the room as the older woman closed the door behind them.

The dozen women already there greeted Miss Langley by her Christian name and regarded Eleanor with surprise, wariness, or concern, depending, Eleanor guessed, upon their own temperaments. One ruddy-cheeked woman burst out laughing. Her hands were chapped and raw, her clothing coarse, but so were those of two other women present, and they sat among the well-dressed ladies as if they might actually be friends. Only two of the women did not seem to notice Eleanor's presence: a dark-haired woman in a fine blue silk dress who revealed her nervousness by tinkling her spoon in her teacup in a manner that would have earned the Lockwood girls a reprimand at home, and an elderly lady who sat by the stove in the corner smiling to herself.

Miss Langley apologized for her tardiness and removed her hat. "As you can see, Mary could not leave her little lamb at home today," she added as she took the nearest chair and gestured for Eleanor to sit on the footstool.

"Never mind," said one of the women, who was dressed so much like Miss Langley that Eleanor wondered if she were a nanny, too. "We've started without you."

A deeper voice added, "But we're a long way from finished."

Others chimed in as they told Miss Langley what she had missed. Their friends from upstate needed their help in organizing the demonstration at the capital, but while many of them were eager to assist, others insisted they were wasting their time with state governments and should instead concentrate on reform at the federal level. On the contrary, the others countered, success in one state would ease the way for others.

One debate swiftly flowed into another: Universal suffrage ought also to include coloreds and immigrants, with all impediments such as property ownership and literacy removed. No, they should fight for the rights of white women only unless they wanted to jeopardize the very structure of their society.

"Is that not precisely what we seek to do by seeking the vote for ourselves?" inquired Miss Langley, setting off another debate.

Eleanor followed the back-and-forth, fascinated. These women looked so ordinary but they talked like confounded radicals. Even Miss Langley. If Father could hear them, his eyes would bulge and the little blue vein at his temple would wriggle like a worm on hot pavement.

Then the woman in blue silk set aside her tea. "My husband has spoken to his colleague in Washington."

The voices hushed.

"A certain influential senator has promised his public and unwavering support if we compromise on our demands."

"What's he mean, exactly?" said a dark-haired woman in a thick, unfamiliar accent.

"He would limit suffrage to women who owned substantial property."

The caveat made laughter echo off the walls of the dingy room, and the ruddy-cheeked woman laughed loudest of all. "I'd like to see him tell that to the girls on my floor," she said, wiping a tear from an eye. "They'd drown him in their dye pots."

"We cannot abandon any of our sisters," said Miss Langley in her clear, precise tones. "A laundress may have as much reason as the wealthy woman who employs her. We cannot deny the workers their voice."

The ruddy-cheeked woman applauded but the woman in blue silk looked to the heavens and sighed. "Reason, but no education. Do we want the ignorant masses determining the fate of our nation?"

Miss Langley fixed her with a level gaze. "You sound very much like the men who argue that no woman should vote."

"You care more about your workers than the rights of women."

Voices rose in a cacophony that hushed at a quiet word from the elderly woman in the corner. "Women who own substantial property are so few in number that their votes would scatter like dandelion seeds on the wind." Her voice was low and musing. "No, it must be all women, including colored women, including those who cannot yet read and write or even speak English. Yes, they should learn, and we must see they are taught."

She sipped her tea, but not one of those listening would have dreamed of interrupting. "Our emancipation must be twofold. We must have the vote, but we will not be truly independent until we are independent economically as well as politically."

"Hear, hear," said Miss Langley quietly, as the others murmured their assent.

The elderly woman smiled fondly at her. "And to that end, you must continue your work."

Miss Langley nodded.

The elderly woman went on to say that she hoped they would attend the demonstration, and she would express their concerns to the others in her organization. Then she rose, bid them farewell, and departed, accompanied by one of the younger women in the group.

The meeting broke up after that; Miss Langley spoke quietly with a few of the others, then took Eleanor by the hand and led her back down the creaking staircase and outside. Eleanor pondered the strange gathering as they walked back to the train station, so absorbed in her thoughts that she forgot the cramp in her side and her labored breathing. She was sure she heard Miss Langley tell the ruddy-faced woman something about a union and something more about a strike.

As the station came into view, Miss Langley broke her silence. "You were a good girl, Eleanor." Then she laughed, quietly. "I imagine today was quite an education for you."

Eleanor nodded, but she didn't think she had learned very much because she had so many questions. She had understood enough, though, to realize Miss Langley would be discharged if Eleanor's parents discovered her activities.

"Miss Langley," she ventured as they boarded the train, "who was that woman, the one everyone listened to?"

Miss Langley did not reply until they had seated themselves in an unoccupied compartment. "We call her Miss Anthony. She is the leader of an important organization, and the rest of us were honored by her visit."

"When she said you must continue your work . . ." Eleanor hesitated. "She didn't mean being my nanny, did she?"

"No."

Eleanor waited for her to explain, but when she said nothing, Eleanor asked, "Are you a confounded radical?"

Miss Langley burst into laughter. "I suppose some people would call me that, yes."

Eleanor did not think that was such a terrible thing. Even Mother wanted to vote. Eleanor had heard her confess as much to Harriet, although she would never mention such a shocking thing to Father or Mrs. Newcombe. But she did not understand the rest of it.

She took a deep breath. "You're not the one trying to get a union at Father's store, are you?"

"Eleanor, listen to me." Miss Langley took her hands. "Unions are important and just. Only when all the workers speak with one voice can they hold any leverage against the owners. The influence of power and money are too great otherwise." She gave Eleanor a wistful smile. "But I am not organizing at your father's store. I would be recognized."

"Somewhere else, then."

"Yes, somewhere else."

Miss Langley settled back into her seat, and Eleanor rested her head in her lap. They rode in companionable silence until they reached the station nearest to home. The carriage waited for them outside, and the driver's eyes grew wide at the sight of Eleanor.

"There's a lot of trouble for you at home, miss," he said to Eleanor, then removed his cap and addressed Miss Langley. "The missus has her eye on you. You best pretend we found Miss Eleanor on the way home."

"Thank you, but I shall not lie." Miss Langley smiled kindly at the driver and helped Eleanor into the carriage.

"Maybe he's right," said Eleanor as the carriage began to move. "I could get out a block away and walk home. I could say I was hiding. I could say I was mad about the luncheon."

Miss Langley shook her head. "We will tell the truth and accept whatever comes of it."

❧

Mother met them at the door, frantic. When Miss Langley tried to explain, Mother waved her to silence, ordered the nanny from her sight, and told Harriet to take Eleanor to her room. "You should be ashamed of yourself, giving your poor mother such a fright," scolded Harriet as she seized Eleanor's arm and steered her upstairs. "We thought you had been kidnapped or worse."

"I was fine."

"Ungrateful, disobedient child. It's that Langley woman's influence, I know it."

"Leave me alone," shouted Eleanor, pulling free from Harriet's grasp. She ran to her room and slammed the door. She stretched out on the bed and squeezed her eyes shut against tears. She listened for Miss Langley on the other side of the wall until fatigue overcame her.

She woke with a jolt as the first shafts of pale sunlight touched her window. She ran to Miss Langley's room. The nanny opened at Eleanor's knock, and in a glance Eleanor took in the bulging satchel, the stripped bed, the missing quilts.

Eleanor flung her arms around her. "Please don't go."

"I have no choice."

"I hate her. I hate them both."

"Don't hate them on my account." Miss Langley hugged her tightly, then held her at arm's length. "I knew their rules and deliberately broke them. I made a choice, and I am prepared to accept the consequences. Remember that."

Eleanor nodded, gulping air to hold back the tears. "Where are you going?"

"I have a friend in the city who will take me in for a while, until I can find a new situation. Maybe I'll stay in New York. Perhaps I'll return to England."

"I thought you couldn't go back to England because of the baby."

"What baby?"

"Yours. Your baby."

Miss Langley regarded her oddly. "I never had a baby. Whatever gave you that idea?"

Eleanor couldn't bear to repeat Abigail's tale. "The baby footprints on your Crazy Quilt. I thought you traced your baby's footprints and embroidered them."

"Eleanor." Miss Langley cupped Eleanor's cheek with her hand. "Those are your footprints, silly girl."

Eleanor took a deep breath and scrubbed her eyes with the back of her hand. Miss Langley sighed, reached into her satchel, and handed her a handkerchief. Eleanor wiped her face and tried to compose herself. "Will I ever see you again?"

"That's up to you." Miss Langley closed her satchel. "When you're a woman grown and free to make your own decisions, I would be very pleased if you called on me."

"I will. As soon as I'm able."

Father's carriage was waiting outside, the rest of Miss Langley's belongings already inside. At first Eleanor was surprised to see it, but naturally Mother would also not have it said that the Lockwoods allowed a woman, even one discharged in disgrace, to struggle on foot into the city, unescorted and encumbered by baggage.

"I'll write as soon as I'm settled," said Miss Langley as she put her satchel into the carriage and climbed up beside it. "Take care of Wildrose."

"I will."

Miss Langley closed the door, and the carriage gave a lurch and moved off. Eleanor followed in her bare feet, waving and shouting good-bye. Miss Langley leaned out the window to blow her a kiss, but then she withdrew from sight, and Eleanor could do nothing but watch as the carriage took her through the front gates and away.

"Come inside," called Mother from the doorway. "Goodness, Eleanor, you're still in your nightgown."

"You should not have sent her away."

"On the contrary, I should have done so long ago. You're too old for a nanny, especially one with no regard for your safety."

Without another word, Eleanor went inside and upstairs to the nursery, where she flung herself on the sofa, aching with loneliness. Only anger kept her from bursting into tears. Every part of this room held a memory of Miss Langley, but they would make no more memories here.

After a long while, Eleanor sat up, and only then did she realize she still clutched Miss Langley's handkerchief. She opened it and traced the embroidered monogram with her finger: An A and an C flanked a larger L. She knew the A stood for Amelia, but she did not know what the C was for.

She was tucking the handkerchief into the pocket of her nightgown when her gaze fell upon the window seat. Less than a day before, she and Miss Langley had concealed her Crazy Quilt diamond beneath it. Eleanor had been correct to suspect they would not continue their quilting lessons, but she never could have imagined the reason why.

She crossed the room and lifted the window seat. There, under a faded flannel blanket, she found her Crazy Quilt diamond—but something else lay beneath it. Wrapped in a bundle of muslin were the rest of the fabrics Eleanor had used the previous day, the two crazy patch diamonds Miss Langley had made, and her favorite sewing shears, the silverplated, heron-shaped scissors.

Eleanor held them in her lap a long while before she closed the window seat, seated herself upon it, and cut a diamond foundation from the muslin. She appliquéd a green silk triangle to the center, then added another patch. She added a second patch, and a third, working toward the edges as Miss Langley had showed her.

Then Harriet entered. "Your mother wants you to get dressed and come to breakfast."

"I'm not hungry."

Harriet waited as if hoping to receive some other reply, but Eleanor did not look up from her work. Eventually Harriet left.

Within a few minutes, Abigail replaced her. "Mother and Father want you to come to breakfast," she said. "So do I. Won't you please come down?"

"I'm not hungry."

"But you didn't have any supper."

"I said I'm not hungry."

"All right. I'll tell them," said Abigail. "I'm sorry about Miss Langley."

Eleanor snipped a dangling thread and said nothing.

Soon after Abigail left, Mother herself appeared. "You're too old to hide in the nursery and sulk. Come down to breakfast this instant." She watched Eleanor sew. "What are you doing?"

"I'm making a Crazy Quilt." Eleanor embroidered a seam of velvet and wool with a twining chain stitch. "I will eat breakfast when I'm hungry, and after that, I'm going outside to ride Wildrose."

"Absolutely not. It's not safe. You know nothing about riding."

"Abigail will show me."

"She will not. I will forbid her. I forbid *you*."

Eleanor smiled to herself and worked her needle through the fabric, embellishing the dark velvet and wool with a chain of white silk thread, each stitch another link.

Chapter Three

Their suitcases and supplies were stowed away in the motor home, Sylvia had the map spread out on her lap, and Andrew had just put the key in the ignition when Sarah ran out the back door waving at them. Agnes had just called and was on her way over with something she insisted she must show Sylvia before they departed.

Andrew pocketed the keys, and he and Sylvia returned inside, where Sylvia put on a fresh pot of coffee. Agnes usually sought rides from Diane, who would likely crave a cup or two this early in the morning.

Sure enough, when Agnes and Diane arrived, Diane barely mumbled a greeting on her way to the coffeepot. Agnes, on the other hand, was bright-eyed and pink-cheeked with excitement. "I found it," she said, waving a thick, battered notebook in triumph. "It was with my old tax returns. Thank goodness I remembered the year."

"Found what?" asked Andrew.

"Nothing that couldn't have waited an hour," groused Diane, heaping sugar into her cup. "Even if it does mention your mother's quilt."

"What?" exclaimed Sylvia.

Agnes beckoned Sylvia and Andrew to the table. "I had forgotten all about this notebook. I started it when Richard went off to war, to keep track of news from home to include in my letters. After he was killed, I continued it for myself, as a place to put down reminders, appointments, and so forth."

Agnes opened the notebook to a page marked with a scrap of blue gingham fabric. "The entry for Thursday, March twentieth, 1947, includes my mother's birthday, reminders to write letters to two creditors, and the name and address of a caller who had come to buy a certain quilt," she said. "Claudia was out, and when I told the woman I had no idea which quilt she meant, she left in a huff and ordered me to have Claudia contact her promptly if she didn't want to lose a sale. I assumed Claudia planned to sell her own quilts. If I'd had any idea she meant to sell your mother's, I never would have given her the message."

"I know you wouldn't have," Sylvia reassured her.

"Wait just a second," said Diane, reading over Agnes's shoulder. "Is that who bought the quilts? Esther Thorpe? From right here in Waterford?"

"Not all of the quilts," said Agnes. "Just the appliqué quilt."

"The Elms and Lilacs quilt?" gasped Sylvia. It was impossible to believe she would ever see any of the missing quilts again, but if Agnes's recollection of her notes was correct, the Elms and Lilacs quilt had been sold to a neighbor.

Then Sylvia noticed Diane shaking her head in dismay, or maybe disgust. "Just my luck. It had to be Esther Thorpe."

"What's wrong with Esther Thorpe?" asked Andrew.

"Nothing's wrong with her, not anymore. It's her family I'm worried about, the people who would have inherited her quilts after her death. Esther had a daughter named Nancy Thorpe Miles, and Nancy had a daughter—"

"Oh, dear," said Agnes. "I see."

"I don't," said Sylvia. "Would someone care to enlighten me?"

"Esther Thorpe was the grandmother of Mary Beth Callahan."

Andrew looked around the table, baffled. "And Mary Beth Callahan is . . . ?"

"My next-door neighbor," said Diane. "And my nemesis."

"Oh yes, of course," said Sylvia. "The one who turned you in to the Waterford Zoning Commission when you built that skateboard ramp in your backyard."

"I didn't build it; my husband did," Diane shot back, then nodded, chagrined. "Yes, that's Mary Beth. The one who has been president of the Waterford Quilting Guild for going on fifteen years now."

"She must be doing a fine job, or the guild members wouldn't elect her each year," Agnes pointed out.

"No, they're just intimidated. She has an incumbent's power plus the grace and subtlety of a bulldozer. If she has your mother's quilt, you'll be lucky if she lets you look at it through the window."

The others laughed. Sylvia knew Diane had her own personal grudges against Mary Beth, and she couldn't deny that Mary Beth might have earned every bit of Diane's enmity, but she did not see any cause for alarm.

"We'll stop by and see her on our way out of town," she said. "It's our only lead, and I won't pass it up simply because you two don't get along."

"Don't say I didn't warn you," said Diane. "At least send Andrew in alone if you mean to buy the quilt back. Mary Beth might not recognize him, but she knows you and I are friends. She'll triple her price just to infuriate me."

Sylvia promised to consider it, but she couldn't help feeling a thrill of anticipation at the thought of seeing the Elms and Lilacs quilt after so many years. Mary Beth could triple or even quadruple her price, and Sylvia would pay it—as long as she didn't have to mortgage Elm Creek Manor to do so.

After encouraging Diane and Agnes to stay and help themselves to breakfast, Sylvia and Andrew bid their friends good-bye. Soon the motor home was rumbling across the bridge over Elm Creek and through the leafy wood surrounding the estate.

They reached the main road and drove another fifteen minutes to Diane's neighborhood, a few blocks south of the Waterford College campus. Professors, administrators, and their families resided in the graystone and red-brick houses on the broad, oak tree–lined streets, but in the distance, the low, thumping bass of a stereo reminded Sylvia that Fraternity Row was not far away.

Andrew carefully maneuvered the motor home into Diane's driveway, nearly taking out a shrub near the mailbox. Sylvia raised her eyebrows at him, but didn't criticize. "Diane won't miss a few leaves," Andrew said as he set the parking brake.

Mindful of Mary Beth's reputation, they went a few extra steps out of their way to stay on the sidewalk rather than walk on her lawn. Mary Beth herself answered their knock and gave them one quick, suspicious glance before the motor home caught her attention. Her eyes widened, and for a moment she seemed to have forgotten the couple on her doorstep. "If she thinks she can park that monstrosity there—"

"No need to worry," Sylvia broke in pleasantly. "That monstrosity is ours. We parked in Diane's driveway to avoid blocking the road."

"Oh." Mary Beth frowned at Sylvia as if wondering whether to believe her. "I suppose that's all right. I'm not the sort to complain, but we do have an ordinance against that kind of thing."

"Of course you do," said Sylvia. "I don't know if you remember me, but we've met before. I'm Sylvia Compson, and this is my friend, Andrew Cooper."

"Fiancé, actually," said Andrew, offering Mary Beth his hand.

She shook it warily, her eyes still on Sylvia. "Of course I remember you. Every quilter in Waterford knows you."

"Not every quilter, surely." Sylvia made her voice as cheerful as she could, considering Mary Beth's viselike grip on the front door. "I'm sorry we didn't call first, but we're on our way out of town, and I needed to see you rather urgently."

"If it's about that skateboard ramp—"

"Heavens, no."

"Well . . ." Mary Beth glanced over her shoulder, then at her watch. "I guess I have a few minutes, but I can't invite you in. We just had the carpets cleaned."

"That's quite all right," Sylvia assured her, and decided she did not envy Diane her neighbor. "I recently learned that years ago, your grandmother purchased one of my mother's quilts from my sister. I hoped you might know what became of it."

As Sylvia described the quilt, Mary Beth listened, frowning and chewing her lip. Then suddenly she brightened. "Oh, *that* quilt," she said. "Of course. I saw it when I was a little girl."

"Not more recently than that?"

"No, not since my grandmother died and my mother got rid of all her junk before selling the house." Mary Beth rolled her eyes. "Was *that* ever a chore. It took us a week to sort through her stuff. Grandma called herself an art collector, but she had terrible taste. My mother kept some of the antique furniture and a few other things of sentimental value, but she sold everything else to an auction house. She told my father she was surprised we didn't have to pay them to haul the stuff away."

Sylvia smiled tightly. "I don't suppose my mother's quilt had sentimental value to your family?"

"No. Why should it have? My grandmother owned many quilts. If she had made them, we would have kept them even if they didn't go with our decor, but since she just bought them here and there, and they weren't even valuable antiques—"

"Funny thing is," Andrew remarked, "they might be, by now."

"I'm sure your mother's quilt was very pretty," said Mary Beth hastily, "but we didn't have room enough to keep everything."

"So you got rid of the junk," said Sylvia. "I heard you."

Mary Beth opened her mouth and closed it without a word, pinching her lips in a scowl.

Andrew asked, "You wouldn't happen to know the name of that auction house, would you?"

"Not off the top of my head." Then, reluctantly, Mary Beth added, "My mother might remember. I suppose I could call her and get back to you."

"We'd appreciate it," said Andrew. "Thanks very much for your time."

He prompted Sylvia with a tiny nudge, but Mary Beth closed the door so quickly Sylvia had no time to thank her anyway. She shook her head at the closed door. "Be a dear and remind me of this moment if I ever accuse Diane of exaggerating when she complains about her neighbors."

Andrew chuckled. "I'll do that."

"Junk, indeed." Sylvia took Andrew's arm, but when he headed for the sidewalk, she steered him directly toward the motor home. She hoped that unpleasant woman was spying on them from behind the curtain as they trod on her carefully manicured lawn. Mary Beth was fortunate that Sylvia knew how to control her temper, or she might have marched right through the marigold bed.

❧

Andrew drove west on I-80, pleased they had managed to get an early start despite their detour to Mary Beth's house. "By the time we get home from California, I'll bet she'll have the name of that auction house for you," he said.

"She'd better have it sooner than that," retorted Sylvia. "It's the least she can do, considering how she insulted my mother's quilts."

Andrew agreed, but Sylvia couldn't help wondering if Mary Beth's dismissal of the Elms and Lilacs quilt was a response to its condition rather than its artistic merit. The Bergstroms had taken excellent care of it when it was theirs, but as Mary Beth had so gracelessly pointed out, the quilt had held no sentimental value for her family. Heaven only knew how they had used the quilt. Every quilter of Sylvia's acquaintance had her own horror story of quilts lovingly made and given as gifts only to be dreadfully mistreated by their new owners. As for herself, Sylvia had learned not to look too closely at the dog's bed or the rag bag with the cleaning supplies when visiting the recipients of some of her quilts.

They stopped for lunch outside of Youngstown, then drove on across

Ohio. Just west of Toledo, Andrew asked her to check the guidebook for a suitable place to spend the night. Sylvia eyed him curiously but obliged. Ordinarily he preferred to drive well past dusk, especially on the first day when he was fresh, but if he'd had enough driving for one day, she wouldn't press him to continue. Driving wore her out, too, although she wouldn't admit it, since it seemed ridiculous that sitting down in a comfortable seat should fatigue her. Besides, Andrew enjoyed the freedom of traveling by the motor home, and she wouldn't dream of spoiling his fun.

The registration office at the campsite had a phone, so after they had settled in, Sylvia called home. Sarah answered and reported that Summer was working on their submissions to the Missing Quilts Home Page, and her mother's quilts ought to be on-line by the end of the week. Mary Beth Callahan had not called. Sylvia had not really expected to hear from her so soon, but she still returned to the motor home rather disgruntled. Andrew was already asleep on the fold-out bed, so Sylvia changed into her nightgown as quietly as she could. She kissed him on the cheek before turning in herself, but he did not stir.

In the morning, she woke to find breakfast ready and Andrew sipping coffee and reading a newspaper he had purchased at the office. Soon they were on the road, heading west to Andrew's son and his family in Southern California.

As the days passed, they crossed Indiana—with a detour to the Amish community in Shipshewana so Sylvia could visit friends and shop for fabric—and Illinois. In Iowa they spent a day with one of Andrew's army buddies, then stayed over another night to avoid driving in severe thunderstorms. Sylvia checked in with Sarah every other day, although with camp not in session for the season, her young friend had little business to report. Sylvia wondered if Sarah suspected the truth, that checking in on Elm Creek Quilts was really just an excuse to hear Sarah's voice and to let her know she and Andrew were fine. She knew Sarah and Matt worried about them, two old folks on the road alone. Sylvia might worry, too, if she didn't have absolute faith in Andrew's familiarity with the route and his diligence in maintaining the motor home. "Most accidents happen close to home," she had told Sarah cheerfully the one and only time Sarah had expressed concern. "The farther we go, the safer we are."

She knew her logic was flimsy, but at least Sarah dropped the subject.

Sometimes Sarah did have news when Sylvia called: The new brochures had come back from the printer with an error and had to be redone, Elm Creek Quilt Camp was going to be the subject of an article in an upcoming issue of *American Quilter,* Sylvia had been invited to speak at next year's Pacific International Quilt Festival. Other times, the news from home made Sylvia rather glad she was not there. Judy DiNardo had found the perfect wedding gown in a bridal magazine, Sarah had ordered several catalogs from which Sylvia could choose the invitations, and all the Elm Creek Quilters had taken a tour of the local bakeries to sample wedding cakes. Well, Sylvia was sorry to have missed the wedding cake audition, but she was glad to have avoided the other nonsense.

When Sylvia called from Colorado, Summer answered with unexpected and welcome news: She had received fourteen e-mails from people across the country with leads on the missing quilts.

"Fourteen," marveled Sylvia. "I never thought we'd receive such a response so soon."

"Now will you lose your silly e-mail prejudice?" teased Summer. "I wish you had a laptop so I could forward these e-mail messages to you. Several had photos attached, but you're the only person who can make a positive ID."

"You sound like a detective."

"I feel something like one," said Summer, laughing. "Anyway, since I can't e-mail you, grab a pencil and paper. Most of the tips will have to wait until you return, but you'll pass by some of the locations."

Sylvia fumbled in her purse for something to write with. "Hold on a moment, please."

"There's something strange about these responses, too. Statistically I would have expected the responses to be equally distributed among the five quilts, but ten of them were about the whole cloth quilt."

"That is rather odd. I expected the Ocean Waves and the Crazy Quilt to receive the most, since those patterns are more common and there will be more look-alikes to cause false alarms." Suddenly Sylvia had a thought. "Unless you mean all ten of those e-mails mentioned the same location?"

"Sorry, no. I should have been more clear. Ten unique locations."

"That's not a very good sign." At last Sylvia found a pen. "All right, dear, I'm ready to take dictation."

"First for the good news: One of the sightings of the whole cloth quilt was at a library in Thousand Oaks. That's close to Santa Susana."

"Very close," said Sylvia, delighted. "I recall seeing signs for Thousand Oaks on the freeway near Andrew's son's home. My goodness, can you imagine? We might actually come home with one of my mother's quilts."

"Or more, if you're lucky. Have you reached Golden, Colorado?"

"Golden is more than four hours behind us."

"Too bad. Someone claims she saw the New York Beauty at the Rocky Mountain Quilt Museum."

"I knew I should have paid them a visit," exclaimed Sylvia. "I would have, except I didn't want to give Andrew another excuse to stop."

"You can investigate on the way back. I have an antique dealer in Iowa and a family in Indiana you should check out on the return trip, too. The only sighting between you and California is a quilt shop in Nevada." Summer hesitated. "And when I said you'll pass by these places, I didn't mean they're right on your route. You'll have to take a few detours."

"I'd go hundreds of miles out of my way if it meant finding those quilts." As Sylvia wrote down Summer's information, it occurred to her that she ought to prepare herself to go even farther—literally and otherwise.

❧

One of the responses had come from a Las Vegas woman who said she had seen an Ocean Waves quilt fitting Sylvia's description in a quilt shop in a nearby town.

"It's not far out of our way," said Sylvia as Andrew turned off I-15 onto the highway that led to Boulder City.

"It's no trouble," said Andrew. "I don't mind the delay."

"I almost wish you did."

"Hmm?"

"Never mind." Sylvia unfolded the map and put on her glasses.

They followed Summer's directions into the historic Old Town district of Boulder City and located Fiddlesticks Quilts with little difficulty. Andrew dropped Sylvia off in front of the shop and promised to return for her after checking over the motor home at a filling station. "Don't buy too much fabric," he teased as she climbed down from her seat.

"If that's the kind of husband you're going to be, we're keeping separate checking accounts," Sylvia retorted, but she smiled as she shut the door.

She entered the shop eagerly, pausing only to return a saleswoman's greeting. Over the shelves of fabric, notions, and books hung quilts of all different sizes and patterns. Her first glance took in Irish Chains, samplers, and children's appliqué quilts—and one Ocean Waves. Her heart quickened as she made her way through the aisles toward it, but she was still half a room away when she realized this was not her mother's quilt. While the ecru background fabric could have been mistaken for aged white cloth, the other triangles were green, purple, and black as well as blue, and the quilting had been completed by machine. She continued across the room with a sinking heart, knowing a closer look would reveal the same disappointing truth.

"Do you like it?" asked the saleswoman. "It's available as a pattern or a kit."

"It's lovely, but no thank you, dear. You wouldn't happen to have any other Ocean Waves quilts, would you? An antique, perhaps?"

She knew before the woman shook her head what the answer would be. Sylvia thanked her and pretended to study a nearby bolt of fabric as the saleswoman returned to the cutting table. How on earth could anyone have mistaken this modern quilt for her mother's? Even someone unfamiliar with the intricacies of quilting should not have missed the obvious differences. After all, blue was blue, not purple or green or black. Honestly.

She soothed her indignation with a bit of fabric shopping, so by the time Andrew came back, her good humor had returned. When Andrew eyed her shopping bag askance as she climbed into the motor home, she protested, "I could hardly visit a new quilt shop without buying something."

"I guess not. By the look of it, you didn't do too much damage."

"That's because the rest of my bags are around back at the loading dock."

A look of such alarm appeared on Andrew's face that Sylvia burst out laughing. He grinned sheepishly. "You had me going there for a minute."

"Well, Summer's friend from the Internet had *me* going." She told him what the search of the store had yielded. "I had such high hopes for this visit, much higher than warranted, obviously. I hate to think I'll be forced to investigate every single Ocean Waves quilt in the country simply because people can't read descriptions carefully enough."

"They're probably so eager to help, they'd rather raise a false alarm than pass over a potentially important clue," said Andrew. "But if you buy consolation fabric each time we hit a dead end, we'll have to add another wing to the manor to store it all."

Sylvia laughed, and they drove on for a while, lost in their own thoughts.

"What do you say we stop soon?" Andrew suddenly asked.

"For supper?"

"For the night."

"But it's only four o'clock."

Andrew shrugged. "If you don't want to—"

"No, no, that's all right. You're the driver. If you're—" She almost said tired, but she caught herself. Andrew wouldn't like her to believe him so easily fatigued. "—bored, we can stop."

"I didn't say I was bored. Who could be bored with you around?"

Sylvia decided to take that as a compliment—and to be direct with him. If they were going to be married, she had the right to straight answers. "Well, then, what is it? I like a leisurely drive with pleasant company as much as the next person, but you're dawdling, as much as it is possible to dawdle in a motor home on the interstate. Are you feeling poorly? The drive seems to be taxing you more than usual."

"The drive doesn't bother me as long as the weather's good."

"I see. Then the only logical explanation is that you don't want to get to California any sooner than necessary."

"What do you mean?"

"Don't tease me with the innocent act. I know you too well. You're not in any hurry to tell your son we're getting married." She sat back in her seat and folded her arms. "If I didn't know any better, I'd think you were getting cold feet."

"What? After I hung in there all those years, still hoping, still proposing, even though you kept turning me down and ordered me not to ask you again?"

"You probably thought I'd never say yes, so it was perfectly safe to keep asking. It required absolutely no courage on your part."

"I'm not getting cold feet. They aren't even lukewarm. And you're wrong about my driving, too. This so-called dawdling is just your imagination."

"I can tell time and count miles," she retorted, but Andrew just shook his head and smiled. Still, he drove on well into evening before asking her if she wanted to stop for supper. This time she was the one who had had enough of the road for one day, but he seemed more than willing to stop for the night after she suggested it.

It was not her night to check in, but Sylvia called home anyway to report that their search of Fiddlesticks Quilts had turned up nothing. Sarah thought that the search might be made easier if Sylvia had pictures of the quilts to show, so she offered to send several printouts of Summer's computer illustrations to Andrew's son's home.

When Sylvia asked if they had received any more responses to their posts on the Missing Quilts Home Page, Sarah told her that they had—two more sightings of the whole cloth quilt. "Mary Beth Callahan phoned this morning, too," she added. "She gave us the name and address of the auction house that bought the Elms and Lilacs quilt from her mother."

"That's wonderful news," said Sylvia. "And very welcome, too, after today's disappointment."

"Mary Beth said her grandmother also bought quilts at a consignment shop in downtown Waterford. She thought Claudia might have sold some of your mother's quilts through them, too. The shop closed in the sixties, but the owner's son still lives in Waterford. He runs the coffee shop on the square in downtown Waterford."

"I'll get in touch with him as soon as I return," said Sylvia. "I wouldn't have believed it of Mary Beth, but she turned out to be quite helpful after all. Don't tell Diane or she'll be terribly disappointed."

❦

The next morning, they continued their journey at the usual pace, and Andrew gave Sylvia no more reason to suspect him of deliberately delaying their arrival. A few days later, they drove through the rocky, sun-browned hills of the Santa Monica Mountains into Santa Susana. They left the freeway and passed neighborhoods of houses with stucco walls and red tile roofs. Sylvia had visited Andrew's son and his family several times before, but she still had not become accustomed to the small lots separated by high fences, and the houses seemed rather crowded together.

Andrew parked the motor home in the driveway of his son's ranch house and sat for a moment before rousing himself and helping Sylvia down from her seat. "Don't look so grim or they'll think we have bad news," she teased as they carried their suitcases to the front door. They heard happy shouts from within, and before they could knock, the door swung open.

"Grandpa," cried ten-year-old Kayla as she burst outside, her strawberry blond ponytail streaming out behind her. She flung her arms around Andrew. "What took you so long?"

Andrew gave her a hug so strong Kayla's toes lifted off the ground. "I missed you, too, sweetheart."

"Be careful, Kayla." Andrew's daughter-in-law appeared in the doorway, a red pencil tucked behind her ear as if she had been interrupted while grading papers. "You'll knock Grandpa over."

"No, I won't." Kayla released her grandfather and peered shyly at Sylvia. "We have more oranges so you can pick your own for breakfast, like last time."

"How thoughtful of you to have them ready for me," said Sylvia. "I've never had better oranges than those you grow here. You've spoiled me for anything from the grocery store."

Kayla grinned as another strawberry-blond girl squeezed past her mother. "Hi, Grandpa."

Andrew's eyebrows shot up, and Sylvia suspected hers had, too. When last they saw Angela, she had worn her hair cut short, and it was all her parents could do to get her to wear anything but gym clothes and basketball shoes. In the few months since their last visit, Angela had gained at least two inches in height, had grown her hair past her shoulders, and had discovered lip gloss and nail polish. She wore a silver ring around one of her bare toes, tight white Capri pants with the waistband folded down to expose her navel, and some sort of halter top that had more in common with a bathing suit than any blouse Sylvia had ever worn.

"Angela, that is a sports bra, which means it belongs under a shirt, not in place of one," said Cathy wearily. "And pull up your pants or I'll do it for you."

Grumbling, Angela took Andrew's and Sylvia's suitcases and disappeared into the house. "What happened?" asked Andrew in a low voice as Cathy ushered her guests inside.

"An unfortunate collision of interests in boys and Britney Spears. Honestly, I don't know what to do with her sometimes."

Sylvia figured any young woman thoughtful enough to carry their suitcases without being asked was far from a truant, but she refrained from saying so. She had not raised any children, so it was not her place to offer unsolicited observations.

Cathy led them through the house and out a sliding glass door to the back patio, which overlooked the steep, scrub-covered sides of Wildwood Canyon. Kayla brought them both tall glasses of lemonade—freshly squeezed, with lemons from their own tree, she told Sylvia proudly—and a more modestly attired Angela soon joined them, carrying a flat cardboard mailer. "This came for you yesterday," she said, and handed the parcel to Sylvia.

"Summer's pictures, I presume," said Sylvia, noting the return address as she opened the package. Inside she found computer-generated illustrations of the five missing quilts, ten copies of each. She told Cathy and her daughters about the search, but despite her own pessimistic predictions about the likelihood of finding even one of the quilts, she found herself painting a much rosier picture for her listeners. She managed to recast her disappointment in Boulder City as an opportunity for sightseeing they otherwise would have missed, and made pursuing the other Internet tips seem like an intriguing quest.

Cathy was not convinced. "Isn't that a lot of driving around for something you might not find?"

Andrew shrugged. "We like to travel, so we'd be on the road anyway."

"Maybe now, but it's going to be winter soon. What if you don't find the quilts before then?"

"They've been missing a long time," said Sylvia with a laugh. "I'm certainly not going to quit looking for them after only a few months."

At that, Cathy seemed even less at ease, but she smiled when Andrew teased her and promised they wouldn't risk their lives in a blizzard or any other natural disaster for a quilt.

Sylvia set the pictures aside and admired the view of the canyon as they caught up on the news since their last visit. Kayla's inquisitive sweetness was thoroughly charming, and once Angela forgot her affectations of adolescent disinterest, she became as friendly and engaging as her sister. Sylvia suddenly realized that soon she would be related to these girls, and to their parents. For so many years she had mourned the passing of her family, but once she married Andrew, she would gain another. She would be a stepmother, of all things, and a stepgrandmother. She wondered if Kayla and Angela would call her Grandma or if they would feel that would dishonor their real grandmother's memory. Sylvia thought she would like to be called Grandma, and she wondered how she would go about suggesting it.

When Bob returned home from work, he greeted his father with a joke and a hearty embrace and had a hug and kiss for Sylvia, too. Andrew's son was a taller, sturdier version of his father, with the same warmth and gentleness, the same ready grin. He pulled up a chair, eager to hear about their trip, but before long Cathy reminded him that Andrew and Sylvia were probably hungry after their long drive. Bob promised them a home-cooked meal that would beat anything they could whip up in that motor home. "Would you believe he sold our childhood home to buy that thing?" he asked Sylvia. "All so he could wander the country and make us look bad."

The girls laughed, and Andrew said, "Make who look bad?"

"Me and Amy, of course." Bob crossed the patio to light the grill. "People think we won't take in our homeless father."

"I'm not homeless," Andrew called after him. "My home's in Pennsylvania."

"But, Dad . . ." Cathy hesitated. "That's Sylvia's home, isn't it? And you can't really call your RV a home."

Bob added, "What Cathy means is—well, we know we've been through this before, but it can't hurt to try again. You know we'd be honored if you'd consider making our house your home."

Cathy leaned over to Sylvia and confided, "We hoped you would help us convince him."

Speechless, Sylvia could only raise her eyebrows at Cathy. Before she could fumble for a response, Kayla squealed, "You mean Grandpa's moving in?"

Cathy reached over to settle her down. "We have to discuss it first."

"There's nothing to discuss," said Andrew.

Bob returned to the table and rested his hands on his wife's shoulders, his handsome face creased in concern. "Dad, you know you can't stay on the road forever, and when that time comes, you'll want to be with family."

"Sylvia's home is my home," declared Andrew, missing Sylvia's warning look, "and she's going to be my family, too, as much as you are, so you can stop this nonsense about moving in. I love you very much, but I already have a home and I like it just fine."

Bob and Cathy stared at him.

Sylvia sighed and gazed heavenward, wishing Diane were present to break the shocked silence with a witticism.

Andrew shifted in his seat and reached for his lemonade, but did not drink. "This wasn't how I planned to tell you."

A slow smile of delight spread over Angela's face. "Grandpa, are you getting married?"

Andrew took Sylvia's hand, glanced at his son, and said, "Yes, sweetheart, we are."

Angela and Kayla burst into cheers. They bolted from their chairs and showered Andrew with hugs and kisses. "Can I be a bridesmaid?" asked

Kayla. "Please? My best friend was one in her mother's wedding, and she got to wear the prettiest dress."

"Don't ask me. I'm not in charge of the bridesmaids. Ask the bride here."

Kayla turned to Sylvia, hopeful. "Can I? Please? I'll do a good job."

"I'm sure you would," said Sylvia, wanting to add that she wasn't certain she was any more in charge of the bridesmaids than Andrew. Likely that role now belonged to Diane or one of the other Elm Creek Quilters. She wanted to assure the girls that they would play an important role in the ceremony, but at the moment she was more concerned about Bob and Cathy, who sat silent and immobile in their chairs.

"I suppose this comes as a bit of a surprise," said Sylvia.

"Maybe a little," Cathy managed to say.

Andrew's expression grew serious. "Thank you for your good wishes, girls," he said to his granddaughters. "Sylvia and I know this is unexpected, but we also know you care about us and our happiness, and so even if this is unsettling, you're going to be happy for us."

"It's not unsettling," said Kayla.

Bob patted Cathy lightly on the shoulders until she also rose. "Congratulations, Dad," said Bob, rounding the table to hug his father. As Cathy embraced Andrew in turn, Bob hugged Sylvia and lightly kissed her cheek. She thanked him, but as he drew back to allow Cathy to hug her, Sylvia thought she saw tears shining in his eyes. When Bob abruptly announced he was going inside for the steaks, Cathy stammered an excuse and hastened after him.

Sylvia smiled brightly at Andrew. "That went well."

Andrew managed a rueful smile. "Now you know why I wanted to tell them in person."

"Oh, my, yes. The look on your son's face when he heard the news is sure to become one of our fondest memories of our engagement."

"I like the part where they ran into the house better," said Angela. When Andrew and Sylvia looked at her, she added, "What? It's not like I don't know why they're freaking out."

"They're not freaking out," said Kayla, a trifle too forcefully, then asked, "Is everything going to be okay?"

"It will be," said Sylvia, when Andrew said nothing. "Once everyone has a chance to get used to the idea."

They all turned at the sound of the screen door sliding open. Cathy and

Bob returned to the patio, their expressions somber, and the steaks nowhere to be seen. "Girls, will you please go to the kitchen and fix the salad?" asked Cathy. The girls nodded and hurried inside.

"Dad." Bob sat down beside Andrew. "I'm sorry for my reaction. Really. I'm very happy for you. For both of you."

"We should have known you two would have other plans," added Cathy, with an apologetic smile for Sylvia. "You've grown so close over the years."

"We also should have known you wouldn't want to move in with us," said Bob. He forced a laugh. "In a way I'm glad. We won't have to give up the computer room."

"But—" Cathy hesitated.

Andrew's eyebrows rose. "But?"

Cathy steeled herself with a deep breath. "This isn't easy to say—"

"Then maybe you should keep it to yourself."

"Dad, have you really thought this thing through?" said Bob. "I mean, you and Sylvia are both in good health now, but what if she—if either of you— well, what if your circumstances change? Have you thought about what that will mean?"

Andrew looked from Bob to Cathy and back, his expression darkening. "Are you trying to say we're too old to get married?"

"No," said Cathy. She and Bob avoided looking at Sylvia. "Of course you're not."

Sylvia heard the inadvertent emphasis on the word "you're," and stiffened.

"Our wedding vows will say 'in sickness and in health,' same as yours." Abruptly Andrew rose. "We're going to make those vows, and keep them, the same as you. Whether you like it or not."

He stormed into the house, closing the sliding door with a bang.

"I wish I could put your minds at ease," said Sylvia. "Your father and I visit our doctors regularly and we're both fit as fiddles. I certainly wouldn't marry Andrew if I thought I would become a burden to him."

"I'm sure your friends at Elm Creek Manor find that as comforting as we do," said Cathy.

❧

By the time supper was ready, Andrew's temper had cooled, but a tension hummed in the air around the picnic table as they ate. Cathy engaged Sylvia in polite conversation about Elm Creek Quilt Camp while the men ate with silent deliberation on opposite ends of the table, looking anywhere but at each other. The girls' eyes darted from one adult's face to the next, anxious. Sylvia felt sorry for them, so when the meal was finished, she began collecting the dishes and asked for their help. She ushered them inside to the kitchen, thinking to give Andrew an opportunity to talk to Bob alone. Within minutes, however, Andrew joined them in the kitchen, shaking his head, his eyes glinting with anger. His granddaughters pretended not to notice.

Together they tidied the kitchen and went into the living room to play cards. Bob and Cathy came in soon after, their expressions somber. Cathy made coffee and served dessert, and the family spent the rest of the evening playing games and chatting politely and cautiously on inoffensive topics. This seemed to relieve the girls but irritated Sylvia, who knew all too well what little good came of ignoring conflicts.

Later, Sylvia and Andrew bid their hosts good night and went to the guest room where Sylvia customarily slept. Andrew barely waited to close the door before dropping his facade of affability. "I thought they might have a problem, but not because of some ridiculous concerns about your health." He sat down hard on the bed, a muscle working in his jaw. "I won't have it. I won't be patronized like that."

"They love you. They worry."

"They can show their concern some other way. We are not too old to get married. After all, John Glenn went into outer space at seventy-seven."

"And after that, marriage would seem easy," said Sylvia lightly. "Not that Bob would agree. I thought you said he would be the easy one."

"My prediction stands."

"Well, I can't say you didn't give me fair warning, but spare us the wrath of Amy. You do realize there's always the phone, or we could write."

"I'm tempted, but then I'd have to explain why I told her brother in person but not her. No, when you have two kids, you have to keep things equal." Andrew sighed and rose, pulling Sylvia gently to her feet. "You do know it's not you, right? They like you."

"I realize that," said Sylvia. "They just don't think I'm qualified for the position of stepmother."

"None of this changes how I feel about marrying you. I still know I'm the luckiest man in the world."

Sylvia gazed heavenward. "Oh, please, Andrew. Not the luckiest. Perhaps if you had caught me in my prime—"

He put a finger to her lips, then kissed her. "As far as I'm concerned, you *are* in your prime."

After he left for the fold-out sofa in the computer room, Sylvia felt a sudden pang of homesickness, tempered only by the sight of the familiar Glorified Nine-Patch quilt on the bed. She had made it for Bob and Cathy after they had admired a similar quilt featured on an Elm Creek Quilts brochure. Cathy must have known how it would comfort her—and honor her quilt-making skill, since by tradition a family reserved for guests their best and most beautiful quilt.

Still, when she drew the quilt over herself in the darkened room, she wondered if she might not have preferred the sort of comfortably worn quilt one would give to a member of the family. And as she mulled over Andrew's parting words, she wondered what his son and daughter-in-law had said to make him feel he had to reassure Sylvia of his love.

She wondered which one of them most needed reassurance.

ﷺ

Even this far inland, night mists off the ocean flowed into the valleys, so dense that Sylvia could barely make out the fence from the patio door. When Kayla took her outside to pick an orange, Sylvia shivered in her thin cardigan and was glad to pluck a dew-covered fruit from the tree and hurry back inside. Later, at the breakfast table, she peeled the orange and reflected upon the canyon, which on a morning like this would be invisible until a passerby was nearly upon it. She thought of the first Europeans who had come to California, the Spanish missionaries and the farmers and ranchers who had followed, and wondered if any had come to a dangerous end mere yards from where she now sat, believing the landscape ahead of them to be as gentle and bountiful as that which they had already traversed, never suspecting the truth until they stumbled into it.

"Angela," asked Sylvia as they cleared away the breakfast dishes. "Can you drive?"

"Not yet," said Angela. "I can't get my learner's permit until next year."

"Then if I drive, could you direct me to the Thousand Oaks library?"

"Can I come, too?" asked Kayla.

"Of course, dear." She smiled brightly at Cathy. "Now all we need is a car. Would you mind lending me yours? I'm not as handy with the motor home as Andrew."

The truth was she had only driven it once, and that was in the parking lot behind Elm Creek Manor.

"Of course," Cathy stammered out, just as Andrew said, "I can drive you."

"There's no need. The girls and I will play detective. You stay here and catch up with Bob and Cathy." Quickly she sent Angela for the car keys and Kayla for her purse and the envelope of pictures Summer had sent, then herded the girls out the door before the others could stop them.

"That was close," said Angela as she climbed into the front seat beside Sylvia.

Sylvia nodded and put on her glasses. "For a minute there, I thought they might figure out what I was up to."

"Are we leaving them alone so they can fight?" asked Kayla.

"So they can talk," corrected Sylvia, starting the car. "Just talk."

The morning mists had burned off and traffic was light, so Sylvia felt quite comfortable behind the wheel, especially with two bright girls navigating for her. Twenty minutes later they arrived at the Thousand Oaks City Library. Sylvia had expected another Spanish-style stucco building, but the library was quite modern in design, with an exterior of white stone and dark tinted glass, and unusual jutting angles that reminded her of the Sydney Opera House. When she commented on the architecture, Angela said, "People either love it or hate it. I like it, but Mom says it looks like a stack of books that fell over."

Inside, the building was open and spacious, with a fountain trickling near the sloping front entrance. The girls led Sylvia down into the center of the library to the reference desk, where Sylvia asked for the librarian who had e-mailed Summer. They waited while she was paged, but Sylvia could not keep still knowing her mother's quilt might be hanging somewhere in that building. She went off to search for it, instructing the girls to stay together and to find her as soon as the librarian returned.

Within minutes Angela and Kayla came after her, bringing the smiling librarian with them. Sylvia apologized for not waiting. "It's been decades since I've seen my mother's quilt," she explained with a laugh. "One would think I could control my impatience for five minutes more."

The librarian's face fell. "Oh, I'm so sorry. I thought I explained in my e-mail, but perhaps I wasn't clear. We don't have the quilt in the library."

"You don't?"

"I'm afraid not. We only have the pattern."

"The pattern?" But the whole cloth quilt was her mother's original design. There should not be a pattern. She forced herself to smile through her disappointment. "I'm afraid there must be some mistake. Thank you very much for your time, but I believe we're talking about two different quilts."

"I don't think so," said the librarian. "I'm a quilter myself, and the drawing in the pattern is strikingly similar to the one on your Web site."

"Similar, but not identical?" asked Angela.

The librarian smiled. "Similar enough that I think it's worth a look."

"Yeah, let's at least look at it," urged Kayla, tugging at Sylvia's hand. "What kind of detectives would go home without studying the clue?"

Sylvia could not argue with that, so they followed the librarian to a computer terminal, where she soon brought up archived editions of the *Ladies' Home Journal* on CD-ROM. "Here it is," she said, rising, and motioned for Sylvia to take her seat.

Sylvia frowned at the screen, then drew back with a gasp. "My goodness. It's very like my mother's quilt."

"Here." Angela retrieved one of the drawings from the envelope. "Let's compare them."

Sylvia held the illustration up to the computer screen. The two images were fundamentally the same, with a few minor inconsistencies that could easily be explained by Summer's interpretation of Sylvia's description or gaps in Sylvia's memory. "This quilt is enough like my mother's that one must surely be the source for the other," said Sylvia.

"This magazine was published in October 1912," said the librarian. "When did your mother complete her quilt?"

"Around that same time, but I couldn't tell you whether it was before or after." Sylvia sighed, removed her glasses, and rubbed her eyes. "Of all her quilts, why did she have to leave the date off this one?"

"There may be other clues," said the librarian, and pointed to the screen. "Have you ever heard of the woman given credit for this design?"

Sylvia slipped on her glasses again and read the name. "The name is familiar, but I can't place it. Was she a well-known designer for her era?"

The librarian didn't know, but she offered to make a list of resources Sylvia could investigate. She also printed out a copy of the pages from the *Ladies' Home Journal* for Sylvia to take with her, but despite the stack of papers, Sylvia felt as if she were leaving empty-handed.

"I'm sorry you didn't find your quilt," said Kayla as they drove home.

"Me, too," said Angela.

"Me, too," said Sylvia with a sigh.

"You still found some interesting stuff, though," remarked Angela. "Don't you think this magazine pattern's an important clue?"

"I do, but I'm not so sure I like what this particular clue suggests." She did not remember if her mother or another member of the family had told her that that quilt was her mother's original design, but someone had, and she did not like to think that someone, especially her mother, had lied about its origin. Still, this would not be the first time she had discovered errors in the stories handed down through the family.

"Do you think they're done fighting yet?" asked Kayla from the backseat.

"Talking," said Angela before Sylvia could respond. "Don't worry. They're just talking."

But when they returned home to a stony silence, Sylvia knew something had gone terribly wrong. The adults maintained a courteous front before the children, but as soon as Andrew and Sylvia were alone, he said, "We're cutting the trip short. We're leaving Sunday."

"You can't mean that," protested Sylvia. "We drove too far to go home so soon. What will the girls think?"

"Let Bob explain it to them."

"Don't make the children suffer for your stubbornness. Whatever happened today, let's resolve it before it worsens."

Andrew shook his head, grim. "It's not something I'm willing to resolve in any way that would satisfy them."

Sylvia studied him, heartsick. She could not bear to think she was the cause of any ill will between Andrew and his son. "What would satisfy them?" she asked, and when Andrew did not respond, she knew.

Chapter Four

Mother refused to leave her bedroom, so instead of retreating to her study to enjoy Miss Langley's letter, Eleanor spent the morning with Abigail and the dressmaker. Abigail looked nearly as pale as the white satin of her wedding gown as the dressmaker adjusted the bodice and the drape of the train.

"You will be the most stunning bride New York has ever seen," said Eleanor, but Abigail's face took on an even more sickly cast. Oblivious, Harriet clucked approvingly and reached up to place the headpiece. Abigail shrank away, her eyes locked on her reflection in the mirror.

"We need to check the length of the veil," said Harriet, trying again. "Be a good girl and let me—"

"I don't want it."

"Don't be silly. Of course you do."

Eleanor took the headpiece. "Later, Harriet."

"Your mother said to make sure everything is perfect," said Harriet peevishly. "What would she think if she walked in and saw that we didn't check the veil?"

"I don't think we have to worry about that, do you?" Briskly Eleanor gathered up the length of tulle and satin. "She fought with Father only this morning, and she usually needs at least a day to recover."

Harriet gave her a tight-lipped scowl, but the dressmaker said, "I could come back tomorrow."

"That might be best," replied Eleanor in an undertone. The expression on Abigail's face worried her. For someone who had spent every moment of the past four years planning for her wedding day, Abigail seemed a rather reluctant bride. Perhaps she had no idea what she would do with herself once she was finally married.

Harriet and the dressmaker left, and, like an obedient child, Abigail allowed Eleanor to help her change clothes. "You and Edwin were mentioned in the society pages again this morning," said Eleanor cheerfully, troubled by her sister's strange silence. "They're calling this the wedding of the year. Mrs. Newcombe is absolutely furious, since her daughter—"

"Do you still want to become a nanny?"

Eleanor's fingers froze on Abigail's buttons. "What?"

"When we were children you used to talk of becoming a nanny someday. Do you still wish to?"

Eleanor resumed unfastening Abigail's gown. "That was a little girl's wish. I don't think of it anymore."

"Why not?"

"Because someone must remain home to take care of Mother, and it can't be you since in four days you're going to have a husband to look after, and children, too, before long."

"It's not fair to you."

"Perhaps not, but it's my own fault for confounding our parents by forgetting to die. They have no idea what else to do with me."

"You might have wanted to have a husband and family of your own, but they never gave you that choice." Suddenly Abigail took her hand. "You would like that, wouldn't you? Nothing would be so bad as long as you had that, don't you think?"

Eleanor forced a laugh. "If you're trying to make me jealous, you can save your breath. I'm perfectly content with my books, my horse, and my study. And when Mother finally passes from this earth, I'll live with you and be your children's nanny so you can be a proper society lady and spend all your time dancing at balls with your handsome husband."

"But you would want more than that, even then. This house would seem so big and lonesome with just you and Father."

Eleanor felt a pang. Surely Abigail was not too distracted to realize that Father would have sold their home just as he had the summer house if not for Mother, the necessity to maintain appearances, and his refusal to acknowledge his insurmountable debts. Eleanor could only imagine how he was financing Abigail's wedding. He had called her a "scolding shrew" when she asked him outright, saying only that the long-awaited partnership with the Corvilles would restore their good fortune.

"Father will be fine," said Eleanor. "And I will be fine."

"Father will not be alone, even if you were to leave," said Abigail in a voice so devoid of emotion Eleanor felt a chill. "He will not be without Mother. Nothing afflicts Mother but a terrible temper. She will outlive us all."

"None of us will die any time soon, not even me," said Eleanor firmly. "Unless you slipped poison into the soup, in which case I shall have to warn our guests."

At last Abigail showed a flicker of a smile. "Am I being morose?"

"If not for the gown and the enormous cake Mother ordered, one might think you were planning a wake, not a wedding."

"That won't do." Abigail took a deep breath and looked determinedly into the mirror again. "Father has enough to bear without my jeopardizing my engagement."

"Father? What about you?"

Abigail did not answer.

🌼

When Abigail said she wished to rest before their guests arrived, Eleanor went upstairs to her study, pausing first to rap on her mother's door. "Will you join us for supper tonight?" she called. "We will have guests."

There was a long silence, and then, "Horse people."

Eleanor suppressed a sigh. "Yes, Mr. Bergstrom and his son will be there, as well as your future son-in-law and his parents. Won't you please come down?" She paused. "The Corvilles might think it strange if you don't."

A lengthier silence, and then, "If I am not too ill."

"Thank you, Mother. Abigail will be grateful." She hesitated. "Do you need anything?"

"If I do, I will summon Harriet."

"Very well." Eleanor pressed her fingertips to the door, gripped by a sudden ache of regret. Abigail was right; illness was Mother's euphemism for anger. Her bitterness at Father had worsened through the years, increasing at the same pace as their debts and expenses. Lately Mother had feigned illness so often that Eleanor feared her imagined symptoms would become real. By then, no one would believe her.

When Mother said nothing more, Eleanor continued upstairs to her study. Everyone else still called it the nursery, though the dolls and toys had disappeared long ago, and Father's oak desk and second-best leather chair from the summer house had replaced those she had studied at as a child. A basket of fabric scraps sat between the treadle sewing machine and the wooden quilt frame Eleanor had purchased with money saved from birthdays and Christmases. The noise of the two deliverymen porting them up the stairs had roused Mother from her bed, and she had stood silently watching from the doorway of her room. She had learned the futility of complaining about her daughter's quilting.

A burgundy, green, black, and white Rocky Mountain quilt lay half-finished in the frame. Eleanor had intended it as Abigail's wedding gift, but the wedding preparations had kept her too busy to complete it. She had selected the pattern after the couple chose their honeymoon destination—or rather, after Edwin chose it. Abigail, who had never traveled farther west than Chicago, wanted to explore the West by train, journeying through the Rocky Mountains and along the coast of California. Edwin laughed at his fiancée's "little fancy" and told her they would be going to Europe, because every newly married couple of their position went to Europe. Abigail knew this was not entirely accurate, and even if it were, she did not care. She had been to Europe three times and wanted to see something new. Edwin assured her he might take her to the West someday, but not now, and made arrangements for a tour of the great European capitals.

Eleanor, who had never traveled farther west than Philadelphia and who had only dreamed of seeing Europe, found Edwin's condescending dismissal of his bride-to-be's wishes baffling and a troubling sign of how he would make decisions in the future. When she failed to persuade Edwin to change his mind, Eleanor decided to give her sister the only Rocky Mountains she could offer, although she knew a symbol stitched into a quilt was a poor substitute for what Abigail truly wanted. That the quilt pattern was also known as Crown of Thorns was an appropriate secondary meaning Eleanor kept to herself.

Ruefully noting the amount of work left to be completed, Eleanor reluctantly decided that the quilt would have to be an anniversary gift instead. She had already become quite attached to it, however, and by next year, she would not be able to part with it easily.

She curled up on the window seat and retrieved Miss Langley's letter from her pocket. The postmark indicated it had been mailed from Boston, where Miss Langley had lived for the previous four years as the boarder of a certain Mr. Davis. She had not worked as a nanny since leaving the Lockwood family, and she was as vague regarding how she made her living as she was about her relationship with Mr. Davis.

June 12, 1907

My Dear Eleanor,

As you no doubt surmised as soon as you beheld this letter, my parting for England has been indefinitely postponed, much to the chagrin of factory owners throughout Massachusetts. Too much work remains to be done here, and Mr. Davis simply cannot manage without me. I cannot shirk my duty simply to indulge my sentimental heart, which is why I must also decline your kind invitation to attend Abigail's wedding. Do not think for a moment that I decline because your family is unaware you invited me, which, although you did not say so, I assume is true. Please give Abigail my kind regards and tell her I will think of her on her special day.

I will also think of you, dear Eleanor, for I wonder what will become of you when you no longer have your sister's company. I do hope you will reconsider continuing your education. We have fine colleges here in Boston and a scholarly community you would find quite invigorating. You could live with us; we all work to help support the household and share all things in common, and I know you would make yourself quite useful. I cannot believe your father would deny you the tuition. He may have come upon hard times, but he is neither unkind nor imprudent, and he would see the wisdom in sending you to college if his pride were not in the way.

Now, on to your questions. As to the first, yes, I am certain that women will eventually obtain the right to vote. It might not come in my lifetime, but it will most assuredly come in yours. It will come to no woman, however, unless we fight for it. You must do your part as I must do mine.

As to your second question: I agree that you must tell Mr. Bergstrom the truth. Some might say that misleading a man is not as grievous a sin as lying to him outright, but in my opinion, deception is deception. If you are certain, then you do no one any good by allowing Mr. Bergstrom to persist in his misunderstanding. Your integrity is at stake, my darling girl, and I know you will do what is right. Let Abigail throw herself on the sword of filial loyalty if she must, but you have sacrificed too much of yourself already.

I must believe myself still your nanny to lecture you so. Please forgive my ramblings and remember that I am always

Your Affectionate Friend,
Amelia Langley

PS: Thank you for the thoughtful gift of fabric. I shall make lovely warm quilts of the scraps from Abigail's trousseau. Please give her my thanks and tell her many immigrant children will sleep more soundly soon because of her generosity. The white and the rose satin are truly lovely, but I have no idea to what use I shall put them. They would be quite attractive in a Crazy Quilt, but I think my time for making impractical luxuries has passed. However, I am confident I will recognize what useful work they are meant for in time.

Eleanor folded the letter and returned it to the envelope. She could almost hear Miss Langley's voice as she read her words, but that only emphasized how great a divide separated them. Miss Langley could never return to the Lockwood home, and Eleanor was nearly as unlikely to visit Boston. Eleanor was loath to admit it, but they would probably never see each other again.

College, of course, was out of the question. Even if Father did not think education wasted on a woman, he would not go deeper into debt for such a poor investment, especially since the recent threat of another Panic. Even if their financial situation improved dramatically after the wedding, Mother would still need her. Eleanor had been given no choice, as Abigail had reminded her. She ought to resign herself to her future and be grateful that she had lived long enough to see one.

More troubling was Miss Langley's opinion on the subject of Mr. Bergstrom. Now that Miss Langley concurred with Eleanor's opinion, Eleanor had no excuse to delay telling him the truth, although this meant she would never see him again. He and his father traveled to New York from their horse farm in central Pennsylvania only infrequently, but he was one of the few people who did not treat Eleanor like an invalid. She had known him since she was nine years old, and she felt oddly hollow when she thought this weekend's visit would be his last.

He would arrive soon, if he had not already. Eleanor hid Miss Langley's letter in her desk—she had caught Harriet snooping for Mother more than once—and hurried downstairs to her bedroom. She brushed her hair, debating whether to change her dress, and decided she would not. Later she would dress for supper, but the clothing she wore was good enough for a visit to the stable, regardless of who waited there.

Her step quickened as she approached the stable and saw Frederick Bergstrom putting a dark brown horse through its paces in the practice ring under Father's watchful eye. Nineteen, dark-haired, and tanned from many hours outdoors, Mr. Bergstrom sat a horse as comfortably as if he had been born to it, which in a sense he had, for his family raised some of the finest Thoroughbreds in the world, and had for generations. The senior Mr. Bergstrom, who until recent months had always accompanied his son, was nowhere to be seen.

Mr. Bergstrom spotted her and grinned as she approached. "Miss Lockwood, would you help me convince your father that this magnificent animal is worthy of his stables?"

"If my father cannot tell that by the sight of him, nothing I say will make any difference."

"It's a fine animal," Father conceded, "but not suited for Abigail. This is not a woman's horse. Next time you see your father, I'd like you to ask him why he would send me such a temperamental, high-strung horse for my eldest daughter."

Eleanor had a sharp retort ready, but Mr. Bergstrom said, "I'll ask him, but I already know what he'd answer."

"And what's that?"

He grinned. "Those New York women must be exceptionally delicate if they can't handle a sweet-tempered stallion like Diamond."

"I suppose they are," said Father, chuckling. "The most strenuous activities our refined ladies engage in are dancing at balls and spending my money at the dressmaker's. The harsher environment of your part of the country requires greater strength of your women, a strength, I regret to confess, that has atrophied in our ladies."

"Oh, for heaven's sake," snapped Eleanor, entering the corral. The stallion stepped back and snorted as she took the reins from Mr. Bergstrom. "Pennsylvania isn't the Wild West."

Father eyed her as she began to shorten the left stirrup. "What are you doing?"

"I should think it's rather obvious. Mr. Bergstrom, I would be obliged if you would do the other side."

"Eleanor, don't be a fool," said her father as Mr. Bergstrom complied.

Eleanor gave him a long, wordless look as she gathered up her skirts and climbed on the horse's back. Then she dug in her heels, chirruped, and set Diamond into a canter. As soon as they cleared the gate, they broke into a run.

She ran him the entire length of the estate and back, skirts pulled up past her knees, corset squeezing uncomfortably. The horse's hooves thundered on the grass, but he flowed like silk thread through a needle as they raced over the wooded ground. She slowed him to a steady trot as they returned to the corral, where the two men stood watching her, Father speechless in consternation, Mr. Bergstrom trying to hide his amusement.

He took the reins from her, and she slid to the ground. "He doesn't seem temperamental to me," she said, breathless. Perspiration trickled down her back, her hair had come loose and tumbled in her face, and she desperately wanted to give her corset a yank.

Her father glowered. "Temperamental is a relative quality."

"What do you think of him?" asked Mr. Bergstrom.

"Lovely to look at, remarkable speed, good health," said Eleanor as she inspected the horse. "However, he is not as fine as some of the others you have shown us."

"In what way?"

"I'm sure you know." She stroked the horse's flank as if to apologize for her criticism. "His gait is merely acceptable, as is his endurance." She glanced at her father. "And he is a trifle high-strung. The mare you brought us two months ago was far superior. And . . ."

"What else?"

"I know I've never ridden him, but I'm certain I've seen him before."

"What's the meaning of this?" Father demanded. "Don't tell me you Bergstroms are bringing around horses I've already rejected. Play me for a fool at your peril, young man."

"I assure you," said Mr. Bergstrom in a cool voice, "neither I nor my father has ever shown this horse to you."

"I didn't mean to suggest such a thing," said Eleanor, glaring at her father.

"Fine, fine," said Father. "You can't blame me for wondering if you and your father have grown impatient with my strict standards for horses. I admit it would have been a clever joke if I purchased a horse I had rejected before."

Mr. Bergstrom's expression suggested he did not agree. "That would not have been possible, since as I said—"

"Yes, yes, you have never shown me this horse before. But that is not the only reason. It would not have been possible because I have no intention of purchasing him." He drew out his pocketwatch. "The Corvilles should arrive soon. Eleanor, since you apparently bear this horse a particular affection, I will leave you to help Mr. Bergstrom care for him. Mr. Bergstrom, I look forward to your company at supper."

Eleanor was too humiliated and angry to take notice of Mr. Bergstrom's reply. Father knew very well how he had insulted her by leaving her alone with a young man. If confronted, Father could protest that she was hardly unchaperoned, since her parents, sister, and servants were within the house, but the fact of the matter was that she and Mr. Bergstrom would be unobserved within the stable. She knew what her father meant to tell her: No young man would be interested in attempting anything that might ruin her, and furthermore, her reputation was not valuable enough to preserve from scandal.

She took hold of Diamond's bridle and tugged until the horse followed her into the stable. "It seems you have wasted another trip to New York."

"On the contrary, I'm always pleased to visit your family."

Eleanor busied herself caring for the horse. Mr. Bergstrom fell into place beside her, his every motion assured and gentle. "Is your father well? I'm surprised he did not accompany you."

"He's fine, just too busy to leave Elm Creek."

"What a shame. He'll miss the wedding of the century."

"You're not jealous?"

"Of course not," said Eleanor, regretting her words. "I'll just be glad when all the excitement is over. I'm afraid we're all under a bit of a strain."

Mr. Bergstrom grinned. "I guess that means you have something less elaborate in mind for your own wedding."

Eleanor felt a flash of surprise, then anger, and for a moment she wondered if he were mocking her. "I don't have any plans for my own wedding," she finally said. She picked up her curry comb and went around to the horse's other side.

They worked in silence, and gradually Eleanor's anger ebbed. In the eight years she had known him, Mr. Bergstrom had never once treated her as if she were frail or sickly. For all she knew, no one had told him about her weak heart, and he might truly believe her as marriageable as Abigail. She wanted to apologize, but she did not see how she could without revealing the truth.

All at once, she remembered Miss Langley's letter.

"Mr. Bergstrom." She took a deep breath and plunged ahead. "I have something to confess to you. Something . . . rather unpleasant, I'm afraid."

"You won't dance with me at your sister's wedding?"

"No. I mean, that's not what I had to say. I—I would be pleased to dance with you." If he would still attend after what Eleanor had to tell him. "But I'm afraid my father has no intention of buying any of your horses."

"That's the big secret?"

"I don't just mean today. Not ever. When I think of how many times you and your father have come here and how far you've traveled . . ." She steeled herself. "I am ashamed to disclose this about my own father, but I am even more ashamed that he has deceived you. He wants a Bergstrom Thorough-bred, but he does not have the means to purchase one. He hoped your father would give him a horse as a wedding gift for Abigail, assuming that my father would reward his extravagance with loyalty—that, and the purchase of numerous Bergstrom Thoroughbreds for himself."

"Miss Lockwood—"

"I know what you must be thinking—"

"We gave up on your father as a customer a long time ago."

Eleanor stared at him. "What?"

"For years he's visited our farm and we've showed him our finest horses. For the last fourteen months, we've brought them to him. We're persistent, but not stupid. My father suspected your father was angling for a gift, and the invitation to Abigail's wedding confirmed it."

They had known for months. "Then why . . ."

"Miss Lockwood, do you really think I'd travel all this way so often just to convince a man to buy a horse?"

Eleanor had thought exactly that. "You and your father are known as very good businessmen."

"It's not very good business to bring one horse after another such a great distance except for a proven customer. Most of our customers come to us."

Eleanor let out a small gasp. "I was so upset about my father I never thought of the poor horses."

"Don't worry too much about this one." Mr. Bergstrom slapped the horse's flank affectionately. "He's a Bergstrom Thoroughbred I borrowed from a local customer."

"I knew I had seen this horse before," exclaimed Eleanor, then his meaning sank in. "How dare you lie to us! You deliberately deceived my father."

"I did not lie," said Mr. Bergstrom, emphatic. "I said I had never shown him this horse before, not that he had never seen it. I wouldn't have done it except I knew he wasn't buying."

"I suppose it's foolish for me to defend him after he tried to deceive you." Eleanor let out a shaky laugh. "What would you have done if he had made an offer?"

"I would have told him to take it up with Herbert Drury."

"This horse belongs to Mr. Drury?"

Mr. Bergstrom nodded. "He's one of our best customers. I should have asked someone else, but when Drury offered, I couldn't resist. It was a risk, though. If Abigail had seen—"

"How would Abigail have recognized Diamond when I did not?" asked Eleanor, indignant.

"I assumed she visited the Drury place more often than you. She's frequently there when my father and I visit, and you never are."

Eleanor knew Abigail had befriended the eldest Drury daughter at school, but it never occurred to her that Abigail might have called on her without their parents' consent. As far as Eleanor had known, Abigail had seen the Drury home only once, five years before, when the Lockwoods went to pay their respects to the family after Mrs. Drury's death. Even Father had put aside his animosity that day.

"I don't think my mother and father will be pleased if they learn Abigail has been to the Drury home."

"I won't say a word. Not about Abigail, and not about your father."

Eleanor looked away. "You must think I'm terribly disloyal, Mr. Bergstrom."

"You couldn't be more wrong, Miss Lockwood. And would you please call me Fred? You used to."

"We were children then."

"We've known each other too long to persist with the formality of titles. Every time you say 'Mr. Bergstrom,' I think you're addressing my father."

"Very well. I will call you Fred, if you will call me Eleanor." Hastily, she added, "But only when no one can overhear."

Mr. Bergstrom laughed, but he agreed, and Eleanor realized that she had implied she wanted to be alone with him again. She did, but she did not want him to know it, or to think that she valued her reputation as little as her father did. As soon as they finished caring for the horse, she went back to the house, alone, keeping to a brisk walk in case Fred was watching. Once inside, she hurried upstairs to her study. Only when she had shut the door on the rest of the house did she feel safe, but her heart raced.

She pressed a hand to her forehead and paced the length of the room. As impossible as it seemed that someone could care for her, surely Mr. Bergstrom—Fred—had not meant merely to be kind to the poor invalid. Mere kindness could not explain all he had done simply to have an excuse to visit the Lockwood family. To visit *her*.

"I cannot think about this," she said to the empty room. Pushing Fred from her thoughts, she sat down at the quilt frame and threaded a needle with shaking hands. She popped the thread through the three layers twice before she was able to fix the knot in the batting, then slipped her thimble on her finger and quilted a feathered plume in the background of one of the Rocky Mountain blocks. She waited for the familiar, repetitive motions to soothe her, but her thoughts remained an unsettling mix of pleasure and despair. Abigail, not Eleanor, was the beauty of the family, the cherished daughter who inspired affection in all who saw her. Abigail was the one who was meant to love and be loved, to leave home and have a family of her own—

At a flash of pain, Eleanor gasped and withdrew her left hand from beneath the quilt to find a spot of red on her fingertip. If she had stained the back of her quilt, she would never forgive Fred.

She bit back a sob and flung her thimble across the room. Blinking away tears, she fumbled for her handkerchief and pinched it against her fingertip. Fred's affection for her—if it was affection, and she had not in her loneliness allowed herself to misinterpret his friendship—changed nothing. Her health rendered her unfit for marriage, and Mother still needed her. Whatever Fred's intentions were, Eleanor could not fulfill them.

❧

By the time she returned to her room to dress for dinner, she had regained her composure and had resolved to distance herself from Fred. She could not bring herself to tell him to stay away, but eventually he would make that decision for himself.

As Eleanor went downstairs, she heard voices from the parlor. When she entered, Fred rose from his armchair near the window and gave her a warm smile, which she could not return. On the opposite side of the room, Abigail and Edwin sat on the divan, their parents and Edwin's two sisters arrayed around them. Mother, who had apparently decided that impressing the Corvilles was more important than nursing her wounded feelings, broke off her conversation at the sight of Eleanor. "Where on earth have you been?" she exclaimed. "You missed Edwin's gift to his bride."

Abigail's hand went to her throat, and only then did Eleanor see the beautiful string of pearls that encircled it. "It's exquisite," she said.

"It is not half as lovely as the woman who wears it," said Edwin, his eyes earnest behind his glasses.

"Well said, young man," said Father gruffly, and Abigail flushed pink.

They were summoned to supper; Abigail murmured something and rose to walk out with Father. In a flash of panic, Eleanor feared Fred would escort her, but to her relief, Edwin fell in step beside her instead. "I brought a gift for you, too," he told her, producing a wrapped parcel from behind his back.

"For me?"

"Of course. You are going to be my sister-in-law, aren't you?" They stopped in the corridor and allowed the others to continue on past them. Eleanor carefully unwrapped the colored paper and discovered a fine leather-bound book. "*Bleak House,*" she said, reading the spine. "Oh, Edwin, you know how much I enjoy Dickens."

"It's a first edition." Edwin opened the cover and pointed. "Inscribed by the author."

"How on earth did you find this? Thank you. I believe I'm going to enjoy having you for a brother-in-law."

Edwin laughed and said he certainly hoped so, and they continued on to the dining room together.

As the first course was served, Eleanor did her best to ignore Fred. She made every effort to join in the conversation, but as the meal progressed, she realized only the Corvilles seemed perfectly at ease. Father sat stiff and tense in his chair, and Eleanor had no doubt that if it were up to him, he would have rushed off to find a minister to marry Abigail to Edwin that very hour rather than risk letting the partnership fall through. At the foot of the table, Mother chatted with her guests, so energetic and merry that the Corvilles, at least, seemed thoroughly charmed. Fred gave the appearance of polite engagement, but frequently he looked Eleanor's way, a thoughtful expression on his face. Abigail did not eat a morsel, but sat pensive and anxious in her chair, so distracted that she did not respond to the conversation until prompted.

Afterward, as the men retired to the drawing room and the women went off to the parlor, Fred surprised Eleanor by taking her by the elbow and murmuring close to her ear. "What's wrong? Are you afraid I'll step on your feet when we dance on Saturday?"

"Of course not."

"Then what's wrong? Tell me what it is or I'll follow you into the parlor and call you Eleanor in front of all those women."

She whirled to face him. "You wouldn't dare." Then she thought of Mr. Drury and Diamond. "Please don't. I—I regret that I might have misled you in the stable earlier today. Let me make myself plain: My feelings for you extend no farther than friendship. I hope you will forgive me for any misunderstanding."

"There is nothing to forgive," he said. "Of course, I still expect to dance with you at Abigail's wedding."

"Did you not hear a single word I said?"

He held a finger to her lips. "I heard you, and if you're not careful, everyone else will, too. I traveled a long way to dance with the maid of honor at the wedding of the century, and I'm not going home until I do. That's a promise."

With that, he left her and stormed down the hall to her father's study. His touch lingered upon her lips.

❦

Later, alone in her study, Eleanor stitched on the Rocky Mountain quilt until her eyes teared from the strain. Once Harriet called through the locked door that her mother wished her to come to the parlor immediately, but Eleanor sent her back with her apologies and the excuse that she was not feeling well. Sometime after midnight, someone tested the doorknob but did not knock. Eleanor assumed the others had gone to bed hours ago, so she froze in her chair until she heard footsteps moving off down the hall. She did not know if the would-be visitor was Harriet again, Mother herself, or Fred, but she put away her sewing tools quietly just in case she—or he—had doubled back on tiptoe and waited outside. Only when she was certain she was alone did she steal down the stairs to her bedroom, where she soon drifted off into a troubled sleep.

She woke not long after dawn to soft rapping on her door. "Eleanor," called Harriet softly. "Wake up."

She could not bear to see Fred after what she had said to him. "I don't want any breakfast. I'll come down when the dressmaker arrives."

"Get up and go to your mother at once. She needs you."

At the fear and alarm in the maid's voice, Eleanor bolted out of bed and threw a dressing gown over her nightdress. "What is it?" she asked, opening the door. "Where's my mother?"

"Downstairs. Be quiet or you'll wake the Corvilles." Then Harriet's sharp eyes darted to the floor. "What's this?"

Eleanor looked and discovered a small white envelope. It must have been slipped beneath her door while she slept. She reached for it, but Harriet was quicker. "Someone obviously meant that for me," said Eleanor sharply, thinking of Fred.

Harriet tucked it into her pocket. "It may be your door but it's your mother's house. You can have it if she says you might."

They hurried downstairs. Mother paced in the foyer, wringing her hands. At the sight of Eleanor, fury sparked in her eyes. "You put her up to this, didn't you? Where has she gone?"

Eleanor took in her mother's red-rimmed eyes, the note of hysteria in her voice. "Where has who gone?"

"Your sister." Mother resumed pacing, wringing her hands. "As if you didn't know. She took a horse, the bridal silver, and most of her clothes, but she left the pearls Edwin gave her."

"She also left a note." Harriet handed Mother the envelope. "In Eleanor's room."

Mother quickly withdrew a sheet of Abigail's monogrammed stationery. "Dear Eleanor," she read aloud. "I hope someday you will see that this is best for both of us. Edwin is a good and kindly man. I do not leave because he would not be a good husband, but because I love someone else. Please pray for me. Please forgive me. Your loving sister, Abigail."

"Give me that," said Eleanor, snatching the note.

"Why should she ask *you* to forgive her?" demanded Mother. "She should be begging me for forgiveness, me and her father."

"Where is Father?"

"Searching," said Harriet. "He'll call at the homes of all the young men Abigail knows. If he doesn't find her, at least he'll find out who else is missing."

"You're the only one she saw fit to bid farewell," said Mother. "You must have helped her. You must know the man."

"I don't." Eleanor was at an utter loss for a single likely name. "She has been distracted lately, but I thought she was just nervous about the wedding. I knew nothing of her intentions. You read what she wrote to me; you ought to see that."

Mother stopped short, a hand to her throat. "Merciful God, what if they have run off, but not married?" She inhaled sharply, drew herself up, and resumed pacing. "No matter. In fact, that might be best. We can bring her back. We will watch her so she cannot run off again."

"Mother! Whatever else Abigail has hidden from us, she clearly does not wish to marry Edwin."

"Do not cross me today, Eleanor. I will see them married, and you will keep quiet."

"Even if you could find Abigail and convince her to go through with it, you would be making a terrible mistake. Edwin would eventually learn of the deception. The scandal would force him to divorce her."

"Rumors. He would hear rumors only, and those will fade with time. The Corvilles want this marriage as much as we do. They will ignore what they do not wish to see."

Suddenly the door burst open and Father strode in, his face a thundercloud. Mother reached for him, but he brushed her aside. "We couldn't find her," he growled, "and none of the young men are missing."

Mother groped for his arm. "You were discreet? We cannot have your inquiries stirring up rumors."

"For God's sake, woman, we are beyond fearing rumors."

"Abigail's missing?"

Eleanor turned instinctively, but she knew Fred's voice.

"This does not concern you," said Mother, waving at Fred as if she could shoo him back up the stairs.

Father barked out a bitter laugh. "It is his concern. It was his horse Abigail stole."

Fred and Eleanor exchanged a look, and she knew they shared the same thought. "Did you inquire at the homes of Abigail's girlfriends?" she asked her father.

Mother clasped her hands together, a new hope appearing in her eyes. "Then you believe her letter was meant to send us searching in the wrong direction? Then perhaps there is no other man. Perhaps all will be well."

"Mr. Lockwood," said Fred, "I will need to borrow a horse. I know where we should continue the search."

The men left too quickly for Eleanor to call Fred back. Regardless of the consequences to the family, Eleanor did not want Fred to assist in Abigail's recapture.

❧

Eleanor half expected Mother to take to her bed, but instead she set herself to the task of keeping the Corvilles ignorant of Abigail's flight. Mother hid the letter and the necklace and instructed Harriet and Eleanor to say that Father, Fred, and Abigail had gone riding to see if Abigail approved of the horse the Bergstroms intended as their wedding gift.

Eleanor remained silent rather than lie, but Mother's explanation was enough to satisfy the Corvilles. After breakfast, Edwin and his father went into the city on business and Mother amused Mrs. Corville in the parlor. Eleanor withdrew to her study, but she was too heartsick to quilt, so she sat in the window seat and watched the front gates. Some time later, Edwin and his father returned from their errand; surely when they found Abigail still gone, they would grow suspicious. The Drury estate was close enough that Father and Fred could have made the round trip twice by then. What could be keeping them?

At last, the front gates swung open and two riders on horseback approached the house. She raced downstairs and out the front door just as Father and Fred dismounted and handed off the reins to a stablehand. Father stormed past Eleanor and into the house without a word, more furious than she had ever seen him.

"Was Abigail with Mr. Drury's daughter?" she asked Fred.

"No. She was with Mr. Drury."

For a moment Eleanor did not understand, then the shock of it struck her. She placed her hand on her heart and took a deep breath. "Are they married?"

"They will be before the day is out. Your father and I convinced him it would be prudent to do so."

Eleanor sank down upon the top step. "Oh, Abigail."

Fred climbed the stairs and sat beside her. "She asked me to give you a message. She begs your forgiveness and hopes you will call on her at her new home when the uproar has settled down."

Eleanor let out a bleak laugh. "Once again she asks for my forgiveness."

"She must realize what a scandal she's created. She left you here all alone to deal with the consequences."

"She and Mr. Drury will have consequences of their own to face." But at least Abigail would have a home, and the affection of the man she loved, while the Lockwoods would be ruined. "And poor Edwin. She should have told him. Leaving him like this is cruel."

"I'll tell him."

"No, Fred." She placed a hand on his arm to stop him from rising. "It should be someone from the family."

"I saw your sister at the Drury place often. I should have realized what was happening, but I didn't. Let me at least do this much."

Wordless, Eleanor nodded. Fred went into the house.

Eleanor hugged her knees to her chest and wondered what to do next. She dreaded going inside and facing the ugly scenes that were sure to unfold. She closed her eyes and wished she, too, could leap on a horse and flee to the side of the man she loved.

There would be no wedding, she suddenly realized, no dance with Fred. And now that Father knew of Fred's deception with Mr. Drury's horse, no Bergstrom would be welcome on Lockwood property—if any property remained to the Lockwoods now that the partnership with the Corvilles would dissolve.

She waited long enough for Fred to deliver the unhappy news before returning inside. The door to her father's study was closed, but she found Mother in the parlor conversing in hushed tones with Harriet. They broke off at Eleanor's entrance. "Sit down," commanded Mother, her face drawn but determined.

"Did Mr. Bergstrom—"

"Yes, he told Edwin, and somehow he managed to make the circumstances seem less dire than they are." She sighed and touched her hair. "I suppose I ought to thank him."

Eleanor frowned and sat down. "I suppose you should."

"Oh, do be quiet," snapped Mother. "Today of all days you must try to be pleasant."

The front bell rang. Harriet leapt up to answer it, and returned to inform them that the dressmaker had arrived.

"She came to finish fitting Abigail's gown." Eleanor rose. "I'll dismiss her."

"I told you to sit. Harriet, have the dressmaker wait for us in the conservatory, then fetch Abigail's gown. I will meet you there shortly."

Harriet nodded and fled from the room.

"Eleanor," said Mother. "We must have a wedding."

Eleanor felt the blood drain from her face.

"If Edwin and his parents agree, you will marry him in Abigail's place on Saturday."

"Even if he does agree, which I sincerely doubt, there will be no wedding because I will never consent to it. Edwin loves Abigail, not me."

"He is very fond of you."

"As a sister, and I think of him as a brother."

"Good marriages have been based upon less."

Eleanor stared at her mother in disbelief. "It is incomprehensible."

Mother's voice was acid. "Your father's business is so deeply in debt that without this partnership, we will not survive another year. We will have no home, no means of support."

"Father will find other work," said Eleanor, her voice shaking. "I will find work."

"You? What would you do? Do you think someone would pay you to read books or stitch quilts?"

"Perhaps—perhaps Abigail and Mr. Drury—"

"Absolutely not. We will take nothing from them." Mother rose and grasped Eleanor by the shoulders. "You must fulfill the obligations your sister abandoned."

"I cannot marry. You know this. I'm sure Edwin knows."

"The doctors have been wrong about you before. They thought you would die as a child, and yet here you are, as well and strong as any of us."

"That is not true."

"You are healthy enough for Edwin." Mother squeezed Eleanor's arms painfully. "What would you sacrifice in marrying him? A life alone with your books and your needle? Edwin loves books as much as you, so he will spare you ample time for reading. He will come to accept your patchwork fetish as well. You will have a husband and a home of your own. Don't you want that?"

"Mother—" She did want that; of course she did. But she was not Abigail, and the idea that she could simply step into her sister's place as easily as donning her wedding gown sickened her.

"Think of the alternatives. You may enjoy satisfactory health for years. Do you want to spend them impoverished and hungry?"

Eleanor tore herself away. "It would not come to that. We have friends, relations—"

"You will see how much affection our friends bear us when we are ruined."

"If I marry, it will be for love."

"*I* married for love," said Mother venomously. "And you can see what good it has done me. Never marry for love. Marry for position and security, as your father did. As I should have done. That is the only way you will not be disappointed. That is the only way you will receive exactly what you were promised."

Eleanor could endure no more. She turned and fled from the room, but before she could reach the stairs, Father exited the drawing room and closed the door behind him.

"The Corvilles have agreed," he told her. "You are a very fortunate girl."

Eleanor gaped at him. "How am I fortunate?"

"You have narrowly escaped the shame of spinsterhood. Do you need any other reward for fulfilling your duty to your parents?"

"What of my duty to myself? And what of Mother? For years you have told me it is my obligation as the unmarried daughter to care for her in her infirmity."

"Your obligations have changed. Once you marry Edwin, we will be able to hire a score of nurses to care for your mother."

"You are both mad." Eleanor picked up her skirts and fled to the sanctuary of her study. Once inside, she locked the door and barred it with a chair. She felt faint. She lay on the sofa and buried her face in her hands, anguished. Now she understood the reason behind Abigail's apologies. Abigail must have anticipated how her decision would affect her sister. She had known, and yet she had still run off.

A knock sounded on the door. "Eleanor, it's me."

"Edwin." Eleanor rose and opened the door. Edwin stood in the hallway with his hands in his pockets. "Oh, Edwin, I'm so sorry."

He tried to smile. "Was the prospect of marrying me so horrifying that she had to run off without a word? And for a man twice her age." He shook his head. "I thought she loved me. She never said so, but I assumed she was just being modest. I found it charming. She agreed to marry me, so I assumed she loved me."

"Of course you did," said Eleanor, though she had long known the truth. "Anyone would have."

He nodded and looked off down the hall. "I suppose." He cleared his throat. "I do wish her well. I hope she will be happy with the life she has chosen."

Eleanor's heart went out to him. "That's very generous of you."

"Generosity is a fine quality in a husband, or so I am told."

"Then you've spoken to my father."

He nodded.

"Edwin, surely you don't wish to marry me. I am not my sister."

"I know that, but I am very fond of you. We have much in common—more, I think, than Abigail and I had. I would be a good and faithful husband, Eleanor. I will provide for you and your family, and when the time comes, I will ensure the stability and growth of the business your father founded."

"In other words, you want my inheritance, not me. I thought better of you than that."

"Don't think ill of me for promising to safeguard my wife's fortune. That's all I meant." He reached for her hands, and with some misgivings, Eleanor allowed him to take them. "I've been nearly a part of your family for years, long enough, if you'll forgive me for saying so, to know there are no other suitors. We are friends now, and I'm confident we will grow to love each other deeply in time." He caught her eye and smiled. "I've heard that can happen, haven't you?"

Eleanor thought of Mother and shook her head. "How can I simply step into my sister's role as if I were an understudy in a play? Won't you be ashamed to stand with me at the altar before those hundreds of people because the sister you wanted ran off with another man?"

"Far less ashamed than I would be to notify those same hundreds that there will be no wedding at all," said Edwin. "We both have a duty to our families. It is best for everyone if we marry."

"I lack your confidence."

"Then why not rely upon my judgment? We have nothing to lose and a great deal to gain."

"I usually prefer to rely upon my own judgment," said Eleanor, knowing they had a great deal to lose. But she could not find words to tell him it was out of the question. He had borne too much humiliation that day. She could decline tomorrow, and perhaps, after the immediate pain of Abigail's flight had lessened, Edwin would see their circumstances more rationally. In the light of a new day, Eleanor's refusal would come as a relief.

"I cannot answer you now," she said.

"Of course not. You need time to grow accustomed to the idea, to discuss the situation with your parents."

Eleanor nodded, although she wanted nothing less. Her mother's words still haunted her. Eleanor yearned for a husband, a family, a home of her own—but she did not wish to obtain them under these circumstances. Nor was Edwin the man who had figured in her wistful imaginings.

Still, she had learned to compromise in other difficult situations. All her life, she had been forced to make do with the scraps she was given. She had even managed to piece together some contentment for herself.

"I will give you my answer tomorrow," she told him.

He nodded and quickly kissed her cheek before releasing her hands and disappearing down the hallway. Eleanor shut the door and leaned back upon it, closing her eyes. She wished she could run to Miss Langley's embrace and pour out all her grief and worry as she had done as a child. If Miss Langley were here to offer advice, she would tell Eleanor to do what was right. But what was right?

A knock on the door startled her out of her reverie. "I told you I would give you my answer tomorrow," she said.

"You can't mean you're seriously considering marrying him."

Fred. Eleanor flung open the door and he stormed in. "I have to consider it," she said. "You don't know what is at stake."

"I do know that you aren't property to be bartered between families."

Eleanor turned her back on him before he could perceive how he had wounded her. His words had laid plain what she already knew, that the woman Eleanor Lockwood mattered little in the upcoming nuptials. Her parents said she could not marry—except when they needed a bride to seal a contract. They said she could not leave home—except when saving Father's business took precedence over tending to Mother. They did not care how agreeing to marry Edwin would degrade her, and they craved their own comfort and security more than her happiness.

But she loved them, and she could not bear to be the agent of their misery. "I am not being bartered. It is my decision whether to accept or decline."

"Are you sure?"

"They cannot force me. On the other hand, if my choices are between marrying a decent man and seeing my family rendered destitute, I suppose there is only one choice after all."

"There are other alternatives."

"Such as?"

"If you're going to marry, marry for love. Marry me."

For a moment she couldn't breathe. "What makes you think I love you?"

He spun her around to face him. "Why did you tell me your father never intended to buy my horses?"

"It's not fair to answer a question with—" Then he kissed her, and she clung to him for a moment before pulling away. "I can't. My family needs me."

"Only because Abigail broke her promise, not that I blame her. Your parents will have to make their own way."

"I cannot bear children. Do you still wish to marry me?"

For an instant, pain flashed in his eyes, but he said, "I do. We'll have so many nieces and nephews around that it will be as if we have children of our own."

She did not believe any man would be satisfied with that. "How could I refuse Edwin and then marry you?"

"Because I love you. Edwin does not."

"Love is not the only factor to consider. Edwin cares for me in his way."

For a moment he just watched her. "If that's good enough for you, then there's nothing more I can say."

He went to the door. "Fred—"

"Try on your sister's wedding gown," he said roughly. "Maybe I don't know you as well as I thought. Maybe it'll fit you."

He slammed the door behind him.

❧

Fred's visit had shattered the serenity of her study, so as much as Eleanor longed for solitude, she composed herself and returned downstairs. Mother met her on the landing and steered her to the conservatory, where the dressmaker had been waiting all morning. Numb, she allowed herself to be undressed like a doll. Her corset was tightened, a cloud of white satin was thrown over her head—and there she stood, a pale beauty motionless in the mirror, just as Abigail had been.

"Who would have thought she was so pretty after all," marveled Harriet.

The dressmaker assured Mother the gown would be ready by Saturday morning.

The day passed in a blur. Eleanor was only vaguely aware that Edwin hovered in the background and Fred avoided her altogether. Occasionally she overheard snatches of conversation—her mother and Mrs. Corville quietly discussing how their guests should be informed, her father touting the strength of Lockwood's to Mr. Corville, Harriet asking Mother what she should pack for Eleanor's honeymoon. Not a word was spoken of Abigail, and as she had been the dominant subject in their discourse for months, her absence was conspicuous, and made their talk seem to Eleanor as if they spoke a foreign language.

At supper she discovered Mr. Bergstrom was gone. From the conversation, she learned he had lingered for hours before departing abruptly and without the apologies he owed them for his part in concealing Abigail's true affections. Eleanor could not believe how easily he had left her. She sat at the table without speaking or eating, and when the meal was over, it occurred to her that eventually there would be no distinguishing between herself and her sister.

She passed the evening in the parlor with the women and allowed Mother to escort her to her bedroom afterward.

"Your father and I are pleased you have come to your senses," said Mother as she turned down Eleanor's bedclothes. Eleanor could not remember her ever having done so before.

"I don't know that I have. I still haven't given Edwin my decision."

Mother turned away from the bed and regarded her with something very like pity. "You don't really believe you have a choice, do you?" She strode from the room, and with her hand on the doorknob, she said, "Marry Edwin. How will you pay for your physicians if you are destitute?"

She shut the door.

Shivering, Eleanor sat down on the bed. She saw at once how the rest of the week would unfold. She would go nowhere unaccompanied; she would be watched and threatened and scolded until her wedding day. Her parents could not force her to marry Edwin, but they could make it impossible for her to refuse.

She lay back and stared up at the ceiling. For hours, while night fell and the house grew still, she tried to convince herself to marry Edwin. She reminded herself of her duty, of her illness, of Edwin's promises to make her happy. Fulfilling those needs might be enough. She reminded herself that Fred had abandoned her.

She could not do it.

Mother was wrong. Eleanor did have a choice. Miss Langley would take her in. Somehow Eleanor would find a way to help her parents, but not by marrying Edwin.

She glanced about and spotted the suitcase Harriet had begun packing for the honeymoon. Eleanor hastily added a few more necessities. She snatched up her jewelry box, which contained the valuables her grandmother had bequeathed her and what little money of her own she had managed to accumulate, and tucked it in with her clothes. Hefting the bag, she slowly opened the door and stole into the hall. The darkness seemed watchful and accusing as she descended the stairs. Any moment she could be discovered, any moment—

She stopped short. Once she left that house, she could never return. She could not leave behind every cherished thing.

She hid the suitcase behind a statue on the landing and hurried upstairs again, heart pounding as she entered her study for what she knew would be the last time. There was no time to reason out what she could carry. She pulled the Rocky Mountain quilt from the frame and gathered it like a sack. Into it she bundled her sewing kit, the Crazy Quilt, and the box containing Miss Langley's letters. She could not look at the shelves full of beloved books without wanting to weep. She added the diary she had kept as a child, her first embroidered sampler, a silk shawl that had belonged to her grandmother, and, with a pang, a photograph of her family. Then she slung the awkward bundle over her shoulder and left her beloved sanctuary forever.

Eleanor descended the stairs at a near run, as fast and as silently as her burdens allowed. Already she mourned precious belongings left behind: the smooth stones from the shore near the summer house, the notebook in which she had written the addresses of her school friends, the sewing machine that had brought her so much pleasure. Eleanor pushed the thoughts from her mind and quickened her pace. She reached the door and fled outside—and froze at the edge of the porch in shock.

An automobile was slowly creeping up the drive.

As she stood rooted in place, staring, it slowed and stopped. Fred got out and ran to her. "Are you leaving?"

She nodded, thoughts of Boston and Miss Langley fading.

"Do you need a ride?"

"Yes, thank you," she said. Before the words left her mouth, Fred snatched up her suitcase and bundle and strode back to the automobile. Eleanor hurried after him as he tossed her things inside. He helped her into the passenger's seat before taking the wheel, and in moments, they were under way.

Eleanor did not want to look back, but something compelled her. As they passed through the front gates, she glanced back and saw the house, dark and silent, as if no one lived there anymore.

She shuddered and turned forward. "They will come after me, as they did my sister."

"I hope they won't know where to look. They may think you ran away on your own."

Then Eleanor understood why he had left the Lockwood home earlier that day. "You knew if we were both missing in the morning . . ."

"This way, Elm Creek Manor won't be the first place they look."

"Likely they'll think I ran off to Abigail." Then she shot him a look. "I thought you lived on a horse farm."

"I do."

"Elm Creek Manor is a rather grand name for a farmhouse."

He did not look at her, but even in the darkness she detected his broad smile.

They went to the train station, where Fred and Mr. Drury had agreed he would leave the automobile. Fred purchased two tickets for the next train west and they waited for their train, for pursuers. Eleanor's absence would be discovered by sunrise.

The train arrived first. She and Fred found two seats in an empty compartment and stowed her belongings. Exhausted, Eleanor rested against Fred and closed her eyes.

"Try to sleep if you can," said Fred. "We'll have to change trains in Philadelphia."

"You should rest, too. The conductor will wake us before our stop."

"I couldn't sleep a wink, but I'll try if you insist."

She assured him she did, and she left her seat to take down her belongings. She transferred the items from her bundle into her suitcase, unfurled the Rocky Mountain quilt, and, returning to the comfort of Fred's arms, she spread the quilt over them.

"It's not finished yet," she said, "but I think I have all the needles and pins out of it."

"It's beautiful."

It's our wedding quilt, Eleanor almost said, and realized she had always known it would be.

Chapter Five

Sylvia and Andrew drove east through the foothills of the Rockies toward Golden, Colorado. Andrew had said little about Bob and Cathy since the motor home pulled out of their driveway, as if he preferred to pretend the visit had never occurred. Apparently, despite his concerns about informing his children of their engagement, he had still hoped for a much happier reaction to the news.

She sighed and glanced at her map. The enthusiasm of Sarah and the other Elm Creek Quilters would have to compensate for what Andrew's children lacked, or their wedding would be a dismal occasion indeed.

"We just passed a sign for Golden," said Andrew. "Can you direct me from here?"

"Absolutely." Sylvia had last visited in 1993, when Golden had celebrated its first Quilt Day, but the landmarks were too remarkable to forget. "Just follow the M and the arch."

"Beg pardon?"

In response, Sylvia smiled and pointed out the window to a large letter M on one of the more prominent mountains. "Head that way, and turn south on Washington."

Andrew grinned and complied. "Is that M for 'museum'?"

"I think of it that way, but it's actually for the Colorado School of Mines."

They drove into downtown Golden, a charming place that, in Sylvia's opinion, looked exactly as a Western town should. The distinctive flat-topped mountains in the near distance resembled something straight out of a movie about the Wild West, and Sylvia would not have been surprised to see men on horseback kicking up a cloud of dust as they raced along the slopes.

They passed a statue of Buffalo Bill in the median strip, and just ahead, they spied a sign on an arch over the street. "'Howdy, Folks,'" Andrew read aloud. "'Welcome to Golden, Where the West Lives.' And to think I left my six-shooter at home."

"I want you on your best behavior," scolded Sylvia. "I don't see why anyone here should help me find my mother's quilt if you're going to joke about their town."

"Sorry, ma'am," said Andrew meekly, but his eyes twinkled and he tugged at the brim of an imaginary cowboy hat. "I guess this must be the arch you mentioned."

"It is indeed. The museum entrance is almost directly beneath it. Park wherever you like."

"You mean wherever I can," said Andrew. He twisted around in his seat to view the street behind him. "The kids were right about one thing. Sometimes this behemoth is more trouble than it's worth."

"Only when you have to parallel park."

"And when I have to fill up the tank." Andrew grimaced as he maneuvered the motor home into a place across the street from the museum. "Sometimes I wish I'd settled for a nice SUV."

They left the motor home and crossed the street hand in hand. They entered through the front double doors and paused in the foyer long enough for Sylvia to help herself to some of the pamphlets in the rack of brochures. Andrew sniffed the air. "Sure doesn't smell like a museum. Smells like lunch."

"There's a Chinese restaurant on the lower level. We could stop by for a bite to eat later." She smiled slyly and took his arm. "Or we could try the Buffalo Rose."

"You mean that place a few doors down? From the name, I figured it was a florist."

Sylvia erupted in peals of laughter. "I don't think you should tell them that. It's a biker bar."

"Chinese sounds good," said Andrew hastily. He held open the door and ushered her inside.

Sylvia eyed the gift shop with interest as they passed, but she was too eager to find her mother's quilt to be distracted long. They entered the first gallery and were greeted by two docents, who provided them with brochures about the exhibits and invited them to sign the guest book. "Waterford, Pennsylvania," one of the women said, reading upside down as

Sylvia handed the pen to Andrew. "Did you ever attend the quilt camp there?"

"She's one of the founders," said Andrew.

The second woman spun the guest book around, and her eyes lit up at what she read. "You're Sylvia Compson?"

"She sure is." Andrew put an arm around her proudly.

"I love your quilt, Sewickley Sunrise," the second docent said, adding that she had a print of it hanging in her office.

Sylvia and Andrew thanked the docents and moved deeper into the gallery. Andrew trailed after her as Sylvia approached the first quilt, an appliquéd scene of the first moon landing, nearly lifelike in its realism. "I don't think we'll find your mother's quilt here," said Andrew, and read aloud from the brochure. "'A retrospective of the works of Colorado quilter Alexandra Grant, age ninety-seven, who used intricate appliqué and surface embellishment to depict the most significant historical events of her lifetime.' That's some lifetime. Do you think you'll still be quilting when you're that age?"

"God willing," said Sylvia, and moved on to the next quilt, a collage of images from the civil rights movement, fluid and vividly colored scenes of hope and triumph. Hanging next to it, in stark contrast in monochromatic grays and browns, was a three-panel work depicting the World Trade Center, the Pentagon, and rolling hills Sylvia immediately recognized as the countryside of her own beloved state of Pennsylvania. A single bright color illuminated each panel: a brilliant blue sky over the Pentagon, a lush green forest for Pennsylvania, a firefighter in a yellow coat against a background of rubble in Manhattan.

Sylvia could hardly bear to look at it, and at the same time she longed to touch it, to find comfort in the soft fabrics even as the images caused her pain. She reached for Andrew's hand instead. He held it in both of his, and let her linger a moment longer before drawing her away to the next quilt.

Before long, Sylvia lost herself in the beauty of the quilts and the poetry of their stories. Andrew's prediction proved true, however, as Sylvia had assumed it would; not even a novice quilter or a very poor historian would have confused Eleanor Lockwood's pieced New York Beauty quilt with the appliquéd pictorial works of Alexandra Grant. They left the first gallery and went upstairs to the second, although one glance at the sign outside the exhibit indicated they were not likely to find her mother's quilt there, either.

"'Agriculture Quilts,'" Sylvia read aloud. "It's a long shot, but if we have time, I'd prefer to check anyway, if only to be sure."

"Maybe they have quilts in here that aren't part of the special exhibit," said Andrew, escorting her into the gallery. "Besides, if we don't look, I'll spend the whole drive home wondering what in the world an Agriculture Quilt is."

They quickly discovered that Agriculture Quilts were quilts inspired by farming. Some artists had used pictorial quilts to create fabric snapshots of farm life, much as the artist featured in the lower gallery had done for historical events. Others had approached the theme more whimsically, resulting in works such as the Pickle Dish bed quilt pieced from cow print fabrics and the Corn and Beans quilt with the Farmer's Daughter border. Sylvia's favorite was an Attic Windows wall hanging pieced from vintage feedsacks. She peered at the quilt closely to study the fabric, then nodded, satisfied that the fabrics were not reproductions. Genuine vintage feedsack fabrics were scarce and highly prized by some collectors, and whenever Sylvia saw the charming works modern quiltmakers had created from the scraps they had found, she remembered with misgivings how many sacks of horse feed must have come to Elm Creek Manor in her childhood. Her thrifty mother would not have simply discarded them, but since she had not cut them up to make quilts as far as Sylvia could recall, Sylvia had no idea what had become of them.

They returned downstairs. Andrew said nothing, but he still held Sylvia's hand, so she knew he was sorry for her sake that their second lead had turned out no more successfully than their first. "There must be other rooms we haven't seen," said Sylvia, unwilling to give up so easily, not after driving so far and hoping for so much.

They returned to the first gallery, where Sylvia showed the docents Summer's computer illustration of the New York Beauty quilt and asked if they recalled seeing it. To Sylvia's dismay, the women studied the picture and shook their heads. "Are you certain?" she asked. "A recent visitor to your museum says she saw it here. We already checked the galleries, but might it be somewhere else in the museum?"

The docents exchanged a look, and Sylvia could see they were reluctant to disappoint her. "It's not in any of the staff offices," said the first docent, "or in the classroom. Did you ask in the gift shop? We do sell some antique quilts. Your friend might have seen it there, although I know it isn't there now."

Sylvia nearly gasped. "You mean it might have been here—but was sold?"

"Most likely not," said the second docent quickly. "We'll ask Opal. She's been with the museum since its founding. If your quilt has ever been here, she'll know."

Sylvia nodded, but as the docent led them back upstairs to the museum's administrative office, she envisioned a clerk closing a cash register and handing a satisfied customer the New York Beauty in a plastic bag. How on earth would she find it then?

Opal turned out to be a cheerful, curly haired woman who greeted them warmly and listened with interest to Sylvia's explanation about her search for her mother's missing quilts. "Your Internet correspondent says she saw your quilt here?" asked Opal, accepting the picture Andrew handed her.

"She did, but unfortunately, she didn't say when."

Opal studied the illustration, shook her head, and returned the paper to Sylvia. "It's not one of ours. We never sold a quilt resembling this one in our quilt shop, and I know we don't have it in storage."

"Storage?"

"Why, yes. We have more than two hundred and fifty quilts in our permanent collection, and when we aren't displaying them, we keep them in protected storage."

"If you don't mind, could we please look for ourselves?" asked Sylvia. "I don't mean to be a bother, but if there's any chance you might have my mother's quilt, I would kick myself later for not asking."

Opal smiled sympathetically. "Unfortunately, that's easier said than done. Ordinarily, we don't even open this room to the public, but I think we can make an exception for the founder of Elm Creek Quilts."

She led them next door to a locked room. Inside the air was cool and dry, and along one wall Sylvia discovered shelves and shelves of quilts, each wound around a long carpet roll and wrapped in a clean cotton sheet. "Oh, dear," said Sylvia. "I suppose looking at these quilts would be more difficult than I thought."

"I'm afraid so," said Opal. "But I've been through this collection many times, and I know we don't have any in the New York Beauty pattern. I would definitely remember such a striking quilt."

She offered to post pictures of the New York Beauty on their announcements board in case any of their other visitors had seen it. Perhaps, she suggested, Sylvia's Internet correspondent had seen the New York Beauty elsewhere in the area and was mistaken only in regard to the specific location. Sylvia appreciated the thread of hope, however thin, and gratefully gave Opal illustrations of all five quilts.

"Strike two," said Sylvia as she and Andrew returned downstairs.

"Don't get too discouraged," said Andrew. "We make progress with every lead we follow, even if the trail doesn't seem to go anywhere."

"I won't feel like we're making progress until we find one of the quilts."

Andrew chuckled. "Come on. I'll cheer you up at the gift shop."

Sylvia raised her eyebrows at him, but allowed him to steer her into the QuiltMarket. She had enjoyed exploring the museum despite the unsuccessful search, but she wasn't about to tell him so. If he wanted to console her with a present, it wouldn't be right to spoil his fun.

❧

By the time they reached Iowa several days later, Sylvia had read her new book on the Agriculture Quilts exhibit from cover to cover twice, and Summer had received nine more responses from the Missing Quilts Home Page. None of these new sightings were on the route home to Pennsylvania, however, which suited Sylvia just fine. After their disappointments in Boulder City and Golden, she and Andrew had decided that it would be wiser to contact future prospects by phone first to rule out obvious false leads rather than put so many extra miles on the motor home for nothing more than another dead end.

But since they were driving through Iowa, anyway, they saw no reason not to turn north at Des Moines and investigate a promising e-mail message sent by the proprietor of Brandywine Antiques in Fort Dodge. Not only had he seen an Ocean Waves quilt fitting Sylvia's description, he actually had it in his possession.

"He inherited the business from his grandfather," said Sylvia as they paused at a gas station to fill up the tank and purchase a map of the city. "His grandparents used to travel to Pennsylvania to buy Amish quilts, but they bought others, too, and he believes this Ocean Waves quilt might have originated in Pennsylvania."

"Why would they go all the way to Pennsylvania for Amish quilts?" said Andrew. "There are Amish communities much closer."

"Perhaps he had a fondness for Lancaster. I certainly do."

"Well, sure, but you're from Pennsylvania. Why would an antique shop be interested in new Amish quilts, anyway?"

"Heavens, Andrew, how should I know? Perhaps they bought antique Amish quilts. You'll have to ask—" She glanced at her notes. "You'll have to ask this George K. Robinson when we arrive."

Andrew shrugged and said he might do just that.

They located the street on the map and, with slightly more difficulty, found it in the city as well, but the shop itself eluded them. "3057 Brandywine Drive," said Sylvia, checking her notes. "Perhaps I wrote down the wrong number."

"Could be. This strip mall is the entire 3000 block, and I don't see a sign for Brandywine Antiques."

Neither did Sylvia, and they had passed the strip mall three times. Andrew drove the entire length of the street once, and again, scanning every sign and building they passed, but they could not find it. They did discover one antique shop, but not only was it not the one they were searching for, the owner claimed there were no other antique shops in that part of town.

"Of course he would say that," said Sylvia as Andrew helped her back into the motor home. "He doesn't want us to visit the competition."

She didn't really believe that, and she knew Andrew didn't either when he suggested they return to the strip mall and inquire at whatever business occupied 3057 Brandywine Drive. If they didn't know where the mysterious antique shop was, Sylvia could phone Summer and verify the address.

They parked in the strip mall lot and strolled the length of the shops. "I hate to think we made this trip for nothing," Sylvia remarked, when Andrew suddenly stopped in his tracks in front of a Letters et All store.

"This is it."

"This can't be it. This is one of those shipping and mailing services." Then Sylvia understood. "There's no store. It's just a mail drop."

Andrew nodded and pushed the door open.

"But that doesn't make any sense," she said, lowering her voice as she followed him inside. "I don't care how much mail a business receives. It wouldn't be practical to send someone to pick it up each day instead of having it delivered to the store."

"Exactly." Andrew strode up to the queue. "I think you might have been right when you said there is no store."

Sylvia had no time to reply, for the smiling young woman behind the counter beckoned them forward. "May I help you?"

"I hope so," said Andrew. "We're looking for a business called Brandywine Antiques. They gave this place as their address."

The young woman's smile vanished. "They must be one of our mail clients." She nodded to a wall of metal post office boxes on the opposite wall.

"We need to find the shop itself," said Sylvia. "Do you have another address?"

The young woman glanced at a middle-aged gentleman behind the counter. He had not appeared to be listening, but he looked up at Sylvia's question and said, "I'm sorry. We can't give out any personal information about our clients. It's a corporate privacy policy."

"We aren't asking for personal information," said Andrew, "just the address of a business."

"I'm very sorry, folks." He looked past them to the next customer in line. "May I help you?"

Andrew scowled, and the young woman gave them a look of helpless apology. "Come along, Andrew," murmured Sylvia, taking his arm. "We haven't hit our dead end yet."

They left the shop and retraced their steps until they came to a pay telephone Sylvia remembered passing earlier. They searched the weathered telephone book, but Brandywine Antiques was not listed in either the yellow pages or the alphabetical business directory. "I suppose it's time to call home," said Sylvia, digging into her purse for change. "Perhaps Summer said Fort Dodge, Indiana, or Ohio. Or maybe the city—"

Andrew placed a hand on her shoulder. "Hold on. I think I see help coming."

Sylvia followed his line of sight and discovered the young woman from Letters et All hurrying toward them, glancing furtively over her shoulder. "Here," she said, and handed Sylvia a scrap of paper. "The owner of the box gave this as his address. Just please don't tell anyone where you got this. I could get fired."

Sylvia glimpsed a hastily scrawled address. "Are you sure, dear?"

She nodded. "This is the third time senior citizens have asked about him in two weeks. I think he's up to something, and I don't like it."

"Thanks very much, miss," said Andrew. "We appreciate your help—and we can keep a secret."

The young woman gave them a quick smile and dashed back to the store.

Sylvia studied the address. "Well, Andrew? Do you feel like playing detective?"

Within minutes they were back on the road, following their map away from the business district into a residential area. When they stopped in front of a two-story colonial house on a pleasant, tree-lined street adjacent to a park, Sylvia shook her head in disbelief. "I suppose our Mr. Robinson might run the business out of his home."

Andrew snorted, skeptical.

A woman who looked to be in her late forties answered the doorbell, wiping her hands on a dish towel.

"Oh, dear, I hope we didn't interrupt your supper," said Sylvia, giving the woman her most disarming smile.

"Oh no, my son isn't even home from school yet," she assured them. "He's a junior at the local college. Is there something I can help you with?"

"I hope so. We're looking for Brandywine Antiques."

The woman looked puzzled. "Brandywine Antiques? There's a Brandywine Drive near the mall . . ."

"Yes, we're quite familiar with that," said Sylvia. "I don't suppose you know a George K. Robinson?"

Behind them, a car pulled into the driveway. Sylvia and Andrew turned to see a bushy-haired young man in baggy clothes climbing out of a bright blue hatchback.

"I'm afraid I don't," said the woman. "My son might. He has me at my wit's end most of the time, but he does know the neighborhood."

"Hey, Mom, did I get any mail?" he called, sauntering up the front walk.

"Two packages on the hall table. Jason, do you know the Robinson family?"

"Who?" he asked, brushing past Sylvia and Andrew on his way to the front door.

"These nice people who you didn't even say hello to are looking for someone named George Robinson."

"George K. Robinson, to be precise," said Sylvia.

"Or his company, Brandywine Antiques," Andrew added.

Jason froze. "Never heard of him. Or—or it. That company. Whatever you called it."

"That's a shame," said Sylvia. "Brandywine Antiques is supposed to have a quilt that belonged to my mother, and we were willing to spend quite a lot of money for it."

Sylvia and Andrew bid his mother good-bye and turned to go.

"Just a sec," said Jason, with a furtive glance at his mother as he followed them down the stairs. "I do all my business over the Internet, see? You can only buy my stuff through AsIsAuctions dot com. I don't have a storefront yet."

"What?" his mother said. "Since when are you an antiques dealer?"

"You told me to get a job," protested Jason. He turned a pleading gaze on Andrew and Sylvia and lowered his voice. "I'm saving up money to buy a store, but until then, I'm running my business out of the house. Really. What was it you said you were interested in again?"

"A quilt," said Andrew, loud enough for Jason's mother to hear. "The pattern's called Ocean Waves. It's made up of lots of blue and white triangles."

Jason nodded, but before he could reply, his mother called, "You mean that raggedy old thing you got at the Hixtons' garage sale?"

Jason managed a weak grin. "You'd be surprised where great finds turn up."

"Great finds? That's no antique. Mr. Hixton's mother made that quilt, and you know it. I heard her tell you myself."

Jason held up his hands, begging Sylvia and Andrew not to leave. "Let me just run inside and get a contract. Once you sign that, I can show you the quilt."

He hurried back up the stairs, but his mother blocked the doorway with her arm before he could duck past. "Sign a contract before they see what they're buying?" Her eyes narrowed. "Just what kind of business are you running, anyway?"

With his mother's help, Sylvia and Andrew eventually dragged the truth from him.

The young man had indeed been running a business out of the house—a shady business Sylvia considered to be just this side of fraud. He trolled Internet Web sites such as the Missing Quilts Home Page and eBay to find potential customers. With a list of the desired items in hand, he rummaged through garage sales and flea markets until he found similar products. Then he would contact the potential customer with the good news that he might have what they were looking for. "The key word is 'might,'" said Jason, glancing from his mother to Sylvia and Andrew apprehensively. "All my sales were through AsIsAuctions. They clearly state in their service agreement that all items for sale are as is. It's the buyer's responsibility to inspect the item in person if they want. All sales are final, so you can't get a refund unless you never get your product or you can prove the seller lied about it."

"You certainly lied to us about this quilt," declared Sylvia.

"I didn't lie." Jason turned to his mother and quickly added, "I didn't."

Andrew frowned. "You said you believed this quilt might have come from Pennsylvania."

"Exactly. I said 'might.' That also means it might *not* have come from Pennsylvania."

"But you knew for a fact that it did not," exclaimed Sylvia. "And what about your alias, George K. Robinson? There is no such person."

"Everybody uses fake names on the Internet. It's for personal privacy, that's all."

"Young man," said Sylvia, shaking her head, "you have such a gift for double-talk I'm sure you're destined for a career in politics."

Andrew folded his arms and regarded Jason sternly. "If you're such an honest dealer, why did you pretend to know nothing about Brandywine Antiques?"

Jason hesitated. "I didn't want my mom to get mad. I knew she wouldn't want me to run a business out of the house."

"A business I could handle," said his mother sharply. "A scam, on the other hand . . ." She shook her head and gave Sylvia and Andrew an appraising look. "The question is, what are we going to do about this?"

Sylvia was reluctant to involve the police, but she and Andrew were both resolute that Jason should not be allowed to perpetrate his scheme any longer. They also insisted that he make restitution for any past customers he might have deceived and write every one of them a letter of apology.

"Oh, he'll do that, all right," said his mother. "If I have to stand over him while he writes every word."

They all agreed that Jason should be denied access to the Internet at least until his obligations to his customers were fulfilled, and that AsIsAuctions must be informed. If all those measures were followed, Sylvia and Andrew would be satisfied, and they would not press charges.

"Do you think that's enough?" Sylvia asked Andrew as they resumed their journey east.

"Nothing short of shutting down this AsIsAuctions place would be enough for me," said Andrew. "They're just as guilty as he is. But I guess this will have to be enough unless we want to have Jason prosecuted for fraud."

"He's just a boy. I hate to ruin his life when all we lost was a few hours of our time and the cost of gasoline."

"We wouldn't be ruining his life. He did it to himself. And I don't know how we can rely on his mother to punish him when she didn't even know what was going on under her own roof."

The harshness in Andrew's tone surprised Sylvia. "She seemed furious. I'm sure she'll see to it he can't swindle anyone else."

Andrew shook his head. "Remember what the girl from the mailbox place said? This is the third time seniors have asked about Brandywine Antiques. Jason's targeting old folks, and that shows calculation and contempt. He's a crook, Sylvia. A young crook, but still a crook, and he's just going to get worse. Mark my words."

Sylvia did not know what to say. They drove on in silence until they stopped for the night, just west of the Illinois border.

❧

Two days later they arrived in Silver River, Indiana, just outside Fort Wayne, to pursue the last of Summer's Internet leads between them and Elm Creek Manor. Although he didn't complain, Sylvia knew Andrew just wanted to get the visit over with and go home. She could hardly blame him. Her anticipation had lessened with each dead end. She might have considered abandoning the search altogether if not for a sense of duty to her mother—and if not for her proud proclamations that she would not give up the search until every lead had been followed to its end.

"At least they're expecting us this time," Sylvia said as Andrew drove through town, keeping an eye out for the Niehauses' street. Sylvia had phoned them the previous night, for while it was perfectly acceptable to stop by a museum or antique shop unannounced, she would not dream of intruding on a private residence that way. Mona Niehaus herself had answered the phone, and when Sylvia explained they were in the area, Mona invited them to come see the quilt for themselves. Her description sounded so much like Sylvia's mother's Crazy Quilt that Sylvia allowed herself to hope their luck would take a turn for the better here.

They parked in front of a sky-blue Victorian house with a white picket fence and a minivan in the driveway. In the front yard, a sudden gust of wind rustled the boughs of a pair of maple trees, sending a flurry of brilliant gold and orange leaves dancing to the ground. Dried cornstalks adorned a black lamppost in front of the house, and on the wraparound porch stood a white stone goose dressed in blaze orange and camouflage, a wooden duck decoy propped up against its booted feet. It was such a typically idyllic autumn scene that Sylvia would have been thoroughly charmed if not for their sojourn in Fort Dodge.

"Reminds me of Jason's house," remarked Andrew, echoing her own thoughts.

"Don't be ridiculous," said Sylvia, unfastening her seat belt. "His house was brick, and they had no picket fence."

She spoke mostly for her own benefit, however, and tried to prepare herself for the worst as they climbed the porch stairs and rang the doorbell. A boy of about seven opened the door halfway and greeted them in a very formal manner. When they asked for Mona Niehaus, he said, "She's my grandma." At that moment, a girl about two years younger peeped shyly around the door. "I'll get her."

"Thank you, darling, but I'm right here." The door opened all the way, and a tall, thin woman with salt-and-pepper hair pulled back in a batik scarf stood before them. Silver bracelets jingled as she placed her hands on the children's shoulders and steered them back into the house. "You must be Sylvia and Andrew. I'm so pleased you could come."

She welcomed them into the living room, where the two children played with a jumble of unrelated toys in the center of a woven rug. Sylvia took the seat Mona offered, an overstuffed armchair with legs shaped like lion's feet, and glanced about the room for the quilt. She saw heavily embroidered pillows on the sofa, all manner of candles on the mantel, and framed photographs and other eclectic pieces covering so much of the walls that she could barely see the flowered wallpaper behind them. She saw no quilts.

Mona excused herself and returned with a tray. "Please help yourselves," she said as she placed the tea and sandwiches on the coffee table and hurried back out. In a moment they heard the creaking of footsteps on stairs.

Sylvia and Andrew exchanged bemused looks, but Andrew shrugged and piled several sandwiches on a plate. Sylvia knew she was too nervous to hold a teacup, so she merely sat fidgeting in her chair, watching the children play. "No, the engine goes in here," the little boy told the girl, handing her a small wooden block, but what sort of vehicle the engine was meant to propel, Sylvia had no idea.

Before long they heard footsteps again, and then Mona returned with something draped over her arm. "This is the quilt I contacted you about," she said, unfolding it carefully. "I hope it's the right one. It would be a shame if you came all this way for nothing."

"We were passing by on our way home from California anyway," Andrew said, but Sylvia merely nodded. Involuntarily, she straightened in her chair and held her breath.

Mona held up the quilt, and Sylvia was struck speechless.

"As you can see, it definitely is a Crazy Quilt." Mona regarded Sylvia inquisitively, awaiting a response. "And it has the identifying marks you listed on the Web site. Although some of the stitches have come out, you can still see an embroidered spiderweb in this corner. Here is the appliquéd horseshoe, and if I'm not mistaken, this patch here is from a linen handkerchief. Do you see the monogrammed ALC?"

"Sylvia?" prompted Andrew.

"That's it," said Sylvia. "That's my mother's quilt."

"How wonderful," exclaimed Mona. She draped the quilt over Sylvia's lap. "I hoped it would be. You must be thrilled."

Sylvia hesitated before touching the delicate fabrics, as if they would dissolve like the memory of a dream. She had not seen her mother's Crazy Quilt in more than fifty years. The colors were not as bright as she remembered, and some of the fabrics had unraveled so that only the embroidery stitches held the quilt together, but she did not remember when she had ever seen anything so lovely.

"Mona," she said, "I am so far beyond thrilled that I don't think they've invented a word to describe how I'm feeling."

Mona clasped her hands together and beamed. "I couldn't be happier for you. And to think, I never would have known to contact you except for my daughter-in-law." She indicated the children with a proud nod. "Their mother."

"She's a dentist," the boy piped up. "Grandma plays with us when she works."

"Yes, and we have a lovely time, don't we?" Mona turned back to Sylvia. "She's a quilter, and she heard about the Missing Quilts Home Page at her guild meeting. When she read the description of your lost Crazy Quilt, she immediately recognized mine."

Sylvia felt a pang at Mona's last word, though she was right to use it. The quilt did belong to Mona. "I'm very grateful you contacted me," she said. "I'm also quite curious. How did you come to own it?"

"By a very circuitous route," said Mona with a laugh. "This quilt has had an eventful life since leaving your household.

"On your way through town, you passed a lovely old brownstone called the Landenhurst Center. It was refurbished into an office building during the eighties, but back in the sixties and seventies, it was a theater for the performing arts. A lovely place, too—velvet curtains, ornate paintings and carvings, two balconies, and private boxes for the local gentry—but the acoustics were far from ideal and the roof leaked, and after the new civic center opened, its time had passed.

"The founders of this theater, Arthur and Christine Landenhurst, were rising stars in vaudeville at a time when vaudeville was going the way of the buggy whip. They traveled from town to town performing their comedy act on a variety of stages—nothing terribly grand, of course, but fame and fortune seemed only the next performance away. They had both been married to other people, people who were not performers and thus did not understand them at all, or so Arthur and Christine thought. They fell passionately in love with each other, and one night, after a particularly successful performance in front of a scout from a New York theater who promised them they could be headliners, they ran off to New York, where they divorced their spouses, married each other, and eagerly anticipated their coming stardom.

"Not long after their arrival, they discovered that the theater this scout worked for was not one of the most prestigious. According to the story, it was one of the seediest in the city. Christine and Arthur needed a year to get out of their contract, and almost another year to find a better one, but that, too, was short-lived. Both tried to find work on Broadway, never managing to get more than bit parts, but they persisted, until one day they realized they were ten years older and not one step closer to becoming headliners than the day they had arrived in New York.

"They must have realized their big breaks might never come, for when Christine was offered a role in a traveling production, she took it, and Arthur accompanied her. Eventually he won a part in the cast, too, and together they toured throughout the East Coast and parts of the Midwest, enjoying every minute on stage, but hating the travel and the unpredictability of their profession.

"They were heading West after a performance in Harrisburg, Pennsylvania, when the train was delayed for repairs. The entire company found themselves stranded in a small town with nothing to do but wait and try to enjoy the unexpected time off. Arthur and Christine decided to explore the quaint shops downtown, which is where they found your mother's quilt."

Mona reached for the quilt, and Sylvia reluctantly allowed her to take hold of one edge. "They bought it, of course," said Mona, regarding the quilt with amused fondness. She nodded to the patch cut from a linen handkerchief. "Actors are notoriously superstitious, and when they saw the monogram—the same as their own, ALC for Arthur and Christine Landenhurst—they saw it as an omen of change. I imagine they were ready to give up the road anyway, but finding this quilt gave them the push they needed. So they resumed their journey with the company and waited for another sign.

"The production was in its final week in South Bend when the sign finally came. A childhood friend of Arthur's had driven all the way from Fort Wayne, where he was a college professor, to see the couple's performance. As it happened, this friend was in a position to offer Arthur a job as a drama teacher. Arthur accepted, and so he and Christine moved to Fort Wayne."

"Arthur became a drama professor at the college?" asked Andrew.

"Well, not exactly. The job was at the local high school. But there Arthur discovered a love for teaching, as did Christine, who became a music instructor and vocal coach. Eventually they joined the college faculty, and wouldn't you know it, their acting careers finally took off. They both made numerous appearances in university theater productions, and later, they became quite popular hosts of a local television variety show. They founded the Landenhurst Theater here in Silver River, where they made their home, and they were very well regarded as patrons of the arts and pillars of the community."

"They sound like very interesting people," said Sylvia. Suddenly she didn't mind quite so much that they had owned her mother's quilt. They had purchased it honestly enough, and by its appearance, they had cared for it properly.

"That explains how it ended up in Silver River, Indiana," said Andrew, "but not how you became its owner."

"Oh yes. Please go on," said Sylvia. "Are you related to the Landenhursts?"

"No, but my husband was acquainted with them. Arthur Landenhurst died in 1984, and Christine passed away two years later. They had no children, and except for a modest percentage for the general scholarship fund at the college, they left their estate to a trust to help fund the Landenhurst Theater in perpetuity. Most of their possessions were sold to establish this trust, but others—their substantial collection of costumes and musical scores, for example, autographed photos and scripts from actors they had met, various items that seemed to have little fiscal worth but could be used as distinctive stage props—those remained in the theater, in the safekeeping of the theater board.

"Regrettably, after some time, the theater ran into financial problems, which were augmented, I'm sad to say, by the board's poor management of their finances. The board held an auction of the Landenhurst's remarkable collections in an attempt to shore up the trust, but they held off their troubles for only a few more years." Mona sighed and gathered up the quilt, and Sylvia forced herself not to cling to it. "The theater sold to a business development group. At first there were some sporadic protests from local preservationists who wanted the building to remain a theater, but even they realized it would cost a fortune to bring it up to modern standards." Mona stroked the quilt. "I have wonderful memories of that theater. Now all that remains is its name, most of its original exterior, and those belongings of the Landenhursts that were sold at auction."

"The Crazy Quilt was one of those?" asked Sylvia.

Mona smiled. "Yes. It was a prop in numerous plays over the years—*Little Women* and *Arsenic and Old Lace,* among others. It was also used in *You Can't Take It with You,* in which my eldest son appeared. He went on to become a theater major at Yale, and now he's a director."

"I can see why you wanted to keep this quilt as a memento," remarked Andrew.

"Well, everyone around here knows the legend of how the Landenhursts came to Silver River, but only a few know the story of this particular quilt, or I suspect the bidding would have gone far beyond my reach."

"How did you happen to hear the story?" asked Sylvia, with a sudden fear that Mona's tale might be no more than hearsay.

"My late husband was a lawyer," said Mona. "He was also, at one time, a member of the theater board. When Arthur and Christine updated their will to create the Landenhurst Trust, my husband met frequently with them and their counsel. They shared quite a few stories of how they came by certain items of great sentimental value." She gave Sylvia a long look of understanding. "I suppose the only person who valued this quilt more than they did would be you."

Sylvia tried to smile. "In my case, 'sentimental value' would be an extreme understatement."

"That's why although I might own it, it truly belongs to you. To me it will never be more than a beautiful object d'art, a fond remembrance of pleasant occasions and two people I greatly admired. To you, every piece of fabric, every stitch, every thread contains a memory of your family, of your mother. This quilt is a part of you in a way it will never be a part of me, however attached to it I might have become." She smiled. "That's why you are the only person I could conceivably sell it to."

Sylvia felt a catch in her throat. "You would let me buy it?"

Mona appeared to consider it for a moment, and then she shrugged. "For what I paid for it, and oh, perhaps a little something extra."

"I expect you to make a fair profit, of course." Sylvia worried far less that the price would be out of her reach than that Mona might change her mind.

"That's not what I mean," said Mona. "Did I mention my daughter-in-law is a quilter?"

❦

Sylvia and Andrew began the last leg of their journey home, their spirits light. Sylvia rarely let the quilt out of her hands. She could still hardly believe that Mona had been willing to part with it for the few hundred dollars she had spent at the Landenhurst auction and the promise of a free week at camp for her daughter-in-law. "I hope you offer classes in making Crazy Quilts," said Mona wistfully as they parted. "Perhaps you can encourage her to make me a replacement."

"I'll do my best," promised Sylvia, although they both knew nothing could replace this particular quilt.

As they drove east to Pennsylvania and Elm Creek Manor, the precious quilt on Sylvia's lap, she could laugh at all her worries of the past few weeks. Her disappointment over the earlier false leads suddenly seemed insignificant. Even Bob's and Cathy's lack of enthusiasm for the news of their engagement no longer troubled her quite as much as before.

Cradling her mother's legacy in her arms, she renewed her resolve to search out the remaining four quilts wherever the trail would take her. Now that she had found one, nothing could dissuade her from pursuing every lead. Nothing could diminish her high hopes, not after the impossible had come to pass.

Nothing, she thought, until they arrived home at Elm Creek Manor and found Andrew's daughter waiting for them.

Chapter Six

Eleanor sat alone in her study on the third floor of Elm Creek Manor. The unfinished quilt in her lap was too small to warm her, but she scarcely noticed the chill. If she acknowledged a discomfort as trivial as the cold, she would then have to feel all the other pain. Far better to allow her fingers to grow numb in the draft from the open window. Far better for her to grow numb everywhere.

She stroked the quilt, though she barely felt the soft cotton beneath her hands. She should have set it aside, as she had two years earlier when her hopes had last been shattered. This time, although her morning nausea had almost certainly revealed her secret weeks before she and Fred had told the family, she had waited until nearly halfway through her time before taking up the quilt again. Within a month she had quilted nearly every feathered plume, every wreath of elm leaves, every crosshatched heart, every delicate ribbon in the quilt's pure, unbroken white surface before she lost the child she had so longed to cuddle within its soft embrace.

She would set the quilt aside again, and complete it when she again had reason to do so. If she ever again had reason.

She heard the door open. "I felt a draft all the way down the hall," said Lucinda. "Why on earth is that window open?"

Because Eleanor longed for some scent of spring on the air to remind her of the promise of life. Because she no longer had any reason to take extra precautions regarding her health. Because she might see Fred, and he always reminded her that although God had denied her a child, he had given her a husband who loved and cherished her. He had brought her into a loving family, and that ought to be enough.

Instead she said, "I wanted some air."

"Then you should have accepted Fred's invitation to walk outside with him this morning rather than let all this winter chill into the house."

"Winter's over, Aunt Lucinda."

Lucinda was her father-in-law's youngest sister, only four years older than Eleanor herself, but the Bergstrom family firmly believed in using the honorific. In the five years she had been married to Fred, Eleanor had grown accustomed to their habits.

"In Pennsylvania, April does not necessarily mean the end of winter." Lucinda crossed the room and shut the window firmly, then grasped Eleanor's hands, warming them in her own. "We've had snowstorms in April that rival any in the heart of winter."

"I know. All the more reason to stay indoors." Eleanor tucked her hands into the folds of the quilt. "You forget how long I've lived here."

"No, you forget." Lucinda's voice was gentle, but resolute. "You could not be more a part of this family than if you had been born into it. You do not grieve alone. Don't shut yourself away up here, away from everyone who loves you."

Eleanor choked back the threat of tears. "To think, in my parents' home, I was so eager to turn the nursery into a study. Now I would give anything to turn this study into a nursery."

"If you mean to stay up here until such a need arises, you will be waiting a very long time. That sofa is much too narrow for both you and Fred."

Eleanor was so shocked she forgot to stifle a giggle. "Only you would joke at a time like this."

"It's a pity more people don't realize that jokes are most necessary precisely at times like this." Lucinda took Eleanor's hands again and pulled her to her feet. Eleanor felt only the slightest dull ache in her abdomen. "Come downstairs and quilt with us. If not for you, then for Clara."

Eleanor gently folded the little quilt and nodded. For reasons she could only guess, Fred's seven-year-old sister admired her and imitated her in nearly everything. Eleanor knew that all she did in these dark days would teach Clara how to respond when, inevitably, her own life was touched by sorrow.

She was about to leave the quilt behind when Lucinda said, "Bring it. It's too beautiful to go unfinished."

Wordlessly, Eleanor tucked the quilt under her arm and followed Lucinda from the room. Lucinda would not raise her hopes with false promises that someday her quilt would cuddle a little one, and Eleanor found her frankness reassuring in its familiarity. She would take her comfort wherever she could find it, for she now knew that while she had defied her childhood doctors by living far beyond their estimates, their predictions about her ability to withstand the rigors of pregnancy had thus far proven all too true.

Lucinda slowed her steps so Eleanor could easily keep pace with her as they descended the carved oak staircase in the front foyer of the manor. Her home for the past five years was nearly as grand in its own way as anything she had seen in New York, and its pastoral setting and German flavor only enhanced its beauty. It seemed ages ago that she had assumed her Freddy lived on a humble horse farm. Her parents still believed it, based on what Eleanor could interpret from her mother's brusque responses to the letters Eleanor still dutifully sent them.

They had just reached the bottom of the stairs when Eleanor heard rapid footsteps coming from the west wing. Clara burst into the foyer and dashed across the black marble floor. "Louis went for the mail," she said, breathless, and to Eleanor, added, "You have two letters. One is from New York and the other's from France!"

Eleanor would have been delighted to hear of the second letter had the first not filled her with foreboding. The letter from France must be Abigail's; she and her husband had been touring the Continent for the past month. The letter from New York was equally as certain to be from her mother, and almost as certain not to be a letter at all, but a news clipping—a society page account of a gala event where Edwin Corville and his wife had danced and dined with foreign royalty, a business report of Corville's lucrative expansion throughout the Eastern seaboard. Mother rarely added anything in her own hand except in spite and unless the article discussed Drury-Lockwood, Incorporated, which was, if Mother's caustic notes were to be believed, a misnomer.

"We'll meet you in the west sitting room," said Lucinda, drawing a disappointed Clara away. The girl had never ventured farther from home than Philadelphia, and she loved to hear stories from far-off places. She seemed to believe Eleanor had visited the locales she had only learned about from books, no matter how often Eleanor told her the truth.

Alone, Eleanor sat down on the bottom step and decided to open her mother's envelope first, to dispense with whatever insult it contained. Fred said she ought to discard them unopened, but Eleanor could not bear to risk destroying a letter of forgiveness, should it one day come.

She withdrew a newspaper clipping and read only enough of the article to learn that Mr. and Mrs. Edwin Corville had been blessed with a baby boy. Her heart pounded as she read what her mother had appended to the bottom with bold strokes of black ink: "What has your husband given you but shame and grief? What have you given him?"

Eleanor crumpled paper and envelope and, resisting the urge to fling them aside, tucked them into her pocket. She would put them on the fire at the earliest opportunity. She would not have Fred see them for the world.

How foolish she had been to hope that her mother's anger would lessen with the years. Did she send the same hateful letters to Abigail? Abigail had never mentioned any, but of course, Mother had no need of letters when she could make her anger apparent in person. Abigail had written of at least a dozen society engagements where Mother and Father had departed as soon as she and Mr. Drury arrived. Abigail wrote little more of their parents, even when Eleanor asked for news, filling her letters instead with tales of her life as mistress of the Drury household.

April 2, 1912

Dear Eleanor,

By the time you receive this letter, Herbert and I may be on our way home. Do not worry; my health and that of your niece or nephew is quite good, but my condition is becoming too noticeable for me to enjoy our tour of the Continent much longer. I do not mind cutting our trip short as much as you might think, as I will find much to console me in decorating the nursery.

Paris was beautiful, as lovely as I remembered. I can almost hear you laugh at that, since my last visit occurred in the height of spring, a season that, as I write this, has only just begun to appear. You will say that my view of this romantic city has been colored by my delight in my husband and my anticipation of our child. Well, all I have to say to that is . . . you are absolutely correct. I find more joy in a sky full of rain now than I ever did on the balmiest summer day before I married. I have no doubt you know exactly what I mean. You are the only person in the world who understands what it was like to live in that cold house. If not for you, I never could have borne it. And this may sound contradictory, but if not for you, I also could not bear being shut out of it forever.

If you had any idea how much I worried about you and ached to hear from you when you left home, you would forgive me every thoughtless thing I ever did to you. I know you have long ago forgiven me for abandoning you when I left home. I suppose that came easily to you, since if I had married Edwin, you probably never would have married Fred! If only Mother and Father would follow your example. Father gets a good living from Herbert. One would think he would be grateful, but of course that is not Father's way.

Please promise me you will come to see me when the child is born. Five years is too long for sisters to be apart when modern conveniences have made travel so safe and comfortable. Bring Fred if you like; Herbert is fond of him, and I would like to know him better. If you wish to avoid Mother and Father, that is easily done; our parents avoid engagements they suspect I might attend. Will gifts tempt you? If so, know that I have a liberal allowance and spent it freely on the Champs-Elysées. If you want your gifts, I insist that you collect them from me yourself.

I have so much to tell you about our travels that I have no patience to put it into a letter, so you must come to me so I can tell you everything. There is one incident I must share now, however, because it amused and yet so affronted me that I hardly know what to make of it. In Germany we attended a ball to honor a certain count who had been awarded a great honor by the Kaiser—I do not recall the name of either the count or the honor, and I make no apology for my ignorance because both were in German. I do not believe even you comprehend a word of that language, although on second thought, perhaps you have acquired fluency living with Fred's family.

At this ball, I was introduced to an old dear from a very respected and influential English family, good friends of the Drurys, who told me she was very pleased to see me again. I knew we had never met, but rather than offend her by saying so, I merely smiled and steered the conversation elsewhere. She spoke to me quite kindly whenever our paths crossed that evening, and when Herbert and I were about to depart, she clasped my hand and said, "I was so sorry to hear your mother passed. I was very fond of her."

You can imagine my shock upon discovering in this manner that our mother had perished—and now I realize that I may have given you that same fright! Eleanor, dear, our own mother is alive if not well; the "mother" the Englishwoman mourned was Herbert's first wife. The dear lady thought I was his daughter! I wanted to laugh although I was mortified, for my condition was apparent then if not so obvious as now, and since she did not know Herbert was my husband, she must have wondered if I had one at all! Still, her remark was innocent and not offensive, unlike those of many Americans we have encountered in our travels, who seem to find my condition scandalous even when they know full well Herbert and I are man and wife.

How much more I would enjoy confiding these secrets to you in person than through the post. Do promise you will come and see me when the baby's arrival is imminent. If gifts will not tempt you, then perhaps you will think instead of what a coward I am and how I dread the travail that awaits. If you could be by my side, lending me your strength as you always have, I think I shall be able to endure it. You may think me cruel to play to your sympathetic heart so, but if guilt shall speed you to my side, then I must be cruel!

I am not accustomed to writing such long letters, and my hand has grown weary, so I must close. Tomorrow we are off to England, where I shall be certain to collect a vial of earth from the home of Jane Austen, as you requested. You do ask for such silly things. I think I shall buy you a tea service as well, though you did not ask for it. You will never see it, of course, unless you return to New York. Please do ask Fred if you might come.

So tomorrow to England, and after a week, from Southampton to home. Would you be so kind to have a letter waiting there for

Your Loving Sister,
Abigail

Eleanor smiled as she returned the letter to its envelope, warmed by Abigail's happiness but well aware of how it cast her own sorrow into greater relief. She wished she could unburden herself to her sister, but Abigail had scolded her after she lost the first two babies and would certainly be even more vehement if she learned Eleanor had not abandoned her hopes for a child. In Abigail's opinion, Eleanor knew the doctors' warnings and ought to heed them. "If Fred loves you as much as you say," she had written, "I cannot believe he would demand a child of you if it might cost you your life."

Eleanor had hastened to assure her that Fred had never made any such demand, but the news of her first pregnancy had so delighted him that she knew he longed for a child as much as she did. He had responded to her subsequent pregnancies with guarded optimism and comforted her tenderly when they ended in grief. This time, however, he had also gently suggested that they resign themselves to their childless state rather than risk her health again.

She wondered if she could ever resign herself. She longed for a sympathetic friend in whom she could confide, someone who might advise her. She would have turned to Miss Langley, but her former nanny agreed with Abigail regarding Eleanor's yearning for a child. Moreover, she was not especially receptive to any talk of Fred, since although she approved of Eleanor's decision to flee her parents' home, she could not hide her disappointment that Eleanor had married instead of pursuing her education. The only other women Eleanor knew well enough to confide in were members of Fred's family, and somehow, even sharing her worries with Lucinda seemed a breach of his confidence.

She gathered up the unfinished quilt, slipped Abigail's letter into her pocket, and tried to close off her grief in a distant corner of her mind as she went to join Lucinda and the others. She passed through the kitchen on her way to the west sitting room, and Mother's news clipping quickly turned to ash on the fire.

Fred's mother, Elizabeth, looked up and smiled encouragingly as Eleanor took her usual chair by the window. Maude and Lily broke off their conversation and studied their needlework intently, giving Eleanor only quick nods of welcome. In a surge of bitterness, Eleanor wondered if her sisters-in-law feared they might suffer her same unhappy fate if they acknowledged it. Even Elizabeth, the most superstitious woman Eleanor had ever met, did not believe that.

Clara left her mother's side and seated herself on Eleanor's footstool. "Would you like me to thread a needle for you?"

Eleanor smiled and thanked her. She let Clara borrow the heron-shaped shears Miss Langley had given her and slipped her thimble on her finger.

"I'm pleased you're going to finish your quilt," said Maude. She had married the second eldest of the Bergstrom sons, Louis, the previous spring, and with her first anniversary approaching, she had decided to learn to quilt to make an anniversary gift for her husband. Elizabeth had encouraged her to choose a simple Nine-Patch, but after seeing a picture in the *Ladies' Home*

Journal, Maude had fallen in love with a stunning appliquéd Sunflower quilt designed by renowned quilter Marie Webster. Privately, the other women of the family agreed she would be lucky to finish even a small fraction of it in time, but no one wanted to discourage her newfound interest in their beloved craft, and since Maude did not want to settle for a simpler block, they decided to let her go her own way.

"Perhaps she will learn better, learning from her mistakes," Elizabeth had said with a sigh.

"Perhaps," Lucinda had agreed, "and perhaps this quilt will be a gift for their tenth anniversary instead of their first."

Eleanor had joined in the laughter. It had been so much easier to laugh then, when she had just begun to feel life stirring within her womb and every stitch she put into the soft, white whole cloth quilt was another prayer for the health and safety of the precious child she carried.

Eleanor gazed at the quilt. "I don't like to leave work unfinished." In a flash of inspiration, she added, "I've decided to give this to my sister when her child is born."

"You can't do that," said Lily in dismay. "You've worked so hard on it, and you're going to need it yourself someday."

Eleanor smiled fondly at her sister-in-law, her earlier bitterness forgotten. Lily's characteristic optimism was as welcome as Lucinda's frankness. "Perhaps I will," she said, "but my sister has such a good head start that her child will definitely be born first, and I have no quilt for him. Or her. The only other quilt I have under way is the Turkey Tracks—"

"Absolutely not," said Elizabeth, not even looking up from her work. "Under no circumstances should a child be given a Wandering Foot quilt."

Lucinda caught Eleanor's eye and grinned. "She said Turkey Tracks, not Wandering Foot."

"You know very well that they are one and the same." Elizabeth looked up from her work and realized they were teasing her. "Suit yourselves, then," she said, shrugging. "If you want to condemn a poor innocent child to a lifetime of restlessness and wandering, then I can't stop you."

"Quilt or no quilt, I would not be surprised if the child has a bit of wanderlust," said Lucinda. "It seems to run in the family."

The other women laughed, and even Eleanor managed a smile.

❧

Later that evening, after she prepared for bed, she read Abigail's letter again, hungry for news of their parents. Mother was alive if not well, Abigail had written, but Eleanor had read enough similarly derisive comments to know that the remark pertained to Abigail's general opinion of their mother and not to her current health. She was not surprised to hear that their parents still avoided Abigail in society, or that Abigail still seemed genuinely astonished that their parents did not appreciate how she had resolved their financial difficulties. Within months of marrying Abigail and the dissolution of any possible agreement with the Corvilles, Mr. Drury had purchased Lockwood's and had assumed responsibility for Father's debts. He had made Father a vice president, and in an overture of reconciliation that Eleanor had found remarkable at the time, he had kept the Lockwood name in the title of the new company. Since then, as she pieced together the scraps of information her sister let fall, Eleanor had come to believe that Mr. Drury's ostensible generosity had masked one last stab of revenge against his former rival. As best as Eleanor had been able to determine, Father had been given very little work to do, and although he received an impressive salary, he had no influence whatsoever. Sometimes Eleanor wondered if Father would have preferred to go into bankruptcy with his pride intact, but she knew her mother never would have allowed it. It was bad enough that their position in society had been irreparably damaged by the scandal; they should not also have to endure financial ruin.

Eleanor had pen and paper in the nightstand; she could write to Abigail and ask outright how their parents fared, and satisfy both her curiosity and Abigail's request for a letter at the same time. She would have, except she knew Abigail would ignore her questions or respond so breezily that she might as well not have bothered.

She climbed into bed and blew out the lamp, pulling the Rocky Mountain quilt over her. She and Fred had slept beneath it every night of their marriage, even when it was not yet complete. Lately she had fallen asleep beneath it alone more often than not.

She was not sure how many hours later Fred inadvertently woke her as he pulled back the covers. When she stirred, he kissed her and murmured an apology. "It's all right," she said as he lay down beside her at last. "I'm glad you woke me. I haven't seen you all day, except at supper."

"I'm sorry. I've been busy."

"Doing what?"

"You could come outside and see for yourself tomorrow."

"Or you could simply tell me, if you weren't so stubborn."

"Oh. So I'm the stubborn one." He kissed her gently and shifted onto his back, settling against the pillow. He let out a long sigh.

Eleanor knew he was exhausted, but she could not let go just yet. "I heard from my sister today."

"Is she well?"

"She is. She and Herbert are returning from Europe soon." She steeled herself. "She wants me to come when her child is born. I thought I might go. If I can be spared."

She did not mean if Bergstrom Thoroughbreds could do without her. Although everyone was expected to contribute to the family business, the others would divide up her work so that her absence would be little noticed. She meant if Fred could spare her, if the man who had sworn never to leave her side would willingly or eagerly let her go so far away.

"That would be in the middle of August?"

"Unless the child is early. I thought I should be prepared to leave at the beginning of the month, if necessary."

"That's not a good time for me to be away."

"Well, no," said Eleanor, surprised. "I assumed I would go alone. Perhaps Clara could accompany me."

"My sister's a level-headed girl, but she's still just a child," said Fred. "I was thinking of someone who might look after you."

"I'm perfectly capable of looking after myself."

"I know you are," he said quickly. "Well, Clara would be thrilled, and she's a good helper. How long will you be gone?"

She had not decided. "A month, perhaps more."

"That long?" He drew her into his arms. "Maybe I can get away for a few days and visit you in New York."

"That would be nice."

"We could see your parents, if you like."

"I don't think we would be welcome."

"Would they turn us away at the door?"

"I doubt they would even let us pass through the front gates."

He stroked her hair and held her close. "Then we'll leave them alone."

❧

Clara was as thrilled by the upcoming trip to New York as Fred had predicted, and Elizabeth readily granted her permission to accompany Eleanor. The women of the family agreed that at such a time as Abigail would soon face, no woman fortunate enough to have a sister wanted to be without her. "Or without her mother," added Lily, and blushed, remembering too late the state of affairs among the Lockwood women.

"I cannot imagine my mother would be much comfort," said Eleanor, smiling to show Lily she had not taken offense.

"Then you must go, as much as we will miss you," said Elizabeth. "Have you ever assisted in childbirth?"

"No, but fortunately Abigail won't need to rely entirely upon me," said Eleanor with a laugh. "A doctor and at least one nurse will be present. I don't plan to do anything more than comfort my sister and be one of the first to cuddle the newborn."

"Even the best doctors sometimes overlook important remedies," said Elizabeth. "Or rather, they dismiss them as silly folk tales. If you do arrive in time for the delivery, remember to place a knife beneath your sister's bed. That will cut the pain."

"Cut the pain?"

"Will any sort of knife do, or does it have to be a special knife?" inquired Lucinda. "What would happen if you used a spoon instead?"

"Tease me if you must," retorted Elizabeth, "but there was a knife beneath my bed for every child I bore except for Louis, and his birth was by far the longest and most painful."

"Of course it was," said Maude. "He was nearly ten pounds."

"He's your husband, so your children will probably be large, too. You'll be begging for a knife then, and it would serve you right if I made you do without."

"I'll put a knife under your bed for you, Maude," said Clara loyally, but after glancing at Eleanor, added, "Maybe it doesn't help, but it couldn't hurt, either."

Clara spent the next several days in the library, reading everything she could find about New York City. Within a day she had composed an impressive list of all the sights she wished to see, and Eleanor was pleased to discover that many of her favorite museums and landmarks were included.

"We'll have plenty of time for sightseeing," Eleanor promised one evening later that week as the women of the family gathered in the west sitting room for a last bit of quilting before bed. "Unless I can't finish this quilt in time and have to sneak away to complete it while Abigail tends to the baby."

"A whole cloth quilt is the perfect choice for a baby's first quilt," said Elizabeth. "Its unbroken surface suggests purity and innocence. Whole cloth quilts are well suited for newborns and for brides."

"What does it matter, as long as the quilt is pretty?" asked Lily.

"It matters a great deal," said Elizabeth. "Think of the symbolism, the omens in a quilt. What would you think if a bride pieced her wedding quilt in the Contrary Wife or Crazy House or Devil's Claws pattern? It would be far better for her to choose something like Steps to the Altar or True Lover's Knot."

"You're absolutely right," said Lucinda.

Elizabeth regarded her with surprise. "Why, this is a novelty. You agree with me?"

"Of course," said Lucinda. "Can you imagine, for example, if a bride chose Tumbling Blocks? That pattern is also called Baby Blocks, and everyone would gossip about why she had to get married."

"Lucinda," said Elizabeth over the others' laughter, "if you weren't my dear husband's baby sister, I would give you the scolding you deserve."

"Don't let that stop you." Lucinda shrugged. "What do I care what pattern a bride chooses for her wedding quilt, so long as it isn't yet another floral appliqué with bows and birds and butterflies and—oops. Sorry, Maude."

"This isn't my wedding quilt," said Maude primly, struggling to put a sharp point on the petal of another Sunflower block. "And while I might add a few butterflies if I am so inclined, you won't find any birds or bows here. Not that I'd let you influence me. If it's good enough for the *Ladies' Home Journal*, then it's good enough for me, and it would be good enough for you, too, if you weren't so prideful."

"Who's prideful?" protested Lucinda. "I like the *Ladies' Home Journal*. I like it even more now that they're going to publish Eleanor's whole cloth quilt pattern."

"What?" exclaimed Eleanor.

"Now look what you made me do," Lucinda complained to Maude. "It was supposed to be a surprise."

"It is a surprise," said Eleanor. "Believe me, it is."

Maude shook her head. "This must be another one of Lucinda's jokes."

"Not at all," said Lucinda. "I thought we could all use a bit of cheering up around here, so I copied Eleanor's pattern and sent it to the editor. It's such a beautiful, original design, so I thought, why not share it with the world?" She smiled kindly at Eleanor. "I didn't know if you would have the heart to finish your own quilt, and it seemed a shame not to have someone, somewhere completing it."

Eleanor reached out and clasped her hand. "That was thoughtful of you."

"Not really. I just wanted to brag about my famous niece."

Clara said, "Eleanor's going to be famous?"

"Of course," said Lucinda. "This is the *Ladies' Home Journal,* after all. Eleanor's name will be right up there at the top of the page with the picture of her quilt, just like Marie Webster and that Sunflower quilt Maude is making."

"Will her picture be there, too?"

"I don't think I want my picture in a magazine," said Eleanor, a nervous quake in her stomach. "Or even my name."

"Why not?" asked Clara.

Eleanor forced a laugh. "I suppose so no one will know where to send their criticism. Can't they show my quilt without mentioning me?"

She regretted her words when she saw the disappointment in their faces. "I suppose I should have asked your permission first," said Lucinda. "But I'm sure they would let you use merely your initials, or a pseudonym, if you prefer."

"Aren't you proud of your quilt?" asked Clara. "I think you should be."

"I am proud of it," said Eleanor. "And I'm very grateful that Lucinda thought enough of my quilt to send it to the magazine. And I'm thrilled that it's going to be published. However, I would prefer to be all those things and anonymous, too."

She saw from the looks they exchanged that they did not understand, but they let her be. Elizabeth would think her too modest; Maude would think it false modesty and another sign of her pride. Lucinda and Lily would respect her decision, but they would wonder why she had made it. Dear, insightful Clara would probably figure out the reason before anyone else, perhaps before Eleanor herself.

She wondered what Fred would think.

❧

Fred worked through supper and missed Lucinda's announcement to the rest of the family. The other men congratulated Eleanor and agreed that publication in a national magazine was quite an accomplishment, although her father-in-law looked bemused and remarked that he thought quilters did not like others to duplicate their unique designs. "My mother, especially, was adamant about not copying other women's quilts," said David. "Though I remember my Aunt Gerda once whispered to me that my mother had done her fair share of copying when she was a new quilter."

"Everyone learns to quilt by copying other quilters' patterns," said Lily. "Just like painters learn by studying the old masters."

Louis and William guffawed at the comparison, earning themselves frowns from the quilters at the table. Those for William were milder because he was only a few years older than Clara; Louis, however, knew better, as his wife's steely glare made clear. Eleanor hid a smile and wondered if Maude would now consider adding a few Contrary Wife blocks to her Sunflower quilt.

"Perhaps copying another quilter's work without permission is wrong," said Eleanor, "but duplicating her quilt with her consent is another matter entirely. I wouldn't allow my quilt to appear in a magazine if I didn't want other quilters to make it."

In fact, now that the shock of Lucinda's surprise had passed, she was becoming more excited about the thought of opening a magazine and seeing a picture of her quilt inside. She knew, too, that Abigail would be all the more thrilled by the gift, knowing that her baby's quilt had been featured in a national magazine. Eleanor's desire for anonymity would be thwarted in New York, at least, for Abigail was certain to tell everyone she knew.

For a very brief moment, she considered sending her mother a clipping with a note pointing out that none of Mrs. Edwin Corville's quilts had ever received such an honor, but given her mother's distaste for quilting, that would only prove how low Eleanor had fallen.

After supper, she finished quilting the whole cloth quilt and trimmed the batting and lining even with the scalloped edges of the top. For the binding, she cut a long, narrow strip of fabric along the bias rather than the straight of the grain so that the binding would ease along the curves and miters of the fancy edge. Fred came in as she was pinning the binding in place, hair windblown, hands dirty from working outdoors, but he had only stopped by to say hello, so there was no time to tell him her good news. He kissed her on the cheek and told her he wouldn't be late, then left the room as quickly as he had entered.

❧

Later that night, Fred roused Eleanor just moments after she doused the lamp. "Come with me," he said. "It's done. Let me show you."

"Show me what?" she asked. "A new fence? That addition to the stable you and your brothers are always talking about?"

"No, something much better." He pulled back the quilt and took her hands. "At least I hope you'll think so."

Curious, she climbed out of bed and dressed for the chilly spring night. Quietly, Fred led her into the hallway past his siblings' rooms, and as they descended the stairs, Eleanor was struck by a sudden remembrance of another night five years earlier and another flight of stairs she had stolen down in the darkness. Eleanor wondered if Fred ever thought of that night and wished her family had awakened and prevented her from leaving with him. She did not doubt his love for her, but he would have had children if he had married any other woman.

He led her across the foyer, into the west wing of the manor, and paused at the west door. This had once been the front entrance of the Bergstrom home, before Fred's father had added the grand south wing with its banquet hall and ballroom. Fred took both of her hands in his and watched her expectantly. "Are you ready?"

"Of course," she said, but as he opened the door, she dug in her heels. "Fred, no. It's so late. It's too dark and cold now. You can show me in the morning."

"Eleanor." His voice was gentle, but commanding. "You're coming outside."

With no other choice, she took a deep breath and stepped outside—but instead of bare earth, her foot struck smooth stone. A patio of gray stones nearly identical to those forming the walls of the manor lay where rocky soil and sparse clumps of grass had been only weeks before. Surrounding the expanse of stone were tall bushes and evergreens, enclosing the intimate space completely except for one opening through which Eleanor spied the beginning of a stone trail winding north.

"That path leads to the gazebo in the gardens, and to the stables beyond them," said Fred. "The lilac bushes don't look like much now, but when they flower in the spring, this place will be so pretty—you'll see. We'll have flowers before then, though." He gestured to the freshly turned earth lining the patio. "Those are dahlias and irises, and these over here are gladiolus. They'll come up before September."

"I love lilacs," she said, slowly turning and taking in the patio. It felt enclosed, sheltered. Safe. "Dahlias, too."

"Look over here." He knelt and pointed to the northeast corner of the manor. "That's the cornerstone of Elm Creek Manor. The entire estate was founded on this very spot."

"'Bergstrom 1858,'" Eleanor read aloud, and as Fred continued to describe the features of the garden he had created just for her, Eleanor could picture in her mind's eye how lovely it would be in midsummer when the bulbs bloomed, and how the evergreens would bring a spot of color to the landscape even in the depths of winter. A year hence, the lilacs would fill the air with their fragrance.

"I'll make some chairs next," said Fred. "I also thought about putting some benches along the two sides, or maybe along the house. What do you think?"

"Why, Fred?"

He pretended not to understand. "So we can have some place to sit."

"No, Fred. Why? Why did you do all this—for me?"

"Because I love you, and I can't stand to see you making the house into your prison. I would make you a thousand gardens if that's what it took to get you to come outside again."

She stared at him. "I have no idea what you're talking about."

"Don't you? Eleanor, you haven't set foot beyond the foyer since the day we lost the baby. You've wondered why I wouldn't tell you what I was working on all this time. I had hoped your curiosity would compel you outside. Two months ago, you never would have watched from the windows instead of coming out to see what I was doing."

"I've been tired." Her voice shook, and she turned away from him. "I'm still recuperating."

"I'm not asking you to work with the horses yet, just to leave the house for a while." He spun her around to face him. "Eleanor, it's not your fault. You heard what the doctor said. You didn't do anything to harm the baby."

"But I did. I did. I should have rested, I should have taken care of myself—"

"You took excellent care of yourself."

"No. No. I didn't. I came outside, I took walks, all for selfish reasons. I wanted to see the new colts, or I wanted to play in the snow with Clara . . . I should have stayed inside, in bed or by the fire—"

"Nothing you did hurt the baby. My own mother rode horseback and worked the farm when she—"

"But your mother had never lost a child. I had, so I should have known better. After I lost our first two babies, I should have done everything—everything—to make sure I didn't fail you again."

"My God, Eleanor, you didn't fail me." He reached out for her, but she avoided his embrace. "You nearly died. Do you think I could ever be angry with you after that? Do you think I care more about being a father than about spending the rest of my life with you?"

"I'm so sorry, Fred."

"Listen to me. You didn't do anything wrong. Maybe we aren't meant to have children. If that's true, we still have each other, and that's all I ever wanted."

"Fred." She steeled herself. "I told you before we married that I did not think I could bear children. You said it didn't matter, but it does. If you want to divorce me—"

"Never." For the first time, she heard a trace of anger in his voice. "Don't ever say that again. Did you marry me only to become a mother?"

"I—" No. She had thought only of him, of choosing her fate instead of letting her parents and Edwin Corville determine it for her. But the assumption that she could not have children mattered less to her as a girl of seventeen than it did now that she had built a life with the man she loved. "I married you because I loved you."

"The reasons we married are reasons to stay married. Please don't ever suggest we divorce unless it's what you truly want."

"It will never be what I want."

She buried her face in his chest and wept as she had not when she lost the last baby, for she had been too stunned for tears, too unable to comprehend that God could visit this same terrible grief upon her a third time.

Fred held her and murmured words of comfort, but his voice trembled, and she knew he also wept.

"Life goes on, Eleanor," he said. "I know it sounds trite, but it's true. Life goes on not only for us, but for our family."

She nodded. A faint hope kindled in her heart. Life went on—Fred's siblings would have children. Abigail's child would enter the world by late summer. Life would go on, and she and Fred would be a part of those lives.

"We've already been through the most difficult, most painful times we will ever face," he said. "From this point forward, we don't have to fear anything, because we've already survived the worst."

"I hope you're right." She prayed he was right.

❧❧

Less than a week later, she sat on the smooth stone of the cornerstone patio enjoying the first truly warm, sunny day of that rainy spring. She sat with the women of her family chatting and planning for the summer, for the summer and beyond. She put the last stitch into the binding of the whole cloth quilt and held it up for the others to admire. They praised her, and Eleanor felt warmth returning to her heart as she imagined cradling her little niece or nephew within its soft folds.

Clara sat by her side, working on her most difficult quilt yet, and Eleanor was so engrossed in helping her with the appliqué and answering her questions about New York that a few moments passed before she realized that the others had fallen silent. She looked up to discover Louis whispering into his mother's ear; Elizabeth suddenly went pale, and her hand went to her throat.

"What is it?" asked Lucinda as Louis raced off down the stone path toward the stables.

Elizabeth pressed her lips together tightly and fumbled for her handkerchief, lowering her head so none of them could meet her gaze. Louis rode into town each day for the mail and the papers; he must have brought home terrible news. Clara's face was full of worry. Eleanor stroked her hair reassuringly and tried to resume their conversation, but Clara was too distracted to respond.

Eleanor grew faint when, barely minutes later, Louis returned with Fred. Both men's faces were grave, but behind Fred's eyes she saw a pain she had not seen since her last baby died.

"What is it?" she tried to ask, but the words dried up in her throat.

"Eleanor." Fred knelt beside her and took her hands in his. They felt almost unbearably warm against the ice of her skin. "Your sister sailed from Southampton on the tenth, isn't that right?"

"Yes." She looked from him to Louis and back. "They're probably still at sea. Why?"

"Do you remember the name of her ship?"

"I—I don't recall. I would have to check her letters. Why? What has happened?"

"Two nights ago, a ship sailing from Southampton to New York struck an iceberg and sank in the North Atlantic. Only a few hundred souls were spared."

"No. No." She shook her head. "That could not be Abigail's ship. She wrote me—Herbert told her it was a marvel of engineering. It was designed to be unsinkable. It could not be Abigail's ship. Mother would have sent a telegram." Despite their estrangement, Mother would have sent word, Eleanor repeated silently to herself, though she knew such things took time, and if the accident had only just happened, there would be passenger lists to be sorted out, next of kin to notify— Abigail. Abigail and her baby.

"Eleanor." Fred's voice called to her, quietly insistent. "Was her ship called the *Titanic*?"

"I don't remember." She did not want to remember. She could not believe it; she would not believe it. She took a deep breath and closed her eyes to clear her head of dizziness. It swept over her, crowding out her resolve to forget the name of her sister's ship for as long as possible, and in the space between breaths she went from believing that Abigail's ship was not the one that sank to praying that Abigail had been among the handful of survivors. Women and children were always the first into the lifeboats; surely a woman in Abigail's condition would have been among the very first even of these. Surely Mr. Drury, with his wealth and influence, would have seen to Abigail's safety.

❧

In the days and weeks that followed, Eleanor would read reports of women who refused seats in half-filled lifeboats rather than leave their husbands behind. She would hear rumors that near the end, survivors had witnessed a beautiful, golden-haired woman sitting on the first-class deck, staring out at the sea with unseeing eyes, one hand absently stroking her swelling abdomen, her husband weeping on her shoulder.

Eleanor prayed for a miracle she knew would not be granted.

The family gathered in the parlor on the day the passenger manifest they had requested finally arrived. With it was the list of survivors. Abigail and her husband were not among them.

"Why did she not leave when she had the chance?" said Eleanor. Fred's arm was around her, sustaining her; the whole cloth quilt lay upon her lap. She had scarcely let it from her grasp since first learning of the disaster. The papers from the White Star Line lay on the floor where they had slipped from her fingers.

"Her love for her husband was too great," said Lily in a soft voice. "She could not bear to be parted from him."

"Not even for their child?" Eleanor could not believe it of Abigail; she could not bear to believe it. Perhaps Abigail refused to take her place in the lifeboat because she did not fully comprehend the danger. Perhaps she thought her child more at risk on the open sea. Perhaps by the time she understood, it was too late. "I know my sister," said Eleanor firmly, though her voice trembled. Instinctively, she clutched the quilt to her chest. "She would not have chosen death with her husband over her child's life. Never."

"Will you let go of that thing?" shrilled Elizabeth. Before Eleanor could react, Elizabeth had crossed the room and snatched the quilt away. "I will throw this wretched thing on the fire. You should have destroyed it after you lost the first baby."

"Give that back to me."

"I won't. Don't you see? Every baby you intend it for has died. It's bad luck."

"Mother," said Fred, rising, "this quilt had nothing to do with any of these tragedies."

"Elizabeth, you don't know what you're saying." David's voice was calm, but firm, as he addressed his wife. "Return the quilt to Eleanor at once."

Elizabeth clenched her teeth against a low moan, but she did not struggle as Fred and David pried the quilt from her white-knuckled grasp. Eleanor examined the quilt for rents and folded it with shaking hands. Her heart pounded, and a sudden flash of pain left her breathless.

"Destroy it or I will," Elizabeth choked out. "I swear to you, no grandchild of mine will ever sleep beneath that quilt."

"Be quiet, Elizabeth," commanded Lucinda. To Eleanor, she murmured, "Get the quilt out of her sight until she comes to her senses."

Eleanor nodded and fled upstairs to her bedroom to hide the quilt, knowing the light of day would not shine on it while Elizabeth lived. The risk that she would destroy Eleanor's only remembrance of Abigail's child was too great. Her heart ached as she buried the quilt at the bottom of her cedar chest, blinded by tears. Oh, Abigail. How could she have spurned the lifeboats, knowing that her death meant the death of her child?

The pounding ache in her heart subsided, and a fire kindled within

Eleanor as she locked the trunk and wiped her eyes, her resolution stronger even than that which had compelled her to leave her parents' home forever. She would have a child, and she would live for that child. And Abigail's name would not be forgotten.

No telegram from her parents ever came.

Chapter Seven

S he knows," said Andrew as he and Sylvia watched through the windshield as Amy approached the motor home.

"I'd imagine so," said Sylvia dryly. "I thought you said Bob can keep a secret."

"He can. I don't understand it. He promised me he wouldn't tell."

"Did you remember to get that same promise from Cathy?"

Andrew drew in a breath and winced. "Put your seat belt back on. We're getting out of here."

"I'm afraid it's too late for that." Sylvia rose, shouldered her tote bag with the Crazy Quilt and library printouts inside, and nudged Andrew to his feet.

Amy met them halfway to the house, her arms crossed, her mouth a thin, worried line.

"Amy, dear," said Sylvia. "I suppose it's too much to hope that you've come all this way to congratulate us."

In lieu of an answer, Amy reached for one of the suitcases her father carried. "Let me help you with that."

Andrew set one of the suitcases on the ground, but he continued on to the manor without a word for his daughter. Sylvia gave Amy an apologetic look and fell in beside him.

Amy trailed after them. "Dad, I want you to be happy. I want to be happy for you, but . . ."

"But what?"

"This isn't a conversation I wanted to have in front of Sylvia."

Sylvia did her best to conceal her annoyance. "Pretend I'm not here."

Amy frowned and shrugged as if to say Sylvia had been fairly warned. "Dad, we all know you care about Sylvia."

"I don't just care about her. I love her."

"Of course you do. We understand that." Amy reached for his hand, but Andrew merely opened the back door and waved her inside. "But we wonder if you've thought about what marriage would mean."

"Considering I was married to your mother for more than fifty years, I think I have a good idea."

"I think maybe you have a selective memory," countered Amy. "You and Mom were very happy for a long time, but think about those last three years. Dad, we can't bear to see you go through that again."

Andrew took the suitcase from her and set the pair down with a heavy thud in the hallway. "You mean when your mother had cancer."

"You never complained, but we know how difficult it was to care for her." Amy glanced at Sylvia, then quickly looked away. "Do you really want to put yourself through that again?"

"Sylvia does not have cancer."

"No, but she's already had one stroke and could have another any—"

"All right. Enough," said Andrew. "Sylvia is in excellent health, and so am I, but even if that were to change tomorrow, I would still want to marry her. That's what marriage is about—in sickness and in health, remember?"

"You've already grieved for one wife. You shouldn't have to mourn a second time."

"How do you know that I will? For all you know, Sylvia will outlive me."

Amy gave Sylvia a guarded look. "Maybe she will. We all would love for you to have many, many years together. But the end is going to be the same."

Andrew shook his head. "And it's the same end you and Paul are going to face, and Bob and Cathy. Does that mean you shouldn't have gotten married? If being by your mother's side throughout her illness taught me anything, it showed me that nothing matters but sharing your life with the people you love. Your mother had a great love of life. I'm ashamed that in her memory, you want me to curl up in a corner and wait to die."

Amy flushed. "That's not what I meant—"

"Listen—and you can pass this along to your brother—I don't know how many years I've got left, and neither do you. I'm going to spend them with Sylvia with or without your approval."

"Dad—"

"I love Sylvia, and my feelings aren't going to change. I'm going to mourn her whether she's my wife or my friend, so she might as well be my wife." He strode down the hall, but paused at the door. "I'm going to get the rest of our gear and check the engine. Amy, you're a good girl and I love you, but you ought to know better. You're welcome to stay as long as you like, but I expect you to treat Sylvia with respect. Your mother and I didn't raise you to be rude to people when you don't get your own way."

Amy's cheeks were scarlet as she watched her father depart.

Sylvia sighed and reminded herself it would be unwise to take Amy's reaction personally. Andrew's children would be just as difficult if he were engaged to a woman half her age—in fact, in that case, they might be even more upset. She doubted, however, that telling Amy to count her blessings would help matters.

"Amy dear," said Sylvia carefully. "I have no intention of becoming a burden to your father. Yes, I did have a stroke several years ago, but my doctor assures me I am in good health. However, should that change, I have resources enough to ensure that the burden of my care will not fall upon your father. Sarah and Matt are like my own children, and they will see I am looked after."

"It's not just the caregiving. It's the emotional toll of losing you that we're most worried about."

Sylvia raised her eyebrows. "So you would prefer for him to lose me now? I'm sorry, dear, but that's not living. Your father and I have each lost a beloved spouse. We know—better than you, I think—what we're risking. We also know what we stand to lose if we let fear paralyze us."

"We understand all that," said Amy so quickly that Sylvia knew they didn't understand at all.

"Then let's not have any more of this nonsense." Sylvia smiled sympathetically to show she did not hold Amy's words against her. "I'm sure you mean well, but we've made our decision, and I'm afraid you're going to have to live with it."

❧

In answer, Amy regarded her in silence for a moment, then turned and left through the back door. Sylvia went into the kitchen and sank down upon the bench, deeply troubled. Amy had always been so kind to her—a bit chilly when they first met, perhaps, but she had certainly seemed to warm to Sylvia as they had become more acquainted over the years. Sylvia had even taught her to quilt. She never would have expected Amy to look upon her as if she were the enemy.

She roused herself and rose to fix herself a cup of tea. She must not blow Amy's remarks out of proportion. Amy might not relent easily or soon, but eventually she would see reason. Right now she was still dealing with her surprise, and perhaps some hurt, too, at hearing the news secondhand. After they had some time to adjust, the children would accept their marriage for Andrew's sake. What alternative did they have?

"Sylvia?"

Sylvia started at the sound of Sarah's voice. "Oh, hello, dear."

"Welcome home." Sarah hugged her warmly. "I heard the end of Amy's rant. I was stuck on the phone when you pulled into the driveway or I wouldn't have let her tear into you the minute you got out of the motor home. I'm sorry."

"It's not your fault. I suppose I should have been prepared for something like this after the way Bob and Cathy took the news."

"How can you prepare for something so bizarre?"

"I suppose I could have been more delicate. Telling Amy she would just have to live with it was too blunt."

"You were more polite than she was." Sarah reached into the cupboard for Sylvia's favorite mug and set it on the counter. "To hear her tell it, you and Andrew are a hundred and ten years old and hooked up to life support."

"I hate to imagine what kind of nonsense she's filling his head with at this moment," said Sylvia. "For someone who's so concerned with his health, she doesn't seem to mind sending his blood pressure through the roof. I do hate to see him at odds with his children."

"You haven't done anything wrong," said Sarah firmly. "His kids just need an attitude adjustment. Be resolute, and they'll cave in long before June."

"June? What's in June?"

"Your wedding."

"Oh. I see. So you've set our wedding date, then?"

"Not me. Diane. She had to coordinate it around the Elm Creek Quilters' vacations. She and Gwen almost came to blows before they settled on June nineteenth."

Sylvia looked heavenward. "Well, thank goodness I'm finding this out now. It would have been quite embarrassing not to know until the invitations are sent out. I assume I will be invited?"

"Sure. Bring Andrew, if you like."

"Thank you. I will." Sylvia dried her hands and returned the dish towel to its hook. She glanced out the window and saw Andrew checking under the hood of the motor home while Amy made an impassioned argument by his side. She wondered, briefly, if Andrew regretted asking her to marry him, but just as quickly pushed the thought aside.

Rather than dwell on Andrew's children any longer, Sylvia showed Sarah the Crazy Quilt and told her the story of its journey from Elm Creek Manor to the Indiana home of Mona Niehaus. Sarah admired the quilt, then led Sylvia upstairs to the library, where the responses to Summer's Internet inquiry awaited.

Twelve more e-mail messages and four letters had arrived since Sylvia had last spoken to Summer. While Sarah booted up the computer, Sylvia opened the first envelope and skimmed enough of the letter inside to learn that the writer had purchased a whole cloth quilt at an estate sale. The writer had enclosed two snapshots, one of the quilt draped over a chair, and the other a closeup of the central motif.

Sylvia was so surprised she had to sit down, and the nearest place was the arm of Sarah's chair. "This is it," she exclaimed, holding out the letter to Sarah. "I know the stitches don't show up very clearly in this first picture, but the detail shot proves it, and so does that scalloped edge. No one but my mother used that particular design."

Sarah hesitated. "Before you get too excited . . ."

"What?"

Sarah rose and beckoned Sylvia to take her seat at the computer. Sylvia complied, curious, as Sarah leaned over and clicked the mouse to open the e-mail file. The first message appeared on the screen, and Sylvia gasped. Following a few paragraphs of text there was a picture of another whole cloth quilt, identical to the one in the photo Sylvia held except for a slightly darker hue of fabric and a different pattern of wear and tear.

Sylvia sank back into her chair. "I see."

"I'm afraid that's not all."

One by one, Sarah opened seven more e-mail messages, each with another photo of a whole cloth quilt attached. Sylvia saw quilts draped over bassinets and held up by proud owners, quilts in pristine condition and quilts with water stains and tears, quilts that had aged from white to every shade of ecru and cream—but each was quilted in the same pattern of feathered plumes, entwining ribbons, and crosshatched hearts, and each boasted the same scalloped border.

"I don't need to look at any more," said Sylvia as Sarah tried to hand her a small stack of letters. She tossed the unopened envelope she still held on the desk. "I don't even want to open this one."

"Mind if I do?" asked Sarah. Sylvia waved at the envelope dismissively, so Sarah picked it up. "This one is about the Ocean Waves quilt. They sent a picture."

Her hopes renewed, Sylvia took the photo, only to slap it down on the desk after a glance. "For goodness' sakes. I have this same fabric in my own stash. It's from the late nineties, no earlier, and my description specifically said my mother made her quilt during World War I. Is it too much to ask for people to read carefully?"

"Maybe they hoped you wouldn't be too particular," said Sarah, her eyes on the letter. "She'll sell this one to you for six hundred dollars, or custom make you one in the size and fabric of your choice."

"I wouldn't give her six cents for it. That's not the quilt I'm looking for, and if she read Summer's Internet post, she knows it. She's just trying to make a sale."

Sarah reminded her of the other messages that did not include pictures; they might yet prove to be worthwhile leads. Thanks to Mary Beth Callahan, they also now had the name of the auction house that had purchased the Elms and Lilacs quilt, which just the day before Sarah had discovered was still in business in Sewickley, Pennsylvania. Mary Beth's tip about the now-defunct consignment shop in downtown Waterford was also worth investigating, Sarah said, as were the rest of the e-mail messages.

"So we're down but not out," said Sylvia, and she agreed to see the remaining responses. Two people had written to say they spotted the Crazy Quilt in their states; those claims, Sylvia could safely disregard without further investigation. One e-mail message located the New York Beauty quilt at the San Jose Quilt Museum, while another writer's apologetic note explained that she knew she had seen that exact quilt at a museum, but she could not remember which one.

Those leads seemed more promising, especially when coupled with the mistaken sighting of the New York Beauty at the Rocky Mountain Quilt Museum. Perhaps this most recent writer was not the only one to have forgotten which museum possessed the quilt. Fortunately, one of Sylvia's closest friends was a master quilter living in San Francisco. Sylvia knew Grace Daniels would be happy to investigate this lead for her, and since Grace was also a museum curator, Sylvia could rely on her expert evaluation of whatever she found.

Since the computer was already turned on, Sylvia used the Elm Creek Quilts account to send Grace an e-mail explaining the quest and asking for her help. "I hope Grace receives this," she said as she sent her note off into cyberspace, already feeling misgivings that she was trusting a matter of such importance to something as ephemeral as electrons rather than the comforting solidity of paper and ink. "If you don't hear back in a few days, I'll call."

"She'll receive it," Sarah assured her. "In the meantime, let's check out a lead closer to home."

They went downstairs and met Andrew and Amy in the west hallway. Sarah could not possibly have missed the anger sparking between father and daughter, but she summoned up some cheerfulness and told them about their errand into downtown Waterford. "You're welcome to come with us if you like," she said. "We can get a bite to eat at the coffee shop while we talk to the owner."

Amy began, "I don't think—"

"Sure," declared Andrew. "Let's all go. I have an errand of my own downtown."

Amy's mouth tightened, but she went upstairs for her purse and returned wearing lipstick, her hair brushed neatly back into her barrette. She offered to drive her rental, but Sarah declined, explaining that they would have more room in the company car.

The company car was actually a white minivan emblazoned on both sides with the Elm Creek Quilts logo. During the spring and summer it was so often in use shuttling campers back and forth from the airport or on shopping trips into Waterford that its reserved parking place was rarely occupied except overnight.

Amy kept her attention on the passing scenery as Sarah drove through the woods and into Waterford proper. They turned down a service alley and parked behind a row of stores lining the main street that separated the downtown from the campus of Waterford College; Elm Creek Quilter Bonnie Markham had three spaces reserved for Grandma's Attic employees, but since these days only she and Summer, and occasionally Diane, worked at the quilt shop, she let her friends borrow the leftover space.

They stopped by the quilt shop to say hello to Bonnie before continuing around the corner and up the hill to the square, a green with benches and a bandstand bordered by shops, restaurants, and city government buildings. The Daily Grind, a coffee shop next to the small public library, was a favorite with students and professors; lone figures hunched over coffee cups at tables strewn with papers and books, crumpled napkins, and plates of half-eaten muffins and biscotti.

They joined the queue. When Sarah reached the front of the line, she placed their order, gave her name, and asked to speak to the owner. "He's expecting us," she said. The clerk nodded, disappeared into the back, and returned with the message that Norman would meet them at their table.

Like the rest of his staff, Norman wore a green apron over his jeans and flannel shirt, and his thick black hair and beard gave him a wild look tempered by a good-humored smile. He pulled up a chair beside Sylvia as Sarah made introductions. At nearly six and a half feet tall, he towered over them even sitting down, but what captured Sylvia's attention most was the thick ledger he carried under one arm.

"I called my dad in Florida," said Norman to Sylvia, opening the ledger. "He remembers you and your sister, and he's positive Claudia sold some items through the store in the postwar years, but he doesn't remember the specific transactions."

"I expected as much," said Sylvia. "It was a very long time ago, and he had so many sales."

Norman grinned. "Not too many, unfortunately, or the shop wouldn't have closed. Then again, if it hadn't, he wouldn't have started his second business, and I'd much rather run a coffeehouse than a consignment store." He carefully turned to a page near the back of the ledger. "My father kept good records, and there's a lot of information here once you decipher his shorthand. See, here's your sister's account."

Sylvia slipped on her glasses and read her sister's name, printed in small, neat handwriting on the title line. The same handwriting filled nearly three quarters of the page, which was divided into five columns. Norman ran his finger down the first and stopped at one of the last entries. "These are the dates items were left with the shop, and these apparently random combinations of letters and numbers are my father's descriptions. See this QLT? That's his code for quilt, and believe me, that was one of the easier ones to figure out."

"What about the rest of it?" asked Andrew. "What's the BLUW/L stand for?"

"BLU indicates that the item was blue. The W means white. The information after the slash usually refers to the item's size or its era."

"A large blue-and-white quilt," said Sylvia. "That could be the Ocean Waves. Did your father keep more detailed records so we could confirm this? Did he take any photographs of the items in his inventory?"

Norman shook his head. "Only if the clients requested an appraisal, and they typically only did so for valuables or antiques because of the additional expense. If your sister had asked for one, there would have been a note."

Sylvia pursed her lips and nodded. Claudia would have done so if she had thought an appraisal would raise the price, but if she had understood the quilts' true worth, she never could have sold them. Sylvia gestured to the check mark in the third column beside the code for the blue-and-white quilt. "I assume the check mark indicates the item was sold?"

"It does," said Norman. "A dash instead of a check means the client reclaimed the item before it sold. In the fifth column, the two numbers separated by a slash are the price of the item and my father's commission, and the fifth column is the date the item left the store."

Sylvia had already guessed as much, and she studied the entry with a pang of regret. Fifty dollars. Claudia had parted with their mother's Ocean Waves quilt for fifty dollars, and nowhere on that page did Sylvia see any indication of who had purchased it.

"Why are there blank spaces for some of the items where the checks or dashes should be?" asked Amy. "What happened to the things that didn't sell and weren't reclaimed?"

Sylvia and Andrew exchanged a look, surprised to see her taking an interest.

"If the third column is empty, the item was still in the shop when my father retired," said Norman. "He tried to contact his clients so they would pick up their goods, but not everyone responded. He donated what little inventory remained to charity." He pointed to the last entry on the page. "Which brings me to this."

Sylvia, Andrew, Sarah, and even Amy leaned closer to get a better look at Claudia's last transaction with the consignment shop. On November 22, 1959, she had placed another quilt with Norman's father, one identified as QLT W/S.

Sylvia sucked in a breath and sat back in her chair. A small, white quilt. The whole cloth quilt. And the third column was blank.

"Do you have any idea what charity your father donated his inventory to?" she asked.

"He gave to several—Goodwill, St. Vincent de Paul, a few other local groups that aren't even around anymore, but he didn't keep a record of how the items were distributed, just one receipt from each organization with an amount for his tax deductions."

"May I?" Sarah asked, reaching for the ledger. Norman slid it across the table. She paged through it and eventually shook her head. "Did your father keep a separate record for his accounts receivable? This book tells us how much he paid out and to whom, but not what his customers paid the shop."

Norman winced. "One of my father's failures in the business was that he was always more interested in the contents of the store's shelves than its cash register. He was so disinterested in actually selling anything that I think he would have been happier running a museum." He rose. "I can show you the rest of his records, such as they are. I don't think he'd mind."

He led them behind the counter and through the kitchen into a small, cluttered office. Floor to ceiling bookshelves stuffed with books, magazines, and coffee mugs lined one entire wall, while the others were plastered with movie posters. Someone had taken a pen to them, Sylvia noted, contributing mustaches, eye patches, and blackened teeth as well as dialogue balloons with rather more colorful language than filmmakers typically included in their advertising. A dusty computer sat on a small desk, but there was no chair, and the desk calendar was set to April of the previous year. She and Sarah spotted the filing cabinet bursting with papers and exchanged looks of dismay; looking for records in this place would be nearly as bad as searching the attic of Elm Creek Manor. But Norman merely said, "Excuse the mess," took a key from the desk drawer, and led them back down the hall.

He unlocked the door to a narrow storage room and shoved it open as far as it would go, which was barely enough room for him to reach inside and flip on the light. Sylvia peered past him, noted the several large filing boxes that had impeded the door's progress, and wished they were searching the office instead.

Norman glanced down at her and chuckled. "Not all of this stuff is my dad's." With effort, he shoved the door open wider and squeezed his torso through the narrow opening. "Most of this is for the coffee shop."

"I hope you don't ever get audited," said Sarah, taking in the scene. "You'd need a team of accountants to sort out this mess."

"What?" Norman seemed genuinely bewildered as he looked from her to the room and back. "Oh. Yeah, I guess it's a little untidy, but I know where everything is."

Andrew looked dubious. "All I see are piles of paper."

"But each pile has a purpose." Grinning, Norman hauled four filing cartons into the hallway and lined them up along the wall. "You'll wish my dad was that organized before you're through."

He removed the first carton's lid, and Sylvia heard Sarah stifle a groan as they took in what appeared to be nothing more than a box of the street sweepings after a ticker-tape parade.

"Accounts receivable, I presume?" asked Sylvia, accepting Andrew's assistance as she knelt beside the carton.

"Accounts receivable and miscellaneous," affirmed Norman. "With the emphasis on miscellaneous." Then he apologized and explained that they would have to search on their own, for he had to return to work. He encouraged them to look as long as they liked and offered the use of his photocopier to duplicate any documents that would aid them in their search.

"I hope no one has any plans for the afternoon," said Sarah after Norman left.

Andrew hesitated. "I still need to run that errand."

"Well, there are four of us and four boxes." Amy seated herself on the floor beside another carton and removed the lid. "We shouldn't need more than a few hours."

Behind her back, Sylvia and Andrew exchanged speculative glances, then Andrew shrugged and made his way to the last carton. He patted his daughter on the shoulder as he passed.

Sylvia sifted through the first few layers of paper in her carton, uncertain what she ought to be looking for and doubtful she would recognize it when she found it. Sarah advised them to look for anything with Claudia's name on it, of course, but also bank records or store receipts for purchases made on the date the Ocean Waves quilt was sold. If Norman's father had not written the item code on the receipt, they could still identify the quilt by comparing the total on the receipt to the price listed in the ledger.

Their work was painstakingly slow, and working on the floor added to their discomfort, but within the first half-hour Andrew made a fortunate discovery: an envelope containing receipts for donations to five local charities, dated the same year Norman told them the shop had closed. "We'll phone them as soon as we get home," said Sarah, placing the envelope on a nearby shelf for safekeeping. "I admit it's not likely they still have the whole cloth quilt, but they might know where it ended up."

"Not unless their records are much better than Norman's father's," said Amy as she thumbed through a stack of canceled checks bound by a stack of rubber bands. Wisps of hair had come loose from her barrette, and she absently tucked them behind her ears as she set the checks aside.

Despite the exasperation of the unnecessary labor Norman's father had inflicted upon them, as she sorted through the contents of her carton, Sylvia began to sympathize with him. She had only rarely visited his store as a young woman and its closing had passed her by unnoticed, but the ledger and those haphazard files revealed a man happy in his work, one who had cultivated a close relationship with his customers. He had often scrawled notes on claim tickets, reminders to set an item aside for a customer who would particularly appreciate it or to inquire about the health of an ailing relative. One note brought tears to Sylvia's eyes. "Tell her no more quilts," he had jotted in black pencil on the back of the claim ticket stub for the Ocean Waves quilt. "Hate to sell them. Should keep."

Someone, at least, had recognized that the true measure of the quilts' worth was not in what price they could fetch but in the story they told of the woman who had so lovingly crafted them. But did the ambiguous message mean that Norman's father would like to keep the quilts for himself, that Claudia ought to keep the quilts because she hated to sell them, or that he hated to sell them because he believed Claudia ought to keep them in the family? Sylvia knew her sister's selfishness well, and yet part of her longed to believe that Claudia had sold off their mother's legacy only because she had no other choice. If Sylvia could never reclaim those precious heirlooms, their loss would be easier to accept if she knew Claudia had not parted with them easily.

Their search gleaned one other tantalizing clue, and Amy was the one who discovered it: a bank statement listing a check whose date and total matched the ledger entry for the Ocean Waves quilt.

A thrill ran through Sylvia as she examined the check, crumpled from its long storage, the ink of the signature fading, but with the printed name and address of the account holder still legible. Even Sarah's warning that they ought to examine the ledger in the unlikely event that a second item had sold that same day for the exact same amount did not weaken her confidence that this was the check that had purchased her mother's quilt.

"It's more than fifty years old," said Amy. "That woman may no longer live at that address."

"I'm certain she doesn't," said Sylvia. "I know this woman, or rather, knew her. She was my mother's age."

"Were they friends?" asked Sarah.

"Whatever else Gloria Schaeffer may have been, she was no friend to our family. You may recall, Sarah, that I told you how Claudia and I were kicked out of the Waterford Quilting Guild during World War II because of silly rumors that we Bergstroms were German sympathizers. It was utter nonsense, of course, but Gloria thought our presence disrupted the harmony of our meetings, and since she was guild president . . ." Sylvia shrugged. "I figured if they didn't want me, I wanted no part of them, but Claudia took our dismissal hard. What I don't understand, though, is what Gloria Schaeffer would want with a Bergstrom quilt."

"Maybe she didn't know it was your mother's," suggested Andrew.

"Unlikely. My mother and Gloria were both founding members of the guild. They would have seen a good deal of each other's work, both complete and in progress."

"Maybe she wanted to help Claudia financially," said Sarah. "Out of guilt for what she did."

Sylvia admitted it was possible, but perhaps she still harbored some resentment for that long-ago offense, for she could not believe Gloria would wish to assist any Bergstrom. More likely, Gloria had taken a perverse glee in the downturn in the family's fortunes and could not resist parting them from one of their treasured heirlooms.

"Gloria had two sons," said Sylvia, setting the canceled check aside with the charity receipts and the Ocean Waves claim ticket stub. "Assuming Gloria is no longer among the living, one of them may have inherited the quilt." They would be in the phone book, if they still lived in Waterford.

Several hours and cups of coffee later, they finished wading through the detritus of the consignment shop without finding any more clues to the whereabouts of the missing quilts. Still, with Gloria Schaeffer's last known address in hand, Sylvia felt somewhat optimistic, despite her growing concerns about the whole cloth quilt, of which they still knew very little.

Sarah photocopied the relevant documents while the others returned the cartons to the storage room. Then they found Norman out front and thanked him. As they left the coffee shop, Andrew glanced at his watch. "It's four-thirty. If we hurry, we can take care of that errand before the office closes."

"Goodness, Andrew, I completely forgot." Sylvia turned up the collar of her coat and tucked her arm through his. "If I had known we would spend so much time at the Daily Grind I would have suggested we take care of your errand first. Where to, then? The bank? The hardware store?"

"The county clerk's office," he replied, "and it's not my errand. It's our errand. Don't tell me you forgot."

"I'm afraid I did," said Sylvia, smiling at his eagerness.

"How could you forget? What were we talking about ever since the Ohio border? What did we say we'd take care of as soon as we got home?"

With dismay, Sylvia remembered. "Oh, let's worry about that another day, shall we?" Her arm in Andrew's, she began strolling down the sidewalk toward Grandma's Attic and the van. "After all that work, I have absolutely no interest in waiting in a long line."

Andrew stopped short. "There won't be a line at this hour. Besides, we're right here."

"Sylvia's right," said Sarah. Sylvia doubted she had caught on, but she could usually sense Sylvia's moods and must have realized there was a problem. "Anyway, it's my turn to make supper, so I need to get home."

"This won't take long," said Andrew. "All we have to do is fill out a form and show our IDs. It's not that hard to get a marriage license."

Amy looked at her father, expressionless.

"Andrew, please," said Sylvia quietly. "Let's go home."

"The county clerk's office is right across the street. We're here, so we might as well stop by. If there's a long line, we'll come back another time."

"You had to do this now," said Amy. "You couldn't wait until I went home."

"You mean sneak around, as if I'm doing something shameful? I'm proud that Sylvia's marrying me, and I'm not going to hide that from anyone."

"Andrew, please," murmured Sylvia.

"I'm not asking you to hide."

"What, then? Should I pretend that we're not getting married rather than offend you?"

Amy threw up her hands. "Listen, Dad, you do what you have to do. Just don't pretend you're not baiting me, and don't expect me to stand around and watch while you do it."

She stalked off. Andrew glowered, and Sylvia started to follow her, but Sarah caught her by the arm. "I'll stay with her," she said quietly. "We'll meet you at the van."

Sylvia agreed and watched as Sarah hurried down the sidewalk after Amy. Amy paused when Sarah approached, and they exchanged a few words before continuing on together. Neither one looked back.

"Are you coming?" asked Andrew after the pair rounded the corner and vanished from sight.

Sylvia nodded.

Andrew was right in one respect: The county clerk's office was not busy at that hour, and they waited only a few minutes before their number was called. They filled out the proper form, paid the forty dollar fee, showed their driver's licenses, and accepted the clerk's congratulations when he told them they could pick up their license in three days. Soon they were back outside on the sidewalk in the fading daylight. Sylvia returned Andrew's kiss when he told her how happy he was, but she shivered in the cold and tucked her hands into her pockets instead of taking his arm.

They walked in silence toward Grandma's Attic. "Well, that's one more task to cross off our list," said Andrew.

"True enough."

He gave her a sidelong glance. "But?"

"But we could have put it off until later."

"Don't tell me you're siding with Amy."

"The very fact that you would make this an issue of choosing sides tells me you know you're in the wrong."

"What?" He placed a hand on her arm to bring her to a halt. "You're the one insisting we have to go on about our own lives without worrying about their concerns."

"Yes, but that's altogether different from flaunting our decision in your daughter's face. We could have come downtown any day, and you know it. Why did it have to be today, especially after Amy was so helpful sorting through those dreadful files? She was trying to give us a chance, and I think if we had given her more time, we might have won her over. But now . . ." She shook her head and resumed walking. "Now we're worse off than before."

After a moment, Andrew caught up to her. "I wasn't trying to goad her. Honest."

Sylvia could manage only a shrug. She wasn't sure she believed him.

Sarah and Amy were not waiting in the van when Sylvia and Andrew arrived, but they appeared fifteen minutes later carrying shopping bags from Grandma's Attic. Sylvia was thankful that Sarah had attempted to distract Amy until tempers cooled, but there was no mistaking Amy's lingering anger. She barely looked at her father or at Sylvia as she climbed into the van, and she made only monosyllabic replies to Sylvia's attempts at conversation. As they pulled up behind Elm Creek Manor, Sylvia heard Amy quietly offer to help Sarah prepare supper. Sylvia quickly volunteered herself and Andrew, but Amy frowned, and Sarah told her that they were entitled to a rest after their long trip. "You have some phone calls to make, too," she pointed out.

Andrew wanted to unpack, so Sylvia went alone to the library, welcoming the relief of solitude after the tension that had marred their homecoming. She seated herself at the desk that had been her father's and flipped open the phone book to the business pages. She found numbers for Goodwill and St. Vincent de Paul easily, but Lutheran Outreach and St. Michael's Society were not listed. There was a St. Michael's Catholic Church, so Sylvia hoped for the best and dialed.

The young woman who answered the phone had never heard of St. Michael's Society, but she offered to ask around and call Sylvia back. Sylvia thanked her and hung up, and then, although she was reluctant to tie up the line, she called Goodwill. As she had feared, they told her it was highly improbable that they would still have her mother's quilt after so many years. "But you never know," said the woman on the other end of the line, and offered to search for it. This time Sylvia said she would hold, and about ten minutes later, the woman returned to report that the only quilts currently in their possession were pieced or appliquéd, and since they did not maintain detailed records of individual purchases, there was no way to know who had bought the quilt, or when. She promised to call Sylvia if any whole cloth quilts were donated to their collection site in the future. Sylvia appreciated her helpfulness and her sympathy, but as she recited her phone number, she doubted the woman would ever have reason to call it.

Her luck was no better at St. Vincent de Paul, except to rule out one possible destination for the quilt. The man who took her call noted that back when Norman's father would have made his donations, their branch had handled only large durable items like furniture and appliances, and customarily had advised donors to take items such as clothes and bedding to other charities, such as Goodwill and Lutheran Outreach. Sylvia said that she had spoken to Goodwill but could not locate the Lutheran Outreach; the man told her that they had closed down in the early seventies, and that as far as he knew, no one affiliated with the organization remained in Waterford.

Disappointed, Sylvia thanked him for his time and hung up; she was crossing St. Vincent de Paul off her list when the phone rang. The young woman from St. Michael's Catholic Church had called back to report that the parish priest knew of St. Michael's Society, a community service and social justice organization founded in the early 1960s by a group of Waterford College students. For nearly fifteen years, they had served impoverished families, especially single mothers of young children, throughout the Elm Creek Valley, and eventually had become an official organization of the college and was still in existence under a different name. "One of the founders is the emeritus director of Campus Ministry," said the young woman, and since he was also one of their most active parishioners, she didn't think he would mind if she gave Sylvia his name and number.

To Sylvia's delight, he was home when she called, but while he seemed to be a thoroughly charming man and his tales about St. Michael's Society were intriguing, he had no information on the whereabouts of the whole cloth quilt. "All donations were either passed along to needy families or sold to raise money to purchase necessities," he explained.

Sylvia's heart sank, but she persisted, inquiring whether the campus organization might have some record of the donations from the consignment shop. No such records existed, she was told, and he regretted that he could not help her.

Sylvia assured him he had been very helpful, and hung up the phone with a sigh. She fingered the list of crossed-off names and phone numbers for a moment before tossing it on top of the responses to Summer's Internet posts. She studied the pile before beginning to leaf through it, and as she worked her way through the letters, each promising her the whole cloth quilt, frustration and disappointment stole over her. Last of all, she examined the printouts she had obtained at the Thousand Oaks Library, and as she did, she forced herself to accept two unavoidable conclusions she had been trying her best to ignore ever since the discovery of the pattern.

The Mrs. Abigail Drury identified in the magazine as the designer must have created the whole cloth quilt pattern. What Sylvia had always thought of as her mother's original design was nothing more than a reproduction of someone else's work. That surely explained why Mother had neglected to embroider her name and the date on this quilt alone, out of all those she had completed over the years.

Worse yet, since the pattern for the quilt had been published in such a popular magazine, hundreds if not thousands of quilters must have stitched quilts indistinguishable from her mother's. Even if Sylvia purchased every one of these she could track down, she would never be able to determine which one, if any, had belonged to her mother.

No matter how long she searched, the lovely whole cloth quilt would remain forever lost to her.

Later, at supper, she did not share her realization with her friends, because she could not bear to hear them agree with her conclusion. As the meal ended, Sylvia rose from her chair with relief, longing for a good night's sleep. She noticed, too late, that Amy alone had remained in her chair. "If you don't mind," she said quietly, fingering her water glass, "I have something to say."

Sylvia shot Andrew a warning look, but he knew enough to keep quiet until Amy had a chance to speak.

"I'm leaving in the morning."

"Why?" asked Andrew. "Honey, I'm sorry about this afternoon. I didn't intend to taunt you."

"It's not just that." Amy caught Sylvia's gaze and held it. "With all due respect, what you're doing is wrong. You're asking too much of my father, and I simply can't support your decision to marry. Under those circumstances, I no longer feel comfortable accepting your hospitality."

"Please stay," urged Sylvia. "In the morning we'll have a good talk and sort this thing out."

"What's to sort out?" Amy shook her head and rose. "I don't approve of your marriage. I can't. Please don't ask me or my family to witness it."

"Amy, please—" Andrew reached out for her, but she waved him off and hurried from the room. He turned to Sylvia, stricken. She took his hand in both of hers, dumbfounded and heartsick, and utterly at a loss for what to do.

Chapter Eight

With Claudia squirming on her lap, Eleanor tore another long strip from the faded sheet and rolled it into a tight, neat bundle. Claudia crowed and grabbed at it, knocking it from Eleanor's hand. It bounced across the floor, unrolling in a long, narrow streamer that ended at Lucinda's feet.

"I swear she unrolls one bandage for every two you finish," said Maude. "Why don't you just set her on the floor, for heaven's sake?"

Eleanor spread Claudia's Four-Patch quilt on the rug and gently placed Claudia on it. No one argued with Maude anymore, and not even Lucinda retorted when her tongue grew too sharp. Louis's death had left Maude bitter and angry, as if he had not died in a muddy trench in France but had abandoned her. She seemed to believe he could return to her if he wanted to.

Eleanor could almost understand it; even now she found it difficult to imagine handsome, mischievous Louis choking on mustard gas. But she *could* imagine it, so she had come to believe it. Her heart went out to Maude, who could not, and to poor Lily, who could imagine her own husband's death too vividly. Richard had been the first of the brothers to enlist and the first to die, barely three days after his arrival at the French port of Bordeaux. He had gone off to war so proudly, so eager for adventure. Lily had not wanted him to become a soldier, but she could not deny him the chance to distinguish himself when he wanted it so badly. Soon, as patriotic fervor swept over the nation, his elder brothers found their own reasons to battle the Hun. First the Waterford Chamber Orchestra announced they would no longer perform any works by Bach or Beethoven. Then Waterford College suspended the teaching of the German language. Then Eleanor was turned away by the cobbler who muttered that he would not work his craft for any friend of the Kaiser.

Eleanor did not care what an ignorant cobbler said or did. She could not bear for her darling husband to sacrifice himself to pride. She begged him not to go; she implored him not to leave her now that their longing for a child seemed likely to be fulfilled at last. But he was resolute. "No one must ever doubt the loyalties of the Bergstrom family," he had said as he and Louis went off to enlist. "We are not German, but American, and we will fight for America."

Louis died within weeks of Richard. The family prayed for Fred's safe return and thanked God that William was too young to fight and that Clara was a girl. These children, at least, could be protected. They would be safe, and so would Claudia, the only Bergstrom grandchild to remain at Elm Creek Manor after Lily took her boys back to her own family and the home of her youth. Eleanor missed Lily's gentle innocence and the laughing, tumbling happiness of her sons. She did not expect they would ever return.

When Claudia realized her mother no longer held her, she waved her limbs frantically in protest, her face screwing up in scarlet fury. "Hush, my angel," murmured Eleanor, stroking her downy hair. Clara joined them on the floor and playfully dangled a strip of fabric within the baby's reach, bringing it close and then far. Claudia squealed with delight when she managed to seize the end in her tiny fist.

Eleanor returned to her chair, hungry for the joy that watching her beloved little girl brought her. Claudia was nearly five months old and had never seen her father—might never see him.

That was why Eleanor rolled bandages instead of escaping into the solace of quilting. What if Fred were wounded and perished for the lack of a single bandage? What if he faltered from hunger and cold when he most needed strength? She knew, logically, that nothing she did could directly preserve her husband. Her bandages would go to other wounded; the sugar she did not buy would feed other doughboys. And yet she knew, too, there was connection in the greater whole; she sensed it as she doggedly rolled bandages and bought Thrift Stamps and war bonds and conserved every scrap of food and fabric. She could not wield a gun, but she would do all she could to put wind in the sails of the Allied victory and hasten her dear Freddy's safe return home.

"I think Claudia looks like Fred," said Clara suddenly, picking her up. "They have the same eyes."

Lucinda snorted. "She has the Bergstrom chin, but other than that, she's the very image of her mother."

"What did Fred think when he saw her picture?" asked Elizabeth. Like Maude, she was clad all in black, but she had faced the death of her two sons with more resignation than Eleanor thought she could manage in her place.

"He thought she resembled me," said Eleanor, and felt heat rising in her cheeks. Along with the photograph of the baby, she had sent a picture of herself holding up her most recent quilt. She had chosen the Ocean Waves pattern for the ocean that separated them, blue and white fabrics for the crashing storm he faced abroad and the churning sea her life seemed without him. "Hurry home and help me use this, darling," she had written on the back, blushing as she imagined how his buddies would tease him. The photo did not do the quilt justice, but he had written back that it was her most magnificent creation next to the baby. In fact, he liked it so much that when he returned, he might stay beneath it for a month straight, assuming she would keep him company. After all, he had written, they needed to get started making Claudia's baby brother.

Eleanor had implied that no one would use the quilt until his return, and knowing that the idea held special meaning for Fred, it was difficult to look across the room at Elizabeth without embarrassment. Fred's mother was nursing a head cold, and she sat in her favorite chair with the Ocean Waves quilt draped over her, sipping lemon tea sweetened with honey. To ward off a sore throat, she had wrapped her neck with a poultice of her own invention. It smelled like burnt licorice, but Eleanor had no desire to learn its true ingredients. Lucinda decried Elizabeth's remedy as useless for anything but frightening away unwelcome guests, and David slept in a spare bedroom whenever she wore it, but Elizabeth insisted that it worked.

Elizabeth made no such testimonials for Eleanor's Ocean Waves quilt, but she seemed to place at least as much faith in its curative powers. She asked for it whenever she felt unwell, and had done so ever since she had fallen asleep beneath the unfinished quilt as Eleanor sewed on the binding and woke released from a day-long headache. To believe that a quilt could heal the sick was ridiculous, maybe even blasphemous, and perhaps Elizabeth realized this, for she never proclaimed the powers of the quilt as she did her various poultices and charms.

Ordinarily, Eleanor tried to humor Elizabeth's superstitions, especially now, with the war and the losses of Richard and Louis to put her harmless eccentricities in perspective. But what if Elizabeth fell ill in the night and came to Eleanor's and Fred's bedchamber for the quilt at the very moment they were beneath it endeavoring to give Claudia a baby brother? Elizabeth might not be deterred by a locked door if she thought her health was at stake.

Heat rose in Eleanor's cheeks that had less to do with embarrassment than with the scene she imagined Elizabeth interrupting. She lowered her head and tried to appear focused on the bandage she was rolling, but Lucinda's sharp eyes missed nothing. Lucinda appeared about to speak, but at that moment, the front bell rang. "I'll get it," said Eleanor, rising and hurrying from the room with only one quick glance over her shoulder to reassure herself that Claudia was content playing with Clara. By the time she returned, Lucinda would have found someone else to tease.

As she had hoped, Frank Schaeffer, the postman, stood at the front door. "You should not have come so far out of your way," Eleanor scolded him cheerfully. "One of us would have come to the post office eventually."

"It's no trouble at all," Frank assured her, as he always did. "By the time you got around to it, the pile would have been so deep I would have had to help you haul it home anyway."

He handed her two letters, but even before she scanned the envelopes, his sympathetic look told her neither had come from Fred. Despite his thick shock of gray hair, Frank was barely a year older than Fred and widely regarded as the best marksman in the Elm Creek Valley. His greatest shame was that, as a sleepwalker, he had been declared unfit for military service. Privately, his wife Gloria had told Eleanor that she never imagined she would praise God for her husband's most irritating habit.

"I'm sure you'll hear from Fred soon," said Frank. "He's probably too busy to write much."

"I'm sure that's it," said Eleanor, though her stomach clenched when she thought of all the horrors that could prevent him from writing. She bid Frank good-bye with a forced smile and a reminder for his wife that their blocks for the guild's charity quilt were due in two weeks.

She read the return addresses on her way back to the west sitting room, her pace quickening in delight. The first letter was from Lily; the family would be overjoyed to hear from her. The second was from Miss Langley.

She gave Lily's letter to Elizabeth to read aloud, but months had passed since she had last heard from her former nanny, and she was impatient to learn the reason for her silence. Promising herself she would read Lily's letter later, she quietly tore open Miss Langley's envelope and withdrew two sheets of ivory writing paper.

September 6, 1918

My Dear Eleanor,

Please accept my apologies for my long delay in responding to your letter, but as you will learn, my recent circumstances have rarely been conducive to the sort of quiet contemplation required for thoughtful writing, and when they were, I chanced to be bereft of paper and ink.

I do fear my confession will shock you. Eleanor dear, please do sit down and hand the baby to someone else.

I did not write to you sooner because I was in prison.

You will assume my arrest resulted from my activities organizing the union among the mill workers. A sensible deduction, since the factory owners often use their influence with local law enforcement to harass those who strive for the liberation of the laborer, but incorrect. Instead I was prosecuted for a more villainous crime: speaking my mind too frankly where unsympathetic listeners could overhear.

You are aware, of course, of the law making seditious utterances a crime. I, too, could not claim ignorance of the law as an excuse, although the passionate enthusiasm of the crowd at a labor rally did make me forget it for a moment. It seemed natural to me to divert from denouncing one great wrong to demanding an end to a second, but evidently some among my audience will more readily decry a greedy factory owner than a cruel war.

I was arrested the day after the rally and charged with criticizing the war policies of the United States government. I was convicted, as was to be expected given the current climate of this nation, and was sentenced to a year in prison and deportation. That was the worst part of it, that I should be exiled from my adopted land when so much work remains to be done.

So that my mind would not grow despondent and dull in idleness, I endeavoured to make the best of my confinement by establishing a law library within the prison and organizing a literacy program. Perhaps my imprisonment was a blessing in disguise, for I had not understood the shameful state of the penal system until I was myself subjected to it. I resolved that if I were somehow able to remain in this country after my release, I would fight to reform the prisons as I had fought to improve its factories.

You are a bright young woman, and I am sure you have already perceived some ostensible contradictions in this account. Clearly this letter was posted in Boston, while I ought to be either in prison or in England. As it happens, I did not serve out my year-long sentence, nor was I deported. These remarkable consequences came about through the agency of Charles Davis, who has been my dear friend and comrade for years, almost ever since I departed the Lockwood household. Faced with the prospect of never seeing me again, he proposed marriage, and once assured that unlike many of his sex he would remember we would remain equals after we wed, I consented.

The parole board was greatly impressed by this apparent reformation and domestication of my character, and as I had been a model prisoner, and as no one had been injured nor any property damaged by my speech, I was released after only six months. Moreover, now that I am married to an American, I cannot be so easily deported.

The parole board admonished me to be on my best behavior, which I agreed to do, although I am sure we would define that differently. Thus, upon regaining my freedom, I resumed my union activities. I now forgo criticism of the war except among friends, though I hate to see our Freedom of Speech so abused. I did not forget the promises I made to myself during my incarceration, either, and I have returned to that same prison as a teacher. When I see my students struggling proudly with their lessons, I cannot help wondering how they may have never seen the inside of a prison if only they had been granted a solid education in their youth. I do not romanticize these inmates; many of them have committed abhorrent, unspeakable crimes. Yet while living among them I learned that desperation and fear drove them to these terrible acts far more often than greed or rage did, and they might have chosen another path if it had been made clear for them.

Unfortunately, my enlightenment came with a price, and I do not speak of my temporary loss of freedom. Eleanor dear, I am so sorry I could not be present at the birth of your daughter as I had promised.

My only consolation is knowing that you were surrounded by women who love you, and I am sure they were a great comfort. I am pleased little Claudia likes the quilt, and I am very glad I finished it early and sent it to you before the tumultuous events of the past few months could have interfered.

I so longed to see you, and still do, which makes this next part the most difficult to write. Eleanor, you must not come to Boston. There is an illness spreading throughout the city, and although the authorities claim the matter is well in hand, I have my suspicions that the situation will worsen before it improves. Apparently the sickness first appeared in the Navy barracks at Commonwealth Pier, and even now it seems to afflict primarily sailors and soldiers, but yesterday, a friend who is a nurse at Boston City Hospital told me they have admitted civilians afflicted with the same disease. The bewilderment and fear in her expression when she confided the details of her cases filled me with considerable alarm. The onset of the illness is sudden, intense, and cruel; I will spare you a description of the symptoms, as my friend's yet haunts my nightmares and I do not wish to burden you with it.

I do not tell you this to alarm you, only to convince you to stay away until this illness has run its course. Perhaps you will still be able to visit this autumn, before the weather worsens, or perhaps I could visit you. That might be better in any case; I am sure my husband and my pupils can spare me, and I would so enjoy seeing the places and people you have described in your letters. Otherwise we will have to wait until spring. Chin up! We have waited nineteen years; we shall survive another few months.

Please take good care of yourself and give sweet Claudia a kiss from

Your Affectionate Friend,
Amelia Langley Davis

"Eleanor?" said Clara.

Eleanor looked up from the letter, startled. "What is it?"

The others were watching her, concerned. "You're as white as a sheet," said Elizabeth, and coughed into her handkerchief. "Is it bad news?"

"I'm afraid so," said Eleanor, quickly composing herself as she returned the letter to its envelope. "Miss Langley—or I should say, Mrs. Davis, for she has married—has asked us not to come."

"Why not?" asked Maude. "Not that I ever thought you should go. The baby is much too young to travel so far."

"There has been an outbreak of illness in Boston." Eleanor fingered the envelope, a fist clenching in her belly. "It sounds a great deal like the three-day fever Fred said afflicted the soldiers overseas in the spring, but . . ."

"But what?" asked Lucinda sharply.

Eleanor smiled and shrugged. "I was going to say more virulent, but you know how Miss Langley exaggerates."

Miss Langley did not exaggerate, and Lucinda had heard enough stories about Eleanor's nanny to know that. Lucinda gave her a long, steady look before glancing down on the floor where Clara played with Claudia. "Mrs. Davis, you mean," Lucinda said, taking up another strip of cloth.

"Mrs. Davis. I must remember that, although it will be difficult after so many years of calling her Miss Langley."

Eleanor scooped up Claudia and held her close.

❧

A week passed with no more visits from Frank Schaeffer, which meant no letters from Fred. Eleanor wrote to her husband nearly every night, a few paragraphs telling him about her day, about Claudia. Maude scolded her for wasting paper and postage on so many letters instead of writing one longer letter once a week, but when Eleanor thought of the hazards her fragile letters would pass through, she decided that sending many separate envelopes would increase the chances that at least one would reach Fred.

Frank still had not returned to Elm Creek Manor by the following Saturday afternoon, the date of the Waterford Quilting Guild's monthly meeting. Eleanor drove into town with Lucinda and Clara, who at thirteen was too young to be an official member but had been granted special permission to attend meetings. Eleanor and Lucinda were two of the four founders of the guild, after all, and even the fussiest members tolerated Clara's presence rather than offend Elizabeth and risk being excluded from the quilting bees at Elm Creek Manor, which were a welcome diversion during the long Pennsylvania winters.

Eleanor had made sure they left home early so she could mail her letters before the meeting. Clara had filled an entire book of Thrift Stamps and was eager to exchange it for a War Bond, so while Eleanor ran her errand, Clara and Lucinda went to the bank.

At the post office, Eleanor joined the line to buy stamps, her thoughts drifting to Fred. She wondered if he was still in France. It was not like him to be silent so long between letters. He must not be able to send mail from wherever he was. If he had been killed, she would have been notified by now.

As she waited, she was at first only distantly aware of the hushed, worried voices around her until snatches of conversation broke through her reverie:

" . . . hundreds by now, and more dying every day . . ."

" . . . dropped dead, right on the street corner . . ."

" . . . Spanish flu, but I say it's German in origin . . ."

"I beg your pardon." Eleanor touched the shoulder of in the man in front of her in line. "What did you say?"

"It's nothing, miss," the man said, and the man with whom he had been speaking nodded. "Nothing for you to worry about."

"You said people are dying."

"Well, yes, I suppose I did." The man hesitated. "They're calling it the Spanish flu."

"Influenza?" Eleanor was not quite sure she believed him. She and Elizabeth had both had influenza in the spring. Only the very old and the very young died from it. "Hundreds are dead from influenza?"

"Yes, miss, but as I said, you shouldn't worry. It's all happening very far away from here."

By force of habit, Eleanor placed a hand on her heart to still its pounding. "Boston isn't that far away."

A long look passed between the two men before the first said, "I was speaking of Philadelphia."

"You could have been speaking of any city east of here," a sharp voice broke in from behind them. Eleanor turned to find a stout woman with her arms full of parcels. "My daughters in New York City say the undertakers are running out of coffins."

Eleanor's heart leapt in alarm; the two men exchanged uneasy glances. "It's true," the woman insisted. "That why I'm sending my girls my best remedies as quick as can be. Wish I could go there and tend to them myself, but this time of year my rheumatism troubles me terribly when I travel."

Eleanor nodded in sympathy, but as the sharp-voiced woman went on to describe her various concoctions, her thoughts raced to Miss Langley—Mrs. Davis—in Boston, to her parents in New York. She must send word to them right away and invite them to wait out the illness in the safety of Elm Creek Manor before they succumbed to it themselves. Mr. Davis, too, of course, and any of their friends who wished to take precautions.

She murmured her excuses to the woman and left the line, retrieving paper and pen from her purse with trembling hands. By the time she finished the letters and rejoined the line, the woman and the two men had left. Others had taken their places, but the newcomers continued the anxious murmurs: The disease had spread as far west as St. Louis; no, it had halted at the Mississippi; no, it ravaged the nation from coast to coast. It was an affliction caused by unsanitary conditions and overcrowding, which is why it afflicted soldiers and the poor. It was simply the same flu they saw every season, nothing to fear. It was a deadly germ released on the Eastern seaboard by spies put ashore from German U-boats.

Eleanor finished her errand and fled.

Outside, Lucinda sat on a bench reading the paper while Clara read over her shoulder. "Lucinda," Eleanor began, and hesitated. She did not wish to alarm Clara. "It seems the sickness has spread beyond Boston."

"It was never confined there." Lucinda folded the paper and tucked it under her arm. "It's everywhere, or it will be soon."

"But the paper says the doctors have it 'well in hand,'" said Clara.

"I know, dearie. I was reading between the lines." Lucinda rose and strode off in the direction of the public library, where the quilting guild met.

Eleanor and Clara hurried to catch up with her. "There's no flu in Waterford," said Clara, a question in her voice.

"Not yet there isn't," said Lucinda. "As far as we know."

Clara looked up at Eleanor, anxious. "Don't worry," Eleanor said quietly, placing an arm around Clara's shoulders. "It's just the flu."

The meeting had already begun when they arrived, ten minutes late, so they quietly found places in the back. Gloria stood at the podium calling for nominations for the next year's slate of officers. One of the women in the front row called out, "Since she's not here to object, I nominate Eleanor Bergstrom as president."

There was a murmur of assent. Gloria grinned at Eleanor and shrugged as if to say she was powerless to object. "Wait," began Eleanor. "I—"

"I second the nomination," declared another.

"But I've already been president," protested Eleanor. "Twice."

"And you did a wonderful job. That's why we all want you back." Gloria regarded the two dozen quilters inquisitively. "Any other nominations?"

The women shook their heads, and a few turned around to smile at Eleanor, who suppressed a sigh.

"It looks like you're running unopposed again," called out a friend of Elizabeth's.

Over the ripple of laughter, Eleanor said, "At least keep the nominations open until next month. Perhaps someone who isn't here today would like to run."

"Everyone's here," the guild secretary noted. "Everyone comes on nomination day."

"That's because if they don't, they'll find themselves president," said Eleanor, but she smiled to show she would be glad to resume the office.

The rest of the guild's business was quickly concluded, for everyone was eager to work on the charity quilt. Each woman had pieced a block in her favorite star pattern using red, white, and blue fabrics; in the Bergstrom family, where several quilters shared the same dwindling supply of precious fabric scraps, necessity had compelled them to adapt their patterns to make the best use of the available materials, but Eleanor was proud of the results. The five blocks representing the Bergstrom family were among the prettiest presented at the meeting, but what mattered most was that when the quilt was completed, the guild would raffle it off to raise money for the county chapter of the Red Cross.

The women pushed two tables together and placed all the blocks upon it, each contributing her opinion as to the most pleasing arrangement. The blocks were shuffled, considered, and rearranged until all but Gloria and Lucinda were satisfied, and their disagreement came down to the placement of two particular blocks. Lucinda wanted to exchange a LeMoyne Star block in the center of the quilt with a Sunburst block along one of the edges, explaining that the more intricate design would make a better central focal point. Gloria insisted that the two blocks should remain exactly where they were.

"She cares more about herself than the quilt," said Lucinda in an undertone only Eleanor could hear. Then Eleanor realized the LeMoyne Star block was Gloria's.

"If she cares about it so much, let her have her way," Eleanor murmured back. "Honestly, what does it matter?"

Lucinda's eyebrows rose, since Eleanor never settled for less than perfect where her own quilts were concerned. Still, Lucinda gave up the battle, and the women separated into smaller groups of friends to stitch the blocks into rows.

Eleanor expected the conversation to focus on this mysterious outbreak of disease in the East, but instead the women chatted about more ordinary things closer to home. Hungry for news, Eleanor introduced the subject herself, but no one volunteered anything she had not already heard at the post office. The general consensus seemed to be that the illness could not be as dire or spread as swiftly as rumor had it, and that they were fortunate to live in a pleasant little hamlet like Waterford, where they were spared the evils of the cities.

But the rumors did not die out, and swiftly the voices of authority gave them credibility. State health officers advocated the wearing of gauze masks. Eastern governors warned their Western counterparts to start making coffins. All the while, the disease stole closer, creeping along the highways and rivers. Thousands of cases reported in Philadelphia, hundreds more in Harrisburg. The first case in State College. And then the first case in Grangerville, only ten miles down the state road.

Hours after this announcement came, an emergency meeting was called at the town hall. Eleanor, David, and Lucinda attended, along with so many others that the meeting was moved to the Lutheran church on Second Street. As they squeezed into a pew, Lucinda remarked that this was the most unruly crowd in the church's history. David chuckled, but Eleanor was breathless from anxiety and unable to smile at the joke. Her eyes locked on the mayor as he entered and went to the front, followed by three men: Robert Cullen and Malcolm Granger, Waterford's two doctors, and a third man Eleanor did not recognize. He was tall and slim with a neatly trimmed black mustache, and he sat slightly apart from the two doctors, who were engaged in an urgent, whispered conversation.

The room quieted as the mayor took the pulpit. A portly, jovial man, he thanked them for coming and got straight to the point: No cases of Spanish influenza had yet occurred in Waterford, and he meant to keep it that way. A collective sigh of relief went up from the crowd, and as the murmurs rose into a crescendo of questions, the mayor raised his hands for silence and announced the formation of the town's first Health Committee. The two doctors had agreed to serve on it, and the third man, a professor of social sciences at Waterford College named Daniel Johnson, would direct their activities as Health Officer.

The mayor stepped down and was replaced in turn by each of the members of the Health Committee. The elderly Dr. Cullen took the pulpit first and somberly described the symptoms of the disease to a suddenly silent room. Once infected with the influenza germ, the patient's descent from robust health to incapacitation was sudden and savage. Raging fever. Racking coughs producing green pus and blood from the lungs. Gushing nosebleeds. Delirium. Pneumonia. Bluish or even purple skin, followed within hours by death. If anyone suspected the onset of these symptoms, they must report to his clinic at once.

"What will he do for us once we get there?" asked Lucinda in an undertone, but David said nothing and Eleanor could only shake her head.

Malcolm Granger spoke next. As he approached the pulpit, Eleanor took comfort in the reassuring presence of her own physician despite the scattered throat clearings and shuffling of feet that greeted him. Doctors from the Granger family had served the people of Waterford respectably since before the Civil War, but none had been as controversial as the youngest Dr. Granger, who was praised as a modern thinker by some and disparaged as a dangerous fraud by others. No one questioned his ability to set a broken bone or deliver a baby, but his ideas about disease aroused skepticism even among his own faithful patients. Eleanor trusted him, not because his ancestors had cared for Bergstroms since their arrival in America, but because under his care she had given birth to a healthy daughter. Furthermore, while Dr. Granger acknowledged that her heart did appear to have sustained damage, he also said that neither he nor any physician could truly know if it would cut her life short, so she would do well to discount any dire predictions and instead embrace each day as a gift. His advice brought tears to her eyes each time she recalled it, so it was little wonder she had become one of his most loyal defenders.

Dr. Granger addressed the treatment of the disease. The germ of influenza was thought to be a bacterium, perhaps Pfeiffer's bacillus, perhaps something else. Until a vaccine could be developed, the only treatment was rest, fresh air, cool baths and compresses to reduce fever, and fluids to replace those lost in the body's natural responses to the affliction. Make the patient comfortable and pray for the best, he told them, and remember that since the disease seemed nearly always fatal, the best remedy was prevention.

A rumble of protest and disbelief followed Dr. Granger to his seat, and Eleanor wished he had not spoken with his characteristic bluntness and brevity. He had spoken for less than half the time Dr. Cullen had, and he had left his listeners with little hope.

"And just how are we supposed to keep from getting sick?" a man shouted from somewhere in the crowd. "It's knocking strong young soldiers flat on their backs. What chance do we have?"

Amid the chorus of agreement, the Health Officer rose. "I believe I can address that."

He took the pulpit and regarded his listeners coolly. As his gaze swept over the crowd, over Eleanor, she had the sensation of tallies made and percentages calculated, a feeling reinforced when he began to speak. Professor Johnson had observed bubonic plague in San Francisco and other epidemics both at home and abroad, but if the reports were true, this Spanish flu was more virulent and more deadly than anything he had experienced. The only way to prevent Waterford from succumbing as Boston and Philadelphia and New York had was to make sure the germ of influenza never entered the town.

As of four o'clock that afternoon, he declared Waterford under quarantine. No one not currently within the city limits, whether stranger or lifelong resident caught away from home, would be allowed to enter until the danger of contagion had passed. All citizens must wear gauze masks or handkerchiefs over their noses and mouths. All indoor public gathering places, including schools, restaurants, taverns, and churches, were closed until further notice.

At this the grumbling rose to a roar. "We can't close down the churches when we need them most," called out a man to Lucinda's left.

Near the back of the room, a young man with a jauntily loosened tie stood and shouted, "What of the students? If there's a crisis, our families may need us. You can't expect us to stay in our dormitories instead of going home."

Professor Johnson waited for the shouts of affirmation to fade. "The quarantine functions in only one direction," he said. "You may leave any time you wish, but you may not return."

The mayor hurried to the podium, raising his hands for quiet. "These measures are only temporary."

"How temporary?" a woman shouted. "My son works for the railroad. Are you saying he can't come home?"

"That's precisely what I'm saying," the professor said. He looked to the rest of the Health Committee for support. A muscle in Dr. Cullen's jaw tightened. Dr. Granger nodded.

The mayor withdrew a handkerchief from his pocket and mopped his brow. "Listen. I don't like it any more than you folks, but we have to take drastic measures if we want to stay alive. We've all had news from friends to the east. Do you want your neighbors dropping dead on the streets? Do you want coffins stacked chest-high on our sidewalks? Do you want your loved ones flung into mass graves because there aren't any more coffins? Well, I don't, and since I'm the mayor of this town, what these gentlemen have decided stands."

He flung his handkerchief on the floor and stormed out.

The people were shocked into silence for a heartbeat before their voices rose in a cacophony of anger and alarm. Eleanor took a deep breath and felt Lucinda's hand close around hers as her father-in-law urged them to go. Rising, they steadied one another in the rush for the doors, barely keeping their feet. Outside, the crowd quickly dispersed, and among the men and women hurrying home, Eleanor spotted several who had already knotted handkerchiefs over their faces. Only their eyes were visible, wide and frightened above the white cloth.

❧

The following morning, more than thirty people reported to Dr. Cullen's clinic fearing they might have contracted the Spanish flu before the quarantine was enacted, but after examining them, the doctor declared that not one suffered from anything worse than a bad case of nerves and a head cold. The next day, half their number appeared and were sent home with the same diagnosis. On the third day, only a handful came, and on the fourth, none. Two mask slackers were fined fifty dollars apiece. The newsstand parted with its last out-of-town newspaper. A week passed, and it seemed that thanks to the foresight of the Health Committee, Waterford might be spared.

The next time Eleanor went into town, the streets seemed unusually quiet, the shops nearly empty, filling her with a sense of unease that the beautifully mild October day could not dispel. She completed her errands and, ignoring the inner voice that urged her to hurry home to baby Claudia, she found herself wandering through town. Before long she realized she

had been searching for news, only there were few passersby and little conversation to overhear, and that much muffled by masks. Some people wore
gauze masks like her own, given to her by Dr. Granger, others wore bright
scarves or fine white handkerchiefs. Eleanor's mask moved as she breathed
and made her feel as if she could not fill her lungs completely.

She wandered down by the riverfront. The wharf was almost deserted,
and the few boats tied up at the docks looked as if they had been there a
while. She walked to the end of the nearest dock and read the sign nailed to
a piling: WARNING! THE TOWN OF WATERFORD IS QUARANTINED. ENTRY FORBIDDEN
BY ORDER OF THE MAYOR.

She walked on, leaving the riverfront and the downtown behind until she
had reached the only road bearing east out of Waterford. The heaviness in
her breasts warned her she had been gone too long; Claudia needed her.
Yet she continued until she found the sign posted by the road, identical to
the one on the dock but for the additional line printed in smaller letters: FOR
PITTSBURGH AND PARTS WEST, TAKE DETOUR FROM GRANGERVILLE 5 MILES BACK.

A westbound automobile or carriage would have little choice but to turn
around and take the detour, for two overturned wagons blocked the road in a
spot bordered by deep ditches. A traveler on horseback could circumvent the
barrier if he were a skilled rider, and a man on foot would encounter no difficulty at all. The people of Waterford would have to pray that the word quarantine would be interpreted to their advantage, and that all who read the sign
would assume that the sickness was worse within the town than without.

Eleanor stared at the sign, catching her breath, her hand on her heart.
On other days she could have hoped for a ride back into town, but no one
passed now.

The signs were working.

❧

By mid-October, churches resumed Sunday services in defiance of the law.
Masks disappeared. Merchants and their customers wondered when the
quarantine would be lifted; how would they know when the danger had
passed if they did not? Someone should venture out to Grangerville and investigate. Everyone thought so, but no one wanted to be the envoy in case
he would not be allowed to return home.

Eleanor hungered for news, news of the sickness, of the war, of Fred. The
Bergstroms resumed their normal activities out of necessity, but they rarely

left the farm and had few callers. Sometimes their nearest neighbors would come to see if the Bergstroms had any news, bringing little of their own to report, and twice Gloria Schaeffer had shown up in tears to beg Elizabeth to allow the quilting guild to meet at Elm Creek Manor. The Health Committee had banned gathering in public places, not private homes; the Bergstroms had room enough to comfortably accommodate the whole guild and they were unlikely to attract attention here on the outskirts of town. Gloria argued that they needed to work on the charity quilt, but Eleanor suspected Gloria was simply desperate for something to distract her thoughts. She was frantic with worry for her husband, who had been delivering the town's mail to Grangerville when the quarantine signs went up.

The Bergstroms needed no such distractions, for the farm and Bergstrom Thoroughbreds kept them so busy they rarely had time to think of anything but the tasks before them. Sales had dropped off with the start of the war, but with his oldest sons gone, David needed the help of everyone else in the family just to take care of the horses. Eleanor spent most of her days rushing from the nursery to the stable and back, so that at night when she finally crawled into bed, she was too exhausted to lie awake worrying. She ached for Fred every moment she was awake, so sleep was a blessing.

She and Clara were weeding the garden while Elizabeth played with Claudia on a blanket nearby when she heard a horse coming up the road. She sat back on her heels and shaded her eyes with her hand.

"Who is it?" asked Elizabeth.

"I don't know," said Eleanor, and then suddenly she recognized him. "It's Frank. Merciful God, it's Frank! It's over!"

She scrambled to her feet and ran toward him, laughing and shouting his name. He pulled up and grinned down at her. "I knew I'd get a warm welcome here, but I didn't think it would be this warm."

"I can't tell you how good it is to see you," she gasped, trying to catch her breath. "When did you return?"

"Just this morning." He reached into his bag and pulled out a letter. "This is my first stop. I haven't even been to the post office yet."

"Thank you, Frank. God bless you for this." She took it from his hand with a laugh, her joy dimming only slightly when she read the New York postmark. Now that mail had resumed, she would surely hear from Freddy soon. "When did they lift the quarantine?"

"You mean those signs? They're still up. I guess we won't be seeing any strangers in town any time soon."

Eleanor went cold. "The quarantine is still in force?"

"Well, sure, as far as Gloria knows, anyhow. She hasn't left the farm much. Says there hasn't been any reason." He studied her, puzzled. "Those signs aren't for me, Eleanor. They're for strangers."

"They're for anyone who wasn't in Waterford at the time."

"But I live here," he protested. "And I was in Grangerville all that time and didn't have so much as a sniffle."

"Frank, please don't go into town."

He laughed as if she had told a joke, but when he realized she was in earnest, he spoke to her as if she were a child awakened by nightmares. They were safe in Waterford, he assured her, as safe as any place on earth.

✿

Frank Schaeffer was the first to fall ill. Gloria was the next, and then the other postal clerks, and then, it seemed, nearly everyone.

Soon every bed in Dr. Cullen's clinic was occupied by a feverish, coughing man or woman who only hours before had seemed whole and strong. Dr. Granger raced from house to house, caring for those too sick to come to the clinic. His father came out of retirement at eighty-five to assist him on his rounds, though neither man had any remedy to offer their patients. There was no cure for influenza.

Rumors spread, ignited by fear. A father of six had ridden for help when his oldest child could not be roused from unconsciousness; he returned home with a nurse to find all six children and his wife dead. An ailing husband and wife had tried to drive into town to the clinic; their horse arrived pulling the wagon bearing their corpses. Everywhere Professor Johnson went, the people of Waterford begged him to lift the quarantine so that doctors from the cities might aid them, bring them medicine. "Every doctor who can hold a thermometer is already in service to the sick elsewhere," he told them. "And there are no medicines for anyone to bring."

But there had to be something; the alternative was unthinkable. In the absence of medicine from the doctors, the people of Waterford developed their own: plasters made of mustard and turpentine. Quinine and aspirin. Vinegar scrubs. Tobacco smoke. Poultices of every description. None worked. Nothing prevented Spanish influenza from sweeping through Waterford like fire through straw.

When every chair and even the hallway floors of Dr. Cullen's clinic overflowed with the sick and the dying, Professor Johnson turned the primary school into a makeshift hospital. Lucinda and Eleanor were among the volunteers who set up cots and sewed muslin partitions from old sheets. Then, at Dr. Cullen's request, they joined the teachers working in the kitchen preparing meals to be delivered to the bedridden. They worked late into the night before returning home to Elm Creek Manor, almost too exhausted to eat the meal Maude had kept warm for them, and too drained to describe the horrors they had witnessed passing by the sickrooms throughout the day.

The following morning, Eleanor could hardly bear to leave Claudia in the care of Elizabeth and Maude as she and Lucinda returned to the school. They took the wagon, leaving the strongest horses for David and William, who at Elizabeth's urging spent the days helping their stricken neighbors. They rode from one farmhouse to the next, calling out from a safe distance to ask whether the people inside needed anything. Sometimes their neighbors needed food; often David and William heard a weak voice call out that the cows needed to be milked and the livestock fed. They returned home after dark as exhausted as Lucinda and Eleanor, reluctant to report which of their neighbors had died overnight.

On their fourth day in the kitchens, Dr. Granger strode in; later Eleanor learned that he had just returned from the Waterford College infirmary where he had found more than fifty students, the doctor, and the two nurses all dead from influenza.

His mouth set in a grim line, his eyes shadowed and glittering, he tore into the cupboards and pulled out a large stockpot. "Mrs. Bergstrom," he called, without looking in her direction. "To me, please."

Eleanor quickly washed her hands and dried them on her apron as she joined him. "How can I help?"

"Find me herbs that will smell and taste like medicine when mixed with this." His voice was low as he withdrew four tall bottles of liquor from his overcoat. He set the bottles on the counter and filled the pot with water. "I have some bottles in the clinic. They will need to be brought here and boiled."

Eleanor nodded and sent Lucinda for them. By the time Lucinda returned, Eleanor and Dr. Granger had cooked up a dark, vile-smelling brew that resembled the worst medicine Eleanor had ever seen. "But it is not medicine," she said as they poured the mixture into bottles. The other women were studiously ignoring them, but she kept her voice to a murmur nonetheless.

"If they believe it is medicine, it may help them." He raked his hair out of his face, and only then did she see that his eyes were feverish, his face flushed. "You are wasted in the kitchen, Eleanor. You and Lucinda will be more useful tending to the sick."

"But we are not nurses," said Eleanor faintly.

"You are the closest thing we have to them." He corked the last of the bottles and carefully filled his pockets with them. The rest he placed in the cupboard. "Ask for Dolores Tibbs in the clinic. She is in charge of the nurses now."

Eleanor nodded. She knew Dolores well; the librarian was the fourth founding member of the Waterford Quilting Guild. Dr. Granger rushed off without another word, and Eleanor watched him go, her hand on her heart.

"Eleanor," said Lucinda. "I don't think I can."

Something in her voice made Eleanor turn sharply. Lucinda was pale and shaking, her teeth chattering. She clutched the counter as if it alone kept her upright.

Eleanor pressed a palm to Lucinda's forehead; her skin radiated heat. "We must go after Dr. Granger."

Lucinda nodded in reply. Eleanor helped Lucinda to a chair, then raced through the school searching the sickrooms for Dr. Granger, Dr. Cullen, anyone who might help. A white-faced girl too young to be a nurse interrupted her duties long enough to say that they had no more beds left and that Eleanor would be better off taking Lucinda directly to Dr. Cullen's clinic rather than waiting for a doctor to return. Eleanor hurried back to the kitchen, pulled Lucinda to her feet, and helped her outside, past classrooms hung with blackboards and cheery pictures that now looked down on the dead and dying.

When they reached the clinic, they could not approach the front door for the crowds of afflicted men and women trying to enter. A man stood in the doorway at the top of the stairs shouting that they were too full to accept new patients, and that anyone who could make it that far should go to the Waterford College gymnasium, where Dolores Tibbs was arranging another hospital. "I can make it," Lucinda murmured. So Eleanor turned and half-carried her back down the hill toward the campus, trying not to think of what would become of those who could not walk so far or had no one to take them.

Inside the gymnasium, volunteers were arranging cots in rows, and where they had run out of cots, they had placed mattresses on the floor. Patients filled the makeshift beds as soon as they were available. At the back of the room, dozens of sufferers waited to be examined. Some sat slumped against the wall, others lay upon the floor alone, as if fearful relatives had abandoned them there and fled. One young mother cradled a baby and a young boy in her lap. She called desperately for a doctor, but her children were motionless in her arms, and the scurrying volunteers could not stop to comfort her.

Eleanor stared at the scene in shock before swallowing hard and scanning the room for Dolores. She spotted her among the crowd at the back, bending over a patient, calling out orders, gesturing and pointing. Eleanor knew Dolores would not hear her over the din, so she made her way to her friend's side, still bearing up Lucinda. "Dolores," she began. "Dr. Granger—"

Dolores glanced at her and turned to another patient. "You'll need to wait in line by the door."

"Dolores—" Eleanor stumbled as Lucinda slumped against her. "Dr. Granger sent me to help you."

Dolores looked over at Lucinda quickly. "Then get your friend into a bed and come back."

Eleanor nodded and half-carried Lucinda through the rows of mattresses, looking about for an open bed. Just then, two men passed her carrying a body draped in a sheet. Eleanor looked back the way they had come and found an empty mattress on the floor two rows down. Swallowing hard, she hurried to claim it and helped Lucinda onto it.

"I'll be back soon," Eleanor promised, and raced back to Dolores. Dolores did not seem to recognize her, so Eleanor repeated her offer to help.

Dolores studied her and nodded. "You're new, you're still fresh. You can help with triage. Most of these people would be better off at home, but they won't listen when you tell them that, so save your breath. Send those whom we can still help to a bed. Leave the rest here."

"Wait," said Eleanor as Dolores turned to go. "How will I know which is which?"

"Check their feet. If they're blue, the person won't make it."

Eleanor nodded, but Dolores had already spun away.

Eleanor hurried back to Lucinda. Quickly, before fear could stop her, she removed Lucinda's shoe and stocking, and forced herself to look. The sole of her foot was pink and healthy.

Swiftly she returned stocking and shoe. "Come on," she said, grunting from the effort as she pulled Lucinda to her feet. "You're going home."

"Don't be stupid," said Lucinda faintly. "I can't risk carrying this illness home to the family."

Eleanor knew that, but she also knew if Lucinda stayed in that makeshift hospital, she would die. "There are too many patients here and not enough nurses. Dolores herself said people like you would be better off at home." She draped Lucinda's arm over her shoulder and breathed a sigh of relief when Lucinda walked along beside her, supporting much of her own weight. "When we get home—"

"No. You're needed here. The horses know the way home, and Elizabeth can care for me."

As they left the gymnasium, Eleanor reluctantly agreed, and they made their way back to the wagon. Eleanor warned her always to wear her mask and to allow only Elizabeth to care for her, to limit the risk to the others. She watched Lucinda ride off, slumped with exhaustion but steady in her seat, and hoped it would be enough.

Then she raced back to help Dolores.

She did not know how long she worked before another volunteer helped her, stumbling, to a chair to catch a few minutes of sleep. One day blurred into another. She knew many of the sick at least by sight, while many others were unfamiliar and young, probably students of the college. She could not think about friends and neighbors left by the wall and strangers directed to beds; she could not give special consideration to anyone, except for children and mothers carrying babies. She did not care if they had to be carried to their cots, they were assigned them.

Once she passed Dr. Granger administering his concoction to a middle-aged man. She had to turn her face away when he swallowed the bitter liquid and gazed up at the doctor, his eyes shining with gratitude. Too busy to acknowledge her, the doctor swiftly moved on to the next patient, but something compelled Eleanor to follow. "Dr. Granger," she said. "Will the Health Officer lift the quarantine and send for help?"

"Professor Johnson was buried this morning. In the trench." Dr.

Granger's voice was hoarse, his gaze haggard. "There is no help to send for, Mrs. Bergstrom. We have only ourselves."

He hurried away. Eleanor stood there dumbly nodding, her ears ringing. The trench. She had heard whispered rumors about the mass grave, but she had not wanted to believe them true.

"Eleanor." She felt a hand on her arm. "Eleanor, dear."

Slowly she turned. Elizabeth stood beside her. "You must come home at once," she said. "We need you."

Eleanor felt a fist close around her throat. "Lucinda?"

"She lives yet, but others fell ill even before she returned to us." Elizabeth put her arm around her daughter-in-law and guided her to the door. "My husband. Maude. Clara. William."

"Claudia?"

"We must hurry," said Elizabeth, her anguish like a knife in Eleanor's heart.

❧

Eleanor felt as if she tended her family at a dead run. First to Claudia to try to get her to nurse, then to Lucinda to change her bed linens, soaked through with perspiration, then back to Claudia to coax her to sleep in her cradle, then to the kitchen to prepare a sustaining broth, and then back to Claudia. Always back to Claudia.

Maude was the first to die. Two days after Eleanor's return, her sister-in-law slipped away before the sun rose. Through the frenzy of nursing those who yet lived, Eleanor watched Elizabeth with a sort of detached amazement as she arranged for her daughter-in-law to be buried on the family estate. Maude was her son's widow, and Elizabeth would not see her interred in a mass grave with strangers.

David, Clara, William, and Claudia hung on. Once Clara came out of her delirium enough to beg Eleanor for the Ocean Waves quilt, and she was inconsolable until Eleanor found it, draped it over her, and assured her it was there. Eleanor sat beside her and stroked her sweaty hair until she drifted off to sleep.

That night, Claudia screamed in pain until she was too exhausted to do more than whimper. She lay so limp and silent in her cradle that Eleanor's last bit of control finally shattered. She broke down in sobs and gathered her child in her arms, but Claudia did not even blink at the tears that fell upon her hot skin. Eleanor carried her into her own bed and lay beside her;

Claudia took her nipple in her mouth but had no strength to suckle. "You will be all right," whispered Eleanor, kissing her, knowing that Claudia would probably not survive the night. She murmured soft words of comfort, all the while silently praying: Please, Lord. Please. You took all of my babies but Claudia. Please don't take her from me now. I will never again ask you for more children. I will never again ask you to spare my dear Freddy. Please Lord. Take whomever else you want, take me, but let my child live.

Eleanor fell asleep to the rhythm of her desperate prayer. She woke late the next morning to find Claudia breathing beside her, the Ocean Waves quilt spread over them.

She sat up, startled. Claudia let out a soft cry and rooted for her, so Eleanor lay back down and gave her the breast. Claudia never opened her eyes as she nursed, and fits of coughing forced her to spit out more milk than she swallowed, but she did not cry as she released the nipple and drifted off to sleep. Eleanor pressed a hand to Claudia's forehead; she felt cooler, if only slightly.

Carefully Eleanor gathered up the Ocean Waves quilt and stole from the room, whispering a prayer as she closed the door. She met Elizabeth in the hallway on her way to Clara's room. She looked haggard, but she must have seen something in Eleanor's face to give her hope, for she asked, "How is the baby?"

"She nursed, and I think her fever has broken," said Eleanor. She saw no point in saying how little Claudia had drank, or how weakly she had suckled. "You should not have let me sleep so late. How are the others?"

"I let you sleep because you needed your rest. David is sleeping. William asked for something to eat. Lucinda drank some broth, but I had to force her. Clara . . ." Elizabeth shook her head. "Clara is the same."

"I'll tend to them while you rest."

Elizabeth nodded, but stopped Eleanor before she went two paces. "Where are you going with that?"

"To Clara." Eleanor indicated the quilt in her arms. "She asked for it yesterday. Thank you for returning it, but I don't need it."

"I didn't bring it for you." Elizabeth took the quilt, and Eleanor was too surprised to stop her. "Claudia may still need it."

"Surely you don't believe the quilt will cure her."

"You yourself said her fever broke," Elizabeth countered. "What does it matter to you what I do? I've heard you say my superstitions are harmless. The quilt will not harm her, even if you don't believe it will help."

"I don't believe it, but what if Clara does? She asked for this quilt for a reason. What if you've taken her hope from her?"

"Clara herself insisted I give it to Claudia. She said the baby needs it more than she does."

Eleanor heard the note of hysteria in her mother-in-law's voice and could not bear to prolong the argument. "If Clara asks, we must give it back to her at once," she said. Elizabeth nodded distractedly as she hurried off to Claudia, the quilt in her arms.

Clara never asked for the quilt. Within hours she sank into an unceasing, feverish sleep in which she screamed and cried and babbled nonsense. Then, suddenly, she grew still. While Eleanor tried to rouse her, Elizabeth fled from the room and returned with the Ocean Waves quilt. Weeping, she flung the quilt over the bed and threw herself upon her daughter's silent body, moaning her name.

Finally Eleanor had to gently pull Elizabeth away.

William insisted that he be the one to dig his sister's grave. Though his legs wobbled beneath him when he rose from his sickbed, Elizabeth was too heartsick to object. She had not left Clara's side since fleeing to retrieve the quilt. "Too late," she whispered, rocking back and forth on her chair and staring straight ahead at nothing.

When the time came to bury her, Eleanor gently asked Elizabeth if she felt well enough to join them and say a prayer over the grave. Elizabeth did, but she said not a word until the end, when she fixed Eleanor with an icy stare. "My daughter gave her life for your daughter," she said. "Never forget that."

She took Claudia from Eleanor's arms and returned to the manor.

Slowly David, William, and Lucinda recovered, and as they did, the absence of their loved ones became a tangible pain. Elizabeth held Claudia almost constantly, and Eleanor, remembering how Elizabeth had already lost three of her children and might yet lose her eldest son, could not bear to take the baby from her.

No word came from Waterford. In the bleakest hours after Clara's burial, Eleanor sometimes wondered if all there had perished, if they alone had survived the plague.

"Someone needs to go into town," said David, still in his sickbed.

"I'll go," said his son. At fifteen, William seemed a shriveled old man with sunken cheeks and hollow eyes.

Elizabeth grew frantic and insisted that none of them must leave the manor, especially William, who was still too weak to sit a horse. They placated her, but they knew that eventually, someone must go.

The thought of news from town reminded Eleanor of a letter she had never opened. Frank Schaeffer's appearance had so unsettled her that she had forgotten all about the slender envelope that had brought him, and the contagion, to Elm Creek Manor. She found it where she had left it weeks ago, a relic from a different age. She hesitated before opening it, gripped by the sudden fear that she would unleash more disease upon her family like Pandora lifting the lid to her box of evils.

Within the envelope Eleanor found a single clipping from *The New York Times,* her father's obituary. He had died in September of influenza.

Days passed. When still no one came to Elm Creek Manor, Lucinda insisted that Eleanor, ironically now the strongest of the family, go into town. Even Elizabeth did not object.

Eleanor rode alone. She did not wear her mask; she did not know what miracle had protected her and Elizabeth when all around them had fallen ill, but she assumed it protected her still. She did not stop at any of the other outlying farms and passed no one on the road or working in the fields. She saw no one at all until she reached Tenth Street. The people she encountered waved excitedly, smiling and laughing. They wore no masks. She wondered at their rejoicing. Perhaps they were merely happy to be alive.

From far away she heard voices crying out in joy. When she rounded the corner of Main Street, she saw that the square between the library and town hall was filled with people. From everywhere came the sounds of celebration—music, raucous cheering, firecrackers, voices raised in song and laughter.

Someone called to her; she searched but could not find the speaker in the crowd.

"Eleanor!"

Then she saw the frantic waving; it was a woman from the quilt guild. Eleanor knew her name but could not call it to mind; all she could think of was the Starburst block the woman had made for the charity quilt.

"Eleanor!" the woman shouted again, crying tears of joy. "Did you hear? It's the armistice! The war is over!"

The war was over.

Freddy was coming home.

Chapter Nine

November was one of the busiest months of the year for Elm Creek Quilts, rivaled only by the first month of the new camp season. Although summer probably seemed a long time away for their campers, Sylvia and her colleagues were already deciding what classes and seminars to offer, assessing their staffing needs, printing up brochures and registration forms, and running new marketing campaigns. Sylvia wondered why they bothered to advertise since hundreds of registration forms had already arrived, but Sarah insisted the investment would pay off later. Sylvia shrugged and decided to have faith in Sarah's and Summer's judgment. She couldn't argue with their success, and besides, the activity kept her friends from talking about wedding gowns and bouquets day and night.

When she could spare time from Elm Creek Quilts, Sylvia continued the search for her mother's quilts from behind her father's oak desk in the library. The flood of letters and e-mails in response to Summer's post on the Missing Quilts Home Page had slowed to only one or two a week, but Sylvia followed each trail until she was sure it had reached a dead end. Unfortunately, virtually all the newest leads did so, for whenever Sylvia called or wrote to verify certain details, her questions brought forth new information that confirmed the quilt in question could not be her mother's.

Other leads that had once seemed promising had faded away. Even her friend Grace Daniels, the quilt historian from San Francisco, responded to Sylvia's e-mail with bad news.

TO: Summer.Sullivan@elmcreek.net
FROM: Grace Daniels <danielsg@deyoung.org>
DATE: 10:10 AM PT 6 Nov 2002

SUBJECT: Your Quilt Investigation

(Summer, please print out this note for Sylvia.)

Sylvia, I'm sorry it took me so long to get back to you, but I'm afraid I have bad news. I checked the San Jose Quilt Museum as you requested, but they do not have any New York Beauty quilts on display or in storage. I also called my contacts at the New England Quilt Museum and the Museum of the American Quilter's Society with the same result. We'll keep spreading the word and eventually some better information will surface.

I wonder if you might want to modify your inquiries to include the alternate names for the pattern. As you probably know, the New York Beauty did not acquire that name until the 1930s, when its pattern was included in the packages of a certain brand of batting. Until then, it was known as Rocky Mountain, Rocky Mountain Road, or Crown of Thorns.

I'll talk to you soon, and remember, don't give up!

Grace

PS: You really ought to get your own e-mail address.

Sylvia had never heard of the alternate names for the New York Beauty pattern, but when she searched her memory, she was forced to admit she could not think of a single occasion when her mother had referred to her version as anything but her wedding quilt. Sylvia's earliest memory of the name was a time several years after her mother's death, when Great-Aunt Lucinda showed Sylvia's father a similar quilt in a magazine and remarked how appropriate it had been for Sylvia's mother to choose that pattern for her bridal quilt, as she had been a New York beauty herself. Tears had come to her father's eyes, and he had agreed.

Sylvia doubted that adding the alternative names to the description of her mother's missing quilt would help where an illustration had failed, but with so little else to go on, she decided it wouldn't hurt to try.

The only clues that still gave Sylvia any hope were the check Gloria Schaeffer had used to buy the Ocean Waves quilt, the name of the auction house that had purchased the Elms and Lilacs quilt from Mary Beth Callahan's mother, and—despite Grace's disappointing reports—the few responses that placed the New York Beauty quilt in a museum. Although none of these responses named the same museum, Sylvia still believed she could not afford to dismiss them. She theorized that the quilt was or had been part of a traveling exhibit, which was why those who spotted it did not agree on the location, and why none of those museums now had the New York Beauty in its possession.

The one quilt Sylvia had abandoned her search for was the whole cloth quilt. Without her mother's embroidered initials and date, and with so many virtually identical quilts in existence, Sylvia reluctantly had to admit that identifying her mother's version would be impossible. Why, then, did the name of the quilt's designer sound so familiar? At first she assumed that she must have seen other examples of Abigail Drury's work, but Summer searched the Waterford College Library's databases and Sylvia pored over her many quilt books and magazines without finding a single mention of her name besides the October 1912 issue of *Ladies' Home Journal.* It seemed unlikely that a quilt designer of her considerable talent would have published but a single pattern in her entire career.

The frustration of this unsolved mystery urged Sylvia on to likelier prospects. The auction house in Sewickley kept excellent records, including who had purchased the Elms and Lilacs quilt and when, but it also had a strict confidentiality policy and would not release the name of the current owners without their permission. After a few anxious days, the auction house called back to inform her that the owner's niece, who had inherited the quilt upon her aunt's death, had agreed to take Sylvia's call. The niece traveled often, so Sylvia left several messages on her answering machine before finally reaching her, only to learn that the niece had sold the Elms and Lilacs quilt two years before.

"I hated to give it up," the young woman said. "Unfortunately, in her will, my aunt left the quilt to me and my husband. Ex-husband. She never thought we would split up or she would have left it to me alone. Our divorce negotiations dragged on for months longer than necessary just because he would not give up that quilt."

"He must have been very fond of it."

"Not at all. He preferred the duvet. He just wanted to hurt me."

"I suppose you're better off without him, then."

"You have no idea. Eventually I just couldn't deal with the struggle anymore, so I offered to sell the quilt and divide the money. He considered that a victory since I would lose my quilt. We agreed to have an independent appraiser from some organization, the Association of Quilters of America or something—"

"The National Quilters Association?"

"Yes, that sounds right. Would you believe she said the quilt was worth three thousand dollars? I'll never forget my ex's face when he heard that. He practically danced around the room with dollar signs in his eyes and cash registers ringing in the background." The young woman sniffed. "But he wasn't laughing long.

"I offered to find a buyer for the quilt, and since in addition to being a jerk my ex is also lazy, he agreed. I took it to the quilt shop in downtown Sewickley, but they were having financial problems and weren't buying quilts. From there I went to two different antique stores. One offered me a thousand and the other, two."

"But you knew it was worth much more."

"That wasn't the point. So I took it to Horsefeathers."

"Where?"

"The Horsefeathers Boutique. It's a funky arts and crafts store in downtown Sewickley. The owner is a local artist and you would not believe the stuff she makes. I showed her the quilt, she oohed and ahhed and agreed it was beautiful—and offered me thirty dollars for it."

"That's all? Did you tell her about the appraisal?"

"No, I told her it was a deal. I handed over the quilt, she gave me the cash and a receipt. Then I drove right over to the apartment my ex was sharing with his new girlfriend and gave him his fifteen bucks."

Sylvia closed her eyes and sighed. "I suppose I can understand why you did that, but it sounds like a bitter triumph to me."

"So it wasn't my proudest moment. At least I showed him he couldn't walk all over me and get away with it. He knew I loved that quilt, and that's why he took it from me."

"If you cared for it so much, why didn't you buy it back after the terms of the divorce negotiations were satisfied?"

"I couldn't. That quilt became a symbol of everything wrong in our marriage." Suddenly her tone shifted. "This doesn't mean you'll never find your mother's quilt. It might still be at Horsefeathers, and if not, they'll know who has it."

Unless it had changed hands once again. "I'll try to contact them right away. Thank you very much for the information."

"No problem. Oh, one more thing."

"Yes?"

"When you make out your will, don't leave something to a couple when you really just mean for one of them to have it. And if you know anyone who's getting married, your grandchildren or whatever, make sure they have a great prenup."

"Thanks," said Sylvia. "I'll be sure to keep that in mind."

Sylvia had lived in Sewickley for many years, but she had never heard of the Horsefeathers Boutique, and she would have sworn there was a toy store at the street corner the young woman had described. Still, she knew better than to rely upon her memory alone, and sure enough, when Summer searched on-line, she found a phone number and address for the store. When Sylvia called, the owner was not available but the sales clerk said the Elms and Lilacs quilt sounded familiar. Sylvia decided to take this as a good if ambiguous sign. She left her name and number and asked for the owner to call her at her convenience.

Following the trail of Gloria Schaeffer's check proved easier. Gloria's old phone number was no longer in service, as Sylvia had expected, and the house and land had been razed decades ago to make way for a shopping mall. Fortunately, one of her two sons still lived in Waterford and was listed in the phone book. When Sylvia called, she reached Philip Schaeffer's wife, Edna, a friendly woman close to her own age. She seemed fascinated by Sylvia's tale of the search for her mother's quilts and explained that the two sons had divided up the quilts they had inherited from Gloria. "My husband and I don't own any quilts that sound like your Ocean Waves quilt, so it must have gone to his brother, Howard," said Edna. "He lives in Iowa now, but he and his family are coming here for Thanksgiving. I'll ask him to bring the quilt if he still owns it, but I'm afraid I can't promise he'll sell it to you."

"I understand," Sylvia assured her, and they made plans for Sylvia to stop by on the Friday after Thanksgiving. She could not expect everyone to part with their quilts as readily as Mona Niehaus had. The Schaeffers had owned the Ocean Waves quilt for more than fifty years, longer than the Bergstroms themselves. They likely considered it one of their own family heirlooms by now. After the disappointment of the whole cloth quilt, Sylvia would be satisfied just to see the quilt again and to know it was treasured.

As Thanksgiving approached, Sylvia waited for Andrew and his children to decide how they would spend the holiday. Sometimes Sylvia and Andrew joined his children and their families at Amy's home in Connecticut, but on alternate years, Sylvia invited everyone to Elm Creek Manor. She enjoyed those celebrations the most because Sarah's mother and Matt's father also joined them for the weekend, and the other Elm Creek Quilters always found time to stop by for some coffee and pie. This year was supposed to be Sylvia's turn to play hostess, which Sylvia considered especially fortuitous because she knew she would have few opportunities to make peace with Andrew's children before the wedding. Welcoming them into her home would, she hoped, show them how much she cared about them and their father.

But as the days grew colder and shorter, and the first light snow fell, Andrew said little about the upcoming holiday. When Sylvia pressed him, he would say that they had not had a chance to discuss it, or that his children had not made up their minds. Finally Sylvia insisted that he call them and make a decision, because in a few days she would either need to buy a turkey or pack her suitcase and she would appreciate a little advance notice. Andrew apologized and went off to the parlor to phone them, but returned shaking his head.

"They're not coming?" asked Sylvia.

"Not this year. It's too far to drive round trip in four days and they don't want to fly. Since they know it wouldn't be fair to ask me to choose between them, they thought it best if we all spend Thanksgiving at our own homes."

Sylvia heard Amy's voice echoed in Andrew's words. "I can't believe Bob is afraid to fly," she said. "If your children want to get together with you at Amy's, I'll stay home. I don't want to rob you of a holiday with your family."

"Absolutely not." He put his hands on her shoulders. "Like I told Amy when she was here last month, you're my family."

He kissed her, and Sylvia knew he meant what he said, but she felt sick at heart thinking about the widening divide between Andrew and his children. She thought of his grandchildren and wondered how the holiday plans would be explained to them. She wondered what excuses they would invent for Andrew's absence, year after year, if the disagreement grew into estrangement.

A shadow darkened their Thanksgiving feast that year, and not even the presence of Sarah's mother and Matt's father could lift it entirely. Sylvia knew that Andrew missed his family; he glanced at the clock throughout the day, as if imagining what his children and grandchildren were doing at that moment. He left shortly after dessert to call them, but he returned a mere fifteen minutes later to say that they were well and that they gave Sylvia and her friends their best regards.

Privately, Sarah tried to reassure Sylvia that the disagreement would not last long. The chill must be thawing already, or Andrew wouldn't have phoned Amy and Bob at all. "By Christmas everyone will be on good terms again," she said, giving Sylvia a comforting hug. "You'll see. We'll invite everyone here and have a wonderful time. We'll wine and dine the adults and slip the kids candy when their parents aren't looking. Before long they'll start to see the advantages of having you as a stepmother."

Sylvia had to laugh. "You're absolutely right. Why didn't I resort to bribery long ago?"

She was joking, of course, but although she wouldn't admit it to a soul, she might have tried to win them over with gifts if not for her pride—and her certainty that it wouldn't work. Nothing Sylvia could do or say or give could change the facts that she was seven years older than Andrew and had once had a stroke. It would be easier to persuade his children to give the marriage their blessing if they merely disliked her.

The next morning, Sarah drove Sylvia to Edna and Philip Schaeffer's house, a red-brick ranch with two large oak trees in the front yard and four cars parked in the driveway. Three young children ran through scattered leaves on the lawn, shouting and laughing, while an older boy, rake in hand, called out orders they ignored. The four watched with interest as Sylvia and Sarah got out of the Elm Creek Quilts minivan and approached the front door. "Hewwo," called the youngest, a boy not quite two.

"Hello, honey," Sarah replied, waving. The little boy grinned and hid behind the eldest girl.

"You could have one yourself, you know," said Sylvia as she rang the doorbell.

"Please. You sound just like my mother." Sarah rolled her eyes, but she smiled as she spoke, with no hint of the resentment that used to surface whenever her mother was mentioned. Their relationship had been strained for years, but they had reconciled while both women helped Sylvia recover from her stroke. She should take comfort in their example, Sylvia told herself. If Sarah and Carol could find a way to accept their differences, surely Andrew and his children could. She just hoped they wouldn't require an unexpected calamity to push them forward.

A woman who looked to be in her mid-eighties answered the door. "You must be Sylvia Compson," she said, opening the door and beckoning them inside. "I'm Edna Schaeffer, as you probably guessed."

Sylvia thanked her for allowing them to interrupt her holiday and introduced Sarah. "Did your brother-in-law have a safe trip?" she asked, surreptitiously scanning the room for the quilt.

Edna's face assumed an apologetic expression that had become all too familiar to Sylvia since she had begun the search. "He did, thank you, but I'm afraid he didn't bring your mother's quilt with him."

"I see," said Sylvia.

"I'm sorry, dear." Edna patted Sylvia's arm sympathetically. "It's a long story and he wanted to tell you himself, or I would have called and saved you the trip over. Howard's been looking forward to seeing you."

"Has he?"

"Oh, my, yes. Phil has, too, but don't worry. I'm not the jealous type." Edna smiled and led them into the living room, where two older gentlemen and several younger men and women sat talking and watching a football game on television. The two older men stood as the women approached. "This can't be little tagalong Sylvia," boomed the taller of the two. "What happened to all those dark tousled curls?"

"I'm afraid they're long gone." Smiling, Sylvia shook the men's hands. "And I beg your pardon, but I was never a tagalong."

"That's not what Claudia told us," said the other man, his voice a quiet echo of his brother's. He had to be Philip, the younger of the two Schaeffer boys. He had always been more bashful than Howard.

"My goodness, that's right. I had forgotten you two were in the same class." Sylvia pursed her lips and feigned annoyance. "I suppose I shouldn't be surprised that she told tales on me."

"I was sweet on her," said Phil, with an embarrassed shrug and a glance at his wife, who patted his arm and laughed. "I hung on every word she said, but she only had eyes for Howard."

"Until Harold Midden came to town," said Howard, shaking his head. "Claudia used to kiss me behind the library after school, but once she met Harold, she tossed me out like yesterday's trash."

"She didn't," said Sylvia, shocked. "She told us she went to the library to study."

Howard shrugged. "We sometimes fit in a little studying afterward. Anyway, I always knew it wouldn't have worked out between us in the long run."

"Why not?"

Edna gestured to two chairs near Sylvia and Sarah. "Why don't we all sit down and hear the whole story?"

"Our mother wouldn't be pleased if she knew we were telling you this," said Phil ruefully as they seated themselves.

Sylvia, who had learned that some of the most important stories began with the revelation of a secret, sat back and smiled to encourage him to continue.

"I guess you know our mother disliked yours," said Howard.

"Why, no, I never knew that," said Sylvia, looking from one brother to the other in surprise. "I knew she didn't care for me and my sister, but neither did the entire Waterford Quilting Guild or they wouldn't have let her kick us out."

"Didn't your mothers found the guild together?" asked Sarah. "They must have been friends at one point."

"You never knew our mothers were enemies and we never knew they were friends," said Phil. "We grew up hearing how awful the Bergstroms were, how selfish, how they had cost our father his life."

"What?" exclaimed Sylvia.

"Now you can see why I knew my relationship with Claudia would never go anywhere," said Howard. "Mother would have fainted if I had brought her home."

"That probably added to Claudia's appeal," teased Edna.

"Let's get back to your father," said Sylvia. "Why on earth did your mother blame mine for his death?"

Howard and Phil exchanged a look before Howard said, "Well, first let me say that even as boys we knew our mother and her friends were jealous of your mother. We knew why, too. Your mother was the prettiest woman in Waterford, and she was so gentle and kind that of course every man and boy in town had a crush on her. She wasn't from around here, either, and that made her seem mysterious and exotic."

"Exotic?" said Sylvia. "My mother? She was from New York, not the other side of the world."

"To people who had never left the Elm Creek Valley," said Phil, "New York might as well have been the other side of the world."

"We were like all the rest," added Howard. "We admired your mother, but we felt guilty about it because we knew we were betraying our mother."

"She always thought our father liked your mother a little too much," said Phil. "Not that she ever thought he cheated on her—"

"Not with my mother he didn't," declared Sylvia. "My mother was devoted to my father. She would never have considered such a thing."

"Our father felt the same way about our mother," said Howard. "At least that's what our other relatives told us. I was just a boy when he died, and Phil here was just a baby."

"How did your father die?" asked Sarah.

"In the influenza epidemic of 1918," said Howard.

"So did several members of my own family," said Sylvia.

Phil grimaced and nodded. "We were well aware of that. Mother never let us forget it. You see, as soon as the people of Waterford realized that the disease was coming closer, they quarantined the town."

Sylvia nodded. Her great-aunt Lucinda had told her stories of those terrible weeks when nearly the entire family had been stricken, and Great-Aunt Maude and young Aunt Clara had died. Claudia, too, had nearly lost her life, although no one but Aunt Lucinda ever spoke of it.

"The town stayed free of the disease for a while," said Phil. "But it didn't last, and our father was the first to catch it."

"And the first to die," said Howard. "He was the town mail carrier. He delivered a letter to your mother, and according to our mother, he caught the flu there."

"Our mother fell ill next, and then it was everywhere," said Phil. "Our mother recovered, but she was never the same. She told everyone that my father had caught the disease from the Bergstroms, and that your family had broken the quarantine in order to buy and sell your horses. If not for the greed of the Bergstroms, she said, Waterford would have been spared. The hundreds who died here would never have suffered so much as a runny nose."

Sylvia clutched the arms of her chair. "I don't believe it," she managed to say. "My family never would have risked other people's lives for money."

"Of course not." Sarah reached out and touched her arm, frowning at the Schaeffers. "With all due respect, your mother wasn't a doctor, and no one knew about viruses back then. She couldn't have known for certain where your father contracted the disease, and unless she personally witnessed the Bergstroms crossing the quarantine line, she had no right to accuse them."

Edna held up her hands to calm them. "Please, boys, tell them the rest."

"I'm sorry I upset you," said Howard. "We just wanted you to hear the story we grew up with."

"We know your family didn't bring the flu to Waterford," said Phil. "Our father did."

"He was delivering the town's mail to the postal center in Grangerville when the quarantine signs went up," said Howard. "He stayed in Grangerville, but when people began dying right and left, he got scared and beat it out of town. He holed up in a hunting shack for a while, but when he ran out of food, he came home."

"Mother was so glad to see him that she cried," said Phil, "but she knew he had endangered the town. She came and went as usual rather than arouse suspicions, but she made him stay indoors with the curtains drawn for four days until they were both certain he wasn't sick."

"After that, they figured he was safe, so he acted as if he had never left Waterford," said Howard. "A few close friends knew he had been away, but my parents invented some story about him being laid up with a sprained ankle at an outlying farm, and that in all the confusion, Gloria never received word. Only one other person knew he had knowingly crossed the quarantine line."

"Sylvia's mother," said Sarah.

"Exactly."

"Our mother was horrified that she and our father had infected the town," said Phil. "Frankly, I think it would have come anyway. The Spanish flu was so contagious and the quarantine so easily breached that it was only a matter of time. The fact is, however, that our parents introduced it into Waterford, and my mother couldn't handle the shame. She was terrified that people would find out and condemn her."

"So instead she condemned my family," said Sylvia.

The two men nodded.

"She regretted that all her life," said Howard. "But once she started the lie, it got out of her control. She told herself that people would forget, but although they didn't talk much about the flu itself, everyone remembered to mistrust the Bergstroms long after they forgot the reason why."

"We knew nothing of this until the week before she died," said Edna. "The guilt of what she had done ate away at her for the better part of fifty years. She had bought your mother's quilt as a way to help your sister financially, and at the end of her life, her greatest concern was that we return the quilt to you."

"She wasn't content to return it to Claudia because she was afraid your sister would just sell it again," said Howard.

"If the secret bothered your mother for roughly fifty years, she must have passed away in the 1960s," said Sarah. "Why didn't you return the quilt to Sylvia as your mother requested?"

Sylvia thought she knew the answer, and Phil confirmed it. "No one knew where Sylvia was. Claudia didn't know, and the rest of the Bergstrom family had either moved away or passed on. We always assumed she would return to Elm Creek Manor some day, and we planned to return the quilt to her then."

"As the years went by, we all sort of forgot about it," said Edna apologetically.

"Then I moved away to Iowa." Howard frowned and shook his head. "I should have left the quilt here, but it was packed away with other things my mother had left me, and I never gave it a second thought. I found it when I was clearing out the basement after my wife passed away. I knew it ought to be in Waterford in case you came home, but I didn't want to ship it, so I decided to bring it the next time I came to visit."

And yet here he was, without the quilt. "What happened to it?" asked Sylvia.

Edna said, "I'm sure you heard about all that terrible flooding in the Midwest a few years back."

Sylvia could guess the rest, but she nodded.

"I lost nearly everything when the Mississippi crested," said Howard. "I'm sorry, Sylvia, but your mother's quilt couldn't be salvaged."

❧

"It was so waterlogged and encrusted with mud that they didn't recognize it as a quilt," Sylvia told Andrew when she and Sarah returned home. "They discarded it with the rest of the soiled clothes and bedding."

"There probably wasn't anything you could have done to restore it even if they hadn't thrown it away," said Andrew.

"Probably not," she admitted, but she still wished they had saved it. Soiled or not, it was still the work of her mother's hands, rare and precious, if only to her.

On the Monday after Thanksgiving, Sylvia and Andrew drove west in the Elm Creek Quilts minivan, which they favored over the motor home when the twists and turns of the Pennsylvania roadways were dusted with snow. Sylvia preferred not to travel in foul weather at all, but she was impatient to pursue this lead, and the owner of the Horsefeathers Boutique had not returned her calls. Sylvia wanted to believe that the owner either never received the messages or had been too swamped by the Christmas sales rush to call her back, but it was equally likely the owner had not called because she no longer had the quilt. Sylvia would have waited another week before going to see the shop in person, but the drive to Sewickley was reasonable and her need for answers urgent.

Sylvia's anticipation grew as they approached Sewickley. She had lived there for nearly forty years, from the time she first accepted a teaching position in the Allegheny School District until the lawyer called with news of her sister's death. When Sylvia went to Waterford to settle her sister's affairs, she had planned to sell Elm Creek Manor, return to Sewickley, and live out her days there. She never imagined she would return to Sewickley only to sell her house.

She happily pointed out her former home as they passed by it on Camp Meeting Road. "Goodness, they painted it robin's egg blue," she said, twisting in her seat and staring out the window. "When I lived there, the house was a deep brick red, with black shutters. It used to disappear into the trees."

"No danger of that now," said Andrew, carefully maneuvering the minivan down a steep, curving hill. Sylvia directed him to turn left on Beaver Street and into the downtown area, where several blocks of Victorian homes, shops, and restaurants were already decorated for Christmas, with colored lights in the storefronts and holly twined about the lampposts.

The familiarity of the sight warmed her, which was why the changes to her former hometown struck with unexpected surprise. Her favorite café had become a men's clothing store, she saw as they passed, and the old Thrift Drug store was now a Starbucks. "The quilt shop is gone," she exclaimed with dismay, staring in disbelief as they passed a shoe store.

"They probably went under after you moved away," said Andrew. "What you spend on fabric could keep three or four quilt shops in the black."

"Just for that, I'm not treating you to lunch," Sylvia teased. "And I know all the best places around here."

They parked the minivan in a public lot and put on their coats and gloves, for although Horsefeathers was just around the corner, the wind blew cold and the air smelled of snow.

"I'm surprised they're allowed to use that color," Sylvia remarked as they approached the fuchsia storefront.

"I'm surprised anyone would want to."

"No, I mean I believe they have a board that regulates those sorts of things. At least they did when I lived here. The downtown district tries to maintain a certain aesthetic. You should have seen the uproar when McDonald's tried to move in."

By then they were close enough to read the bright gold letters painted on the storefront window. "HORSEFEATHERS BOUTIQUE. ART FROM FOUND OBJECTS," read Andrew. "That disqualifies your mother's quilt, since it's a lost object."

"One person's lost is another person's found," said Sylvia absently. Her hand was on the doorknob, but the assortment of oddities displayed in the window had captured her attention. A chandelier made of antique doorknobs. A men's trench coat pieced from velvet Elvises. Several picture frames embellished with everything from coins to insects trapped in amber. The whimsical collection had been arranged to set off each piece to its best advantage, obviously by someone quite fond of her creations.

"Whoever the owner is," said Sylvia, pulling open the door, "she must have a sense of humor."

Inside, the shop was almost too warm, but the heat was a welcome respite from the cold wind. Sylvia removed her hat and tucked it into her pocket, looking around in amazement. The aisles were stuffed with items that defied description—a sculpture made from stacks of old newspapers, a refrigerator transformed into a grandfather clock, a dress sewn from small, white rectangles of fabric that appeared to have printing on them. Sylvia leaned closer for a better look, and laughed. "'Under penalty of law this tag is not to be removed except by the consumer.'"

"That doesn't look very comfortable."

"I don't think that's the point, do you? I'm sure the artist was making a statement." She paused. "What sort of statement, I honestly couldn't say."

Andrew found the price tag. "An expensive one. This will set you back six hundred bucks."

"And here I was going to put it on my Christmas list." Sylvia looked around the shop. She didn't see any quilts amid the clutter, but a stout woman in a purple caftan had emerged from a backroom and was making her way toward them. Her dark brown hair hung nearly to her waist and, unless Sylvia's eyes were deceiving her, her earrings were made from pasta embellished with silver paint and glitter.

"Can I help you find something?" the woman asked.

"I hope so," said Sylvia. "Are you Charlene Murray? My name is Sylvia Compson. I left a message—several messages, actually—about an antique quilt that I believe may be in your possession."

"A quilt?" The woman's brow furrowed, and then she brightened. "Wait. Are you the woman from Waterford?"

"Yes, that's right."

"I'm so glad you stopped by," exclaimed Charlene. "I meant to call you back, but I lost the sticky note with your phone number."

"Maybe you sewed it into a pair of pants," offered Andrew.

Sylvia nudged him. "Your associate said that the quilt sounded familiar. Did she tell you about it? It was made in the medallion style, with appliquéd elm leaves, lilacs, and intertwining vines. The hand quilting is quite superior, fourteen stitches to the inch, except in a few places where my sister and I helped." She tried not to, but she couldn't help adding, "My stitches were nine to the inch back then. Any larger than that were my sister's."

"I know exactly the piece you mean." Charlene beckoned for Sylvia to follow her deeper into the shop. "It wasn't in the best condition when I took it on, but it was fabulous material, and it cleaned up nicely in the washing machine."

Sylvia winced. "I hope you used the gentle cycle. It *is* an antique."

"No, I just threw it in with the rest of my laundry," said Charlene airily. "I had to treat it as I know my customers would to see if it would hold up. No one hand washes anymore, no matter how many times I tell them this is wearable art and not something they picked up at the Gap."

"But you do have the quilt, right?" asked Andrew.

Charlene beamed. "I do, and wait until you see what I've done with it." She stopped at a clothing rack, pushed aside a few hangers, and gestured proudly to a quilted jacket. "You're in luck. This is the last one."

Sylvia took in appliquéd flowers and leaves, exquisite quilting— "Good heavens."

"Thank you. It's absolutely one of my favorites. I already sold one size small, two larges, and an extra-large." She removed the jacket from the hanger and held it up to Sylvia. "I was tempted to keep this one for myself, but it's a medium, and as you can see, I'm not. It should fit you, though."

Sylvia closed her arms around what remained of her mother's quilt and tried to think of something to say. All she could manage was, "Why?"

Charlene's laughed tinkled. "I get that question all the time. I take my inspiration from many sources, but I admit this one is a little more pragmatic. I had a friend who fought with her sisters over a quilt their late mother had made. Since they all wanted it and no one was willing to let the others have it, they took a pair of scissors and cut it into four pieces. My friend doesn't sew, so she asked me to repair the edges of hers so the filling wouldn't fall out. But since her little quarter of a quilt wasn't big enough for a bed anymore, I made her a vest instead."

Sylvia wanted to bury her face in the jacket and weep. "She let you do that?"

"Are you kidding? She was thrilled. Two of her sisters had me do the same thing to their pieces." Charlene peered at her inquisitively. "Do you want to try it on?"

Sylvia shook her head, but Charlene pretended not to notice and within moments had Sylvia out of her winter coat and into the jacket. She led Sylvia to a full-length mirror, where she gushed about how much the jacket suited her. Sylvia ran her hands over the jacket. It fit her well, and her mother's handiwork had retained much of its beauty despite its transformation. But the jacket was less than what the quilt had been, and Sylvia could not speak for the ache in her heart.

Charlene's chatter had ceased, and she regarded Sylvia with perplexed worry that deepened as the awkward silence dragged on. Finally, Sylvia took a deep breath. "Did you save the rest of it?"

"You mean the scraps from my sewing?" Charlene shrugged. "I saved all of the filling and some of the fabric, but it's long gone now, used up in other projects."

"And the other jackets—do you know where they might be?"

Charlene chuckled, flattered but bemused. "Why, are you planning to outfit a basketball team?"

"Please, do you know how I might find them?"

She shook her head. "My records aren't that detailed. I could ask my assistants if they remember, but we get mostly tourist traffic in here. The jackets most likely weren't purchased by anyone from Sewickley."

Sylvia's hopes of reassembling the quilt faded.

"What do you want for it?" asked Andrew.

Sylvia fumbled for the price tag dangling from her sleeve. "Four hundred." She shrugged off the jacket and handed it to Charlene. "Quite a return on your investment."

"It might seem expensive, but it *is* a one-of-a-kind work of art."

Andrew regarded her, stern. "By my count you made four others."

"Not in size medium, and the appliqués are arranged differently on each jacket," countered Charlene, but she looked sheepish. "Okay, I'll tell you what. Since you came such a long way, I'll give you ten percent off."

"I'll take it," said Andrew.

"No, Andrew," said Sylvia, thinking of his pension. "Let me get it."

But he insisted, and within minutes she was on her way back to the minivan, one arm tucked in Andrew's, the other clutching the handles of a shopping bag with the quilted jacket inside. A light snow had begun to fall. Andrew steadied her so she would not slip on the pavement, and she burrowed her chin into her coat when a sudden gust of wind drove icy crystals into her face.

Once they were in the car, Andrew asked, "Do you want to head home or find a place to stay overnight?"

Sylvia had lost all interest in Christmas shopping. "Would you mind if we went home, or is that too much driving for one day?"

He assured her he was up to the trip if she was, and as he pulled out of the parking lot, she spread the jacket on her lap and sighed, running her hand over lavender lilac petals and faded green elm leaves, tracing a quilted feathered wreath with a fingertip. Considering the fate of the whole cloth quilt and the Ocean Waves, she was fortunate to find any part of the Elms and Lilacs. "I suppose a mutilated remnant of my mother's quilt is better than nothing at all."

"Hey," protested Andrew. "Is that any way to talk about a man's Christmas present?"

"I'm sorry, dear." Sylvia hugged the quilt to her chest and managed a smile. "I am glad to have it, and it was good of you to get it for me."

"That's more like it." He glanced at her for a moment before returning his gaze to the road. "What's that writing on the inside?"

"This? It's just the size tag."

"Not that. On the left front, where the chest pocket would be."

Sylvia opened the jacket and gasped at the sight of a faded bit of embroidery. "It's my mother's initials, and two numbers, a nine and a two. That must be part of the date. I know my mother completed this quilt in 1927." She hugged the quilt, then leaned over and kissed Andrew. "Charlene was right; I am lucky. I would have purchased any one she had in the shop, but only this one had the embroidery."

"That's lucky."

"It is, indeed. And you know what else? I think it's a very good sign. I believe I will find the New York Beauty quilt before long."

She settled back into her seat, content for the first time in days.

"Maybe it's a sign for something else, too," said Andrew.

"Oh?" She raised her eyebrows at him. "Such as?"

"Maybe we should get married here."

"Instead of Waterford?" She frowned. "Then all our friends would have to travel—"

"No, they won't. I mean here and now."

Sylvia stared at him. "Now? As in right now?"

"As soon as we can find a minister or a judge or a justice of the peace. Come on, Sylvia, what do you say? We already have our marriage license. This way we could avoid all the conflict with the kids. They'll have to stop complaining and start getting used to the idea if we just go ahead and do it."

"That would put an end to my friends' plans for an extravagant wedding," mused Sylvia.

"We can still have a party. That way our friends can't say we cheated them out of their celebration."

Sylvia laughed. "I don't know if that will be good enough, but I suppose they'll forgive us eventually. She paused, considering. "Very well. Let's do it."

Andrew turned the minivan around.

They drove to the county clerk's office, where they learned a justice of the peace could marry them, but not until the following day. They made an appointment for ten o'clock the next morning and set about finding a place to stay for the night. Sylvia remembered a charming bed-and-breakfast on

Main Street, and since it happened to have a rare vacancy, Sylvia and Andrew checked in and concluded this was another happy omen.

They unpacked their overnight bags and, disregarding the chill in the air, ventured back toward the shops. Sylvia didn't want a fancy wedding gown, but she certainly wouldn't marry in the casual travel clothes she had brought for the ride home, and she could only laugh at Andrew's suggestion that she wear the Elms and Lilacs jacket. To her delight, she found a lovely plum suit on sale, suitable for a wedding and yet something she could wear again, at Christmas. She insisted Andrew pick out something nice for himself as well and steered him toward a charcoal gray suit in which he looked quite distinguished. "This is your Christmas present," she retorted when he protested about the price, and bought him a pair of shoes to go with it.

Afterward, they hurried through the falling snow to a jewelry store, where they selected their wedding bands. They told the bemused jeweler that they needed the rings right away and would wait while he engraved them.

They celebrated their wedding eve supper at the finest restaurant in downtown Sewickley, and strolled hand in hand back to their bed-and-breakfast, full of anticipation for the morning. They kissed good night and teased each other about oversleeping and missing their important date, but each knew the other would not miss it for the world.

Sylvia hummed to herself as she hung up her new suit and got ready for bed, but just before she turned out the light, her glance fell upon the telephone, and she wondered if she ought to call Sarah, at least, and ask her and Matt to witness the ceremony. She could hardly invite them and ignore Andrew's children, however, so she turned out the light and went to sleep.

The next morning she woke before the alarm and lay in bed, listening to the wind blow ice against the windowpane. The dim light made the day seem younger than it was, but she heard Andrew stirring on the other side of the wall, and she knew she could not linger on such an important day.

Andrew had risen early, and he met her at breakfast with a small bouquet of flowers. It was lovely, and his face beamed with happiness as he kissed her and pulled her out of her chair. Their host and hostess were thrilled to discover they had a bride and groom at the table, and soon all the other guests were offering them congratulations and toasts of coffee and orange juice.

Andrew enjoyed every moment, but Sylvia found she had no appetite. When Andrew asked her if she felt ill, she assured him she was fine, just a little nervous from all the excitement. Andrew closed his hand around hers and held it while he ate, and by the time he finished, she felt much better. She even managed to swallow a few bites of her scrambled egg and drink most of her tea.

The sun had come out, chasing away the unseasonable cold, and nearly all the snow from the previous day had melted. They found a parking place right in front of the city clerk's office. "Another good sign," said Andrew, as he helped her from the minivan.

She clutched her bouquet and took his arm. "Do you have the wedding license?"

He touched his coat pocket. "Right here."

"And the rings?"

He stopped, frowned, and patted all his pockets in turn until he smiled and withdrew the two small velvet boxes from his front suit pocket. "They're here, too."

"Good. I have the strangest feeling we're forgetting something." Sylvia felt breathless. "Should I hold your ring?"

He smiled. "As long as you promise to give it back."

He gave her the ring box and offered her his arm again. She took it, smiled up at him, and allowed him to escort her inside.

Her heart pounded as they walked down the corridor toward the city clerk's office. People they passed spied her bouquet and grinned. Sylvia flushed and smiled back at them, then held her head higher and strode purposefully forward. She loved Andrew. She wanted to marry him. And yet . . .

She stopped short in the corridor, bring him to a halt. "Andrew—"

He looked down at her, his dear face full of concern. "What's wrong?"

"We can't do this. We shouldn't marry here, far from home, with strangers as witnesses." His face fell, but she knew in her heart what she said was true. "We should marry surrounded by people we love, or not at all."

He stared at her for a long, silent moment. He released her hands, turned away, and stood, head bowed, his back to her.

Hesitantly, she reached out and touched him softly on the shoulder. "Andrew?"

"You're right." He inhaled deeply, then turned to face her. She had never seen him more full of regret or resolve. "You're right. Let's go home."

Chapter Ten

The weight and thickness of the envelope told Eleanor that it contained more than a simple news clipping. Her mother's mailings had grown less frequent since Father's death; six months had passed since the last. If the return address of the Manhattan brownstone had not been written in her mother's own hand, Eleanor would have assumed the elderly cousin with whom she lived had sent notice of her mother's death.

Inside the envelope was a sheet of ivory writing paper edged with a quarter-inch black border. Her mother's note took up barely half the page.

May 8, 1927

Dear Eleanor,

Cousin Claire has died and her late husband's property now belongs to his brother's children. They intend to live here themselves and would not keep me among them even if I wished to stay, which I do not. I do not expect you to take me in. If you felt for me the respect and concern a daughter owes her mother, you never would have left us. However, I have no one else, so I must turn to you and hope that time has softened your selfish heart. I am to be evicted at month's end, and unless I do not hear from you, I will have no choice but to take up residence in an asylum for destitute women. If you wish to spare me from that disgrace, respond promptly to

Your Mother,
Gertrude Drayton-Smith Lockwood

Eleanor kept the letter in a bureau drawer for a day before showing it to Fred and Lucinda. She would have consulted Elizabeth first, as the eldest and nominal leader of the family, but since her husband's death five years before, Elizabeth did little but rock in her chair and quilt and murmur bleak predictions about the future. Claudia laughed at her behind her back, but seven-year-old Sylvia would turn her dark eyes from her grandmother and lead Richard away by the hand as if the mournful words could not hurt him if he did not hear. The solemn girl seemed to believe it was her responsibility to protect her younger brother from all dangers, real and imaginary.

Her darling boy was little more than a year old but already as headstrong and spirited as his father. If she could have given Fred another son, she would have named him after the other brother he had lost in the war, but she knew her heart could not withstand another pregnancy. When she first thought she might be pregnant again, Dr. Granger had scolded her when she went to him, glowing with joy, to confirm her secret hope. After she nearly died in child-birth, he had exhorted her—and Fred, too—not to risk another. But Eleanor did not need the doctor's warnings or her husband's white-faced pleading to convince her. She had not recovered from Richard's birth the way she had with the girls. She had lost something she could not define, and she knew another baby would kill her. She had been blessed with three beautiful, beloved children, and she so wanted to see them grow up that she would cling to life with her fingernails for one more day with them.

Fred read the letter, snorted, and handed it to his aunt. Lucinda scanned the lines and barked out a laugh. "Dear Eleanor," she paraphrased, holding out the page to Eleanor. "I am so sorry that for almost forty years I was a hateful old hag to you instead of a loving mother. Now that I am impoverished in my dotage, won't you please take care of me?"

"I know better than to expect an apology," said Eleanor, returning the letter to its envelope. "She thinks I owe her one."

"We'll send her money," said Fred. "A monthly allowance so she can maintain her own household in New York. We don't have to bring her here."

"I don't think she will accept charity."

"Isn't inviting her to live with us charity?" asked Fred. "I can't forget how she mistreated you. I won't allow her to hurt you in your own home."

Eleanor touched his cheek. "I have you. I have the children. She has lost the power to injure me."

She smiled at him, and he placed his hand over hers and regarded her fondly, but there was a tightness around his eyes that none of her reassurances could ease. She had tried to hide her increasing weakness, but he knew her heart labored to sustain her life. He would fight against anything that would sap her remaining strength, even if it meant abandoning his mother-in-law to her own fate.

Nevertheless, she was Eleanor's mother, and Eleanor did have a duty toward her. If her mother-in-law agreed, Eleanor would invite her mother to Elm Creek Manor.

Elizabeth gave her permission, but not without misgivings. "I admire your willingness to forgive," she said, shaking her head, "but if she says one cruel word against you or my son, I will slap her."

Lucinda laughed, but Fred grimaced and Eleanor wondered if she had made a mistake. She could not bear it if her mother's presence brought more grief to a family that had seen too much mourning.

Before writing back to her mother, she told the children. Claudia clapped her hands, delighted that she would be able to meet Grandmother Lockwood at last. Eleanor forced a smile and stroked her eldest daughter's glossy curls. She had told Claudia stories of her childhood in New York, of pretty dresses, glamorous balls, beautiful horses, and the summer house. She had allowed Claudia to believe the fairy tale, reserving the truth for when she was older. Even after so many years, the thought of telling those stories pained her. Now, perhaps, she would not need to. Once Claudia met Grandmother Lockwood, she could decide for herself.

Sylvia, apparently, already had. "Why is she coming now, after so many years?"

"Someone else owns her home now, and she has to move," said Eleanor, knowing better than to dissemble with Sylvia, who would reproach her with dark, silent looks when she discovered the truth. "Naturally she would turn to family at such a time."

Sylvia looked dubious, and Eleanor held her breath, certain Sylvia would ask why Grandmother Lockwood had not turned to them before, such as when Grandfather Lockwood died, but Sylvia said only, "When is she coming?"

"I don't know," said Eleanor. "I will ask her. Now, off you go to the nursery. I have letters to write."

Sylvia gave her a curious look, but she picked up Richard and went off after her sister. Eleanor watched them climb the stairs, longing to run after them as she once had. Lately climbing the stairs tired her so much that she remained on the first floor from breakfast until retiring for the night. Fred had to help her, and more often than not, he simply lifted her into his arms and carried her upstairs, effortlessly, as if she were one of the children.

After she had transformed her study into a nursery, the library had become her favorite place to linger over a book or compose a letter, but over the past year she had moved her favorite books and writing papers to the parlor. She was not surprised to find the room empty at that time of day, since Elizabeth preferred the sitting room off the kitchen and everyone else was working outside, tending to the horses, absorbing her former duties into their own. She had not ridden in ages. Even the walk to the stables exhausted her now.

At the bottom of her stationery case, Eleanor found a few sheets of black-edged paper left over from when Fred's father passed away. She would observe the rituals out of respect for her mother. Mother would expect it.

She rehearsed her words in her head rather than waste paper and ink searching for the appropriate phrases. Mother was easily offended, and her present circumstances would render her even more sensitive. But after twenty unproductive minutes, Eleanor steeled herself and wrote the first words that came to mind, as quickly as she could.

May 14, 1927

Dear Mother,

The Bergstrom family is honored that you would consider coming to reside at Elm Creek Manor. You will have a comfortable room and bath of your own and all the privacy you wish. Your three grandchildren will be thrilled to finally meet you.

I have indicated the nearest train station on the enclosed schedule. Please let us know when you shall arrive so Fred and I may meet you.

I would be grateful if you would extend our sincere condolences to Cousin Claire's family.

Your Daughter,
Eleanor Lockwood Bergstrom

She read the letter over as the ink dried. Despite her attempts to sound cordial and welcoming, the words were as stiff and remote as anything her mother could have written.

The second letter was easier to write, for all Eleanor regretted the need to do so.

May 14, 1927

Dear Mrs. Davis,

Now it is my turn to instruct you to sit before reading on. I believe I have news that will give you one shock to equal all those you have sent me throughout the years.

My mother is coming to Elm Creek Manor, not merely to visit, but to live. I still cannot quite believe it, but she would not have asked unless she was in earnest, and I have her request written in her own hand.

She must vacate her current residence by the end of the month, so I suppose she will be among us by June. I tell you this not to warn you away but to prepare you. Promise me you will not cancel your visit on her account. You would not visit me at my parents' house because of her, but this is my home, not hers, and you will always be welcome in it. I will lock her in the attic if you cannot bear the sight of her, but please do not deny me the pleasure of your company. With my mother in the house, I am certain I will need you more than ever.

My children do not believe you are real and never will unless they finally meet the former nanny of

Your Affectionate Friend,
Eleanor

PS: If you simply cannot bring yourself to visit with my mother here, please consider coming before her arrival. We still have two weeks left in May. What more can I say to persuade you? Tell me and I will say it.

Eleanor sent off her letters, hoping for the best. When Mother arrived, everything would change. She would have to shield the children from Mother's cutting tongue. Claudia was lovely and usually obedient and thus might earn her grandmother's grudging approval, but Mother would shudder at Richard's noisy play and proclaim him incorrigible within minutes of meeting him. As for Sylvia, she stood little chance of earning her grandmother's favor. Bright and moody and perceptive, she was everything her grandmother disliked in a young lady, and her appearance was unlikely to help. Her hair always seemed a tangle no matter how often Eleanor instructed her to comb it, and she could not step out of doors without getting grass stains on her dress and dirt on her face.

She was seeing them through her mother's eyes, Eleanor realized, but those very things that her mother would find so offensive were what endeared them to Eleanor most.

All that week, she waited anxiously for replies to her letters. As before, as always, she found solace in quilting. Not in the way Elizabeth did, numbing her pain with the repetitive motions of the needle, but in the act of creation, in piecing together beauty and harmony from what had been left over and cast aside. Her art would not endure as long as painting or sculpture, but it would outlive her, and every time her descendants wrapped themselves in one of her quilts, she would be with them, embracing them.

Months ago, Fred and William had moved the quilt frame into the nursery so that she might quilt while she looked after the children. That was the excuse she made, but in truth, she did not want Fred to see the quilt she worked upon, a gift for their twentieth anniversary. Once she had not thought it possible she would live twenty years, and in a few weeks, she would have been married that long, more than half her life. It was a miracle, and she had Fred's love and God's grace to thank for it. She did not have the words to tell her Freddy what those twenty years had meant to her, so she stitched her love, her passion, her longing into the soft fabric, which was as yielding as they had learned to be with each other, and as strong, as closely woven together. She was the warp and he the weft of their married life, two souls who had chosen each other, not knowing the pattern their lives would form.

One morning she climbed the stairs to the nursery, resting every three steps before continuing upward. The children were surprised to see her; the girls ran to hug her, and Richard toddled after them, crowing with joy. Sylvia begged Eleanor to read them a story, which she did, then gathered them all into her arms for one big hug and asked them to play without her for a while. They were so glad to have her in the nursery again that they did not complain.

Eleanor removed the sheet she had placed over the quilt to keep off dust and sticky fingers. Two years in the making, the Elms and Lilacs quilt was truly her finest work. She had appliquéd each lilac petal and elm leaf by hand, using fabrics in the new lighter hues that were coming into fashion. She had quilted around the floral motifs in an echo pattern, as if the leaves and petals had fallen into a pond and sent out gentle ripples. In the open background fabric, she had quilted feathered plumes over a crosshatch. Every stitch and scrap of fabric she had put into that quilt had a meaning she knew Fred would understand. The elms came from Elm Creek Manor, of course, but everything else symbolized the cornerstone patio. As Freddy had given it to her, so would she share it with him.

Only the last corner of the quilt, a square less than a foot wide, remained unquilted. When it was complete, she would need to finish the scalloped edge with binding. A straight edge would take less time, but in such situations she preferred to sacrifice her deadline to her design.

She threaded a needle, slipped her thimble on her finger, and soon was engrossed in her work, the children's play a happy murmur in the background. Then Richard toddled over and demanded to be picked up. She laughed and settled him on her lap, but she put only two more stitches into the quilt before he began to squirm. "Richard, darling," said Eleanor, sliding the heron-shaped scissors out of his reach, "this will work only if you hold still."

"Let Mama quilt," said Claudia. "Don't be naughty."

"He's not being naughty," said Sylvia. "He's just being a baby. That's what babies do."

"But Mama needs to finish her quilt."

"I need to play with Richard, too," said Eleanor quickly, before the fight could escalate. Claudia could be as imperious as Abigail had once been, but Eleanor had known to ignore Abigail's bluster and let her have her way. Sylvia ought to do the same with her sister, but she would rather be right than give in to get along.

"We could take turns," said Sylvia, brightening. "One of us could quilt while the other two play with Richard. This way he gets to play with everybody and the quilt still gets finished."

Claudia regarded her with scorn. "You just want to work on Mama's quilt."

"So what if I do? As long as Richard's happy and the work gets done—"

"That is the point, isn't it?" interrupted Eleanor. "I think it's a fine idea. I've already taken my turn, so Claudia, would you like to quilt next?" Claudia nodded, and Sylvia, who had already reached for the spool of thread, snatched her hand back. She shot Eleanor a look of protest, but Eleanor shook her head to remind Sylvia she did not reward bickering.

"Mama, *pay*," beseeched Richard, tugging on her hand. "Pay bock."

"Very well." Eleanor allowed herself to be led away, with only one glance back at Claudia and her quilt. "Let's go play with your blocks."

Sylvia joined her, helping Richard stack his wooden blocks and building towers for him to knock over. Sylvia threw herself into their play, pretending to have forgotten her sister, but after ten minutes she looked up at Eleanor with such woebegone hope that Eleanor agreed she could take her turn. Claudia relinquished the needle with only a small pout, and though she dragged her heels a little, she brought over one of Richard's favorite storybooks and offered to read it to him. He climbed into her lap, stuck a finger in his mouth, and stared at the pictures while Claudia told him the story. Eleanor sat back and watched, grateful for the chance to rest. The tranquil scene made her forget the time until Claudia set the book aside and reminded her Sylvia's turn was over.

Sylvia traded her place at the quilt frame for Richard's storybook, and she continued reading from where Claudia had left off. Eleanor studied her daughters' handiwork, pleased to discover that both girls had used their very best quilting. Claudia, especially, had far surpassed her usual efforts, so that her stitches were virtually indistinguishable from her sister's, even though Sylvia's work was ordinarily finer. Freddy wouldn't care even if their stitches were an inch long and uneven, of course; he would be prouder of a quilt bearing his daughters' imperfect stitches than a flawless quilt they had no part in making.

The climb upstairs to the nursery must have taxed her more than she had realized, for she was ready for a rest when Claudia's turn came again. Claudia took the needle eagerly and set herself to work with enthusiasm, the tip of her tongue visible in the corner of her mouth.

Sylvia's turn came once more, and then Eleanor's, and then Claudia's again. The girls no longer made faces when Sylvia took over for Claudia, and Richard was content, enjoying play time with all three of them. Eleanor was congratulating herself for resolving the latest in her daughters' long series of disagreements when Claudia suddenly shrilled, "What is she doing?"

"Hmm?" Eleanor looked up from Richard's wooden train in time to see Sylvia quickly set down the scissors. "What's wrong?"

Claudia stormed over to the quilt frame. Sylvia folded her arms over her work, but Claudia shoved her aside. "She's ruining my work," cried Claudia. "She picked out all my stitches."

Sylvia thrust out her lower lip. "I didn't ruin her work."

"Liar! She did!" Claudia pointed at the quilt. "Come and see for yourself."

Suddenly Eleanor felt too exhausted to do anything more than pull Richard onto her lap. "Sylvia, did you remove Claudia's stitches from the quilt?"

"Only the bad ones," said Sylvia. She glared at her sister. "I can't help it that most of them were bad."

Claudia shrieked and Sylvia shouted back. Eleanor closed her eyes and kissed the top of Richard's head. "Stop it." She covered the baby's ears and raised her voice. "Girls! Stop it. Sylvia, that was a very naughty thing to do—"

"But it's a present for Daddy," said Sylvia, chin trembling. "It should be just right."

"My quilting is just as good as yours," said Claudia.

"Now who's the liar?"

"Sylvia," said Eleanor, stern. "What you did was wrong, and being saucy about it only makes matters worse. Apologize to your sister, and go to your room."

Sylvia shot her a look of shame and frustration before mumbling something that might have been an apology and fleeing from the nursery. Eleanor sighed and sank back into her chair, patting Richard to soothe him, although he seemed not half as troubled as she.

The room fell silent. Eleanor closed her eyes and felt weariness overtake her. She had almost fallen asleep when she heard Claudia say, "I'm finished now. Do you want a turn?"

"No, thank you, darling."

She heard Claudia's chair scrape the floor and soft footsteps. Then, near her ear, Claudia whispered, "Richard's asleep."

Eleanor nodded. Even with her eyes closed she had known, not only by the sound of his breathing, but because only when asleep did her son hold still for so long.

"Shall I take him downstairs to his crib?"

"Would you, please?" Eleanor opened her eyes and allowed Claudia to take him. "Be careful on the stairs."

"I will." Claudia regarded her curiously. "Mama, are you all right?"

Eleanor smiled. "I'm just tired."

"Why don't you go to bed and take a nap? I'll get Richard if he cries."

She was tempted, but the thought of all those stairs was too daunting. "I think I'll just rest here for a moment and then quilt some more."

Claudia looked dubious, but she nodded and carried Richard away, sleeping on her shoulder.

When the door closed behind them, Eleanor curled up on the sofa, pulled an old scrap quilt over herself, and drifted off to sleep.

⁂

Eleanor's mother sent a telegram: "June 2, 3:15 PM."

From the moment the terse reply arrived until the hour Eleanor and Fred went to meet her at the station, Eleanor felt an urgent need to warn her family about her mother, to instruct them how to behave in order to divert her wrath. In the end, she said nothing. She could not find the words.

Fred held her hand as they waited on the platform. As the passengers began to disembark, Eleanor scanned the faces and wondered how she would recognize her mother after twenty years, how Mother would recognize her. Then Fred squeezed her hand. "There," he said, and nodded. Eleanor looked, her throat constricting with emotion—apprehension, anticipation. Hope. Her eyes met her mother's, and hope faltered.

Gertrude Drayton-Smith Lockwood wore black from head to toe; even the ostrich feathers bobbing on her hat had been dyed black to match the black wool of her coat. Her mouth hardened into a thin line as she descended from the train and gestured for the porter to fetch her trunk and satchel. The soft plumpness that had given her girlish beauty had been burned away, so that her features and dark eyes stood out sharp and prominent against her pale skin. She clasped her gloved hands and waited for Eleanor and Fred to come to her, her mouth displeased, her shoulders squared in long-suffering resignation.

Eleanor could not move until Fred gently guided her forward. Should she embrace her? Apologize in advance for everything Mother would find wanting in her new home? The crowd parted, and before Eleanor could force a smile, she found herself face to face with her mother.

"So." Mother eyed her, ignoring Fred. "I can see you're not well."

"It's good to see you, Mother." Eleanor kissed the air near her mother's cheek. She smelled of rose water. "I trust you had a pleasant journey."

"I abhor trains, and this one in particular was crowded and uncomfortable and unsanitary, but since you could not be troubled to come to New York for me yourself, I had little choice."

An icy smile played on Eleanor's lips. Her mother had had a choice: Elm Creek Manor by train or the asylum for destitute women on foot. That choice remained.

"The rest of the way will be more comfortable," said Fred

Mother grunted as if she certainly hoped so but doubted it. She bent stiffly and reached for her satchel, but Eleanor picked it up first. Fred moved to lift her trunk, but Mother pretended not to see him and waved for a porter. Fred wisely said nothing, but dismissed the porter with a shake of his head and carried the trunk himself.

Mother sniffed at the sight of their car and refused the front seat beside Fred to sit in the back with Eleanor. "My goodness, this is provincial," she muttered, peering out the window at the passing scenery.

"It is, isn't it?" responded Eleanor, ignoring the insult. "It's very restful after the noise of the city. You'll adore the town. It's quaint, very charming."

"I doubt I'll find much charm in it." Her mother folded her hands in her lap and turned her head away from the window, but glanced back again as if forcing herself to accept her new, diminished circumstances. Her frown deepened as they left the town behind, and she drew in a sharp breath at the sight of a herd of cows grazing in a pasture. Eleanor wanted to assure her Elm Creek Manor was not some mean farmhouse, but even more, she wanted to shake her mother and ask her how she could be so blind to the amaranthine sky, the rolling green hills, the lush forests that in autumn would be ablaze with color, breathtaking in their beauty.

Instead she sat back in her seat and watched the landscape roll by.

When Elm Creek Manor came into view, Mother straightened in her seat for a better look. She sat perfectly still, then she arched her brows and gave a derisive sniff that somehow lacked conviction. Fred parked the car, opened the door, and offered her his arm, which she ignored, or perhaps this time she truly did not see him, for her gaze was fixed on the manor.

Eleanor led her inside, and only then did Mother speak. "Well, Eleanor," she said, inspecting the grand front foyer. "I see you did not entirely come down in the world after all. Perhaps there was more calculation than romance in your choice."

Eleanor stiffened, and she was about to snap back with all the anger she had kept in check since leaving the train station when she heard footsteps pattering on the black marble. Lucinda and Elizabeth ushered in the children, freshly scrubbed and dressed in their second-best. Eleanor hid a smile, imagining Elizabeth and Claudia debating their wardrobe and deciding that their very best might seem too formal and off-putting, while second-best would acknowledge Mother as a member of the family while still marking the significance of the day.

Elizabeth came forward, smiling warmly, and kissed Mother on both cheeks. She had shed her mourning clothes for the day, and in her dark blue appeared almost festive next to Mother. "Mrs. Lockwood, how good it is to meet you at last," she said. "I'm Elizabeth Bergstrom, Fred's mother. I cannot tell you how grateful we are that you let us keep Eleanor to ourselves so selfishly all these years. We hope you will let us make it up to you by making our home your home."

With some satisfaction, Eleanor noted that Elizabeth's graciousness had utterly confounded Mother. "Thank you," Mother managed to say, and nodded to Aunt Lucinda as Elizabeth introduced her sister-in-law.

Claudia, who had been shifting her weight from foot to foot, could wait no longer. "Welcome to Elm Creek Manor, Grandmother," she said, throwing her arms around her. "I'm Claudia. I'm the oldest. I'm so glad you're going to live with us. Mama's told me all about you."

Mother started and patted Claudia awkwardly. "Has she, indeed?"

Sylvia hung back, holding Richard by the hand, until Eleanor surreptitiously beckoned her forward. "Welcome to Elm Creek Manor, Grandmother," said Sylvia, her voice a hollow echo of her sister's. "I'm Sylvia, and this is Richard."

"Yes. Well." Mother pried herself free from Claudia and caught Eleanor's eye. "I believe I would like to be shown to my room now."

❧

At least Mother did not complain about her rooms, not even at the sight of a patchwork quilt on the bed. Perhaps hard times had forced her to reconsider her disdain for the beauty of thrift.

Eleanor oversaw dinner preparations with care, supervising the reproduction of her mother's favorite French recipes while Elizabeth and Lucinda attended to the best table linens and silver. William snatched an éclair on his way through the kitchen and remarked that he hoped that they ate like this every night of her mother's visit.

Elizabeth shooed him away with a wooden spoon. "It's not a visit. She's here for good, and those are for dessert," she added in a shout as he grabbed a second éclair and ran.

"Please tell me we aren't going to eat like this every night," said Lucinda, frowning at a spot of tarnish on a salad fork.

"Just tonight," promised Eleanor. Tonight, and then perhaps tomorrow, at breakfast. By then, first impressions would be over and Mother would have made up her mind how she felt about them. Little could alter her opinions after she had formed them, so these first few hours were crucial. Elizabeth seemed to be faring well, as did Claudia, but Fred might as well not exist as far as Mother was concerned.

Claudia offered to call Mother for dinner, and Eleanor gratefully accepted, wanting a few moments to freshen up. All was ready in the formal dining hall, which Eleanor usually regarded as cold and imposing, but tonight it seemed just the thing. If Mother's favorite foods failed to impress her, the china and silver and crystal would not.

But when Mother entered on Claudia's arm, carrying her satchel, she did not seem to notice the tokens of wealth she once thought she could not live without. Fred rose to pull out her chair, but she waved him off and gestured for Claudia to assist her. An uncertain smile flickered on Claudia's face, as if she was proud to be chosen but dismayed that her father had been slighted.

Conversation was careful, polite, and stilted. Only Richard seemed perfectly content, banging his spoon on his high chair and stuffing his mouth with potato and sweet peas. Suddenly he reached into his mouth, scooped out a handful of chewed vegetables, and dropped them on the floor. "All done!"

"Yes, darling, I see that," said Eleanor, bending over to wipe up the splatter. Sylvia giggled.

"Disgraceful," said Mother.

Eleanor sat up quickly. For that moment, she had forgotten her mother's presence. "What is?"

"That urchin of yours, wasting good food when so many in the world go hungry." Mother set down her fork and pushed her plate away. "I cannot abide such rich dishes. A clear broth would have been much better."

"That's easily granted," said Elizabeth, smiling. She rose and left the room to speak to the cook.

"I thought you loved French cuisine," said Eleanor, wiping Richard's face.

"I did, once, before we had to let our cook go after we lost the business." Mother sighed and dabbed at her lips with her napkin. "We lost everything, but I suppose you knew that."

"I did not," said Eleanor. "I thought Father became Mr. Drury's partner."

"In name only, but I am not talking about the merger. This happened later, after Mr. Drury died and his children inherited the company."

"The entire company?" asked Fred.

This time it suited Mother to acknowledge him. "Of course. After all, Mr. Drury owned the entire company, for all that he retained the Lockwood name at the stores. He only did that to profit from our good reputation, since he had ruined his own by seducing an innocent young girl into betraying her family."

Her words were met with silence.

"Well?" inquired Mother, eyebrows raised. "What did you think would happen? Did you think ownership of the company reverted to your father?"

"That is what I assumed," said Eleanor.

Elizabeth returned with Mother's broth. Mother tasted it and set down her spoon. "Even if your sister had lived to bear Mr. Drury a child, the children from his first marriage still would have been the primary beneficiaries of his estate, since he failed to make a new will. If he had preceded her in death, she would have been left destitute unless his children were generous enough to provide for her, which, considering how they treated us, seems unlikely." She took another sip of broth. "So as you can see, Mr. Drury betrayed Abigail in the end, just as he betrayed us."

"He did not betray her." Eleanor's voice shook with anger. "He would have seen she was provided for. How could he have been expected to predict such a disaster?"

"He did not have to. All he had to do was take stock of his own mortality, as every responsible husband should. Five years they were married before they died, and yet he could not spare one day to change his will. Either he was shamefully negligent or he never intended to change it."

"He must have made other arrangements."

"Nonsense. You simply can't bear to see the romance tarnished. You ought instead to take heed of his poor example and see to your own affairs. If I am not mistaken, you have little time to waste, for all you have exceeded the doctors' expectations until now."

Someone gasped. Claudia blanched, and Sylvia turned to Eleanor, stricken and confused. Eleanor felt the blood rushing to her head. She tried to speak, but could not.

"That's enough," said Fred, his dark eyes glimmering with anger. "You've said enough for one evening."

Mother looked incredulous. "You haven't told them?"

"Told us what?" asked Sylvia in a whisper.

"The children may be excused," said Elizabeth. "Eleanor?"

"Yes—yes, of course. The children may be excused." Clumsily, she lifted Richard from his high chair and handed him to Claudia, but Sylvia had not left her seat. Her dark eyes went from Eleanor to her grandmother and back, questioning and afraid.

"Don't send them away before dessert," said Mother. "I brought presents."

"We don't want any presents," said Claudia in a small voice.

"Nonsense. What child doesn't want presents? Give the baby back to your mother like a good girl and come here."

Obediently, Claudia returned Richard to her mother's arms, but before she could take a single step, Fred spoke. "There's a little matter to clear up first. You made a careless remark that obviously frightened the girls. Why don't you explain to them what you meant?"

Mother's hand flew to her bosom. "You want me to be the one to tell them?"

"You're the one who misspoke." Fred's voice was ice. "In this family, whoever makes the mess cleans it up."

Mother's eyebrows arched. "Misspoke?" She forced out a brittle laugh, but she could not hold Fred's gaze long. She glanced at Eleanor, but just as quickly looked away. Perhaps something in their expressions reminded her that the train ran east as well as west.

"What I meant to say, children, was that we all have our time," said Mother. "We—we—sometimes we pass on before we are prepared. That's all I meant to say, that your parents should be prepared."

Claudia was visibly relieved, but Sylvia's eyes remained steadily fixed on her grandmother. "Who is Mr. Drury?" she asked. "What did he do to our grandfather?"

"Goodness, don't they know anything about our family?" asked Mother. Eleanor could see Claudia wanted to assure her that she, at least, knew something, but whatever stories Claudia repeated would only reveal her ignorance of the truth.

When no one answered her, Mother waved her hand impatiently. "Never mind. Now that I am here, I will remedy that. You will learn all I can teach you about the Lockwoods, and my gifts will be a fine start."

Claudia almost smiled, but Sylvia's expression hardened, a reflection of her father that seemed too old for such a little girl. Eleanor knew at once that Sylvia had resolved never to listen to her grandmother's stories, never to learn about the Lockwood family history. Eleanor felt a twinge of grief, but she had turned her back on the Lockwood family, and she could not expect Sylvia to embrace it.

"Ah." From her satchel, Mother withdrew a small, white box. "Come, Claudia. This is for you."

Claudia left her mother's side and took the box from her grandmother. When she lifted the lid, her eyes widened in surprise and admiration.

Mother smiled. "Do you like it?" Claudia nodded and reached tentatively into the box, glancing up at her grandmother for permission. "Of course you may pick it up, silly girl, it's yours." Eleanor caught a glimpse of silver flashing in her daughter's hand. It was her mother's silver locket, an heirloom passed down to her from her own mother.

Claudia opened the locket. "Who are these people?"

"The woman is my mother, and the man, my father. I will tell you all about them. Would you like to try it on?" When Claudia nodded, Mother fastened the locket about her neck. "There. It suits you."

Claudia fingered the locket and smiled. "Thank you, Grandmother."

"You're quite welcome." Mother reached into her satchel and produced a small parcel wrapped in brown paper and tied with string. "Be sure you take good care of it. Sylvia, this is for you."

When Sylvia did not leave her chair, Mother handed the parcel to Claudia and gestured for her to take it to her sister. Sylvia slowly unwrapped the gift, and when the paper fell away, Eleanor saw a fine porcelain doll with golden hair, dressed in a gown of blue velvet. It was a beautiful doll, but Sylvia did not care for dolls. She never had.

"Thank you, Grandmother," said Sylvia, solemn, and hugged the doll.

"She was your mother's. They were inseparable until she decided she was too old for dolls. Then she sat on a shelf in the nursery gathering dust, the poor, neglected thing."

"I didn't neglect it," said Eleanor. "You're thinking of Abigail. That was her doll, not mine."

"That's not so," said Mother. "I recall very clearly giving it to you for Christmas when you were four."

"That was Abigail. She said Santa brought it." Eleanor could still see Abigail cradling the doll, brushing her fine hair, dressing her in the frocks Miss Langley sewed. "When Abigail no longer wanted her, she gave her to me, but by then I was not interested in dolls, either."

"You would have liked them still if Abigail had." Mother turned her gaze on Sylvia. "Well, my dear, it seems I've given you the doll no one wanted. I suppose you, too, will abandon her."

Sylvia shook her head.

Mother studied her for a moment, assessing her, then frowned and reached into her satchel. "This is for you, Eleanor, if you want it." Mother placed a black, leather-bound book on the table. "It was to go to Abigail, as the eldest girl . . ."

She left the sentence unfinished. Eleanor knew what the book was, but she was immobile, unable to rise from her chair. It was Claudia who, unasked, brought it to her.

"What is it, Mama?" asked Sylvia, who always took interest in a new book.

"It's the Lockwood family Bible." Eleanor traced the gilded letters on the cover, then turned to the first few pages, to the records of births, baptisms, marriages, and deaths her father's mother had begun. With a pang of sorrow, she noticed that her mother had not written in either of her daughters' marriages, or Abigail's death.

"I leave it up to you to complete the record," said Mother. "You are the only one who can."

She meant, You are my only surviving child. There is no one else. But Eleanor understood that, and what it meant that her mother had given her this inheritance now. "I will not complete it, merely continue it," she said, closing the Bible. "As Claudia will continue it after me."

"Why Claudia?" asked Sylvia. She had placed the doll on the table and had leaned closer to her mother for a better look at the Bible, but at the mention of Claudia's name, she sat up.

"That's the tradition," explained Eleanor. "The family Bible always goes to the eldest daughter."

She regretted the words when she saw the smug look Claudia gave her sister, and the resentful glare Sylvia gave her in return. She remembered how the unfairness of the custom had stung when she realized the Bible would belong to Abigail one day, and not herself. Now she would give almost anything to be able to place it in her sister's hands, and sit by her side as she wrote down the names of all of their children in her round, girlish script.

"I have no gift for you, Fred," said Mother. "But I have already given you my daughter, and my children were always my greatest treasures."

Fred inclined his head, a gesture of respect, of recognition. Eleanor wondered if Mother had prepared her remarks on the train or if she had spoken them as an afterthought, a token of gratitude for Elizabeth's generosity.

The rest of the meal was subdued, but Eleanor was thankful enough that the hostility had passed, and that the girls had apparently forgotten their grandmother's cryptic references to her health. Mother retired immediately afterward, without a good night to anyone, much less the thanks anyone else in her position would have gratefully offered. Elizabeth made the excuse that she was surely exhausted from her long day of traveling, but they all knew better, and Lucinda told Eleanor that her rudeness was the first of many bad habits they would rid her of for the sake of family harmony.

"I forgot something," Lucinda added, handing Eleanor an envelope. "This came for you while you were at the station."

Its postmark read Lowell, Massachusetts, where Miss Langley had resided for the past six years.

May 28, 1927

My Dear Eleanor,

I am so sorry I did not respond sooner, but your letter arrived while I was traveling, and I only just received it. Please accept my heartfelt apologies, but I must decline your kind invitation. I will come to visit you as soon as your mother departs, for New York or the great hereafter, whichever comes first.

All the reasons that delayed my travels in the past seem trivial now that our separation has been extended indefinitely. I regret all the missed opportunities, all the postponements, as I am sure you do, but we must not dwell on them. I am resolved to see you again, Eleanor, or I am not

Your Affectionate Friend,
Amelia

She was not coming. Eleanor crumpled up the letter and put it in her pocket. If Miss Langley would not come now, when Eleanor needed her the most, she would never come.

❧❧

The next morning, Eleanor served her mother a delicious breakfast she barely touched. Eleanor offered to show Mother the estate, but she declined, saying that she would spend the morning finishing her unpacking.

"When do you expect the rest of your things to arrive?" asked Eleanor, accompanying her mother upstairs, fighting to conceal how the effort drained her.

Mother fixed her with a withering glare. "There are no other things."

Eleanor flushed. "I didn't realize—"

"What? That I did not exaggerate when I said we lost everything?" Mother reached the top of the stairs and waited for Eleanor to join her. "You grew up in a beautiful house full of lovely things, and if you had married Edwin Corville, you would have inherited them all one day."

"Instead I married the man I loved, and now I have my own house full of lovely things." Eleanor spoke coolly, but felt a sudden stab of sympathy for her mother as she imagined her selling off the accumulated treasures of generations of her family. The sympathy faded, however, when she recalled all that Mother and Father had been prepared to do to hold on to that way of life rather than accept the limits of their fortune and live within their means.

They walked down the hallway in silence. "Obviously your marriage, or this climate, or something out here in the country agrees with you," Mother said when they reached her door. "You lived much longer than anyone expected."

Eleanor gave her a tight smile, but would not acknowledge the question in her eyes.

Mother dropped her gaze and reached for the doorknob. "In any event, you are surely more fortunate than Mrs. Edwin Corville. I'm sure you heard how she caught her husband in bed with that opera singer."

"That is one news clipping you neglected to send me," said Eleanor. "Are you saying you admit I made the right choice?"

"I will not say that, and I will never say that," declared Mother. "Abigail certainly did not, for look where it got her. Dead, at the bottom of the sea. You, on the other hand, have done quite well for yourself."

"Please don't speak of Abigail that way."

"You always were afraid of the hard truths of life. You know you are more ill than anyone in your family perceives. And that Abigail sealed her own fate by betraying her father and me. And that you resent her for abandoning you to a choice that never should have been yours to make."

"I don't resent her."

"Of course you do. That's why you treat your daughters so differently."

Eleanor stared at her. "What on earth do you mean? I love my daughters equally."

"I said nothing of how you love them, only how you treat them. You prefer Claudia, and while Sylvia seems to be made of strong enough stuff to bear it—"

"You met them for the first time less than a day ago," snapped Eleanor. "I don't see how after twenty years you can presume to know anything about me or my children."

"I simply say what I observe. It is for your own good, and theirs. I do not want you to repeat my mistakes."

"See to it first that *you* do not repeat them." Eleanor paused to catch her breath. Her heart was racing. "If you intend to live in this house, you will treat everyone in it with respect, including my husband, including me. If you ever criticize my children again, call my son an urchin or say he is a disgrace, I will put you on the next train east if I have to carry you to the station on my back. Do you understand?"

Mother studied her, mouth pursed. "This is your home, not mine. I assure you I will show you and your family all the respect you showed me when you lived under my roof."

She went inside her room and shut the door.

❧

Mother did not come down for lunch. Lucinda left a tray outside her door, and half an hour later, she went upstairs to retrieve it. "So she does eat," she said with satisfaction, placing the empty dishes in the sink. "That will give us some leverage over her."

"We are not going to starve Eleanor's mother into being more sociable," scolded Elizabeth. "Be patient. She needs time to adjust to us."

After Eleanor put Richard down for his afternoon nap, the thought of her own bed tempted her, but she had too much work to do before the girls came home from school, even if her churning thoughts would allow it. Twenty years before, in her mother's house, Eleanor would have sought comfort in the solitude of her study. Now she climbed the stairs to the nursery, but by the time she reached the third floor, she felt light-headed and nauseous from exertion.

Eleanor seated herself in the chair by the window, where she had left the Elms and Lilacs quilt the last time she worked upon it. She had finished the quilting and had begun binding the three layers, but more than half the binding remained to be sewn in place, and tomorrow was their anniversary. If she worked on it for the rest of the day, she might finish by evening, but while Elizabeth and Lucinda would gladly give her that time to work, she did not have the strength to quilt for hours on end as she once had.

Freddy would not mind sleeping beneath an incomplete quilt, Eleanor told herself as she slipped her thimble on her finger. In fact, it would be more fitting that way, as the first quilt they had shared had also been a work in progress. So much had happened since that night on the train when they dreamed beneath the Rocky Mountain quilt together.

She sewed until her eyes grew too tired to see the stitches clearly, then rested before resuming her work. An hour passed. Richard would be waking soon, the girls were due home from school. They would be expecting her to chat with them as they had their afternoon snack. She knew she should join them, but if she descended those stairs she doubted she would be able to climb them again until Freddy carried her upstairs for bed.

That she would not let her mother see.

"Mama?"

Eleanor lifted her head to find Sylvia in the doorway. "Yes?"

"Were you sleeping?"

"No, just resting."

Sylvia crossed the floor and leaned against the armrest of Eleanor's chair. "Why didn't you come down for a snack? Weren't you hungry?"

"No, dear. I'm sorry I didn't keep you company. But as you can see . . ." She smiled ruefully and lifted the quilt. "I'm running out of time."

Sylvia studied it. "It looks like you're almost done."

"It might seem so, but I have to complete the binding, and then embroider my initials and the date." Eleanor sighed and adjusted the folds of fabric on her lap. "I often feel like a quilt is never truly finished, that there's always a little something more I ought to do. Your great-aunt Maude used to say I was too fussy."

"That's not true. You're not the least bit fussy." Sylvia hated to hear anyone she loved criticized, unless she herself was doing the criticizing. She
watched Eleanor work for a moment. "Can I help?"

"'May I.'"

"May I help?"

"Of course you may."

Sylvia pulled up the footstool, threaded a needle, and began sewing the
unattached end of the binding opposite her mother. They sewed toward the
middle in silence. Sylvia looked up the first time Eleanor paused to rest, but
she resumed her work without questioning her. Eleanor watched her small
dark head bent over the quilt and wondered if any of her children would
ever understand how deep, enduring, and profound was her love for them.

"Why did you give the Bible to Claudia?" asked Sylvia, without looking
up.

"I have not given it to her yet," said Eleanor gently. "It belongs to the
whole family."

"But Claudia will get it someday."

"Someday. Years from now."

"Why Claudia? Why not me?"

"Because she is the eldest daughter. That is the tradition."

"You weren't the eldest daughter," Sylvia pointed out. "Neither was your
father."

Eleanor had to laugh. "No, he certainly was not, but he was an only child,
so his mother had no daughters to leave it to. In my case, the Bible would
have gone to my sister if she had not died."

"Why don't you ever talk about her?"

"I don't know." Eleanor sat back and thought. "I suppose because I miss
her very much."

"Maybe if you talked about her, you wouldn't miss her so much."

Eleanor smiled. "Perhaps."

"Mama?"

"Yes?"

Sylvia set down her needle and took a deep breath, and, in a flash of
panic, Eleanor realized she was going to ask if Eleanor was going to die. She
dreaded the question, but she would not lie.

Sylvia's eyes were on her face, searching.

"What did you want to ask me, Sylvia?"

"Nothing." Sylvia picked up her needle and bent over her work. "Will you tell me about your sister?"

Eleanor took a deep, shaky breath. "Of course.

"Your aunt Abigail was four years older than I," she began, and as she spoke, she recalled what her mother had said earlier that morning. Mother was wrong. Eleanor did not favor Claudia out of guilt for any long-buried resentment, but because she had almost lost her. The image of her darling baby suffering from influenza made her choke back reprimands and punishments even when they were deserved.

If there was a grain of truth in Mother's accusation, it was that Claudia did remind Eleanor of Abigail, with the gifts their parents had not nurtured and the faults they had allowed to flourish. Claudia needed Eleanor's guidance more than her younger sister, who reminded Eleanor of herself, except that Sylvia was strong and resilient and beautiful.

❧

With Sylvia's help, Eleanor finished the Elms and Lilacs quilt by late afternoon.

They hurried downstairs, late for supper, to hide the quilt in Eleanor's bedroom closet. Later that night, while Fred slept beside her, Eleanor stole from bed, carefully lifted away the light coverlet they slept beneath on warm summer nights, and tucked in her beloved husband beneath his anniversary gift.

Something woke her before dawn—a noise, a stillness, a touch on her hair. She opened her eyes to find Fred sitting up and gazing at the quilt with shining eyes.

"Happy anniversary," she whispered, and reached out for him.

He brought her hand to his lips. "It's beautiful."

"The girls helped."

He grinned. "I'm sure they did."

He lay down beside her again and held her. They reminisced about their first years together as husband and wife, marveling at how swiftly twenty years had passed. They talked about the children, the funny and heartbreaking things they had done, muffling their voices so their family would sleep on, undisturbed, leaving them this time to themselves. They left other memories unspoken—their arguments, their angry bursts of pride, the demands that had seemed so important once but now stood plain and bare for what they were, a senseless squandering of precious time, moments they longed to go back and collect and spend more wisely, like shining silver coins fallen from a tear in a pocket.

They talked until the sun began to pink the sky. Then Fred kissed Eleanor and told her to get dressed so he could give her his gift.

She did, quickly, and though she was not tired, he lifted her up and carried her downstairs, across the marble foyer she thought too grand, into the older west wing of the manor and out the door to the cornerstone patio, and on, until they reached the stables.

With the sure skill of a man who loved horses, he saddled his own stallion and a mare Eleanor had long admired but had never ridden. Her heart quickened, but she hesitated. "Freddy—"

"Have you forgotten how to ride?"

"Of course not."

"Do you want to ride again?"

"Of course I do," she said. "I long for it. I dream of it."

He held out a hand to assist her. "Then what's stopping you?"

"I shouldn't. The doctors say—"

"Eleanor, if you and I did no more than what was allowed, then right now you would be Mrs. Edwin Corville of New York and I would be an old lonely bachelor with only these horses to keep me company."

Eleanor smiled, but her heart ached with sorrow. "You would have married someone else."

"That's where you're wrong. You are the only woman I ever could have loved, Eleanor. I knew that from the time I was fourteen and I saw you tearing around the corral on a horse."

She felt tears spring into her eyes. "You could have loved someone else." She took a deep breath, and, instinctively, placed a hand on her heart to calm it. "You still could love someone else."

His face darkened. "No, Eleanor. Not on our anniversary."

"You are still a young man, Fred. The children will need a mother."

"They have a mother. You."

"I heard you talking to Dr. Granger."

He held perfectly still, and when he spoke, his voice was quiet. "What did you hear?"

"That I will be lucky to live another year."

Fred busied himself adjusting her horse's bridle. "Doctors," he said gruffly. "According to your doctors, you've been at death's door for almost thirty-eight years."

"We have to talk about this. We have to prepare the children."

"Nothing will prepare them. How could anything prepare them for life in a world without you?"

His voice broke, his pain was laid bare, but she knew she must say what she needed to say, for they might never broach this subject again. She had tried too often to tell him what he would not hear. "I want you to know you have my blessing if you should choose to remarry."

"I don't want your blessing," he said helplessly. "I want you. Twenty years is not enough. It went too fast."

He bowed his head and turned away. She went to him and brushed away the tears he had not wanted her to see.

He pulled her into an embrace. The time for words had passed, she thought, but it would come again. She would make him hear her, and if it could not prepare him it would at least ease her own passing. She would tell him that twenty years had not been enough. She would tell him that she would not have traded these twenty years with him for a hundred lifetimes without him. She would tell him she was grateful for every single moment of her life.

She blinked away her tears, smiled, and reached for the mare's reins.

In the meantime, she was going to live.

Chapter Eleven

Sylvia and Andrew did their utmost to convince Amy and Bob to bring their families to Elm Creek Manor for Christmas. It was the most central location, they argued. They had plenty of room for everyone. The snowfall was particularly excellent that year for cross-country skiing and tobogganing, and if that didn't interest the older grandchildren, Waterford had plenty of theaters and clubs that would be open even while the college was on semester break. More important, if Andrew and his children did not spend the holidays together, it would be the end of a tradition that had endured since Amy and Bob were babies. The Coopers always celebrated Christmas as a family, no matter what distances separated them, no matter the demands of their jobs and school. Until this year, it had been a tradition each of them had been happy to keep.

By the second week in December, their persistent invitations had worn away at Bob and Cathy's resolve, and they promised to come if Amy would. When Amy's resistance seemed to weaken at this announcement, Andrew appealed to her husband, Paul, for help. He seemed a likely ally, since he had added a note beneath Amy's signature on their Christmas card congratulating Sylvia and Andrew on their engagement. Moreover, the last time Andrew spoke to him on the phone, Paul had told him he wished his late father, a longtime widower, had found a "neat lady" like Sylvia with whom to spend his golden years.

Andrew called Paul to find out how close Amy was to changing her mind, and what, if anything, they could say to bring her around. Paul confided that she had been very unhappy on Thanksgiving without them, and that as recently as two days ago, she had told him she regretted giving her father an ultimatum. Unfortunately, he added, "You know Amy. Once she thinks she's right, she refuses to back down. She's afraid that if she agrees to see you, you'll think she approves of your marriage."

"We respect her right to disapprove of us," said Andrew. "We don't understand it, but we accept it. What I can't accept is being shut out of her life, especially when she admits she wants to see us."

"She won't be able to keep this up for long," Paul consoled him. "No one in your family has the stomach for a long-drawn-out fight. Give her more time. She'll come around long before June. I hate to give up on Christmas, but I don't see any way to convince her by then."

"It's not just about Christmas," said Andrew. He glanced helplessly at Sylvia, who stood nearby, listening in on the cordless extension. She nodded, and as they had arranged beforehand, Andrew asked Paul how he and Amy would feel about having the family gather at their home in Connecticut instead. It would throw their arrangements into an uproar, but it was their plan of last resort, and they were running out of time.

Paul asked them to hold on, and they waited anxiously throughout the long silence until he returned. They were not surprised to learn that Amy had refused. Not only that, she came to the phone herself to tell them that she, Paul, and their children had decided to spend a quiet family Christmas at home, and she would appreciate it if they would accept this as the last word on the subject.

"Maybe next year," said Andrew.

"Maybe," said Amy softly, and hung up.

"She's as unhappy about this conflict as we are," Sylvia told Andrew afterward.

"Then why doesn't she just bury the hatchet?" grumbled Andrew. "Honestly, Sylvia, she's so stubborn, you'd think she was your daughter instead of mine."

"Who are you calling stubborn?" asked Sylvia indignantly, then added, "Well, I suppose I am—stubborn enough to insist that we have a merry Christmas anyway. I have no intention of altering our plans, as long as you don't."

"I don't," Andrew assured her. "I just wish the kids would be here to celebrate with us."

Sylvia did, too, but what could not be changed had to be endured. On Christmas Eve, at least, they would not be alone. Sarah and Matt as well as all the Elm Creek Quilters and their families would celebrate at Elm Creek Manor, as they did every year.

❧

On the morning of Christmas Eve, Sylvia and Sarah rose early to finish their preparations for the party. At times like these, Sylvia was especially grateful for Sarah's business skills; a week before, when Sylvia told her how important this particular party would be, Sarah had made up lists and menus and schedules so that they could accomplish everything and still have a little energy left over to enjoy the party themselves. Only once did Sarah grumble that Sylvia could have given her a little more notice, but she soon got so caught up in organizing and planning that she forgot Sylvia's small offense.

By late afternoon, a light snow had begun to fall, but there was no sign of the roaring blizzard Sylvia had feared would keep their friends at home. A half hour before the first guests were to arrive, Sarah ordered Sylvia out of the kitchen and upstairs to put on the plum suit she had purchased in Sewickley. "Matt and I can take care of the rest," said Sarah, who had somehow found time to change earlier, and now wore a green-and-red plaid apron over her dress.

Sylvia complied, and as she hurried upstairs, she met Andrew coming down, wearing his new suit. "You look very handsome," she told him in passing.

He laughed. "No time for a kiss?"

"You'll get your kiss later," she promised, and hurried off to her room.

Her suit lay on the bed, freshly pressed and waiting. Beside it sat a small bouquet of ivory roses tied with a plum velvet ribbon. "Oh, Andrew," she said, smiling. He had not left a card, but only Andrew would have thought to give her flowers.

She dressed quickly, but took time for powder and lipstick. She put on earrings and a pearl necklace that had once belonged to her mother, and fussed with her hair longer than usual. She was not vain, but tonight she wanted to look her best. She scrutinized herself in the mirror, frowning critically. "That will have to do," she said, but she gave her reflection a nod of approval. She thought she looked rather nice, if a trifle flushed from the excitement.

She returned downstairs, smiling with delight when she saw the Christmas tree lit up in all its splendor. Sixteen feet high, it would have seemed enormous in any other room but the grand foyer. Andrew and Matt had needed a day to string the small white lights upon it, and the better part of another to decorate the boughs with ornaments. Ordinarily Sylvia preferred a smaller tree, just the right size for the parlor, but this year called for something special.

At that moment the front door opened. Matt appeared in the doorway, stomping his feet to clear the snow from his boots. He spotted Sylvia and grinned. "There's still time to put up the blinking colored lights if you like."

"Not on your life," retorted Sylvia, taking his coat as he came inside. "How's the driveway?"

"It's clear. The snow wasn't too deep," said Matt. "Don't worry, Sylvia. The weather's fine. Everyone will be here."

"Not quite everyone," said Sylvia, rueful. But it could not be helped.

Matt had other chores to attend to before the guests arrived, so Sylvia left his coat in the cloakroom and went alone to the ballroom, where Sarah had just finished lighting the last hurricane lamp centerpiece, blowing out the match as she inspected her work.

Sylvia took a few steps toward her and stopped short, enchanted by the transformation candles, poinsettias, ribbon, and evergreen boughs had wrought on the ballroom. Andrew had built a fire in the large fireplace at the far side of the room, and nearby was the Nativity scene her father had brought back from a visit to the Bergstroms' ancestral home in Baden-Baden, Germany. Earlier that day, Summer had stopped by to set up her CD player at one end of the dance floor, and Christmas carols wafted on air fragrant with the scents of pine and cinnamon and roasted apples. Just across the dance floor, the cook and two assistants—his daughter and her best friend, or so Sylvia had overheard—were placing silver trays of hors d'oeuvres and cookies on a long table, and preparing the buffet for hot dishes still simmering in the kitchen. Someone had opened the curtains covering the floor-to-ceiling windows on the south wall, and snowflakes fell gently against the window panes.

Sarah joined her as Sylvia took in the sight. "What do you think?" she asked.

"It's absolutely splendid," declared Sylvia, putting her arm around her young friend. "I can't imagine a lovelier or more festive place to spend a Christmas Eve."

"If you had given me more time, I could have done more."

"Nonsense. It's perfect the way it is." Sylvia hugged her. "Thank you, dear."

Sylvia had Sarah show her to her seat so she could leave her flowers at her place. She wanted to seek out Andrew so they could share a moment alone before the festivities began, but just then, the front bell rang, and a few moments later, their guests began to fill the ballroom. First Summer arrived with her boyfriend and her mother, Gwen, and then Judy entered with her husband and young daughter. Next came Diane, stunning in a black crushed velvet dress, accompanied by her husband and two teenage sons. Bonnie and her husband followed close behind; with them were a number of young men and women Sylvia recognized as their adult children and their spouses. The precious bundle cradled in the pink-and-white Tumbling Blocks quilt was surely Bonnie's new granddaughter, and in her eagerness to meet the baby, Sylvia forgot all about finding Andrew.

More guests arrived, including the rest of the Elm Creek Quilts staff and faculty and their families, other friends from Waterford, college students Sylvia had befriended while participating in various research projects, and Katherine Quigley, a prominent local judge. As soon as Katherine and her husband arrived, Sylvia made a point of welcoming them to Elm Creek Manor and thanking them for coming. Since the Quigleys were not a usual part of Sylvia's circle of friends, Sylvia had been concerned about making them feel comfortable, but when nearly a dozen people called out greetings the moment Katherine entered, Sylvia had to laugh at her worries.

Cocktails were served, and then a delicious meal of roasted Cornish game hen with cranberry walnut dressing that reminded Sylvia all over again why some quilters claimed they came to Elm Creek Quilt camp for the food alone. Afterward, Summer put some big band tunes on the CD player and led her boyfriend, Jeremy, onto the dance floor. Other couples joined them, and soon the room was alive with laughter, music, and the warmth of friendship.

As the first notes of "Moon River" played, Andrew found Sylvia chatting with a few of the Elm Creek Quilters and asked her to dance. "You're so popular, I've hardly had a moment alone with you," he teased.

Sylvia laughed. "You've never been the jealous type. I certainly hope you don't plan to start now."

He promised he wouldn't, and she closed her eyes and touched her cheek to his as they danced. He had become quite a fine dancer since the previous summer, when he had promised to learn to dance if she would learn how to fish. She still hadn't caught anything, but Andrew said, "Fishing isn't just about having a trout on the fire at the end of the day." She replied that she felt exactly the same about quilting.

"I don't think I've ever had a happier Christmas Eve," said Sylvia. "I hate to see it end."

"Is that so?" He regarded her, eyebrows raised. "Does that mean you've changed your mind?"

"Of course not," she said, lowering her voice as the song ended. "In fact, I was just about to suggest we get started."

He brought her hands to his lips. "I was hoping you'd say that."

Sylvia signaled to Sarah, and while her young friend found Judge Quigley in the crowd, Sylvia picked up her bouquet and met Andrew at the opposite end of the dance floor from where the judge waited with Sarah and Matt. Sylvia took a deep breath and swallowed.

"Nervous?" asked Andrew, smiling.

"Not at all," she said, and cleared her throat. "I just hope our friends will forgive us."

Andrew chuckled. "They'll have to, once we remind them that you and I never said anything about waiting until June."

"May I have everyone's attention, please?" called Sarah over the noise of the crowd. Summer turned down the volume on the stereo. "On behalf of Sylvia and Andrew and everyone who considers Elm Creek Manor a home away from home, thank you for joining us on this very special Christmas Eve."

Everyone applauded, except Andrew, who straightened his tie, and Sylvia, who took his arm.

"It is also my honor and great pleasure," said Sarah, "to inform you that you are here not only to celebrate Christmas, but also the wedding of our two dear friends, Sylvia Compson and Andrew Cooper."

Gasps of surprise and excitement quickly gave way to cheers. Sylvia felt her cheeks growing hot as their many friends turned to them, applauding and calling their names.

"You said June," said Diane, her voice carrying over the celebration.

"No, *you* said June," retorted Sylvia.

"But I already bought my dress," wailed Diane, "and picked out your gown!"

The gathering of friends burst into laughter, and, joining in as loud as anyone, Sarah held up her hands for quiet. "If you would all gather around, Andrew would like to escort his beautiful bride down the aisle."

The crowd parted to make way for them, and Summer slipped away to the stereo. As the first strains of Bach's "Jesu, Joy of Man's Desiring" filled the air, Sylvia nodded to Andrew, and they walked among their friends to where the judge waited.

To Sylvia, every moment of the simple ceremony rang as true as a crystal chime. They pledged to be true, faithful, respectful, and loving to each other until the end of their days. They listened, hand in hand, as the judge reminded them of the significance and irrevocability of their promises. They exchanged rings, and when they kissed, the room erupted in cheers and applause. As Sarah and Matt came forward to sign the marriage license, Sylvia looked out upon the gathered friends wiping their eyes and smiling and knew that she and Andrew had wed surrounded by love, exactly as they knew they should.

If only Andrew's children and grandchildren were there to share this moment. If only they were as happy for Sylvia and Andrew as their friends were. Sylvia looked up at her new husband and saw in his eyes that he shared her wistful thoughts.

She reached up to touch his cheek. He put his hand over hers and smiled.

❧

Sylvia woke Christmas morning in the arms of her new husband.

She watched him as he slept, reminiscing about the previous night. It had truly been a marvelous wedding, exactly the sort of celebration she and Andrew had wanted. Even the Elm Creek Quilters had enjoyed themselves too much to complain that their own plans for the wedding would now have to be abandoned. "I feel sorry for Judy's daughter," Summer had confided to Sylvia as the celebration wound down. "The Elm Creek Quilters are going to do the same thing to her that they did to you, and they won't be fooled by a surprise early wedding twice."

"Emily?" echoed Sylvia. "I'd be more concerned about yourself."

"I think I'll elope," said Summer, blanching. "Or stay single."

"Good luck, dear," Sylvia had told her, knowing Summer was unlikely to escape that easily.

Sylvia muffled a laugh at the memory and carefully sat up in bed. Andrew slept on, undisturbed, warm and snug beneath her old Lone Star quilt. It suited the master suite perfectly, just as Sarah had assured her it would. Except for moving their clothing and other personal items into the suite they would share, Sylvia and Andrew had decided to keep their old rooms as they were. Everyone needed a private retreat every now and then, even newly married sweethearts.

She put on her glasses, slipped on her flannel robe and slippers, and seated herself at the desk near the window. More snow had fallen overnight, but the flakes were fluffy and light, and once the snowplows made their rounds, the roads ought to be safe for travelers.

The family Bible lay on the desktop where she had left it the previous afternoon after moving her things into the new room. First, she read the story of the Nativity from Luke, a Christmas tradition of her own.

She reflected on the words, then glanced at Andrew, smiled, and retrieved a pen from one of the desk drawers. She turned back to the front of the Bible, to the record of important milestones in the Lockwood family written in several different hands. The last entries were in her mother's small, elegant script. She had recorded her own marriage to Sylvia's father, her sister's marriage and death, her parents' passings, and the births of all three of her children. No one had written in the date of Sylvia's mother's death, nor those of the loved ones who had followed.

The familiar melancholy that stole over Sylvia whenever she contemplated the record touched her only lightly that morning—and then, as she took a second look at a name that had caught her eye, it vanished entirely.

"Herbert Drury?" she exclaimed. "Abigail Drury is Aunt Abigail?"

"Who's what?" asked Andrew sleepily, sitting up in bed with a yawn.

"The quilt designer, the one from the magazine. The woman whose name seemed so familiar. My goodness, she was my aunt. My mother's sister. I didn't recognize her married name."

Andrew grinned and put on his robe. "You forgot your own aunt's name?"

"I did, and I'm not ashamed to admit it. She died long before I was born, and my mother always referred to her as her sister, or Abigail, but never Abigail Drury."

"So your Aunt Abigail designed the whole cloth quilt." Andrew pulled up a chair and stroked her back as he read over her shoulder. "That's one more mystery solved."

"No, I don't think so," said Sylvia. "My mother told me on several occasions that she was the only quilter in her immediate family. An aunt or a family friend taught her. I can't recall which." Sylvia thought for a moment. "I'll bet half my fabric stash my mother designed that quilt and gave her sister the credit."

"Why?"

"Well . . ." Sylvia considered, then indicated the record of her aunt's death. "I suppose because Aunt Abigail had died only a few months before the pattern's publication. Perhaps my mother used her sister's name in tribute, to immortalize her, in a sense."

Andrew leaned closer for a better look. "April fifteenth, 1912. Did you know that's the same date the *Titanic* sank?"

"Of course I know. No one in my family could ever forget. Of course, we're not sure whether Aunt Abigail died on the night of the fourteenth or the morning of the fifteenth."

Andrew stared at her. "Your aunt died aboard the *Titanic*?"

"She and her husband, yes."

He shook his head in amazement. "Now, that's a Bergstrom family story I haven't heard."

Sylvia supposed it was, but since her mother had told her only those few spare details, she had little more to share with Andrew.

Andrew touched the page where the date of Aunt Abigail's death was written. "This is your mother's handwriting?"

"Yes."

"Your grandmother didn't pass on until several years later. Why didn't she make this entry? Come to think of it, she should have put down your mother's and aunt's weddings, and the births of you and your siblings, but it looks like your mother did those, too."

"My grandmother abandoned the record after both of her daughters ran off to marry against her wishes," said Sylvia lightly.

"Your grandmother didn't approve of your father?" asked Andrew, incredulous. He had admired Sylvia's father since childhood. "Why not?"

"I don't know. My grandmother never spoke an ill word about him in my presence. Of course, I know little more about her than about Aunt Abigail. I met her for the first time when I was seven years old and she came to live with us. She died less than two months after her arrival."

"All this talk about death, marriages the family doesn't approve of . . ." Andrew shook his head and gave her a rueful smile. "This isn't a very cheerful project for the first morning of your honeymoon."

"Don't you worry," she told him, smiling. "I believe it will have a happy ending."

She took up her pen and finished the record her mother's great-grandmother had begun. Her mother's death, a date she would never forget. Her marriage to her first husband, James. The death of James and her beloved little brother, on the same day in the same tragic accident far from home. Claudia's marriage and passing, which she should have witnessed, but learned of through letters from mutual friends.

She concluded her entry by recording her marriage to Andrew. Then she set the pen aside. She did not know who, if anyone, would continue the record after her. She would not be dismayed if no one did. It would not bother her in the least if the record ended on a note of joy and promise, the union of two dear friends.

❧

When Sylvia and Andrew finished packing, they went downstairs for breakfast. Sarah and Matt were lingering over coffee in the kitchen, waiting to wish them a Merry Christmas and safe journey before leaving for Sarah's mother's house. Sarah and Matt had prepared the newlyweds a special breakfast: blueberry pancakes with maple syrup, a pot of lemon tea for Sylvia, and good strong coffee for Andrew. And as they sat down to eat, Sarah placed a brightly wrapped box on the table. "Your Christmas present," she explained. "It's a wedding gift, too."

Inside Sylvia discovered a digital camcorder. "My goodness," she exclaimed.

"It's to record all your honeymoon memories," said Sarah.

"Maybe not all of them," said Matt, winking at Andrew. Sarah rolled her eyes. "What? The poor man didn't even get a bachelor party. I think I'm allowed one tasteless joke."

"That's the best you can do?" inquired Sylvia. "I've heard worse at your average quilting bee."

They all laughed, and Andrew, who loved gadgets, eagerly opened the box. "This is great, kids. Thanks."

"Yes, thank you," added Sylvia, though the device looked so complicated she decided not to touch it until she read the manual. "We'll enjoy documenting our travels for you."

"Will you spend your whole honeymoon in the Poconos?" asked Matt.

"No, just tonight," said Sylvia. "Tomorrow morning we're continuing on to New York."

Sarah's face lit up. "To see some Broadway shows? To go shopping?"

"That, and we're going to visit my mother's childhood home. I've never seen it. I wrote to the current residents, and they graciously offered to give us a tour."

Andrew caught Sylvia's eye and smiled. "After that, we're going to Connecticut."

Sylvia smiled back at him. If Amy wouldn't come to them, they would go to her.

When the last bite of Sarah's delicious pancakes was gone and the dishes were washed and put away, they exchanged the rest of their gifts. Then, to put their young friends' minds at ease, Sylvia wrote down their itinerary, including the number of her new cellular phone, a Christmas present from Andrew.

Sarah and Matt helped them carry their luggage to the Elm Creek Quilts minivan. "Will you call me at my mother's house when you get to the inn?" asked Sarah.

"If you promise to stop worrying," said Sylvia, climbing into the passenger's seat and shutting the door. Andrew started the engine, and Sylvia waved good-bye through the window.

"Get a shot of us pulling away from the manor," said Andrew as they crossed the bridge over Elm Creek.

"Oh, for heaven's sake," grumbled Sylvia cheerfully, but she took the camera from its case. "I hope you won't have me doing this the whole way there."

"Of course not," said Andrew. "The batteries will run down."

Even so, she did spend quite a bit of time behind the camera as they traveled, sometimes at Andrew's request, sometimes on her own initiative, when a particularly lovely valley or snow-covered mountainscape inspired her. When they stopped for lunch or to stretch their legs, Andrew took his turn, and to Sylvia's amusement, he spent more time training the camera on her than on the sights of the journey.

"I'm coming with you," she teased when he had her stand right in front of a historical marker, so that no one watching the video would be able to read why it was so important. "You don't need a picture of me."

He replied that he was capturing their honeymoon memories, as instructed, and whenever she tried to step out of the way, he followed her with the camera. She eventually gave in, realizing that if she didn't play along, their entire vacation video would consist of her complaining and ducking out of camera range.

They arrived at the Bear's Paw Inn by early afternoon. The proprietors, Jean and Daniel, were pleased to see them again, and were thrilled to discover that they were on their honeymoon. They showed Sylvia and Andrew to their usual room, where they relaxed until suppertime.

They joined their hosts and two other vacationing couples in the dining room, and Daniel began the meal by offering a toast to the newlyweds. The food was delicious, the company pleasant, and eventually the conversation turned to quilting when a new guest inquired about the quilts displayed throughout the inn. Jean, an avid collector, was pleased to entertain them with stories of how she had acquired her favorite pieces and what she knew of their history. For Sylvia, the details of the quilts' makers and prior owners called to mind her own quest to find her mother's quilts. Thinking of what those fragile heirlooms had endured reminded her how fortunate she was to have found the Crazy Quilt whole and sound, and how generous Mona Niehaus had been to part with it. She was grateful to have the Elms and Lilacs quilt, too, for despite its altered condition, her mother's love for her family and willingness to endure any hardship for their sake was still evident in every stitch. While the Ocean Waves quilt had been lost forever, its beauty would survive in her memory, and she would learn from the example of Gloria Schaeffer's sons and not put off acts of healing and forgiveness. The whole cloth quilt, too, was beyond her reach, but knowing her mother had created it after all, and that she had lovingly offered it to the world in her sister's name, brought her as much comfort as the quilt itself would have done. And while the New York Beauty quilt still eluded her, she would continue to search. That was one lesson her mother had taught her well: Persevere, hope, and do all things with love, for then the attempt would be successful even if it fell short of the goal.

"Have you ever been to the New England Quilt Museum?" one of the new guests asked Sylvia.

"Indeed I have," said Sylvia. "Although not recently."

"If you have a chance to visit again soon, you should," said Jean. "We spent Thanksgiving with our son in Boston, and we made a day trip out to Lowell. The museum had just set up the most beautiful exhibit of Christmas quilts. If you're heading east, it's definitely worth going out of your way."

"Lowell's only about two hours northeast of Amy's house," said Andrew.

"Some of their quilts are even closer than that," said another guest, an avid quilter who had come running into the inn when she returned from a day of skiing to discover the Elm Creek Quilts minivan in the parking lot.

"The Penn State branch campus in Hazleton has some pieces from the New England Quilt Museum in their library gallery. It was a special themed exhibit called—oh, what was the name again?"

"The Art of Women Pioneers," offered her husband.

"Yes, something like that. There were quilts, of course, but also other needlework, pottery, weaving, and other media, all on loan from museums across the country. The stories of the women who made those pieces were fascinating. I highly recommend it."

Sylvia nudged Andrew. "Not only recommended, but highly recommended. Surely you don't expect me to resist that."

"I don't, but we already passed Hazleton. Should we see it on our way home?"

"That sounds like a fine idea."

"I wish my film wasn't still in the camera," the other guest lamented. "I took a picture of an absolutely stunning quilt in a pattern I had never seen before. I'm sure you would be able to identify it."

"Perhaps I still can," said Sylvia. "Describe it for me."

"Well, it looked to me like a cross between the Sunflower and the Grandmother's Fan pattern. Imagine a quarter circle with narrow spires branching out from it like sunbeams—"

"Were the blocks separated by sashing?" interrupted Sylvia.

"Very distinctive sashing, as a matter of fact. The strips had spires similar to those in the blocks, and at the junction of the sashing strips were small pieced stars. Do you know the pattern?"

"I do," said Sylvia, nearly breathless from excitement. "In fact, I think I may know the very quilt. Do you recall how long the exhibit will be there?"

She shook her head. "I don't, sorry. We just stopped by on our way north from Harrisburg."

"I would hate to miss it," said Sylvia, giving Andrew a significant look. "I simply can't miss it. By the time we come home, the pieces in the exhibit might have been returned to their owners."

"I don't mind a detour if you don't," said Andrew, with a good-natured grin. "After all, you are the bride."

❧

The next morning, they bid their hosts good-bye and backtracked west for an hour through a light flurry of snow, then turned south. As they drove, Sylvia mulled over the other guest's words. A special themed exhibit, she had called it, comprised of pieces from several different museums. While Grace Daniels's contact at the New England Quilt Museum had confirmed that there were no New York Beauty quilts on display or in storage, Sylvia had not thought to have Grace specifically inquire about pieces on loan to other galleries.

Sylvia laughed, and when Andrew asked her why, she said, "I couldn't find the New York Beauty quilt among large quilt collections or even on the entire Internet, and yet here I am hoping it will be among these few quilts."

"You never know," said Andrew. "Stranger things have happened."

"Not this strange," retorted Sylvia, and yet she could not shake a sense of hope that ran contrary to all common sense. Her mother was not a pioneer, so her work would not even fit the exhibit's theme. It was too much of a coincidence that Sylvia would happen to stay at the same inn as a woman who happened to see her mother's quilt, and who just happened to mention it in passing conversation. And yet it might not be such a coincidence after all. The other guest had sought out the Hazleton exhibit because she loved quilts, and she and Sylvia had both selected the Bear's Paw Inn for that same reason. Indeed, tracking down her mother's quilt by chatting with other quilters was similar to Summer's search on the Internet, only on a much smaller scale. Was it really so wrong for Sylvia to hope, as long as she didn't set her expectations so high that she forgot to enjoy what was right before her?

"It will be a lovely exhibit either way," she said firmly. Andrew grinned and shook his head as if she had spoken her entire argument with herself aloud.

Following the directions the couple from the inn had provided, Andrew drove on to the campus and found the library with the help of a graduate student trudging along the snow-dusted sidewalk, bent over from the weight of his backpack. They parked in an empty lot just as the wind began to pick up and the flurries turned into a light but steady snow shower. Sylvia pulled up the hood of her coat and put on her gloves as Andrew came around to her side to help her from the minivan.

They spotted the sign posted on the glass door from the sidewalk. "That can't be good," said Sylvia, glancing over her shoulder at the empty parking lot. Sure enough, when they drew closer to the sign, they learned that the library would be closed for another week for the semester break.

"That's too bad," said Andrew. "We can still visit the museum in Lowell, though."

"That New York Beauty quilt won't be in the museum," Sylvia reminded him. "I'm not giving up yet, not after turning back especially to see this exhibit. I had my heart set on seeing some quilts today, and I'm determined to do so."

"We could drive around town until we found a quilt shop," suggested Andrew, but Sylvia cupped her hands around her eyes and pressed them against the glass. She thought she saw a light coming from one of the rooms on the other side of the front desk.

"Come on," she said. She made her way along the sidewalk for a few paces, then stepped off into ankle-deep snow.

"Careful," Andrew said, and gave her his arm.

They circled the building, stopping to look in each window. Andrew worried aloud that a security guard might haul them off for trespassing, but Sylvia figured the risk was worth it. "Who would pick on two senior citizens on their honeymoon?" she teased, peering into what must have been a staff lounge. "Aha! Look on the counter, beside the refrigerator. See that red light? Someone made coffee this morning."

"Or they left the pot on from the end of the semester."

Sylvia knew he could be right, but was unwilling to admit it. The next two windows looked in upon shelves of books, but the third revealed a large cluttered office containing several computers, carts of tagged books, and one young woman sipping from a coffee mug as she collected sheets of paper emerging from a printer.

Sylvia tapped on the window. The woman jerked her head up, her long blond braid slipping over her shoulder. Sylvia smiled and waved, but the woman shook her head, mouthed some words, and turned back to the printer.

"I think she said they're closed," said Andrew.

"That would be my guess, too." Sylvia rapped on the glass again, and when the woman looked up, Sylvia beckoned her to come closer.

The woman sighed and came over to the window. "We're closed," she called, her words barely audible through the glass but her meaning unmistakable.

"Please?" shouted Sylvia. "We won't take but a moment of your time."

Sylvia wasn't sure if the woman understood, but after a moment, she nodded and pointed toward the front of the building. "Hurry," said Sylvia, taking Andrew's arm again. "Before she changes her mind."

The woman was waiting for them inside the front foyer. As they stomped their feet to shake off the snow, she unlocked the door and held it open. "May I help you with something?"

"We understand you have an art exhibit here," said Sylvia, breathless from racing around the building. "May we please see it?"

"I was hoping you just wanted to use the bathroom," said the woman. "I'm afraid the library's closed until next week."

"We won't be here next week," said Andrew. "We're just passing through on our way to New York."

"We heard your exhibit is not to be missed," said Sylvia. "May we just take a brief look at the quilts, if nothing else? We won't disturb your work."

"We're on our honeymoon," said Andrew.

The woman blinked at him. "You're what?"

"We're on our honeymoon," he repeated, and Sylvia nodded.

"No kidding." The young woman eyed them. "Congratulations."

"Thank you, dear," said Sylvia. "Now, I'm sure it's against the rules, but it's cold out here and we've come a long way. May we please come inside?"

"We promise we won't touch anything," said Andrew.

The woman hesitated, then pushed the door open wider. "Oh, all right," she said. "I can give you fifteen minutes. But if anyone catches us, I only let you in to use the bathroom."

They thanked her and wiped their feet thoroughly on the foyer mat so that they would leave no trace of their visit. The young woman introduced herself as Claire and led them into the library gallery.

Sylvia glimpsed paintings, woven baskets, silk embroidery, pottery, but mindful of the limited time, she continued to search the room instead of admiring them. "The quilts are along that wall," said Claire, pointing, at the same moment Sylvia spotted them.

Sylvia could only nod in reply.

The Crazy Quilt had caught her eye first, for it was so like her mother's, composed of unusual diamond-shaped blocks. It had held her attention for only a moment, though, for beside it hung a New York Beauty quilt.

The colors were right. That much registered as Sylvia crossed the floor, slowly, as if in a dream. The number and arrangement of blocks were right. So was the pattern of hand-quilted stitches flowing in feathered wreaths and plumes as only her mother could have worked them.

She felt Andrew's hand on her elbow just before she ran into the velvet rope stretched before the display. "That's the one, isn't it?" he asked softly.

Sylvia nodded.

Claire had followed them across the room. "Isn't it beautiful?"

"Yes." Sylvia cleared her throat. "It is indeed. What do you know about it?"

Claire shrugged. "Only what I read in the brochure and heard from the art professor who arranged the exhibit."

"I'm afraid I have bad news for your professor," said Sylvia. "I know for a fact that this is not a pioneer-era quilt."

"Oh, he knows that," said Claire, with a laugh. "We use the term 'pioneer' metaphorically. All of the artists featured here were pioneers in their fields—medicine, psychology, child development, politics, and in this woman's case, social reform."

Sylvia's eyebrows shot up. "I beg your pardon?"

"Social reform. She was a key figure in the women's suffrage and labor rights movements. Hold on a moment. Let me get an exhibit guide." Claire hurried off and returned holding a small booklet, which she handed to Sylvia. "Her name was Amelia Langley Davis."

Sylvia accepted the guide, shaking her head at the unfamiliar name. She turned the pages until she came to a brief biography of the artist credited with her mother's work. Amelia Langley Davis was born in England, immigrated to the United States, and worked as a nanny for several years in New York, where she became involved in the workers' rights movement. Upon moving to Boston, and later, to Lowell, Massachusetts, she played a key role in the labor union organizing among garment workers. After serving a prison sentence for "seditious utterings" at a labor rally, she devoted herself to improving the conditions for incarcerated women, including the establishment of several "residential workhouses," where recently released female convicts lived and learned a trade as they adjusted to life outside prison walls.

"She sounds like a remarkable woman," said Sylvia when she finished reading, "but I assure you, she did not make this quilt."

"I know," said Claire, regarding her curiously. "I guess you heard. Well, you're not the only person to think this quilt doesn't belong in this exhibit. I thought so, too, until I heard the story behind it and had some time to think it over."

She turned the page in the exhibit guide and indicated that Sylvia should read on.

NEW YORK BEAUTY QUILT
Pieced, cotton and wool c. 1920–1930

This item is unique among those selected for The Art of Women Pioneers exhibit in that it was not made by the artist, but is instead a piece that she owned and treasured. While the identity of the actual quiltmaker is not known, she is believed to have been one of Amelia Langley Davis's earliest students, most likely a former convict who resided in the first residential workhouse Davis established in Lowell, Massachusetts. It is not certain if Davis supervised the making of this quilt, but the style, pattern, color design, and material selection suggest that she was influential in the quiltmaker's development, almost certainly as her teacher.

According to Davis's journal for April 4, 1950, she acquired the quilt in the town of Waterford, Pennsylvania, from the quiltmaker's daughter. Only one cryptic reference confirms that Davis and the artist knew each other: "It was with a heavy heart that I at last traveled to Waterford, knowing I had delayed my journey too long. I came too late to see her, but I did meet one of her daughters, the eldest. The brother was killed overseas and the other sister's whereabouts are unknown. The eldest sells off her family's possessions. I managed to purchase the New York Beauty, which I knew at once from her letters, although she called the pattern Rocky Mountain. I would have rescued more but her daughter had none left to sell me. It is a cold comfort that at least my dear friend did not live to see her children estranged, her handiwork scattered."

It is known that Davis kept the New York Beauty quilt with her throughout the rest of her life, but the story of its creation has been lost. This piece was included in this collection not because it was precious to her, however, but because it represents Davis's commitment to her students, a crucial facet of the art in which she was a pioneer.

Sylvia looked up from the guide, her gaze fixed on the New York Beauty quilt, but her thoughts far away. Whoever this Amelia Langley Davis was, she must have known Sylvia's mother. The details from her journal could not possibly have referred to any family but the Bergstroms. But if she was such a "dear friend," why had Sylvia's mother never mentioned her—or had she, and had Sylvia carelessly allowed the stories to pass by unheard?

Her mother had confided little about her life before coming to Elm Creek Manor—but Amelia Langley Davis had also lived and worked in New York. Could she have been Sylvia's mother's nanny? Could she have been that distant relative or family friend who had taught her to quilt?

Grief came over Sylvia, for the stories lost, for those pieces of her mother's life she would never know. Now only her quilts remained, silent and steadfast testaments to the woman she had been.

And yet one other part of her legacy remained: Sylvia herself, and all that she recalled, and all that she had yet to discover.

Gazing at the quilt that had so long eluded her, Sylvia resolved to gather the precious scraps of her mother's history and piece them together until a pattern emerged, until she understood as well as any daughter could the choices her mother had made. She had no daughter to pass those stories along to, but she had Sarah, and she had Andrew's children, and among them she would surely find one who would listen, so that her mother's memory would endure.

She would begin by setting the record straight.

"Your booklet is incorrect," Sylvia told Claire. "I don't know for certain how your Amelia Langley Davis knew the quiltmaker, but I do know who she was."

She turned back to face the quilt, her grief forgotten. She had found the New York Beauty at last, and with it, a small portion of her mother's history. For years and years to come, the New England Quilt Museum would share her mother's quilt with the world, and soon, also, the story of the woman whose hopes and dreams and longings still lingered in the soft fabric, in the gentle colors, in the intricate stitches, like the last fading notes of a song.

"My mother made this quilt," said Sylvia, and though Claire regarded her skeptically, Sylvia smiled, knowing that in a moment, Claire would turn over the quilt to reveal the initials and date Eleanor Lockwood Bergstrom had embroidered so many years ago, as if she had known this day would come.

❧

Acknowledgments

This book would not have been possible without the expertise and guidance of Denise Roy, Maria Massie, Rebecca Davis, and Christina Richardson. It is a privilege and a pleasure to work with such talented women.

I am grateful to the Wisconsin Historical Society for providing an outstanding collection of historical resources and for thoughtfully locating it in Madison. Thanks also to Lisa Cass and Christine Lee for playing with my boys while I worked.

Many thanks to the incomparable Anne Spurgeon for reading an early draft of this novel, for the research assistance, for the Monday lunches, and for her friendship.

Thank you to the friends and family who continue to support and encourage me, especially Geraldine Neidenbach, Heather Neidenbach, Nic Neidenbach, Virginia and Edward Riechman, Leonard and Marlene Chiaverini, Rachel and Chip Sauer, and the Tuesday morning moms: Mia McColgan, Leah Montequin, Jane LaMay, and Lori Connolly.

Most of all, I am grateful to my husband, Marty, and my sons, Nicholas and Michael, for everything.

To Marty, Nicholas, and Michael,
with all my love.

CHAPTER ONE

Sarah

January 7, 2002

Dear Friends of Elm Creek Quilts,

Wedding bells rang at Elm Creek Manor much earlier than any of the Elm Creek Quilters could have predicted! While Sylvia Compson's friends were helpfully—we thought—planning her wedding to Andrew Cooper, Sylvia and Andrew made plans of their own. Friends and family gathered at Elm Creek Manor to celebrate Christmas Eve and found ourselves unsuspecting guests at the union of two very dear friends.

The bride was beautiful, the groom charming, the ceremony moving, and the celebration joyful (although admittedly a few of us spent most of the reception recovering from shock). It was a perfect wedding save one glaring omission: Sylvia's bridal quilt. We had not yet sewed a single stitch!

Diane says Sylvia deserves to go without, but the rest of us know that that would be a cruel punishment for someone who has brought quilting into the lives of thousands of aspiring quilters. That's why we're asking all of Sylvia's friends, family, former students, and admirers to help us create a bridal quilt worthy of everyone's favorite Master Quilter.

If you would like to participate in this very special project, please make a 6-inch pieced or appliquéd quilt block using green, rose, blue, gold, and/or cream 100% cotton fabrics. Choose any pattern that represents how Sylvia has influenced you as an artist, teacher, or friend.

Please mail your blocks so they arrive at Elm Creek Manor no later than April 1. If you have any questions, contact Sarah McClure or Summer Sullivan at Elm Creek Manor. Thanks so much for your help, and remember, this is a surprise! Let's show Sylvia we can keep a secret as well as she can.

Yours in Quarter-Inch Seams,
The Elm Creek Quilters

"Did Diane really say that?" asked Summer as she read over the draft.

"No," admitted Sarah, "but it sounds like something she would say, and I thought it was good for a laugh. Should I delete it?"

"No, leave it in. Just don't send her a copy."

Sarah and Summer exchanged a grin, imagining Diane's reaction. Diane had been the last of the Elm Creek Quilters to admit that the Christmas Eve surprise wedding had been truly wonderful—and that was not until a week later, and only grudgingly. For all they knew, maybe Diane had indeed declared that Sylvia deserved to go without a bridal quilt for not sharing her secret with her closest friends.

"Don't you think Sylvia will get suspicious when dozens of blocks start piling up in the mailbox?" asked Summer.

"I'll ask Bonnie if we can have the blocks sent to Grandma's Attic," said Sarah. Bonnie would probably be able to find room in her quilt shop to store the blocks, too, rather than leave them lying about Elm Creek Manor where Sylvia might discover them.

A phone call to Bonnie and a few revisions later, Sarah saved the final version of her letter and began printing out copies for every former camper, every quilt guild that had invited Sylvia to speak, and everyone in Sylvia's address book, hastily borrowed for the cause. She needed to refill the paper tray twice and replace the toner cartridge before the last letter emerged from the printer. Summer seemed to think they would receive dozens of blocks, but Sarah was less certain. Quilters were generous, helpful people, but they also tended to be quite busy. For all their good intentions, most might not be able to contribute a block by the deadline.

With all those hundreds of requests, surely they would receive the 140 blocks Bonnie had calculated they would need for a queen-size comforter. As

Sarah affixed stamps to the envelopes, listening carefully for Sylvia's footsteps in the hall outside the library, she reflected that they might be fortunate to settle for a ninety-six-block lap quilt.

✢

The bridal quilt was Sarah's idea, but the other Elm Creek Quilters were just as enthusiastic about the project—even Diane, who now only rarely complained about having to return the "perfect summer dress" she had purchased for the anticipated June wedding. Sylvia was the heart and soul of Elm Creek Quilt Camp, the business the eight friends had founded, jointly owned, and operated each year from spring to autumn, and not only because Elm Creek Manor was her ancestral home. Sylvia's passion for the artistic, historical, and social aspects of quilting so permeated the quilting retreat that the campers felt her influence in every class, every lecture, and every late-night chat with new friends that took place within the manor's gray stone walls. She had earned the respect, admiration, and affection of every quilter who had passed through the doors of Elm Creek Manor, yet she alone seemed unaware of this. Whenever Sarah tried to explain, as she did on each anniversary of the founding of Elm Creek Quilts, Sylvia cut her off and dismissed her praise as "preposterous." This bridal quilt would finally tell Sylvia what she would not allow Sarah to say.

To Sarah's delight, the first quilt block arrived only a week after the letters went out. The next day, Bonnie phoned with news that two more blocks had come in the morning mail, and after that, packages came so frequently that Bonnie stopped calling to report them. When she offered to bring them to their upcoming business meeting, Sarah couldn't resist. She and Bonnie told all the Elm Creek Quilters except Sylvia to meet in the kitchen thirty minutes early. Sarah figured that would give them plenty of time to examine the blocks, read the accompanying letters, and return the packages to Bonnie's car before Sylvia expected them in the formal parlor.

That Thursday evening, Bonnie arrived first, hustling through the back door and into the kitchen with a Grandma's Attic shopping bag in her arms. "Maybe this was a mistake," she said as Sarah eagerly took the bag and set it on the long wooden table in the center of the room. Bonnie shrugged off her coat and sat down on one of the benches. "All Sylvia has to do is look out the window at the parking lot and she'll know we're here."

"Sylvia's room faces the front of the manor," Sarah reminded her, emptying the bag onto the table. "It's twenty degrees outside, so the windows are shut and the furnace is running. She won't hear the cars pull up."

Bonnie raked her fingers through her close-cropped dark hair and glanced at the doorway. "Even so, we should keep our voices down."

"We're here," Diane sang, strolling into the kitchen, her blond curls bouncing. "Do we have to wait for everyone or can we see the blocks now?"

"Diane, hush, dear," warned white-haired Agnes, following close behind. Her blue eyes were exasperated behind pink-tinted glasses. "Stealth, remember?"

"She's about as stealthy as a thirsty elephant at the only waterhole on the savanna," remarked Gwen, peering in over Diane's shoulder. "You're also blocking the doorway."

"Well, excuse me, professor," Diane shot back, but she took a seat beside Sarah and reached for the envelope on top of the pile.

"Is Summer coming?" Sarah asked Gwen as she helped Agnes with her coat. "I sent her an email, but she didn't write back."

"Who knows what my daughter's up to anymore?" said Gwen. "I've had more meaningful conversations with her answering machine than with her lately."

"Summer has already seen most of the blocks at the quilt shop," said Bonnie. "But I'm sure she'll be here for the meeting."

"Summer never misses them," added Judy as she hurried into the kitchen, removing her gloves. "Unlike some of us. I honestly didn't think I'd make it tonight. When did juggling the schedules of two parents and an eight-year-old become so complicated?"

"When was it not?" asked Bonnie.

Sarah glanced at her watch and opened an envelope. "Let's keep an eye on the time, everyone."

"And keep one ear pointed toward the door," added Judy.

They agreed in whispers and soon were engrossed in passing the blocks around the table, praising them in hushed voices, silently reading the letters their makers had sent. Little Giant, Mother's Favorite, Three Cheers, Trip Around the World—the blocks were as imaginative and as varied as the women who had made them; while Sarah usually couldn't decipher the hidden meaning at first glance, the letters never failed to explain what the blocks represented. Sarah's favorite was a Spinning Hourglass block, which the maker wrote was inspired by a conversation she and Sylvia had participated in over dinner one evening at camp. One of the women at the table had complained that she never had time to quilt at home and had to cram an entire year's worth of quilting into the one week each summer she spent at Elm Creek Manor. "We make time for the things that are important to us," Sylvia had remarked, and she listed several activities people typically participated in out of habit rather than necessity or enjoyment.

The writer said that Sylvia's words resonated with her and when she returned home, she scrutinized her routine to see where she could make better use of her days. After cutting out mindless television watching and delegating some household chores to her husband and teenage sons, she found several hours each week that she could devote to her own interests, including quilting. "Sylvia showed me that although we never have enough time for all the things we want to do," she concluded, "if we simplify our busy lives, we can keep them from spinning out of our control."

Sarah tucked the block and letter back into the envelope, ruefully running through her mental checklist of daily activities and wondering which she could sacrifice.

"Sarah?" called a distant voice. "Where is everyone?"

They scrambled up from the benches. "Quick," Gwen hissed, but the others were already returning the quilt blocks and letters to their envelopes and tossing them into the bag.

"Someone stall her," whispered Sarah frantically just as someone thrust the bag into her arms.

"Sarah?" Sylvia's voice came louder now, her footfalls swiftly approaching. "I don't have time for hide-and-seek."

Sarah flung open the pantry. She threw the bag inside and slammed the door just as Sylvia entered the kitchen.

"Sarah—" Sylvia stopped short in the doorway and eyed the gathering. "Well, for goodness' sakes. Why are you here so early?" She fixed her gaze on Sarah. "And why are you clinging to that door for dear life?"

"Because—" Sarah opened the door and retrieved the first item her hand touched. "They came early to help me make brownies. I was just getting the mix. Do you know if we have eggs? I was going to stop at the store, but—"

"You need six people to make brownies?"

"Sarah's never been much of a cook," offered Diane.

"Nonsense," said Sylvia, and gestured to the cellophane-wrapped plate on the counter. "She made lemon squares this morning."

"Should we get started?" asked Judy, reaching for an apron hanging on a peg beside the pantry door.

"Don't be ridiculous," said Sylvia, glancing at the clock. "We have a lot to cover tonight. We shouldn't waste time preparing extraneous desserts."

"Chocolate is never extraneous," said Gwen, but the others quickly agreed with Sylvia, eager to get her out of the kitchen.

They gathered in the formal parlor, where the original west wing of Elm Creek Manor intersected the south wing, added when Sylvia's father was a boy. The antique Victorian furnishings might have seemed stuffy if they were not so comfortably worn. Sylvia had once mentioned that her paternal grandmother had brought the overstuffed sofas, embroidered armchairs, beaded lamps, and ornate cabinets to Elm Creek Manor upon her marriage to David Bergstrom. No one else in the family had cared for the young bride's tastes, so they had arranged the furniture in a spare room and proclaimed it too fine for everyday use. Thus the newest member of the family had not felt slighted, and the Bergstroms were able to keep the west sitting room, their preferred place for quilting and visiting, exactly as it was. In more recent decades, the Bergstroms had grown more fond of the room, but even now the only nod to modernity was a large television in the corner, concealed by a Grandmother's Fan quilt whenever it was not in use.

Sarah began the meeting with an update on registration for the coming season. Enrollment was up fifteen percent, and there were so many requests for Gwen's Photo Transfer workshop that they had decided to add a second weekly session. "If you're up for it," added Sarah, glancing at Gwen.

Gwen shrugged. "Why not? Once the spring semester ends, I'll have plenty of time."

"Bonnie, I also thought we should add a few extra shuttles into town so campers can shop," Sarah continued. "Since they'll want to visit Grandma's Attic, we'll arrange them for when you can be fully staffed, okay? I wouldn't want one person to get swamped."

"Oh. Great." Bonnie hesitated. "Do you need to know the best times of the day now? Because I'm not really sure—"

"Just get back to me whenever you know." Sarah gave Bonnie an encouraging smile. She knew the quilt shop owner appreciated the extra business Elm Creek Quilt Camp sent her way, but she always seemed embarrassed by it, as if she thought she was taking advantage of their friendship. "You'll probably want your camp course schedule first."

Bonnie nodded, so Sarah glanced at her notes. "Oh. One more thing. This goes for everyone. Please remember to charge anything you use in your classes to supplies, not overhead. If we ever get audited—"

"I'm here," said Summer, rushing in red-cheeked from the cold and struggling out of her coat. "I'm sorry I'm late."

"Relax," said Diane. "This isn't the first time."

"Yes, but your tardiness has been increasing lately," mused Sylvia. "I can't imagine what has been keeping you so busy."

Summer draped her coat over the back of a chair and sat down. "What did I miss?"

"Sorry, Sylvia," said Judy with a laugh. "I don't think Summer wants to discuss her boyfriend."

Everyone except Summer laughed, but she managed a wry smile. "Fine. I was having supper with Jeremy. Satisfied?"

"You guys spend so much time together you might as well live together," said Diane.

"Don't suggest such a thing," protested Agnes. She patted Summer's hand. "She meant after you get married, dear."

Summer blanched, and Gwen said, "Married? Are you crazy? Don't go putting thoughts of marriage in my daughter's head. Or of living together. My daughter has more sense than that."

"As a newlywed myself, I object to the implications of that remark," retorted Sylvia. "Sometimes getting married makes perfect sense."

Agnes nodded, but Bonnie said, "Sometimes marriage makes no sense at all."

"Can we please get back to business?" begged Summer, throwing Sarah a pleading look.

Sarah promptly returned to her agenda despite grumbles from Diane, who apparently found teasing Summer far more interesting.

Midway through the meeting, Sylvia offered to return to the kitchen for refreshments, but Bonnie leapt to her feet and announced that it was her turn. She returned with the lemon squares, coffee, and a look of relief so plain that Sarah knew the quilt blocks were safely hidden away in her car.

That night, as Sarah and her husband prepared for bed, she told him about the afternoon's mishap. Matt laughed and said, "Why didn't you just go to Grandma's Attic and look at the blocks there?"

"Because every time I say I'm going downtown, Sylvia asks to come with me. I can't very well ask her to stay in the van while I go into the quilt shop."

"No, I guess not," Matt acknowledged. "And I guess delaying your trip downtown until you could go alone was out of the question?"

Sarah drew back the quilt and climbed into bed. "Absolutely."

Matt grinned and shook his head as he joined her. "Sorry to be the one to have to tell you this, but there's no way you're going to keep this quilt a secret very long."

"What do you mean?"

"You've never been good at keeping secrets."

"That's not true," Sarah protested, nudging him. "My friends trust me implicitly. I could tell you stories—but of course I *won't*."

"Not other people's secrets. Your own. You have this overwhelming need to confess."

"I do not."

"I bet Sylvia will know about this bridal quilt before the first day of camp."

"And I know for a fact she won't." Sarah propped herself up on her elbows and regarded him. "Okay, if you're so sure, let's do it."

"Do what?"

"Make a bet. I say that Sylvia won't know about the quilt until we give her the pieced top. You can say whatever dumb thing you like, because you're going to lose."

"I'm not going to lose," said Matt firmly. "Okay. You have a bet. What am I going to win?"

"Nothing, but I'm going to win breakfast in bed for a week. Prepared by your own hands, so don't pass the work off on the cook."

"It won't be a problem, because I'm going to win five new apple trees for my orchard."

"Five? Then I get two weeks of breakfast, with the newspaper and a foot massage."

"Done." Matt held out his hand. "Shake on it?"

Sarah smiled, took his hand, and pulled him close. "I'd much rather kiss."

❧

For the next two weeks, Sarah resisted the temptation to invite Bonnie to bring the most recently arrived blocks to Elm Creek Manor, resigning herself to hasty descriptions over the phone and Bonnie's assurances that if this pace continued, they would have all the blocks they needed well in advance of the deadline. Nearly three weeks passed before Sarah finally managed to sneak away to Grandma's Attic after dropping off Sylvia at her hairdresser.

Sarah drove the white Elm Creek Quilts minivan onto Main Street, which marked the border between downtown Waterford and the Waterford College campus. She tried to park in the alley behind Grandma's Attic, but an unfamiliar car already occupied the space reserved for Bonnie's employees. Because Bonnie's only remaining employees were Diane and Summer, she invited the Elm Creek Quilters to use the extra space, since downtown parking was scarce. But none of the Elm Creek Quilters owned the gleaming luxury sedan parked beside Bonnie's twenty-year-old compact. In fact, only a few of them could have afforded the payments.

Apparently a customer had discovered the secret parking space. Sarah hoped the driver liked to spend as much on fabric as she did on transportation. Bonnie never complained, but Sarah suspected the competition from the large chain fabric store on the outskirts of town had been siphoning off her revenues more than usual. Grandma's Attic had sometimes dipped dangerously into the red, but even then, Bonnie had managed to keep any hint of trouble far from her customers' view. Lately, however, Sarah noticed she had begun rearranging her shelves to conceal gaps in her inventory rather than restocking them.

Sarah found another spot not far away on Second Street and hurried down the hill to Main, turning up her collar and thrusting her hands in her pockets since she had forgotten her scarf and gloves. In the front shop window, beneath the familiar red sign with the words GRANDMA'S ATTIC printed in gold, hung several sample quilts Bonnie and Diane had made as demonstration projects for their classes at quilt camp. The front bell jingled when Sarah entered, but a glance at the cutting table in the center of the room and a quick survey of the aisles told her Bonnie was not in the main store area. "Bonnie?" Sarah called over the folk music playing in the background, just as she glimpsed her friend through the window of the back office. Bonnie was speaking earnestly—or heatedly—with a man in a well-tailored coat of rich black wool, who at that moment turned his back on her and strode briskly from the office. Something about his smug, self-satisfied grin plucked at Sarah's memory and, as he passed her and nodded on his way to the door, recognition struck her with the shock of cold water. She spun around and watched the door swing shut behind him, then turned back to Bonnie, who had followed him from the office.

"Wasn't that Gregory Krolich?" asked Sarah. Bonnie nodded and sat down on a stool behind the cutting table. "I knew it. The real estate business must be treating him well. He's driving an even more expensive car than the last time I saw him."

"You know him?"

"Barely. I haven't seen him in years, not since I first moved to Waterford. He wanted to buy Elm Creek Manor and raze it so he could build a few hundred student apartments on the property."

"Obviously he didn't," said Bonnie. "So he's just a lot of threats and bluster in a nice suit?"

Sarah shook her head. "On the contrary, I'm sure he would have gone through with it if Sylvia hadn't found out about his plan. She refused to sell to him once she learned the truth."

"Oh." Bonnie studied the cutting table for a moment. "So. Do you want to see the blocks?"

"Of course," said Sarah, removing her coat. "I have about twenty minutes before I need to pick up Sylvia."

Bonnie disappeared into the storage room and returned with a large cardboard box, which she said contained thirty-four blocks. She seemed so pleased that Sarah hid her dismay. A month into the project, and they had received only a small fraction of the blocks they needed. As Bonnie separated the newest packages from the ones Sarah had already seen, Sarah reminded herself that they were averaging one new block a day, and that contributors typically provided their blocks either right away or at the very last minute. Surely in the last week before the deadline, Grandma's Attic would be inundated with blocks. If not, Sarah would work overtime at her sewing machine to make up the difference.

"Look at this," Sarah marveled as she opened the first envelope and found an exquisite Bridal Wreath block. "I will never be able to appliqué this well."

"Only because you won't practice."

Sarah returned the block to its envelope and opened a second. "Queen Charlotte's Crown? It's lovely, but what does it have to do with Sylvia?"

Bonnie watched as Sarah put the block away and reached for another. "Why don't you read the letter and find out?"

"Can't. Sylvia expects me back at twenty past, and if I'm late, she's sure to ask questions." Sarah admired a Steps to the Altar block. "She'll know if I'm lying, too."

"Well, you can't leave without reading this one." Bonnie handed her a package somewhat thicker than the others. "You know the quilters who sent it."

Intrigued, Sarah took the thick padded envelope and withdrew two blocks, a Grandmother's Pride and a Mother's Delight. "I'm guessing these two are related," she said, unfolding the letter.

February 6, 2002

Dear Elm Creek Quilters,

Thank you so much for inviting us to participate in this gift for Sylvia. We know it will be a spectacular quilt and look forward to seeing it when we return to camp for our annual reunion of the Cross-Country Quilters.

Deciding to participate was easy, but choosing appropriate blocks proved far more difficult. Fortunately, we see each other frequently, so we have been able to share our thoughts. Sylvia has inspired us with her courageous attitude toward life, her insistence upon excellence, her steadfast dedication to her craft, and in so many other ways that we're sure it's evident why no single block could express what we feel for her. So instead we decided to focus on how Sylvia most directly influenced our lives simply by creating Elm Creek Quilt Camp.

Vinnie, as you recall, was one of the first campers of Elm Creek Quilt Camp's inaugural season. Recently widowed, she wanted to attend camp during the week of her birthday rather than try to celebrate in the home she had so recently shared with her husband. At quilt camp she found friendship and fun, and discovered in Sylvia a fellow widow, but one with a far more tragic past. Sylvia's story of how she had lost her husband in World War II reminded Vinnie that she should not dwell upon what she had lost, but cherish and be thankful for the many decades she and her husband had spent together.

A few years later, Megan first attended quilt camp and, although she did not then realize it, meeting Vinnie would prove to be one of the most important moments of her life—and not only because Vinnie is as remarkable and inspirational as Sylvia herself. Vinnie was eager to find a sweetheart for her favorite grandson, Adam, and with a little meddling that Megan failed to appreciate at the time, she finally succeeded in arranging for the two to meet. The couple had the usual ups and downs (and a few that were not at all usual) on the path to love, but six months ago, Adam and Megan were married in St. James of the Valley Church in Cincinnati, with Megan's son, Rob, as best man. Adam, Megan, and Rob are all thrilled that in July a new baby will join their family. Rob says we should name the baby Sylvia if she is a girl and Elmer if he is a boy, because this child never would have come into the world if not for Elm Creek Quilt Camp.

How can one or even two quilt blocks adequately represent what Sylvia has done for our family? We admit no single pattern could, but we think Grandmother's Pride and Mother's Delight come close.

Please let us know if we can do anything more to help complete Sylvia's bridal quilt. If you need additional blocks, Vinnie has six all ready to put in the mail to you!

> Love to you all,
> Vinnie Burkholder and
> Megan (Donohue) Wagner

❧

At the bottom of the typed page was a postscript added in spidery handwriting: "I'm sure you can tell Megan wrote this letter and kindly allowed me to add my name to it. It doesn't sound like me at all! I never would have bragged I was as remarkable and inspirational as Sylvia, not that anyone would have believed it anyway! I hope the baby is a girl, not just because I don't care for the name Elmer but because I've already made her a pink-and-white Ohio Star quilt. Hugs and Kisses from Vinnie."

"Megan and Vinnie's grandson got married!" exclaimed Sarah. "Sylvia will be thrilled."

"Don't tell her yet," said Bonnie, taking the blocks and the letter. "You'll have to explain how you know, and you're a terrible liar."

"I suppose you're going to tell me I can't keep secrets, either."

Bonnie winced. "No offense. I trust you with my secrets—most of them— but when it comes to your own—"

"You can stop there. I've heard it before, from Matt."

"Sorry."

"Frankly, it's not the worst thing in the world to be a terrible liar. At least everyone knows when I'm telling the truth."

"Even so, you'd better think of a convincing story pretty fast," advised Bonnie, nodding to the clock.

It was already a quarter past eleven. Sarah glanced about in dismay and put her hand on the nearest bolt of fabric. "Cut me a yard of this, would you?"

Bonnie rang up the charges quickly, and within two minutes Sarah was hurrying back to the minivan. As she rehearsed her cover story on the way to the salon, she realized Sylvia would never believe she had spent the entire time in the quilt shop only to emerge with a single yard of fabric. She took a sharp left at the town square and parked in front of the Daily Grind. Sylvia might more readily accept that Sarah had lost track of time in a coffee shop.

The early lunch crowd was just beginning to gather as Sarah joined the line. She bought herself a large latte and ordered a hot cocoa with whipped cream to appease Sylvia. As she stirred sugar and vanilla into her steaming cup, she glanced up and saw a familiar figure at a corner table. She didn't have time to chat, but just as she turned to go, Judy caught her eye and froze.

Sarah smiled and waved, but Judy appeared so discomfited that Sarah realized her friend must have noticed her attempt to avoid her and wondered at the cause. A cup in each hand, she made her way to the table Judy was sharing with a shaggy-haired man in a business suit.

"Judy, hi," she said, smiling at Judy and her companion in turn. "I thought I'd get my caffeine fix while Sylvia's getting her hair done."

"You must have had a late night," said Judy, noting the two cups.

"Oh, no, this one's a peace offering for Sylvia. I'm late."

"Sorry you can't join us," said the man with a smile.

With a start, Judy quickly introduced him as a colleague visiting from the University of Pennsylvania. Sarah set down her coffee long enough to shake his hand, then made a hasty exit. She would be even later now, but at least she had a truthful and, better yet, believable excuse.

To Sarah's surprise, when she arrived, Sylvia wasn't waiting by the front door in her coat and hat. Sarah found her in the back of the salon with her hands beneath a nail dryer. "Sarah, dear," Sylvia greeted her. "You were so late they talked me into a manicure."

Sarah apologized and offered her the hot cocoa, which Sylvia couldn't pick up at the moment anyway. Sarah rambled through an account of Grandma's Attic and the Daily Grind, which was mercifully cut short by the timer on the nail dryer. "Do you know I never get my nails done?" said Sylvia, admiring her hands. "Quilting is so hard on them that I usually don't bother, but the young lady was so persuasive. You showed up just in time or they would have convinced me to let them do my toes, too."

Sylvia paid the manicurist and gave her a healthy tip, then happily took her cocoa. She lifted the lid and inhaled the fragrance of the still-steaming chocolate. "If this is real whipped cream, don't you dare tell Andrew."

"It's the real thing and I wouldn't breathe a word."

Sylvia laughed and tucked her arm through Sarah's and, to Sarah's deep satisfaction, nothing in her manner suggested she doubted Sarah's ability to keep their little secret. It wasn't until they were halfway home that Sarah realized she had forgotten to ask Bonnie what Greg Krolich had been doing in Grandma's Attic. She resolved to phone Bonnie that evening and inquire, but at supper, Matt quickly made her forget all about the unexpected encounter.

"You look great, Sylvia," he began as he passed the bread basket to Andrew. "Did you do something different with your hair?"

Sylvia touched her hair, pleased. "Why, thank you for noticing, Matthew. My stylist talked me into some highlights."

"Take a look at those nails," said Andrew. Sylvia obliged by regally extending a hand. "My bride's gotten herself all dolled up, and I keep scratching my head wondering what special occasion I forgot."

Sylvia laughed. "The only special occasion is that Sarah was late picking me up."

Matt turned to Sarah, his eyes wide with false innocence. "Sarah, late? Usually she's the one keeping us all on schedule. What kept you?"

"Nothing, sweetheart." Sarah gave him a look of warning. "I stopped for some coffee—"

"And fabric," added Sylvia. "You can't forget that, although why you left with such a small purchase I honestly don't know. Bonnie could use the business."

"That is strange," exclaimed Matt. "What were you doing at Grandma's Attic all that time if you weren't shopping?"

"You know how it is. I got started talking with Bonnie, and then, well, I looked up at the clock and I barely had enough time to get coffee before Sylvia expected me." Sarah set down her fork and glared at Matt. "If it bothers you so much, I'll go back tomorrow and spend all the money for your Valentine's Day present on fabric for myself."

Matt could barely hide his grin. "You don't have to go that far."

"Sarah, dear, relax," said Sylvia, astounded. "Goodness. Everyone's allowed to be late once in a while. He's only teasing you. There was no harm done."

"You're right." She smiled sweetly at Matt so that he would be sure to know the real harm was yet to come. "I'm sorry, honey."

Sylvia seemed satisfied, but Matt could only manage a weak grin.

She cornered him by the kitchen sink after Sylvia and Andrew retired to the parlor to watch the news. "All right," she said, snapping a dish towel at him. "We're adding a codicil to our wager. If Sylvia finds out about the quilt because of you, it doesn't count."

"I'm not going to tell her," he protested.

"That's not good enough. If you force the truth out of me in front of her, or trick any of our friends into revealing the secret, or accidentally on purpose leave one of the quilt blocks on her chair, I win the bet." She extended her hand. "Shake on it."

He took her hand gingerly. "No kiss?"

"Not this time."

"Does this mean you're not getting me a Valentine's present?"

"Oh, no. You'll get exactly the present you deserve."

Two days later, a still-contrite Matt brought Sarah breakfast in bed, and he gave her a thorough foot massage while she read the paper. Only afterward did he mention that he was trying to make up for all the breakfasts in bed she would not receive once he won the bet. Sarah didn't take offense. Instead she made him a Dutch apple pie to compensate for the apple trees she had no intention of buying him.

✿

The first day of the new season of quilt camp was rapidly approaching, and Sarah's days were filled with the minutiae of the business: processing registration forms, scheduling classes, ordering supplies, mailing out welcome packets, assigning rooms and sometimes roommates. Amid the chaos, Sarah wondered how the campers could not fail to notice how she scrambled to make everything run smoothly. Summer assisted her by planning evening entertainment programs and inviting guest speakers, and together they wrestled with the problems of last-minute course adjustments. Already it seemed apparent that Gwen's Hand-Dyeing and Agnes's Baltimore Album courses would not be filled throughout March, while Diane's class for beginners and Judy's seminar in computer design were in heavy demand. It was no small feat to adjust the schedule in a way that would please everyone.

When Sarah and Summer decided they had done the best they could, Summer phoned the instructors involved to see if they would agree to the changes. In the meantime, Sarah went through invoices and contacted the distributors who—for reasons they could not explain—had still not delivered supplies Sarah had ordered months before. Summer hung up the phone in defeat long before Sarah had sorted out her own problems. "What is wrong with everyone this year?" asked Summer, dropping into a chair in front of the library fireplace, which still held a few logs in cynical mistrust of the calendar. "Agnes was home, of course; you can always count on Agnes. But Diane, Judy, and my mom are incommunicado. My mom won't even pick up her cell phone."

"She's probably in class."

"Not all day. She ought to be in her office by now." Summer let her head fall back against the cushions. "People could try to be a little more accessible at this time of year."

"Diane's so stressed out about Todd's college acceptances that she's probably too jittery to sit by the phone. Judy's either at work or with Emily, and you know better than anyone how busy your mom is."

Summer snorted in grudging acceptance.

"Besides, if anyone's inaccessible, it's you," remarked Sarah. "You rarely answer your email anymore and never answer your phone. All anyone can ever get is your machine. By the way, I think it might be broken. There's no outgoing message anymore, just a beep."

"Oh. Thanks. I'll look into it."

"You should. Last week I called three times in a row just to make sure I had the right number." Sarah leafed through a pile of registration forms and sighed. "How does Agnes feel about canceling her appliqué class?"

"She'd rather not. She doesn't care if there are only four students. If they want to learn to appliqué, she's willing to teach them."

"I guess we should keep it on the schedule, then." Better that than writing apologetic letters to the four campers and trying to squeeze them into their second-choice classes.

"Did you know Agnes started piecing the top for Sylvia's bridal quilt?"

Sarah set down the forms, instantly attentive. "No. Does that mean we have enough blocks?"

"Not quite. She's adding an elaborate pieced border to compensate."

Sarah smiled ruefully. "I had hoped to receive a better response."

"We still might. There's a whole month before the deadline. Agnes just wanted to work ahead since camp starts in almost three weeks." Summer studied the unlit fireplace. "Have you decided what block you're going to make?"

"I have no idea." Sarah had been so preoccupied with the other blocks that she had never given her own a thought. She had not even checked her fabric stash to see if she had the right colors. "What pattern did you choose?"

"I was hoping to steal some ideas from you." Summer rose and stretched. "Back to work. Maybe my mom's in her office by now."

Sarah nodded, lost in thought.

What block could possibly convey all that Sylvia meant to her?

❧

Either Summer was unable to reach her mother or she forgot that she was supposed to contact Sarah with Gwen's response, because Sarah did not hear from either woman until their business meeting the following Thursday evening. In the past Gwen had protested any cuts in her teaching schedule, insisting that holding a class with only one student was far preferable to disappointing the one camper who had registered. Sarah and Gwen had gone through the same debate so often that this time Sarah came prepared with documented evidence proving that one-student classes, while good enough in theory, could be a financial disaster. But when she took Gwen aside before the meeting and recommended that they cancel her dyeing workshops for the first two weeks of camp, Gwen merely shrugged. She added something vague about possibly directing a seminar on the sociopolitical implications of quilt contests instead, but she drifted off to the parlor before waiting for Sarah's response.

Throughout the meeting, Sarah gradually realized that Gwen was not the only one who seemed inordinately distracted. Bonnie looked tired and pale, as if she had not slept in days. Agnes, too, must have noticed, for she watched Bonnie all evening with a look of carefully muted concern. Summer paid more attention to her watch than to Sarah's updates about enrollment, and twice Judy left the room to take calls on her cell phone. Their behavior was puzzling, but Diane's was downright irritating; she stormed in twenty minutes late muttering about admissions counselors and tuition payments, then spent the rest of the meeting tapping her pen against her notebook and scowling.

Finally Sarah had had enough. "While we're on the subject of guest lecturers, Jane Smith has agreed to speak to our campers in August. That's perfect timing because, as you know, Jane is the world-famous Naked Quilter, and she requires that all of her lectures be conducted entirely in the nude. Students included. I decided we should make all of Elm Creek Quilt Camp go naked for the whole week so her students don't feel self-conscious. Matt, Andrew, and the rest of the male staff should wear fig leaves so our more sensitive campers aren't offended."

Everyone but Sylvia nodded absently. "Are you out of your mind?" Sylvia gasped.

"What?" said Summer. "What did she say?"

"If any of you had been listening, you would know." Sarah took a deep breath and made herself count to ten. "Look. I realize you're all busy and that you have lives and jobs outside of camp. But it seems to me that you're beginning to take Elm Creek Quilts for granted. I realize we've been very successful very quickly, but contrary to appearances, this camp does not run itself. I can't do it without you, so please, while you're here, really be *here*, okay?"

Abashed, the Elm Creek Quilters nodded and murmured apologies.

"Jane Smith, the Naked Quilter, indeed," said Sylvia. "I suppose there is no such person. Pity. That certainly would have been an interesting week."

"Jane Smith the who?" said Diane.

"No one." Sylvia shrugged. "Serves you right for not listening."

As far as Sarah could tell, they hung on her every word for the rest of the meeting.

❧

Whenever Sarah could find a spare moment from the frenzy of camp preparations, she pored through Sylvia's library of quilt-pattern books trying to find the perfect block. With no time to idly admire the illustrations, she began with the index and read through the names, trying to find one that was suitable. A block called Homecoming evoked Sylvia's return to Elm Creek Manor after a fifty-year absence and also the launch of Elm Creek Quilts, but one glance at the pattern told Sarah it would be too difficult. Many blocks incorporated the word *Friendship* into their names, but while Sarah liked several of the designs, she suspected everyone else would be looking for some sort of "Friendship" block, too, and she wanted her choice to be more distinctive. With only one week before the first day of camp, Sarah finally settled on Sarah's Favorite, for Sylvia was certainly Sarah's favorite quilter and ran a very close second with Matt for her all-around favorite person. The approaching deadline nagged her, but as the organizer of the project, she figured she could extend the deadline if circumstances warranted. Readying Elm Creek Manor for its first guests of the season certainly qualified.

Sarah found a perfect rose-colored floral print in her stash and stopped by Grandma's Attic to pick up a few coordinating fat quarters in blue and leaf green. She cut the squares and triangles that same day and sewed the pieces together late at night, after Sylvia retired.

"Nice," Matt remarked a few evenings later, when she had nearly finished. He had come to the sitting room adjoining their bedroom, Sarah's de facto sewing room, to see when she planned to come to bed.

Sarah thanked him and sighed as he began rubbing her shoulders. She hoped her block would be good enough. It was well made—she'd had an exacting teacher—but most of the blocks sent to Grandma's Attic were far more elaborate.

"You know," she mused, "I think I might want shoulder rubs on alternate days rather than foot massages for the entire two weeks."

"I still have two more days to win this bet."

Sarah laughed. "I admire your confidence, misplaced though it is."

"You have to admit you skewed the odds in your favor with your codicil."

"And you have to admit that dropping hints to Sylvia would have been unfair."

"Explicitly telling her about the quilt would have been cheating," Matt acknowledged. "But hints would have been fair. Tricking you into revealing the secret would have been the best of all."

Sarah turned in her chair and regarded him. "Why are you so eager for Sylvia to find out about our surprise?"

"I'm not. I just want those apple trees." Matt paused. "Want to play double or nothing?"

"When I'm this close to winning? No, thanks."

"You'd turn down four weeks of breakfast in bed? You must be closer to spilling the truth than I thought."

"Hardly. What are your terms?"

"Double or nothing, Sylvia will find out about the quilt before it's finished."

"Finished as in all the blocks sewn together or as in quilted and bound?" They were planning to set up the pieced top in Sylvia's quilt frame on the ballroom dais so campers could contribute stitches throughout the spring and summer. Sarah had planned to present the pieced top to Sylvia before then, for they would be unable to conceal it and still allow the campers to work on it.

She hid her glee when Matt said, "I want to pick out my trees soon, so let's say until all the blocks are sewn into a top. But I want more leeway with this codicil."

"Sylvia can't learn about the quilt from you," Sarah warned.

"But anything else is fair game."

For four weeks of breakfast in bed, why not? Since Agnes had already begun to assemble the top, surely Sarah would only need to keep the quilt secret until mid-April, at the latest. "You have a deal." She extended her hand, but the words had barely left her lips before Matt bent down and kissed them.

❧

A week of late nights and early mornings followed. Sarah finished her block on the last evening before quilt camp and spent most of that night lying awake, running over last-minute details in her mind. She fell asleep sometime after three and stumbled down to the kitchen the next morning, bleary-eyed and yawning, to find Sylvia, Andrew, and Matt already seated at the kitchen table. As Sarah took her seat beside Matt, the cook, recently returned from his annual monthlong vacation, placed steaming plates of blueberry pancakes before them.

"Sarah, dear, you look exhausted," said Sylvia.

"She should," said Matt. "She stayed up half the night quilting."

"I did not."

"Sarah," scolded Sylvia gently. "You should have gotten more rest. Today's a busy day."

"That's what I told her, but she kept at it," said Matt.

"What on earth was so important that you had to finish last night?" asked Sylvia. "It couldn't have been a class sample. You aren't teaching this week."

Sarah took a hasty bite of pancake. "These are delicious," she called to the cook.

"Sarah?"

"Oh, Sylvia, don't believe a word Matt says. I was done sewing by ten-thirty and in bed by eleven. You know how it is when you see a new quilt pattern and just have to try it out right away."

"Hmph." Sylvia looked dubious. "Well, do I get to see this amazing quilt block?"

Matt shot Sarah a look of triumph, but she did her best to sound unconcerned. "Sure. Later. If I remember." It was the first day of quilt camp. She would have abundant excuses to forget.

Satisfied, Sylvia let her off with a warning that she should make sure to go to bed early that night. Sarah laughed, knowing how impossible that would be, but assured Sylvia she would try. As the conversation turned to other matters, Sarah raised her eyebrows at Matt, smug. He lifted his coffee mug to her to acknowledge his defeat, but she suspected he considered it a temporary setback. Matt wanted those apple trees, and he intended to fight dirty.

At twelve o'clock, the first sixty quilters of the new camp season began to arrive. The Elm Creek Quilters had gathered well before then to arrange registration tables in the grand front foyer and to go through the guest rooms to be certain no detail had been overlooked. Agnes and Diane arranged fresh flowers from the cutting garden on each bedside table to assure every guest received a proper welcome, while Judy and Gwen checked with the cook to be sure all was ready for the Welcome Banquet. Bonnie and Summer gave the classrooms one last inspection, as Sylvia helped Sarah set out forms and organize room keys. Matt and Andrew stood ready to assist arriving guests with their luggage, while the rest of the staff bustled about, filled as they all were with the expectation and excitement that heralded each new season of Elm Creek Quilt Camp. As far as Sarah could discern, the distraction that had afflicted her friends earlier that month had completely disappeared.

A few minor problems surfaced during registration: Two friends who had wanted to room together had been paired with total strangers, and a woman who had registered for the following week had shown up early, totally unaware of her mistake. Sarah and Sylvia resolved these minor crises before anyone had time to become too anxious, and once again Sarah marveled at their illusion of flawless service. No wonder people assumed the camp ran itself!

The Welcome Banquet was the best one yet, and the Candlelight ceremony at sunset on the cornerstone patio was like a warm embrace, drawing campers and faculty alike into a close circle of friendship. After the last guests retired for the night—or, more likely, gathered in neighbors' rooms to renew old friendships and initiate new ones—Sarah returned to her library office to go over a few last-minute details for the classes that would begin the following morning. She could not keep the smile off her face as she listened to footfalls going from room to room and laughter muffled behind closed doors. Elm Creek Manor had become her home and she loved it in any season, but it truly came to life when it was filled with quilters.

Sarah did not get to bed as early as she had promised Sylvia, but Matt was even a few minutes later. As the manor's caretaker, his workload increased exponentially when the estate was full of visitors. He seemed so content, though, that Sarah knew he had come to enjoy his role in the company as much as she did hers.

Still, as they lay down beneath the sampler quilt she had made for him as an anniversary gift so many years before, she could not resist teasing him. "I sure hope camp runs as smoothly as Sylvia's bridal quilt project," she said, exaggerating a yawn. "Agnes finished her pieced border, and is just waiting for the last blocks to arrive so she can sew it all together."

Matt feigned sleep, punctuating Sarah's remark with a snore.

❧

Sarah's alarm woke her at half past six, and by seven she was descending the carved oak staircase and hurrying to the kitchen. The cook and his two assistants had breakfast well in hand—and seemed surprised and even hurt that Sarah had felt it necessary to check—so she returned to the banquet hall to join Matt. Sylvia and Andrew, both early risers, had already finished eating and were nursing cups of coffee and chatting with a group of campers. Matt had joined them, so Sarah hurried through the buffet and took the seat he had saved for her. So many enthusiastic campers came by to greet her that Sarah had barely managed to take a few quick gulps of coffee before she was summoned to the phone.

She grabbed half a bagel and munched on it as she hurried to the nearest private phone, in the formal parlor. Judy was on the line, breathless. "Sarah, I'm so sorry to do this—"

"What's wrong?"

"I have to go out of town, so I can't teach my classes today or tomorrow. I might be able to make it back by Wednesday, but I won't know until later today. I'm sorry I can't at least teach my ten o'clock today, but I have to leave for Philadelphia by nine—"

"Is your mom all right?"

"Yes, yes, she's fine. It's for work. I have to meet with some professors at Penn."

"But it's spring break." They always scheduled the first week of camp to coincide with spring break, to lighten the burden on Judy and Gwen.

"It's Waterford College's spring break, not Penn's. I'm so sorry for the short notice. I just found out five minutes ago. Apparently they sent a letter, but I never received it."

"That's all right," said Sarah bleakly. "These things happen. We'll find someone to cover for you."

"Thank you, Sarah. Thank you. I swear I'll make it up to you. Look, I have sample quilts for display and handouts and lesson plans. I'll drop them off on my way."

"That would be great." It was as far from great as Sarah could imagine, but what else could she say?

Judy thanked her profusely and hung up. Sarah tossed her bagel in the trash and raced upstairs to the library. Ordinarily she could recite the teaching schedule from memory, but at the moment, she couldn't think of a single available instructor. She rifled through her files, found the weekly class schedule, and let out a moan. Judy's morning workshop was Bindings and Borders, and only Diane was free from ten o'clock until noon. Judy's class taught participants how to draft original pieced borders and how to finish the quilted tops in unusual fashions—scalloped edges, spiral bindings, contrasting piping, prairie points. While Diane might be able to handle the drafting-borders segment of the class, she had never attempted the unusual bindings. For that matter, neither had Sarah.

She sank into the high-backed leather chair and spread the papers out on the desk. Judy's afternoon class was a weeklong program in computer-aided design. Summer knew how to use that software—Sarah shuffled some pages—and she was free from four until five every day that week except Wednesday, when she worked a longer shift at Grandma's Attic. Agnes had that afternoon off, as did Bonnie and Gwen. Gwen. Perfect.

The door opened and Sylvia entered. "I thought I'd find you here." She crossed the room and set a steaming cup of coffee on a coaster on the desktop. "When you didn't come back to breakfast, I made some inquiries and discovered you had been spotted racing upstairs, a look of sheer panic on your face."

Sarah filled Sylvia in on Judy's abrupt cancellations and her attempts to adjust the schedule. "The afternoon class should be fine, as long as Summer and Gwen agree. As for this morning—" She folded her arms on the desk and buried her face in them. "I don't see how to resolve this."

"It's simple, really," said Sylvia, patting Sarah's shoulder. "I'll teach it. I've made all of those bindings and borders more times than I could count."

"You? But you have . . ." Sarah sat up and shifted around some papers. "You have your Hand-Quilting class from ten to eleven. Do you mean change the seminar from eleven until one? Because we can't. We need the classroom, and the students will need time for lunch."

"No, dear, that's not what I mean. I'll take over Judy's seminar. You'll teach my Hand-Quilting class."

"Me?"

"Why not? You're a fine hand-quilter."

"But I've never taught that class before." She had only taught Beginning Piecing and Quick Piecing, and she always planned the classroom time down to the minute and would rehearse for weeks in advance. "There must be someone else."

"I'm sure Andrew would do it if we asked, but since he's never quilted before, I'm confident the students would much prefer you."

Sarah tried to laugh, but it came out as a whimper. "Maybe we should cancel."

"Out of the question. There are twelve eager campers waiting to learn hand-quilting, and we can't disappoint them. You'll do just fine. Just go in there and teach them everything I taught you. What could be easier?"

Canceling the class, for one, but Sarah took one look at Sylvia's raised eyebrows and folded arms and decided against saying so. Sylvia would never admit that Sarah might not be up to the task, perhaps because she honestly believed Sarah capable of it. Worse than disappointing the twelve students would be disappointing Sylvia by not even trying.

"After I call Summer and Gwen, I'll run downstairs and bring back some breakfast," said Sarah, resigned. "I'll start preparing while I eat."

"You go ahead and get ready," said Sylvia. "I'll fix you a plate myself."

Sylvia did more than that; before leaving for her own nine o'clock lecture, she helped Sarah outline the topics she should cover the first morning and gather the appropriate supplies. Sarah went over her notes until the very moment class began, and although the students seemed disappointed by Sylvia's absence, the lesson went better than Sarah had expected.

She spent most of the rest of the day in the office catching up on all the work set aside that morning. She joined the faculty and guests for supper, and later that evening assisted Summer with the evening program, a slide show of antique quilts from the Waterford Historical Society's Quilt Documentation Project. She was too exhausted to join the rest of the Elm Creek Quilters for a celebratory cup of hot chocolate afterward, as was their tradition. She might have joined them if she could have her cocoa laced with rum, but as it was, sleep seemed the preferable option.

In comparison, the next day went remarkably well, with a broken slide projector and an overscheduled Machine Quilting workshop the worst crises she had to solve. She joined in the evening program, Games Night, with her old enthusiasm, and by Wednesday morning, the familiar excitement and anticipation of the first week of camp had returned. She went to the office cheerfully, the stress of Judy's last-minute cancellation faded, her confidence in her ability to manage Elm Creek Quilt Camp restored.

It was nearly eleven o'clock, and Sarah was considering returning to the kitchen for another cup of coffee when she heard someone running in the hallway. The library door opened suddenly and Matt rushed into the room. "Honey," he called. "There's a problem."

Sarah was already on her feet. "What happened?"

"Summer sent me to tell you Bonnie never showed for her ten o'clock workshop. Her students waited for twenty minutes before leaving. Those that weren't too angry just joined other classes, but the others . . ." He shrugged.

Sarah sank into her seat. She had been within arm's reach of the phone since breakfast and had checked the voicemail only fifteen minutes before. Bonnie had not called.

She glanced at the clock. There was still an hour left in the workshop. If Matt helped her gather the students, Sarah could teach the class. She could extend it past noon so they received the full two hours they had paid for, if the students didn't have scheduling conflicts, if the classroom space was available . . .

She scrambled for the schedule. Bonnie's workshop was on sewing tailored quilted jackets. Sarah could barely hem a pair of pants.

"We'll refund their money," said Sarah. She closed her eyes and rested her head against the soft leather chair.

Wherever Bonnie was, she had better have a very good excuse.

CHAPTER TWO
Summer

Summer would have stayed to help Sarah revise the letter for Sylvia's bridal quilt, but Jeremy had just returned from semester break the night before, and she had not yet had a chance to see him. After suggesting a few changes—most importantly, having participants send their blocks somewhere other than Elm Creek Manor—she hurried outside to her car and drove downtown to Jeremy's apartment.

She parked behind his apartment building, a three-story red brick walk-up on the opposite end of Main Street from Grandma's Attic. Jeremy's car was in the lot, but he walked to and from campus, and a glance at his darkened windows confirmed he was not yet home. She retrieved the groceries from the trunk and hurried upstairs to the third floor. After two weeks apart, Jeremy would be as eager to see her as she was to see him, and she wanted to get dinner started in case he came home early.

She let herself in with the key Jeremy had given her after his roommate moved out upon graduating at the end of fall semester. A pile of unopened mail sat on the table and a snow shovel was propped up beside the front door. Summer hung up her coat and went to the kitchen, where she found a bottle of wine chilling in the refrigerator. She smiled and put a pot of water on to boil.

Not half an hour later, she heard the door open. "Summer?"

She set down the spoon. "In here," she called, hurrying out of the kitchen. Jeremy met her in the doorway, where she flung her arms around him.

"I missed you," he said, hugging her. He had cut his curly dark hair and was wearing the organic aftershave she had given him for Hanukkah.

"You better have," she teased, kissing him.

"I don't want to spend this much time away from you ever again."

"Does this mean no more locking yourself away in the library for days?"

He picked her up, and she wrapped her legs around him as he carried her to the sofa. "I'd gladly flunk out first."

"That's what you say now." She ran a hand through his dark curls. "We'll see what happens when you're closer to defending your dissertation."

"Please don't remind me. My advisor doesn't expect it until September."

"I bet you spent your entire break writing."

"I should have spent it here with you."

Summer wished he had; most graduate students stayed close to campus during breaks. But Jeremy's parents had been surprised and disappointed when he suggested remaining in Waterford, so he'd loaded his car with books and research notes and driven home.

She gave him a long kiss. "You're here now."

He smiled and stroked her arm. "Yes."

The timer went off in the kitchen. "Hope you're hungry," Summer said, climbing off him. "I made gnocchi with rosemary and sun-dried tomatoes."

Jeremy followed her into the kitchen. "No sprouts and tofu?"

"Not tonight. It's a special occasion." She emptied the gnocchi into the colander in the sink and motioned for him to set the table. "It's still vegetarian."

"It smells great." He gave her a sidelong look. "I promise I won't do anything as tacky as to ask what's for dessert."

After supper, which to Summer's satisfaction was perfect, from the tender gnocchi to the crusty Italian bread, they sat on the sofa finishing the bottle of wine and catching up on the time they had spent apart. "I missed you," Jeremy said, setting their empty wineglasses on the assemblage of milk crates that passed for a coffee table.

"So you've said."

"I meant what I said about not wanting to be apart from you ever again."

She kissed him, then lay down on the sofa, resting her legs in his lap. "After two weeks without you, I feel the same way."

"Then move in with me."

She stared at him. "What?"

"Move in with me."

"I heard you. I'm just surprised."

"Surprised?" He looked hurt. "The only real surprise is why you haven't moved in already. Officially. You practically live here as it is."

She sat up. "Not quite."

"Come on. It makes perfect sense." He took her hand. "I have to get a new roommate to share the rent anyway, and your lease is up at the end of the month."

"I was planning to renew."

"But if you move in here instead, we'll see more of each other."

He was so earnest that she almost laughed despite her discomfort. "Yeah, maybe more than we want."

"This way we won't have to drive back and forth between apartments. We won't have to play phone tag just to arrange to have dinner together."

"If you think I'd cook like this for you every night, you're out of your mind."

"That's not what I expect at all." He put his arm around her shoulders and held her close. "You'd have your own room, your own space. Anytime you want to shut your door and be alone, I won't bother you."

Summer found that hard to believe, but instead of saying so, she said, "Let me think about it."

"Okay. Sure." He was clearly disappointed. "I guess you want to check with your mom first."

Sharply, she asked, "Why would I want to do that?"

He shrugged. "To see if she approves. Or more accurately, to see if she disapproves too much."

"There's a guy sharing my apartment now."

"Yes, but you're not dating him, and there are two other women." He grinned. "Anyway, I don't think she'll object, do you? From what you've told me, your mother was pretty wild when she was younger. I don't think she'd argue about propriety."

No, Gwen would object on entirely different grounds. "Whatever decision I make, my mother will have nothing to do with it."

❧

Summer's copy of the bridal quilt letter arrived three days later, the same day she met Jeremy for coffee and told him she would move in at the end of the month. She could use a change, anyway; the neighborhood of fraternities and undergraduate apartments had seemed exciting when she was a student, but now that she was almost five years out of college and holding down two jobs, the party atmosphere was more of a nuisance than a pleasure. By moving, she would save almost seventy dollars a month on rent for a newer building with its own laundry and free parking. And the company was much better.

Jeremy wanted to start packing at once, but Summer laughed and reminded him that he had to study and she had to work.

"Elm Creek or Grandma's Attic?" asked Jeremy.

"Both. Grandma's Attic until two, then I'll be at home working on some lesson plans for camp."

"Did you tell Bonnie yet?"

"Not yet. But I will."

"The sooner you tell her, the more time she'll have to find someone else."

Summer knew that, but she also knew circumstances were more complicated than Jeremy thought. She had worked at Grandma's Attic since she was sixteen, and Bonnie had hinted that since none of her children were interested in running a quilt shop, she intended for Summer to take over upon her retirement. Once, Summer would have been happy to do exactly that, but her responsibilities at Elm Creek Manor had expanded more than she had anticipated. She could no longer divide her attention and remain sane, and since Elm Creek Quilts was without question the more promising opportunity, she had chosen it.

Grandma's Attic would be fine without her, Summer told herself. If, despite their diminishing sales, Bonnie thought she needed the extra help, she could hire one of her loyal customers or expand Diane's job to full-time. But telling Bonnie would be much easier if Summer didn't feel as if she were abandoning her friend when Bonnie needed her most.

Bonnie was in such good spirits when Summer arrived that she immediately decided not to spoil it. "Holiday sales were better than we thought," Bonnie told her. "We made a profit for the month of December."

"That's fantastic." Summer tucked her backpack away on the shelf beneath the cutting table. "How much of a profit?"

"Enough to pay off all the overdue ninety-day invoices and some of the sixty-day."

"Great," said Summer, with somewhat less enthusiasm.

"If this keeps up, we'll be able to get out of debt by March."

Summer nodded and began straightening bolts of fabric. It wouldn't keep up, and if Bonnie weren't so indefatigably optimistic, she would admit it. The year-end rush of quilters seeking materials for holiday projects and husbands seeking gifts for quilting wives had ended with Christmas. "We could get out of debt faster if you pressured some of our delinquent customers to pay their bills."

Bonnie shook her head and began cutting a remnant bolt into fat quarters. "We've been through this."

"If they want to buy on credit, they should use a credit card."

"And pay seventeen, eighteen percent interest if they can't pay off their cards in full?"

"If they can't pay off their cards, they shouldn't buy more stuff."

"Summer . . ." Suddenly Bonnie looked tired. "Customers expect that kind of service from a shop like mine. If I don't keep them happy, they'll shop at the Fabric Warehouse instead."

Yes, Summer thought, *where they would pay with cash, check, or credit card.* Granted, customers were fickle and sustaining their loyalty was important, but in Summer's opinion, Bonnie could well afford to lose a few of those so-called loyal shoppers. Summer could name at least twenty who owed Grandma's Attic much more than two hundred dollars each. If they were any more loyal, they would sink the shop so deeply into the red that Bonnie would never drag it out.

Summer would just have to figure out some other way to generate more revenue. Then she might be able to leave with a clear conscience.

At least her three roommates took her news without complaint. One even confided that their real worry had been that Summer would invite Jeremy to move in there. Aaron, the lone male in the household, said he had a friend who would be glad to take over the lease. Karen, who had been her friend since their undergraduate days, asked, "What will your mother say?"

"Probably something to the effect that I must be crazy to sacrifice my independence and autonomy for a guy."

"Really." Karen folded her arms and regarded her with interest. "My mother would be more concerned about all the implied sex."

Aaron, on his way from the kitchen with a bag of chips, added, "Your mom's going to let you move in with a guy?"

"Let me?" echoed Summer, incredulous. "I'm twenty-seven years old."

"Well, yeah, but you know. You and your mom . . ." Aaron shrugged.

"My mom and I what?"

"Ignore him," said Karen, glaring at Aaron in disgust. "Don't worry. Tell your mom when you're ready to tell her. We'll cover for you until then."

Summer thanked her and frowned at Aaron, who managed a sheepish grin before backing away. Things were worse than she expected if even her friends questioned her autonomy. She had learned to expect that from the Elm Creek Quilters, who had known her most of her life and who, despite their assurances to the contrary, still thought of her as little Summer in pigtails with her stuffed bear in the basket of her bike. If she had gone away to college or had found work in a far-off city after graduation, her mother and the other Elm Creek Quilters would have been forced to acknowledge her as an independent adult long ago. The tuition waiver Waterford College offered the children of faculty had been too persuasive, however, and once she had earned her degree she had not wanted to leave her mother or the fledgling Elm Creek Quilts, despite tempting offers from graduate schools. Often Summer wished she had experienced life in other places, experiences deeper and richer than the few glimpses that vacations and one semester of study abroad had afforded. Sometimes she even envied Jeremy, who within a year would be leaving Waterford College with his doctorate for an exciting job somewhere. She wondered what it would be like to have no idea where she would be living or what she would be doing this time next year.

❧

For the next three weeks, Summer concentrated on the details of moving, and on the last day of January, Jeremy borrowed a friend's pickup truck and hauled Summer's belongings to his apartment. Summer left behind her answering machine in case someone called for her during the few days the phone company insisted they needed to switch over Summer's number to her new home. Jeremy had agreed to leave the outgoing message on his answering machine blank. "We just have to remember the different rings so we only pick up for our own calls," Summer reminded him as they stacked her books on shelves in her new room.

"Or we could just tell your mother you moved in, and not worry about who answers the phone."

"She wants me to come for supper on Sunday. I'll tell her then."

She worried that Jeremy would ask to accompany her, but he simply wished her good luck, adding, "And the next time you see Bonnie, you can tell her you're leaving Grandma's Attic at the end of March."

Summer agreed. She might as well offend everyone in the same week.

By Sunday morning, Summer had finished unpacking and was growing pleasantly accustomed to having Jeremy around, although she still felt like a guest in his apartment rather than an occupant of her own space. While making room for her soy milk and herbal teas in the kitchen and rinsing the tiny black hairs from his morning shave down the bathroom sink, Summer told herself the feeling would pass in time.

As suppertime approached, Summer prepared her mother's favorite three-bean salad and kissed Jeremy for luck. A light snow fell as she drove to her mother's neighborhood, the streets shrouded in midwinter dark despite the early hour. She parked in the driveway and steeled herself as she approached the front door. Her mother admired her independence and trusted her ability to make her own decisions—or so she said. Now was her chance to prove it.

"Mom?" she called, opening the front door. There was no reply. Summer set down the bowl on the hall table and removed her coat and boots when something else struck her: She detected no aroma of her mother's lentil and brown rice soup.

Hurrying into the darkened kitchen, Summer called out again and was rewarded with a muffled reply. She found her mother in her office, eyes fixed on the computer screen, papers strewn across the desk, academic journals scattered all over the floor.

"Hi, kiddo," said Gwen, frowning at the computer. "What's up?" She gasped and spun around in her chair. "Oh, no. Supper."

Summer grinned and tapped her watch. "Sunday at five o'clock."

"I completely forgot." Gwen absently smoothed her long auburn hair, the same shade as Summer's but streaked with gray. "We could send out for pizza."

"I brought a salad. If you have sandwich makings, we'll be fine."

As Summer set the table, Gwen layered Gorgonzola and crushed walnuts on sourdough bread spread liberally with pesto. "That's the best I can do on the spur of the moment," she said as she set one on her daughter's plate.

Summer assured her it was delicious, then couldn't contain her curiosity any longer. "What are you working on in there? Something for the conference?"

Gwen shook her head and loaded her fork with three-bean salad. "I don't want to talk about it. It's too depressing. This is fabulous, by the way."

"It's your recipe. What's too depressing?"

"As it happens, I'm not going to be in charge of the conference after all."

"Why not? I thought the new department chair always ran things." Her mother winced, and Summer guessed the rest. "You weren't made department chair?"

"Nope."

"But you seemed so sure you would be."

"I was." Gwen took a bite of her sandwich, her expression hardening. "The outgoing chair informed me, on behalf of the committee, that they needed someone with solid academic credentials in, and this is a quote, 'substantial, hard research.'"

"What's wrong with your research? You publish at least three articles a year. The book you edited with Laurel Thatcher Ulrich is coming out this fall. Your last conference paper was quoted in *The Washington Post*. What could that committee possibly object to?"

"My topics."

Summer shook her head, uncomprehending.

"I write about quilts."

"Well, yeah. Quilts as cultural and historical artifacts. You've written about what certain quilts tell us about American society in particular eras. What else would they expect a professor of American Studies to do?"

"Write about a less frivolous art form, apparently."

"They said that? They used the word *frivolous*?"

"Merely implied, but the outgoing chair did encourage me to turn my attention to sculpture or painting or architecture if I'm that fixated on art."

"Let me get this straight," said Summer. "It is not okay to study quilts, which happen to be made primarily by women, but other arts are perfectly acceptable, especially those dominated by men?"

"You have an extraordinarily clear grasp of our conversation."

"That's outrageous!"

"You put it more eloquently than I did." Gwen tore the crusts off her sandwich, frowning. "I told him that for a card-carrying liberal and someone who claims to be devoted to the pursuit of knowledge, he had an obvious and detestable bias for 'manly' topics. I also asked him when he turned into a Republican."

"You didn't."

"Unfortunately, I did."

"Oh, Mom."

"I know."

Summer sat back in her chair. "How can they say your work isn't substantial? What about how your analysis of the dyeing processes used in those New England quilts indicated how the settlers interacted with the Native Americans? What about your paper on those Confederate quilts and how their fabrics reveal the disruption of trade routes?"

Gwen shrugged and continued eating.

Summer had lost her appetite. "I can't believe a college, of all places, would discourage an intellectual investigation because the subject is 'women's work.'"

"Believe it, kiddo. I'm afraid it's all too true."

Summer reached across the table and took her mother's hand. "I'm sorry, Mom. You deserved that chair. You were robbed."

"Everyone knows being the department chair is a thankless job, anyway."

Maybe so, but Summer also knew it would have given Gwen the prestige she deserved, professional clout she had earned, and a not insubstantial increase in salary for the duration of her term. "Can you protest their decision?"

"I could." Gwen's reluctance told Summer that she had considered that idea and dismissed it. Summer didn't need to ask why. Through the years, she had learned enough about the politics of academia to know her mother had to choose those battles wisely.

"So what were you working on?" asked Summer. "A new paper on a new topic?"

"I'll let you read it when it's done."

Summer nodded, concealing her disappointment. She had hoped that Gwen would tell her she would study whatever topic she thought relevant, regardless of her colleagues' disapproval. Her secrecy obviously meant she would no longer study quilts.

"When your book comes out this fall," Summer said, "and when it becomes a best-seller, and when you and your coeditor are nominated for the Pulitzer, those idiots in your department will eat their words."

Gwen managed a laugh. "I'm counting on it, kiddo."

❧

Gwen's rejection astonished Jeremy, who said that the committee's reasoning would never pass scrutiny in the history department. To Summer's relief, he readily agreed when she suggested waiting until Gwen had adjusted to her disappointment before telling her about the move.

Unfortunately, that excuse would not work with Bonnie. Two days later, Summer arrived for her morning shift at Grandma's Attic with a lump in the pit of her stomach. Bonnie was sitting at the cutting table sorting the morning mail. She wore her purple-and-green Pineapple quilted vest, which she seemed to choose whenever she needed extra courage to get through the day.

"Four more packages arrived today," she said. "Sylvia's bridal quilt is going to be gorgeous."

"Can I see the new blocks?" asked Summer, slipping out of her coat. She resolved to phone Sarah and assure her the project was on schedule. Sarah seemed unnecessarily worried about the bridal quilt, certain they would not receive enough blocks. Summer thought it more likely they would receive too many and would have to wrestle with the more difficult problem of deciding which blocks to include and whose to reject.

Bonnie had already inspected the newest blocks, so she handed the padded envelopes to Summer and turned her attention to the rest of the mail. "Bills," she muttered as she edged her stool closer to the table.

Since there were no customers, Summer lingered over the accompanying letters explaining the quilters' inspiration for their pattern choices. A woman who had sent a Rocky Road to Dublin block explained that Sylvia's investigation into the lives of her ancestors had compelled her to learn more about her own forebears, a search that eventually led her to Ireland and some long-lost relations. A Blazing Star block was pinned to a three-page letter extolling Sylvia's accomplishments and praising her with phrases like, "the brightest star in the firmament of the quilting world," and "truly the most gifted and giving quilter of her generation."

Summer smiled as she returned the letter and block to their envelope. Sylvia wouldn't be able to read through half a page before setting it aside in embarrassment.

The next envelope contained a simple Variable Star and a note apologizing for its simplicity. "I hope this is good enough to be included," the maker wrote. "I'm just a beginner. I took my first lesson at Elm Creek Manor last summer. As you can see, Sylvia has inspired me not to give up! It might not look like it, but I've made a lot of progress since the Nine-Patch I made at camp."

Summer recognized the name of a frequent camper on the last envelope.

February 1, 2002

Dear Elm Creek Quilters,

I was thrilled to hear about Sylvia and Andrew's wedding. I wish I could have been there, but I suppose they couldn't have invited every former camper without giving away their secret. And not even Elm Creek Manor is large enough to host a reception that big! I guess I'll just have to congratulate them when I see them again in August.

Thanks for inviting me to participate in Sylvia's bridal quilt. I sat down and made my block right away rather than add this project to my growing list of UFOs. My reason for choosing the Quilter's Dream pattern is probably obvious: Sylvia herself is the friend and teacher every quilter dreams of, and she has turned her home into a wonderful haven where quilters' dreams can come true.

I don't think I ever told Sylvia this, but I started quilting because I saw a picture of one of her quilts in the newspaper when she came to Minnesota to speak at a quilt show twenty-three years ago. I was expecting my first child, and I knew right then and there that I had to make my baby a quilt. I took the article to the nearest fabric shop and begged them for lessons. Apparently, that happens a lot, because half the women in their beginner's class were pregnant!

Twenty years later, I attended Elm Creek Quilt Camp for the first time. I went for two reasons: to finally meet my long-time Internet friend in person, and to avoid meeting my daughter's future in-laws. The friends I met at camp that week convinced me to trust my instincts that the marriage was a mistake. With their support, I was eventually able to convince my daughter to leave what I did not yet realize was an abusive relationship.

Sylvia is a wonderful role model for women of all ages. She is self-reliant and makes those of us who know her want to be that way, too. When we come to a situation where we will either sink or swim, we think of Sylvia and start paddling.

I'm pleased to say that my daughter has been doing wonderfully ever since I taught her what Sylvia taught me. She loves film school at USC and, thanks to another one of my quilt camp friends, has been able to work on several well-known feature films. My younger daughter is a freshman at the University of Wisconsin in Madison where she is studying pre-law. It's hard to have both of my girls so far away, but I'm so proud of both of them and I don't want to hold them back from following their dreams.

As for me, for the past year I have been volunteering at a local shelter for abused women. We were able to take in our daughter when she left her fiancé's apartment, but many women have nowhere to go, and often they bring children with them. The shelter provides women with a safe place to stay until they can make their own way, and it also directs them to whatever counseling or work placement assistance they need. I admit the work is stressful sometimes, but when I think of what might have happened to my daughter, I stick to it and do what needs to be done. I think that's what Sylvia would do.

This is probably more information than you wanted about why I chose that block! Thanks again for letting me be a part of this quilt. I can't wait to see it.

Sincerely Yours,
Donna Jorgenson

"How totally cool," said Summer as she put away the block and the letter. "I wonder what movies her daughter worked on. Maybe we've seen some of them."

Summer looked up when Bonnie did not reply. In one fist, she held a crumpled envelope, in the other hand, a crisp sheet of paper.

"What is it?" asked Summer. A list of their angriest creditors flashed through her mind.

"The building's been sold. All tenants have to sign new leases if we want to stay."

"Of course you'll stay," said Summer, aghast. "Where do they expect you to go? They won't raise the rent, will they?"

"The letter doesn't say."

"But you have a lease. They can't change anything until that lease is up, can they?"

"A new owner takes precedence over existing leases. That's city law." Bonnie had once belonged to the Waterford Zoning Commission; she would know. "I wonder what this means for the condo."

Bonnie and her husband lived in the flat directly above the shop. "You guys own that, right?"

"We do, but our landlord owned the building as a whole. It's complicated." Bonnie looked up from the letter. "Do you know anything about University Realty?"

"A little. They manage my old apartment building."

Bonnie's eyebrows rose. "Old apartment?"

"Yeah. I mean, you know, my apartment. It's old. Not that old. Just older than this."

"The new owner says he'll be around to meet all the current tenants and discuss the transition." Bonnie smoothed the crumpled envelope and returned the letter to it. "I'll just have to wait to hear what he says."

"I guess so," said Summer, and decided one transition was enough for Bonnie to worry about at the moment.

Bonnie took the letter into the back office. Through the window, Summer watched her file it and sit down in front of the computer. She did not emerge until the end of Summer's shift, and Summer could tell from her expression that she didn't want to discuss the sale.

After work, Summer stopped by her old apartment to collect her answering machine. Her former roommates apologized for forgetting to tell her about the eight messages on the tape, but they assured her they had not revealed anything to Gwen the time she stopped by on her way to work. Summer thanked them and wondered why her mother had not mentioned the visit.

Jeremy came home later than usual that evening bearing Thai takeout since it was his night to cook. Over Phat Thai, Summer told him about Bonnie's situation, the exasperation of her roommates' forgetfulness, and Gwen's visit to the old apartment.

"She probably thought you spent the night at my place," said Jeremy.

"I know. I didn't want her to."

"Why not? It's the truth, sort of."

Summer sighed and toyed with her chopsticks. "Jeremy, your parents must be incredibly accepting for you to be so clueless about why this bothers me."

"Are you kidding? My mother would faint if she ever finds out the truth." He quickly added, "I'm kidding. They already know."

"They don't mind?"

"That's the benefit of being the youngest of four. They've already been through everything with my sisters and brother."

"Great," said Summer dryly. It was far too late to hope for any siblings to help share her burden of maternal attention.

❧

Throughout February, Summer managed to rationalize away several more opportunities to mention the move to her mother or give notice at Grandma's Attic. She had even begun to forget her anxieties enough to feel at home in Jeremy's apartment until one evening during supper when three hang-up calls on the answering machine convinced her that Gwen had figured out the truth. Summer waited a reasonable interval before calling her mother on some camp-related pretext only to find her engrossed in her new research project.

Relieved, she hung up and wondered aloud who had called, but Jeremy was annoyed that Summer had not gone ahead and unburdened her obviously troubled conscience. That led to their first fight as roommates. They made up that same night, but not before Jeremy told her that if she was so ashamed to live with him she ought to move out, and Summer retorted that she had considered it.

The next morning they lingered in bed and shared a leisurely breakfast, still apologetic and careful, wanting reassurances that everything was fine between them before they parted for the day. Despite her late start, Summer managed to get to work on time since Jeremy's apartment was only a five-minute walk from Grandma's Attic. She arrived to find the quilt shop dark, the sign in the front door still turned to CLOSED. Bonnie should have unlocked the door an hour earlier. Summer fumbled in her backpack for her key and let herself in.

"Bonnie?" she called, flipping the sign. She turned on the lights and the music system, taking advantage of the opportunity to slip in one of her favorite CDs instead of Bonnie's usual hammered dulcimer and flute. She restocked the empty shelves with what little was left in the storage room, but when another half hour passed with no sign of Bonnie, she phoned upstairs. The answering machine picked up; Bonnie's husband's voice announced that she had reached the home of Craig Markham and that he would return her call later. Summer hung up without leaving a message.

At that moment, the door burst open and Diane came in. "Oh, hi," she said, taking off her coat. "I thought no one else was working today."

"I work every Friday when camp isn't in session," said Summer, puzzled. Diane knew that. "Bonnie should be here, too, but she didn't show up this morning. I'm worried. No one answered the phone upstairs, either."

"She's not coming in today." Diane hung up her coat on a peg on the back wall and stored her purse under the cutting table. "Agnes called and asked me to open the store. I guess she didn't know you would be here."

"Agnes? Why would Agnes have called?"

Diane shrugged. "I have no idea. I imagine Bonnie asked her to."

"But Bonnie knew I was working and she would have called you directly."

"Well . . ." Diane paused. "I don't know. But I'm here, so I'm going to work. I need the hours. Todd is still holding out for Princeton. Do you have any idea how expensive that is? Thank goodness Michael decided to go to Waterford College so we could take advantage of the family tuition waiver."

Summer nodded. Michael had been something of a troublemaker since the fifth grade, but as his former and favorite baby-sitter, Summer tended to see harmless mischief where others saw an inmate-in-training. When Michael enrolled at Waterford College, Diane had been so relieved that she would have paid any amount of tuition without complaint. Now completing his sophomore year, Michael seemed to be thriving as a Computer Sciences major. When the time came, Summer hoped he would find a job outside of Waterford so that, unlike herself, he would be accepted as the adult he had become instead of perpetually seen as the child he had been.

The morning passed with no word from Bonnie. When a call to Agnes went unanswered, Summer considered phoning Bonnie's husband at work, but she had carried on only a handful of strained conversations with Craig in all the years she had known the Markhams. She didn't want to risk making trouble by bothering him at his office. If something was seriously wrong, he wouldn't be there, anyway. He would be with his wife.

A slow but steady flow of customers kept Summer and Diane too busy to have much time to chat, but it tapered off long enough for them to go to lunch. After Diane's turn, Summer went to the Daily Grind for coffee and a salad. Judy was there, an empty plate on the table beside her laptop. Summer did not want to interrupt her work, but when she stopped by to say hello, Judy invited Summer to join her. Summer agreed and, as she seated herself, she couldn't resist a glance at the computer screen. She glimpsed what looked to be lecture notes before Judy shut it down.

They chatted about quilt camp while Summer ate and Judy nursed a cup of black coffee. "Have you started your block for Sylvia's quilt yet?" Summer asked.

"I confess I forgot all about it," said Judy. "I don't even have the fabric yet."

"If you run out of time you could always buy one of those bargain kits at the Fabric Warehouse," teased Summer, and had to laugh at her friend's stricken expression. "I'm just kidding. You have plenty of time. I haven't started my block, either."

"I don't know what's more insulting," said Judy, tossing her straight black hair over her shoulder and feigning moral outrage. "That you think I have such poor time management skills or that I'd take my business anywhere but Grandma's Attic."

Summer assured her she knew otherwise on both counts.

She would have stayed to talk longer, but she couldn't linger with a clear conscience knowing Diane was at the store alone. Judy encouraged her to stay, but she had her computer switched back on before Summer pushed in her chair. On her way out, Summer passed two young men joining the line at the counter, digging in their back pockets for folded bills. She recognized the tall blond on sight, although she hadn't baby-sat Diane's sons in years. The younger of the brothers, Todd was handsome, athletic, and therefore popular, and his companion seemed much the same. The boys laughed and talked loudly like the lords of the local high school class that they were, wanting and expecting to be noticed, oblivious to the utter lack of interest of the college students and professors who had no idea how important they were among their peers. Summer smiled and left the coffee shop. She shouldn't be so hard on Todd and his friend, who looked vaguely familiar. Troubled Michael had always been her favorite, and Todd couldn't help that his perfection made him so annoying.

Back at Grandma's Attic, the stream of customers slowed to a trickle by midafternoon, and despite Bonnie's absence, Summer considered leaving early. Quilt camp would begin in almost three weeks, and Summer should have been at Elm Creek Manor helping Sarah. Out of guilt for her intended resignation, she had not reduced her hours at the quilt shop as she usually did by that time of year. Sarah rightly could have complained, but she probably had everything so well under control that she barely noticed Summer's absence. Even so, come Monday, Summer would revert to her camp season hours. Maybe that would provide a natural transition into leaving permanently.

Eventually customer traffic slowed so much that Diane suggested that to pass the time they read the letters accompanying the blocks for Sylvia's bridal quilt. Summer agreed, but thoughts of her enormous workload nagged at her so much she could not enjoy herself.

Just as she was about to ask Diane if she would mind closing on her own, the front bell jingled. A customer entered wearing a red wool coat trimmed with black fur, and black pumps rather than the snow boots nearly everyone else in Waterford favored this time of year. She removed a black fur hat and smoothed her platinum blond pageboy with a leather-gloved hand. "Isn't Bonnie here today?"

"No," said Diane abruptly, sitting down at the cutting table with her back to the woman and unfolding another letter.

"Diane," whispered Summer, incredulous.

"Don't worry. She's not a customer."

Diane's voice dripped with disgust, but fortunately she had spoken too softly for the woman to overhear. Suddenly Summer recognized her. She had been a brunette the last time Summer had seen her, but she was unmistakably Mary Beth Callahan, the perennial president of the Waterford Quilting Guild and Diane's next-door neighbor.

Summer decided to avoid giving Diane another opportunity to address Mary Beth, since their mutual loathing was legendary. "Bonnie's not here, but may I help you?"

"I suppose so. You're Summer, right? Summer Sullivan?"

"That's right."

"Your name is in the letter, so I guess you'll do." Mary Beth withdrew an envelope from her purse and unfolded it. "I believe this was sent to me by mistake."

She held out the envelope until Summer took it. One glance told her it was the invitation to participate in Sylvia's bridal quilt.

"We definitely meant to send it to you," Summer assured her. "Actually, to the entire guild. You're listed as the guild contact, so we sent it to your home, hoping you would announce it at your next meeting."

She tried to return the letter, but Mary Beth waved it away. "Oh, no, I couldn't do that."

"Why not?" asked Diane.

"I couldn't impose on my fellow guild members like that. They'd probably feel obligated to participate, and that isn't fair. Sylvia is not a charity case. If I endorse your project, where does it stop?"

"We're not asking you to endorse it, just announce it," said Diane. "Just tell them about the quilt and let them decide whether they want to help."

Summer raised a hand to quiet her friend. "I understand your concerns, but many of your guild members have known Sylvia for years. Don't you think they would want to know about her bridal quilt?"

"Don't you think once they see the finished quilt they'll be ticked off that you kept them from participating?" Diane added.

Mary Beth regarded her sourly. "If those few members of my guild are such good friends of Sylvia's, I'm sure you have their addresses and can contact them individually. Our guild happens to be very busy, Diane, so regardless of their feelings for Sylvia, we would appreciate it if nonmembers didn't come around begging for blocks."

"How would you know if you never ask them?" said Diane. "If they don't want to participate, fine, but you won't even give them the chance to refuse for themselves!"

Mary Beth ignored her. "Make sure to take our address off your mailing list," she called to Summer over her shoulder as she departed.

"Gladly," retorted Diane as the door closed behind her. "Can you believe that woman? What is her problem?"

"I have no idea." Summer tossed the letter into the trash. "She seems easily threatened."

"Absolutely. Remember how she freaked out when I opposed her for guild president? I would have been elected if she hadn't reminded everyone that I had never won a ribbon in a quilt show."

"Winning lots of ribbons can't make someone a good president," said Summer. "You need an entirely different set of skills." She didn't point out that the Waterford Quilting Guild apparently believed Mary Beth possessed them or she wouldn't be elected every year. Diane would merely argue that she ran unopposed because everyone feared her wrath.

"She's deliberately trying to ruin Sylvia's quilt," said Diane, opening and closing her rotary cutter with an ominous glint in her eye.

"Why would she do that?" Summer gently guided Diane to the cutting table. "Remember, that's to cut fabric, not throats."

"Because she's jealous of Sylvia's success. And Bonnie's. And mine, too, probably."

Summer couldn't dispute that, but said, "She can't ruin Sylvia's quilt. It would have been nice to have some contributions from more local quilters, but we'll have enough blocks without them."

"Oh, really? The mail came while you were at lunch. The three blocks we got today brings us to a grand total of fifty-eight. We need one hundred forty." Diane frowned and tapped the rotary cutter on the table. "Think about it. Mary Beth has had our letter since the beginning of January. Why would she wait two months to tell us she can't announce it at the guild meeting?"

"I imagine you're about to tell me."

"To make sure we couldn't get around her, that's why. Even if we do send letters to someone else in the guild and ask her to make the announcement, and even if she manages to sneak it past Czarina Mary Beth, the guild members won't have enough time to make any blocks."

Summer had to admit that Diane's explanation of Mary Beth's motives sounded plausible, but she couldn't believe that one spiteful woman could ruin the entire quilt. They had plenty of time. She had not started her own block yet, but she would definitely complete it before the deadline.

❧

Summer left shortly afterward, making Diane promise to call her if she received word from Bonnie. Over the weekend she worked on sample projects for a new course she hoped to teach later that season, and on Sunday afternoon, she phoned Bonnie to remind her she intended to cut back her hours in preparation for camp. She left messages at Bonnie's home as well as at Grandma's Attic, but Bonnie did not return them.

Before driving out to Elm Creek Manor Monday morning, Summer dropped by Grandma's Attic just in case Bonnie failed to show. To her relief, the quilt shop was open, and Bonnie was inside helping a customer. Summer stopped in just long enough to remind Bonnie about her changed schedule—and to notice the dark circles beneath her friend's eyes. Bonnie apologized for not returning her messages but offered no explanation for her silence, and with a customer listening in, Summer could not ask.

Summer spent the rest of the day in the library of Elm Creek Manor helping Sarah prepare for the start of the new camp season. After several hours arranging and rearranging the course schedule, they finally acknowledged that they would have to cancel a few classes. Summer volunteered to phone some of the Elm Creek Quilters to confirm schedule changes, wanting to spare her overworked friend that unpleasant task. Summer contacted Agnes, but could not track down her mother, Diane, or Judy.

Frustrated, Summer hung up and flung herself into a chair in front of the library fireplace, complaining about their friends' inaccessibility. Sarah laughed and as usual offered a logical explanation for their absence, then added that Summer was the least accessible of them all. "All anyone can ever get is your machine. By the way, I think it might be broken. There's no outgoing message anymore, just a beep."

"Oh," said Summer guardedly. "Thanks. I'll look into it."

"You should. Last week I called three times in a row just to make sure I had the right number."

Summer nodded. So Sarah was the mysterious caller.

That evening, Summer told Jeremy what she had learned, making light of the misunderstanding and the argument that had followed. Jeremy laughed with her about it, adding, "I don't want another fight over something so stupid. Record whatever message you want. My callers will just have to get used to it."

"No, you record it. If my mom calls, problem solved."

His eyebrows shot up. "Are you sure that's the best way for her to find out?"

"No, it's not. Now I'll have some incentive to tell her soon."

She resolved to do so before the Elm Creek Quilters' next business meeting.

On the following Thursday, she tried all day to reach Gwen and offer her a ride out to the manor. They could talk in the car. Summer would time it so she delivered the bad news just as they were crossing the bridge over Elm Creek. Gwen would have to settle down for the meeting, and by the time Summer drove her home, she might be better able to conduct a rational discussion. Unfortunately, Gwen did not cooperate with her daughter's plans. She did not respond to calls to home, office, or cell phone, so eventually Summer gave up and drove to the meeting alone. She still hoped for a few minutes alone with Gwen beforehand, but Gwen arrived just as Sarah opened the meeting.

"Mom, hi," whispered Summer, edging her chair closer. Sarah frowned slightly but continued speaking. "Listen, can we talk after the meeting?"

"Hmm? Oh, hi, kiddo. Sure, if things wrap up before eight-thirty. I have to get back to the library before it closes."

So that was where she had been hiding. Summer hoped Sarah would get through the meeting with uncharacteristic brevity. She willed Sarah to quicken her pace, instinctively checking her watch every time Sarah paused between topics, but as the minutes passed, her thoughts wandered from Gwen to Jeremy to Bonnie's still unexplained absence from Grandma's Attic. Summer would have asked for an explanation, but considering her own secrets, it seemed hypocritical—

"Are you out of your mind?" Sylvia cried out.

"What?" said Summer, looking from Sarah to Sylvia and back. "What did she say?"

"If any of you had been listening, you would know." Clearly distressed, Sarah begged her friends to pay attention. Summer, who already felt guilty over helping Sarah less that year than in the past, resolved to concentrate on Elm Creek Quilt Camp for the rest of the meeting. When Sylvia and Diane exchanged a few quips about some naked woman, Summer paid no attention and nodded at Sarah to encourage her to continue.

The meeting concluded at eight twenty-five. "What did you want to talk about, kiddo?" Gwen asked as she put on her coat.

"Nothing." Nothing they could discuss in five minutes. "I just wanted to catch up. Let's talk on Sunday, okay? Want to try supper again?"

Gwen agreed, gave her a quick hug and kiss, and hurried out the door. Summer was reaching for her own coat when she felt a hand on her arm. "Summer, dear," said Sylvia. "Do you have a moment?"

"Sure."

Sylvia beckoned her to take a seat and waited for the others to leave the room. "I hope you won't think me a nosy old biddy, but I wonder how you're doing these days. You seem somewhat troubled."

Summer forced a smile. "I'm fine."

"I see. Apparently I was mistaken, then, when I assumed all was not well with your, shall we say, domestic situation."

"What do you mean?"

"I phoned yesterday and was greeted by a pleasant young man's voice on the answering machine. A familiar voice—Jeremy's, I believe."

"Oh. Right." Summer tried to sound nonchalant. "Actually, I moved in with Jeremy in February."

"In February? Goodness, you can keep a secret. I assumed this was a much more recent development."

Feeling foolish, Summer said, "I have my own bedroom."

"Of course you do," said Sylvia, without missing a beat. "I assume you haven't told your mother?"

"I haven't told anyone except you." Summer hesitated. "I guess you're going to tell her?"

"Oh, my, no," said Sylvia with a little laugh. "I'm afraid that's in your hands. It's not my place to tattle on you, nor to judge. However, as your friend, and as someone who cares about your well-being, I'm compelled to ask why you would choose to do anything you're ashamed for your mother and your friends to know about."

"I'm not ashamed." Summer slumped against the backrest. "But I know how everyone will react and I'm not looking forward to it. They still think of me as a little kid."

"Some of our friends would object to your living with Jeremy whether you were twenty-seven or fifty-seven. It's not a question of age, but of marital status."

"They have a right to object," Summer countered, "but I have the right to make my own choices."

"So you do," said Sylvia, nodding. "Then you believe Jeremy is 'the one'?"

"I don't know. I suppose not."

"My understanding is that moving in together is often a precursor to marriage."

Summer shook her head. "Jeremy has to know that isn't possible. My life is here, right?"

"Are you asking me or telling me?"

"My career, my mom, my friends are all right here in Waterford," said Summer firmly. "I couldn't leave if I wanted to."

Sylvia's eyebrows rose. "Couldn't you?"

Summer let the question pass. "Jeremy will eventually get his Ph.D. and move on to some faculty position elsewhere. He knows I can't come with him."

"Are you certain he knows? Men have a way of ignoring what they don't want to see."

Summer couldn't argue with that. She toyed with a loose string on her shirtsleeve. They had never discussed marriage or made any long-term plans. Summer loved Jeremy, and she would be brokenhearted when he left, but she knew it would happen and accepted it. He occasionally mentioned different colleges he aspired to work for after receiving his degree, and Waterford College was not among them. Even if he did prefer a small, rural school, departments seldom hired their own Ph.D.s for tenure-track positions. It was just the way things were.

"I know our time together is limited," said Summer. "One of the reasons I moved in with Jeremy was to make the most of that time."

"I see."

"He has less than a year before he graduates." Summer forced a laugh. "Most couples break up sooner than that. Jeremy and I probably will, too, and so none of this will matter."

"If none of this matters, why haven't you told anyone? And if you honestly believe you're going to break up anyway, isn't it rather foolish to move in with him?"

Summer had no answer for her.

Sylvia reached over and patted Summer's hand. "I believe you two should have had this discussion before you gave up your old apartment, but you should still have it. Better late than much too late."

Summer nodded. Sylvia was right, but that meant one more discussion she loathed to have. Speaking to Gwen seemed easy in comparison.

ಞ

On Sunday, Summer decided to get it over with.

She waited until after supper, then, in a calm, controlled voice, told Gwen she had moved in with Jeremy. She omitted a few details, such as when the move had taken place and her former roommates' assistance in deceiving Gwen. She waited for her mother to respond, but finally prompted, "Mom?"

"Why?" Gwen choked out.

With barely a tremor, Summer carefully went through the reasons again. Jeremy needed someone to share the rent. She was tired of her old place. The new apartment was better in every respect, including rent. She loved Jeremy and wanted to spend more time with him, something their busy schedules would not permit otherwise.

"But you've only been dating since last summer," said Gwen, with remarkably less hysteria than Summer had anticipated. "How could you give up your freedom, your independence?"

Summer couldn't help it; she rolled her eyes. "I knew you would say that.

I'm not chained to the kitchen table. Jeremy doesn't shove a toilet brush into my hand when he leaves for campus in the morning."

Gwen shook her head. "I can't believe you didn't discuss this with me first."

"I'm not a teenager, Mom."

"But apparently still not mature enough to understand the consequences of your decisions."

Gwen rose and began to clear the table, refusing Summer's offer of help. Summer carried plates to the sink anyway and tried to change the subject by asking about Gwen's progress on her new research project. Gwen told her she did not want to stir up more negative energy that evening, and maybe they could talk about it another day, when Gwen felt less hopeless.

Summer did not know what else to do, so she went home, where Jeremy was waiting to hear how it had gone. She told him both better and worse than she had expected, and left it at that. He gave her a searching look, but left his books and papers to make her a cup of her favorite chamomile tea.

Summer drank it curled up on the futon with a book that could not hold her attention. Her mother's reaction was a disturbing echo of Sylvia's. Summer trusted her own instincts, she was comfortable making her own decisions, and she enjoyed living with Jeremy. Still, somehow she wished she had talked to someone before making the move.

"Jeremy," she finally said, "do you think moving in together has changed things?"

"You mean, between us?" A book closed. "Of course. For the better. Don't you?"

She chose her words carefully. "I'm happy with the way things are right now."

"So am I."

"But you know, they can't stay like this forever."

A pause. "No, I guess not, but I love you, Summer, and when the time comes to take the next step, we'll take it."

She could only nod in reply. She wondered what he thought that next step was when they both knew he would be leaving Waterford someday.

❧

The remaining two weeks before the first day of camp passed in a flurry of activity. The Elm Creek Quilters were too busy to spare much time for gossip, so Summer's news spread more slowly than it would have at any other time of the year. Judy was the first to find out; she expressed surprise, but like Sylvia maintained a non-judgmental front. When Summer admitted she had waited more than a month after moving to tell her mother, Judy seemed more impressed than shocked. "How did you keep it a secret for so long?" she asked admiringly. "The Elm Creek Quilters tell each other everything."

"Not everything," said Summer, thinking of Bonnie. One secret was enough to keep from Bonnie, Summer decided, so she mentioned her change of address casually during her next shift at Grandma's Attic. Bonnie stared at her for a long moment before saying, "Are you sure you know what you're doing?" When Summer assured her she did, Bonnie studied her for a moment before finding an excuse to work in the storage room. Later she emerged, forced a smile, and told Summer that she was probably right to test the relationship before making a more permanent commitment. Summer managed not to flinch as she nodded.

Summer knew Agnes had been told when the older woman began studying her mournfully when she thought Summer unaware. She became so flustered in Summer's presence whenever certain words came up—*apartment* and *boyfriend*, of course, but also unavoidable words such as *together*, *living*, *trouble*, and *wrong*—that they could no longer carry on a conversation. Summer tried to put her at ease, but Agnes's disappointment in her was so apparent than it became easier to avoid her. Dreading that Sarah, Diane, and the rest would share Agnes's feelings, Summer decided to let them find out on their own rather than telling them herself. One friend's dismay was difficult enough to bear.

Then the deadline for Sylvia's bridal quilt, once so distant, was only a week away. Summer thought of all the blocks she had ever made, but none of the names captured what she felt for Sylvia. Unlike the quilters who had mailed blocks to Grandma's Attic, she knew Sylvia too well to pick out one particular conversation or encounter that had transformed her life. She found the perfect fabrics in her stash—better organized than in years past, now that she had a room to herself—but the inspiration she waited for did not come.

On the morning of the first day of camp, Summer decided to ask for an extension. Surely the deadline was somewhat flexible for Elm Creek Quilters, and maybe the block choice guidelines were, too.

Summer made it to Elm Creek Manor by eleven, her worries momentarily forgotten in the excitement of the first day of camp. Sarah buzzed about the grand front foyer setting up tables and delegating tasks, her frenzy barely tempered by Sylvia's reassuring confidence. When Sarah asked Bonnie to inspect the classrooms, Summer quickly volunteered to assist, determined to talk to her alone.

As they checked the classrooms for equipment and furnishings, Summer asked Bonnie why she had not shown up for work on the first of March. When Bonnie hesitated, Summer prompted, "Did it have something to do with the building?"

Bonnie busied herself with testing a sewing machine. "Yes, I guess you could say that."

"Are they going to raise the rent?"

"Oh, sure, but only by seventy-five percent."

"Seventy-five?" Summer dropped into a chair. "They can't do that."

"They can, and they're going to."

"How do they expect you to pay that much?"

"They don't. They want me out."

"Why? It can't be that easy to find a new business to fill the vacancy."

"Oh, they have big plans for the building. They're going to turn it all into student apartments."

"Even the condos?"

Bonnie nodded.

"They can't," said Summer, although she was beginning to wonder about the limits of their power. "You own the condo. They can't force you to sell."

"They assume I'd prefer that to living surrounded by partying sophomores. And these days I'm not too attached to the condo, so moving wouldn't be the end of the world." She paused. "But it is my one bit of leverage over University Realty. They want me to sell the condo, but they know I'll dig in my heels if they force me out of my store. As long as we're still holding on financially, I'll never give up Grandma's Attic."

Summer clasped her hands together in her lap. "I know one way you can cut your expenses."

"I know." Bonnie nodded, resigned. "It's awful, but it's the most obvious solution. I have to fire Diane."

"What? No, not that! I'll resign."

"Oh, Summer. It's sweet of you to try to save Diane's job, but I couldn't manage without you. Your ideas are what have kept us afloat this long."

"I was planning to quit anyway. I can't keep holding down two jobs, and Elm Creek Quilts is my first choice."

Bonnie managed the first smile Summer had seen from her all day. "I appreciate what you're trying to do. I know Diane's concerned about paying for Todd's tuition—"

"That's not it." Summer placed her hands on Bonnie's shoulders and looked her directly in the eye. "Let me make this as clear as I know how: I quit."

Bonnie patted her hand and rose. "I'm glad people like you still exist in this world. Believe me, I'm in no hurry to fire my friend. I'll tell you what. I'll keep Diane on for another month. If we can turn things around by then, I won't let her go. If not . . ." She took Summer's hand and pulled her to her feet. "Come on. We still have three classrooms. Sarah probably thinks we ran off."

❧

"She wouldn't let you quit?" Jeremy asked as they prepared for bed that evening. He had waited up for her to hear how the banquet and Candlelight welcoming ceremony had fared.

"It's not that she wouldn't let me. She didn't believe that I wanted to." Summer vigorously brushed her long auburn hair. If she had quit weeks ago, she wouldn't be in this mess. Neither would Diane.

"Put it in writing," said Jeremy. He lifted her hair off her shoulders and kissed the nape of her neck. "Then stop showing up for work."

"I still have a month to save Diane's job," she reminded him, but resolved to write a letter of resignation first thing in the morning.

The next day, she had just kissed Jeremy good-bye and was settling down at her computer with a cup of tea when Sarah phoned. "Would you mind teaching Judy's four o'clock Computer Design class this week?" Sarah asked. "I know you're busy Wednesday afternoon, but I thought your mom could sub then."

"Sure," said Summer, puzzled. She had arranged that schedule herself and knew she had not overlooked a conflict. "What happened to Judy?"

"She had to go out of town unexpectedly on business." Sarah sounded even more frazzled than usual. "I think we have her other class covered, though."

"Are you sure?"

Sarah let out a bleak laugh. "Unfortunately, yes." She said something about needing to prepare for some hand-quilting, said a hasty good-bye, and hung up.

Summer shook her head, hung up the phone, and typed her letter of resignation. She rehearsed what she would say on the drive to Elm Creek Manor. Bonnie spent her mornings at Grandma's Attic, so Summer didn't bother to look for her until after the morning sessions. She found her at lunch engaged in an animated conversation about quilted clothing over burritos and margaritas. "I'm sure you understand how much I regret this," said Summer, jumping into a momentary pause in the discussion. She handed Bonnie the letter and smiled at the assembled campers, who looked on curiously. "This is to prove I'm serious."

Bonnie laughed and tucked the letter into her pocket without reading it. "Sure you are. Remember, you work the closing shift on Wednesday."

Summer frowned. And Sylvia said *men* ignored what they did not want to see. She left to grab a sandwich before her afternoon classes. Obviously Bonnie would not wish to discuss her resignation in front of the campers but, like it or not, she would have to accept it.

Summer's classes were full of fun and over too soon, reminding her again why, when forced to make a choice, she had chosen Elm Creek Quilts over Grandma's Attic. Her students' energy and enthusiasm rekindled her own passion for quilting and reminded her anew why she had first begged Gwen to teach her the art.

Except for Judy's absence, camp seemed to be off to a fine and unusually smooth start, from classes to evening entertainment programs to the mundane details such as laundry and parking. Summer thought so as late as Wednesday morning, as she began the third day of her weeklong workshop in color theory. At half past ten, she noticed two students lingering in the doorway, but they moved on when they realized she had seen them. Then, five minutes later, three other students slipped into the room and quietly took seats in the back. A murmur of voices came from the hallway, rising, falling, and yet another student entered the room. Apologizing to her students, Summer quickly went to see what was happening.

The source of the commotion was the room next door; Summer had to wait for two students to exit before she could enter. Six students remained within, talking irritably. They fell silent when they caught sight of Summer. "Are you our new instructor?" one woman asked.

"What happened to Bonnie?" demanded another.

"I don't know," said Summer. "Did she have to leave?"

"She never showed up," said another peevishly. "I've never seen anything so unprofessional in my life."

"Oh, hush up, Phoebe," said a third student. "Emergencies happen. She was so nice to us at lunch yesterday."

"Let me see what I can do," said Summer, and hurried from the room. She ran from the ballroom into the front foyer, where through the tall double doors she glimpsed Matt working outside. She called him over and asked him to run upstairs and inform Sarah what had happened. Then she hurried back to her own students and carried on with the class.

At noon, Summer found Sarah in the foyer on her way to the banquet hall with an armful of schedules and other papers. She had no idea what had become of Bonnie. "She never called," said Sarah. "I've tried Grandma's Attic and her home, but all I get are answering machines. Something strange, though. Craig seems to have recorded over Bonnie's family greeting on the home machine."

"It's probably nothing," said Summer, thinking of her own answering machine problems. "Their youngest moved out years ago. They were overdue for a change."

Sarah nodded dismissively. "You're right. I don't know why I even mentioned it. We have enough to worry about."

"I'm going to Grandma's Attic right now," said Summer. "I'll call you as soon as I find out what's wrong. Maybe she just had car trouble."

"Car trouble *and* phone trouble?" said Sarah. "Unlikely."

In response, Summer nodded and ran up to the office for her backpack. In a few minutes she was driving through the leafy wood surrounding the estate on her way downtown. She wished she had her mother's cell phone so she could try to reach Bonnie. Why had she failed to call—again?

Fifteen minutes later she pulled into the employee parking space behind Grandma's Attic and ran around the block to the front entrance.

Parked in front of Grandma's Attic were two police cars.

Summer stopped short for a heartbeat, then caught her breath and hurried inside.

"Bonnie?" she cried, searching for her friend. The quilt shop was a shambles. Notions were scattered across the floor, bolts of fabric knocked from their shelves and unrolled in a snarl of color, books and patterns flung about as if by a great wind.

Bonnie looked up from a far corner of the room, her face ashen, but she did not break off her conversation with the two uniformed officers before her. She leaned against an empty bookcase as if she might faint without its support.

"I'm afraid you can't come in, miss," said a third officer Summer had not noticed. "This is a crime scene."

"What?"

"We had a break-in," said Bonnie, picking her way across the room. Her eyes were filled with unshed tears, but she held out her arms to comfort Summer.

Summer embraced her. "What did they take?"

"Everything in the cash register." Bonnie clung to her, trembling. "Last night's deposit. I didn't have time to take it to the bank after closing."

Why didn't you take it upstairs? Summer almost cried out, but she held back the instinctive criticism. It was pointless.

"Some rotary cutters and scissors, pens, a sewing machine." Bonnie's voice was distant, disbelieving. "And the quilt blocks."

"What?"

"All of the blocks for Sylvia's bridal quilt, except for those I had already given to Agnes." Bonnie shook with sobs. "They're gone."

CHAPTER THREE

Gwen

As soon as the spring semester began, Gwen began checking her office mailbox twice daily for official notice that she had been named chair of the Department of American Studies. She waited, but in the first three weeks of January, the most interesting piece of mail she received was the invitation to participate in Sylvia's bridal quilt, and she had already known about that. Of course, she already knew what the committee's letter would say, too, but before she told all her friends and celebrated, she wanted official confirmation of the hints and veiled promises the outgoing chair had dropped during the past year and a half.

They would have to reveal their selection soon. Although the official transition would not take place until the end of May, the incoming chair traditionally assumed some of the duties by the end of January. Every summer the Society for the Study of American Culture held a four-day conference at Waterford College, which the department chair directed. A good portion of the work had already been completed, but the incoming chair would be expected to take over just in time for reviewing paper submissions, scheduling speaking times, and making sure Food Services remembered to order enough alcohol for the opening reception, which never failed to set the tone for the entire conference. Gwen had seen chairmen's careers falter over too little wine or the wrong brand of beer.

"Chairmen" was the accurate term to use, too, even for someone who generally eschewed gender-exclusive language. Only three women had directed the department in its entire history, and the last had retired fourteen years earlier. The department was long overdue to select another woman, but Gwen considered herself the strongest candidate regardless. She had seniority over the other professors who had not yet served, her record of publications was outstanding, her graduate students performed well and consistently found tenure-track positions in respected universities, and her undergraduate teaching evaluations were excellent. So why did the committee's reticence trouble her so much?

Because, she admitted to herself, she had been a tenured member of that faculty for too long not to have been chair already. Twice before she thought she deserved the job at least as much as the person who was eventually named. If she were passed over again, she would have to consider seriously whether she ought to spend the rest of her career at Waterford College.

The news finally came one Wednesday morning when a knock sounded on her office door. "Gwen?"

"Come on in, Jules," Gwen called. The door opened and one of her graduate students entered. "Ready for the candidacy exam?"

"Almost. Ask me again next month." Jules settled his lanky frame into the opposite chair. "How are you doing?"

"Me?" Gwen turned away from the computer to find him peering at her, his expression guarded. "I'm fine. Why wouldn't I be?"

"So you haven't heard? Or is it just a rumor?"

"Is what a rumor?"

"One of Professor Brannon's grad students says she's going to be chair."

For a moment Gwen just stared at him, absorbing this. "There hasn't been any official word yet. It's a bad idea to spread rumors. Or to listen to them."

"I know. I know. But this rumor's spreading fast, and no one's refuting it." He hesitated. "We wanted to see how you were taking it."

He meant the rest of her grad students had sent him in to gauge whether it was safe to approach or if they ought to avoid her for the next few days. "Thanks for keeping me in the loop." She saved her document and rose, adding with forced confidence, "I'll get this cleared up."

Bill's assistant buzzed her in to the department chair's office with little delay, with a look of sympathy that spoke volumes. She had probably known the committee's decision weeks before Bill did.

When Gwen entered, Bill rose and offered her a seat. His atypical politeness so unsettled her that she almost involuntarily dropped into the chair. "I think I know why you're here," he said, scratching a graying sideburn.

"I've heard some rumors."

"Annette Brannon has been appointed department chair."

"I see." She inhaled deeply but held his gaze. "Based upon our conversations of the past two years, it was my understanding that I was first in line."

"If it makes you feel any better, you were our next choice if Annette refused."

"No, it does not make me feel any better." No one who would consider refusing was ever offered the position. "Why? What happened?"

He spread his palms. "The same process that happens every three years. The committee scrutinized a number of relevant factors and determined that Annette was the best choice."

"I have been a member of this department for nearly sixteen years." Gwen studied the photos on his desk: Bill and his wife in tuxedo and gown, his wife alone, Bill and William, Jr. wearing identical Pittsburgh Steelers sweatshirts. When she was calm enough, she said, "Annette joined us five years ago. She has one book out, her dissertation. I have four and another slated for the fall. She has not yet led so much as one department committee to my six. Compare our journal publications and you'll find—"

"Gwen. Please. The decision's been made." Bill glanced at his watch discreetly, but not discreetly enough. "Maybe next time will be your turn."

This time was supposed to have been her turn, and she was not about to go through this same humiliation three years hence. "I'd appreciate hearing how the committee reached its decision since you didn't dispute my comparison of our qualifications."

"Maybe you should take it up with the committee."

"I've had a little too much bureaucracy for one day, so I'd prefer to take it up with you." Gwen reminded herself to be civil. "I'd appreciate it, especially since, inadvertently or not, you led me to believe I would be offered the job."

"Annette is the most appropriate choice for the department at this juncture," said Bill. "You're focusing on quantity of work and ignoring quality. The committee felt the department needed someone with solid academic credentials in substantial, hard research, and Annette is that person."

The implication stung, but Gwen let him continue unchallenged.

"Undergraduate majors have been declining over the past decade. We've lost students to history, government, and women's studies at alarming rates. Annette's research is cutting-edge and well regarded, and the political angles have caught students' attention. Her teaching evaluations are off the charts. She's brought in two six-figure grants. She'll invigorate this department at a time when we desperately need it." He rose to indicate the conversation was over, but added, "Does that clear up the situation?"

"Almost. One more question. Are you saying my work is not 'hard, substantial research'?"

"Gwen—"

"What is soft and insubstantial about my research?"

"Is that a rhetorical question? You study quilts. That's nice, but it's not politically or socially relevant."

"Haven't you read any of my papers? How can you say art is not politically or socially relevant within a culture?"

"Art? Come on, Gwen. Quilts aren't art. My mother-in-law makes quilts." He came out from behind his desk and rested his hand on the doorknob. "I know you're disappointed. Personally, I think you'd make a fine chair. Here's some advice if you want to improve your chances in three years. If you want to study the arts, study the arts that matter—architecture, maybe. Sculpture or painting."

He opened the door and gave her a sympathetic grimace.

Somehow his attempt to be helpful infuriated her even more. "For a card-carrying liberal and someone who claims to be devoted to the pursuit of knowledge, you and your committee have an obvious and detestable bias for 'manly' topics. Since when did you all turn Republican?"

He looked wounded, but she did not linger to apologize. She stormed from his office and back to her own, ignoring the curious glances from colleagues and students alike.

Jules had wisely not waited for her return. Fuming, Gwen shut down the computer and packed books and papers into the quilted satchel she used as a briefcase. "The arts that matter," she muttered, locking the door behind her. If Bill had read any of her research—for that matter, if he had any common sense—he would realize that home arts and folk arts revealed more about a culture than the isolated, esoteric pieces preserved in museums for the benefit of the elite. She was sick and tired of having her work dismissed as frivolous because it centered on a largely female occupation. If most quilts had been made by men, no one would question her interest in exploring the role of quiltmaking in American history.

She crossed the wooded campus carefully, her footsteps unsteady on the snow-covered sidewalks. A snow squall had struck while she was in class, too recently for the maintenance crews to have cleared the icy dusting from anything but the main roads. Two men, one probably a student, were shoveling snow from the steps of the Computer Sciences building when she arrived. The older man greeted her by name as she climbed to the front door. She did a double take before she recognized Bonnie's husband, Craig. She smiled and made some joke about his getting out of his office to enjoy the fine weather, but he didn't get it. "We're understaffed," he replied instead. "Everyone has to help out."

Gwen had never particularly liked Craig, so she merely smiled again, nodded, and went on her way rather than explain. Bonnie and Craig were a prime example of opposites attracting, although Gwen had never figured out what Bonnie found so appealing. Of course, she found little to admire in the institution of marriage, so she probably wasn't looking hard enough.

She found Judy in her lab studying a long printout of rows and columns of numbers and letters—incomprehensible to Gwen, but apparently holding Judy and two of her graduate students spellbound. When Gwen asked if she had a moment to talk, Judy handed the printout to one of her students and led Gwen into an adjacent office. The room, though small, had a window, two laptops, and a color laser printer Gwen had coveted ever since Judy unpacked it. The walls were lined with bookcases—the shelves so full they bowed in the middle—and on the back of the door hung a quilt designed from a fractal pattern.

"What's going on?" Judy asked, leaning against the edge of a desk and gesturing to a seat.

Gwen sank heavily into it. "I wasn't named department chair."

"I thought the committee had all but given you the keys to the office."

"Never again will I believe anything until I see it in writing."

Judy shook her head, her long black hair slipping over her shoulder. "So they chose another man after all."

"No, they cleverly rendered me unable to complain on those grounds. The woman they chose is bright, capable, and only five years out of graduate school. She doesn't even have tenure, but her work is hip, political, and socially relevant, which mine isn't."

"Since when?"

"Since I started concentrating on textiles, apparently." Gwen's head throbbed. She buried her face in her hands and massaged her forehead. "And naturally I had to make everything worse. I couldn't just take the news stoically and write up a well-reasoned, formal protest after I regained control of my temper. I had to storm into Bill's office and demand an explanation."

"How did that go?" When Gwen hesitated, Judy winced. "Never mind. I can guess." She reached out and squeezed Gwen's shoulder. "I wouldn't worry about it. He's probably more embarrassed than you are, no matter what you said. He must be ashamed of the committee's ridiculous excuses."

"I doubt it. He seemed sincere when he told me to switch to studying 'the arts that matter' if I hope to be considered three years from now."

"So what are you going to do?"

"I might write him a letter of apology."

"Sounds like overkill to me. I meant, what are you going to do about your research?"

"I don't know." She wanted to pursue research that fascinated her, but had her passion blinded her to the obvious? Was her work irrelevant? She never wanted to become one of those academics who churned out journal article after journal article that no one would ever read. For a time, a time she had enjoyed enormously, studying the lives of women in history had been celebrated as the archiving of the almost forgotten past of an enormous, disenfranchised population. When had the climate shifted?

"You have tenure, so they can't fire you simply because they don't like your research," Judy reminded her. "But they can prevent you from advancing within the college and otherwise make your life miserable. I suppose you have to ask yourself which is more important: impressing the committee or continuing your current research, which until an hour ago you couldn't have imagined abandoning."

"I could always return to it after my term as chair."

"That's true, but three years is a long time to study something that bores you."

Gwen doubted she could stand even one year bored out of her mind simply to make a point. Worse yet was the idea of herself humbled, acquiescent, willingly switching research topics to please the selection committee. She might be able to do so if she accepted their assessment of her work, but she did not. "Not all departments believe that women's stories are irrelevant," she said.

Judy shrugged. "It is possible to outgrow a college. You can be happy for many years, but one day, you realize you've gone as far as you can go. Sometimes the best and only way to pursue your research is to pursue it somewhere else."

Gwen would hate to leave Waterford College, Elm Creek Quilts, Summer. But she was a long way from retirement and refused to be shuffled off to her rocking chair where she could work on her girlie projects while younger women like Annette were celebrated for their important work.

She had to find a middle ground. If her ongoing research wouldn't impress the department, she would find something new, but she would not abandon quilts simply because some stuffy old men didn't understand their significance. It was her job as an educator to make them understand.

But it wouldn't hurt to find something that would also win her a grant.

❧

Gwen managed to avoid Bill and Annette the next day, but she found little comfort in the sympathies of the two American Studies professors who stopped by her office once the official announcement was made. Her grad students, perhaps warned away by Jules, did not seek her out, so she left campus right after her last class. She would work at home until it was time to leave for the weekly business meeting at Elm Creek Manor. Bonnie wanted them to arrive early so she could show them the first blocks of Sylvia's bridal quilt.

Was it any wonder Gwen preferred the energy and camaraderie of the manor to the suspicious temper of the Liberal Arts building? Elm Creek Quilts was collaborative, cooperative, and—she dared to say—matriarchal, while academia was still a rigid hierarchy despite the varying political winds that drifted across it, altering its surface without changing the deeper layers. As an idealistic student, she had thought the university was a place where the love of learning and the sharing of ideas were celebrated; now she knew that argument and backbiting were the norm, the egalitarian exchange of knowledge an afterthought.

Or maybe she was just bitter. Judy never seemed to encounter politicking and backstabbing. All she ever complained about was inadequate funding and too many boring department meetings.

The gray stone manor was a welcome sight as Gwen crossed the bridge over Elm Creek. She parked near the middle of the lot, where a patch of snow-covered grass encircled two towering, bare-limbed elms. Summer's car was not there, but inside Gwen found Bonnie, Agnes, and Diane, and Judy soon joined them. Gwen wished Summer was there; she never failed to help Gwen put her disappointments in proper perspective. Still, Gwen joined in the usual banter and admired the blocks until Sylvia's sudden arrival sent them scrambling. Fortunately, Sarah managed to fling the blocks into the pantry before Sylvia saw them, but her feeble cover story made Gwen cringe. Miraculously, Sylvia believed it, or pretended to, and the Elm Creek Quilters went to the parlor to begin the meeting.

Sarah began with the good news that enrollment for the coming season was up fifteen percent. "Your Photo Transfer workshop is especially popular, Gwen," she added. "Summer and I thought it would be a good idea to offer a second session each week. If you're up for it."

Gwen shrugged. "Sure. Why not? Once the spring semester ends, I'll have plenty of time." Much more time than she had intended or hoped, but she needn't tell Sarah that. No one but Summer and Judy knew how much she had counted on that appointment.

Not long into the meeting, Summer burst in, slipping out of her coat and full of apologies. She wore her long auburn hair in a loose knot at the nape of her neck, and if Gwen wasn't mistaken, she had secured it with a number-two pencil. "Relax, kiddo. You're not that late," whispered Gwen, but Summer was too distracted by the others' teasing to hear. Naturally they assumed she was late because of her boyfriend, which Gwen thought ridiculous until Summer confessed they were correct.

"You guys spend so much time together you might as well live together," said Diane.

Agnes looked horrified. "Don't suggest such a thing. She meant after you get married, dear."

Summer blanched as Agnes patted her hand.

"Married? Are you crazy?" said Gwen. "Don't go putting thoughts of marriage in my daughter's head. Or of living together. My daughter has more sense than that."

She gave Summer a reassuring grin. The other Elm Creek Quilters still felt cheated out of planning Sylvia and Andrew's wedding, and they saw Summer as the most likely candidate for matrimony. They obviously hoped to nudge her closer to the altar so their investigation of local florists and bakeries wouldn't go to waste. What they could not possibly understand was that Summer was just like her mother in her need for personal freedom. Summer was too wise to commit to anyone when she had so much of her own life to live first. No one would ever accuse her of either settling or settling down.

The teasing subsided when Sarah resumed the meeting. Afterward,

Gwen stopped Summer before she could put on her coat. "Kiddo, can we talk?"

"About what?" said Summer, wary.

"Nothing important." Gwen forced a smile. Clearly Summer was in no mood for a heart-to-heart. "It can wait. Can you come for supper on Sunday?"

"Can we make it the following week?" Summer tugged on her coat and wrapped her scarf around her neck. "I'm swamped until the end of January."

Puzzled, since January was far from their busiest season, Gwen agreed and promised to make the lentil and brown rice soup Summer loved. Summer thanked her with a quick kiss on the cheek and bounded out the door, and Gwen watched her go. It was hard to believe that Gwen herself had once been so slender and lovely, but she had the photographs to prove it. Summer would accomplish much more with her life than Gwen had, though, because she was brighter and braver than Gwen had ever been.

"You must be very proud," remarked Sylvia as she cleared away the cups and plates left over from their midmeeting snack.

"Proud beyond reason," said Gwen with a laugh.

She stayed behind to help Sylvia tidy the room, and as they carried the dishes to the kitchen, she found herself telling the older woman about her disappointment at work. Sylvia put on a fresh pot of tea and they sat at the kitchen table while Gwen confessed the whole sorry tale.

"I spent most of my teaching career trying to convince people quilting was art," said Sylvia when Gwen had finished. "Now you're trying to persuade them it's a relevant art. I suppose that's progress of a sort."

"At that rate, in another forty years, no one will have these arguments anymore." Gwen stared glumly into her teacup, wishing she could read the leaves. "Just in time for my great-grandchildren."

"The woman they chose instead—what is her field of study?"

"Media and the political process, mostly. How campaigns have changed over time, the role of debates in elections." She forced herself to add, "I have to admit it's interesting work."

"I'm sure it is, but that doesn't make your work dull or irrelevant." Sylvia drummed her fingers on the tabletop. "I wish I could think of a quilt that figured heavily in politics, but I'm afraid nothing comes to mind. The closest I can come is the time Mrs. Roosevelt was presented with the prizewinning quilt from a contest held at the 1933 World's Fair in Chicago."

Gwen set down her teacup. "Eleanor Roosevelt?"

"That's right. This was the biggest quilt competition ever held, before or since. Nearly twenty-five thousand quilters submitted quilts, and my sister and I were two of them." Sylvia chuckled. "We bent the rules a little by making our quilt together. When we signed the form saying that the quilt was entirely of our own making, Claudia wrote, 'Claudia Sylvia Bergstrom.' That was her idea. I thought no one would believe a mother would name her child Claudia Sylvia, but they must not have noticed, because we made it to the semifinals."

Gwen laughed. "Sylvia, I'm shocked. You cheated in a quilt competition?"

"Only in a sense," she protested. "Keep in mind, I was only thirteen and my sister fifteen. If we combined our ages we were still younger than most of the other participants, so we decided we weren't really cheating."

Sylvia explained that they weren't the only participants to interpret the rules liberally. The woman who claimed the grand prize had not put a single stitch into the quilt submitted in her name. Instead she sent the fabric and pattern to one woman who pieced the top, while another added beautiful stuffed work, and still others contributed the exquisite, sixteen-stitches-to-the-inch quilting. The winner paid her team of helpers a modest fee for their labor, but refused to share any of the prize money with them after she won. "They were poor women, too, and it was the Depression," said Sylvia disapprovingly. "The grand prize of one thousand dollars was an enormous sum in those days, more than a year's salary for most people. I never understood why she wasn't more generous."

"How does Eleanor Roosevelt figure in this story?"

"After the World's Fair, the grand prize quilt was presented to her and kept at the White House. It has since disappeared. Now, that would be a project worth researching. I'd give a lot to know what happened to that quilt." Sylvia sipped her tea, thoughtful. "But whatever happened to it, and however one regards the woman who won, that's not what I think of when I recall that quilt show. The theme of the fair was 'A Century of Progress,' and the interpretations those quilters produced were simply remarkable. There were quilts that celebrated advances in technology, transportation, industry, women's fight for equal rights—and remember, this was at a time when the nation was truly struggling. To see all those expressions of optimism and hope when we had so recently seen the worst of times in the Great War and were now mired in the Depression—well, it certainly impressed me, even at my age."

"You saw the quilts? In person?"

"Yes, indeed. My father took my sister, my brother, and me to the World's Fair that year. It was a long journey to Chicago with three children in tow. I can't imagine what he was thinking, but I'm glad he did it." Sylvia rose and inclined her head to the doorway. "I saved a box full of souvenirs, if you would like to see them."

Gwen wouldn't have dreamed of doing otherwise, so she followed Sylvia up the oak staircase to the third floor, where Sylvia gestured to the narrow set of stairs leading to the attic. She declined to accompany Gwen farther, but she described the old walnut bureau so well that Gwen found it easily, halfway down the west wing. Gwen retrieved an engraved tin box from the bottom drawer and dusted it with her sleeve as she carried it down the creaking staircase.

They went to the library, where the embers of an earlier blaze still glowed in the fireplace. Sylvia seated herself nearby, but Gwen sat on the floor at her feet, the better to spread out the box's treasures. Inside she found brochures, ticket stubs, programs, photographs, and other items that must have been added later—newspaper articles from around the country featuring local quiltmakers whose entries had made it to the finals, advertisements from Sears Roebuck announcing their sponsorship of the contest, commercial patterns taken from prizewinning quilts, a tattered ribbon with writing in faded ink naming Claudia Sylvia Bergstrom as the first-place winner from the Harrisburg Sears.

Before long Gwen became so engrossed in examining the artifacts that she hardly remembered to thank Sylvia when the older woman rose to go to bed, telling her to stay as long as she liked. Alone, Gwen lost track of the hours as she pored over the yellowed newspaper articles and studied the show catalogue. The picture that emerged from the fragile scraps of history was not the little-known anecdote from the life of Eleanor Roosevelt that Gwen had hoped to find, but something far more intriguing. The quilts entered in the 1933 World's Fair contest had captured the national mood during a time of extreme trial. Granted, the theme "A Century of Progress" would have encouraged more optimistic interpretations in those days than in Gwen's ironic era, but even if the quiltmakers had been steered toward a rosier perspective, their quilts still could be considered an accurate record of how those women defined progress.

This was it, Gwen realized. This was her new book.

She surveyed the orderly groupings of souvenirs on the floor all around her. Sylvia's treasure trove of information was surely just the beginning. If nearly twenty-five thousand quilts had been submitted, surely there were more newspaper articles about the women who had made them, more scandals like the one surrounding the dubious honor of the grand prize winner, more mysteries such as the disappearance of the winning quilt—and, of course, the quilts themselves. A few hundred or even a few thousand of them might still exist, and if their makers were still around or had left diaries behind or had told their children stories—

"Sylvia's quilt," Gwen suddenly exclaimed. Sylvia had shown her the souvenirs, but not the quilt she and Claudia had made. She scrambled to her feet, left the library, and hurried down the hall to Sylvia's room. She rapped softly at the door and drew back when Andrew opened it, squinting.

"What's wrong?" he asked in a hoarse whisper.

"I'm sorry. Did I wake you?"

His brow furrowed. "Of course. It's ten after one."

"What?" She should have checked her watch. "Never mind. It can wait until tomorrow."

"Is this a quilt thing?"

"What else would you expect at this hour? I'm sorry, Andrew. Go back to sleep."

He shrugged as Gwen pulled the door shut softly. It was probably good she had woken him instead of Sylvia. Gwen doubted she herself could have managed so much tolerant humor in Andrew's place. He was a rarity among his sex, the sort of man she could understand a woman wanting to marry.

She returned the souvenirs to the box and placed it carefully on a bookcase away from the fireplace and windows. As she drove home, her mind raced with possibilities. Tracking down her primary source materials would be a challenge, most likely involving travel—which meant finding grants to pay for it.

❧

The next morning, she arrived at her office so jubilant that when Jules came to see her—once more either the bravest of her graduate students or the one who had drawn the short straw—he looked at her as if unsure whether she had indulged in some mind-altering substances more potent than caffeine. She immediately sent him off to the library to search the online newspaper archives for articles on the 1933 Chicago World's Fair. "What about my other assignments?" he asked, halfway out the door.

"Forget about those for now. This is our new project."

He didn't ask why. Gwen supposed the previous day's announcement provided reason enough.

Jules must have spread the word to her two other graduate students that it was safe to approach, because they stopped by before noon for their new assignments. As for herself, she alternated between searching the Internet for leads on funding sources and scanning her reference books of Depression-era quilts for possible Sears National Quilt Contest entries, even if they were not expressly identified as such. In a ten-year-old auction catalogue she found a floral appliquéd medallion quilt with "A Century of Progress" embroidered in a scroll across the top, but nothing in the item's description alluded to the World's Fair contest. It had to be connected, and a bit of research would uncover the particulars. Exultant, she concluded that this lucky find was a positive omen and thanked whatever divine spirit had inspired Sylvia to tell her about the contest.

The rapidly approaching camp season, the deadline for Sylvia's bridal quilt, and even the committee's misguided decision slipped to the back of her thoughts as her new research consumed her time and her imagination. Even her graduate students caught her enthusiasm after she explained the scope of the project and made them swear on the fate of their doctoral dissertations that they would discuss it with no one. Before their weekly business meeting on the last day of January, she and Sylvia arranged to meet at the manor in the afternoon to search for the Bergstrom sisters' entry.

"I know where it ought to be," said Sylvia, huffing slightly as she led Gwen up the narrow staircase to the attic. "My concern is that it was moved during a search for something else."

Gwen switched on the light and sneezed, waving away dust motes. "Is it possible Claudia sold it?" She had sold many other family heirlooms during Sylvia's fifty-year absence from Elm Creek Manor, including their mother's own bridal quilt.

"It's possible, but I doubt it. Claudia rarely won ribbons for her handiwork. I doubt she would have parted with any quilt of hers that earned such recognition. Of course, she never would have made it to the semifinals working on her own."

"Of course not," said Gwen, hiding a smile.

Sylvia directed Gwen to a section of the attic not far from the walnut bureau and gestured to a collection of trunks and boxes. "If it's here, this is where we'll find it."

There they found papers, books, china, clothing, and assorted items Gwen would have tossed out with the trash if they were in her house, but no quilts. When Gwen decided to broaden their search area, she discovered a bundle of Storm at Sea blocks pieced from the pastel cottons common to the late 1920s and early 1930s. Sylvia examined them and announced that Claudia had made them, judging from the poorly matched seams that she never would have permitted in her own work. "You're on the right track, dear," said Sylvia approvingly, and took up the search nearby.

Before long they found the quilt, nestled into a paper box all its own. Gwen held it up so Sylvia could examine it. The quilt was in fine condition for its age, a testament, Sylvia noted, to the excellent care it had received, except during shipping and at the judging venues. Even so, few stains marred the green, lavender, rose, and ivory quilt, which was accented with appliquéd features in bold red, blue, and black.

The design itself was a compromise, Sylvia explained. Sylvia had wanted to create an original pictorial quilt inspired by the "Century of Progress" theme, but Claudia thought they would stand a better chance of pleasing the judges if they used a traditional pattern and devoted their time to flawless, intricate needlework rather than novelty. After an argument spanning several weeks—which would have been better spent sewing—they agreed that Sylvia could design a central appliqué medallion depicting various scenes from colonial times until the present day, to which Claudia would add a border of pieced blocks. "Odd Fellow's Chain," said Sylvia, fingering the border. "Obviously, she chose it for its appearance, not its name."

"Unless she meant to make a statement about contemporary notions of progress."

"Hmph." Sylvia showed a hint of a smile. "Claudia was not that clever. The block did give us the quilt's title, however. We called it Chain of Progress."

Gwen draped the quilt over an upholstered armchair to better examine it. She could see in this early example of Sylvia's work how her tastes and skills had developed through the decades. The uneven quality of the needlework she attributed to the widely differing abilities of the two sisters, but even the worst pieced Odd Fellow's Chain block proved that Claudia could not have been as poor a quilter as Sylvia suggested. The green Ribbon of Merit still attached to the quilt attested to that.

Gwen was imagining how Chain of Progress would look on the cover of her book when Sylvia began folding it. "It's almost time for the meeting. Shall we take this downstairs and surprise our friends?"

"No," Gwen exclaimed. "I don't want anyone to know."

"Why on earth not? If you want to track down other contest entries, the more people who know about your project, the better. You never know who might provide a useful lead."

"I will tell them eventually. Soon," she amended, when Sylvia raised her eyebrows. "First I want to be sure there is a book in this. Then I'll be grateful for help."

"You'll be lucky if you get any, keeping secrets from your friends as if you're afraid they'll steal your ideas," admonished Sylvia. "Whenever the Elm Creek Quilters keep secrets from one another, it always means trouble."

"Not always," said Gwen, remembering Sylvia's bridal quilt and the block she had yet to begin.

🦋

The next day, Gwen received a response to an email she had sent to the Chicago Historical Society. They agreed her idea was worth pursuing and would consider funding a portion of her research if she submitted a full proposal by their annual deadline, February 5.

That left Gwen with only a few days to pull together all the information they needed, but fortunately, she had no plans for the weekend. On Friday afternoon after her last class, she hurried home, turned off the ringer on the phone, and hid her cell phone in a kitchen drawer. She resolved not only to complete her proposal in time, but to write the best, most persuasive proposal the Chicago Historical Society had ever seen. One late night blurred into an early morning, and another, as she feverishly raced to meet her deadline. If she succeeded, it wouldn't be one of Annette's six-figure triumphs, but it would be a start.

"Mom?"

Gwen jumped at the sound of Summer's voice from elsewhere in the house. "In here," she called, typing frantically even when she heard her daughter enter the room. "Hi, kiddo. What's up?" Then she remembered, and she spun her chair around, dismayed. "Oh, no. Supper."

"Sunday at five o'clock," Summer said, grinning and tapping her watch.

"I completely forgot." How could she forget inviting her only child for a meal? "We could send out for pizza."

Summer assured her she would be satisfied with a sandwich to accompany the salad she had brought, and Gwen suddenly realized she had taken nothing but coffee since breakfast. Her refrigerator was shamefully empty, as she had skipped her customary Saturday morning trip to the grocery store, but Summer, as always, was a good sport. She was also always very curious, and she soon asked her mother what she was working on.

Gwen couldn't tell her. She knew her idea would make a fascinating, informative book—but maybe she was not the person to write it. She could not bear to tell Summer later that she had abandoned a brilliant research project because, ultimately, Bill and his committee were correct: She was good enough for what she did, but she need not aspire to anything greater.

Gwen tried to put Summer off, but Summer persisted, so Gwen told her about the committee's decision not to appoint her department chair. Summer's indignation warmed her and reminded her that she had made some important discoveries in her tenure at Waterford College. Too bad Bill lacked Summer's insight—or bias.

Then Summer asked, "So what were you working on? A new paper on a new topic?"

"I'll let you read it when it's done."

Summer nodded, but Gwen knew she was disappointed, despite her light-hearted reassurances about Gwen's forthcoming book. She thought her mother was giving up the study of quilt history to appease the committee.

Gwen wanted to assure her she wasn't, she wouldn't. She wanted to see pride shining in her daughter's eyes again. But she could not commit that hope to words until she knew she would not have to relinquish her new project to a more able scholar.

She tried to change the subject by asking how Jeremy was doing. Summer said he was fine and she saw him often, but offered no more than that. They talked about the upcoming camp season and Sylvia's bridal quilt, but Gwen was too conscious of disappointing Summer to enjoy the rest of the meal.

The next morning, she decided to stop by Summer's place on her way to work. It wasn't really on the way, but Gwen was eager to apologize for her forgetfulness and her evasive behavior the previous night. Karen opened to her knock and told her Summer had left not long before, but Aaron hovered in the background, his expression so alarmed and wary that Gwen knew at once Summer had not spent the night there.

So. Summer must have slept at Jeremy's. Gwen thanked the roommates, who were visibly relieved not to be interrogated further, and departed without leaving a message. She could hardly criticize Summer for doing something many other young women her age did, something she herself had done. She just hoped Summer wouldn't make a habit of it, and build up Jeremy's expectations when she surely had no intentions of leaving with him upon his graduation.

Surely Summer had no such intentions?

With a knot in the pit of her stomach, Gwen continued on to campus, pausing only to drop her grant proposal in the overnight express pickup box.

February passed in a frenzy of classes, research, writing, and the submission of grant proposals, with worries about Summer and Jeremy lingering in the back of Gwen's mind. She would have forgotten Sylvia's bridal quilt entirely if not for the invitation letter pinned to the bulletin board behind her computer, and she had so neglected her preparations for the upcoming quilt camp season that at the first business meeting of March, when Sarah told her they needed to cancel some of her classes, Gwen felt too guilty to argue. That feeling was compounded when Summer, who had asked to speak to her afterward, changed her mind, obviously sensing Gwen's eagerness to get back to work. They made plans to have supper the following Sunday, and this time, Gwen vowed not to forget.

When the evening arrived, she set aside her notes, which were accumulating with reassuring speed, to make a batch of almond cookies to follow Summer's favorite vegetable stir-fry. Summer showed up right on time with pot stickers and spring rolls from their favorite carry-out, and they spent an enjoyable hour eating and talking about Elm Creek Quilt Camp. Summer had some great ideas about new seminars she wanted to try, but she confessed to having no idea which block to make for Sylvia's quilt. "I hope Elm Creek Quilters get an automatic extension," she added. "I'm planning to run my block over to Agnes's house at midnight on the very last day."

Gwen laughed and admitted to her own difficulties. "On the surface it seems like an easy project," she said. "Make one six-inch block. What could be simpler?"

"Adding the condition that it represents all that Sylvia means to us, that's what," said Summer. "The blocks accumulating at Grandma's Attic typically express that in their names. But what if you can't find a block with an appropriate name? What if you'd rather express yourself visually?"

"Exactly," said Gwen. She and Summer never failed to find the same bandwidth. "I've decided the only way to resolve the problem is to design an original block. I know it's taking the easy way out—"

"I doubt it, Mom," said Summer, laughing. "It won't be easy to invent a completely original pattern."

"At least I can name it whatever I like."

Summer agreed that Gwen's method had its merits, but she planned to keep looking. Then, suddenly, she hesitated. "Mom, remember last Thursday, when I said I needed to talk to you?"

Gwen recalled that Summer had said she *wanted* to talk, not that she *needed* to talk, a significant difference in mother-daughter parlance. Suddenly she thought of Jeremy, then Jeremy in his doctoral hood clutching a diploma under his arm as he helped Summer load a moving van.

"Sure, kiddo." She steeled herself. "What's up?"

"You know that Jeremy and I are very close." She paused so long that Gwen realized she was supposed to nod, so she did. "Well, his roommate moved out at the end of fall semester, and he needed to find someone to share the rent. Remember how great his place is?"

It was nice enough, for a student apartment. "He's having trouble finding someone?"

"No, actually. He found someone. Me." Summer took a quick breath and plunged ahead. "It's so much more convenient than my old place, and much less expensive, too. I don't even have to pay for parking anymore, and I *so* don't miss all the partying every weekend."

She continued, but what registered in Gwen's mind was, first, that Summer was not planning to leave Waterford with Jeremy in the immediate future, and second, that she was speaking in the present tense. She had already moved. Without seeking Gwen's advice, without giving Gwen a chance to talk some sense into her.

"Mom?" Summer prompted, worriedly.

All Gwen could say was, "Why?"

Summer repeated the list of reasons almost verbatim, as if she had rehearsed many times. Gwen forced herself to remain calm, then pointed out—quite reasonably, given the circumstances—that Summer and Jeremy had not been together very long, surely not long enough to know whether he was worth the sacrifice of her independence. Summer rolled her eyes, a gesture Gwen loathed; it signified that she was an old-fashioned, closed-minded throwback to the olden days rather than the hip mom of the twenty-first century she liked to imagine herself.

Summer was twenty-seven, old enough to make her own decisions. Gwen knew that. She wasn't sure, however, if Summer understood the entirety of the decision she had made.

Give her your blessing, Gwen told herself. But she held back. Summer had made decisions Gwen had disagreed with before, and her announcements had always come with a hint of concern that Gwen would not approve. This time Gwen sensed something more, that Summer sought her approval in order to convince herself she had not made a mistake.

What bothered Gwen most of all was that despite her obvious uncertainty, Summer had not talked it over with her before making her choice.

✌

A few days later, Gwen took a break from her research to shop for fabric. Grandma's Attic was cheaper than therapy.

Although she had chosen one of Summer's afternoons off, Gwen still glanced around from the doorway before entering the quilt shop to make sure her daughter was not there. Bonnie was in the back office, looking morose as she paged through a folder. She happened to glance up as Gwen entered the shop, then mouthed something inaudible through the glass as she put away the file and rose to meet her.

"Keep working if you want," said Gwen as Bonnie exited the office, wondering what in that file had the power to make her optimistic friend look so glum. "I'll just browse for a while."

Bonnie sighed and seated herself on a stool by the cutting table. "No, I could use a break."

"If you don't mind my saying so, you're looking rather grim today."

"Thanks. I can always count on my friends to cheer me up with praise." But Bonnie managed a wan smile and indicated the office with a nod. "This should be a profitable business. Even with high rents and a competitor undercutting me at every turn, I should be in the black every month. What am I doing wrong?"

"You're too nice," said Gwen, recalling many conversations with Summer on that subject. "People take advantage."

"Customers, friends, husbands, children—I know, but what can I do?" She peered at Gwen. "You know, you're looking rather grim yourself."

"Funny you should mention children," said Gwen dryly. "I just found out Summer moved in with Jeremy."

Bonnie said nothing.

Gwen stared at her. "You knew?"

"Only since yesterday."

"Oh." At least Gwen wasn't the last to know; that was something. "At first I thought she was crazy. Then I decided it was a delayed form of rebellion. My current theory is ignorance."

"Ignorance?"

"Ignorance of what she's getting herself into."

Bonnie looked dubious. "Maybe that's what she wants to explore, I mean, before she gets in any deeper."

"Don't tell me you approve."

"Actually, I'm surprised you don't. Isn't this better than rushing into marriage?" She rubbed her chin absently. "If I had lived with Craig before marrying him, I might have decided against it."

"Then it's a good thing you didn't, right? Anyway, that doesn't always work. I lived with Summer's father before we got married, and we split up soon after."

"You lived in a van with a bunch of other flower children," Bonnie reminded her. "And you were probably high most of the time."

"I was not," Gwen retorted. "That's slander. Pot gave me migraines."

"So you say." Bonnie sighed. "Listen. If I had found out before you, would you have wanted me to tell you?"

"Absolutely. I would have counted on it." Gwen studied her, then, with some effort, hopped up to sit on the cutting table. "Why? What else do you know?"

"This isn't about Summer."

"But clearly it's about someone we know, so spill it."

Bonnie hesitated. "I was in the liquor store the other night—"

"Rough day?"

"You have no idea. Anyway, you'll never guess who I saw buying beer."

"Who?"

"Michael."

"Michael? Diane's son Michael?"

Bonnie nodded. "He showed the clerk an ID, but it must have been fake. Michael saw me, too, and froze right there at the counter. I gave him a look, you know, like he'd better watch out, but I didn't say anything. Should I have? He just bought the beer and left as fast as he could. Should I have stopped him, told the clerk, something? What would you have done?"

"I don't know." Gwen pondered the question. "I think I would have been too startled to react. I probably would have done the same as you."

"You mean, done nothing." Still, Bonnie looked somewhat relieved. "So what should I do now? Should I tell Diane?"

"How old is Michael, anyway? Nineteen?"

"Twenty."

Gwen shook her head. "I don't know. He can drive, he can join the military, he can vote—who are we to say he can't drink?"

"We aren't saying it. Pennsylvania state law says it." Bonnie let her hands fall into her lap, helpless. "He could get into a lot of trouble, if not with the drinking, then with using a fake ID. Aren't friends supposed to keep an eye out for each other's kids?"

"Maybe just thinking you'll tell Diane will keep him honest."

Bonnie shrugged, unconvinced. "I don't want to turn a blind eye. If he should get hurt, I'd never forgive myself. Diane would never forgive me, and I wouldn't blame her."

"Then why haven't you told Diane already?"

"Well, like you said, he is twenty years old."

"You don't have to tattle to Diane," said Gwen. "You could talk to Michael himself."

"What would I say?"

"You're a mom. You know what to do. Tell him what you're worried about. Remind him he's breaking the law." Gwen grinned. "And then threaten to tell Diane if he doesn't clean up his act."

Bonnie said she would think about it.

With Bonnie's help, Gwen searched the shelves until she found several bold geometric prints in the appropriate hues for Sylvia's bridal quilt. She bought twice as much fabric as she needed with the excuse she might attempt several different designs in her search for an original pattern. Bonnie gave her a sidelong look, but she said nothing to indicate she knew Gwen was trying to alleviate Bonnie's financial worries one yard of fabric at a time.

Gwen decided she would set aside fifteen minutes each day to work on the block, but her resolve quickly eroded under the mounting pressures of her new research project and the upcoming camp season. With only a week to go, she scrambled to revise her lesson plans, assemble samples, and gather materials, glad for the activity to consume time she otherwise would have spent worrying over Summer.

It took an all-nighter, but somehow she managed to finish by the first day of camp, which only involved registration and welcoming ceremonies, not the more challenging and enjoyable work of teaching. The second day of camp had a less promising start, with an early-morning phone call from Sarah asking her to take over an afternoon class for Judy later that week. Gwen agreed, wondering what was going on and why Judy had not told her about the trip to Philadelphia. Guiltily, she reflected that she had not stopped by to chat with her friend since the day she had found out about the department chair. They usually got together for coffee or lunch at least once a week. The last few times they had spoken at business meetings, Gwen had not even remembered to ask how Judy's mother was recovering from a serious bout of pneumonia that had afflicted her throughout January. She would have to apologize when Judy returned.

Gwen's quilt camp seminars went well, as she expected, and she didn't regret the one that had been canceled. Mindful of how she had neglected friendships and camp responsibilities of late, she gave herself a few days' vacation from her research. It was spring break, after all, and her grad students needed the time off even if she didn't. Besides, the first week of camp usually brought with it a few unexpected surprises. She needed to be flexible in case of another curveball like Judy's absence.

The wild pitch came out of nowhere on Wednesday. At lunchtime, she found Sylvia, Sarah, Diane, and Agnes sequestered at a table at the back of the banquet hall rather than scattered among the campers as usual. She joined them, only to find her friends huddled over the daily schedule.

Sarah looked up at her approach, harried. "Could you emcee the quilted clothing fashion show for the evening program tonight?"

"Sure," Gwen said with a shrug. "I thought Bonnie was doing it."

"Maybe she will, but she didn't show up for her workshop this morning, so I thought I should have a backup plan."

"Didn't show up?" Gwen sat down. "Why not?"

"No one knows," said Agnes, fingering her beaded necklace worriedly. "She didn't call in, and no one's answering the phone at the store."

"You tried her at home, right?"

"Well, yes, but—well, she's not there, either," said Agnes.

"Summer drove to Grandma's Attic a few minutes ago," said Sylvia. "She'll call us when she learns anything."

Gwen nodded. Summer worked an afternoon shift at the quilt shop on Wednesdays. If Bonnie had not shown up for work there, either, Summer would be unable to look for her elsewhere and too busy to call.

As soon as her afternoon workshop concluded, Gwen found Agnes in the hallway and told her she was on her way to Grandma's Attic. She parked behind the store next to Summer's car, then hurried around to the front entrance. The door was locked, the sign in the window turned to CLOSED several hours ahead of time. She cupped her hands around her eyes and peered inside.

Summer and Bonnie worked amid overturned shelves and piles of scattered cloth and notions, deliberately, wearily, battling the mess.

Gwen gasped and pounded on the door. Bonnie started, but quickly recognized Gwen and carefully made her way across the room. "What happened?" Gwen exclaimed after Bonnie let her in.

"We had a break-in." Without pausing to elaborate, Bonnie returned to work.

Gwen stood rooted in place, stunned, until Summer came over and hugged her. "Come on, Mom," she murmured. "We could use the help."

Gwen nodded and joined her. Quietly, Summer explained the little she knew as they tried to restore unwound yards of fabric to their bolts. Surprisingly little had been taken. Money and tools. A sewing machine. Several packs of Pigma pens. Blocks for Sylvia's bridal quilt. The police had spent all morning and most of the afternoon combing the store for clues, dusting for fingerprints, questioning Bonnie and Summer, taking photographs. They had found no evidence of a forced entry, so they suspected an inside job.

"What?" said Gwen, astounded. An inside job meant someone with a key: Bonnie, Summer, Diane, possibly Craig. "That makes no sense."

None of it made any sense. Why take Sylvia's blocks instead of an extra sewing machine? Why trash the place instead of fleeing with the most expensive merchandise? The bizarre scene suggested vengeance—or a horrible prank.

"Someone must have left the door unlocked," she told Bonnie later as together they struggled to right an overturned bookcase. "Some college students must have passed by on their way home from the bars and found it open. Drunken kids have a sick idea of fun."

"I locked the door myself." Bonnie's mouth set in a hard, worried line. "No college students did this. There are three keys. I didn't do it, and I know Diane and Summer didn't, so it must have been someone with access to one of our keys. At first I thought—"

"Thought what? Who?"

"Nothing. Someone who as it turns out wasn't anywhere near a key." Bonnie glanced at Summer on the other side of the room and lowered her voice. "Then I remembered."

"What?" Gwen glanced worriedly at Summer. Surely Bonnie didn't suspect Jeremy—or herself.

"Last Friday I ran into Michael. I warned him about the dangers of alcohol abuse, of breaking the law—you know, the standard mom lecture."

Gwen nodded, heart sinking.

"I also told him to give me his fake ID or I'd tell his parents what I had seen him do with it." Bonnie took a deep, shaky breath. "He gave it to me, but he was furious. He stalked off without another word, but he gave me a look over his shoulder I'll never forget. Gwen, now that ID is gone."

"How can you be sure, with this mess?"

"I'm sure."

"We've known Michael since he was a baby," said Gwen in a whisper, glancing at her daughter. Summer used to baby-sit Michael and his brother. She defended him against all criticism, especially when he most deserved it. "He's made mistakes, but he would never do anything like this."

"Wouldn't he? Remember when he was in the ninth grade, and he vandalized the school?"

Gwen could not reply. Until that moment, she had forgotten the incident.

Bonnie scrubbed a hand through her short hair and glanced about as if desperately seeking another answer amid the debris.

Quietly, Gwen asked, "Did you tell the police?"

"No," said Bonnie, shaking her head. "Not yet."

Chapter Four

Bonnie

Craig was gone when Bonnie woke, but she knew he had come home because the bed in the guest room had been slept in. Still in her flannel nightgown, Bonnie made the bed and plumped up the pillow. When Craig had first stopped sharing the master bedroom, Bonnie had been troubled, even hurt, but she had grown accustomed to his absence. It was easier than lying beside him wondering what she could do to inspire some affection in him, wondering if it was worth the bother.

There was a time when Craig would have called to let her know he was working late. There was a time, Bonnie thought ruefully as she showered and drew on her bathrobe, when he would have turned down overtime in his eagerness to come home to his family. That time was so long ago it preceded the children, Grandma's Attic, her first gray hairs.

At least with Craig gone she could eat breakfast in her bathrobe without snide comments about her appearance. At least she could read the newspaper without worrying about irritating him by getting the sections out of order. In many ways his absence was preferable to his silent presence. Even that was far better than their one-sided arguments, in which Craig complained and criticized and Bonnie simply let his words wash over her. He didn't really mean it, she would tell herself, until a particularly harsh jab provoked her into reminding him that someone who had been forgiven for a cyber affair had little room for error. He would explode then and accuse her of not really forgiving him, of enjoying her grudge, of finding a perverse pleasure in taunting him forever for his one mistake.

But it was not his one mistake; it was simply his biggest mistake. As far as she knew. And wasn't that part of the problem, that she would never know and always wonder?

He probably had worked late. The Office of the Physical Plant was understaffed, and winter meant sidewalks to clear of snow and frozen pipes to thaw. But Craig could very well have decided that anyplace was preferable to home. Bonnie often felt that way.

Grandma's Attic was her haven. She could not imagine how she would have endured the past few years without it. The quilt shop was one sign that she had not wasted her life, that she was not a failure. Her children were the other. But they were so far away and visited so rarely that they probably had no idea that an equally vast distance separated their parents.

Bonnie put on a warm pair of slacks and her oldest but most favorite quilted vest, made from miniature purple-and-green Pineapple blocks. She'd had to rip out many a seam during the months it had taken her to complete it, and she wore it whenever she needed a reminder that even the most difficult times would eventually pass.

She opened the shop and worked in the office until customers arrived. She dreaded looking at the accounts. Holiday sales had boosted their gross income, allowing her to pay off their worst debts, but January sales were down from the previous year, and February seemed to be matching that disappointing pace. She was not surprised. She could hardly open the *Waterford Register* without seeing an advertisement for the huge chain fabric store on the outskirts of town. If not for Summer's help, Bonnie would have been forced to close the shop years before. Whenever Grandma's Attic teetered on the brink of bankruptcy, Summer would somehow come up with an inspired idea for bringing quilters into the shop. Sales would surge for a time, then dwindle as the novelty of their innovation faded. The one exception was their virtual quilt shop on the Internet, which had garnered consistently strong sales since its inception. One day, Bonnie surmised, email orders might account for the majority of their profits.

A few customers came in, some merely to browse, drawn inside by the colorful display in the front window. Then morning mail arrived, and with it, more bills. Bonnie set those aside and opened the larger packages, which contained more contributions for Sylvia's bridal quilt. They were lovely, but Bonnie would have been grateful for them even if they were only half as well made. At their current pace, they would have only enough blocks for a modest lap quilt, although she wouldn't admit that to Sarah until absolutely necessary.

Summer arrived moments later and, as always, her confidence and good cheer made Bonnie glad she would be leaving the quilt shop in such good hands after her retirement. Summer greeted her as she slipped off her coat, her eyes lighting up at the sight of the packages on the cutting table. "Can I see the new blocks?" she asked. Bonnie handed them over and forced herself to sort through the rest of the mail. Good news rarely came to Grandma's Attic in a business-size envelope.

The phone bill was lower than usual; Bonnie congratulated herself for keeping to her resolution to use email whenever it would save her a long-distance call. The power bill was higher, as expected, due to the recent cold snap. She sighed and opened the last envelope, something from University Realty, most likely an advertisement. Anything but another bill.

February 1, 2002

Dear Ms. Bonnie Markham:

I am pleased to announce that Waterford Commercial Properties has sold your building to University Realty, Inc. Welcome to the University Realty family. A fixture in the Waterford community since 1957, University Realty is the area's finest resource for commercial and residential properties.

Within the next week, a representative from University Realty will visit your business in order to discuss the terms of our rental agreement for any tenants who wish to remain in their current location. The visit for Grandma's Attic is scheduled for Tuesday, February 12, at 10:45 A.M. If this is not convenient, please contact our office. However, please note that new leases must be signed within ninety days of the sale to University Realty, after which expired tenants risk eviction.

Again, thank you for joining the community of properties owned and operated by University Realty. We look forward to a long and rewarding relationship with you.

Sincerely,
Gregory H. Krolich
Vice-President

Bonnie read the letter a second time, disbelieving. How could something like this happen without any word to the tenants? What would this mean for the condo upstairs? She could not recall all the clauses of their purchase agreement. Surely University Realty could not touch their home, and even if they raised the rent on the shop, they couldn't afford more than a modest increase. Far too many storefronts in downtown Waterford stood empty already. The new owners had to offer competitive rents or risk losing all their tenants.

"What is it?" asked Summer, watching her with concern.

"The building's been sold. All tenants have to sign new leases if we want to stay."

"Of course you'll stay," said Summer. "Where do they expect you to go? They won't raise the rent, will they?"

"The letter doesn't say." But Bonnie was sure the rent would go up. Why else would Gregory Krolich have included that vague, threatening line about the dangers of missing her scheduled meeting and becoming an "expired tenant"?

She tried to answer Summer's questions about the stipulations of her lease, but she was too upset, her thoughts a swirl of confusion. The last thing she needed, what with Craig so distant and the shop already in financial trouble, was to have to worry about the expense and hassle of moving.

She spent the rest of Summer's shift in the office, going over books, paying the utility bills, and ordering products from the few suppliers who had not yet suspended her credit. At the end of the day she closed the shop, walked to the corner grocery for milk and coffee, and went home. On her way upstairs she checked the mail, only to find a second envelope from University Realty. She set it on top of the pile of bills and advertisements on the counter and started supper, taking a chance on making enough for two. So far Craig had never stayed away for more than a day without calling.

When the chicken was in the oven, Bonnie steeled herself and opened the envelope. Inside she found a letter announcing the sale in slightly more cordial tones than before. This time Gregory Krolich expressed his hopes that the Markhams would consider selling the condo to his company so that they might make it available for "other residential purposes." He promised to phone within the next few days to arrange a meeting.

"You have a different attitude when you want to buy, don't you?" muttered Bonnie as she tossed the letter on the counter. Did this Gregory Krolich even notice he had written to her twice? Perhaps not; the condo was in Craig's name, too, while the shop was in Bonnie's alone. Still, if Krolich wanted them to sell their home, he ought to be more civil regarding her shop—and more flexible about the new lease.

With the first stirring of hope she had felt since morning, Bonnie finished preparing supper. She did have some leverage after all. Though the thought of lying to Krolich made her uncomfortable, she could not allow him to believe she might sell the condo until they had settled on the terms of their new rental agreement for the shop. She would do anything to save Grandma's Attic. If she could consider firing one of her closest friends, she could mislead Krolich for a few weeks. Businesspeople did that sort of thing all the time. Just because she was new at it—

The outside door opened and shut. Craig did not call out, but she knew it was her husband from the familiar sounds of snow boots thumping on the linoleum and the closet door squeaking as he put away his coat. "Supper will be ready soon," she said without turning around when she heard him enter the kitchen.

"What are we having?"

"Baked chicken, the kind with parmesan cheese in the crust. Mashed potatoes and peas."

He grunted his acceptance and took a beer from the refrigerator. She waited, but he said nothing about his absence. She vowed not to ask, but she did a slow burn as she set the table and served the meal.

They ate in silence, Craig's face hidden behind the newspaper.

"We received some interesting mail today," she said eventually. "Our building has been sold. The new owners want to buy our condo."

"What?" said Craig. She repeated herself, and he set down the paper. "What was their offer?"

"They weren't that specific." Bonnie wished she wasn't so pleased that she finally had his attention. "I'll also have to sign a new lease for the shop."

"They'll probably raise your rent."

"Yes, I rather expect them to."

He shrugged and picked up the paper again. "Maybe now's a good time to get out, then."

Bonnie stared at him, hard. "Why would I want to get out?"

He glanced at her, his expression full of disbelief and exasperation, as if he could not believe he had to argue the same points again when he had made himself perfectly clear many times before. "When's the last time you made a profit? It's a hobby, not a business. Everything you earn from Elm Creek Quilts goes into keeping that store afloat. We have better uses for the money." He wiped his mouth and dropped his napkin onto his plate. "If you'd let go of that place, we could finally move into a real house."

"You want to leave our home?"

He glanced around, taking in with impatient distaste the rooms she had decorated so lovingly. "Did you ever think we'd stay here this long? Maybe you don't care, but I've always wanted my own house with my own yard. Do you realize I never got to play ball with my own sons on my own lawn? If I'd wanted this kind of lifestyle I would have moved to the city, but that store of yours has always come first."

"How dare you," said Bonnie, incredulous, furious. "I never put the store before my children."

"Well, you put it ahead of other things. Other people."

She almost laughed. "You blame Grandma's Attic for our problems?"

"Maybe. Yes. I don't know." He pushed back his chair and rose. "I don't know. Give me the letter and I'll find out what they're willing to offer us for the condo."

"I don't want to move."

"Where's the letter?" He rifled through the stack of mail on the counter. "Never mind. I'll find it and call them tomorrow."

"I don't want to move," Bonnie said again, but Craig found and pocketed the envelope. He indicated the conversation was over by leaving the room. A moment later, she heard the door to the guest room close.

❧

In the week that passed between the arrival of the letter and her appointment with Gregory Krolich, Bonnie saw little of Craig and spoke to him even less. He offered scant explanation for his erratic comings and goings. "By the time I know I won't be coming home," he said, "it's too late to call."

"You won't wake me," she said. "I'm usually awake wondering where you are. Where do you go, anyway? You must be sleeping somewhere."

"I catch a few hours on the sofa in my office."

Bonnie found that hard to believe. She had seen the furniture he picked out when he redecorated after his last promotion, and it looked as uncomfortable as it was worn. She assumed he had bought used rather than new to save money, but she never understood why he did not at least have it re-upholstered and refinished. He said he would get around to it when he had time, but Bonnie doubted it since the furniture resembled some antique pieces they had seen in the President's House on the Penn State campus. Craig was a fervently loyal alumnus, and Bonnie had expected him to be pleased when she had remarked upon the similarities, but instead he had grumbled something about never wasting hard-earned money on designer stuff and ushered her from his office. Still, even if he had intended the resemblance, Bonnie was not convinced he could actually sleep comfortably there.

"Where do you shower and shave?" she asked him.

"I don't," he said, as if it were obvious. "The guys don't care."

On the day of the meeting, Bonnie went to Grandma's Attic carefully attired in her one suit rather than a quilted jacket, determined to make a strong, businesslike impression. The shop was remarkably busy that morning, so that when a man in a black wool coat arrived promptly at ten forty-five, a group of cheerful, well-satisfied customers passed him on the way out. "You must be Mr. Krolich," Bonnie greeted him, pleased that his first impression of Grandma's Attic was that of a lively, thriving business.

"Please call me Greg," he said, removing a leather glove and shaking her hand. "Are you Ms. Markham?"

"Bonnie. Yes."

He glanced around the room, but Bonnie suspected his quick glance took in much more than it appeared. "Is there somewhere we could talk undisturbed?"

The shop was now empty, but Bonnie led him into the back office and offered him the best chair. He removed his coat and sat down, smiling all the while. "Based upon my conversations with other tenants, my guess is this sale came as something of a surprise."

"Shock is the word I would use," said Bonnie, managing a laugh. She seated herself, her hands clasped tightly in her lap.

"I trust you began considering your options when you received our letter."

"Well—" What options? "I think I'll be more able to make an informed decision once I see the rental agreement."

"Of course." He opened his briefcase and withdrew a sheaf of paper in a clear plastic binder. "We have several attractive properties in the downtown area, some within walking distance of your current location. However, I've taken the liberty of highlighting one I think you'll find ideal." He opened the binder and placed it on the desk before her.

At the top of the page was a color photocopied picture of a store in a strip mall. BUTTONS AND BOWS was painted in blue and pink on a window that displayed frilly lace frocks and blue sailor suits. Beneath the picture was a detailed description of the property—square footage, available utilities, address—which Bonnie skimmed before realizing what Greg had assumed.

"Thank you, but I don't intend to move," said Bonnie, smiling apologetically and closing the binder. "I want to see your rental agreement for this location."

"Oh." Greg's expression turned puzzled and alarmed. "You want to stay." "What's wrong?"

"Basically, you're the first of our tenants who wasn't grateful for the opportunity to find a more suitable location." He turned a winsome smile on her and opened the binder again to the correct page without glancing at it. "I understand change can be difficult, but if you drive out and inspect this property, all you'll want to know is how soon you can move in. That's immediately, by the way. The current tenant is retiring."

"I don't need to drive out and see it. I don't want to move Grandma's Attic away from downtown, especially not there. That's right next door to our biggest competitor."

"Exactly. Traffic into the Fabric Warehouse would naturally drift over to you, and if you don't mind my saying so, you look like you could use more business."

More likely Bonnie would lose even more customers to the chain store, but she kept her voice even and asked, "May I please see the new lease for this shop?"

Greg frowned and dug in his briefcase. "Here," he said, slapping it down on the table.

Bonnie skimmed the first page before she stopped, aghast. "This increase in the rent—it must be close to seventy percent!"

"Seventy-five, to be exact." He smiled, and for the first time, Bonnie detected a smug satisfaction in his manner. "Please also note that our leases are for six months and the rent may increase semiannually. It's safe to assume that it will."

Bonnie returned to the document, afraid to ask if seventy-five percent was the standard increment. Some clauses sounded similar to those in her current lease; others seemed to tack on fees for everything from late payment of rent to improper use of the trash receptacles to new distribution of parking in the back alley. She tried to absorb it all, but her mind was fixed on the rent, that outrageous, impossible rent.

"I can't afford this," she finally said, returning the lease. "I suspect none of my neighbors can, either, and that's why they're leaving. I used to serve on the Waterford Zoning Commission and I can tell you these rates are unreasonable for this area in this economic climate. You're going to end up with an empty building and a lot of angry business owners, who might have something to say at the next public review of your business license."

He blinked, clearly unprepared for a challenge from a nice little middle-aged quilt lady. He recovered quickly, but all pretense of helpfulness vanished. "An empty building would be ideal," he said. "We already have plenty of commercial properties. What we need are more student rentals."

Bonnie stared at him. Other buildings on her street had been transformed from offices into apartments, but her building would require extensive remodeling for such a drastic change in purpose. Except for the condos. Suddenly Bonnie pictured her home surrounded by wild undergraduates, the shop, her haven, thrust into the middle of a twenty-four-hour fraternity party.

"You'd be amazed at what students are willing to pay for housing directly across the street from campus," remarked Greg. "Or, rather, what their parents are willing to pay."

"I have no intention of moving," Bonnie said, but less firmly than before. "From the shop or from my home."

His perplexed frown deepened into a scowl as he made the connection. "You've already admitted you can't afford the rent," he said, rising. "Your husband might not find living among college kids as appealing as you do."

"My husband and I stand together on this."

"We'll see." He put on his coat and nodded toward the binder. "Keep that. Like it or not, you're going to need a new location. If you don't like the one I picked, choose for yourself, but choose fast. All of the other tenants have the same binder."

"I already said I'm not moving." She thrust the binder at him. "And if I were to move, I would never rent from you."

"We would have offered you a good price for the condo and an excellent rent in another building." He returned the binder to his briefcase, shaking his head. "Now you'll have to take what you can get."

He picked up his briefcase and strode from the office. "I'll do just fine, thank you," she said, but he ignored her. Beyond him she saw Sarah standing in the middle of the store.

Sarah turned to watch Greg leave, then spun back around to face Bonnie, eyes wide. "Wasn't that Gregory Krolich?"

Bonnie nodded, drained, and sank onto a stool behind the cutting table. What was she going to do? What could she do? She could not have afforded that outrageous rent even in the shop's best days.

"I knew it," declared Sarah. "The real estate business must be treating him well. He's driving an even more expensive car than the last time I saw him."

Suddenly it registered that Sarah had identified him by name. "You know him?"

"Barely. I haven't seen him in years, not since I first moved to Waterford. He wanted to buy Elm Creek Manor and raze it so he could build a few hundred student apartments on the property."

"Obviously he didn't. So he's just a lot of threats and bluster in a nice suit?"

"On the contrary, I'm sure he would have gone through with it if Sylvia hadn't found out about his plan. She refused to sell to him once she learned the truth."

"Oh." Bonnie dropped her gaze and tried to compose herself, her momentary hopes swiftly fading. She would have to come up with a plan, and Craig would have to help her. Even if he did want to move, even if he was no longer in love with her, surely pride would compel him to intercede when someone tried to intimidate his wife and drive them from their home.

But that evening Craig did not come home, nor did he call. The next morning Bonnie phoned his office from Grandma's Attic, but his assistant said his morning was booked solid with staff meetings and maintenance on campus to supervise, and that he would probably not return until lunch. "Should I have him call you before he leaves for his appointment?" she asked.

"What appointment?"

"I don't know. He just told me he has to leave for an appointment at four." His assistant chuckled. "Maybe he's planning a big surprise for Valentine's Day."

If he was, it was not for Bonnie. She hung up and eyed the store's displays of pink, red, and white fabric and ribbon with distaste. They should have reminded her, but she had forgotten today was the fourteenth. She had probably blocked it out. Craig seemed to every year.

She searched the storage room for their St. Patrick's Day decorations and selected green and white fabrics from the shelves so that she could expunge all signs of the romantic holiday from her shop first thing the next day. As she worked, pausing to assist the occasional customer, the idea that Craig might be planning a Valentine's surprise for someone else gnawed at her. He was obviously up to something. A man didn't stay away from his wife that long without cause. While she longed to believe he had been staying up nights planning that second honeymoon in Paris they once talked about, she knew they had moved well beyond any chance of that. It was a bitter truth to accept, but she forced herself to be realistic.

He had planned to cheat on her once. He might have cheated on her since.

She had to know what this appointment was about.

When Diane came in at two, Bonnie made an excuse about needing to leave early. Diane assured her she would be happy to close the shop alone, so at three-forty, Bonnie bid her good-bye and hurried across campus on foot. She wished she had departed earlier. If his appointment was far away, he might have left already. Then another realization stopped her in her tracks: He might have already returned home for his car. He never drove to work; the employee parking lot was farther from his building than their home. She had not checked for his car before leaving.

She would just have to wait outside the Physical Plant building and hope for the best, she told herself, and resumed walking at a brisker pace. She rounded a copse of snow-shrouded evergreens and nearly crashed into a couple engrossed in an intense discussion.

"Excuse me," she mumbled, hurrying on.

"Bonnie?"

Bonnie stopped short and whirled around. She recognized Judy before her friend lowered her scarf. "Oh, hi. Hi, Steve."

"Hi," said Judy's husband, smiling. "Where are you going in such a hurry?"

"Oh, well—" Bonnie fumbled for an excuse before realizing she didn't need one. "I'm going to see if I can catch Craig before he leaves work. You didn't happen to see him pass this way?"

They shook their heads. "If we do, should we tell him to meet you somewhere?" asked Steve.

"No, that's all right." Bonnie forced a smile and backed away. "I'd better hurry."

"See you tonight at the business meeting," said Judy. As Bonnie turned to go, she heard her ask Steve, "Do you think she overheard?"

Bonnie understood at once that she had interrupted an argument and wished with all her heart she had not. If the happiest married couple she knew argued, what chance did she and Craig have if he made her resort to spying?

She reached Craig's building with ten minutes to spare and brushed snow off a bench partially concealed from the front entrance behind the bare limbs of a lilac bush. She sat down and waited, mittened hands clutching the tote bag on her lap. Students passed on their way to and from classes, but just then she glimpsed a familiar burly figure in a blue Penn State coat and blaze-orange knit hat exiting by a side door. Bonnie tracked him with her eyes as he hurried across the quad toward downtown, but not in the direction of home.

She waited as long as she thought she could afford before pursuing him. She almost lost him trying to cross Main Street, but his blaze-orange hat stood out among the crowd on the other side. Once across, she had to run to close the distance between them. When she was within two blocks, Craig turned down an alley lined with bookstores and coffeeshops, then headed south. He was on his way to the residential area, Bonnie guessed, but he turned again and climbed the stairs of a three-story Victorian, one of the many former private homes on that street converted to offices. Outside, a steel blue-and-gray sign read UNIVERSITY REALTY.

Out of breath from the chase, Bonnie gasped and ducked behind a street sign. Her heart pounded; her face burned. What was Craig doing here? He must be meeting with Krolich, and not to demand an apology for the way Krolich had treated Bonnie.

Bonnie pulled up her hood and hurried away before either man chanced to step outside. Craig could have come to find out what University Realty was prepared to offer for the condo, but a phone call would have sufficed for that information. Bonnie paused, glanced back at the office, then crossed the street and entered a coffee shop. She ordered a mocha latte and found a seat by the front window with a decent view of University Realty. Her cup was empty by the time Craig emerged. He descended the steps with a jaunty gait. He appeared to be whistling.

Sick at heart, Bonnie gathered her coat and purse and left.

She took the long way home, longing for the comfort of Grandma's Attic but too stricken to face Diane, too distracted to think of an explanation for her unexpected return. Exhaustion weighted her footsteps as she climbed the stairs to the condo. Craig was not there.

She wanted to crawl into bed and sleep until spring, but she went to the kitchen and cut up vegetables and leftover turkey for soup. The latest *Contemporary Quilting* magazine had come in the mail. She curled up on the sofa beneath a flannel Lady of the Lake quilt and read while the soup simmered.

At six she decided Craig wasn't coming home, so she warmed a few slices of sourdough bread in the oven and ladled soup into a single bowl. The door opened just as she began to eat. "That smells great," Craig called from the hallway as he hung up his coat.

It was the kindest thing he had said to her in weeks. Tears sprang into her eyes, but the automatic thank-you died on her lips. He bustled in, cheeks red, rubbing his palms together for warmth. Bonnie sipped her soup and pretended not to notice how he hesitated at the sight of her eating alone.

"Bread smells good, too," he said on his way to the kitchen. She heard him fishing a spoon from the drawer, taking a bowl down from the cupboard, opening a beer. A few minutes later he joined her at the table.

She ate without looking at him, waiting for him to speak. Oblivious to her silence, he ate with his eyes glued to the paper. Bonnie returned to the kitchen for seconds, then sat at the table swirling the barley and thick slices of carrot without tasting a mouthful, realizing only then that she was no longer hungry. She had refilled her bowl only to prolong the meal.

Finally she said, "Don't you have something you want to tell me?"

He set down the paper and studied her for a moment. "Oh. Right. Happy Valentine's Day."

"That's not what I'm talking about."

"What were you expecting, chocolates and a dozen roses?"

It was all Bonnie could do not to fling her bowl at him. "I have a meeting," she said, rising, clearing away her dishes. "Please put the leftovers in the fridge when you're done. I'm taking the car. Don't wait up."

"Don't worry."

Fighting off tears of rage, she grabbed her tote bag and left. She endured the meeting, finding no comfort in her friends' presence or their anticipation of the upcoming camp season. Then it was time to go home, but Bonnie dreaded the discussion—the argument—that would inevitably follow her return. She had to confront Craig; if he intended to tell her why he had met with Gregory Krolich, he would have done so over supper. Whatever secrets he kept could not be good for their home or Grandma's Attic. Or their marriage.

When she pulled into the parking space behind their building, all the second-floor windows overlooking the back alley were dark. Inside, she found the pot of lukewarm soup sitting uncovered on the stove. Craig was gone, and so was the large duffel bag that once carried his workout clothes, but had sat on the floor of his closet, unused, for most of the past year.

❧

He stayed away for three days. In the meantime, Bonnie called University Realty and left a message on Krolich's voicemail declaring that the Markham home was not for sale. She wrote lessons for camp. She pored over the shop's finances and concluded that she would have to cut her employees' hours in half or let one of them go. Summer was out of the question, so it would have to be Diane. Reluctantly, she spent Sunday morning with the classifieds circling ads for commercial properties. There weren't many choices, since three-quarters of the listings belonged to University Realty.

On Sunday afternoon Craig finally returned home. He ignored her as he went down the hall, tossed the duffel bag into the guest room, and continued on to the bathroom.

She went to the kitchen to fix a cup of tea. Eventually Craig came to the kitchen for a beer. "We need to talk," she said, but he pretended not to hear as he rooted in the refrigerator. He left the kitchen and in a moment she heard a basketball game on the television.

She followed him into the living room and sat down. "I know you met with Gregory Krolich."

He raised the can to his lips, eyes fixed on the television screen.

She clasped her hands around her mug of tea. "I want to know why."

"So he could make an offer on this place."

"I already told you I don't want to sell."

"It's a good offer. Better than we could get if we tried to sell on our own."

"I don't want to sell."

"It's not up to you."

"Yes, it is." Her hands shook so badly she had to set the mug on the table. "It's up to both of us."

"You're a spoiled brat." He looked at her with such venom that she shrank back into her chair. "You won't admit this is the best opportunity we're likely to see. Ever. You won't admit you can't afford the new rent for the shop. You can't admit you should close that place before it sinks us any deeper."

"Grandma's Attic means the world to me," said Bonnie. "I still have many loyal customers who would hate to see it go. For them, and for me, I won't close it short of total bankruptcy."

"Then we won't have long to wait."

❧

After that, Bonnie no longer noted when Craig slept in the guest room or how many days he stayed away. A week after their confrontation, she was vacuuming the carpet when words came into her mind, so suddenly that it shocked her, so clearly that she knew she had been considering them for weeks.

I want a divorce, she thought, then said aloud, "I want a divorce."

She shouldn't. He didn't beat her. He had not, as far as she knew, been unfaithful. He had been a reliable if critical father to their children. Maybe he was right and she was a spoiled brat. But she could not endure the current situation. Spending the rest of her life in a state of perpetual animosity was unthinkable. She didn't think she loved him anymore; she barely even liked him most days. She was tired of the tension, tired of feeling at her worst when he was around, tired of feeling inconsequential when he did not even bother to tell her he wasn't coming home.

Whatever happened with the store, with their home, they had to try marriage counseling again. It had helped them reconcile five years before when she had discovered and thwarted his planned rendezvous with a woman he had met on an Internet mailing list. They simply could not throw away a shared history of thirty years. Things had never been worse between them, but she had to believe they still had a chance.

She wrote him a short but heartfelt note asking him to please come home for supper so they could discuss resuming counseling. She left it on the pillow of the guest room. It was gone by the time she returned home from work the next day, but Craig left no reply behind, and he did not show up for supper.

The last day of February was cold and overcast, with gusty winds that sent newspapers and trash scuttling down the alley behind their building. Bonnie rose early to pay the household bills before going to Grandma's Attic, where she would have to complete the same chore. Craig's paychecks were direct-deposited into their joint checking account at the end of each month; usually he brought home a pay stub telling her the amount, but this week he had not left the familiar envelope by the computer. Bonnie wasn't sure how many of his late nights had actually been overtime, so she estimated conservatively when she entered the deposit into the account. She would inquire at the bank for the actual amount when she withdrew funds on her lunch break.

The ATM was down when Bonnie arrived, but she had beaten the midday rush and used her brief time in line to fill out a withdrawal slip. "Could you check on a deposit for me?" she asked the teller while he counted out her bills. "It was made by direct deposit either this morning or yesterday afternoon."

The teller entered a few keystrokes, frowned at the monitor, and shook his head. "Sorry. The last deposit was on the twelfth for twenty-two seventy-eight."

"That can't be right. My husband's paycheck comes by direct deposit from the college at the end of each month."

"Yeah, I know. They all come the same day." The teller, freckled and far younger than her children, pressed another key. "The last direct deposit was on January thirty-first."

"Maybe the college delayed their transfer for some reason. A computer glitch or something."

"I doubt it, ma'am. People with Waterford College IDs have been coming in all day."

"Well—" Bonnie didn't know what to think. "What is my balance without that deposit?"

"Oh. Sorry." He handed her the receipt he had forgotten to give her with her cash.

Bonnie stared at the receipt in shock—$215.74. In a moment of confusion she thought the checks she had written that morning had somehow already cleared, then she realized the envelopes were still in her bag. "There's been some mistake," she said. "There should be at least a thousand dollars in this account."

"Um." The teller glanced over his shoulder. "Well, there was a big withdrawal yesterday. I could print out a statement for you, or you can see it online. Do you know about our online banking?"

Bonnie went cold. "What about the savings account?"

"You want me to check the balance?"

"Yes, yes, please."

Her distress motivated him to hurry. "Twenty dollars and fifteen cents," he said, not wasting time on a printed statement. "Just enough to keep the account open."

"I don't understand." But she did understand. Craig. "Can you tell me if the money was transferred to another account? Or was it in cash?"

He studied the screen. "It was a cash withdrawal."

"Did my husband—" She took a deep breath. "Did he open a new account and deposit the money in it?"

"I'm sorry. I can't give you any information about accounts not in your name."

"Please," she said, fighting off tears. "Please make an exception just this once."

His fingers clattered on the keyboard. He glanced over his shoulder again, then said, "I'm sorry. I'm not allowed to tell you that your husband did not open a new account at this bank."

"Thank you." Bonnie forced a shaky smile, which faded when she remembered the bills in her purse. "While I'm here, I need to transfer money from my business account into the checking account."

"Are you sure you want to do that?"

Bonnie stopped short, her hand on the stack of transfer slips. "What do you mean?"

"They're still joint accounts."

Bonnie withdrew her hand, slowly. "No." She ducked her head as she returned her checkbook to her bag. "No. I suppose I don't. Thank you."

He nodded, with more sympathy and understanding than she expected from a boy his age.

Bonnie hurried back to Grandma's Attic, rushed past Diane with barely a greeting, and shut herself in the office. She tore up the checks she had written that morning and wrote new ones drawn on the Grandma's Attic account. Craig could not have touched those funds, she reminded herself after a quake of fear made her hands tremble as she signed the new checks. The Grandma's Attic accounts were in her name alone. Craig did not even know the account numbers. Ordinarily she was scrupulous about keeping her personal and business accounts separate, but this was an emergency. As long as Craig had not taken a plane to the Cayman Islands, she would be able to return the money soon.

Diane readily agreed to close for her that evening. "I'll open tomorrow, too, if you want to sleep in," she offered with a grin.

Bonnie forced a smile and thanked her, but declined. How could she offer Diane more hours one week and fire her the next?

Later, upstairs in the condo, she waited in the living room, hugging her knees to her chest on the sofa, the flannel quilt draped over her, until the winter light faded. She knew she should start supper, but she could not even rouse herself to turn on a light. Finally hunger overcame her immobility, and she went to the kitchen for tea and toast with honey. The clock on the microwave told her it was half past eight.

She waited on the sofa long past her usual bedtime. At eleven she brushed her teeth and put on the evening news. When that ended, she switched between Leno and Letterman, but their jokes seemed inane and the celebrity guests fatuous. She put on the History Channel and tried to concentrate on an account of the Battle of Stalingrad, but the narrator's voice sounded so much like Gregory Krolich's that she finally turned off the television.

Not long after midnight the door quietly opened. She sat in the dark watching Craig remove his boots and hang up his coat. He switched on the dining room light, then turned and nearly leapt into the air at the sight of her. "What're you doing up?"

"I went to the bank today."

He disappeared into the kitchen. "So?"

"So, what did you do with our money?"

There was a long pause in which Bonnie heard the refrigerator door open and the microwave heating something. Soon Craig returned with a beer and a slice of pizza on a paper plate. "*Our* money? I earned it. Everything you earn goes straight into that money pit you call a store."

"That is not true." Bonnie had the ledgers to prove it. "You can't drain our accounts so much without at least telling me. I paid bills this morning, and all those checks would have bounced if I had not happened to go into the bank today."

He shrugged and sat down in his recliner, his mouth full of pizza. He reached for the remote and put on a sports network.

"I think we should try marriage counseling again."

Craig barked out a laugh. "Right, since it was so successful the first time."

"If you won't come with me, I'll go alone."

"Suit yourself, but you're paying for it."

"Craig—" She fought back tears. "I want to sort this out, but if we can't, I think we should separate."

"You mean divorce."

"I didn't say—"

"No one gets a separation unless they really want a divorce. Why don't you just say what you want for a change?"

She stared at him in bewilderment. "Will you please just go?" she said after what seemed an interminable silence. "Pack an overnight bag. Tomorrow—tomorrow, when I'm at work, come back for whatever you want."

He watched her balefully as he chewed his pizza. "Go where?"

She lifted her hands and let them fall into her lap. "Wherever it is you go when you don't come home."

"Why should I be the one to leave? You're the one who wants a divorce."

Didn't *he*? "You hate it here."

"It's not so bad, now that it's for sale. Why don't *you* leave? Go move into that Elm Creek Manor with the rest of the crones. You practically live there anyway."

Her home was not for sale, she thought, but she said, "Please, Craig. Let's not make this any worse. For the kids' sake if not for ours. Please, just go."

He jabbed the remote at the television and shook his head. "If the Penguins keep playing like this, they'll never make the playoffs."

She watched him, but he acted as if she had already left. So she put on her shoes and coat, shouldered her tote bag, and went.

She was so accustomed to walking everywhere except to Elm Creek Manor that she never thought to take the car. It was nearly one o'clock when she rang Agnes's doorbell. After a while she rang again, but no one answered. She was debating whether she ought to walk to Diane's and endure the third degree in warmth or risk freezing to death by spending the night on Agnes's front porch swing when a light went on in a second-story window. A few moments later, Agnes opened the door, squinting without her glasses and holding her fuzzy pink robe closed at the neck.

"Bonnie, honey," she said. "What's wrong?"

"May I spend the night?"

Agnes immediately opened the door wide. "Of course."

The older woman bustled about, showing her to the guest room, setting out fresh towels in the adjoining bath, offering her a cup of tea or glass of milk, but Bonnie refused, clutching a borrowed flannel nightgown to her chest and wanting desperately not to cry. She wanted to kiss Agnes for not asking any questions.

Once alone, she put on the nightgown. It was warm but too snug and it only came down to her knees, so she crawled into bed with her socks on. She fell asleep as soon as her eyes closed and did not dream.

❧

She woke to bright sunlight and felt a moment of contentment before realizing that she was not at home, and then, that she had left her husband. Sick dread filled her as she rose and saw from the clock on the bedside table that it was after eleven.

She showered quickly and dressed in the clothes she had worn the day before. She found Agnes in the kitchen. "I overslept," she said, wondering where she had left her shoes. "I have to get to work."

Agnes smiled and shook her head, gently guiding her to a chair. "Not without breakfast. Do you want scrambled eggs or waffles?"

"But the shop—"

"Don't you worry. I called Diane. She said she'd head over as soon as she could. She probably didn't get there on time, but she got there."

Agnes closed Bonnie's hands around a cup of coffee. Bonnie sank back into the chair as Agnes brought her cream and sugar. "Thank you," said Bonnie.

"I had waffles myself," remarked Agnes, patting her shoulder and returning to the refrigerator. "I like to add cinnamon and vanilla. Have you ever tried them that way?"

"I haven't, but I'd love to."

Agnes nodded and left her to drink her coffee in silence. A few minutes later she set a plate in front of Bonnie and refilled her coffee, then brought a second cup for herself. She sat down as if friends showed up unexpectedly on her doorstep every night.

"I left Craig," said Bonnie.

"For good?"

"I think so."

Agnes nodded, apparently not surprised. Bonnie told her what had happened the night before, and in the weeks leading up to it, and all the months of loneliness and arguing and pretending that everything would be all right eventually if she just weathered the current storm. When Bonnie said she still intended to speak to a counselor, Agnes said, "As long as you speak to a lawyer, too."

Bonnie nodded. She supposed Craig already had.

They washed the dishes together. "You can stay here as long as you need to," Agnes said as she wiped off the table.

"Thanks, but I intend to stay at home tonight." She dreaded the thought of seeing Craig again, but she would not give up her home to him. "He doesn't usually sleep there anyway." She managed a small laugh. "I have to go home, if only to change clothes."

"I'll come with you, if you like."

Grateful, relieved, Bonnie nodded.

They linked arms as they walked, with Bonnie unsure who was supporting whom. The Markhams' parking space was empty, but Diane's car filled the one beside it. Bonnie knew she ought to stop by and thank Diane for coming in on a moment's notice, but not before she changed clothes.

The outside door stuck on a crust of ice. Bonnie shoved it open and led Agnes upstairs to the second floor. She hesitated before slipping her key in the lock, wondering if she ought to ask Agnes to watch for Craig. The key did not turn. Bonnie withdrew it and checked that she had the right key, since it resembled the one for Grandma's Attic. Neither key worked. She tried again, jostling the knob and shoving the door with her shoulder, but it would not budge.

"He changed the locks," she said, not believing it.

She tried the Grandma's Attic key again, but Agnes gently pulled her away. "Come on. We'll go shopping. Buy yourself something nice and send the bill to Craig."

Bonnie pressed her lips together and nodded, holding her breath to fight off sobs. "Please don't tell anyone about this," she managed to say as they emerged in the alley below.

Agnes glanced at her to see if she meant it. "I won't breathe a word."

They walked downtown, past the fancy boutique where five years before Bonnie had tried on expensive, flattering dresses in an attempt to find one that would lure Craig out of his cyber-girl infatuation, to Bonnie's favorite department store. Woodenly she selected slacks, sweaters, blouses, sweats; she would have forgotten undergarments if not for Agnes's delicate reminder. She did not know how much to buy. Ordinarily she never would have purchased so many items for herself, but she did not know when she would be able to go home.

Standing in line, Agnes did her best to amuse Bonnie with a story about how Sarah's husband, Matt, had spied pieces for Agnes's block for Sylvia's bridal quilt in her sewing box. He had been so interested in seeing her current project that she had had no choice but to show him. "Right in front of Sylvia," she said, chuckling, as the clerk rang up Bonnie's purchases and took her credit card. "I know Sarah told him Sylvia's quilt is a secret, but of course he didn't know that particular block was my contribution or he wouldn't have insisted upon seeing it. Fortunately Sylvia wasn't paying attention or the surprise would have been ruined."

"That was lucky," Bonnie agreed, remembering her own half-finished block on the table in her sewing room. It had once been her daughter's bedroom. The kids. What would they think when they learned what had happened? How would Bonnie tell them?

"Ma'am?" said the clerk. "I'm sorry, but your card didn't go through."

"Oh." That bill, still in her purse from yesterday. It was late, but not that late. "Here's my bank debit card. No, wait." She remembered just in time and snatched the card away before the clerk could pick it up. She extended a second card. "Here, use this. May I have the other one back?"

"I'm afraid I can't do that. I have to cut it up. It's been reported stolen."

"What?" said Agnes.

The clerk looked uneasy. "I'm sorry. Your credit card company insists."

"That's outrageous," Agnes began, but Bonnie placed a hand on her arm to silence her. She should have anticipated this. She returned the second card to her wallet and handed the clerk her Grandma's Attic corporate card without a word. The clerk scrutinized it, dubious, but the card cleared. As soon as the humiliating transaction ended, Bonnie snatched up her bags and fled.

Agnes hurried to catch up with her. "Come home with me," she said. "You can change clothes and call your lawyer."

"I don't have a lawyer."

"I do. He's a wonderful young man. His father looked after our affairs for years, and he took over the firm after his father passed."

"Does he handle divorces?"

"If not, he'll know someone who does."

❧

Bonnie took the lawyer's number but did not call. She reminded herself that less than two weeks before she had been cleaning the condo and contemplating divorce. For five years, since Craig's first betrayal, she had struggled to hold their marriage together, but in her heart she knew it was over. It was time to salvage what she could and move on.

And yet she could not bring herself to make the call. She did not know why and did not want to think about it.

She spent the weekend with Agnes, helping her cut fabric for the pieced border of Sylvia's bridal quilt. Agnes arranged for Diane to cover for her at Grandma's Attic on Saturday before Bonnie remembered to ask. On Monday she returned to work as if she had not been away. Summer stopped by in the morning, her concern and curiosity apparent, but fortunately Bonnie was helping a customer so she avoided uncomfortable questions.

"You have nothing to be ashamed of," said Agnes that evening, when Bonnie returned to her house in defeat. She had tried to outwait Craig at the alley door since he would not return her calls, but her resolve faltered as the night grew colder. "Our friends would be a great comfort to you if they knew you needed their support."

"I'm not ashamed," Bonnie said, but she was. Ashamed that she had failed at her marriage, ashamed that she had not heeded the obvious warning signs and left Craig five years before.

On Wednesday, at Agnes's urging, she camped in Craig's office until he showed up for work. She pleaded with him to let her come home, but he said, "You're the one who decided to abandon the property. Now you've got to live with it."

She didn't like his gleeful tone or the odd emphasis he gave the words *abandon* and *property*, but she was too emotionally exhausted to argue within earshot of his coworkers, whom she had known for years and had entertained in their home. She considered it a triumph when he agreed to let her come home that evening to pack her clothes and other necessities. Agnes accompanied her and stood glaring at Craig as Bonnie quickly filled two suitcases and sorted the mail. She left the bills for him to pay, since she had drawn on Grandma's Attic as much as she could afford, but took her magazines and an unopened letter from their daughter.

"I forgot to ask him if the children called," she told Agnes in dismay as they struggled to her house with the suitcases in hand.

"The light on the answering machine was blinking," said Agnes, breathing hard from exertion. "I doubt if he even saw it, buried under all that mail."

Bonnie waited until late the next morning, then called and checked the messages using the remote code. There were three messages, none very important, but Bonnie did learn that Craig had changed the outgoing announcement.

The days passed. Bonnie often felt as if she were watching a dream of someone else's life. She went to work, returned to Agnes's for supper, and spent her evenings helping Agnes with the bridal quilt or working on lesson plans for camp. Some mornings before unlocking the door to the shop, she would stare up at the windows of her home from across the street and wonder what Craig hoped to accomplish by throwing her out and cutting her off from their joint resources. She had no idea what her next step should be, no foresight into what Craig intended. Did he want her to suffer longer before he allowed her to return? Was he keeping her out just long enough to sell their home without interference?

A week and a day after she left the condo, she understood. He had no intention of allowing her to return. He had already divorced her in his heart. The legalities of their relationship he would leave for the lawyers.

New resolve filled her the day she accepted the inevitable. She still dreaded the confrontations to come, the astonishment of the children, the frightening questions of how she would manage financially, but she would no longer pretend these problems would disappear if she ignored them.

Somehow she felt like celebrating—she also felt like weeping, but she was determined not to. She had cried every night since leaving the condo and she felt too wrung out for more tears. After work, she stopped off at the market for a crown roast and all the fixings for a special dinner to thank Agnes for all she had done, suppressing a wave of guilt as she handed over the Grandma's

Attic corporate card. Afterward she passed a liquor store, something of a dive but popular with the students, and decided to stop for a bottle of wine.

She knew next to nothing about wine, but Agnes never criticized anyone except for bad manners, so she could hardly go wrong. She chose a red she had enjoyed at Gwen's last Winter Solstice feast and got in line behind a young man hefting two cases of beer onto the checkout counter. When he dug in his back pocket for his wallet, Bonnie glimpsed his face in profile— and nearly dropped the wine. His hair was shorter than he had worn it in years, but he was unmistakably Diane's eldest son, Michael.

The clerk asked for Michael's ID, and Bonnie held her breath—waiting for Michael to run, for the clerk to call his supervisor, the police—but Michael said, "Sure," and handed him something that looked like a Pennsylvania driver's license. It couldn't have been; at least, it wasn't Michael's. But the clerk looked from the photo on the card to Michael's face and back, then returned the license and rang up the beer. Bonnie watched, dumbfounded, as Michael paid him and pocketed his wallet. He turned to go and stopped short at the sight of her, his expression giving way to surprise and dismay. He left quickly, without a word.

He was nowhere in sight by the time Bonnie exited the store. She had no idea what she would have said to him anyway, had he lingered to shower her in excuses. She must tell Diane, of course. Shouldn't she? She could imagine how that conversation would unfold: "Diane, I saw your underage son buying beer last night. Since I'm managing my own domestic situation so perfectly I thought I should tell you how to raise your son. Oh, by the way, Grandma's Attic is in even more trouble than my marriage, so I'm afraid you're fired."

She didn't tell Agnes about the encounter—Agnes had baby-sat Diane as a child and they had remained close, so she was almost a surrogate grandmother to her boys and could hardly be objective—but she did tell Gwen when she stopped by the shop a few days later. Gwen seemed more concerned with her daughter's perfectly legal decision to move in with her boyfriend than by Michael's breaking the law, but that was not surprising. Gwen did offer one offhand suggestion and, after mulling it over, Bonnie decided it was actually quite good: She could talk to Michael herself. She was no prude, and she knew college students started drinking as soon as they hit campus regardless of age, but that fake ID could get him in serious trouble. Diane and Tim were so proud of how their rebellious son had turned his life around. Bonnie could not sit back and wait for him to disappoint them, or worse.

But first Bonnie had to pay back Grandma's Attic. The following Thursday evening she took a cab out to Elm Creek Manor and found Sylvia in the formal parlor, tidying up for their business meeting. After procrastinating with small talk, Bonnie awkwardly asked her for an advance on her first quilt camp paycheck. "I wouldn't make this request lightly—"

"I know you wouldn't," interrupted Sylvia. "If you say you need the money now, you must have good reason."

"I think I owe you an explanation."

"Well, you don't. Now, let's go upstairs so I can write you a check before everyone else gets here and wants their first paycheck early, too."

Bonnie managed a smile as she followed Sylvia from the room, but as they climbed the stairs, she said, "I left Craig."

Sylvia nodded. "I thought it was something like that. Have you contacted a lawyer?"

"I meet with him tomorrow." Bonnie gave Sylvia a sidelong glance. "You're not surprised?"

"Frankly, no. I've been expecting something like this for the past five years."

Bonnie stopped short on the landing. "Really."

"Of course, dear. Once the trust between a husband and wife is broken, it's very difficult to repair, even with the best of intentions."

Sylvia continued down the hall toward the library, but Bonnie caught her arm. "You're not going to tell me I should try harder?"

Sylvia looked shocked. "I wouldn't presume to. You stuck it out for more than thirty years, by my reckoning. You would know far better than I whether you've done all you could."

"But what about all your talk about forgiveness, about reconciling before it's too late?"

"Oh. That." Sylvia sighed and shook her head. "In an ideal world, your forgiveness would have inspired Craig to mend his ways and be an exemplary husband. You gave him five years to prove himself, which is about four and a half more than I would have managed in your place. If you're still miserable, if you still can't trust him, you're far too young to live that way for the rest of your life."

"I didn't leave because of that woman from the Internet," said Bonnie, and while Sylvia wrote out a check, Bonnie filled her in on the events of the past few months. Sylvia's expression grew more grave as the story tumbled out, and at the end, she gave Bonnie one long, wordless hug. They returned downstairs together, ten minutes late for the meeting.

❧

The next day was unseasonably mild, with sunny skies and warm breezes that promised of the coming spring. Students basked in the sun on the main quad across the street from Grandma's Attic, while others clad in shorts and T-shirts packed their cars for spring break. Business picked up a little that week, as residents of outlying small towns took advantage of the students' absence to venture into Waterford. Bonnie tried to take some hope from this and the fine weather as she locked the door to the quilt shop and walked to her lawyer's office.

She had collected some of the papers he had requested, but the most important documents were unattainable in the condo. Not for long, however, if her new lawyer could be believed. Darren had told her it was unfortunate that she had abandoned the property, but he could argue that Craig gave her no other choice. The echo of Craig's words made her uneasy, but she decided to believe Darren when he said he would have her back in her home soon. She didn't ask where he expected Craig to go.

Scanning front doors for the address, she glanced through the window of a coffee shop and spotted Michael pouring sugar and cream into a to-go cup. She hesitated, then checked her watch and went inside.

Michael eyed her warily as she approached. "Hello, Michael."

"Hi, Mrs. Markham," he mumbled.

She smiled pleasantly. "Do you have any plans for spring break?"

"Stayin' here."

When he did not elaborate, she decided to get to the point. "Michael, I've been concerned ever since I saw you at the liquor store."

"It wasn't all for me," he broke in. "I wasn't going to drive after."

"I'm relieved to hear it, but that doesn't change the fact that you used a fake ID."

"I'll be twenty-one in six months."

"Do you think the police would care? Do you have any idea what would happen to you if you got caught?" He shrugged, and since Bonnie didn't know either, she let the ominous threat hang in the air. "I could tell you all the reasons why you shouldn't drink, but I'm sure you've heard them before. What you might not have considered is that breaking the law so you can drink makes a bad situation worse." His scowl deepened, so she finished in a rush. "I want you to give me that ID."

"What?"

"It's for your own good." She could have cringed; she shouldn't have put it that way. "I haven't told your parents what I know, and I won't, as long as I know you can't do it anymore."

"What if I just promise?"

"If you promise, and if you intend to keep your promise, you won't need the ID." She held out her palm. "Please, Michael. Either give it to me now or to your parents later."

He looked as if he might protest, but then he whipped out his wallet and shoved the card into her hand. He stalked off as she tucked it into her purse, but at the door, he turned and gave her a look of such unmitigated rage that her breath caught in her throat. Then he was gone.

She composed herself and continued on to her lawyer's office, to prepare for another confrontation she did not want but could not avoid.

❧

Two days later, Bonnie and the other Elm Creek Quilters welcomed the first group of campers for the season. It was a scene so customary that it should have comforted her, but instead its sameness in the context of sudden and unwelcome change unsettled her. First there was the excuse she invented for being at Agnes's house when Diane stopped by to pick her up—although she would have been uncomfortable around Diane regardless. Then, when she finally confided to Summer that she would have to let Diane go, Summer actually tried to resign in order to save her friend's job. Bonnie was deeply touched that Summer would offer to make such a sacrifice without even pausing to consider the consequences, and if Summer were not so crucial to the survival of Grandma's Attic, Bonnie might have taken her at her word.

Still, as the Candlelight welcoming ceremony concluded, Bonnie began to fall under the spell of the campers' joy. Even Judy's unexpected absence seemed reassuring as the sort of ordinary emergency the Elm Creek Quilters had learned to expect and absorb. By the end of the first day of classes, Bonnie almost managed to forget her grief over the loss of her marriage, the indignity of having to rely on Agnes for a place to live, her fear that one day soon she might have to lock the door of her beloved quilt shop forever. The familiar rhythms of quilt camp reminded her that she had a life beyond Craig, beyond Grandma's Attic.

True to her predictions, business did pick up slightly as spring break began, so that as she walked to the quilt shop Wednesday morning, she considered that they might just be able to save the store without losing Diane.

But then she reached the front door, and before unlocking it, she knew that she had already lost.

She was too shocked to cry. She stepped carefully over the rubble of her dream, turning around, taking it all in. She could not believe it, but it had to be real. It hurt too much to be a nightmare.

Craig. He had always hated the shop. He had smirked when he said she was close to losing it. She never suspected he would be vicious enough to push her over the edge. Until that moment, she had not understood the depth of his contempt for her.

The cash register was empty, as she had suspected it would be. Then, a shiver of alarm ran through her. In her haste to meet her lawyer, she had stashed the previous day's deposit in a filing cabinet rather than taking it to the bank. She ran to the office, tripping over fabric and spools of thread, but that room, too, had been ransacked, the filing cabinet overturned. The money bag was gone.

With a sob, Bonnie sank down onto a chair. She stared at the disarray, seeing Craig hurling fabric bolts across the room, knocking over shelves, tearing sample quilts from the walls and grinding them beneath his feet, until she remembered she ought to call the police. She fumbled for the phone and made her report numbly. When the squad car pulled up in front of the store, lights flashing, she was picking her way through the mess in a daze, trying to determine exactly what had been stolen.

One officer questioned her and took notes while the other looked around, studying the front and back doors and the windows carefully. They asked what was missing. When Bonnie told them, the second officer's eyebrows rose. "That's all?" she asked.

"As far as I know," said Bonnie, indicating the mess with a wide, despairing sweep of her arm. "It's difficult to say."

They urged her to look around, carefully. Bonnie complied, gradually understanding the reason for their surprise. Common thieves would not have wasted so much time destroying the shop, and they would not have left so many expensive items behind. Whoever had done this had wanted to hurt her. Bonnie wanted to dismiss the thought—it would be easier to believe thieves had struck rather than the man with whom she had shared most of her life—but it became an irrefutable conclusion when she discovered the thief had also taken the carton of blocks for Sylvia's bridal quilt.

Bonnie could no longer stand. She managed to reach a stool and brace herself against the cutting table, but not before the officers noticed. When she told them what else was gone and explained the significance of the project, they exchanged a knowing look she doubted she was meant to see.

The first officer finally asked the question she had been dreading: Did she have any idea who the culprit was? She could not bring herself to speak, so she shook her head. The officer frowned and tapped his pad with a pen. "Do you have any enemies?" he asked. "Anyone who would like to see you driven out of business? Any competitors who play hardball?"

"No," Bonnie said, since the Fabric Warehouse was succeeding in that without destroying her shop. Then she thought of Krolich and gasped.

"What is it?" the second officer asked.

"There is someone . . . I don't want to accuse anyone lightly, but the new owner of the building doesn't want me to stay. He wouldn't need to resort to this, though. The rent he wants to charge is enough to drive me away."

"We should probably talk to him anyway," said the first officer. "Can you tell us how to reach him?"

Bonnie nodded and made her way to the front counter, where the contents of her card file had been scattered on the floor beneath the register. She picked through the pile but she could not find Krolich's business card, and then suddenly she froze, realizing what else was missing.

Michael's fake ID. She had put it in the card file for safekeeping, not quite willing to discard it in case she had to go to his parents after all. A momentary relief flooded her when she realized Craig was not to blame, but the feeling vanished when she thought of what this would mean for Michael, and for Diane.

Then she spotted Krolich's business card and quickly scooped it up and rose before the officers noticed her distress. "Here's his card," she said, handing it to the first officer.

He glanced at it before tucking it into a pocket. "I assume that as the owner Mr. Krolich has a key to the building?"

"I suppose he must," said Bonnie. "Why?"

"There's no sign of forced entry," said the second officer. "It must have been an inside job, if you're sure you locked the door."

"I'm sure, but I really don't think Gregory Krolich did this."

The officers nodded noncommittally and resumed their work.

Krolich would likely have access to a key. So would Michael, but not Craig. Michael could have taken Diane's key from her purse, while Craig had not been within blocks of Bonnie's key for weeks.

Another officer arrived shortly afterward and began dusting for fingerprints and photographing different areas of the store. The officers' questions shifted from points of entry and the motives of her enemies to Bonnie herself, and how she felt about her shop. Bonnie supposed they were trying to put her at ease, but explaining that she and her husband were estranged and admitting that Grandma's Attic was not in the best fiscal health only made her more uncomfortable. Just when she was considering asking them to allow her to sit down for a moment, alone, Summer burst in. The third officer tried to prevent her from entering, but Bonnie was so glad to see her she almost could not tell her what had happened. She clung to her young friend and, finally, let her tears fall when she admitted that Sylvia's blocks were missing. Why would Michael have done that, when most kids would assume losing the expensive sewing machines would hurt her most deeply? How would Michael have known to do that?

It was midafternoon before the officers said she could straighten up the areas they had already searched and photographed. As soon as they departed, Bonnie and Summer got to work. They had made little progress by the time Gwen arrived several hours later. Since Summer had a tender spot in her heart for Michael, Bonnie waited until she was out of hearing to confide her suspicions to Gwen. At first Gwen denied the possibility that the Michael they had known since childhood could have done such a terrible thing, but soon doubt appeared in her eyes.

Bonnie had no doubts.

CHAPTER FIVE

Agnes

Agnes's New Year's resolution was to update her will and get her affairs in order, so after the traditional New Year's Day feast of honey-glazed ham with all the trimmings, she took her two daughters aside and told them if they especially wanted any of her belongings, they should let her know so she could set them aside.

She was not surprised when both of her girls recoiled. "Mom, that's morbid," said Stacy, her eldest. "That's not something you need to worry about yet."

Laura, as always, suspected she had not been told the entire story. "Are you ill?"

Agnes laughed. "Of course not. I'm perfectly healthy, or so my doctor tells me. But I'll be seventy-four in two months, and no one lives forever. I'd like to know things are settled so there won't be any arguments after I'm gone."

"You aren't going anywhere," Stacy assured her, patting her on the arm and guiding her to a seat on the sofa. "Is something else bothering you?"

Agnes sighed. She should have anticipated this, although she wished her daughters would show more respect for her intelligence. She was well aware she would not be the first immortal woman in the history of the species, but the gentle, soothing tones in her daughters' voices suggested they thought they could convince her otherwise. "If there's a certain quilt you would like, for example, or a piece of furniture, let me know so I can put it in writing. Soon," she added, and hid a smile when they exchanged a look of dismay at the implied urgency. They deserved to be needled a bit for patronizing her.

"Just divide up everything fifty-fifty," said Laura. "We won't argue over anything."

"Of course not," Stacy chimed in. "For goodness' sake, Mom, how could we care about *things* when we've lost you?"

Laura nodded, so Agnes merely smiled, patted their hands, and suggested they return to the family room where her sons-in-law and grandchildren were watching football on television. Even as youngsters Stacy and Laura had indeed gotten along much better than the average pair of sisters, but Agnes had witnessed the sad legacy of friends whose children's amicable relationships had fractured into bitter animosity over the ownership of an antique armoire or a set of books worth only sentimental value. She did not want to think of that happening to her girls, nor did she want to stipulate that they sell everything and divide the cash. After seeing what Sylvia had gone through to find her mother's heirloom quilts Claudia had sold off, Agnes was determined to spare her daughters that ordeal.

The girls said nothing of her proposal for the rest of their visit, so two days after they departed, when their absence and the enduring winter made the house seem especially lonely and quiet, Agnes sorted through her collection of quilts with a pad of paper, a pen, and a box of new safety pins by her side. She admired the handiwork of decades, reminiscing about the creation of each quilt and mulling over who might appreciate it best. Each daughter would receive one of her two queen-size Baltimore Album quilts— Stacy the one in pastels and Laura the one in brighter hues. Sarah, who loved samplers, would adore the floral appliqué wall hanging, and the Pinwheel lap quilt simply had to go to Summer, who had encouraged Agnes to piece it from Summer's own favorite vivid Amish solids. Come to think of it, she ought to put Summer's name on the leftover fabric, too, which had sat untouched in her fabric stash since she had completed the quilt five years before.

As for Sylvia—Agnes chuckled as she wrote Sylvia's name on a piece of paper and carefully pinned it to a cheerful scrap Double Wedding Ring quilt. Surely Sylvia would remember Agnes's first quilting lessons, when Agnes, who knew nothing of sewing except needlepoint, decided to learn to quilt in order to pass the time while their men were in the service. Sylvia suggested Agnes choose a simple pattern or a sampler as her first project. Then Claudia drew her aside and told her she would master the skills more quickly and thoroughly if she chose a more challenging pattern. Agnes unwisely took her advice, for the bias edges and curved seams of the Double Wedding Ring proved too difficult for her inexpert stitches, and the resulting half-ring buckled in the middle and gapped in the seams. She never finished that quilt—the news of the men's deaths and Sylvia's subsequent departure brought the quilting lessons to an abrupt end—but twenty years later she had attempted the pattern again. Practice and a more knowing eye for color and contrast enabled her to create a lovely, comforting reminder of how far she had come since leaving Elm Creek Manor to remarry. If Sylvia inherited that quilt, she would be clever enough to understand the symbolism and generous enough to forgive Agnes one parting joke.

For each quilt and each friend or relation, Agnes affixed an identifying tag and added the information to her list. She intended to type up the list, sign it and date it, and keep it with her will in the fireproof box beneath the bed in Stacy's old room. After going through the quilts, she would consider the furniture and other belongings. She had already decided what to do with the contents of her sewing room. Since neither of her daughters quilted, she would bequeath her fabric stash, pattern books, and all her tools to Elm Creek Quilt Camp. They would surely find a good use for them.

Agnes was nearly finished when the phone rang. She climbed to her feet, shook the stiffness from her legs, and picked up in her bedroom. "Hello?" she said, gingerly lowering herself onto the edge of the bed. She should have known better than to sit on the floor for so long.

"Grandma?"

"Why, hello, Zachary," she said. "This is Zach, right, not Norman?" His voice sounded so much like his father's that it was difficult to tell.

Zach laughed. "Yeah, it's me."

"What a lovely surprise. How are you? Are you back at school already?"

"I moved back into the dorm this morning. Classes don't start until Monday," her grandson said. "Grandma, the reason I'm calling is that—well, my mom and dad were talking in the car on our way home from your house last week."

Agnes could guess the topic of discussion, but she said, "Talking about what, honey?"

"About your will. Mom said you asked her and Aunt Stacy what they wanted to inherit, you know, if there was something in particular they wanted."

"I imagine your mother didn't discuss this calmly."

"You know Mom. She was kind of upset, but Dad said it was thoughtful of you to spare them a tough job at what would obviously be a stressful time."

Good old Norman. "What do you and your sister think?"

"Rebecca's like Mom. She thinks if you pretend something can't happen to you, it won't. She made Mom and Dad stop talking about it."

"And you?"

"I didn't like talking about it, either. I don't want to think about you dying, Grandma. I don't want you to ever die."

"I appreciate that, honey."

"But since you asked—" He paused. "I know you just asked Mom and Aunt Stacy, not the kids, but—"

Gently, Agnes asked, "Is there something special you would like?"

"You know that quilt with the different colored triangles and all the black?"

"Of course," said Agnes, surprised. She was not aware he had ever given the quilt a second glance. "Would you like it?"

"Yes, please. And—your journals."

"My what?"

"Your journals. You know, the ones you started keeping during World War II."

Agnes had to think a moment before she understood. Her notebooks. She had begun the first when Richard went off to war to note news from home to include in her letters. After he was killed, she continued out of habit for nearly ten years, filling fifteen notebooks with reminders to herself, appointments, to-do lists, and the like. She wondered when Zach had learned of them, then vaguely remembered an occasion several years before when Laura was filling out a medical form and needed to know if she had ever had a particular illness. Agnes had consulted her notebooks and determined that Laura had been vaccinated at age eight.

"Why would you want those old things?" asked Agnes. "They're not very interesting, just a lot of lists, mostly. They don't read like a story, even a dull one."

"I don't care. They're an important record of our family history."

Agnes had to laugh. Her old grocery lists and hairdresser's appointments, family history? "There aren't any fascinating family stories in those old notebooks, Zach. I should have thrown them away a long time ago."

"That's exactly what you shouldn't do, and that's why I want you to set them aside for me. Someone might throw them away not knowing what they are. You're wrong to think they're trivial or worthless. They're irreplaceable and important, and that's the truth, even if you don't think so."

"Why, if they're that important to you, they're yours, of course," said Agnes, surprised.

He thanked her, and they talked of other, more pleasant matters. After they hung up, Agnes rummaged in the kitchen cabinet until she found a large padded envelope. She located her old notebooks under her sweaters in the bottom drawer of her bureau, frowned ruefully at their battered state, and slipped them into the padded envelope with a shrug. She still couldn't see why Zach wanted them so badly. Likely he would read the first few pages and wonder the same thing. Agnes ought to save him the trouble of discarding them by taking care of the job herself, but she couldn't now, not after promising to save them.

She wrote his name on the outside of the envelope and added her notebooks to the list on the pad. Then she took Summer's name from the Pinwheel quilt and pinned Zach's in its place, marking the change on the list. She would have to find something else for Summer to supplement the leftover Amish solids from her fabric stash. Summer would understand. Friends were dear, but grandchildren came first.

❧

The invitation to participate in Sylvia's bridal quilt had arrived in the meantime, but Agnes already knew the requirements and had not bothered to read the letter thoroughly. When she had finished sorting out the future ownership of her quilts and a few other special belongings, she filed the list and decided to turn her attention to her quilt block. This time she read the letter over carefully, and tsked when she read that Diane had said Sylvia deserved to go without a wedding quilt since the surprise wedding on Christmas Eve had thwarted her friends' plans for an elaborate June affair. Agnes could imagine Diane thinking that, briefly, but not blurting it out where someone might overhear. Despite her sometimes abrasive manner, Diane cared for her friends too much to wish them any disappointment. If she had gone a bit overboard in planning the couple's wedding, it was only from the desire to please them.

It was too late to ask Sarah to change the letter, so Agnes could only hope she and Summer had been wise enough not to send Diane a copy, and not only because she might be hurt. They could not afford to discourage any-one from participating, especially one of their own. While Sylvia had many friends and admirers around the world, 140 blocks were a great many to col-lect in such a short period. Even if Sylvia and Andrew had not surprised them with an early wedding and had married in June, as the Elm Creek Quilters had anticipated, they still should have begun the quilt much earlier, ideally as soon as the couple announced their engagement. Agnes blamed the demise of their weekly quilting bees for the delay. Their business meet-ings were so full of details for Elm Creek Quilt Camp that the friends rarely had the opportunity to chat just about quilting. Finding such a time when everyone but Sylvia was present was even more difficult, since Sylvia never missed a meeting unless she and Andrew were traveling. Agnes considered the quilt camp a great adventure and was thrilled to be a part of it, but she missed some aspects of the old days.

"So many blocks," said Agnes with a sigh as she sorted through her fab-ric stash for hues suiting those described in the guidelines. The other Elm Creek Quilters had gladly accepted her offer when she had volunteered to assemble the blocks into a quilt top, since they knew the task meant much more than simply stitching all 140 blocks together. To avoid a cluttered or chaotic quilt, she might need to separate the blocks with strips of fabric called sashing. If not enough blocks arrived, she would need to employ more elaborate tricks, such as setting the blocks on point or alternating them with squares of solid fabric. Either way, she ought to make a few extra blocks just in case. If, as Summer had predicted, they received enough blocks or more than they needed, she would simply save her extras for an-other project.

Since she could not think of one single block that represented all that Sylvia meant to her, she decided instead to make blocks reminiscent of their shared history. She began with a Bachelor's Puzzle block. How shocked Sylvia would be to learn that Agnes had known about the nickname almost from the time the Bergstrom sisters had bestowed it upon her! Long ago, Agnes and Richard had been unable to send word when Agnes decided on the spur of the moment to accompany him home from school in Philadel-phia for the Christmas holidays, and her presence—and Richard's obvious affection for her—had confounded the sisters. Sylvia, especially, was jealous that someone had stolen away her beloved baby brother's attention, and de-cided to find nothing redeemable in her rival. She saw Agnes as a flighty, spoiled, pampered princess, and nothing Agnes said or did could persuade her otherwise. It was a puzzle, Sylvia said, what Richard saw in her.

Agnes chuckled to herself as she worked on the block, imagining how flustered Sylvia would be to discover her little meanness had not been a secret for decades. So as to not spoil the joke, Agnes would allow Sylvia to believe Agnes had overheard the sisters using the nickname. She would not reveal that while their menfolk were overseas, Claudia had confided the secret in a spiteful attempt to win Agnes to her side after an especially heated argument with her sister.

Next Agnes pieced a Sister's Choice block for Sylvia's rash and oft regretted decision to leave Elm Creek Manor upon learning that Claudia's future husband, Harold, could have saved the lives of Richard and Sylvia's husband, James, but, out of cowardice, had done nothing. Sylvia's decision to abandon her ancestral home transformed her life, her sister's, and the manor itself. Perhaps nothing more than Agnes's own choice to marry into the Bergstrom family had influenced the course of her fate more than Sylvia's departure from the manor. If Sylvia had remained to run the family horse-breeding business, Claudia and Harold would not have driven it into bankruptcy. If the couple had not depleted the family fortune and begun selling off parcels of land and precious family heirlooms, Agnes would not have met the history professor who advised her on antique markets and later became her husband. If she had not married Joe, she would have lived out her days in the manor that had become as full of grief and despair as it had once been blessed with love and prosperity. She would not have become a mother and a grandmother. She would not have known the greatest joys of her life.

Upon completing that block, Agnes somberly began a Castle Wall. Sylvia would know at once why Agnes had chosen the pattern. More than a year after Sylvia's departure, in a rare moment of regret, Claudia had agreed to help Agnes complete a memorial quilt for Sylvia, whom they still believed would soon return. Together Agnes and Claudia had sorted through James's closet, selecting shirts and trousers and ties they knew Sylvia would recognize. From the cloth they cut diamonds and triangles and squares and sewed them into the pattern whose name conveyed all that the founders of Elm Creek Manor had wanted their descendants to find within its walls: safety, sanctuary, family, home. For a year the forsaken sisters pieced the tribute to the husband Sylvia mourned, but Claudia's own marriage had begun to crumble under the strain of grief and guilty secrets, and as she withdrew into her solitary bitterness, Agnes layered the top in the frame and quilted it alone. It had yet been incomplete when she had left Elm Creek Manor to marry Joe. After Sylvia's return to the manor, Sylvia and Agnes had finished the quilt together, and it now hung in the library, where Sylvia and James had spent so many happy hours discussing the family business, planning for a future that would not come to pass.

Rather than evoke only sorrowful memories, Agnes next pieced a Christmas Star in celebration of Sylvia and Andrew's Christmas Eve wedding. That pattern called to mind Sylvia's favorite block, the eight-pointed LeMoyne Star, and all the variations that found their way so often into Sylvia's quilts: Virginia Star, Snow Crystals, Blazing Star, Carpenter's Wheel, St. Louis Star, Dutch Rose, Star of Bethlehem. Once Agnes completed these, she made her own favorites, the appliquéd Whig Rose, American Beauty Rose, and Bridal Wreath.

By the end of February, Bonnie had collected thirty blocks at Grandma's Attic, which she delivered to Agnes so that she might begin planning their final arrangement. To these Agnes added her own twenty-four blocks and arranged them on the design wall Joe had put up for her when she had converted Laura's old bedroom into a sewing room. The pieced and appliquéd blocks clung to the flannel surface where she placed them, and as she admired their beauty and variety, she decided that a border of split LeMoyne Stars would be just the thing to set them off best. She would start on it right away. She could always stitch a few more blocks later, if they were needed.

❧

Agnes dreamed of a balmy summer day, Joe in his shirtsleeves cooking steaks and hot dogs on the charcoal grill, her daughters shrieking with delight in pink and yellow bathing suits as they ran through the sprinkler. She threw the red-and-white checked tablecloth over the picnic table and returned inside for plates and napkins, where she found Zach sitting at the kitchen table reading one of her notebooks. He looked up and smiled. "This is an important family record," he said, grinning. "But what the heck is oleo?"

She opened her mouth to reply but was distracted by a distant ringing. She turned to find Laura, suddenly a grown woman, ringing the doorbell on the screen door. Her expression was solemn and she did not speak. Confused, since the back door had no bell, Agnes watched as Laura rang again.

"You should probably get that," advised Zach. The summer day vanished, and Agnes woke to the dark winter night of her bedroom. She jumped and clutched her quilt, heart pounding, as the doorbell rang downstairs. She glanced at the clock on her nightstand. Good news never came to the door at nearly one o'clock in the morning. She put on her robe and slippers and hurried downstairs, remembering to check through the window before opening the door. What she saw made her fling it open.

"Bonnie, honey," she said, gasping at the sudden cold. "What's wrong?"

Hollowly, Bonnie said, "May I spend the night?"

"Of course," said Agnes, opening the door still wider and ushering in her friend. Her mind raced with questions, but Bonnie seemed dazed, shocked, lost in an uneasy dream. "You must be exhausted at this hour," Agnes said instead, leading Bonnie upstairs to Stacy's old room. "I won't need but a moment to set everything up for you. Would you like a cup of tea while you wait? A nice glass of warm milk? I like to put just a touch of vanilla in it."

Bonnie shook her head, eyes downcast. She seemed to be fighting back tears.

At a loss, Agnes made nervous small talk as she showed Bonnie the adjoining bath and set out fresh towels for her. Bonnie would need a nightgown, she thought, noting for the first time that Bonnie had brought nothing with her. She hurried to her own room and retrieved the largest and warmest nightgown she owned, and hoped it would do. Bonnie took it and shook her head again when Agnes asked her if she wanted to try it on first, if Agnes should look for something better.

It was apparent Bonnie wanted nothing more than to surrender to a dreamless sleep. "I'll say good night, then," said Agnes, lingering with her hand on the doorknob. "Just call me if you need anything."

"Thank you," said Bonnie, stroking the flannel nightgown absently.

Agnes shut the door and went to her own room, where she lay awake in bed listening to floorboards creak, water flowing in the pipes, the settling of bedsprings. When all was silent once again, she drifted off to sleep.

❧

Agnes woke at six, her first thoughts of Bonnie. What on earth had brought her friend to her door, on foot, on a cold winter's night? It could not have been a disaster with the children; Bonnie would have remained at home with her husband and called her friends to her side. Knowing Bonnie, she would have waited until morning to trouble them no matter how she longed for the comfort of their presence. No, the most logical explanation was a fight with Craig. Trouble with a husband was what most often sent a woman from her home in the middle of the night.

Agnes bathed and dressed, then tiptoed downstairs, pausing by Bonnie's door. When she heard nothing, she continued on to the kitchen, where she put on a larger pot of coffee than usual and fixed some waffles. She read the newspaper while she ate, and a large ad for Fabric Warehouse reminded her with a jolt that Bonnie worked on Fridays. She would surely be in no fit state to work today, especially considering that her husband would be right upstairs. Agnes waited until half past seven before phoning Diane and asking her to fill in. Diane agreed, but not before asking too many questions that Agnes evaded with difficulty. Agnes hung up, hoping she had not given Diane any reason for suspicion besides the obvious, calling on Bonnie's behalf when Bonnie typically took care of such matters herself. With any luck, Diane's harried morning rendered her too distracted to notice, which was why Agnes had phoned her instead of the more perceptive Summer.

Still listening for noises above, Agnes washed her breakfast dishes, then crept softly upstairs to her sewing room and gathered the fabrics for the pieced border, her rotary cutter and ruler, and a cutting mat. She set up her tools on the dining room table and cut fabric pieces in silence, working off her worries in the familiar, repetitive motions of measuring and cutting. Shortly after eleven o'clock, she heard Bonnie walking about upstairs, followed by the sound of the shower. Agnes set her work aside and met her friend in the kitchen. Bonnie appeared fairly well rested given the circumstances, but was clad in the clothing she had worn the previous night. Agnes had not thought of that or she would have searched around for an alternative.

"I overslept," Bonnie said. She looked around the room as if she had lost something. "I have to get to work."

"Not without breakfast," said Agnes, leading her to the table, then turning to pour her a cup of coffee. "Do you want scrambled eggs or waffles?"

"But the shop—"

"Don't you worry. I called Diane. She said she'd head over as soon as she could. She probably didn't get there on time, but she got there."

As she returned to the counter for cream and sugar, Agnes watched from the corner of her eye as Bonnie relaxed and sank back into the chair.

"Thank you," said Bonnie softly.

As far as Agnes was concerned, it was the least she could do. She convinced Bonnie to have some breakfast, and while Bonnie ate her waffles, Agnes poured herself another cup of coffee and joined her at the table. Every ounce of willpower she possessed went into appearing nonchalant as she sipped the hot, fragrant coffee and waited for Bonnie to speak.

"I left Craig," said Bonnie suddenly.

Agnes was not surprised, but she wondered if it was rude not to appear so. "For good?"

"I think so."

Bonnie continued with an account of the argument that had sent her to Agnes's for the night, and then the more heartbreaking story of the lonely, angry months that had preceded it. As Bonnie spoke, Agnes could only listen, speechless and sympathetic, her heart aching with one relentless question: Why? Why had Bonnie not shared her anguish with her friends? Each would have rallied to her side, lent her their strength. Worse yet, why had they not noticed how much she was hurting?

When Bonnie's voice trailed off at the end of her story, she stirred her coffee idly and added, "I still have the number of our marriage counselor. I'm going to ask if he can see us—or even just me—as a sort of emergency rescue case."

Agnes hid her astonishment. Nothing Bonnie had just told her suggested the marriage was salvageable. "That's fine," she said carefully, "as long as you speak to a lawyer, too."

To her relief, Bonnie nodded.

As they cleaned up the kitchen and finished washing the dishes, Agnes told Bonnie she was welcome to stay as long as she liked, but Bonnie shook her head and staunchly assured her—or herself—that she fully intended to sleep in her own bed that night. In the meantime, she had to return home for a change of clothes. Agnes offered to accompany her, and prepared to insist upon it, but Bonnie nodded almost before Agnes finished speaking.

But Bonnie's intentions would not be fulfilled. They arrived at the condo to find that Craig had changed the locks; when Bonnie tried to buy new clothes, they discovered he had canceled her credit cards. Agnes would have put the purchase on her own account, but Bonnie handed over the Grandma's Attic corporate card impassively, as if she had expected such vindictiveness from her husband. Agnes was so shocked she hardly knew what to do, but on the walk home, she certainly knew what to say.

"Come home with me," she said. "You can change clothes and call your lawyer."

"I don't have a lawyer."

"I do. He's a wonderful young man. His father looked after our affairs for years, and he took over the firm after his father passed."

"Does he handle divorces?"

"If not, he'll know someone who does."

She gave Bonnie his card as soon as they returned home. Bonnie nodded and took it upstairs with her shopping bags, but when she returned in her new knit pants and sweatshirt, she shrugged when Agnes asked her when her first appointment with the lawyer would be.

"You didn't call him?" asked Agnes.

"I don't feel up to it." Indeed, Bonnie looked as if she needed a good soak in a warm tub, preferably with a huge plate of chocolate chip cookies within reach. Or, failing that, a strong right cross capable of knocking Craig on his rear.

"Bonnie, honey, I don't think you should delay."

"I'm not even sure if I want a divorce. I don't know if I could go through with it."

"Maybe not, but a lawyer could at least tell you what your options are. And your rights."

Bonnie nodded and wandered into the dining room. Agnes followed and found her fingering the strips of fabric cut for the bridal quilt's border. Agnes did not want to add to the pressure already weighing down her friend, but Craig had proven to be more spiteful and cruel than Agnes could have imagined, and she was certain he wouldn't demur when it came to getting a lawyer on his side. "He nearly cleaned out your bank accounts," said Agnes. "He canceled your credit card. He locked you out of your home and gave you nothing to live on. That can't possibly be legal."

"At least the kids are grown." Bonnie picked up a stack of fabric diamonds and set them back down. "If they were still living at home, this would be a hundred times worse."

Agnes figured things would rapidly become a thousand times worse if Bonnie didn't take care. Agnes took her by the shoulders. "I know this is an enormous shock. I know divorce would be a drastic change and you don't want to think about it. But right now you have to do what's in your own best interest. You can be sure Craig is."

Bonnie blinked, then frowned, hard. "I wouldn't doubt it. That's what he's always done."

Finally, Agnes thought with relief. A bit of well-deserved anger. Bonnie would need that if she were to shake off this wounded bewilderment and steel herself for what was likely to be an unpleasant fight. Agnes could see it coming, even if Bonnie refused to look.

❧

Agnes knew that until Bonnie found her bearings, what she needed most was companionship and activity, so she enlisted Bonnie's help in assembling the split LeMoyne Star border. Over the weekend they cut fabric and assembled the four-pointed half stars, taking turns at Agnes's sewing machine. They worked uninterrupted except for meals and sleep, and, without consulting Bonnie, Agnes arranged for Diane to cover at Grandma's Attic. They spent the hours working in tandem, at first conversing little except to discuss the progress of Sylvia's bridal quilt. But as the weekend passed, Bonnie broke the silences more frequently with other dismaying revelations about the Markham marriage—and surprising confessions about the financial status of the quilt shop. Revenues were down, debts were high, and the rent was going up. The building's new owner seemed as unscrupulous as Craig, and Agnes concurred with Bonnie's suspicion that they intended to arrange the condo's sale with or without her consent. Agnes was not sure how that could happen since Bonnie's name was on the deed, but that was all the more reason Bonnie ought to consult a lawyer without delay.

To Agnes's consternation, Bonnie seemed as unwilling to confront this Gregory Krolich fellow as she was Craig. Her friend seemed deflated, skittish; on Sunday evening she sounded reluctant when she told Agnes she planned to return to work in the morning. Agnes quickly assured her she thought that was an excellent idea. Grandma's Attic had been Bonnie's favorite place from the day of its grand opening, and Bonnie's former confidence and optimism were more likely to be restored in familiar, beloved surroundings.

Indeed, early Monday evening Bonnie returned to Agnes's house in better spirits and was more resolute than she had been in weeks. Agnes even managed to persuade her to go to Craig's office and refuse to leave until he allowed her back into the condo. "You need it more than he does," Agnes pointed out, "since he enjoys staying away so much." Bonnie agreed, and on Wednesday morning, after arranging for Diane to open the shop, Bonnie headed for the Waterford College campus. Agnes was so proud of her that she resolved not to let her fight alone.

First she phoned her lawyer herself and told him about Bonnie's situation. He recommended a divorce attorney named Darren Taylor, describing him as smart, honest, and relentless. "Call him soon," her lawyer advised. "He's the best in the county, and you don't want your friend's husband to retain him first."

Uneasy, Agnes decided not to wait for Bonnie to return home from work. She phoned Darren Taylor herself, left a message with his assistant, and worked on Sylvia's bridal quilt impatiently while she waited for him to return the call. At noon the phone rang, and Agnes told the attorney as much of Bonnie's story as she could remember.

"Your friend's husband sounds like a real louse," said Darren. "It's too bad Bonnie had to leave the property, but it's obvious he left her no choice. We'll have a strong case against him if she can document his actions."

"So you're willing to take the case?"

"I'd prefer to speak to your friend first, but I see no reason why not."

"Considering how her husband has frozen her assets, I'd be happy to send you a check myself if it's a matter of your retainer."

"Thanks, but what I really want to know is if your friend truly wants to go through with a divorce."

"She does," said Agnes firmly, thinking, *She will.*

"Then have her call me and we'll set up a meeting. In the meantime, tell her to secure any assets her husband might not have thought of yet—investment accounts, properties, autos—and to go over their bank records very carefully to see if there were any other unexplained withdrawals before the one that all but closed the accounts. He could have been siphoning off money from their joint accounts for years and concealing it somewhere. He acted so quickly I bet he's been planning this for some time."

Agnes quickly took notes as he spoke. "I'll tell her."

"I'm afraid this next business is rather ugly. You said he's spent a lot of nights away from home. Ask your friend if she knows where he's been staying, and with whom. If we can sue on the grounds of infidelity, any claim that she abandoned the property will lose its impact."

"I'll ask," said Agnes, but she doubted Bonnie knew or she would have mentioned it.

"This business with University Realty might prove a difficult knot to untie. Some of my colleagues have dealt with them before, and while they're unscrupulous, they always manage to keep everything nice and legal. If your friend can get me copies of her lease for the store and purchase agreement for the condo, I'll pass them along to our property law specialist."

Heartened by Darren Taylor's confidence—and the fact that they finally had some steps to take—Agnes assured him that everything would be taken care of, and that Bonnie would call him soon.

"The sooner the better," Taylor emphasized.

When Bonnie returned from work, she glowed with accomplishment: She had refused to budge from Craig's office for three hours until he had finally appeared. "And that's not idle boasting," she said with a laugh. "That old furniture in his waiting room is uncomfortable. Craig bought it because it looks like some antiques he saw at Penn State once, not because he cares about the poor visitors who have to use it."

Agnes sniffed. "How typical." Craig's reputation as a cheapskate was well earned.

"I think he would have stayed away even longer except he had to get some papers from his desk for a meeting."

Agnes smiled, proud of her. "Did he agree to move out and let you return home?"

Bonnie's face fell. "No, he didn't. But he did say I could come home to pack a suitcase."

"Well, he's become quite the altruist, hasn't he," said Agnes, and insisted that she accompany Bonnie. She was neither strong nor intimidating enough to defend Bonnie if Craig tried to harm her physically, but experience had taught Agnes that often the presence of an older woman encouraged younger men to be on their best behavior. Furthermore, her conversation with Darren Taylor had put her in a litigious frame of mind, and she thought it prudent to witness Bonnie's visit home. Heaven only knew how Craig would describe it later.

As they walked to the condo, Agnes summarized her phone conversation with Darren Taylor and urged Bonnie to contact him first thing the next morning. Bonnie hesitated and said, "I'll think about it."

What more was there to think about? Agnes wanted to ask, but determined to be a supportive friend, she linked her arm through Bonnie's and nodded.

Having some of her belongings back and wearing her own favorite clothes brought about a marked change in Bonnie's attitude, even greater than her triumph of facing down Craig at his office. Three days after her return to the condo, Bonnie came home from work bearing two grocery bags and a bottle of wine, and announced that she intended to prepare Agnes the best meal she had ever eaten. Agnes was too pleased by her friend's good cheer to ask how she could afford such a feast and instead tied on an apron and offered to help. They had a delightful evening preparing and indulging in a crown roast, sweet potatoes, salad, and a luscious chocolate soufflé for dessert. Agnes even finished off a glass of wine, but what made the occasion truly worth celebrating was that Bonnie announced her intention to contact Darren Taylor and begin divorce proceedings. "I can't be afraid of being alone," she said. "The wrong man is much worse than no man at all."

"Oh, Bonnie." Agnes reached out and touched her hand. "You have so many friends, you'll never be alone."

Tears filled Bonnie's eyes. "Now I just have to explain things to the kids."

"Do they have any inkling of what has been going on between you and Craig?"

"Who knows? I doubt it. To them we're just old mom and dad, fixtures, a unit." Bonnie sighed and swirled the last drops of wine in her glass. "They're old enough to understand the reasons why couples divorce, but I can't imagine they ever thought their own parents would. I wish for their sake Craig and I could keep things amicable, but I think once you've crossed over into hostility, you can't go back."

"You don't have to be nasty, regardless of what Craig does," Agnes assured her, and was rewarded with a grateful smile.

Agnes would take care of the nastiness herself.

❧

On Monday morning after Bonnie left for Grandma's Attic, Agnes waited a suitable interval before setting off on the same route. Rather than enter the quilt shop, she circled around behind the building and ducked into a shallow alcove at the rear entrance of a drugstore just across the alley. The hiding place provided a good view of the back door to Bonnie's building, but no one leaving the building would see her unless they knew to look.

She had arrived just in time; within ten minutes the door banged open and out came Craig, clad in his blue Penn State coat and blaze-orange knit hat, whistling, his hands in his pockets. Agnes sighed with relief as he walked past the car without a glance—she would not have been able to follow him driving—and continued east down the alley. She waited a few moments to see if an overnight guest would emerge a discreet few moments later, but when the door remained closed, Agnes hurried after Craig.

From the mouth of the alley Agnes spotted Craig jaywalking north across Campus Drive and turning east again down Main. She pursued him for several blocks, dodging students and professors hurrying to class, until he pushed his way through the revolving door of The Bistro, a favorite breakfast and lunch spot for locals and faculty, a popular student hangout after six.

Agnes pretended to study the menu posted in the window. She glimpsed Craig inside as he removed his hat and finger-combed his hair. She frowned and sniffed. Primping for his lady friend, no doubt, for all the good it would do him. No amount of grooming would conceal the flaws in Craig's character for long.

As Agnes watched, a man clad in a black wool coat and carrying a leather briefcase joined Craig in line and clapped him on the back. Craig seemed glad to see him, but not surprised; they shook hands like fond colleagues and waited together to be seated. "My," breathed Agnes as she watched, but unless she had completely misread Craig all these years, this particular breakfast companion was not the reason for Craig's nights away from home.

The hostess appeared, menus in hand, and led the two men through a doorway and out of sight. Agnes hastened to a window farther down the sidewalk, but although she rose up on her tiptoes, she could not see where they had been seated. She cupped her hands around her eyes and peered through the glass—and then became aware of the curious and pointed stares of the couple eating pancakes at the table on the other side of the window. Agnes felt her cheeks grow warm. "Sorry," she mouthed, backing away. Then she retraced her steps and entered the restaurant.

She sidestepped the hostess's stand and headed into the main dining area, pretending to be in search of the ladies' room. Suddenly she spied Craig and the man, who had removed his coat to reveal a suit of equally fine quality, chatting up the pretty young waitress as she poured their coffee. The man had opened his briefcase and set a thin sheaf of papers on the table, promptly distracting Craig's attention from the waitress. Agnes strolled by, heading for the REST ROOMS sign on the far wall, but stealing quick glances at the papers as she passed. They were clearly legal documents of some sort; she knew this not because she could read the small print, but because the man uncapped a silver pen and passed both pen and papers across the table to Craig as they spoke. She caught snatches of conversation from the man—"property under contention," "sole resident," and "closing"—and confident assurances from Craig consisting mostly of "No problem."

Agnes reached the hallway to the rest rooms and ducked around the corner. No problem indeed! She would bet her last spool of silk thread that the man in the well-tailored wardrobe was that despicable Gregory Krolich, and the property under contention must surely be the condo. She peered around the corner and watched as Craig capped Krolich's pen and returned it to him. They shook hands, and Krolich gathered up the papers and filed them in his briefcase.

Agnes did not linger to observe what coldhearted snakes ate for breakfast. She marched home, indignant. If she recalled correctly, Sylvia had met with that Gregory Krolich years before, when she still intended to sell her estate. She might be able to confirm his description.

To her disappointment, when Sarah answered the phone at Elm Creek Manor, she reported that Sylvia and Andrew were out running errands. "Oh, dear," said Agnes. "I have a rather urgent question for her. Could you have her call me back as soon as she returns?"

"Of course," said Sarah. "Is there anything I can do in the meantime?"

"Thank you, honey, but I don't think so. I have some questions about a local real estate company and recalled Sylvia had some dealings with them."

"Are you planning to move?"

"No," said Agnes, determined to stay on the fair side of truth. "A friend of mine may be, and she could use some advice."

"Well, the only company Sylvia's dealt with since I've known her is University Realty."

"I thought so. That's the one."

"I can tell you what Sylvia would say: Your friend should run, not walk, to another agency as soon as possible. Did you know one of their people wanted to raze Elm Creek Manor and build student apartments in its place?"

"That was Gregory Krolich, right?"

"That's right."

"Is he tall, dark hair with gray at the temples, would be distinguished if not for the obsequious smile?"

"Expensive clothes, flashy car—that's the guy."

"Thank you, Sarah," said Agnes. "You've been very helpful. Please tell Sylvia she doesn't need to return my call."

How far could Craig proceed with the sale of the condo without Bonnie's consent? The little Agnes had overheard suggested that Craig had implied he had her consent, or at least that she could raise no objections. Krolich had seemed perfectly willing to believe him.

Agnes's sleuthing had uncovered more questions than answers, and nothing she had learned explained who or what had kept Craig away from home all those nights.

She pondered this all day as she worked on Sylvia's bridal quilt and made some last-minute revisions to her lesson plans for her Baltimore Album Appliqué class. Perhaps there was no lady friend. It was possible Craig had spent each night sleeping in his office, alone, but that seemed a great many nights to toss and turn on what Bonnie had called old, uncomfortable furniture, regardless of its resemblance to something finer at his beloved alma mater. Bonnie could not afford to hire a private detective to follow Craig, as a suspicious wife on television would do, nor could Agnes herself stake out the condo every evening.

In Agnes's experience, if a man was having an affair, his best friends knew about it. The betrayed wife usually found out from their wives, if they were close, or from clues the husband carelessly left behind. Bonnie either had found no such clues or had ignored them, and she and Craig did not seem to socialize with other couples much, other than gatherings of the Elm Creek Quilters and their families. Agnes could not imagine Craig confessing an affair to one of the Elm Creek husbands.

The only people who knew Craig as well as his friends were his coworkers, and they probably saw more of him than his family. If Craig was involved with another woman, he had probably conducted the affair from the office rather than home, especially since five years earlier Bonnie had caught him in that awful liaison with that woman from the Internet.

When Bonnie called at five to say she planned to eat takeout at Grandma's Attic for supper while she caught up on some paperwork, Agnes decided to pay Craig an office visit.

First, she stopped by the Grandma's Attic building to see if his car was there and if any lights were on in the condo above. The car was parked in its usual place and the condo windows were dark, so Agnes continued on foot along the most direct route to Craig's building. As she left the back alley, she remembered what Darren Taylor had said about securing other joint assets. She would suggest to Bonnie that she drive the old compact home from work one day and store it in Agnes's garage. Let Craig walk or bum rides from his good buddy Krolich. It would serve him right.

Craig did not pass her on the way across campus. She reached his building at a few minutes to six and checked the directory posted in the lobby for the room number of the director's office. Since students rarely came to the Office of the Physical Plant, the halls were deserted except for an occasional custodian with a cleaning cart. Light spilled through one open doorway at the end of the corridor; as Agnes approached, she saw the sign announcing OFFICE OF THE DIRECTOR posted on the wall beside it. She peered inside and saw three desks bearing computers, papers, and the assorted photos and personal knickknacks that attempted to make the workspaces more homey. Not far from the desks was a waiting area, and Agnes understood at once why Bonnie had commented about it. The pieces were enough alike in design—a sort of hybrid of Shaker and Arts and Crafts—to be considered a set, but the chairs and sofa were upholstered in different fabrics and their wooden armrests and legs had been finished in stains of slightly different hues, as were several tables scattered among them. Their only other unifying features were the dings and scratches of what appeared to be generations of hard use. Unless Craig had more comfortable accommodations in his private office, he surely wasn't spending the night here.

Agnes glanced at the two doors on the far wall; one was closed, light visible through the long, narrow window beside the door. The other was open and, at that moment, Agnes heard the unmistakable sound of a file drawer slamming shut. Before she could duck out of sight, a slim woman, who had short blond hair with a touch of gray, emerged from the room, a stack of files in her arms. "Oh, hi," she said, smiling briefly at Agnes before seating herself at the largest desk with the most impressive-looking computer. "Can I help you with something?"

Agnes forced herself to smile. "No, I just wanted to see who else was working late. Is Craig still in?"

"Of course. We can barely pry him out of this place lately."

Agnes nodded knowingly. "I've heard he has . . . company most nights."

The woman's eyebrows shot up. "Who? Craig? Not unless his computer counts as company. He's too cheap to run up his own Internet bill at home."

"I should have known they were only rumors." Agnes chuckled and gestured at the waiting area. "I guess they would have to be, if the furniture in his private office is as awful as this stuff. No one could sleep—or anything else—on this."

"What do you expect when he insisted on redecorating at his own expense? Between you and me, though, he's roughed it more than once. His wife was here the other day and—" Suddenly her eyes narrowed. "But that doesn't mean I believe those rumors floating around your office. Where do you work, again?"

Agnes made a dismissive gesture. "Oh, I'll bet you can guess. The office everyone hates and everyone fears they'll be transferred to. Thankfully, I'm just a temp, which is probably why you don't recognize me. At least, you don't seem to. Maybe you do. That would be nice."

The woman nodded, her brow furrowed, but Agnes didn't wait for her to puzzle it out. She bid her good-bye and hurried away.

She walked home, too absorbed in what she had learned that day to notice the chill that had descended with darkness. So. Craig stayed up late "surfing the net" as her computer-savvy younger friends liked to say. For a man with his history, that counted as having illicit company, although his assistant seemed certain he was not seeing anyone in the physical sense. Craig did not seem overly fussy, as his choice in new furniture confirmed, and Agnes could picture him being too lazy to do anything more than slouch over to the nearest sofa, lumps and scratches and all, rather than return home after a late night of computer-assisted romance.

That furniture. Something about it . . . Agnes paused and frowned. That unusual hybrid of Shaker traditions and Arts and Crafts. She had read about that style somewhere, or had seen something like it before.

"Likely at a yard sale," she said aloud, and continued homeward. Craig's assistant was right: Craig was cheap and always had been. He would leave Bonnie with nothing to show for their thirty-some years of marriage except for their children and memories unless Agnes found something more substantial than assumptions and intuition to use against him. He'd shake down Bonnie for her pocket change, if he could.

❧

As the last two weeks before the start of the new camp season passed, Agnes learned little more about Craig or the hypothetical computer girl-friend, despite frequent attempts to follow Craig as he left the condo in the morning or work in the afternoon. She did discover that Craig took two-hour lunches at a sports bar near campus at least twice a week, where he sat alone in the clubhouse, had a beer with his sandwich, and watched three separate cable sports networks on the three giant televisions that rivaled movie screens. Her investigation of Gregory Krolich, however, turned up a few important details. Posing as a prospective tenant, she phoned University Realty and inquired about Bonnie's condo, which she had heard was for sale. The pleasant young woman who answered told her that while it was true the current tenants were moving out, all of the condos were going to be converted to student apartments, so unless that interested her . . .

"No, no," said Agnes, laughing to disguise her outrage. "How disappoint-ing, though! It would have been so convenient to live just upstairs from that charming little quilt shop. I've always wanted to learn, you see."

But the quilt shop was moving, too, Agnes learned. They had decided not to renew their lease, and while University Realty was sorry to lose them, they welcomed the opportunity to take over the space themselves. They had outgrown their current building, which like the other businesses on that block had been converted from a single-family home, and they had long de-sired a storefront closer to campus, to better serve the student market.

University Realty was proceeding as if Bonnie had already signed away both condo and shop, but although Agnes made a risky visit to University Realty to obtain a brochure or flyer or something, the receptionist at the front desk told her they had no rental literature yet available, no matter how urgent her grandson's need for a student apartment was, and that despite what she might have heard, they had not yet "finalized" their plans for the building. She also asked, politely but with an edge to her voice, where Agnes had heard otherwise, but Agnes quickly left before turning in the helpful assistant, who had really been a dear and whose name she didn't re-call, anyway.

Without any evidence to back up her suspicions, Agnes reluctantly de-cided to say nothing of her investigation to Bonnie. Passing on rumors would accomplish nothing, only fuel Bonnie's anxieties.

The first day of camp brought a welcome respite from worry. Agnes was glad to see Bonnie preoccupied with the last-minute preparations for the campers' arrival rather than Craig or Grandma's Attic. Indeed, all of her friends seemed cheerful in their work, except for Diane, who spent much of the time she and Agnes were arranging fresh flowers in the guest rooms grumbling about Bonnie's failure to appreciate her work at Grandma's Attic. Agnes hid her exasperation and pointed out that Bonnie might have other concerns on her mind, problems more significant than who worked more hours than whom. Diane snorted dismissively, but she kept her complaints to herself for the rest of the day until she drove Agnes home after the Candlelight welcoming ceremony. Bonnie had insisted on departing the manor later, by cab, rather than reveal that she was staying with Agnes. When Bonnie finally arrived, Agnes encouraged her to reclaim the Markham family car, but Bonnie only laughed and considered her suggestion a joke even when Agnes told her she was in earnest.

Bonnie insisted on returning to Elm Creek Manor separately the next morning to preserve her secret, even though that meant a bus ride that ended at the main road and a rather long walk through the woods surrounding the estate. Agnes urged Bonnie to tell her friends the truth, or at least to confide in Diane so she could ride with her and Agnes, but Bonnie said that telling Diane was like telling the entire town, and she wasn't ready for all of Waterford to know.

For the first few days of camp, Bonnie's arrangements seemed to work adequately well. She got to work almost on time, and returned home only a little later than usual. Then at lunchtime on Wednesday, Sarah came to the table where Agnes sat eating with her four Baltimore Album students and asked Agnes to join her. Sarah's voice was so urgent that Agnes immediately agreed and excused herself, following Sarah to a separate table at the back of the banquet hall where Sylvia and Diane already waited.

"Has anyone seen Gwen?" asked Sarah as she sat down. Sylvia and Diane shook their heads.

Their solemnity sent a shiver of alarm through Agnes.

"Bonnie didn't show up this morning," said Diane. "We've called the shop and the condo, but no one answers."

"Didn't show up?" Agnes looked around the circle of friends, confused. "Of course not. She had to open Grandma's Attic this morning. She isn't due in until her workshop."

"Her workshop began at eleven," said Sylvia.

"Or at least it was supposed to." Beneath Sarah's concern lingered a trace of irritation. "We had to juggle the schedule to cover for Judy, remember? It was Bonnie's idea to close Grandma's Attic for a long lunch."

Agnes did not recall; probably Sarah had been too harried to tell everyone. "Maybe she forgot." But why did she not answer the phone? Likely she had missed the bus and had been forced to take a later one, and even now was en route to the manor. Agnes should have insisted she take her car. What if Bonnie had tried to, and Craig had stopped her?

Agnes tried to disguise her fear. "Someone—one of us ought to go down there and make sure she's all right."

Sylvia patted her hand. "Summer's already on her way."

"Well—I think we should call again anyway. Sarah, may I borrow your cell phone?"

Sarah agreed and showed her how to use it. Cupping the phone in her palm to conceal the display, Agnes quickly dialed Grandma's Attic and then her own home. Only answering machines responded.

She returned the phone to Sarah, who meanwhile had been going over the schedule with the others. "No answer," she said, and pretended to listen as her friends debated how to cover for another absent instructor. They should call the police. Something was dreadfully wrong, and Agnes knew it.

Just then Gwen arrived, and cheerfully admonished them for huddling together rather than mingling among their guests. In response, Sarah asked her to emcee the evening program.

Gwen shrugged. "Sure. I thought Bonnie was doing it."

"Maybe she will, but she didn't show up for her workshop this morning, so I thought I should have a backup plan."

"Didn't show up?" Gwen pulled out a chair and sat down. "Why not?"

"No one knows," said Agnes. But Bonnie had meant to come; they had spoken about her workshop at breakfast. "She didn't call in, and no one's answering the phone at the store."

"You tried her at home, right?"

"Well, yes," stammered Agnes, "but—well, she's not there, either." It was not exactly a lie; she had not wasted a call to the condo, but someone else had tried.

Sarah and the others explained the situation to Gwen, but Agnes sat silently with her own churning thoughts. She should tell their friends what she knew. Craig was a strong and unpleasant man, and he was furious with his wife. Bonnie could be in danger, and Agnes's silence might prolong it.

As soon as Sarah finished with the schedule, Agnes hurried to the parlor, where she took a few deep breaths to calm herself as she flipped through the phone book for the Waterford College listings. She called Craig's office. "Is Mr. Markham in?" she demanded.

"Yes, he is. May I ask who's calling?"

Agnes recognized the voice of the blond woman she had met in the outer office and lowered her voice half an octave. "This is Jane in accounting. He was supposed to return my call. What time did he get in this morning? Did he just arrive?"

"He was here at eight-thirty when I arrived. I'm sorry he didn't return your call right away. He probably didn't realize it was so urgent. Please hold and I'll transfer you."

"Never mind," growled Agnes and slammed down the phone, heart pounding. At least she knew Craig was not driving to Mexico with Bonnie tied up in the trunk of his car, but that did not mean he had not harmed her. Summer was on her way to Grandma's Attic. If there was any sign of foul play, she would call.

Ordinarily Agnes had Wednesday afternoons off, but today she lingered at the manor, assisting Sarah to make up for the absent Judy, Bonnie, and now Summer, who did not call with news. Three times Agnes slipped away to call Grandma's Attic and home, and once she even tried the condo, but Bonnie did not answer. At midafternoon, Gwen passed her in the hallway on her way out the back door. "I'm going to Grandma's Attic if anyone needs me," she said.

"Promise you'll call," said Agnes.

"I will," promised Gwen, with a reassuring grin, "unless the phones have been knocked out."

When Gwen did not call by supper, Agnes figured that was precisely what had happened.

She had no appetite, but Sarah had asked her to stay to disguise the dwindling numbers of Elm Creek Quilters. Diane had already left to feed her family before the evening program, so after the meal, Agnes asked Matt to drive her home in the Elm Creek Quilts minivan. It was almost seven by the time she unlocked her own front door and hurried inside. There was no sign of Bonnie, not downstairs or in the guest room. She returned downstairs to the dining room and, as her glance fell upon the split LeMoyne Star borders she and Bonnie had assembled together, she berated herself for putting Bonnie's desire for secrecy ahead of her safety.

She hurried to the phone and dialed Craig's office again. When only voicemail responded, she called the condo.

He answered on the fourth ring. "Hello?"

"Craig? This is Agnes Emberly."

"Oh. Hi." There was wariness in his tone, but no hostility, no guilt.

"Bonnie didn't come to work today, and we're all a bit worried. I wondered if you might know where she is."

"My guess is she's still downstairs cleaning up the mess."

"Cleaning?" Then she was all right. "What mess?"

"I don't know exactly. Maybe a robbery. There were cop cars parked out front this morning."

"My goodness," exclaimed Agnes. "Are you sure Bonnie's not hurt?"

"Yeah, yeah, she's fine. She and a couple of other Elm Creekers keep coming out back to throw junk in the Dumpster. Looks like a lot of damage was done."

Agnes bristled at the satisfaction in his tone. "It's a pity you can't find it in your heart to sympathize with your wife. You know how much that shop means to her."

"Listen, you don't know anything about me or my wife or how that store has dragged us down. If this is what it takes for her to give up on it, that's fine by me."

"Bonnie deserves far, far better than you," Agnes declared, but he had hung up the phone with a crash.

It was nearly midnight before Bonnie came home. She sank into a chair, wordless, exhausted, as Agnes ran to fetch her a warm quilt and fix a cup of tea. She refused Agnes's offer of food, but Agnes made her a sandwich anyway, and when she brought it to her, Bonnie wolfed it down as if she had not eaten all day.

"I heard there was a robbery," said Agnes, and Bonnie told her the whole story. Agnes listened with tears in her eyes as Bonnie described the destruction.

"The police think it was an inside job," Bonnie concluded dully.

Agnes was not surprised, but she asked, "Why do they think so?"

"Because there were no signs of a forced entry, and because more was ruined than taken."

Agnes took her hand. "Bonnie," she said gently, "do you think Craig is responsible?"

"No." Bonnie shifted in her chair and pulled her hand away. "I know he isn't."

Agnes remembered the satisfaction in his voice as he recounted the crime to her, and Darren Taylor's suspicions that he had been planning the divorce for a long time. "He could have used the spare key in the condo. He's entirely capable of something like this, especially given the circumstances."

"He's capable, all right, but he didn't do it. I gave the spare key to Diane a long time ago so she could open the shop occasionally. He obviously didn't use my key, since he hasn't been near it in weeks."

But before then he had had ample opportunity to duplicate it secretly. "Did you tell the police about the divorce?"

"The divorce, the debts, everything. They had so many questions. I heard Gwen tell them she thinks I forgot to lock the door last night, and they wrote that down, but I don't think they believed it. I know I locked the door, but I wish I wasn't so certain."

"Why not?"

"If the police say it's an inside job, the insurance company might refuse to pay."

Agnes felt a chill. Suddenly she thought of the personal expenses Bonnie had charged to Grandma's Attic in the past few weeks, the "debts and everything" she had confided to the police.

"Everything will be all right," she said, embracing her friend, and wishing she believed it.

CHAPTER SIX
Judy

I f Judy's mother had not come down with pneumonia soon after Christmas, Judy might never have considered leaving Waterford, even though her mother lived alone and the long drive to suburban Philadelphia made frequent visits difficult. Instead Judy had often reflected that one day she might be forced to put her mother in a retirement community or bring her to Waterford to live with them, taking her away from her Philadelphia home and the close, nearly lifelong friendships she had developed within the Vietnamese immigrant community there. But that January—for the fourth weekend in a row—Judy felt as if she spent more time in the car than caring for her mother, and it occurred to her that life would be so much simpler if she, Steve, and Emily were to relocate.

She allowed herself to imagine, for a moment, rainy Saturday afternoons chatting over tea with her mother in the big house where Judy had grown up, Emily and her grandmother on the sofa reading a book together, Steve helping his mother-in-law tend her garden. Then she reluctantly dismissed the notion. She was on track for a promotion to full professor in the Computer Sciences department, Steve enjoyed reporting the local news for the *Waterford Register*, and Emily was firmly attached to her second-grade teacher and circle of friends. Bringing her mother to Waterford was the far more logical solution, but Judy knew leaving her home would break her mother's heart.

The first day of the spring semester, Judy proposed the move to Steve over breakfast, presenting it as a joke. To her surprise, he told her he had entertained similar thoughts, adding that he had long wished for an opportunity to work for a larger paper. Moreover, Emily would benefit from a closer relationship with her grandmother, and Philadelphia was nearer to his family, but still far enough away that they could not visit without advance warning. "I'm all for it if you are," Steve assured her, but he regarded her curiously. "I can't believe you'd be able to leave Elm Creek Quilts, though."

"You're right," said Judy. "I couldn't."

Steve shrugged and finished his cereal so nonchalantly that she doubted he was genuinely disappointed. Still, she wondered why he had never mentioned his desire to work for a larger paper.

Besides, Steve was right. She could never leave Elm Creek Quilts. Her friends would never understand.

❧

Her mother fully recovered and soon insisted that Judy stop dragging her family across the state every weekend just to check on her. Relieved, and guilty because of her relief, Judy agreed, and soon she was too caught up in the busy routine of the new semester to think about moving. She might have forgotten about it altogether if not for an unexpected email from a former graduate-school classmate, now a full professor at Penn. He had read her most recent paper in the *Journal of Theoretical Computer Science* and could not believe she had not applied for the opening in his department, where they were just embarking on a more advanced stage of related research in a new, state-of-the-art facility. Had she missed the advertisement in the *Chronicle of Higher Education*, or was Waterford College really treating her that well?

Judy never bothered skimming the want ads, and Waterford College treated her fine, but she clicked on the link Rick had provided to an online article from the *Philadelphia Inquirer.* Reading the description of Penn's facility made her alternately admiring and envious. Waterford College's computer systems were adequate to her needs, but Penn's read like the catalogue of her wildest dreams. She could shave years of number-crunching from her current projects, which would allow her to develop her theories in ways she never could have otherwise contemplated.

"Rick, you are more fortunate than you know," murmured Judy, recalling the brilliant but unfocused student who had never made it into the lab before noon and who had twice written half a dissertation before scrapping it for a new subject. On impulse, she went to the home page for the *Chronicle* and searched the archives for the ad. Rick was right to contact her; her experience and interests dovetailed with their criteria perfectly. She would be ideal for the job—as would hundreds of other professors at far more prestigious universities, professors who had not spent their entire careers at small, private, rural colleges much better known for their achievements in the liberal arts than anything in the sciences.

It was nice of Rick to think of her, but she was far too busy to apply for a job she had no chance of getting.

She tried to put Penn and its wonderful new research facility out of her thoughts. She didn't even tell Steve about the job, knowing he would insist she apply anyway. Then, two days later, Gwen came to her office, angry and miserable. Once again the search committee had passed her over for department chair, this time with the asinine excuse that her research was irrelevant. As a scientist, Judy was hard-pressed to find any relevance in most of the papers churned out on that side of the campus, but Gwen's research had always seemed to provide valuable, fascinating historical information. Judy wondered if other factors had influenced the decision, but Gwen was so depressed Judy decided not to pester her with questions.

She thought it over after Gwen left and decided her friend might have struck the infamous glass ceiling head-on without realizing it, deceived because the committee had, in fact, chosen a woman. They clearly thought Gwen had gone as far as she could, despite her past accomplishments. The same could one day be said about Judy, once scholars at other schools made advances in her field that her limited resources simply would not allow.

She told Steve about the position that evening, and he agreed that she would be foolish not to apply. Unfortunately, he also insisted she was guaranteed to get the job, which displayed a charming faith in her abilities and an overwhelming ignorance of the competition. "Don't clear out your desk at the *Register* yet," she begged. "And don't tell the Elm Creek Quilters. They'll take it personally. They'll wonder what they did to make me want to leave, when to them, leaving is incomprehensible."

It would also save her embarrassment later when she had to tell them she didn't get the job.

She started assembling her application package that weekend, wishing she had updated her curriculum vitae long ago, wishing she had begun more than six days before the deadline. Unfortunately, she could not work at the office without attracting the attention of her graduate students, who would be dismayed to hear she would consider leaving them. Instead she took her laptop to coffee shops between classes and student conferences, and stayed up long after putting Emily to bed. Caffeine, Steve's encouragement, and images of that gleaming new research facility sustained her until she ran headlong into her deadline. A former professor of hers had a saying: "Better finished than perfect," and Judy repeated his words glumly as she dropped off her application package at the overnight delivery service the day before it was due. She sent Rick a confirming email, and then there was nothing to do but wait.

Wait, and catch up on all the work she had neglected in the meantime. A stack of papers awaiting grades collected dust on her desk, a graduate student needed to discuss his upcoming candidacy exam, and the first day of quilt camp was barely two months away. Judy had taught computer quilt design many times before and would need only to update her materials, but the Bindings and Borders workshop would be entirely new, and she had yet to finish a single sample. The block for Sylvia's bridal quilt was due a week after the start of quilt camp, which Judy considered rather poor planning. They were all swamped at that time of year despite spring break at the college and, given that they had already missed the wedding, it would have been more reasonable to give themselves an extra week.

She knew the perfect pattern to use for Sylvia's quilt, but since the sample quilts were needed sooner, she decided to complete the border examples first, snatching spare moments from her obligations to her family and the college wherever she could find them. On impulse she decided to sew her sample borders into a quilt top of ten horizontal rows and to finish each of the four sides in a different style. Days later, as she draped the completed quilt top on the living room floor for inspection, she couldn't help laughing. It was without a doubt the most eccentric quilt she had ever made.

"What's so funny?" Emily entered the room and took her hand, inspecting the quilt top. "Wow, Mom. That's great."

Judy put her head to one side and studied the quilt top critically. "Do you really think so?"

"Yeah, I like the colors and how every row is different."

"You don't think it's a little too bizarre?"

"Uh-uh. Can I use it in my room when it's done?"

Judy smiled, thinking of how the exotic batiks would clash with the pastel floral decor Emily had selected three years before. "It doesn't really go with your room."

"I could paint the walls. Please? I'll do it myself."

Judy laughed. She should not have been surprised that Emily, who over the past year had developed a keen affinity for German opera with no encouragement from her tone-deaf parents and who had more recently begun wearing her straight black hair in two asymmetrical braids bound by anything from yarn to bread bag twist-ties, would appreciate her quilt enough to redecorate her bedroom to suit it. "No way I'd let you paint your room by yourself," Judy said, "but your dad and I will talk about it." When Emily cheered, Judy added, "Remember, this quilt isn't finished yet, and I'll still need it all summer at quilt camp."

Disappointed, Emily said, "Maybe I can use it before quilt camp. When are you going to finish it?"

"As soon as I can." She glanced at her watch; on Saturdays, Grandma's Attic stayed open until five o'clock. While Emily went off to her room to dress for soccer practice, Judy found Steve working in the computer room and asked if he would mind taking Emily so Judy could shop for backing fabric and batting in the meantime.

Steve agreed, adding, "Are you finally going to use that gift certificate?"

"Absolutely not. You know I can't set foot in the Fabric Warehouse. It's incredibly disloyal to Bonnie. What if someone I know sees me?"

"That's not likely, since none of your friends will shop there, either." Steve grimaced in sympathy. "I know how you feel, but my mother has been bugging me ever since Christmas."

"I wish she had never bought it for me."

"I'm sure to her it seemed like the perfect gift for a quilter. Look at it this way. If you spend the certificate on batting and backing, you'll satisfy my mother without acquiring any fabric you'll use in a quilt top later. The Elm Creek Quilters will never know."

It still seemed traitorous, but Steve's mother had already paid for the gift certificate, so at least Judy wouldn't be giving them any of her own money. As for her guilt and the money she otherwise would have spent at Grandma's Attic, she would just have to make up for them with an extravagant shopping spree that would leave Bonnie gaping in astonishment.

The Fabric Warehouse took up most of a strip mall on the northwest fringes of town. When Emily was a toddler, Judy used to shop at the children's clothing boutique next door, whose windows were now empty except for a sign announcing the space was available for rent. Judy's last trip to the mall had occurred years before, when she and Summer had accompanied Bonnie on a scouting mission during Fabric Warehouse's holiday sale. Bonnie had ordered them to disguise themselves in head scarves and dark glasses, which only drew attention, made Judy feel ridiculous, and probably fooled no one.

Once inside, Judy steered her shopping cart directly to the batting section and chose two large rolls. Determined not to browse, she went straight to the shelves of fabric bolts along the far wall and selected a cream tone-on-tone print similar to one she had seen in Grandma's Attic. Beneath the fluorescent lights, it looked good enough for the back of a quilt, and if her friends happened to see it, they would assume she had purchased it from Bonnie.

She joined the line at the cutting table where two unsmiling employees in long green aprons unrolled bolts of fabric and snipped away at them with shears. The wait troubled Judy less than the realization that she had not seen such a long line at Bonnie's shop since her last fall clearance.

"Don't I know you?"

The voice behind Judy was unfamiliar, so she ignored it and waited for one of the ten people in front of her in line to turn around. Then she felt a tap on her shoulder. Stifling a groan, she turned her head enough to take in a woman in a red wool coat and a platinum blond pageboy. "Hi, Mary Beth," said Judy weakly. "How are you?"

Mary Beth eyed her with suspicion. "Surprised to see you here, that's for sure."

Judy gestured to her shopping cart. "My mother-in-law got me a gift certificate for Christmas."

"I would kill for a mother-in-law like that. Mine's always buying me these horrible tacky sweaters." Mary Beth shrugged, then brightened. "Does this mean you're no longer in with Bonnie Markham and that gang? If that's the case, you're always welcome to rejoin my guild. Those Elm Creekers are so high-and-mighty, don't you think? Expecting everyone to drop everything and make their precious Sylvia a quilt block. What is she thinking, getting married at her age? What is she, eighty-five or something?"

"Not quite," said Judy shortly, turning back around. "And I'm still in with that gang."

"Oh, pardon *me*," said Mary Beth, in a falsely sugary voice. "No offense. Speaking of offense, I wonder what Miss Bonnie will think when she finds out you were shopping here."

Judy said nothing. She should have invented an excuse for her mother-in-law, anything rather than shop the competition. But it was too late now. Let Mary Beth tattle if she felt so compelled. "Bonnie's heard about my mother-in-law. She'll understand why I had to use the gift certificate. She'll understand, and she won't hold it against me. That's what friends do." She couldn't resist adding, "I don't suppose you'd know that."

She sensed Mary Beth seething behind her and heard her storm away. Judy glanced over her shoulder to find Mary Beth halfway to the thread display and the rest of the line moving forward to fill her place.

❧

Two days later, Judy received an email from Rick. He would be passing through on his way home from Pittsburgh tomorrow and hoped she wouldn't mind treating him to lunch. Judy wrote back that she didn't mind and sent directions to her office.

He arrived shortly after ten. His longish red-blond hair had gone gray at the temples and he had put on a good forty pounds, but otherwise he could have been the same perpetual student she had known back in grad school. He had been working on his doctorate for five years before Judy joined the lab at Princeton, and he had remained for at least three years after she had graduated. Rumor had it their advisor called in favors so that Rick would not be dismissed for failing to complete his degree within the required time span, but whenever any of his friends tried to confirm this, Rick grinned and made up even wilder tales.

Judy showed him around her lab, painfully aware of how it must compare to his, but Rick nodded agreeably and demonstrated unusual restraint in his jokes about the age of her computers. Her graduate students were awed to meet the man who had authored so many of the papers Judy distributed as required reading and, to Judy's delight, Rick seemed impressed with their work and how well they discussed it. Suddenly it occurred to Judy that at that moment she could be in the middle of a job interview.

Before he could mention the position in front of her students, Judy got their coats and suggested they go to lunch. They walked a few blocks south of campus to a popular coffee shop with surprisingly good food, where Judy teased, "This is what you get when you invite yourself to lunch at the last minute."

"Next time I'll offer to treat," said Rick, as he eyed the café with mock distaste. Judy happened to know he had virtually camped out in his favorite coffee shop back in grad school, and she doubted he had changed much. Inside, he ordered the largest sandwich on the menu plus a luscious pastry Judy had often been tempted to try but had managed to resist. She settled on the tabbouleh and hummus platter and black coffee.

They grabbed a table in the corner and caught up on the news of their families while they ate. Rick pretended not to remember Steve's name and referred to him as the guy every heterosexual male in the department had hated from the moment he and Judy went on their first date. Judy teased him by pretending to have lost count of his divorces, then was astounded to hear he actually had one more than she recalled, and that he was planning to marry again in October. "Maybe you should quit while you're ahead," she told him, to which he replied that he couldn't stop now, so close to the record.

After he returned to the counter for a second cup of coffee, he took a sip and remarked, "They love you."

"Who?"

"The search committee."

"How much do they love me?"

"You're in the top five."

Her heart thumped, but she forced a nonchalant grin and said, "That's it? Not even the top three?"

He shrugged. "Sorry. I did what I could."

"I don't doubt it." She sat back, taking this in. "What exactly do I owe you?"

"Not a cent. Just accept the job if they offer it, come to Penn, and do brilliant work for the rest of your career."

She folded her arms and regarded him. "Do you help all your old grad school friends like this?"

"No, just those friends who are underserving themselves and the academic community by spending their careers in a backwater when they ought to be at the forefront of their fields."

Judy had to laugh. "You sounded exactly like Dr. Saari when you said that."

"Did I?" For a moment Rick looked guilty. "Would you be offended if I confessed this was his idea? You always were his favorite student. Don't get me wrong. I wholeheartedly agreed with his recommendation; I just can't take credit for it."

"So you're promoting my application as a favor to Dr. Saari."

"I'm promoting your application because you're the best candidate. However, he did remind me that he could have let the graduate school kick me out on a technicality a year before I would have graduated."

"I'll have to thank him, then, not you." She sipped her coffee and found that it had cooled. "Waterford College is not a backwater."

"Not if you're in the liberal arts. Judy, your doctorate is in Computer Engineering. Your undergrad degree is in Electrical Engineering. You can't tell me you're satisfied teaching computer programming. It's not your fault you got knocked up and had to take the first job that came along, but you don't have to suffer for the rest of your life."

"That's not exactly what happened."

"Close enough. If your hubby had had a real job you would have been able to afford another year of grad school while waiting for the job offers to roll in."

"I might have been waiting a very long time. The economy wasn't especially kind to new Ph.D.s that year."

"Which is why you should have waited it out, and would have, if not for Emily, and if not for the instability of Steve's freelance writing income."

Judy reluctantly had to agree, but she refused to admit that to Rick. She looked away, pretending to check the line at the front counter. She was wondering aloud how long she would have to wait for a refill when she spotted Sarah stirring cream and sugar into a carry-out cup. Judy was so startled she could not return Sarah's wave, and she sat riveted in place as Sarah crossed the room to join them.

"Judy, hi," said Sarah, smiling and indicating the two cups in her hands. "I thought I'd get my caffeine fix while Sylvia's getting her hair done."

"You must have had a late night," Judy said, and silently scolded herself for being so nervous. Sarah could not possibly know what she and Rick were discussing.

"Oh, no, this one's a peace offering for Sylvia. I'm late."

"Sorry you can't join us," said Rick, grinning at Sarah.

"Oh. Rick, this is my friend Sarah McClure. Sarah, this is Rick Balrud, an old friend from grad school. He's visiting from the University of Pennsylvania."

Sarah set down one of the cups and shook his hand "Hi. Welcome to Waterford. I'm impressed you were able to find it without a Sherpa or a global positioning system."

"Who says I didn't have both?" Rick's grin deepened and he held her hand longer than necessary.

Sarah glanced at her watch and picked up her cup again. "I'm late. Got to go. Nice to meet you."

"You, too." Rick watched as Sarah hurried away, then turned back to Judy. "She's cute. Married?"

"Yes, happily," said Judy sharply. "This is why you go through so many wives. You always think your true soul mate is right around the next corner."

His eyebrows rose. "Who said anything about my soul mate? I'm not that deep. I'm content with a nice pair of—"

"Don't say it." Judy waved him to silence. "Not about my friend."

Rick feigned innocence. "Eyes. I was going to say eyes."

"You're awful. You always have been."

"I know." He sipped his coffee. "Fortunately, I'm also a genius."

On the walk back to Judy's office, Rick told her she would soon receive a letter asking her to be available to travel during the week of March 24. If she were one of the top three candidates, she would be invited for an interview with the selection committee, comprised of the department chair, several professors, two graduate students, and one undergrad. They would provide the usual campus tour, job placement conference for the spouse, and meals with selected members of the department, which, Judy knew, was where most of the committee members would make up their minds rather than at the formal interview. She would also need to present a graduate-level seminar and guest lecture in an undergraduate class, the topics of which she should send by return mail so that they could match her with suitable courses.

Judy thanked him for the advance warning. She was familiar with the standard interview hoops candidates were obligated to jump through, having served on several search committees herself, but the last job she had applied for was the one she currently held.

Steve was thrilled by the news, although Judy tried to temper his enthusiasm by reminding him she had not made it to the top three yet. "You'll make it," said Steve, kissing her. "Why is it that everyone else is so much more aware of your abilities than you are?"

"You're blinded by love."

"On the contrary, love has opened my eyes."

Judy rolled her own eyes at that, but she was moved and decided to give him an early Valentine's Day treat that night after Emily went to sleep.

Two days later, on the real Valentine's Day, Steve surprised her by showing up at the lab in the middle of the afternoon and inviting her on a walk. Snow had fallen that morning and the wind still blew cold, but Steve looked so earnest that Judy quickly bundled up in her coat and scarf and followed him outside.

They walked arm in arm until the cold compelled them to stuff their hands into their pockets. "I want you to know that I fully support you and your career," Steve began. "Whatever you've wanted to do, I've always backed you up. I've always adjusted."

"I know you have." He didn't need to remind her of that. He had moved to Waterford without knowing if freelancing for the local paper would ever develop into something more permanent. When Emily was younger, he had stayed home to care for her, putting off his writing for weekends and evenings when Judy was home. It made sense, he said whenever Judy told him how much she appreciated him. Judy's work paid more and provided benefits. If their roles were reversed, no one would remark about what a devoted parent Judy was if she stayed home. Judy couldn't dispute that, but she was still convinced that only three men in a hundred would have sacrificed their own careers for their wives' so willingly.

She took a deep breath through her scarf. "Are you telling me you don't want to adjust anymore? I'm overdue to sacrifice for you. I'll turn down the Penn job if you want."

"No. No. That's the last thing I want." He paused. "I sent a letter and a packet of clips to a guy I know on the *Inquirer* editorial board. The editor of the news division wants me to come in for an interview."

"That's great!"

"Thanks. It wouldn't be for some cub reporter position, either. They liked my investigative pieces on the college embezzlement scandal so much that they're considering me for a senior position, not just comparable to what I have now but a significant step up."

"Oh, Steve." She was so proud she flung her arms around him. "I always said you were too good for the local rag."

"They haven't offered me the new job yet, and if they do, it won't mean anything if you don't get the job at Penn. As much as I want to make the jump, I can't justify doing so if it means a commuter marriage."

"It wouldn't necessarily—"

"Judy, you can't quit your job for me." He said this with such resolve that she knew he had seriously considered it. "The cost of living is higher out there, and my increase in salary won't compensate for the loss of your income."

Not to mention Judy's work would screech to a halt if she lacked a research facility. She could hardly build one in the basement. "So where does that leave us?"

"I've thought about it, and—"

At that moment, a plump woman carrying a tote bag appeared from behind a cluster of snowy pines and veered away just in time to avoid crashing into them. As she murmured an apology and hurried on, Judy recognized her fellow Elm Creek Quilter. "Bonnie?" she called out, fumbling with gloved hands to lower her scarf.

Bonnie spun around. "Oh, hi. Hi, Steve."

"Hi," said Steve. "Where are you going in such a hurry?"

"Oh, well—" Bonnie glanced over her shoulder as if searching for an escape. "I'm going to see if I can catch Craig before he leaves work. You didn't happen to see him pass this way?"

They hadn't, but Steve asked if Bonnie wanted them to pass along a message in case they saw him before she did. Bonnie demurred through a shaky smile and told them she had to hurry off.

"See you tonight at the business meeting," Judy called after her, wondering at her haste. "Do you think she overheard?"

"Not a chance."

"But she looked so startled, like she had caught us plotting a political coup."

Steve laughed and put his arm around her as they walked on. "She's probably on her way to a romantic Valentine's Day rendezvous with Craig, and she's embarrassed that we caught her."

Judy knew enough about Craig to doubt it, but she wanted to believe Steve was right. "So," she said, remembering the question he had not yet answered. "What have you been trying to tell me?"

He stopped and took her gloved hands in his. "I want you to try very hard to get that job at Penn. And when they offer it to you, I very much want you to accept."

❧

Early the next week, a letter from the Department of Computer Sciences arrived and warmly informed her that she was one of five candidates for the position of associate professor. Thanks to Rick's warning, Judy was able to assemble the information they requested well in advance of their deadline. As she sent it off via certified mail, she hoped they awarded points for promptness.

A week passed. Judy knew the supplemental information had arrived, but all Rick would say in his email was that the top three candidates would receive information about their campus visits by mid-March. He told her to be optimistic and reminded her to keep the week of March 24 open. The date sounded familiar, and one glance at the calendar confirmed it: The twenty-fourth was the first Monday of spring break, which would have been ideal for any professor not involved with Elm Creek Quilts. Torn, Judy eventually decided against asking Sarah to cancel her classes for the opening session of quilt camp. Her computer design classes had been filled for weeks, and she couldn't ask any of her friends to take over her Bindings and Borders workshop when she had not yet had the chance to work the bugs out of her new lesson plans. Besides, she couldn't cancel without offering an explanation.

Just in case, she revised her lesson plans carefully, making them so detailed that almost any of her friends could pick them up and run the class from scratch. After that, and in between her usual obligations, she worked on her guest lecture and grad student seminar, just in case. She grew accustomed to lifting a fork to her mouth with one hand and typing furiously on her laptop with her other, since her lunch break was the only time she could work unobserved. She felt a twinge of guilt thinking of how long ago she had last arranged to meet Gwen for lunch, but she promised herself she would make up for it after she returned from Penn. If they invited her.

On the first Friday of March, Judy spent an extended lunch break at the Daily Grind revising the last section of her lecture notes for the undergraduate course and wondering how much longer she would be able to endure the twin burdens of waiting for news from Penn and keeping her application a secret from her friends, especially when Steve was bursting to tell his colleagues about his triumphant interview earlier that week. Judy was thrilled for him and glowed when she recalled how the editors had praised his work, but she cautioned him to keep it to himself. If one did not count the transient population of college students, Waterford was like any small town, with at most three degrees of separation between any two residents. It was not easy to keep secrets when everyone knew someone who knew everyone else.

A shadow fell across the keyboard. "Hey, Judy."

Judy jerked her head up, startled by Summer's sudden greeting. "Oh, hi. How are you?"

"Don't worry, I'm not here to interrupt. I just wanted to say hi."

"Don't be silly. It's too hard to find a free table this time of day. Sit down." Judy quickly saved her document and shut down the computer before moving it out of the way. "Are you working at Grandma's Attic today?"

"Yes, I'm working." A slight frown touched Summer's lips, but it quickly vanished. "Diane came in, too. You should come by sometime and see all the new blocks for Sylvia's quilt."

"I'd love to. I need to buy fabric for my block, too." Judy did not mention that she had stopped by the quilt shop on her way to work on that very errand and found the lights off and the door locked. Bonnie would not be happy to learn that her employees had not opened the store on time, but she wouldn't hear about it from Judy.

As Summer ate, they talked about the upcoming camp season and about their progress on Sylvia's bridal quilt, which Judy was embarrassed to admit had completely slipped her mind until the previous evening, when she had come across the invitation letter while cleaning her sewing table.

"If you run out of time you could always buy one of those bargain kits at the Fabric Warehouse," said Summer with a teasing smile.

Judy's heart thumped. They knew. That awful Mary Beth had told on her, just as she had insinuated.

Summer laughed. "I'm just kidding. You have plenty of time. I haven't started my block, either."

Relieved, Judy fought to compose herself and managed a feeble joke about Summer's poor opinion of her. Summer left soon after that, so Judy got back to work before her guilty conscience gave away something more important than anxiety over a quilt block deadline.

As she glanced up to be sure Summer had gone, Judy's gaze fell on two young men waiting in line. When the taller, golden-haired one turned her way, she recognized Diane's youngest son, Todd, but she did not know his friend. They were laughing and joking and jostling each other, heady with the freedom of their off-campus senior lunch privileges. Todd paid for a cup of coffee and two frosted crullers, which he left on the counter while his friend placed his order. Just then, Todd bent over to tie his shoe, and in the moment while the server's back was turned, Todd's friend removed the lid from Todd's cup, poured half the contents into the tip jar, and replaced the lid. By the time Todd rose and the counter clerk placed the friend's drink on the counter, the friend was scanning the bakery case, hands in his coat pockets.

Surprised, Judy watched while the friend paid the cashier and Todd picked up his plate and coffee, tested the weight of the cup, frowned, and removed the lid. Judy could not hear his exchange with the clerk, but it was evident Todd complained and asked for his cup to be filled to the top. The server checked it, frowned in puzzlement, and was about to oblige when the woman next in line spoke up and gestured to the tip jar. The server looked from the tip jar to Todd, his expression stormy, and his voice rose enough for Judy to make out a demand that the two boys clean up the mess. Todd's friend burst out laughing, grabbed his lunch, and made a quick dash for the door. Todd, obviously baffled, hurried after him.

"Don't come back!" the server shouted.

Judy sighed and shook her head as the server took the tip jar to the sink, carefully poured out most of the coffee, and fished coins and soggy bills from the bottom in disgust. Judy wondered what Diane thought of her youngest son's choice of friends. She was probably just relieved Todd got decent grades and kept his record clean, unlike his elder brother. To be fair, though, as far as Judy knew, Michael had given his parents no undue cause for worry ever since he had started college. Judy was thankful Emily was still young enough that she and Steve could exercise control over her social life, though she knew those days wouldn't last.

She frowned, wondering if she should tell Diane about the prank. She would have, except she was so anxious about the campus invitation that had not yet come that she forgot about the young men by the time she left the coffee shop.

Technically the seventh day of March could not be considered the middle of the month even by the most generous estimate, but Judy still fretted over the lack of any word from Penn. She called home every afternoon to ask Steve if the campus invitation had arrived in the mail, even though she knew he would have called if it had. She could have managed more patience if Rick had sent her regular updates, but it would never occur to him to do so.

By the first business meeting of the month, Judy was a mess of distraction and worry. She drove to Elm Creek Manor mulling over her options and decided that the only reasonable choice was to wait until the fifteenth—indisputably mid-March—and contact Rick. In the meantime, she had other work to occupy her thoughts, plenty to do to keep herself from going crazy.

Even so, she had to force herself to concentrate on the business meeting, for every other topic reminded Judy of her job search. Enrollment reminded Judy of the possibility that Emily might enroll in a new school next autumn. Classroom assignments called to mind the wonderful new facility at Penn. The schedule for the first week of camp made Judy wince when she thought that if all went well, she would need Sarah to make additional changes to the plan she had worked so hard to arrange.

Then, suddenly, her cell phone rang. Quickly retrieving it from her bag, aware of Sarah's subtle frown, Judy checked the display. She made a hasty apology and hurried into the hallway. "Steve?" she said breathlessly into the phone.

"Judy? I have great news."

"What is it?"

"They just called. I got the job."

A momentary rush of joy quickly dispersed. "*You* got the job?"

"Isn't that fantastic? They want me to start as soon as I can—do you believe it? If everything goes well, I might even get my own political commentary column within a year." He paused. "Honey?"

"Wow, Steve." She forced more enthusiasm into her voice. "I knew you'd get it. How could they not recognize your talent?"

"There's more, but we can talk about it when you get home. I just had to let you know."

"I'm glad you did." She took a deep breath and closed her eyes, then told him she had to get back to the meeting, but she'd come home immediately afterward.

They hung up, and Judy returned to the parlor with an apologetic smile for Sarah. She assumed a look of interest as Sarah continued on uninterrupted. Of course Steve got the job; he was talented and experienced. He deserved it. How soon would he have to respond? What could he say until Judy heard something from Penn? She had not even been asked to interview on campus yet. She might not be asked. How could she expect Steve to pass up this job when an opportunity like it might never come again?

The phone rang on her lap. She jumped, checked the display, and raced into the hall, treading on Bonnie's tote bag on her way. "Steve?"

"Honey, I'm sorry I got carried away. I shouldn't have interrupted your meeting."

She forced a laugh. "If you know that, why are you doing it again?"

"Because—look, I don't want you to think I have my heart set on this job."

"Of course not," she said, thinking, *Of course you do.*

"If you don't get the Penn job, I'll just tell them no."

"Well . . ." She glanced back at the doorway to the parlor. "Would they let you work from Waterford? Telecommute?"

He hesitated. "I didn't think to ask, but that's an option. I don't think that would be their first choice, but it wouldn't hurt to check."

"Don't ask yet. I might still get the job."

"Yeah." He sounded deflated.

"We'll talk when I get home, okay?"

He agreed. They ended the call and Judy returned to the meeting, pretending not to notice Sarah's glare. She tried to listen carefully for the rest of the meeting, but her thoughts were in turmoil, and within minutes Sarah issued a plea for attention. She addressed the entire group, but Judy knew she was the only one there who had earned the reprimand.

The days passed. Judy prepared for midterm exams and the first week of quilt camp and waited, but the only news she received was Gwen's mournful email telling her that Summer had moved in with her boyfriend. Judy wasn't surprised; although she sympathized with Gwen's tangible dismay, Summer was a grown woman and many grown women made similar choices these days. She tried not to think too much about what Emily would be doing at that age.

She decided a shopping trip to Grandma's Attic would lift her spirits and distract her for a while. She still needed fabric for Sylvia's block, and she also wanted to take Summer's suggestion and examine the other contributors' blocks. If several other people had used the same pattern she had selected, she would prefer to choose something else.

She took a chance on stopping by the quilt shop before work, glad to discover the late opening earlier that month must have been an anomaly. Perhaps that was because Bonnie herself was inside, rearranging a display of spring floral fabrics. She looked somewhat drained, as if it were the end of a busy workday rather than the beginning, but she was neatly attired in a pair of slacks and twin set Judy did not recognize.

"Good morning," Judy said with a smile, hoping to cheer up her friend. "I love that outfit. Is it new?"

Bonnie glanced down at her clothing absentmindedly. "Oh. Yes, it is. Thanks. Agnes helped me pick it out."

"Did she? Maybe I'll ask her to go with Steve next time he shops for my birthday present. Remember that cardigan he bought me two years ago, the one Diane called the lightning bolt sweater?"

Bonnie rewarded her joke with a smile. "Did he ever find out you always changed into something else when you got to the lab?"

"Are you kidding? He thinks it's still in the back of my closet, awaiting the right occasion."

Judy knew it was more likely he had completely forgotten the sweater, which was just an afterthought to the tickets to Vail they had bought for each other that Christmas, but Bonnie laughed, so Judy didn't mind a little exaggeration at her husband's expense. Bonnie herself often joked about Craig's annoying habits until she had the Elm Creek Quilters doubled over in laughter, but come to think about it, Bonnie had not shared any amusing stories about him in a long time. Maybe Craig just wasn't funny anymore.

When Judy asked for Bonnie's help finding fabric for her block for Sylvia's bridal quilt, Bonnie nodded and took her to a collection of fat quarters so perfectly suited to the project and complementary to one another that Judy surmised she must have set them aside for that very purpose. "I suppose many local quilters have asked for these same fabric suggestions," she said.

"Not as many as you might think." Bonnie shook her head. "I hope it's because they already have suitable fabric in their stashes and not because they aren't going to participate. Judging by the lack of local response, we're having a little trouble getting the word out."

"But all the quilters around here know Sylvia, at least by reputation. Should we send a letter to the Waterford Quilting Guild?"

"We tried that. President Mary Beth refuses to read the announcement."

Recalling their unpleasant conversation at the Fabric Warehouse, Judy wasn't surprised. "What does she have against Sylvia?"

Bonnie shrugged. "What does she have against any of us? Except Diane, of course. They've been unfriendly as long as they've been next-door neighbors. It's amazing that their sons are such good friends."

Judy suddenly remembered Todd and his companion from the Daily Grind. "Does Mary Beth's son have dark, curly hair? Shorter than Todd, but good-looking, with a big cocky grin?"

"That sounds like Brent. Why?"

"I think I've seen them around."

"Well, you usually can't miss them." Bonnie held out the basket of fat quarters to Judy. "They're big men on the high school campus, and they want to be noticed wherever they go."

After Judy selected her fabrics, Bonnie brought out a large carton from beneath the cutting table. Inside were sixty-six blocks from all across the country, including two from the United Kingdom and one from Australia. "Sixty-six?" asked Judy, taking a few packages from the top. "Isn't that a bit short?"

Bonnie admitted that she would feel better if they were closer to 140 than that, but they still had time. Judy smiled. Bonnie, the eternal optimist, would not admit defeat long after the other team went home with the trophy.

Although the return addresses on the packages did indeed indicate the conspicuous absence of Waterford's quilters, the blocks that had arrived were as beautiful and as varied as Judy could have hoped. She recognized some of the patterns as techniques taught in camp workshops, and many of their makers as favorite longtime students. One simple but striking block, an apparent variation on the Sawtooth Star, came from a camper who attended every year and could not help being the most recognized quilter there, with the exception of Sylvia herself.

February 20, 2002

Dear Elm Creek Quilters,

A bridal quilt for Sylvia—what an inspired idea! I'm honored and delighted to contribute a block, which you will find enclosed.

If you had told me on my first day of quilt camp that one day I would be asked to participate in such an important project, I never would have believed you. Actually, I probably would have called my agent and had him fax you a request for your terms, and I would have tried to exploit my benevolent donation for as much good PR as I could squeeze out of it, but thanks to friends I made at Elm Creek Quilt Camp, I have undergone a significant attitude adjustment since then.

Sylvia was the first to show me that the aloof, prima donna routine that served me so well in Hollywood would not go over well at Elm Creek Manor. My agent insisted that I take my meals in my room and that Sylvia forbid anyone to speak to me unless I addressed them first. But Sylvia would have none of that, and she told my agent so in her own inimitable style. She was right, and I knew it, but what impressed me most was that she managed to muzzle that arrogant loudmouth without breaking a sweat. This woman, I told myself, is someone to reckon with.

I came to learn later that she is also someone to trust, to respect, and to emulate. Her high standards for herself and her compassion for others inspire those of us inclined to selfishness and narcissism to do better. I can't say knowing Sylvia has entirely cured me of my faults and weaknesses, but she has been an example I have tried to follow ever since I came to know her. Years ago I thought the most I could learn from Sylvia would be enough quilting to pass myself off as an accomplished quilter for a movie role. Now I know she has far more important lessons to offer for those of us not too self-absorbed to learn.

So, we return to the enclosed block. I could not find a block that, as your instructions requested, captured what Sylvia has meant to me. Any blocks that had ideal names were too difficult for me to make, and those I could handle had names that wouldn't do. So I decided to take a simple block and change it just enough to make a unique block. (At least I hope it is. There are so many blocks out there I might have simply taken someone else's design.) I call it Prima Donna, and I mean that in the absolute best sense of the phrase, for Sylvia is truly the First Lady of the quilting world.

Best regards to you all, and I wish you great success in the completion of this grand project.

Affectionately yours,
Julia Merchaud

PS: I hope you have all had the chance to watch my PBS series, "A Patchwork Life," based upon my PBS movie of the same title. I adore the character of Sadie Henderson and hope you do, too, since I have drawn many of her characteristics and behavioral quirks from Sylvia.

Our third season begins in September. Also, if you get the chance, I hope you'll head to the theater to watch me in *Lethal Weapon Eight*. I play Mel Gibson's grandmother (although I think I could pass for his mother) and my nursing home is beset by villains throughout almost the entire film. Wondering what happened to my resolution to appear in only highbrow, arty films? I assure you, making this movie was a momentary sacrifice more than compensated for by the many times I got to kiss Mel during rehearsals, even if it was only on the cheek.

Judy laughed. "Did you read Julia Merchaud's letter?" she asked Bonnie.

Bonnie nodded and, a little mournfully, said, "I would have paid good money to be her stand-in for that role. Of course, we all know I don't have the money, and with my luck, I would have ended up kissing Mel's understudy."

"I bet even his understudy is cute." Then Judy detected an undercurrent of fear in Bonnie's joke. "Are things really as bad around here as that?"

"Think of the worst they've ever been," said Bonnie. "They're worse this time."

She looked away, and no matter how much Judy asked her to explain, Bonnie the eternal optimist would say nothing more than that she would keep the shop open as long as she could.

❧

On March fifteenth, a Friday, Judy emailed Rick to ask if the campus interview invitations had been sent. She did not expect to hear from him over the weekend, but when an entire week passed with no reply, she assumed the worst. After encouraging her so enthusiastically to apply, he would be too embarrassed to tell her she had failed. An assistant would send her a rejection letter soon enough.

"Wait until the end of the month, then call," Steve advised, unwilling to give up, reluctant to turn down his own job offer. Judy agreed, though she knew by that time the top three candidates would have concluded their campus visits, the selection perhaps already made.

The first day of camp came and went in a cheerful flurry of registration and welcoming ceremonies. Judy tried to find satisfaction in knowing she had not let down her friends by missing camp, but whenever she thought of Penn's new computer facility—and when she observed Steve leafing discouragedly through the *Waterford Register* at breakfast—she wished things had turned out differently.

On Monday morning, the first day of classes, the phone rang a half hour before her alarm was set to go off. Steve rolled over with a groan and answered. "Hello?" He paused. "Yes, it is." Another pause. "Yes, still married, and very happily. Do you want to talk to Judy?" He passed her the phone and put his pillow over his head. "It's Wild Man Rick."

Judy sat up and pressed the receiver to her ear. "Hello, Rick?"

"Hey, Jude."

"What are you doing up so many hours before noon?" And why in the world was he calling? To commiserate? To tease her? Most likely the latter. For that, the least he could have done was let her sleep in.

"What are *you* doing still in bed, or still at home, for that matter? I thought you would have spent the night in Philly."

"What are you talking about?"

"You must be as hung over as I am. Your interview, you dunce. Preceded by a lunch at the University Club and a campus tour, and followed by a multitude of other tedious activities. That's not a commentary on your lecture or seminar, by the way."

"You mean I'm one of the three finalists?"

Steve tore the pillow from his head and stared at her.

"Of course. It was all in the letter."

Judy scrambled out of bed and threw on her robe. "I never received a letter."

"I told you you'd hear by mid-March. Why didn't you call?"

"I sent you an email asking if the letters were sent. You never answered."

"Of course not," Rick shot back, but he did sound somewhat abashed, if one knew what to listen for. "And when you never wrote me again to follow up on your unanswered email, I assumed the letter had arrived."

"Rick, I swear—"

"Before you decide to kill me, may I remind you you're wasting time? You can still make it if you leave now."

"I can't leave now! I have to shower and pack, and look after Emily, and make arrangements for my classes—"

"I thought you were on spring break."

"—get directions—"

"Don't worry about those. I'll email them right away." In the background she heard the clattering of keys on a keyboard and a woman's voice, muffled. "Oh. Angie says she can watch Emily if you need to bring her."

"Tell her she's very generous and she deserves much better than you, but Emily's in school and Steve doesn't need the spouse job placement conference, so he's staying here."

Rick sighed. "You're coming alone, and here I am, engaged to someone else. Ow! Sweetheart, that hurt."

"Tell Angie to hit you again for me."

"I'll do that. Send me an email if the directions don't come through."

"Will you bother to answer it?"

"Maybe. You're wasting time, you know."

"I know." She promised—or threatened—to see him later, and hung up. A glance at the clock told her she had just enough time to race through a shower and throw some things into a suitcase. And call Sarah. Her elation dimmed for a moment. She had to call Sarah. But first she bounded back into bed to tell Steve the good news he had already guessed.

CHAPTER SEVEN

Diane

On the first day of March, Diane's phone rang while she was scrambling to get her husband and youngest son out of the house and on their way to work and school. Her assumption that the morning chaos would lessen by one-third when her eldest son started college had thus far proven to be laughably naïve.

She snatched the receiver a moment before the answering machine would have picked up. "Hello?"

"Hello, Diane? It's Agnes. Sorry to call so early, but I'm afraid there's an emergency."

"What's wrong?"

"It's not really an emergency. Let's call it—a situation."

"Call it whatever you like. Just tell me what's up." Diane covered the mouthpiece with her hand as Todd passed, selecting items from the kitchen counter and pantry at random and tossing them into a brown paper lunch sack. "Todd, leave one of those bananas for your father."

"He said he didn't want it."

"Then leave it for me. You ate both of my oranges for breakfast and there isn't any more fruit in the house."

Todd rolled his eyes, but he returned the banana to the otherwise empty fruit bowl. Diane uncovered the phone. "Sorry, Agnes. Where were we?"

"Todd's a growing boy. He needs fruit."

Diane sighed. "Todd," she called. When he turned, she tossed him the banana. "Okay, Agnes. Whatever crisis you called about, it will be over by the time you tell me."

"Bonnie can't make it into work this morning. Are you free to open Grandma's Attic today?"

"Why can't she come in? Is she sick?" Diane paused to kiss her husband, Tim, on his way to the door. "Why didn't she just call me herself?"

"It's a rather long story, and it doesn't sound as if you have time for a lengthy chat."

That was certainly true. Todd waved at her and, with a hopeful expression, held out a pen and a blue piece of paper. Diane scanned it. Oh. Right. That permission slip for the senior trip. She held the phone to her ear with her shoulder and scrawled her signature on the line.

"Thanks, Mom," whispered Todd as he carefully folded the form and tucked it into his backpack. "Come on. We'll be late."

"Just a minute." She glanced at the clock. "I'd be glad to work today, Agnes, but I can't get there right at nine. I have a dentist appointment and some errands I can't postpone."

"That's all right. As soon as you can get there will be good enough. I'm sure Bonnie would be grateful."

Diane wanted to believe that, but sometimes she wondered if any of her work at Grandma's Attic was appreciated or even noticed. "I'll call Bonnie at home when I get in."

"Mom, we have to go."

"Don't bother," said Agnes quickly. "She needs her rest."

"Okay, I won't." Diane nodded apologetically to her son, bid Agnes goodbye, and hung up. "Can you get another ride home?" she asked Todd as she snatched up her purse and followed him out the side door into the garage. "I might have to work late at Grandma's Attic."

"No problem. Brent will drive me."

"Great." Diane managed not to clench her teeth. Since Todd was a little boy, she had tried to steer him toward other children in the neighborhood, but Brent had been his best friend since the second grade. In her own defense, she didn't object because Brent was the son of her worst enemy; she disliked him on his own terms. If Todd were a more rebellious, sullen sort— in other words, more like his elder brother—Diane would have suspected him of befriending Brent merely to annoy her, but Todd genuinely liked Brent and often mentioned his many admirable qualities in what he thought was a subtle attempt to win her over. Tim occasionally pointed out that if

Brent were anyone else's son, Diane would be pleased Todd had chosen for his best friend a well-behaved, pleasant, athletic young man who earned good grades. While Diane couldn't deny the tiny grain of truth in her husband's mild censure, she had overheard Brent mock her eldest son, then turn around and speak to her with the utmost respect through an innocent grin far too many times. What bothered her most, though, was that Todd never defied Brent to defend his elder brother. She didn't like to think of Todd as a conformist follower, especially if Mary Beth's son was the designated leader.

If it were warmer, she would make Todd walk home from school. If Mary Beth had not bought Brent a new car for his sixteenth birthday, Todd would have had no choice. But since Diane could not fairly accuse Brent of poor driving, she could not withhold her permission without seeming unreasonable.

She dropped off Todd at school with time to spare and headed for the dentist. One routine examination later, she was back in the car en route to the post office and the bank. She hurried through her errands as quickly as she could, wondering about Bonnie's absence. It was odd that Agnes had called instead of Bonnie, but not surprising that Agnes had called her instead of Summer. Whenever Bonnie needed extra help around the store, she invariably contacted Diane. Although Diane had originally accepted the part-time job because she did not want to work any more than she had to, with all the extra shifts, she had regularly worked a two-thirds schedule for more than a year. She spent more time in a Grandma's Attic apron than Summer did, but Diane suspected neither Bonnie nor Summer realized that. Diane's name appeared on the official work schedule posted in the back office less frequently than theirs, and the fact that she worked more often escaped their notice.

Not that Diane minded the extra shifts; she welcomed them. It was not only to help Bonnie, although Diane was glad to do anything to take some pressure off her friend who, despite her outward optimism, had seemed shadowed by a cloud of gloom and worry for months. It was also not only because she appreciated the extra money, although she did, especially with Todd impatiently awaiting an acceptance letter from Princeton. She simply liked the job. The work was never boring or stressful, since Bonnie handled all the financial matters herself, and the customers were generally pleasant and not too demanding. Diane felt useful there, which was a good feeling considering that her sons seemed to need her less and less each day, and she enjoyed having shoppers ask her opinion about fabric selections or new patterns. When Todd went off to college, Diane hoped to work full-time officially. The next time she caught Bonnie in a good mood, she would suggest it.

Diane parked in the employee space behind the building and hurried around to the front door. To her surprise it was unlocked, and through the front window she spotted Summer on the phone. Disgruntled, she wondered if Bonnie or Agnes—or both—had called Summer in, doubting Diane's ability to handle the store by herself. If they had that little faith in her, she would be glad to point to the calendar and show them how many times in the past month she had opened and closed the store on her own.

Diane pushed open the door just as Summer hung up the phone. "Oh, hi," she said brightly, shrugging off her coat. "I thought no one else was working today."

Summer looked surprised to see her. "I work every Friday when camp isn't in session. Bonnie should be here, too, but she didn't show up this morning. I'm worried. No one answered the phone upstairs, either."

"She's not coming in today." Diane hung up her coat and put her purse in its usual place, on a shelf beneath the cutting table. "Agnes called and asked me to open the store. I guess she didn't know you would be here."

"Agnes? Why would Agnes have called?"

Diane shrugged. "I have no idea. I imagine Bonnie asked her to."

"But Bonnie knew I was working and she would have called you directly."

"Well . . ." Diane mulled it over, but all she could conclude was that the whole situation was a little odd. "I don't know. But I'm here, so I'm going to work. I need the hours. Todd is still holding out for Princeton. Do you have any idea how expensive that is? Thank goodness Michael decided to go to Waterford College so we could take advantage of the family tuition waiver."

She figured Summer would understand that, because she had attended Waterford College for the same reason. Or so Gwen had claimed at the time. In Diane's opinion, which no one had requested, Summer would have thrived at a larger university with more opportunities. She was certainly bright enough to succeed anywhere, and Gwen could have afforded even private school tuition. Diane had suspected Summer was afraid to leave Waterford and her mother, and that was why she had stayed. Her opinion was confirmed four years later when Summer turned down a generous fellowship to attend graduate school, in favor of Waterford, Grandma's Attic, and Elm Creek Quilts. At least Summer had those to fall back on; other young people who were too intimidated to leave their small town ended up underemployed in dead-end jobs unless they were fortunate enough to inherit a thriving family business. Diane was relieved her two sons had their sights set outside Waterford but, to be fair, she might not feel that way if she had not already made plans for their bedrooms.

Once Diane knew Summer had not come in to supervise her, she was able to enjoy the day. Business was brisk in the morning, more like the old days before the Fabric Warehouse opened. She and Summer even found an interval between customers to look through the carton of blocks for Sylvia's bridal quilt. The only unpleasantness—Mary Beth Callahan—arrived in the afternoon. The Neighbor from Hell apparently had nothing better to do than to complain about the letter Sarah had sent the Waterford Quilting Guild inviting members to participate in Sylvia's bridal quilt. Diane happened to know that quilters enjoyed making blocks for projects like this and were far more likely to be hurt if they were not asked to help than to be annoyed by "block begging" or whatever Mary Beth had called it.

Everything from Mary Beth's gleeful tone to the fact that she had waited two months to respond to the invitation told Diane she was determined to ruin Sylvia's quilt. And Diane knew why. Mary Beth wanted to be Waterford's best known and most respected quilter and, until Sylvia's return to Waterford, only Bonnie and perhaps Gwen had given her any competition. It was not Mary Beth's quilting that set her apart, of course; although she could count on collecting a ribbon at her guild's own quilt show each summer, she had either never aspired to enter the more competitive national shows, or they had rejected her entries. Her role as perpetual guild president, however, had lent her a certain local notoriety for years. Now all the Elm Creek Quilters were better known in the quilting world than Mary Beth—even Diane herself, the least able quilter among them.

Mary Beth couldn't stand it.

Diane usually enjoyed watching her neighbor stew in her jealousy, but she knew that concealed behind Mary Beth's impeccable makeup and designer clothes and perpetual, if insincere, perky smile lay a heart capable of plotting the most malicious vengeance. Diane would never forgive Mary Beth for complaining to the Zoning Commission and forcing the Sonnenbergs to demolish the skateboard ramp they had built in their backyard for

Michael, just as she would never forgive her if she ruined Sylvia's quilt. Diane would not *allow* Mary Beth to ruin it.

After Summer left for the day, Diane fished Mary Beth's discarded invitation out of the trash. She had not received one herself, so once she figured out how to infiltrate the Waterford Quilting Guild, she would read from Mary Beth's. She rather liked the irony.

She unfolded the letter and was about to rehearse reading it aloud when her own name jumped out at her. "'Diane says Sylvia deserves to go without'?" she read, aghast. She had never said that! She had thought it, but not said it, and that didn't count, certainly not enough to be included in a letter sent out to hundreds of people!

She was going to have a little chat with Sarah as soon as she finished with Mary Beth.

❧

When Diane returned home at six, Todd and Brent were watching music videos in the living room, open books and papers strewn on the coffee table before them. "No television during homework," she called out as she set her purse on the kitchen counter.

Todd, who knew the rule and usually obeyed it, turned off the television without complaint, but Brent grinned at her over his shoulder and said, "We're second-semester seniors. Homework doesn't really count anymore."

She returned his grin with a tight smile. "Homework always counts in this house. And yes, I realize colleges won't see your second-semester grades until after they've accepted you."

Brent shrugged and began closing books and collecting papers. "You should just be glad we're doing it at all. Most kids in our class just blow it off."

"If that's true, which I doubt, I'm thrilled you two have a better work ethic." Diane would have added something about wondering what his mother thought of his smart mouth, but just then the phone rang and she snatched it up. "Hello?"

"Hi," a young woman responded. "Is, um, is Todd Sonnenberg there?"

"Yes." She glanced at the clock. Right on schedule. Ever since word got out that Todd and his girlfriend had broken up soon after she received an acceptance letter to a West Coast university to which Todd had not applied, the Sonnenberg phone had rung almost continuously from the end of the school day until ten o'clock at night, when Tim switched off the ringer on each extension. An unusual day of silence meant they had forgotten to turn the ringers back on in the morning. "May I tell him who's calling?"

"Um, it's Shelley from Calculus class."

"Shelley from Calculus," said Diane, holding out the phone to Todd. Brent shook his head and smirked as Todd ran a hand through his hair and straightened his shirt on his way to the phone.

"Hullo," said Todd into the receiver. "Uh-huh . . . Uh-huh . . . Yeah . . . I'm already going. Sorry . . . Okay. Bye." He hung up.

"I hope that conversation was more articulate on her end," remarked Diane as she searched the pantry for the extra box of pasta she was certain she had hidden in the back.

"It would have been more interesting here, too, if you weren't listening." But Todd smiled and patted her on the shoulder as he passed.

"Another invitation to the prom?" asked Brent.

"Yeah."

Surprised, Diane looked up from her search. "I didn't know you already had a date."

"He doesn't," said Brent before Todd could answer. "But he doesn't want to go with Shelley."

Diane kept her gaze fixed on her son. "I distinctly heard you tell that young lady you were already going."

Todd opened his mouth to speak, but once again Brent beat him to it. "You must not know Shelley or you'd get it."

This time Diane was too annoyed to ignore him. "If she's in Calculus, she must be fairly bright."

Brent began to laugh. "Yeah, but she's a dog."

Todd had the decency to look embarrassed, but Diane was nonetheless displeased with him. "Shelley's not so bad, but I want to ask this girl from Physics," he quickly explained, sensing her mood. "She's just as smart as Shelley, and she's on the soccer team. If she says no—"

"She won't," Brent interjected.

"—I'm going to ask Lisa."

Diane's eyebrows rose. "I thought you two broke up."

Todd shrugged. "We did, but we're still friends."

"If Lisa turns you down, can I ask her?" Brent inquired. Todd grinned and shoved him.

Brent finished packing up his things, none too soon as far as Diane was concerned, and before the door closed behind him, the phone rang again. The caller was a young woman from Physics class but not, judging from Todd's expression, the prospective prom date. She claimed to need the homework assignment, a transparent ruse Diane recognized from her own high school days. Only back then the boys did the calling; a girl never phoned a boy unless they were going steady.

Diane flipped through the mail while Todd carried out another brief, monosyllabic conversation. "You got a letter from Waterford College," she exclaimed, withdrawing the thick envelope from the stack as he hung up the phone. "Why didn't you open it?"

"You can, if you want."

She quickly did so. "Todd, this is great news! You got into Waterford College!"

He looked wounded. "You don't have to sound so surprised."

"I'm not surprised you got in." Not with his 4.0 GPA and 1520 SATs. "Just that you don't seem to care."

"You know it's just my safety school. I already got into Penn State, and I'd go there before I'd go to Waterford College."

"Before you stick your nose too far into the air, allow me to remind you that your father teaches at Waterford College."

"Yeah, but that's not where he got his degrees. It's probably a great place to work, but it's not where I want to go to school. Mom, no offense, but I really have to get out of Waterford."

"It's good enough for your brother." That was both feeble and defensive, and they both knew it. Michael would have gone elsewhere if he'd had the grades.

"It's fine for him since they have a good Computer Science department. But if I want to get into a top law school, I have to, you know, aim high. Like you and Dad are always telling me to do."

The argument was stupid and one-sided, so Diane dropped it. "Please don't complain about the college in front of your father or brother. They have their pride, you know."

"I know," he said, and he kissed her on the cheek.

That evening after supper, Agnes called to ask if Diane could work all day Saturday, because Bonnie most likely wouldn't be able to come in. Diane readily agreed and couldn't resist inquiring why Bonnie had not phoned herself, but Agnes promptly found an excuse to end the call. Ignoring Agnes's earlier admonitions not to bother Bonnie at home, Diane dialed her number, but hung up without leaving a message when the answering machine picked up. She didn't care for their new outgoing recording, which, thanks to Craig's brusque delivery, sounded like a suspicious demand for information and would lead a stranger to believe he lived alone.

The next day she enjoyed having Grandma's Attic all to herself. She moved the coffeepot from Bonnie's office to a table near the front of the store so customers could help themselves. She rearranged the shelves to disguise how bare they were, now that Bonnie could not reorder stock as readily as before, and she managed to persuade two of their most negligent customers to make payments on their long-overdue accounts. By the time she flipped the sign in the front window to CLOSED and locked the door behind her, she felt satisfied that she had put in a good day's work. She wished Bonnie had been there to see it, but that would have defeated the purpose of proving how well she could handle the store on her own.

On Sunday, Michael came home to do his laundry, as he did almost every week. When he first proposed that arrangement after moving from the student dorms to a dilapidated rental house he shared with three other students, Diane had balked, certain that what he really meant was that he would dump his dirty clothes in the basement and expect to pick them up later that afternoon, washed and pressed. To her pleasant surprise, a year in a dorm with its own laundry facilities had taught Michael he could handle the work himself, and he actually did a fine job of it, though he still refused to iron. Most of the time Michael sat at the kitchen table studying—actually studying!—between changing loads, but occasionally he had time to sit and talk with her over a cup of coffee, especially if she had baked cookies earlier that day.

On that Sunday, however, he was sweating over a computer programming project and an English paper, both due before spring break, plus he had midterms coming up, so she knew better than to interrupt him once he sat down to work. When he took a break to stretch and put his whites in the dryer, she asked him what his plans were for spring break. She was curious, because by this time last year he had already hit her up twice for a trip to Cancún, requests she had flatly turned down. Still, she was surprised he had not tried again.

"I'm staying here," Michael told her. "I have a major design project due two weeks after spring break, and I've barely even started it since I have all this other stuff to do."

"That seems like poor planning on your professor's part. Does he expect everyone to work through spring break?"

Michael shrugged. "That's better than having it due during midterms along with everything else. College isn't like high school, Mom. You actually have to work."

"Yes, I seem to remember something about that from my own college years, back in the olden days," said Diane, but she was secretly thrilled, so much so that she didn't add a rebuke about how he actually should have worked in high school, too.

Michael turned down her invitation to stay for supper, citing too much work and plans to get pizza with his housemates. It was not until the next morning that Diane discovered he had left two pairs of jeans on the folding table in the laundry room. She knew he would wear the same pair he had worn Sunday every day for a week rather than make an extra trip home for his clean clothes, so she decided to drop them off at his house before her afternoon shift at Grandma's Attic.

She called ahead to warn him, since she and Tim had promised never to visit unannounced. As she drove through Fraternity Row to a street of student rentals as dilapidated as Michael's, she hoped the message she had left with a housemate counted as fair warning.

Michael, who had returned from class in the meantime, answered her knock and welcomed her in out of the cold. She handed him the jeans and looked around with misgivings, wondering how he would react if she raced to the store and returned with a carload of cleaning supplies. "Do you even have a vacuum?" she asked, eyeing the crumbs on the floor.

"No, we leave that to the mice. I'm kidding," he added hastily.

"Sure," she said, not sure at all, and she nodded to the interesting sculpture of empty beer cans on the floor beside a stereo system with enormous speakers. "One of your friends is an art major, I presume?"

Michael grinned. "Not exactly."

Diane snorted and decided to leave before she saw anything else. As she kissed him good-bye at the door, a young man shouted from another room, "Yes! I got it!"

"Great," Michael called back, and shook his head.

"What?" asked Diane.

"There's this girl he likes in his Econ class. She's not listed in the student directory, so he's been looking for her cell phone number."

"You can do that? Find cell phone numbers on the Internet?"

"Sure." Raising his voice for the benefit of the unseen roommate, he added, "And it wouldn't take me two weeks to do it, either."

Suddenly inspired, Diane asked, "Could you get me Mary Beth Callahan's cell phone number?"

"Why?"

"It might come in handy someday."

"You mean like if Todd's out with her and Brent, and you need to contact him? Why don't you just ask her for it?"

"Michael . . ." She sighed. "Sometimes it's best not to ask too many questions. Can you get me the number or not?"

"Yeah, yeah, I can get it." He hesitated. "Can I use that line sometime, about not asking too many questions?"

"Not with me and your father you can't."

He grumbled but agreed, and told her he would have the number by his next laundry day. Diane thanked him and went home, the first fine threads of a plan gathering in her thoughts.

Three customers were waiting in line at the cutting table when Diane arrived at Grandma's Attic, so she quickly stashed her things, put on her apron, and took her place beside Bonnie. "Are you feeling better?" Diane asked as she unrolled a fabric bolt and measured out two yards.

"Hmm?" said Bonnie. "Oh. I suppose. Thanks."

"Was it the flu?"

Bonnie handed the first customer her pile of cut fabric and offered to help the next person in line. "Didn't Agnes tell you?"

"No."

"Oh." Bonnie fell silent as she sliced through a purple-and-green paisley cotton with her rotary cutter. "Well, I guess it was just one of those weekend things. You know."

That sounded rather vague to Diane, but she nodded. "You know," she said casually, "we had quite a few customers on Saturday. We—I should have said I, because I was here alone."

"I hope it wasn't too much for you."

"No, of course not." Diane handed the cut fabric to the customer. "Everything went quite smoothly. It was no trouble at all to open and close by my-self, so if you ever need me to do it again, just let me know."

"Thanks." Bonnie finished assisting the last customer and headed to the cash register to ring up the three women's purchases. Diane rolled up the fabric bolts and returned them to their shelves. By the time she finished, the store was empty except for herself and Bonnie, who had taken a seat on a stool beside the front counter, visibly drained. No doubt she still felt the ef-fects of her illness. "I apologize for imposing on you last weekend," Bonnie said.

"Not at all." Diane leaned back against the cutting table and smiled. She had thought that Bonnie's first day back would be the best time to approach her about going full-time, with her emergency substitution fresh in Bonnie's mind, but the conversation wasn't going as well as she had hoped. "You know how much I enjoy working here. It sure beats volunteering for an-other committee at the high school."

Bonnie's gaze had shifted past Diane to the shelves of sewing machines on the far wall. "Schools need involved parents."

"Well, of course, but once Todd graduates, I won't be a class parent any-more. Did I tell you Todd has pretty much rejected Waterford College? If he chooses Penn State, the tuition won't be that bad, but if he gets into Prince-ton—" Diane laughed. "Let's just say I'd rather work overtime than take out a second mortgage."

Bonnie said, distantly, "I'm afraid I can't afford to pay overtime."

"I know that," said Diane, bemused. "I was kidding."

"Oh. Okay, then." Bonnie rose and walked toward the back of the store.

"Not about working more," Diane called after her as Bonnie entered her office and sat down at the computer. "I wasn't kidding about that part."

If Bonnie heard, she gave no sign.

That evening, Diane drove to Elm Creek Manor to submit her proposed course schedule, already more than a week overdue and probably unneces-sary since Sarah and Summer were well into arranging the master sched-ule. Her conversation with Bonnie ran through her thoughts, making her more displeased with each repetition. She should have been more forth-right. When had delicacy and tact ever served her well? Bonnie had proba-bly left the discussion thinking Diane resented working the extra hours, which meant Diane was now worse off than before.

She found Sarah in the second-floor library, which Sarah often referred to casually as her office, as if she were the only person who worked there. She was seated behind the large oak desk that had once belonged to Sylvia's father, looking every bit the overworked manager despite her jeans and faded purple turtleneck. Although she did not complain, she could not hide her exasperation when Diane handed her the overdue paperwork. "This would have been useful two weeks ago," she said as she leafed through the pages.

Diane knew she was only ten days late, not fourteen, but she said, "I'm sorry it's late. It's pretty much the same as last year, but if it creates any problems with your master schedule, don't change anything for my sake."

"Thanks," said Sarah dryly. "We won't." She set the papers aside and rubbed her eyes. "Diane, I'm sure you're very busy, but I'd really appreciate it if you could pay more attention to our deadlines."

"Sure," said Diane, giving her a tight smile. "You know, if it was that urgent, you could have called."

"It *was* urgent, which is why we gave it a mandatory deadline."

"Right. Got it." Irritated, Diane left the library before Sarah's reprimand could turn into an argument. "We," she muttered under her breath as she descended the grand oak staircase to the front foyer. Just what she needed, another employer who didn't respect her. Employer! What an unpleasant thought. A few years ago, she never would have thought of Sarah as her employer.

Fuming, she turned down the west wing hallway toward the back door. As she passed the kitchen, she heard Sylvia call out, "Diane, is that you?"

"Yes," Diane called back, reluctantly. She was not in the mood for another lecture.

"Would you mind joining me?"

Diane sighed and passed through the kitchen into the west sitting room. Sylvia's private sewing room was upstairs, but she often brought her work downstairs when she hoped for company. From her favorite armchair near the window, she had a fine view of the rear parking lot and, unless the cook and his assistants were raising a clatter in the kitchen, she could hear anyone passing in the hall.

Diane paused in the doorway as Sylvia looked up from the quilt hoop resting on her lap. "I'm afraid I can't stay long. I have to put supper on."

"I won't keep you but a moment." Sylvia smiled and indicated the opposite chair with a nod. "I hoped you might be able to clear up a mystery. You're very perceptive."

Flattered, Diane promptly seated herself. "I'll try."

"That's all I ask." Sylvia removed her thimble and set her unfinished quilt aside. "Tell me, is it my imagination or have people been acting rather strangely around here lately?"

"It's not your imagination," said Diane, thinking of Bonnie's unexplained absences from Grandma's Attic and Sarah's increasingly bossy tendencies.

"Ah! I knew it." Sylvia removed her glasses and let them dangle from the fine silver chain around her neck. "Now, if we can only figure out why. I admit I might not have noticed myself except for Matthew. He's the one who alerted me to everyone's odd behavior, although, come to think of it, he's behaved rather oddly himself. Would you believe I overheard him and Sarah arguing about foot massages and apple trees, of all things? I couldn't make any sense of it."

"Did you ask them what they were talking about?"

"Heavens, no. I would have been forced to confess my eavesdropping." Sylvia frowned. "But that's not all. Ever since that strange meeting where everyone showed up early and congregated in the kitchen, Sarah has been making the most ridiculous excuses why I can't accompany her on her trips downtown. And have you noticed no one talks about their current quilting projects anymore? We haven't had a show-and-tell after our business meetings in weeks. A few days ago, Matt asked Agnes to show him the quilt block in her sewing basket and you would have thought he had asked to see her unmentionables! This, from a group of quilters who usually can't wait to brag." She shook her head, then fixed a piercing gaze on Diane. "Have you noticed it, too?"

"Actually, no," said Diane weakly. "That's not the odd behavior I was talking about."

"Well, now that I've pointed it out, I'm sure you know what I mean. Do you have any idea what's wrong? I wouldn't be so concerned except the first day of camp is only three weeks away. If we have a serious problem, we must root it out before then."

Diane hesitated. It seemed unfair to allow Sylvia to worry when there was a simple explanation. Maybe she could reveal something—not the entire secret, but just enough to assuage Sylvia's fears.

While Diane struggled to decide what and how much she could say, Sylvia leaned forward slightly, her expression suddenly sharp and expectant. All at once, Diane understood. Sylvia had not invited her to chat because Diane was unusually perceptive, but because she was—undeservedly—considered a bit of a gossip.

Indignant, Diane almost accused Sylvia of deceiving her, but remembered just in time that this would only confirm Sylvia's suspicions. "I'm afraid I can't explain," she said. That was the truth; she couldn't explain or the other Elm Creek Quilters would have her head. "But maybe you can help me with another mystery."

"What's that, dear?"

"Do you have any idea why someone might consider me an incompetent employee?"

"Incompetent? That seems rather harsh. I do recall Sarah grumbling about some missing paperwork recently, but she never called you incompetent."

"I wasn't talking about that." Silently Diane berated herself for ignoring the deadline. From now on she would submit everything early if it killed her. "I mean Bonnie. I've been working at Grandma's Attic for years and I don't think she appreciates a thing I do."

Sylvia smiled. "I suspect all employees feel that way from time to time. It must be especially difficult since Bonnie is also your friend."

"It's more than that," said Diane, and confided her entire list of hurts and grievances: her full-time schedule that invariably went ignored; her willingness to work extra hours on a moment's notice that no one appreciated; her good ideas for store displays and promotions for which she received little praise and no thanks; her exclusion from "management meetings" about the shop's future. "Maybe management meetings made sense when Bonnie had five employees," Diane said, "but not when Bonnie and Summer are management and I'm the only managee!"

"That does seem particularly unfair," said Sylvia. "I can't believe Bonnie is deliberately excluding you or ignoring your contributions. Have you told her how you feel?"

"Of course." Diane paused. "Well, actually, no. Not directly."

Sylvia laughed. "I'm not unsympathetic, dear, but how do you expect her to understand your concerns if you don't tell her?"

"I've dropped a lot of hints."

"I'm afraid that's not good enough." Sylvia reached over and patted her hand. "You've been working yourself into a fine state of hurt and resentment when what you needed to do was sit down with Bonnie and tell her what's troubling you, exactly as you've told me. On second thought, not exactly. You might consider shouting a little less."

"How am I supposed to get Bonnie to sit down and listen? Schedule an appointment?"

"That's a fine idea. Bonnie is a very busy woman, and it's clear she's had a great deal on her mind lately. Summer mentioned that the shop's rent is going up, and I can't open the newspaper without seeing an ad for another sale at Fabric Warehouse. I daresay Bonnie might have other worries, too, which have nothing to do with Grandma's Attic." Sylvia mused in silence for a moment, then smiled ruefully. "I suppose I've solved my own mystery. I must have forgotten that my friends have concerns apart from me, from Elm Creek Quilts. What I have perceived as odd behavior is probably nothing more than the actions of people dealing with problems of their own."

"That's possible," agreed Diane, reluctantly. She wanted Sylvia to find another explanation for her friends' recent secretiveness, but not if it excused Bonnie's behavior at work.

"Possible? I think highly probable." Sylvia put on her glasses, frowning. "It remains a mystery, however, why none of our friends have shared those concerns with the rest of us. Once it seemed we knew the most intimate details of one another's lives."

"That's because we used to have weekly quilting bees," Diane reminded her. "Then those turned into quilting bees tacked on to the end of our business meetings. Now the entire block of time is a business meeting. Each season we have more business to discuss and less time to talk about ourselves. Only Agnes bothers to bring handwork anymore."

"Yes, that's true." Sylvia smiled, regretful. "I suppose that's the price of success."

"It won't always be this way," said Diane. "This time of year is especially busy. Things will settle down once camp is under way."

Sylvia shrugged as she took up her quilt hoop and slipped her thimble on the first finger of her right hand. "You may be right. But nothing endures forever, Diane, perhaps not even the closest of friendships."

❧

A week later, Michael came home with a laundry bag full of dirty clothes and a phone number scrawled on a piece of notebook paper. "That's it," he said as he handed it to her.

"Are you sure?"

"Yep." Michael hoisted the bag on his shoulder and descended the basement stairs. "I tested it."

"From a pay phone, I hope," said Diane, pocketing the number with delight. "She might have Caller ID."

"I used my roommate's cell," he called from below. "Jeez, Mom, you watch too much *Law & Order.*"

Maybe so, but Diane was not willing to overlook any precaution where Mary Beth was concerned.

When Michael returned upstairs and began unloading his backpack on the kitchen table, Diane set a plate of fudge brownies within reach. "A little token of my thanks," she said. "Would you like a glass of milk?"

"Sure," he said, helping himself to a brownie. "I hope giving you that number doesn't make me an accessory to a crime. I feel like I've corrupted my own mother."

"Don't be ridiculous. If you found it on the internet, it must be public information, right?"

"Well . . ." Michael hesitated. "Remember what you said about not asking too many questions?"

"Right. Understood." Diane handed him a glass of milk and hoped she had not tempted him into ruining his record for good behavior. She decided not to dwell on it. It was just a phone number; what harm could it do? "I won't ask how you got it, but if you did anything illegal, don't do it again. And thank you."

"I didn't, and you're welcome." He took a bite of brownie, opened a textbook, and uncapped his highlighter. "Um, if you really want to thank me, there's something I wanted to talk to you about."

Here it comes, Diane thought, noting his casual voice, the way he avoided her gaze. The annual Cancún petition. "You mean your mother's gratitude and fudge brownies aren't thanks enough?"

"They're great, but the thing is, I could really use some cash."

She folded her arms. "Michael, we've had this discussion before. Your father and I do not want you to go flying off to some postadolescent paradise for a week of free-flowing alcohol and drunken coeds in wet T-shirts. Cancún is out."

"Cancún?" he asked, bewildered. "Who said anything about Cancún? I need a new computer."

"Oh." She absorbed this. "No you don't. We bought you a computer for your graduation present. What happened? Did you break it?"

"No, but it's two years old. It's obsolete."

"For what we paid, it's not allowed to be." Diane tore a paper towel from the roll and swept brownie crumbs into the sink. "When you picked out the model, you assured us it would last you through college."

"Back then, I thought it would. I didn't know the kind of software my professors would make us use. Some of it is so new it barely runs on my computer."

"If it's a problem with memory—"

"It's not a problem with the amount of RAM; it's a problem with processor speed, peripheral compatibility—" He broke off and let out an exasperated, beseeching sigh. "Mom, I'm a Computer Science major. I need access to a better computer."

"Then use the college's computer labs."

"Do you know how long you have to wait in line for one of those?"

"No, but I imagine if you add up those hours and compare them to how many your father would have to work to pay for a new computer, waiting in line would still seem like a bargain."

He took a deep breath, and when he spoke again, he was clearly trying his best to sound reasonable. "In my major I need frequent access to a top-of-the-line computer, preferably a laptop. Ask Dr. DiNardo. I'm taking her class next fall. She'll tell you she always recommends students bring their own laptops to class."

Diane didn't doubt it. Judy was so fond of computer gadgets she would wait at the factory to catch some new gizmo as it came off the assembly line if the manufacturer would permit it. "If Dr. DiNardo requires a laptop, your father and I will discuss it. However, we spent a lot on the computer you have, and since it's practically new, you'll have to pay for a laptop yourself."

"Where am I going to get that kind of money?"

"Save your allowance. Get a job. Get two. If you start looking now, you'll definitely have something lined up for summer."

"'Definitely'? Have you ever tried to find a job in Waterford? What am I supposed to do, work at the quilt camp?"

"That's a fine idea. Matt might want an assistant caretaker for the summer, and I'm sure the cook will need help in the kitchen. In fact, you probably wouldn't need to wait until summer, since camp starts in March."

"Great," said Michael, disparagingly. "Just what I want. Mowing lawns and feeding quilters." He hunched over his book as if that would slam a wall in place between them.

Diane held on to her temper. "Michael, you know the value of money by now, and you know we can't throw it around just because your perfectly adequate computer doesn't have all the latest bells and whistles."

"Adequate. That's all it is," he muttered, not looking up from his book. "I guess if you don't care about my grades—"

"This has nothing to do with your grades, and you know it." Diane heard her voice rising and forced herself to maintain the appearance of calm. "I'll talk to Judy DiNardo. If she says you must have a laptop, you can buy one. You can earn the money to pay for it yourself. If you haven't saved enough by fall, your father and I will loan you the rest."

Michael said nothing. Diane watched him pretend to study, her irritation rising, until she wanted to snap at him that twenty going on twenty-one was too old to be acting like a spoiled brat. Instead she forced herself to leave the room. He was a bright boy, but he was too angry to see that her offer was entirely reasonable. She would talk to him when time, reflection, and frustration with his two-year-old obsolete computer brought him to his senses.

❧

Michael was still angry a week later when a full laundry sack compelled him to return home but, to his credit, he made an effort to be civil. Typically his grudges lasted a good two weeks, so Diane left him alone while he washed clothes and studied. Neither mentioned their disagreement, but Diane took it as an encouraging sign when Michael asked for a plastic bag so he could share some of her fresh-baked chocolate chip cookies with his roommates.

All she could do was wait until his anger blew over. She couldn't dwell on a ridiculous argument when she had other more immediate concerns: The following day was the third Monday of the month, the regularly scheduled meeting time for the Waterford Quilting Guild.

As Diane drove downtown to the public library, her cell phone, Sarah's letter, and Mary Beth's number in her purse, she reflected that she ought to be nervous. She had no idea whether she could pull off this stunt or how the guild members would react if she did. But she could not afford second thoughts. Mary Beth never expected to see Diane or any of the Elm Creek

Quilters at another guild meeting after they left in protest years before, when Mary Beth's dirty campaign tactics cost Diane the presidency. Tonight, Mary Beth's insufferably smug complacency would work to Diane's advantage.

In order to avoid detection, Diane parked on a side street and entered the library through the children's department. Her anticipation rose as she crossed the main lobby, adjusted her watch to the large clock over the circulation desk, and slipped into a stall in the women's rest room closest to Meeting Room C. She had to time her entrance perfectly. If she went in too early, she would risk recognition as later arrivals scanned the room for their friends, too late and the interruption would ruin the element of surprise. Mary Beth, anal beyond redemption, would begin the meeting at precisely seven o'clock and deliberately ignore the scurrying few who seated themselves at a few seconds past.

At seven o'clock and ten seconds, Diane left the rest room and hurried into the meeting room on the heels of five latecomers. Fortunately they, too, kept their heads down and eyes averted rather than draw Mary Beth's withering glare, so Diane's bowed head and slumped shoulders did not attract attention. She chose a seat on the aisle near the back behind two taller women and sat low in her chair. She surveyed the room quickly, enough to spot a few people who would know her on sight and to estimate the attendance at approximately seventy-five, down from the hundred or more who used to attend back when the Elm Creek Quilters were members. The room was arranged as for a formal business conference rather than a cozy quilting bee, with straight rows of padded folding chairs placed on either side of a broad aisle. At the front of the room, chairs for the guild officers and a second door leading to the hallway flanked a podium, where Mary Beth stood speaking into a tinny microphone. Folding tables lined the wall between the two doors and were stacked with books from the guild library, advertisements for local quilt shows, and back issues of the guild newsletter. Too late, Diane realized that she should have duplicated the letter—after making a certain editorial deletion—and distributed the copies. Reading it aloud would have to suffice.

The format for the meetings had not changed from the old days. Mary Beth introduced herself and the subordinate officers seated behind her, then asked for new members and guests to raise their hands. Those unwise enough to reply were promptly subjected to unexpected public speaking when Mary Beth urged them to rise and say a few words about themselves. The five unfortunates gave their names, mentioned their favorite quilting techniques, and sat down again as quickly as Mary Beth allowed. When no one nudged Diane to her feet or glanced at her as if to ask why she had not introduced herself, she congratulated herself on blending in.

Mary Beth moved on to guild business. The vice president took the podium and read over some proposed changes to the bylaws; the guild members voted and the measure passed. The treasurer came forward and read over the previous month's record of income and expenses. The social chair reminded everyone about the end-of-the-year picnic and urged them to pay their deposits soon or they wouldn't be able to rent a picnic shelter at the Waterford College Arboretum and would have to sit on blankets, which, as everyone probably remembered from last year, resulted in aches and pains for their older members and far too many insects in the potluck buffet.

Diane opened her purse and withdrew her phone, the invitation, and the slip of paper Michael had given her.

The program coordinator took the microphone next and listed the guild events remaining until the summer break and mentioned a few speakers who had already agreed to appear next year. Diane couldn't help rolling her eyes at the excited murmurs and scattered applause that greeted each name. More prestigious quilters than those gladly waited in line for the opportunity to appear at Elm Creek Quilt Camp. Some were so delighted they would offer to trade their speaker's fees for a few extra days at the manor. As a courtesy to the local quilting community, Sylvia always invited members of the Waterford Quilting Guild to attend such special events free of charge. Since few local quilters except those already on the Elm Creek Quilt Camp mailing list ever came, Diane figured Mary Beth had dispensed with those announcements, too.

She allowed the barest of sighs and keyed Mary Beth's cell phone number into her own, resting her thumb lightly on the Send button.

Mary Beth thanked the program coordinator and took her place at the podium. "Before we introduce tonight's speaker," she said, "does anyone else have any announcements?"

Before she completed the sentence, Diane pressed the button.

In the moment between when the call went through and when the faint, synthesized tones of Pachelbel's Canon sounded at the front of the room, it occurred to her that Mary Beth might have turned off her phone out of respect for the gravity of the occasion. But apparently she had not, and from the startled look she shot her musical purse, she had warned her family never to interrupt, and anyone else who might call her was present. Mary Beth raised her voice and carried on, growing flustered as the phone continued to ring, louder and louder with each stanza.

Finally the ringing stopped; simultaneously, a voice sounded over Diane's phone. She quickly covered the speaker with one hand and hung up.

Mary Beth smiled, relieved. "Voicemail," she said, and the guild members laughed in sympathy.

Smiling and nodding with the rest, Diane waited long enough for Mary Beth to repeat her request for other announcements, then dialed again.

This time, at the ringing of the phone, Mary Beth went bright red. "I'm sorry," she said, hurrying back to her chair and snatching up her purse. "It must be an emergency. Sandra, will you take over?"

With that, she raced from the room and the vice president rose.

Diane didn't wait to be called upon; she met Sandra at the podium and seized the microphone. "I have an announcement," she said, smiling brightly. Sandra eyed her curiously but stepped back and gestured for her to continue.

"It's no secret that quilters love to contribute blocks to group quilts," Diane began, unfolding the letter. A few in the audience nodded; a few others, friends of Mary Beth, gaped in recognition. "There's a wonderful project going on right now, right here in Waterford, for a very special quilter who put our town on the map of the quilting world. On behalf of the Elm Creek Quilters, I'd like to invite each and every one of you to participate."

She launched into the letter. By the second paragraph, the vice president shook her head and murmured a complaint, but Diane ignored her. She read with conviction and feeling, omitting only that slanderous phrase about her thinking Sylvia deserved to go quiltless. Mary Beth returned as Diane read the block requirements; she steeled herself and clutched the podium as if she might be forcibly removed from it, but Mary Beth stood fixed in the doorway, mouth open in horror, until Diane finished the letter.

Prepared for a quick exit, Diane nevertheless relished the moment by smiling out at the audience. "Are there any questions?"

A few hands went up, but Mary Beth stormed to the front of the room, hands balled into fists, red-faced and spluttering. "This—this is an outrage!"

"Yes, it is," called out a woman seated in the front. "Why didn't you contact us sooner?"

"You aren't giving us much time," said another, dismayed. "I already have two baby quilts to finish by the end of the month."

A chorus of agreement rose, but Mary Beth wrestled the microphone from Diane and raised one hand for quiet. "May I remind you that this woman is not a member of our guild? She isn't authorized to make announcements."

Someone snickered; Diane looked in the direction of Mary Beth's glare and spotted Lee Kessenich, a frequent customer of Grandma's Attic. She had recently moved to Waterford from Wisconsin, too recently to have fallen under Mary Beth's influence. As Mary Beth shoved Diane toward the door, Diane leaned to the microphone and said, "I'm terribly sorry if I've broken any rules."

"Wait, don't go," another woman cried. "What colors should we use again?"

As others chimed in with questions, Mary Beth shouted, "Ladies, ladies, please! Obviously Diane's only reason for coming here tonight was to create a disturbance. Please just ignore her. If she really wanted you to participate in this quilt, she would have told you about it sooner."

"We tried," said Diane, incredulous. She held the envelope high. "We sent an invitation to the guild, care of Mary Beth. She returned it to us and said you couldn't be bothered. I have the envelope right here if anyone wants to check the postmark and the address."

A murmur of surprise and indignation rose, but Diane looked around uneasily at the guild members and realized that at least some of them were more upset with her than with their president. "Thanks for your time," she called out as she dashed back to her chair for her coat and purse. "If you have any questions, please call me or Bonnie at Grandma's Attic. Thanks!"

She hurried from the room as the chorus of voices swelled behind her.

❧

Diane went home and waited for her neighbor to storm over in a fury. Mary Beth's car pulled into the Callahans' garage twenty minutes later, but there was no furious pounding on the door, no shrill phone call. Diane regretted leaving the meeting so hastily, although it had seemed prudent at the time. She wished she knew what had happened after she left.

Whatever Mary Beth might have done to discourage her fellow guild members from contributing to Sylvia's bridal quilt, it soon became evident that she had failed. All that week, quilters phoned Grandma's Attic to inquire about the guidelines for block size and pattern choices. Every day several shoppers came in specifically to purchase fabrics for "Sylvia's quilt," and a few remarkably industrious quilters dropped off finished blocks. By Saturday they had added twenty new blocks to the collection and had received promises for many more. Bonnie and Summer were mystified by the sudden outpouring of interest. "I suppose Mary Beth had a change of heart," said Bonnie, dubious. "She must have announced the project after all."

"I know for a fact she didn't," said Diane sharply, and was about to explain when Summer pointed out that Mary Beth couldn't have, since she had left her invitation at Grandma's Attic. As if neither had heard Diane speak, Bonnie and Summer agreed that one of the other guild members must have spread the word. Diane was so irritated with them that she went off to alphabetize pattern books without confiding her role in the sudden windfall.

As the last week before the start of quilt camp passed, Diane waited for Mary Beth to exact her revenge, but she saw nothing of her neighbor except what she glimpsed through the windshield of Mary Beth's car as she pulled in and out of her garage. Even Brent, who came over nearly every afternoon to study for midterms with Todd, gave no sign that he knew anything was amiss.

Maybe Diane had so humiliated Mary Beth that she had not told her family. Maybe the guild had turned on her in fury when it sank in that their president had dismissed the Elm Creek Quilters' invitation without consulting a single member of the board. Maybe they would demand a recall election, and finally, finally Mary Beth would be deposed. New leadership might breathe life into that moribund institution, healing the rift between the guild and the Elm Creek Quilters.

For her next trick, Diane decided, she would drive Fabric Warehouse out of business. In the meantime, she had her own block to make for Sylvia's quilt.

Sylvia was one of the few people Diane knew whose sharp tongue could match her own, and she respected that. Somehow, though, Sylvia managed to speak her mind without annoying her listeners, a skill Diane had yet to master. Sylvia knew when to soften criticism with a compliment or humor, but when she was deadly serious, everyone knew it and listened with respect. Diane could sew for the rest of her life without becoming the accomplished Master Quilter Sylvia was, but she could, and did, emulate her way with words. Without Sylvia's example in mind when she crashed the guild meeting, she probably would have insulted everyone present and fled from the library meeting room with an angry mob on her heels. As it was, she had offended only Mary Beth and her inner circle, and that alone deserved commemoration in a quilt block.

Her block was nearly finished by the first day of quilt camp, but then the whirlwind of activity forced her to set it aside. Apparently she was not the only Elm Creek Quilter who had failed to plan well; on the first day of classes, Sarah had to juggle the schedule to accommodate Judy's sudden trip to Philadelphia and wound up teaching a hand-quilting class herself. Gwen ran out of fusible webbing in the middle of her workshop and had to send one of the cook's helpers to Grandma's Attic for more, and Bonnie and Summer had forgotten that running the evening program together left no one to close the quilt shop. Bonnie asked Diane to cover, and Diane agreed, resolving on the drive over to schedule that appointment with Bonnie as soon as the busy first week of camp settled into an easier routine.

Closing the shop meant that she returned home later than usual. Not until she walked through the door and saw Todd and Brent foraging for food in the kitchen did she remember she had agreed Brent could spend the night, and that she was supposed to stop on the way home for pizza and videos. They had heard her enter, so she couldn't sneak back out to her car. Instead she called in the pizza order and drove the boys to the video store to pick out movies for themselves, which meant twice as many DVDs with twice as much carnage as Diane usually allowed. Tim and the pizza delivery man arrived soon after they returned home, so the evening was salvaged despite Diane's mistake.

Diane and Tim went upstairs to bed when the first movie ended, after urging Todd and Brent to remember to get at least a few hours' sleep. Diane heard them moving the sofa to make more room for the air mattresses, so she knew they had at least unrolled their sleeping bags, but the television was still playing when she drifted off to sleep.

She and Tim woke to the alarm clock early the next morning. While Tim took his turn in the shower, Diane went to rouse Todd for school. She had padded halfway down the hall before remembering spring break and the sleepover. With a groan, she returned to bed for a few more minutes' rest, but she could not allow herself to fall back asleep because she had to be at Elm Creek Manor by eight.

After her shower, she went downstairs, pausing by the family room to check on Todd and Brent. They had drawn the curtains and turned off the television the night before, and one of the boys was snoring. Diane crept away to the kitchen, where Tim was reading the paper and finishing his breakfast. She had planned to make pancakes, but the boys were unlikely to wake before she left for work, so she set out a plate of muffins and a few boxes of cereal for them and took a yogurt from the refrigerator for herself.

She kissed Tim good-bye when he had to leave, then hurried back upstairs to finish getting ready. She stopped by the family room again on her way back—still no sign of life from the two sleeping-bag-shrouded lumps on the floor—and went to the kitchen for her purse. Propped up beside it was a course catalogue for Waterford College, folded open to a page where a paragraph had been circled with a yellow highlighter. Diane picked it up and read a description for COMP 326—Advanced Programming, taught by Dr. Judy DiNardo. A sentence underlined in red ink read, "Students are strongly encouraged to obtain a laptop computer for use in class."

Diane sighed and stuck the catalogue between the phone and the answering machine. Trust Michael to arrange it so he would have the last word. She wondered what time he had come home the previous night. She was not aware that she slept that soundly. Perhaps the television had masked the sound of the front door.

Shaking her head, she picked up her purse and dug around for her keys on the way to the garage. They were not in their usual corner of the front pocket, but she always left the car door unlocked, so she got in and searched the main pouch and the change purse, to no avail. Sighing in exasperation, she emptied the entire contents of her purse onto the front passenger seat— still nothing. "This is ridiculous," she muttered, checking to make sure all the zippers and clasps were unfastened before turning the purse upside down and shaking it vigorously. Only a nickel and a crumpled tissue fell out.

Diane glanced at her watch and hastily shoveled her belongings back into her purse. She always returned her keys to her purse—always—and her sons had learned the hard way to follow suit whenever they borrowed the car. She raced back inside and dug around in the kitchen junk drawer for the spare set, blindly groping through birthday candles, address labels, and miscellaneous batteries until her fingers brushed against the Waterford College Wildcats key ring. She pulled it free and shoved the drawer closed as best she could in her haste. The spare set included only the keys for the house and the car, but they would have to do until she could find her own set. Todd might remember where she had put them after they returned from the video store, but she had no time now to wake him and ask.

Fortunately, she was not teaching that morning, merely assisting Agnes and Gwen with their workshops, so she still arrived at Elm Creek Manor in plenty of time. With misgivings, she skipped what was certain to be an excellent lunch in the banquet hall in order to make sure she arrived for her afternoon shift at Grandma's Attic well before Bonnie departed for Elm Creek Manor and locked the door behind her. In passing, Bonnie told Diane she would be coming back later to go over the books, so Diane wouldn't need to close that evening. Diane used this as an excuse not to mention the missing key; she would surely find it before she was asked to open or close the shop again.

Todd was watching television in the family room, alone, when Diane came home to fix supper before returning to Elm Creek Manor for the evening program. "Where's Brent?" she asked.

Todd shrugged and switched off the television. "Hanging out with some ASB guys, I guess."

"I see."

Todd sounded dejected, and more than a little irritated. The Associated Student Body was not the same as student government, which was comprised of the traditional elected positions and actually did represent student interests fairly well. Anyone could join ASB—although no one outside the popular cliques ever did—if they had third period available and were interested in planning pep rallies, fund-raisers, and Homecoming events. Michael, who had mistrusted anything that reeked of school spirit, had avoided all things ASB with a passion, and even Todd, who would have been welcomed gladly, was unwilling to sacrifice an academic period for what he called a social hour with an occasional bit of work thrown in. Kids joined ASB for a break from real work and for something to add to their college applications to impress people who didn't know any better, Todd claimed, and he couldn't stand it when Brent invited his friends from ASB along when they got together. Diane, who had expected Todd to embrace ASB when he first enrolled with Brent as a freshman, had been astonished when he had declined to sign up for the second semester.

Diane asked, "Are the ASB guys going to monopolize Brent for the rest of spring break?"

Todd said he didn't know and that it didn't matter, because he had other plans with some of the guys from the basketball team anyway. Diane nodded, trying to hide her satisfaction. She wouldn't mind being rid of Brent for a while.

To cheer up Todd—and to assuage her guilt—Diane prepared his favorite supper, spaghetti and meatballs. Afterward, Todd and Tim helped her search for the keys, without success. Diane even phoned the video store and the pizza place, although she knew that was illogical, since she had driven home from the video store and the pizza had been delivered. "Did anyone see me toss my keys into the delivery guy's truck?" she asked wearily, when they had given up and sat in the living room, watching the last of Todd's rented DVDs.

"I saw you put them in your purse," Todd assured her for what must have been the tenth time.

"They'll turn up," said Tim. "Eventually."

Diane agreed, but she didn't have until "eventually." Bonnie could ask her to open the store any day, and Diane had too many doubts arrayed against her already without admitting she had lost her key to the store.

She decided to avoid Bonnie as much as she could for as long as she could, which would not be easy considering how frequently their paths crossed at quilt camp. She gave herself until the end of the week to find her keys. After that, she would confess the truth and ask Bonnie for another.

She did not see Bonnie at all the next morning at the manor, but at lunchtime learned that she had congratulated herself for her stealth undeservedly. Bonnie had never shown up that morning, nor had she called.

Diane agreed with her friends that this was troubling and uncharacteristic, but she wondered if any besides Summer knew that Bonnie had not shown up at Grandma's Attic two days in a row earlier that month. Since no one answered the phone at the shop or at Bonnie's home, Summer had driven downtown to investigate. She had promised to call as soon as she had news, but the afternoon classes ended without any word. Afterward, Diane wanted to stop by Grandma's Attic herself, but she did not have enough time between driving home to prepare supper for her family and racing back to the manor to help Gwen with the evening entertainment program. She was only supposed to assist Gwen, who had agreed to fill in for the absent

Bonnie, but Gwen must have forgotten because she was nowhere to be found by the time the quilted clothing fashion show was to begin.

"She went to Grandma's Attic to find out why Summer didn't report back," said Sarah as Diane prepared for her unexpected starring role as fashion show emcee. "Something must be terribly wrong. No one's answering the phones and no one's checked in."

"Well, let's not send anyone else or they'll get sucked into the same black hole," said Diane cheerfully, donning the outlandish quilted and sequined jacket Bonnie had intended to wear. It hung on Diane's slender frame, but she figured that enhanced the humorous effect. "Bonnie's probably just sick or something and forgot to call. When Summer and Gwen found out it was nothing serious, they decided to wait until tomorrow to tell us. If it was something really terrible, someone definitely would have let us know."

Sarah looked dubious but said she hoped Diane was right.

The next morning, they all learned she could not have been more wrong.

Gwen and Summer had worked late into the night helping Bonnie restore some order to the ransacked shop, but so much remained to be done that Bonnie wanted to continue working throughout the day, if the Elm Creek Quilters could spare her. They quickly assented, and listened, shocked, as Gwen and Summer told them what they had seen, what the police had determined.

"They think it's an inside job," said Gwen, shaking her head in disbelief. "I think it's more likely Bonnie forgot to lock the door, but she insists she remembered."

Summer nodded in agreement and said, "What bothers me is that if the police are focused on this theory, they'll ignore other alternatives."

"Wait," said Diane, heart sinking. "Why do they think it's an inside job?"

"Because there were no signs of forced entry," said Summer. "So they assume the culprit or culprits must have used a key."

"Or the door was left unlocked," said Gwen. "They left no fingerprints, either, so they must have worn gloves."

"So the police think they were professionals?" asked Judy, who had missed the anxious waiting of the previous day and seemed even more shocked than her friends by the news that greeted her on her first morning back from Philadelphia.

"Anyone who has ever seen a detective drama on television knows to wear gloves during a robbery," said Sylvia.

"It was cold that night," said Diane, her voice tight. "Anyone going out-side would have worn gloves. So does this mean everyone in Waterford is a suspect?"

They all looked at her, then returned their attention to Summer as she de-scribed the inscrutable lists of what had been taken and what had been left behind. Not surprisingly, all the money in the store was gone, as well as one of the most expensive Berninas, but only one. A handful of rotary cutters and shears. Some fine-point permanent pens. With a meaningful look to Sylvia, Summer added, "They also took blocks Bonnie had been saving for a special quilt."

The bridal quilt? Diane saw her own confusion mirrored in her friends' eyes.

Gwen's brow furrowed as it always did when she grappled with an espe-cially difficult academic puzzle. "It makes no sense. They take some expen-sive things and leave others. They take quilt blocks and leave the computer."

"No, that makes perfect sense," said Summer. "Bonnie's Mac is eight years old, an antique by computer standards. I can't imagine the thieves would have been able to sell it for much, and if they want a computer, the money they stole is more than enough to buy one of the best."

Numb, Diane nodded along with the others when Agnes proposed they make a schedule so that anyone not immediately responsible for a class or workshop could be relieved of other quilt camp duties so they could help Bonnie set the store to rights.

She wanted to weep.

CHAPTER EIGHT

Mary Beth

M ary Beth read the letter a second time, fuming. How dare those Elm Creek Quilters expect the members of her guild to help them with some silly gift for that overrated old Sylvia Compson? How dare they address her guild at all after Diane's vindictive attempt to assume the presidency? Diane had never won a ribbon in a quilt show, and yet she had thought herself fit to manage the Waterford Summer Quilt Festival. She couldn't meet a deadline to save her life, and yet she believed herself capable of organizing a dozen different guild subcommittees. The guild had neither needed nor wanted a "change of pace" or "fresh air to chase away stale ideas," as Diane had promised in her campaign speech, the first in the history of the guild. For ninety-three years members had been content to modestly mention their interest in the office to friends and allow word to spread, then feign surprise when they were nominated. Until Diane, no one had needed to bribe members with promises to invite better speakers or direct new workshops or spend the dues more frugally. Whoever had the most friends won, and wasn't that the democratic way? Mary Beth would never forgive Diane for forcing her to stand at that podium explaining Diane's inadequacies for the job as if she were begging to be reelected. And she would never forget the added humiliation of Diane's walking out of the meeting the evening the results were announced and taking some of the guild's most talented and dedicated members with her. Bonnie Markham owned the only quilt shop in town, Gwen Sullivan actually published academic research on quilt history, and Agnes Emberly could always be counted on to contribute the work of four quilters to the annual service project. Their resignations stung, but the guild got along just fine without them—better, in fact, without Diane to create constant discord—but the shadow they had cast on Mary Beth's presidency that year had rankled her ever since.

"It's just like that Diane to complain about a present for her own friend, too," Mary Beth told her husband and son over dinner. "It's just another sign of her malignant sense of ingratitude. That woman never appreciates anything anyone does for her."

Brent and Roger merely nodded, so Mary Beth took that as encouragement to continue. "Those Elm Creek Quilters think their time is more valuable than ours, do they?" she said, helping herself to more broccoli, cheese, and rice casserole. "They think we have nothing better to do than sew blocks for some stupid bridal quilt, do they? Don't they know we make a quilt a year for a real charity? They ought to try giving back to the community for a change, but with them it's just take, take, take."

"They make quilts for hospitals," said Brent.

She frowned at him. "What?"

"I heard Mrs. Sonnenberg talking once. They all make quilts for the kids' cancer ward at Hershey Medical Center and for the, what's it called, for babies that are born too early—"

"Premature?" volunteered his father. "Neonatal?"

"Yeah, thanks. The neonatal unit at the Elm Creek Valley Hospital."

Mary Beth bristled at the disloyalty, but she hated to criticize her son. "Then they ought to understand how much work projects like that take."

"It's just one quilt square," said Roger tiredly. "It doesn't sound like that much effort."

"It's not the effort. It's the principle." Mary Beth's sour frown shifted into a smile as she turned to her son. "Honey, I'm sure you know better than to mention this conversation to Mrs. Sonnenberg."

His mouth full, Brent shrugged and nodded. Of course he would never tell tales on her to that conniving shrew next door, even though she was the mother of his best friend. Mary Beth had tried to root out that friendship before it spread like stinkweed, but Brent had taken to Todd Sonnenberg despite her best efforts. Mary Beth's only comfort was that Todd seemed a model son, and Brent shared her antipathy for his delinquent elder brother, Michael. Mary Beth saw Diane's attitude reflected in Michael whenever she had the bad fortune to run into him, but Todd's temperament was as unlike Diane's as Brent's or Mary Beth's. Mary Beth would have guessed Todd

was adopted except he did resemble Diane physically. Todd's good characteristics must have come from his father. Tim wasn't that bad, despite his
obviously poor taste in wives.

Mary Beth wished the Sonnenbergs would move away, far away, and
leave the neighborhood in peace, but she had prayed for that for years with
nothing to show for it. Mary Beth was stuck with Diane the way other people were stuck with miserable allergies or chronic lower back pain. There
was no getting rid of Diane permanently, so Mary Beth could only struggle
to hold the symptoms in check.

There was only one way to handle this most recent outbreak of Diane
nastiness: file the invitation in her quilt room and hope no one else in the
guild received one. There were factions in the guild—small and powerless,
but still a presence—that might actually like to participate in the bridal quilt.
Some members had even attended Elm Creek Quilt Camp! When the camp
was in its third year, Mary Beth and her vice president considered adding a
guild-wide boycott to the bylaws, but others on the board pointed out the
rule would be difficult to enforce and might raise the ire of their members.

Mary Beth had been forced to settle for passive resistance, ignoring the
patronizing invitations to activities at Elm Creek Manor and taking her business to the Fabric Warehouse and mail-order companies rather than
Grandma's Attic. Fortunately, since all guild correspondence was sent to the
Callahan home, she could filter out the junk before the other members discovered it.

Mary Beth put the letter out of sight but not out of mind, fuming over it
whenever she saw Diane—which was far too often but inescapable since she
lived next door—or any of the other Elm Creek Quilters. Once when she
spotted Sylvia leaving the hair salon she was tempted to run up and blurt
out the secret, but that tough-looking Sarah McClure was with her and she
didn't dare. An anonymous note would ruin the surprise just as well, but in a
much less satisfying manner. Eventually, since trying to forget the letter
didn't work, she decided to return it and let those annoying Elm Creek people know once and for all that her guild was off-limits.

She waited until the first day of March, exactly one month before the quilt
blocks were due—too little time for the Elm Creek Quilters to find an alternate way to reach her guild members but just enough to make them feel as
if they ought to try. Let them scurry around like ants in a flooded anthill for
the entire month. They deserved it.

Bonnie Markham was a soft touch and still on good terms with most of the guild and, best of all, Mary Beth could reach her in a public place. Grandma's Attic was a tolerable walk from her front door in fair weather, but not when the temperatures hovered at barely above freezing, so Mary Beth drove downtown. It might have been more convenient to leave the letter at Diane's house, but she could only imagine what that psycho would be capable of when provoked on her own property.

Mary Beth strode into the quilt shop and hid her consternation at the sight of Diane and a vaguely familiar auburn-haired girl looking at some quilt blocks spread out on the cutting table. She took off her hat, smoothed back her hair, and, addressing neither of them in particular, asked, "Isn't Bonnie here today?"

"No," Diane shot back rudely. She sat down on a stool with her back to Mary Beth and removed a padded envelope from a large carton on the cutting table. The auburn-haired girl murmured something as Diane took from the envelope another quilt block and what looked to be a letter. Diane muttered a response that Mary Beth could not make out, so she drew closer, suspicious.

The auburn-haired girl, who so strongly resembled a younger and much thinner version of Gwen Sullivan that she had to be her daughter, smiled and said, "Bonnie's not here, but may I help you?"

"I suppose so," Mary Beth said, reluctant. She would much rather deal with Bonnie. "You're Summer, right? Summer Sullivan?"

"That's right."

"Your name is in the letter, so I guess you'll do." Mary Beth produced the invitation and held it out. "I believe this was sent to me by mistake."

Summer took the page, skimmed it, and nodded. "We definitely meant to send it to you. Actually, to the entire guild. You're listed as the guild contact, so we sent it to your home, hoping you would announce it at your next meeting."

Summer tried to return the letter, but Mary Beth would have none of that. She explained as firmly and clearly as she could that the Elm Creek Quilters were out of line to impose on her guild when their members had so many legitimate charities to support already, but Diane kept interrupting with obnoxious objections, which only encouraged Summer to whine and beg for Mary Beth to reconsider. There was no reasoning with them, and since she was outnumbered, Mary Beth decided she had made her point as clearly as they would allow and left after insisting they remove the Waterford Quilting Guild from their mailing list immediately. The consternation and outrage on Diane's face were priceless, and as Mary Beth sailed out the door, she was glad Bonnie had not been there after all. She paused by the front window and peeked inside for one last glimpse and was rewarded with the sight of Summer throwing the invitation into the trash where it belonged.

At supper that evening, she couldn't resist boasting about how she had put Diane in her place. "And those blocks they had scattered all over the cutting table," she said, "I just know those were the blocks for the bridal quilt."

Roger and Brent nodded and continued eating.

"The ones I saw weren't anything special," she mused aloud. "I guess those Elm Creek people aren't the wonderful teachers they consider themselves to be. Or the people who sent the blocks didn't send their best work, which doesn't say much for how they regard Sylvia."

"Or they were beginners," said Roger, reaching for another piece of chicken, "and that *was* their best work."

"That couldn't possibly be the case," said Mary Beth. "Beginners know better than to ruin a group quilt with their sloppy blocks."

"It's a gift to congratulate a bride and groom, not a masterpiece to display in a show. If beginners want to express their good wishes, they shouldn't be criticized for the number of stitches per inch they use."

"Stitches per inch refers to quilting, not piecing," snapped Mary Beth. "Which just shows you don't know anything about it."

Roger shrugged and continued eating without another word.

"Mom, you've been going on about this stupid quilt for months," said Brent. "You should really just forget about it. It's not that big of a deal."

"It is a big deal. Diane and those Elm Creek Quilters think they're the best thing that happened to quilting in Waterford since my guild was founded, and it's not fair. They ignore everything my guild has done for this town as if it never happened."

When she said "my guild," she meant herself, but she didn't want to brag.

Brent shook his head. "I still say you should just forget about it. You're driving yourself crazy."

When he said "yourself," his expression suggested he meant "us," as did the affirming grunt from his father.

Tears sprang into Mary Beth's eyes. "This is what I get for living in a house full of men," she said, voice shaking. She rose and gathered up her dishes. "You couldn't possibly understand."

She saw them exchange a look of distress as she carried her dishes into the kitchen and dumped them in the sink. She worked so hard, for her family, for the guild, and all anyone ever did was criticize.

❧

When she returned downstairs later that evening, she found that the dishes had been loaded into the dishwasher, the leftovers stored in the refrigerator, the table wiped clean. She smiled, seeing their apology in the completed chores.

As the week went by, she tried to take her son's advice and forget the quilt, but she could not shake the uneasy sense that Diane was plotting revenge. Brent said nothing to suggest he had overheard anything unusual at the Sonnenberg home, but Mary Beth wasn't sure if he would recognize the signs of a covert plan if he happened to stumble across them. She could never tell how much Brent absorbed and what he ignored. She might mention an upcoming appointment every night for a week only to return from it and find him genuinely surprised that she had not been home to greet him after school. Other times she might compliment only once, in passing, a book or blouse she had seen in a store, and receive it as her next birthday or Christmas present. Unfortunately, unless she came right out and asked him to spy on Diane, he wasn't likely to uncover anything. She was tempted, but not quite willing to resort to that.

As another week passed uneventfully, Mary Beth's sense of impending confrontation began to ebb. Maybe this time Diane realized that she was beaten, that retaliation was futile. By the third Monday of March, Mary Beth felt secure enough to savor her triumph, and as she dressed for the monthly meeting of the Waterford Quilting Guild, she decided to share her secret victory with Sandra, her closest friend and loyal vice president. Sandra didn't care for those Elm Creek Quilters either, although her spite was reserved for Bonnie, who had refused many requests to hire Sandra to work in her quilt shop, as if it were so grand a place only experienced salespeople could be permitted to don one of those ridiculous aprons.

Not since Diane sought the presidency had Mary Beth felt so at home behind the podium in Meeting Room C of the public library. At two minutes to seven, she tested the microphone and noted the filling seats with satisfaction, then returned to the officers' chairs long enough to bend close to Sandra's ear and whisper that she had big news to share later. She started the meeting at precisely seven o'clock, welcoming the members who were already seated and pointedly ignoring those who scurried in late.

Five prospective new members were in attendance, a number Mary Beth noted with satisfaction. One of her goals for the term was to increase the membership, which for no discernible reason had been declining over the past few years. She hoped the newcomers noticed how efficiently the officers went about presenting the business of their respective offices. When Diane and her crones had been in the guild, the announcements had been periodically interrupted by wisecracks and laughter, which wasted valuable time and almost always added an extra half hour to the meeting. Without their interference, the guild business was attended to in reasonable time, and before long Mary Beth reassumed her position at the podium and asked if any of the other guild members wished to make an announcement.

At that moment, on the chair several paces behind her, her cell phone began to ring. She pretended not to hear it, then pretended it belonged to someone else, but the distinctive tones Brent had downloaded from the Internet were her signature ring and everyone in the room knew it. Come to think of it, all of her friends were in that room, it was too late for a call from Waterford High School, and her boys had been warned never to phone during guild meetings. "Anyone? Any other announcements?" she asked, raising her voice to drown out the phone.

At that moment, the ringing finally ceased. "Voicemail," she said, relieved, and the guild members laughed and nodded in sympathy. She cleared her throat. "Well, if no one has any announcements, our program chairwoman would like to introduce—"

The phone started up again. Mary Beth flushed and hurried back to her chair. "I'm sorry," she said, snatching up her purse. "It must be an emergency. Sandra, will you take over?"

She raced from the room without waiting for a reply. In the hallway she dug through her purse, seized the phone, and pressed it to her ear, all while hurrying away from the meeting room so that her conversation would not distract the guild while Sandra introduced the guest speaker. "Hello?" she barked. When there was no reply, she moved closer to the outside door to pick up a better signal. "Hello?"

Silence. She grimaced and read the display: "You have 1 new number!"

That made no sense; Roger's cell and their home phone were already programmed. She pressed the keys to bring up her Caller ID, but she did not recognize the number that appeared. Probably a wrong number, or worse yet, a telemarketer. She jabbed the key to clear the display, switched off the phone, and tossed it back in her purse.

Mary Beth stormed back to the meeting room, vowing to call that number back and let them have it as soon as the meeting ended. As she drew closer, she heard a lone voice speaking over the portable sound system, but none of the usual oohs and ahhs and applause that accompanied a guest speaker's trunk show. Curious, she tried to return unobtrusively, but she froze just inside the doorway, reeling from the sight of Diane at her podium reading the invitation to participate in the bridal quilt.

At first she was too shocked to do anything, but when Diane smirked, put away the letter, and asked for questions, she flew into action. "This—this is an outrage!" she exclaimed, hurrying forward.

"Yes, it is," someone called out. "Why didn't you contact us sooner?"

Another chimed in, "You aren't giving us much time. I already have two baby quilts to finish by the end of the month."

Other voices swelled, but Mary Beth, horrified, managed to pry the microphone from Diane's grimy fist and tried to regain order. "May I remind you that this woman is not a member of our guild?" she said, ready to remind them under what circumstances Diane had left. "She isn't authorized to make announcements."

Some traitor laughed derisively; Mary Beth ignored decorum and shoved Diane toward the nearest door. "I'm terribly sorry if I've broken any rules," Diane called out with false innocence, leaning close to the microphone.

"Wait, don't go," another woman cried. "What colors should we use again?"

"Ladies, ladies, please," Mary Beth shouted over the clamor. "Obviously Diane's only reason for coming here tonight was to create a disturbance. Please just ignore her. If she really wanted you to participate in this quilt, she would have told you about it sooner."

"We tried," retorted Diane, holding up an envelope. "We sent an invitation to the guild, care of Mary Beth. She returned it to us and said you couldn't be bothered. I have the envelope right here if anyone wants to check the postmark and the address."

Horror-struck, Mary Beth tried to snatch it away, but Diane suddenly blurted a hasty good-bye and sprinted for the door. Suddenly Sandra was at Mary Beth's side, gently taking the microphone from her hand. "Calm down, everyone," Sandra said, returning to the podium, her deep, gravelly voice making little impact on the rising din. "Don't pay any attention to that troublemaker."

"Is it true?" a voice rang out. "Did you deliberately keep that invitation from us?"

Mary Beth held up a hand as if it would keep back the accusing voices. She took a deep breath and willed herself to calm as she joined Sandra at the podium, her station of order. "I did, and I'll tell you why. I know how busy you are already, especially since so many of you have already been so generous with your time and talents for our service project, and I didn't want you to feel obligated to participate in something so, well, frivolous."

She cringed at the incredulous echo of her last word.

"That's for us to decide!" someone shouted.

"I'm the elected president. I had to use my best judgment. If I made a mistake, I apologize." Mary Beth forced a shaky smile. "From now on, I'll be sure to bring you every solicitation the guild receives, but don't be surprised when you're overwhelmed by all the requests."

"I don't care about next time," wailed a woman in the second row. "Sylvia's wonderful. I want to participate in *this* quilt."

Mary Beth tried to look apologetic. "I'm sorry, but as someone has already pointed out, it really is too late."

"There's plenty of time to make one block," said a woman in the back row. She had joined a year ago after moving to Waterford from Wisconsin; Mary Beth couldn't recall her name. Lee something. "I've been on the Elm Creek Quilts mailing list ever since I attended quilt camp last summer. I received an invitation, too, and I'd be happy to make copies for everyone who wants them. Give me your names before you leave and I'll make a list."

A crowd of clamoring quilters quickly surrounded her. "Maybe this can wait until after the meeting," Mary Beth shouted into the microphone. "Let's not forget we have a very special guest tonight, a talented quilter from Boalsburg and a member of the Centre Pieces Quilt Guild . . ."

She trailed off when she realized no one was listening. The crowd around the traitor in the back row thickened. Mary Beth glanced at the guest speaker, who had taken a flyer from the table along the wall and was writing something on the back. Her address, Mary Beth realized, as she rose and carried the paper to the back of the room.

"Sandra." She plucked at the sleeve of her closest friend and ally, who was gaping at the scene. "Take over, will you? I think I'm—I think I should—"

Sandra gave no sign she heard. Mary Beth left the sentence unfinished and stepped away from the podium.

✿

She drove home in a daze. Inside, she clung to Roger and sobbed out the story. Brent had come downstairs to see what was wrong and now sat by her side, listening, wide-eyed and incredulous, as the story of her humiliation spilled from her.

Roger patted her back and sighed. "I guess maybe now you'll finally drop this silly feud with the Sonnenbergs."

"Dad," said Brent. "She's upset."

"That's your response?" Mary Beth pulled away from her husband and groped on the end table for a box of tissues. "Your wife is dishonored in front of all her friends, and that's how you respond?"

"Well, what do you want me to do? Run next door and challenge Tim to a duel?"

"Don't be ridiculous," she snapped, dabbing at her eyes. "This is between me and that—that evil witch. How can you call it a silly feud? It's much more than that, and that woman's behavior tonight proves it."

"All it proves," Roger muttered, "is that you two are equally committed to a to-the-death struggle over very small stakes."

Mary Beth ignored him and blew her nose. "Brent, I don't want you playing with that Sonnenberg boy anymore."

"That's not fair," he protested. "It's not Todd's fault his mom's a nutcase."

Roger gazed at the ceiling. "Why do I suspect an identical conversation is taking place next door?"

"If you can't be supportive, then be quiet," snapped Mary Beth. "I'm sorry, Brent, but that woman is a bad influence. I don't want you anywhere near her."

"I barely even see her when I'm over there."

"That's not good enough."

"But we have midterms coming up. Todd and I always study together. We're partners for the Physics project. Not to mention he's been my best friend since the second grade."

Mary Beth sniffled into her tissue. She hated to see him so distraught. "Well—"

"Please, Mom. This way, I might overhear her if she plans anything else."

"By all means," said Roger. "Let's take the high road. Let's spy on the neighbors."

"If she tries anything else, I'm pressing charges." Still, Brent had a point. "All right. You can still be friends with Todd under one condition: If that woman says a single word against me, you'll defend me." Unlike her husband. She glared at him, but he had let his head fall against the sofa cushions and was shaking his head at the ceiling.

"I promise," said Brent solemnly.

She reached out and drew him into an embrace. "That's my good boy."

Sometimes she thought Brent was the only person who understood her.

✿

Sometimes Brent thought the main reason he and Todd were best friends was that they both had mothers who were certifiable. Still, while his mother was often embarrassing, at least she didn't have a mean streak like Todd's mom. When Brent went to the Sonnenberg house to study the next day, he was so furious he could barely look in her direction, much less speak to her. He ignored her so intently that it was some time before he realized Mrs. Sonnenberg was ignoring him, too. Then, in a flash of insight, he realized that she wasn't acting much different than usual.

She always tried to pretend he wasn't there. It wasn't just because of what happened at the library.

He wanted to talk to Todd about that night at the library, but he didn't know how to bring it up without starting an argument. He would have just let it go except he just couldn't understand what Mrs. Sonnenberg had against his mother. He wrestled with that question, but the answer was irritatingly elusive.

Finally he couldn't stand it anymore. "What's with your mom?" he asked on the Thursday after the quilt guild meeting, as he and Todd studied for their Calculus midterm.

Todd didn't even bother to look up from his differential equations. "What do you mean?"

"You know. Why'd she go off like that at the quilt thing?"

Todd looked genuinely perplexed. "What?"

"You know," repeated Brent, irritably. "The way she barged into my mom's quilt guild meeting and started ordering them around, telling them they had to make a stupid quilt."

"My mom says a lot of stuff about a lot of quilts, but the only quilt guild she talks about are her friends up at the manor."

Brent stared at his friend, head bent over his book, his pencil scratching on paper. Todd really didn't know. Mrs. Sonnenberg had made a fool of his mother in front of all her friends in the one place where she got any respect, and yet Mrs. Sonnenberg had thought so little of it she had not even bothered to tell her kid.

"Never mind," said Brent tightly, picking up his pencil and writing down equations with a vengeance. Sometimes he was seized by the urge to punch Todd in the face until he begged for mercy, but if he ignored it, the feeling always faded.

❧❧

Although he wouldn't get his grades back until after spring break, Brent knew he had aced his midterms. His mom was so pleased that she hugged him, gave him fifty dollars, and agreed that he could spend the night at Todd's. She had smiled so rarely since that night in the library that out of guilt he put off accepting Todd's invitation until Monday. Unaccustomed to a weekday with no classes and no homework, they hung out for most of the day, watching TV, shooting hoops in the driveway, playing computer games, until they grew bored with the abundance of time. Todd halfheartedly suggested they work on their Physics project, but Brent said he would rather stare at a blank wall than spend one minute of his vacation working on an assignment that wasn't due for another month.

Mrs. Sonnenberg was supposed to bring pizza for supper and videos for later, but by five-thirty Brent and Todd were starved, so they raided the fridge and cupboards for pretzels and sodas and a few attempts at sandwiches. Brent suggested they order their own pizza and have it delivered, but Todd didn't have any cash and Brent wasn't about to blow his fifty bucks on food Mrs. Sonnenberg should have paid for, so he said he was broke, too.

It was after seven when Mrs. Sonnenberg finally showed up, with no pizza and no DVDs. Brent shook his head, disgusted, but she was too busy giving them some lame excuse about having to close the quilt shop to notice. She called for a pizza and herded them out to her car to drive them to the video store. When she wandered off to read the display case for some stupid Julia Roberts romantic comedy, Brent picked out three action movies and said to Todd, "You pick some and I'll pick some."

Todd eyed the stack in Brent's hands. "She said we could get two."

"Yeah, but she also said she'd bring them home for us. She's feeling guilty, so take advantage."

Todd shook his head, but grinned as he turned back to the shelves.

Brent nudged him. "Come on. Don't be such a craven poltroon."

Todd guffawed; one of their favorite inside jokes was to work vocabulary words from their SAT prep class into everyday conversation just to prove how awkward they were. But he selected two more DVDs, and when they took them to Mrs. Sonnenberg, she didn't complain.

Todd's parents finally went to bed after the first movie. "It's about time," muttered Brent, shoving the sofa aside to make room for the air mattresses.

Todd came over to help him. "Why? You tired already?"

"Not tired." Brent grinned and headed for the kitchen. "Just thirsty."

During their search for food, he had found where the Sonnenbergs had unimaginatively stashed their liquor, in a cupboard above the refrigerator. Todd realized where he was heading when he picked up a kitchen chair. "Brent, no. That's not a good idea."

"Why not?" Brent set the chair in front of the refrigerator and climbed up. "You don't complain at my house."

"My mom's a human Breathalyzer. She'll know."

"Not if we don't see them until morning." He selected a bottle of vodka three-quarters full, then took out a bottle of rum. "Hey. Rum and Cokes."

"Keep it down," said Todd, peering over his shoulder. "She's a light sleeper."

"So she can check on her widdle baby if he cries?" Brent tucked the bottles under his arm and returned the chair to its place at the table. All the while Todd trailed after him, glancing anxiously toward the ceiling. "Will you relax? Have a drink. That will help."

Todd scowled, but took the bottle of vodka. He retrieved the orange juice from the refrigerator while Brent searched the cupboards for the supersize plastic tumblers their class had sold two years before to raise money for their sophomore trip. They mixed their drinks in silence, listening for footsteps upstairs, then watered down the bottles, wiped them clean, and put them away.

When the harpy didn't come swooping in to bust them, Todd finally relaxed and laughed his way through the *Lethal Weapon* series like always.
They returned to the kitchen off and on, Todd for snacks, Brent to replenish
his drink. "We should go get some beer," Brent remarked as they slouched
on the sofa watching a half-dozen cars collide and explode. "No one cards
during spring break when the students are gone. We can take your mom's
car."

"You're not driving, not after that industrial strength rum and Coke you
just put away."

It never failed to irk Brent that Todd could drink all he wanted and yet
sound as if he were stone-cold sober. "Screw you. I can drive just fine."

"Take your own car, then."

"And wake up my parents getting it out of the garage? Great idea." But
Brent stayed put, not really wanting to drive for beer or break his fifty when
there were other untouched bottles just a room away.

They were half asleep in front of *Collateral Damage* when the sound of a
door opening roused them. "Quick," Todd hissed, bolting to his feet to hide
the evidence although their cups had been empty for at least an hour.

They heard footsteps in the kitchen a moment before the light went on.
They blinked and looked past the breakfast nook to find Michael setting his
backpack on the counter and frowning at them.

"Oh, it's you," breathed Todd, and dropped onto the sofa.

"You better wash out those cups before Mom wakes up," Michael advised, reaching into the cupboard for a glass. "I smelled rum the minute I
walked through the door."

"We will," said Todd, and Brent remembered that spill near the sink he
had been meaning to clean up.

Michael shook his head and poured himself some milk. "If you make a
habit of this, you'll get caught. They'll know if you water down the booze too
much."

"Thanks for your moral authority," said Brent.

"In case you haven't noticed, we can't go to the bars and we don't have
our own apartment like you," said Todd. "And we aren't doing anything you
didn't do."

Michael finished his milk and put the glass in the dishwasher. "I'm just
trying to help."

Todd, bleary-eyed from the alcohol and lack of sleep, remained stubbornly belligerent. "If you really wanted to help, you'd invite us to one of your parties instead of making us sneak around."

"One, no one's making you do anything. Two, Mom would kill me if I gave you alcohol. Three, we don't party at our house as much as you think."

"Four, you're an idiot," said Brent.

"I didn't come here to argue with a bunch of drunk high schoolers." Michael took some papers or something from his backpack and stuck them on the kitchen counter by Mrs. Sonnenberg's purse. "If you're stupid enough to get wasted with Mom and Dad right upstairs, that's your problem."

He zipped his backpack closed, hefted it onto his back, and stalked away. A moment later, they heard the front door softly open and close.

Todd slumped against the sofa and groaned. "Man, I can't wait until I go to Princeton."

Brent felt a stab of jealousy. He had tried early admission for Princeton and had been rejected, though he was still hopeful for Yale. "Does he move back in at the end of the semester? Because if you have to spend the entire summer under the same roof with that loser—"

"He's staying in his apartment." Todd let out an enormous yawn. "And he's not a loser. He's just trying to look out for us."

Brent scowled. "Yeah, I can tell how glad you were to see him."

In response, Todd yawned again. "I'm gonna get ready for bed."

Brent was too irritated to argue. He stalked off to the bathroom, and by the time he returned, Todd had cleaned up the kitchen, turned off the lights, and unrolled both sleeping bags on the air mattresses. He had left the best pillow for Brent. Mollified, Brent climbed into his sleeping bag and said, "Greg and Will are coming over tomorrow. We thought we'd go see a movie and get some beer. Want to come?"

"Where are you going to drink? The arboretum?"

"Where else is there?"

Todd barked out a scornful laugh. "You know, in a year those two are going to be indistinguishable from all the other losers staggering around Fraternity Row every weekend."

"Yeah? How are you going to be any different?"

"I'm going to leave what passes for fun in high school back in high school. I'm not going to be lurking around in the woods chugging beer." Todd thumped his pillow with a fist and rolled over. "And neither are you, once you get out of Waterford. I can't figure out why you like those guys."

One, Brent thought, glowering in the dark, *they don't always have to prove how much better they are than everybody else. Two, they know how to have fun. Three, they understand the importance of friends who stick together no matter what. Four, their mothers didn't treat my mother like something they scraped off the bottom of their shoes.*

Thoughts churning, he lay on his back with his eyes open, but Todd fell asleep before Brent could think of a retort. With a grunt, Brent crawled out of his sleeping bag and groped his way down the darkened hallway to the bathroom. On his way back, he passed through the breakfast nook and spotted Michael's papers or whatever propped up against Mrs. Sonnenberg's purse. He picked them up and opened the refrigerator door to read them, but it was just the course catalogue from Waterford College with a few passages marked. Brent snorted and stuck the booklet back where he had found it, and as he did, he noticed that Mrs. Sonnenberg had left her purse wide open.

He glanced over at Todd, sound asleep on the family room floor. He reached in for her wallet and leafed through the old photos, choking back laughter at one of the two brothers at about eight and ten years old, their arms over each other's shoulders, beaming with gap-toothed grins. He considered taking money but decided against it, since she was such an airhead she probably wouldn't even notice. But she'd notice missing keys, he thought, lifting the ring carefully to avoid waking Todd. She'd be late for that stupid quilt camp, maybe even get fired. She'd have to walk to that quilt store, too, and maybe get fired there, as well.

Biting his lips together so he wouldn't laugh out loud, Brent stashed the keys in his jacket pocket and climbed into his sleeping bag. A few hours of frustration wouldn't make up for what Mrs. Sonnenberg had done, but it was better than nothing. Too bad he could never tell his mom how he had scored some revenge.

❧

When Brent woke, parched and groggy, the clock on the DVD player read 11:18. He groaned and flopped back against the pillow. He would have tried to fall asleep again if Todd had not sat up and asked if he wanted breakfast. Brent nodded, though he felt too queasy to eat. He padded off to the bathroom and, after splashing some water on his face, he felt a little better.

Mrs. Sonnenberg had left a plate of muffins and a few boxes of cereal on the counter, as if she thought they were too stupid to find the cereal themselves. They fixed themselves some breakfast and carried it back to the family room so they could watch the last of their DVDs while they ate. By that time, Brent had realized to his disappointment that Mrs. Sonnenberg had left in her car, so she must have had a spare set of keys. He hoped he had given her at least a few minutes of frustration, if not the frantic screamfest he had anticipated.

After the movie, they put away their dishes and cleaned up the family room. "Are you sure you don't want to hang with me and Greg and Will today?" asked Brent, giving his friend one last chance.

Todd shook his head. "But call me if you want to do something tomorrow."

Brent didn't bother to try to talk him into it. He packed up the rest of his stuff and left.

He told himself it was Todd's loss, and as it turned out, he was right. The movie was great, and three of the hottest girls in ASB were there—without dates, for a change, so they agreed when Will invited them to The Bistro. They managed to make a plate of nachos and another of mozzarella sticks last two hours, annoying the waitress with frequent requests for the free soft drink refills. When they finally decided to go, it was with enormous pleasure that Brent whipped out his wallet, placed the fifty on the plastic tray with the bill, and announced that he was treating the girls. They squealed with delight and thanked him admiringly in a manner that was more than a little attractive, and Ashley, the prettiest of them with her waist-length blond hair and brown eyes, even hugged him.

They left the restaurant with the girls exclaiming that they'd had a great time and that they should do this again before they all went their separate ways to college. The only disappointment was that the girls turned down their invitation to go drinking in the Waterford College Arboretum, but Brent didn't care because he had managed to get Ashley alone for a minute and she had agreed to be his date for the prom.

He felt invincible as they sneaked back to Will's house and raided his father's well-stocked refrigerator in the garage. Stuffing six-packs beneath their jackets, they hiked along one of the lesser known trails through the arboretum until they came to their favorite drinking establishment, as Will called it, a small clearing where a few fallen trees had created tolerable seats. Night fell before they finished off the last beer, but Brent wasn't worried because his parents knew he and Will were sleeping over at Greg's house, but didn't know that Greg's parents, both sociology professors, were off at some conference in Santa Fe. Brent thought they should have just gone straight to Greg's house with the beer—spring break or not, it was still cold at night—but the arboretum was tradition and Greg worried about his parents finding stray empties.

Hungry and wired, they hiked out of the forest, cracking up as they tripped over roots and fallen branches in the darkness. Main Street was deserted, a rarity for the hour even on a weeknight, with most of the college students long gone and the bars virtually empty.

Will stopped at a legendary dive, the one known for carding even gray-haired alumni and for providing free shot glasses to anyone who could drink twenty-one shots on his twenty-first birthday. He cupped his hands around his eyes and peered inside. "Two, three, four," he counted. "Four customers! They're not making enough to pay for the electricity. Why don't they let us in when the students are gone?"

"Because they don't want to lose their liquor license," drawled Greg, pulling Will away from the window.

They continued down the sidewalk with Will pausing to test every locked door. "All we need is one," he said, yanking on the doorknob of a shoe store. "Locked. And I need some new Nikes."

Brent and Greg guffawed and shoved him along. "Locked," said Greg at a bakery, laughing. "And I need some cookies."

"Locked," said Will. "And I need some—some thread."

Greg laughed so hard he doubled over and nearly fell.

Brent stopped short. "Wait." He dug around in his jacket pocket for Mrs. Sonnenberg's key ring, which he had meant to hide someplace bizarre before he left, like the aquarium or a jar of peanut butter, but he had forgotten. "I think we can get in."

His friends scoffed, and jeered him when the first key didn't work, but their laughter ended when the second turned in the lock. "What are you doing?" demanded Greg, looking frantically over his shoulder.

"Nothing." Brent slipped inside; they followed without prompting. "Let's just look around."

"Don't turn on the lights," hissed Will.

Greg yanked his hand away from the switch as if it burned. "I can't see a thing in here," he complained, stumbling into a display of fabric and knocking it on the floor.

For a long moment they smothered their laughter, shushed each other, and listened with hearts pounding for the police or an alarm. When nothing happened, Brent said, "Be careful, you guys," and shoved over a magazine rack.

Greg laughed and with one sweep of his arm cleared a whole counter of pins and other stuff that went pinging to the floor.

Brent laughed and said, "I hope you have your gloves on."

Greg held up his gloved hands and grinned, but Will said, "Wait. How'd you get that key?"

"Todd Sonnenberg's mom works here."

"Her? Say no more." Will strode over to a bolt of fabric, seized the edge of the cloth in both hands, and flung it so it unrolled in the air. Brent and Greg cheered quietly and grabbed bolts of their own. It became a contest: whose fabric streamer went the highest, the farthest, which cardboard roller knocked over the most stuff when it fell.

Then Greg thought to look for a cash register; they rang up a no sale and cleaned it out without worrying about dividing up the money evenly. "Hey, look at this," exclaimed Will, brandishing a large rotary cutter. "You could do some serious damage with this."

So they each pocketed several and some scissors, since they were on the same rack, then shoved the rack itself until it toppled over.

Brent left the others to ransack the store and wandered into the back office. He gave the ancient computer a shove of disgust and tore the place apart looking for better equipment, but not even the scanner was new enough to be compatible with his system. Annoyed, he flung open file drawers and threw their contents on the floor just for the pleasure of watching the paper fly, but then he spotted a bag with the logo of a bank printed on it, took one look inside, and stuffed it into his shirt. What kind of idiot kept that much cash in an unlocked filing cabinet? Unbelievable.

"Brent, come here," called Greg.

He returned to the main room and found his friends studying something in the dim light. "What?" he asked, picking his way across the littered floor.

"It's a fake ID," gloated Will, "and you'll never guess who's on it."

He held it out of reach and tried to make Brent guess, but Brent wrestled it away from him and gaped at the photo. "Michael Sonnenberg," he read. "Man, this gets better and better."

"Maybe we should think about getting out of here," said Greg uneasily. "The bars are gonna close soon. Someone could walk by."

Brent nodded. "In a minute." He looked around, thinking, until with a sudden flash, he remembered something his mother had said. He stumbled over slippery paperback quilting books on his way to the cutting table, then cleared the shelves until he found the largest carton. One glance inside confirmed it. "Here," he said, shoving the box into Will's arms. "You take this."

"Why? What is it?" Will peered inside. "It's just some pieces of fabric. Why don't you carry it if you want it so bad?"

Brent had already gone to the far wall, where he scanned the shelves of sewing machines for the one with the most gadgets and highest price. "Because I'm carrying this," he said, hefting a carton.

"Are we done shopping yet?" asked Greg, peeved and anxious.

Brent looked around. They were done. "There might be a back door," he said, as the urgency not to be caught sank in.

They found it and raced outside to the back alley, muffling their laughter as they stumbled into a run, slowed by the weight of their prizes.

CHAPTER NINE

Bonnie resumed her duties at Elm Creek Quilt Camp on the Friday after the break-in. Grandma's Attic was nowhere near ready for business and would not be until she could repair the shelving units, but the broken glass and debris had been cleared away and the salvageable inventory culled from the waste. Once she accepted that she would not be able to reopen right away, her conscience would no longer allow her to ignore her camp duties, no matter how many excuses her friends made on her behalf.

On Friday morning she walked from Agnes's house to the shop just to check on things, too anxious to trust in the lock anymore. After making sure there had not been another burglary, she switched off the lights and left the sign in the window turned to CLOSED.

Then she went around back, climbed into the family car, and drove to Elm Creek Manor.

Her friends greeted her with hugs and words of comfort, taking care, as Bonnie had asked, to keep the news of her misfortune away from the campers. Once she reopened, she would not want them to stay away out of fear that the shop was in a dangerous location or that she was peddling damaged goods.

At lunch, her friends showed her the schedule they had arranged so that she would have ample help restoring the quilt shop to order. Bonnie's eyes filled with tears when she saw how many late nights they were willing to endure, at a time of year when their workloads were already daunting enough to weaken the wills of lesser women.

"Do you think Craig could get some of his friends from the physical plant to help?" asked Judy. "It might bend a few department rules, but with more hands and the college's tools, we might be able to finish in time to open next week."

"I don't think Craig's coworkers are necessarily his friends," said Bonnie, nonetheless thanking Judy for the suggestion with a smile. "But I wouldn't ask him anyway."

"Why not?" asked Diane.

Bonnie saw Agnes straighten in her chair, alert and waiting.

"Because Craig and I are getting a divorce."

彩

After the Farewell Breakfast on Saturday, Summer headed straight to Grandma's Attic accompanied by the other Elm Creek Quilters. Only Sylvia and Agnes had remained behind, waiting for the last quilt campers to depart.

All that day they cleaned and repaired and did what they could to raise Bonnie's spirits, but Summer didn't see that they were having much impact. How could they hope to, when Bonnie had lost both her marriage and her life's dream? Channeling her rage into her work, Summer labored in silent fury, repairing shelves, cutting damaged fabric into saleable quantities, and wondering if anyone had thought to question Craig before assuming it was an inside job. The police had questioned Summer thoroughly and with complete skepticism until Jeremy swore she had been with him that night, and she assumed they had given Diane an equally hard time. Had anyone bothered to check Craig's alibi after they grilled Bonnie and her employees? Summer had considered him the most likely suspect even before learning of the impending divorce, which only strengthened her suspicions.

Summer was teaching a Kaleidoscope-Piecing workshop at Elm Creek Manor when the insurance claims adjuster came to inspect Grandma's Attic the following Monday. After classes, Summer hurried to the shop to help with the ongoing repairs and to find out how the meeting had gone.

Not well, Bonnie's expression told her, although she said it went fine. "I won't know anything for certain until I receive his official statement," she said. "Maybe I should have waited until after his visit to clean up."

Summer glanced around the shop; despite all their work, Grandma's Attic was still a disaster. "They have the pictures we took the next morning, and those from last fall for comparison," she said. "They also have the police report."

Bonnie gritted her teeth as she tightened a bolt on a bookshelf. "The police report is part of the problem. If they decide it was an inside job, the agent says there's a clause in my policy that absolves them from the need to pay."

"They can't do that," said Diane, who had been listening in nearby.

"I'm afraid they can. It's my own fault for signing the policy without considering all the consequences. I never thought it would matter." Bonnie sat back on her heels, bleak. "But what choice do I have?"

Diane looked away, white-faced.

"You can tell them about Craig," said Summer, glancing at Diane and hoping she would second her. But Diane said nothing. "Bonnie, I know you don't want to accuse him—"

"He didn't do it."

"How do you know? Does he have an alibi?"

"Yes." Bonnie set down the wrench and met her gaze evenly. "He was in his office on the computer, logged on to the Internet. Campus mainframe records confirm it. The police informed me yesterday."

"But—" Summer's fury vanished like an extinguished flame. "Then who? If they think it was an inside job, that leaves you, me, and Diane."

"And we all have alibis." Bonnie took up the wrench again and moved to another bolt, tightening it furiously.

"What, then?" Summer looked from Bonnie to Diane and back, perplexed. "Do they think our alibis are fake? Do they think we hired someone to trash the place?"

"I don't know what they think," said Bonnie. "But I want you both to understand that whatever the police believe, I know in my heart that you two had nothing to do with it."

Her vehemence surprised Summer. Until that moment, it had never occurred to her that Bonnie might have even fleetingly considered either of her employees to be suspects.

Summer returned home late that evening, as she had every day since the burglary. Jeremy had kept supper waiting for her. It was supposed to have been her night to cook. She had completely forgotten.

She told him the latest developments as they ate. Loyal customers had stopped by to express their condolences as if they were attending a wake; the best of them brought food and positive attitudes to sustain the Elm Creek Quilters while they worked or, better yet, rolled up their sleeves and asked Bonnie how they could assist. Even with the unexpected generosity, it appeared that they would not be able to reopen the shop until mid-April at the earliest. Fortunately, a second look revealed that the burglars had ignored the storage room, so Bonnie would have something to put on the shelves, though not much.

"I still think Craig is involved somehow," Summer said, brooding. "If I could just figure out how."

"I thought Bonnie said he had an alibi."

"She did, but I'm not convinced it's airtight. Maybe he logged on to the Internet before leaving his office, then went back and logged out after trashing Grandma's Attic." She poked at the food on her plate, then set down her fork. She had no appetite but had gone through the motions of the meal for Jeremy's sake. "He's resented Bonnie's success for as long as I can remember. He even seemed to resent her failures, because they at least proved she was willing to take risks he lacked the courage to take."

Jeremy leaned forward and rested his elbows on the table. "You're right to say he lacks courage, so would he really be brave enough to break into the shop just to get some revenge? Wasn't locking her out of their home enough to make that point?"

"You think what he did was an act of courage?"

"That's not what I mean. I was just pointing out that he didn't really need to do it, that he lacks a motive. Whereas this Gregory Krolich guy—"

"Why are you so eager to defend Craig?"

"I'm not," said Jeremy, surprised. "I barely know him. I've only spoken to him once or twice at Elm Creek Quilts functions."

"Bonnie was living out her dream, and Craig couldn't stand it," said Summer vehemently. "It's a typical male response to a woman's success. It's obvious to anyone who doesn't ignore the facts."

Jeremy sat back and studied her. Summer could not meet his gaze. She studied her plate, picked up her fork, and set it down again.

Finally Jeremy asked, "What's this really about?"

"Nothing."

"No, it's something. We should talk about it." His eyes were watchful, his voice steady. "Do you think I don't want you to succeed?"

"I wasn't talking about us."

"I think you were."

"Well . . ." Summer hesitated. "Fine. Let's talk about us. What exactly do you expect to happen when you finish your degree?"

He shrugged. "I'll find a tenure-track assistant position somewhere, and a post-doc if none are available. I've already sent out dozens of CVs. You know that. We've talked about this before."

"We've talked about your job, but not about us." Summer took a deep breath. "I am not trying to drag any kind of commitment out of you—"

"Don't worry," he said, frowning. "I know that would be the last thing on your mind."

"What's that supposed to mean?"

"We both know I'm much more committed to this relationship than you are."

"How can you say that? You're the one who's planning to graduate and leave."

"You've known that from our first date."

"When we were just dating it didn't matter."

"I want you to come with me," he said. "That's the truth, and I say it knowing it will scare you off. When I graduate, I want us to leave Waterford together. I want to get married, if your mother hasn't so poisoned you against men that you're afraid to."

Summer pushed back her chair and rose. "How dare you."

"I'm sorry." He followed her into the living room. "That was unfair. I love you, Summer. I want to be with you. But we both know that won't be in Waterford."

"So you do expect me to sacrifice my career to yours," said Summer. He reached for her, but she pulled away. "You're just like Craig."

A muscle in his jaw flexed, but his voice remained steady. "I am nothing like Craig and you know it. I can't believe you're saying these things."

"What's different? You wouldn't destroy a quilt shop, but you would expect me to abandon my dream to yours."

"Is this your dream?" Jeremy countered. "Or is it Bonnie's dream? Sarah's? You're always saying you want to travel. I've seen the look on your face when you talk about your undergraduate research projects. I've heard you debating theories of historical scholarship with the best students in my department. When I tell you about my research you look—I don't know. Almost envious."

"I'm very happy doing what I'm doing."

"That doesn't mean you want to do it forever."

"I had my chance to go to graduate school. A full ride at Penn. I passed it up for Elm Creek Quilts and Grandma's Attic. I think that shows what my dream is clearly enough."

"Maybe the timing was wrong. Lots of people take time off to work between college and graduate school. You weren't ready then, but maybe you are now."

"Maybe." Then Summer turned and waved him away. "But you're saying I wasted a good portion of my life here. You're just saying this to convince me to leave Waterford."

"I'm not saying that at all, and no one could convince you to do anything you don't want to do." He reached for her again; she stepped back. "You're just afraid to accept what you really want to do because it means admitting your earlier decision might have been motivated by something other than the pursuit of your dream."

"Like what?"

"I don't know. Fear? Uncertainty?"

Summer couldn't bear to hear any more. "I am not afraid to admit my mistakes," she retorted, voice shaking. "And I'll prove it to you."

She stormed off to her room and took down her duffel bag from the top shelf of her closet. She threw it onto her bed and began emptying dresser drawers into it.

"Summer—" Jeremy froze in the doorway. "What are you doing?"

She couldn't look at him. "What does it look like?"

"Summer, don't go." He came to her and put his hands on her shoulders, but she ducked away and continued packing. "This doesn't make any sense. Please don't leave over a stupid argument."

Summer returned to the closet and began taking clothes down from hangers. "What was stupid was moving in here in the first place."

"You don't mean that."

"I do." Summer threw the last of her winter clothes into the bag and zipped it shut. "And don't presume to tell me what my dream is or how to spend my life. Ever."

She tried to avoid his eye as she left, but he blocked the doorway. "Summer." He hesitated, visibly struggling for the right words. "Please don't go."

She could barely breathe as she shoved past him and fled the apartment.

❧

The Callahan family sat at the breakfast table, each engrossed in a section of the newspaper. Mary Beth insisted they eat together every morning, but cajoling them into a conversation had proven impossible.

"Here's something you'll enjoy," said Roger, folding his section in half and sliding it across the table.

"What is it?" asked Mary Beth, dubious. She rarely read more of the news pages than the headlines; the national stories were always so depressing and the world news inscrutable. Sometimes she delved into the local news if someone she knew was mentioned, or read the opinion pages if someone had written in about one of her pet causes, but usually she stuck to the features.

In reply, Roger leaned over and tapped a column at the top of the page. Mary Beth frowned and scanned the weekly police report. "What?" Then she saw it: One week ago, Grandma's Attic had been robbed and vandalized.

Why had she not heard this before? Bonnie was no longer a member of the guild, but this was relevant to the Waterford quilting community, and Mary Beth was the center of the Waterford quilting community. She should have been told.

"I heard it was a real mess," Brent offered.

"Well, this is the first I've heard of it." Mary Beth slid the paper back to her husband. "Why on earth would you assume this would make me happy?"

He feigned innocence. "Bonnie Markham's one of those Elm Creek people, right?"

"Yes, but that doesn't mean I'd celebrate her misfortune." She frowned when her husband and son exchanged a look of surprise. Honestly. What kind of person did they think she was?

"You never shop there," said Brent. "You're always talking about how much you hate them."

"And now they'll be too busy to interfere with your quilt guild," added Roger.

"And that quilt for old Mrs. Compson. Now they won't be able to bother you about that stupid quilt anymore."

There was that. Still, Bonnie was the least offensive of the Elm Creekers, and Mary Beth found it unsettling that the criminals had targeted a quilt shop. Why a quilt shop, when robbers usually focused on convenience stores and gas stations? It was unnatural, a strike at the heartland, at home and family and all that quilting represented.

Brent set aside the sports section and rose. On his way to the kitchen with his cereal bowl and juice glass, he said, "I bet Mrs. Sonnenberg is really upset."

Mary Beth considered. "I imagine you're right," she said, and did not try to keep the satisfaction from her voice.

❧

A week after the claims adjuster's visit, Bonnie received the written report from the insurance company. Due to the suspicious nature of the crime, they were withholding payment until such time as the authorities could determine an outside party was responsible for the alleged burglary.

Immediately Bonnie phoned the agent who had toured the shop, too shocked for tears. "I don't understand," she told him, although she understood all too well. "Do you mean I won't get anything?"

"I'm truly very sorry," he said. "If it makes any difference, I did recommend you for full coverage, but the board is strongly influenced by police reports."

"But the police didn't conclude it was an inside job," she said. "They said it was inconclusive."

"Unfortunately, that's enough to warrant this decision."

"Then why have I been paying all these premiums all these years?" Bonnie heard the shrillness in her words and gulped air. She must stay calm. "Please. I didn't destroy my own shop. If that were true, why would I want to rebuild so badly? Isn't there anything I can do?"

"You can file an appeal."

She held back a sob. "How?"

She took notes as he described the process, but even before she hung up she realized that even if the board reversed its decision, there was no way, no way she would receive the payment in time to save Grandma's Attic.

❧

Gwen was shocked to discover that Summer had moved out of Jeremy's apartment. She was less surprised that her daughter had moved into a suite on the second floor of Elm Creek Manor instead of choosing her old bedroom at home.

"Can we talk about this?" she asked one night after the evening program, when Summer headed for the grand oak staircase in the front foyer instead of the back door to the parking lot.

"There's not much to say." Summer forced a shaky grin. "I thought you'd be happy."

"You don't know much, kiddo," said Gwen, embracing her, "if you don't realize that I'm never happy unless you are."

Bonnie's divorce. Summer's unhappiness, whatever its real cause. Gwen mulled over the events of the past two weeks and decided there had been too much secrecy among the Elm Creek Quilters for far too long.

The next day, she told them about her plans for the new book.

As she should have expected, they praised her idea and exclaimed that someone should have written such a book a long time ago. Summer offered to assist her with her research. Agnes recalled an acquaintance who had also entered the World's Fair quilt competition and who ought still to have the quilt and possibly even some photographs of herself standing beside her entry in the exhibition hall. Each of her friends wanted to help; each assured her that publishers would fight over the right to publish her book and each vowed to buy a copy. When Diane offered to plan her book tour, Gwen laughed and said that academic presses typically did not send their authors around the country, but if Diane wanted to arrange something with the Waterford College bookstore or the independent bookstore downtown, she would have Gwen's blessing.

Her friends' sincere praise rekindled her confidence in the potential of her new project—and gave her the courage to tell Bill about it.

When Gwen asked if Bill was available, his assistant waved her right in, barely looking up from the brochures she was assembling for the Society for the Study of American Culture conference. Usually Martha screened the department chair's unscheduled visitors more carefully, but Bill was a lame duck, and three years' worth of dissatisfaction tended to come out in the last weeks of the term.

Bill was on the phone, so when he gestured to a chair, she sat down and looked at the framed photos on the bookcase, feigning indifference to his conversation, something about next year's hiring budget. Bill's wife and William, Jr. smiled down on her.

Before long Bill hung up. "Gwen," he said. "What can I do for you?"

"I've begun a new research project and wanted to run it by you before I submit a request for travel funds."

"Great." He sat back in his leather chair expectantly. "Let's hear it."

She told him about the quilt contest at the 1933 World's Fair, and how

25,000 quilters—which translated to roughly one of every two thousand American women, given the population at the time—had sought the prize. She explained how a chronicle of the competition would provide an analysis of a folk art, but also fledgling advertising and marketing techniques for a growing industry. She described how a study of the pieces submitted for the exhibition would reveal how "progress" was imagined and defined by a people still recovering from World War I and struggling through the Depression. Her book would capture the mood and values of a nation during one of the most difficult periods of its history.

Bill kept his expression impassive as she spoke. Sometimes his eyebrows rose, occasionally he nodded, but he gave no other sign that he shared her enthusiasm. When she finished, he nodded and mused in silence for a long moment. "Well," he finally said, leaning forward to rest his elbows on his desk. "It sounds like you're on the right track, anyway."

"On the right track?"

"I appreciate how much work you've put into your preliminary exploration, but—"

"But what?"

"Let's face it. This isn't much of a departure from your previous research."

"Ah." She nodded and gave him a tight-lipped smile. "I see."

"Don't get me wrong. It's good that you're focusing on the Depression; you'll find numerous forums for publications, lectures, and so forth. I also see what you're saying about how this contest captured the national mood in a critical era and all that. But couldn't you . . ." He rubbed the back of his neck and looked away before giving her a shrug. "Couldn't you find something else that does that just as well? Something other than quilting?"

"Something like what?" asked Gwen. "Architecture, maybe? Sculpture or painting?"

His face lit up. "Yes. Yes. That's brilliant. I'd go with architecture myself. How did the architecture of the era reflect the values and hopes of the nation? How did the availability of materials or lack thereof determine design? How did the rate of new home building reflect the national economy, and was it comparable to how we use housing starts as an economic indicator today? That would be fascinating research."

"Yes, it would," agreed Gwen. "I'd be interested in reading a paper on that subject. But I would not want to write one."

"What?"

"I've already found the route into the national temper of the Depression I intend to pursue." She stood. "If Depression-era architecture fascinates you so much, then you research it."

"Gwen." He rose quickly and stopped her at the door. "Give it some thought. We're talking about your career here. Do you know what the secretaries around here call you? The Quilt Lady. Is that how you want to be known?"

"Why, Bill," she said. "I had no idea you paid any attention to what your support staff says. I misjudged you."

"You must realize you're sacrificing any remaining chance you had of becoming department chair someday."

"It's a sacrifice I'm willing to make."

She bade him good-bye and shut the door behind her.

She paused for a moment to catch her breath. She had told him, he had balked, as she had suspected he might, but he couldn't stop her from studying what she wanted to study. She had worked too hard to obtain tenure to abandon such a promising idea for the sake of some administrative job she would likely never receive and would probably loathe anyway.

On her way through the outer office, she gave Bill's assistant a cheery smile. "He's all yours," she said.

"Great," said Martha, peering at her over the top of her bifocals. "That makes my day."

Gwen glimpsed a familiar tool in her hand and stopped short. Martha was trimming photographs with a rotary cutter. "You'd better not let Bill see you using that," said Gwen with only a suggestion of the sarcasm Bill had earned. "That's a quilting tool. He might ban it from the campus."

"Is it?" Martha inspected it with interest. "Strange. I don't think he minds it so much. He's the one who gave it to me. And the scissors." She nodded to a gleaming pair of ergonomic shears lying on the desk.

"Really." Gwen picked up the shears and turned them over in her hands. Not a single nick marred the blades. "I thought only quilting shops carried this brand. I suppose Fabric Warehouse might, too."

"Don't ask me. I don't sew. And those aren't leaving my offiice." Martha held out her hand for the shears, and Gwen promptly returned them. "Bill got them from his son. They were left over from some project at the high school. The yearbook committee or some such."

"From William Junior?" That seemed odd. "Since when does a public high school let students walk off with brand-new tools?"

"Don't ask me. I don't have kids."

"Right. Thanks anyway."

"There are worse nicknames than the Quilt Lady," Martha remarked as Gwen left the office. "You should hear what we call Bill."

✖

Bonnie could declare bankruptcy. That option came to her as she sat in the office long after her friends had gone home, pondering her future and struggling not to weep. Until she could reopen, she had no cash with which to pay her bills. Until she could pay her bills, she dared not order new inventory. Until she could order new inventory, she could not afford to reopen. Even if she sold every item on the newly rebuilt shelves, she might not earn enough to pay off her debts after deducting Summer's and Diane's wages from the gross income.

There had to be a way. Bonnie blinked back tears and rested her head on her arms on the desk. She could run the sale herself. The lines would be long—if she were lucky—but maybe the customers would grant her a little extra patience considering the circumstances. She would have to take a week off from camp, at least, which she could not afford to do, but her friends would cover for her without complaint. She could sell the computers, the shelves, the light fixtures, the furniture—students were always looking for cheap items to furnish their campus homes. It would not be easy, but it would be possible.

For a moment she allowed herself a wishful thought: The grand closing sale would be such a resounding success that she would earn enough to pay off her debts, order a truckload of new stock, and reopen better than before. The hope was fleeting. The new rental agreement on the desk beside her provided a sufficient reminder of the new reality she faced.

She had not surrendered yet, but Krolich had won. She wished she could believe him responsible for the burglary, but he had too much at stake to resort to violence, especially since his other tactics were already succeeding.

All she had to do was give the police Michael's name. They would do the rest. Their revised report would exonerate her; the insurance company would meet its obligations. All she had to do was destroy her friend and her friend's son.

She could not. Not even for Grandma's Attic.

He might confess. Michael had made great strides since Sylvia had shown faith in him five years earlier by donating a parcel of land to be developed into a skateboard park. She had led the fund-raising effort and had insisted Michael be allowed to advise the designers. That sense of finally belonging to his community, of having a voice that would be heard, had encouraged him to grow from a sullen and troubled adolescent into a young man with a sense of purpose and responsibility. Why had he thrown it away for revenge and a phony driver's license? Didn't he realize she would figure it out as soon as she discovered the confiscated fake ID was missing?

She sat up and wiped her eyes. Of course he had. He had also known that Bonnie would be incapable of hurting Diane by exposing the truth.

Bonnie decided to go home before Agnes phoned, worried about her whereabouts. She gathered her things and locked the door behind her. She headed for Agnes's house, but after a few blocks, she hesitated and returned to the shop to check the door. It was locked, of course, just as it had been the night of the break-in, as she had known it would be.

The next day at Elm Creek Manor, Bonnie took Summer and Diane aside before their afternoon sessions and shared her plan for one last, great sale. "The shelves will be bare when we're through," she said, forcing a laugh. "In fact, if we're really lucky, there won't be any shelves or even lightbulbs to see them by when we're through. But we might just have enough to pay off the last outstanding debts."

"That's a great idea," said Summer, although she looked as if Bonnie had just announced a funeral.

"We'll help any way we can," said Diane. "You know that."

Bonnie nodded. "I know. That's why—" She took a deep breath. "That's the only reason why I can say this. I'm sorry, but I have to ask you to help me as friends. I can't afford to pay you."

Immediately they assured her that was all right, that they had assumed as much, and that they would have shoved their paychecks back into her hands rather than accept them.

"You might as well," said Bonnie, laughing to keep from crying. "They'd bounce."

Diane and Summer laughed and embraced her. She closed her eyes and clung to them.

❧

Three days later, Diane had emptied the last of the bran cereal into her bowl and was crumpling up the box to fit it into the trash can when it made a strange clinking noise. She opened the box, removed the bag, and discovered her key ring at the bottom.

She held perfectly still for a moment, then withdrew her keys and threw the rest away. She wiped off the lingering film of cereal dust and returned the keys to her purse, lost in thought.

The morning passed as she pondered what to do. Tim was out of town at a conference or she might have consulted him, but she knew what he would say. She had to talk to Michael.

The afternoon crawled by as she waited for Michael to come home to do his laundry. Finally, two hours after she was supposed to be at Elm Creek Manor helping to register the latest group of quilt campers, Michael entered, a gray laundry sack slung over one shoulder.

He seemed surprised to see her. "Hey, Mom. Why aren't you at camp?"

"I needed to speak with you."

"Yeah?" He grinned and dropped his laundry bag in front of the door to the basement. "So you saw the catalogue? Did you have a chance to talk to Dad?"

Bewildered, she just looked at him until she realized he was talking about the course catalogue and the highlighted passage about Judy's class. "Yes, I saw it. Your father and I haven't discussed it yet."

He frowned briefly. "Oh. Okay. Will you try to soon? Because if I'm going to get a new computer anyway, it would be great to have one before finals."

"Michael . . ." She took a shaky breath. "Please. I need you to tell me what you know about the break-in at Grandma's Attic."

He shrugged. "I don't know much. Just what you've told me. Why?"

She could not speak.

He watched her in silence for a long moment. "You think I had something to do with it."

"Michael . . ." She did not want to admit it; she did not want to believe it. "My keys were missing when I looked for them on the morning before the break-in. I just found them today."

His voice was hard. "Then you obviously just misplaced them."

"I found them at the bottom of a cereal box." For the life of her she could not imagine why he had put them there instead of returning them to her purse. Had someone suddenly walked in on him? Had he hoped to make her think she had absentmindedly put them there herself? "That catalogue you mentioned—I know you came home the night the keys were taken because you left that catalogue right by my purse."

"Yeah? Well, I'm not the only person with access to your purse, you know. It's not like you keep it in a bank vault." He grabbed his laundry bag and glowered at her. "I bet you leave your purse lying around open at quilt camp all the time. I know you think all quilters are wonderful people, but you don't know them. Who more than a quilter would want a key to a quilt shop?"

She had actually considered that, but the campers would not have known that she had a key to Grandma's Attic, and even if one had, a burglar with an interest in quilting would have stolen far more and damaged far less.

"I didn't do it," he said flatly. "I can't believe you think I would."

He turned and headed for the door.

"Michael," she called, racing after him and touching his shoulder. "Please. Mrs. Markham will lose everything as long as the police believe it was an inside job."

He jerked away from her. "Yeah? Maybe it was. I don't know and I don't care. All I know is I didn't do it."

He tore open the door and slammed it shut behind him.

Diane reached for the doorknob, hesitated, and released it. She had rarely seen him so angry, but she had too frequently seen him lie with the same persuasive vehemence.

She turned around and leaned against the door.

A sudden movement caught her eye; she glanced up to find Todd standing frozen on the stairs. He had heard everything.

Todd. Michael was not the only one with access to her purse. No, it was incomprehensible.

"Mom," said Todd. "Michael wouldn't do something like that."

Diane could not bring herself to contradict him.

❧

Mary Beth sat at the kitchen table going over the social chair's notes for the end-of-the-year picnic. Less than a third of the members had registered, a fraction of the number who had sent in their deposits by this time last year. At the monthly meeting of the guild the previous evening, the social chair had made another beseeching, bewildered plea for people to get their forms in on time, but attendance had been down sharply, so few of the people who needed to get the message were there to hear it. "I don't understand," Dottie whispered, passing Mary Beth on the way back to her seat. "We've never had so many people miss the deadline before."

Mary Beth gave her what she hoped was an encouraging smile, but she doubted two-thirds of the guild had forgotten the date. They simply weren't coming.

"Mom?"

She looked up, startled from her gloomy reverie. Brent was peeking in the doorway, grinning.

"Yes, honey?" she said. "What is it?"

"I know it's early." He emerged from the doorway carrying a large box. "But I know you could use it, so I thought I'd give you your Mother's Day present now."

He set the box on the table, and Mary Beth gasped.

"A Bernina?" She reached out eagerly, then shot him a wry look. "Or it's something else in a Bernina box."

"Open it and find out."

Disbelieving, she unpacked the box to find that it indeed contained a new sewing machine, the sewing machine of her dreams, one with a computer touch screen and more features and attachments than she knew existed. "Brent," she gasped, running her hands over it. "It's wonderful, it's perfect, it's—" She jerked her hands away as if the beautiful sewing machine had scalded her. "How in the world did you afford this? It must have cost you thousands of dollars."

His grin widened. "It's rude to ask the price of a gift."

"Yes, honey, I know, but in this case—" She gazed at the sewing machine longingly. "Is this from you and your brothers? Did your father pitch in?"

"No, it's just from me, and you're still close to the borderline of that rudeness thing."

All at once, she knew. His college fund. "I can't accept this," she said, reluctant. "You can't spend your college fund on gifts for me."

He laughed. "I didn't." He dug in the box for the user's manual and placed it in her hands. "It didn't cost me as much as you think, so just say thank you and read the manual."

"Thank you." Overwhelmed, she hugged him and kissed him on the forehead. "You are such a dear, sweet boy."

He strode from the room, pleased and proud, as she pushed the social chairwoman's notes aside and pulled the shining new sewing machine closer to her place at the table. Then she let out a shriek of delight, tossed the manual aside, and ran upstairs for fabric and thread.

❧

Two days later, Todd slipped into the desk behind Brent, who turned around and said, "Did you get the answer for the third homework problem? I got 2–i, but that can't be right."

"I have a better question." Todd leaned forward and murmured, "Did you trash the quilt shop by yourself or did Will and Greg help?"

Brent blinked, then assumed a quizzical expression. "What the hell are you talking about?"

"I know you did it, and I know how. What I can't figure out is why. What do you have against Mrs. Markham? Or was it just for the money?"

Brent shook his head, a small, incredulous grin playing on his lips. "What have you been sniffing?"

"My mother isn't stupid. She's going to remember you slept over that night, and she'll figure out you took her keys. And then . . ." Todd sat back and shrugged.

At the front of the room, the Calculus teacher began class. Brent shot Todd a vengeful look over his shoulder as he turned to face front.

For the next fifty minutes, Todd took notes and answered questions and grimly watched his best friend, who did not turn around again.

❧

Judy met Gwen for lunch on a Wednesday, the one day that week when neither woman taught at Elm Creek Quilt Camp. They had only an hour, so Gwen raced through an update on her research project so they could discuss Summer's abrupt break-up with Jeremy and Bonnie's plans for a going-out-of-business sale, although neither dared to call it that. Gwen was so forthcoming with her concerns about work and her daughter that Judy was tempted to confide her own secret, but she had not heard anything from Penn since her interview more than three weeks before, so she decided to keep quiet.

When she returned to the office after lunch, her grad students reported that Rick had phoned.

She called him back and left a message on his voicemail, then hung around the lab impatiently waiting for him to return her call. She left to teach her afternoon Introduction to Programming class and raced back to snatch up the ringing phone just before voicemail would have answered.

Mercifully, he delivered the news without a lengthy preamble. "The job's yours if you still want it."

The official offer had gone out in the afternoon mail, he said, but the terms were just as they had discussed during her interview. Rick promised that the letter contained no surprises and that she would not be disappointed.

"Sign the letter of intent and send it back," he urged. "If you know what's good for you. Get out of that hole in the wall and come where the real action is."

"I'll let you know," she told him.

"What? The job of a lifetime gets dumped in your lap and you can't even give me the courtesy of a straight answer?"

"You can wait a few days. You kept me in suspense for three weeks," she reminded him.

"It was a tough decision! Do you think we interviewed just anyone?"

"I know you didn't. Just consider this as a little payback for all the stress you put me through this semester."

She promised to contact him as soon as she had a chance to review the official offer, and then she called Steve.

"Honey," she said as soon as her husband answered, "we have a decision to make."

☙❧

Mary Beth was so shocked to hear Diane's voice on the line that she almost dropped the phone.

"I know I'm the last person you expected," said Diane, and her laugh was, if anything, nervous.

"That's certainly true." Diane had not called the Callahan home in years. Did she intend to apologize? If so, it was a long time coming—one month to the day after she had crashed the quilt guild meeting. Mary Beth waited, wondering why Diane bothered this time when she had never expressed regret for any of her previous insults throughout the years. Because of the severity of her offense? She had certainly jeopardized Mary Beth's standing in the quilt guild, but Diane ought to find that cause for celebration, not remorse.

Then Mary Beth figured it out. Diane wanted the guild's support for that going-out-of-business sale at Grandma's Attic next week. Mary Beth had seen the signs in the store windows, but she remained steadfast in her vow never to cross that threshold again. In a hundred years Diane could not grovel enough to change Mary Beth's mind about that.

After a long pause, Diane said, "I'll get straight to the point, then."

"I do wish you would."

"Have you heard about the burglary at Grandma's Attic?"

"I read the paper."

"Yes, well, I wondered if Brent might know anything about it."

Icily, Mary Beth asked, "What do you mean?"

"I'm not saying he did it, but he might know who did. You see, my key to the shop disappeared after he spent the night here, and the next night the shop was broken into, and there was no sign of forced entry—"

"How dare you?"

"I'm sorry. I know this is a terrible thing to suggest, but—"

"You're darn right it is. I'll have you know that my son was right here at home that entire night. What about your son?"

"Todd was—"

"Not Todd. Michael. He's the troublemaker in this town. Everyone knows his reputation. I bet this wouldn't be the first time he took your keys."

A pause. "You would be right," said Diane, "but he assures me he had nothing to do with it."

"He assures you." Mary Beth snickered. "Oh, that's rich."

"Please, Mary Beth, talk to Brent."

"I'm hanging up now." And she did just that.

She grabbed the back of a kitchen chair for support. That woman, that horrible, cruel, vicious woman. Mary Beth sat down, head spinning. Diane need look no further than her own delinquent son if she was so eager to find someone to blame. Brent was definitely asleep in his own bed that night, not that it mattered because he absolutely could not have been involved, but he was always home on weeknights. Except—Mary Beth tried to remember. The robbery had occurred during spring break. Brent had spent Monday night at Todd's and Tuesday night at Greg's.

She felt a chill but shook it off. She would phone Greg's parents. They would confirm that Brent had spent the entire night beneath their roof.

No one picked up at home, of course. She looked up the Department of

Sociology in the phone book and obtained both professors' office numbers from the secretary. Greg's mother did not answer, but his father did.

By that time Mary Beth had worked out her story. She said that Brent had been missing his watch since spring break and they wondered if he had left it at Greg's house when he spent the night.

"I'll ask Greg if he's seen it," he responded, "but Brent should probably check with Will."

"Why?"

"That's where the boys spent the night."

"Are you sure?" Mary Beth's heart thumped. "I was sure Brent said your house."

"No, it definitely wasn't, because Marcella and I were out of town at a conference. We have strict rules against overnight guests while we're away."

Mary Beth murmured an apology, thanked him, and hung up. She did not call Will's parents. She knew they would cheerfully assure her that the boys had indeed been at Greg's house under his parents' supervision the entire night.

Brent had lied to her. Well, she should not be surprised. No teenage boy told his mother the truth all the time. But just because he'd lied about his whereabouts so he and his friends could have some unsupervised fun, maybe even a party or something, that did not mean he had broken into the quilt shop. It hurt his alibi, but nothing suggested he had anything to do with the crime.

Except for the sewing machine, the early Mother's Day present he could not possibly have afforded no matter what he claimed, no matter how much she wanted to believe otherwise.

The realization sank in like a cold stone into a pond. When she could, she rose and climbed the stairs and knocked on her son's door. He was at his desk studying, stacks of books piled around him.

He smiled so affectionately at her that she faltered, but she forced herself to do what she had come to do. "Honey," she said. "I think there's a problem with the sewing machine. I may—I may need to exchange it at the store. Would you mind giving me the receipt?"

His expression did not change. "I think I threw it away."

"Well, do you have the credit card statement? I know you couldn't have paid cash. The store might be willing to accept an exchange with that."

He shook his head. "I did pay cash."

"Oh." Mary Beth looked away, her palm slick with perspiration on the doorknob. "Well, how? If you didn't take the money out of your college account, where—"

"It's not new," he blurted.

"What?"

"It's not new. I bought it at a garage sale. I passed it on my way back from the library and saw some quilting stuff, you know, stacks of fabric and stuff, and then I saw the sewing machine still in the box. They were only asking fifty bucks for it."

"Fifty?"

"I know. I couldn't believe it either. The lady in charge said it was her mother-in-law's. She got it for her birthday but died before she ever had a chance to use it. That's why her kids were having the garage sale, to get rid of a lot of her stuff."

"I thought I knew all the quilters in Waterford," said Mary Beth. "I didn't hear of anyone passing away."

"She wasn't from around here. Just her kids. She lived in a retirement home in Pittsburgh or something." Brent rose, stricken. "I'm sorry, Mom. I know I should have told you the whole truth, but you were so happy. I wanted you to think I had given you something really great."

She touched his shoulder. "You did. It's wonderful."

"Yeah, except it's broken, and now you can't return it."

"I think maybe I can fix it." Mary Beth forced a smile. "I'll check the manual again. You go ahead and get back to your studying. I'm sorry I interrupted."

He hugged her. "I'm sorry I didn't tell you the whole story right away."

"That's all right," she said, patting his back and holding back tears.

❧

The signs in the window called it a Spring Spectacular Sale, but Summer knew better, and she suspected most of their customers would figure it out when they saw the half-empty shelves and the funereal expressions on Bonnie and her volunteer employees. Bonnie tried to raise their spirits with generous estimates of how much money they might earn over the five days of the sale, but Summer did not need Sarah's accounting degree to know that even if the shelves were bare by Friday afternoon, they would not have earned enough to pay all the bills.

Fifteen minutes before opening on Monday morning, Summer and Diane sat in the back office as Bonnie made coffee and reminded them about a few last-minute price adjustments. "Make sure to tell everyone there will be no refunds," she advised as she filled three mugs with the Daily Grind's house blend.

"What if they ask why?" asked Diane.

Bonnie shrugged and handed around the coffee. "Tell them it's the only way I can afford these low, low prices. Well, here goes." She raised her mug. "Cheers."

"To Grandma's Attic," said Summer.

Diane and Bonnie echoed her, and they clinked their mugs together. They drank, then filed out of the office clutching their coffee mugs as if for warmth.

Through the front window they saw a handful of women already waiting, shopping bags in their arms.

"Summer, would you let them in, please?" asked Bonnie, absently smoothing her red apron.

Summer nodded and hurried to the front door. She welcomed the five waiting women as they entered, but her smile failed her when they halted and eyed the scanty shelves with surprise.

"I know it looks bare," said Summer, "but there are some real bargains here."

"It's a good thing we came early," remarked one of the women. "You're sure to sell out soon."

"Mary Beth wasn't kidding," added the second woman, hefting her shopping bag, which bulged as if it were already full. "You definitely need this stuff. Where would you like it?"

"Mary Beth?" echoed Summer warily. "What stuff?"

"Donations for the sale," said the first woman. The others nodded and indicated their bags. "What, didn't you know? Mary Beth sent out a letter to everyone in the guild asking us to raid our stashes for fabric and notions for Bonnie to sell."

Bonnie gasped.

"Oh, and blocks for Sylvia's bridal quilt, too." Another woman beamed at Diane and withdrew a plastic sandwich bag from her tote. Summer caught a glimpse of colorful patchwork. "I was surprised she urged us to make them, given her reaction to your announcement at the guild, but she did."

"Her what?" exclaimed Bonnie and Summer in unison, looking to Diane in astonishment. Diane shrugged.

The first woman carried her bag to the cutting table. "May I leave this here while I shop?"

"Of course," said Bonnie, hurrying to assist. The other women followed, and soon a pile of fabric, notions, and pattern books covered a good portion of the table. Bonnie, looking somewhat shocked, waved Summer and Diane over. "Sort all this out, would you?" she murmured, watching the women as they browsed the scanty shelves.

Speechless, Summer nodded. She and Diane quickly got to work while Bonnie attended to the customers. It was obvious that the women had not used this occasion to get rid of their scraps and discards. The minimum fabric cut Summer came across was a fat quarter, the fabric selections included only the same fine-quality cloth Bonnie herself sold, and the pattern books still had their templates.

Summer looked up as the bell over the front door jingled and two more shoppers entered carrying bulging totes. Three more women followed close behind. "Mary Beth is responsible for this?" asked Summer, thrilled but disbelieving.

Diane snorted. "Seems like a guilty conscience at work to me."

Summer shot her a questioning look, but Diane said nothing more, so Summer let it go. Diane would never believe any good could come from her longtime nemesis.

The bell over the door jingled again, and Summer felt a spark of hope kindle. With the donations, and with the support of the guild, they might be able to pull it off.

She longed to tell Jeremy.

❧

Gwen suppressed her guilt as she raced through the last batch of papers, telling herself that at least she was reading and scoring them herself instead of dumping the job on one of her grad students. Between her day job, quilt camp, and volunteering at the whirlwind Grandma's Attic had become, she was stretched to her limit.

A knock sounded on her door. "Not now," she called, glancing at the clock in annoyance. It was time for Jules's weekly conference about his dissertation, but she had warned him to stay away.

"Dr. Sullivan?"

The voice was familiar; she halted in the middle of scrawling a pithy remark about a student's disjointed syllogism and said, "Jeremy?"

"May I speak with you, please?"

She hesitated only a moment before telling him to come in. He entered,
unshaven and grim, and took the chair she offered. "Unless you're still looking for the required nondepartmental advisor for your dissertation committee, I assume you want to talk about Summer," she said gently. "I should
warn you I'm biased beyond redemption in her favor on every conceivable
topic."

"I'd talk to Summer instead, but she won't speak to me."

Me either, Gwen thought, but asked, "Did you have a fight?"

"Yes. Maybe. It's hard to say." He ran a hand through his dark, unruly
curls. "We were discussing the break-in when she started tearing into
Craig—who deserved every word of it—but then she accused me of being
just like him. She said I want to interfere with her career success just as
Craig does Bonnie's."

Gwen felt a pang. Jeremy was nothing like Craig, and Summer knew it. "I
imagine you didn't take that well."

"That's a safe assumption. I defended myself, which was a mistake. When
I tried to find out what was really bothering her, she ran to her room and
starting throwing clothes into a duffel bag." His frown deepened. "That's the
short version."

Edited, no doubt, for Gwen's ears. "What would you have me do?"

"I'm not asking you to be my advocate. I don't expect you to plead my
case. But if you could just get her to talk to me, I would be very grateful. Tell
her that I would never ask her to leave Waterford. Tell her that I would
never expect her to sacrifice everything she's built with Elm Creek Quilts."

"But Jeremy," Gwen said, "you know very well that one day you're going
to leave Waterford."

"Not necessarily."

Gwen frowned and shook her head. "We both know how the system
works. If you want a tenure-track position, you have to look elsewhere."

"Then I won't get a tenure-track position. I can still research and write no
matter where I live, no matter what my day job is."

"Jeremy—"

"I mean it. This is not the desperate plea of a lovesick kid. We both know there's no one else like Summer in the world, and for some reason she loves me. I am not going to throw that away."

"It's just as unfair for her to ask you to sacrifice your career as it is for you to ask it of her."

"Sometimes life isn't about what's fair. Sometimes it's about what's right. There are an infinite number of jobs in the world, but only one Summer. I'm not going to lose her."

Gwen studied him. She could wait a lifetime and never hear anyone make such an expression of love and commitment to her daughter. Summer at least ought to know that.

"All right," she said. "I'll talk to her."

❧

Judy looked up from her computer at a knock on her office door. "Do you have time for lunch?" asked Gwen, oddly subdued.

Judy quickly switched on her screen saver to conceal her letter of resignation. She was just toying with it; it wasn't as if she had made up her mind. For every advantage to accepting the job she found an equally compelling reason to remain where she was. "I'm afraid not," she said, but Gwen seemed so morose that she added, "I have to finish up some work before heading over to Grandma's Attic, and then I'm teaching at Elm Creek Manor until evening. But I have time for a chat."

Gwen took her usual chair, unzipped the quilted batik jacket she had completed in one of Bonnie's workshops, and frowned at the floor. Suddenly she looked up and said, "Do you think I've held Summer back?"

"Held her back? What do you mean?"

"Do you think I've frightened her away from life? From leaving Waterford, from having an enduring relationship with a man, from, well, everything?"

Carefully, Judy said, "I think Summer has accomplished quite a lot considering she's still in her twenties. And it's not unusual for a child of divorce to be wary of commitment."

"I know that." Gwen shifted in her seat, and for a moment she seemed close to tears. "But sometimes I look at her and I see someone just going through the motions, someone who's finished what she set out to do and is now just marking time."

"She seems as enthusiastic about Elm Creek Quilts as ever."

"I'm not so sure. She puts her whole heart into her work because that's her nature. She never does anything indifferently. But sometimes I think her enthusiasm is largely manufactured because she doesn't want to feel like she's letting the rest of us down." Gwen hesitated and said, "Did I ever tell you I persuaded her to go to Waterford College instead of Stanford?"

Speechless, Judy shook her head.

"I did, and you're the only one who knows it but me. And maybe Summer, but I'm not sure. I manipulated her so carefully that even now she might not realize that the decision was more mine than hers." Gwen inhaled deeply. "I felt so horrible afterward, even as I rejoiced in knowing I would have her another four years, that I swore I would make it up to her for graduate school. Then when the time came, she turned down a full ride to Penn."

"That was her choice," said Judy. "She wanted to stay at Elm Creek Quilts and Grandma's Attic."

"But I'll never know if she made that decision because it's what she truly wanted or because I had finally convinced her that she couldn't survive anywhere but here."

Judy shook her head. "Summer seems too confident for those sorts of doubts."

"Maybe." Gwen did not look as if she believed it. "I'd like to think so. But even if remaining in Waterford was the best place for her at the time, that doesn't mean it still is. What troubles me most is that she seems afraid to find out."

"It's never easy to leave the people and places you love," said Judy softly. "Even to pursue a dream. Change can be frightening. Severing ties with friends and family can be worse."

"Summer would never sever her ties with me or with anyone at Elm Creek Manor," said Gwen. "They would stretch, but they would never break, no matter how far away she goes."

"That doesn't make it any easier. What if she takes a risk and realizes it was a terrible mistake? A place that seems so perfect from a distance might be filled with dangers she missed at first glance. She might find that she's not as capable as she thought, and fail utterly at the job she's longed for."

Gwen barked out a laugh. "I can't imagine Summer failing utterly at anything. She would find a way to succeed even if it didn't come as easily as she had anticipated. All the Elm Creek Quilters are like that. We couldn't have built Elm Creek Quilts otherwise."

"But we had one another."

"Summer will have us in her heart and mind wherever she goes. Besides, if she leaves Waterford, I doubt she'll be going alone." Gwen rose and zipped up her jacket, her familiar grin restored. "And if it doesn't work out, if she does fail utterly, she can always come home. She'll always be an Elm Creek Quilter."

"You're right." Judy returned her smile, tears in her eyes. "It's a lifetime position. We can't quit, or retire, or be disbarred. And thank goodness for that."

"Don't get all misty yet. We're talking about my kid, not yours. You won't have to go through this for years."

Judy laughed. "You never know."

"I don't even know what Summer's going to do," admitted Gwen, "but I want her to follow her heart, even if it leads her away from me. Telling her so will be the least selfish thing I've ever done. I hope I can withstand it."

Judy hugged her and wished her luck, and then Gwen left. Alone again, she sat down at the computer and thought.

Then she touched fingers to keyboard and finished the letter.

❧

Hours after her mother left, Summer sat looking out the window of her guest suite at the moonlit lawn of Elm Creek Manor. She did not like to think of herself as afraid, just as she did not like to accept that her mother had persuaded her to stay in Waterford out of her own fear of loneliness. But as much as she might like to, she could not ignore the plain and heartfelt truth of her mother's words.

There was so much Summer longed to accomplish, so much of the world she longed to see. She still loved Elm Creek Quilts and was proud of all she had done there, but she felt as if she had finished the task she had set out for herself and was impatient to move on to the next.

She touched her forehead to the glass pane and smiled ruefully. She loved quilting, she enjoyed teaching, and she had relished the challenge of nurturing a business from a dream into reality. Why did she feel something was missing? Why did she keep wondering what was next and feeling disappointed at the thought of a settled, pleasant routine? Sure, as long as she stayed at Elm Creek Manor it would be more of the same, but wasn't that a good thing?

Wasn't she crazy to think of giving this up for something that might not be as good as what she already had? Even if that meant—or especially if that meant—leaving Waterford with Jeremy?

Summer sighed and left the window. She pulled a hooded sweatshirt and pair of sweats over the long T-shirt she usually slept in and padded down the hallway in her stocking feet. Muffled laughter came from behind closed doors as campers gathered with their new friends to share quilting secrets and confidences. A light shone from the crack beneath the library door; inside Sarah was working on the computer, as Summer had expected. They were all keeping late hours to compensate for their shifts at Grandma's Attic.

Sarah looked up and smiled sympathetically. "Couldn't sleep?"

"No." Summer curled up on one of the sofas in the center of the room in front of Sarah's desk.

"Worried about the sale?"

"Not really. We saw more customers today and yesterday than in the last two months combined, and our inventory is fine. The donations from the quilt guild members have filled half the shelves and they're still coming in."

"So are the quilt blocks, I hear."

Summer nodded. In a few months, if the Elm Creek Quilters made several blocks each, they might even be able to make Sylvia and Andrew a nice lap quilt. The loss of the quilt blocks and their stories from Sylvia's friends and admirers worldwide, though, could not be remedied. No one yet had thought of how to tell the contributors about the theft. It was an unpleasant task they were all willing to postpone. Eventually it would probably fall to Sarah, who was typically the one among them most willing to plunge ahead with necessary work they would rather avoid. Summer wished she possessed a fraction of Sarah's determination.

"Sarah," she asked, "how did you decide to leave your job in State College to follow Matt to Waterford?"

"It wasn't that difficult. I wasn't terribly enamored of my old job."

"You thought enough of it to keep it. You weren't looking for a new job in State College."

"That's true," admitted Sarah. "Well, Matt had been out of work for months and was growing more depressed every day. How could I say no when he finally found something?"

"Because it meant giving up your career without knowing if you'd find anything in Waterford. That's a fairly big chance to take for someone else."

"It wasn't just for him. It was for me, too. I wouldn't have felt happier if I had chosen the certainty of my old job over what Matt needed. Safer, yes, but not happier." Sarah shrugged. "It's just something you do when you're married."

"You mean it's something women do for their husbands when they're married."

"No, not in our case. He would have done the same for me."

"Are you sure?"

Sarah considered. "Yes. I am. That probably made my choice easier. I won't pretend I didn't have misgivings occasionally. There were times I was sure I had made the worst mistake of my life moving to Waterford. I'm sure Matt felt the same way when we first moved into Elm Creek Manor and tried to launch the quilt camp."

Summer thought back on some of the couple's all-too-obvious arguments during the early years of Elm Creek Quilts and had to agree.

"It was a risk giving up security for the unknown," said Sarah, spreading both arms to indicate the entire manor and everything the Elm Creek Quilters had established there. "But if I hadn't taken that risk, I never would have found my dream. I never would have known how much more I was capable of doing with my life."

"You took a leap of faith right off a cliff," said Summer.

"But I eventually landed on my feet." Sarah smiled. "And you will, too."

❧

On Friday evening, Bonnie waited two hours past the usual closing time for the last customer to leave before locking the door and turning the sign in the window to CLOSED. Judy and Diane, the last volunteer shift of the last day of the sale, had already begun cleaning up, although the store was so bare there was little to do except sweep the floor and carry empty boxes outside to the recycling bins.

Judy and Diane wanted to stay and celebrate the success of the sale. Indeed, thanks to the windfall of donations from the Waterford Quilting Guild, Bonnie estimated that they had earned at least twice the amount of her most optimistic projections—and that was without selling the lightbulbs and bookcases. Until she completed her final calculations, though, she would not know if a celebration was in order.

She sent Judy and Diane home and, from their disappointed expressions, she knew they had hoped to stay and wait for the results of her accounting. She understood, but she guided them to the door and told them she would let them know at the Farewell Breakfast the next morning.

Then she filled her mug with the last of the coffee and set herself to work.

It took hours, but eventually she tallied the entire income from the sale and deducted all her outstanding expenses. She double-checked her calculations to be sure she had arrived at the correct figure.

She was tempted to check them a third time, but it was nearly midnight and her eyes were tearing from lack of sleep and too much time at the computer. Besides, the first two totals matched.

There was no mistaking it: After paying off her last creditor, she would have exactly $56.48 left. She would not have to declare bankruptcy.

But she would have to close Grandma's Attic.

Agnes was the first to know, and Bonnie didn't even have to tell her. All she did was walk in the front door and Agnes understood. Agnes hugged her and offered her a cup of tea, but Bonnie reminded her of their early appointment at Elm Creek Manor the next morning and went off to bed.

She told the others in passing as she saw them at the Farewell Breakfast the next day. Some, like Judy, seemed heartbroken; others, like Sarah, were angry. All asked if she was absolutely sure, if the last option had been exhausted, if there was not some chance, however small, that she could keep the shop open. Her reply was always the same: Unless some miracle struck within the next few hours, Grandma's Attic would not reopen for business.

No miracle came, and it was not until she left Elm Creek Manor in her reclaimed car that she remembered she could still turn in Michael to the police and collect the insurance money. Grandma's Attic would remain closed while she waited for their check to clear, and she would still need to find a way to cover that exorbitant rent, but eventually she would be back in business.

If she could bring herself to do it.

Instead she drove downtown to the University Realty office building. She went inside and asked to speak to Gregory Krolich. Upon learning he was in a meeting, she left a message: Bonnie Markham will not be renewing her lease. She was halfway down the front stairs when Krolich bounded after her and invited her back inside for coffee and a doughnut while they took care of the paperwork.

The transaction was less painful than she had anticipated. Indeed, she felt numb; she realized that the pain would hit her later, preferably when she was back at Agnes's house, where she could cry and rant and rave, and dear Agnes would sympathize and allow her to drown her sorrows in infinite cups of tea.

Next she drove to her old building—already it seemed a part of her past—and parked in what had once been her usual spot. Craig answered the buzzer so quickly that he must have heard her pull up.

The door buzzed and unlocked; he met her at the top of the stairs, blocking the doorway to the home they had once shared. "So, you brought the car back?" he said, eyeing her warily.

She shook her head. "Not until the lawyers say I have to."

Craig scowled. "What do you want, then? If you're here to divide up the rest of our stuff—"

"I'm here to sign the papers."

At first he just gaped at her. Then a light of immense satisfaction arose in his eyes. "Wait here and I'll get them."

He ducked back inside, and she followed. While he hurried off to the guest room, fairly dancing with glee, she went to the kitchen and rapidly sorted through the stacks of mail. Into her tote bag went a magazine, her alumni newsletter, and two letters from the kids, sent before she had called to explain the situation and give them her temporary address. Listening for Craig, she hurried back to the living room and took several framed photos from the bookshelves. In his triumph, Craig was as unlikely to notice the new bulges in her tote as he was the bare spaces on the shelves.

"Here." Craig returned with a fistful of papers and a pen. He placed them on the coffee table and beamed a triumphant grin at her. "Sign on the dotted line."

Bonnie hesitated. His arrogance was too much to bear, so infuriating and intolerable that she was tempted to walk out. She would still sign—eventually she would have to—but she could drag it out, make him tear his hair out wondering what she intended to do. His grin faltered as she watched him, and she realized she had no desire to put up a fight for something she knew she had already lost, something she no longer wanted anyway.

It was time to move on.

She took the pen and read the agreement slowly, more to make Craig fret than to look for the details her lawyer had warned her about. Then she signed the agreement to sell the condo to University Realty.

Craig snatched the papers away as soon as she added the date. "Nice doing business with you," he said with an insufferable smirk. "If you'd signed this months ago, we could have had the cash right away. Now the lawyers will wrangle over it and take their cut."

"You're lucky I signed it at all, and we both know if I'd signed it earlier I'd never see my half. We also both know we're not as broke as you claim."

He spread his palms and feigned innocence. "You're the one holding going-out-of-business sales. If you can find some cash I've overlooked, naturally I'll split it with you."

Bonnie turned and went to the door without wasting another word on him.

He followed and called to her as she descended the stairs: "By the way, I told the kids you left me. They're furious with you."

She almost laughed. "Whatever you say, Craig."

She waved at him over her shoulder and left.

❧

Two days later, Agnes strode across the Waterford College campus, so determined that towering undergraduates a third of her age jumped out of the way at her approach. Her outrage had not lessened one iota since Bonnie had told her she had signed off on the sale of her home, and Agnes was about to unleash her temper on that despicable man if she had to kick down his office door to do it.

Bonnie had told her not to bother. She was at peace with her decision, and nothing Agnes could say to Craig would change the situation. Maybe not, but Agnes was still determined to show Craig he had made a grave error in judgment when he chose this particular path to divorce. If he thought leaving Bonnie virtually penniless and homeless would make her cower, he was dead wrong. Bonnie was not going to buckle to a bully, not with staunch friends to support her and see her through to the end.

She stormed into the director's office and almost crashed into the same blond assistant she had encountered before. "I'm here to see Craig," she muttered, and tried to duck past her.

"Wait." The woman cut her off. "Do you have an appointment?"

Agnes glowered and nudged her aside; the woman was too startled or too wary about manhandling a senior citizen to interfere. Just before she reached the door, she heard the sharp click of the lock. "Craig Markham," she called out, turning the doorknob in vain. "Get out here and face me like a man, you coward!"

"He's not in," said the blond assistant, alarmed.

"Yes, he is. I see him through the window. Craig!" She rattled the doorknob again. "Don't think you can get away with driving Bonnie from her home. I happen to know she has an excellent lawyer. You'll get what's coming to you!"

"Please, ma'am." The woman moved as if to wrestle Agnes away from the office, but was still reluctant to lay hands on her. "Don't make me call security."

"You go right ahead," said Agnes primly. She had embarrassed Craig and delivered her message. She actually felt much better. "I'll tell anyone who cares to listen the truth about that man."

She turned, and her gaze fell once again upon that distinctive furniture, that unusual combination of Shaker and Arts and Crafts, too worn and mismatched to really suit a professional office. With a frown, she dodged the assistant, set her feet, and gave one of the armchairs a fierce shove.

"Now, really," complained the assistant as the chair toppled over onto its side. Agnes ignored her and got down on hands and knees to examine the bottom of the seat. In addition to a spiderweb and a bright pink piece of chewed gum, she discovered a manufacturer's mark burned into the wood: an intertwined W, K, and M encircled by a wreath of ivy.

Just then the assistant seized her elbow and heaved her to her feet. "Thank you, dear," said Agnes brightly. "I'll show myself out."

She left the office with all haste.

❧

"I don't care how," hissed Brent, glancing around. No one could overhear him in the din of the cafeteria, but if his former best friend happened to spot him speaking so urgently to Will and Greg, he would figure out what Brent planned and turn him in before he could act. Brent had no idea why Todd had said nothing so far. It obviously wasn't to save their friendship, which was so far gone it had flatlined.

Will and Greg exchanged a look. "Get rid of everything?" said Greg.

"You heard me. And soon."

"But—" Will gaped at him, stricken. "I gave some scissors and one of those circle cutter things to my dad."

"You moron," Brent seethed. "Get them back. I don't care how. Get them back and then lose them permanently."

He shoved back his chair and stalked away from the table.

Brent didn't bother to stop at his locker before leaving campus. He had just enough time to drive home and take care of the sewing machine before his fifth-period class. His mom had some appointment, a haircut or something, but she would be home after school. He might not get another chance.

He parked in the driveway and ran inside to his mom's sewing room, where he shoved some fabric pieces out of the way, unplugged the sewing machine, and put it on its side. There was no time for elegance. He opened the case and pulled a few wires, then raced to the bathroom for a cup of water, which he poured over the electronic components and the touchscreen. He dried his hands carefully before closing the case and plugging in the cord. There were no sparks, no smoke, when he turned it on, just a blank touchscreen and a sluggish whirring sound when he pressed the foot pedal.

Quickly Brent returned the sewing machine to its place, wiped up the spilled water, and raced back to his car. He had to run a few stop signs and sprint from the parking lot to make it to class, but he slipped into his usual desk a few seconds before the bell. He caught his breath and ignored his ex–best friend's curious stares.

Later that afternoon, he returned from school to find his mother seated in front of the sewing machine, her hands in her lap. She jumped when he greeted her from the doorway. "Hi, sweetheart," she said, her face oddly drawn. "Did you have a good day?"

"Uh-huh." He entered the room and pointed at the machine. "What's wrong? Is it busted again?"

"It appears so." She touched the sewing machine gingerly. "I don't understand. It was working fine this morning."

Brent let out a loud sigh of exasperation. "I knew that deal was too good to be true. I never should have believed that story about some sweet old dead granny who never touched her Christmas present."

"Yes," said his mother. "It does seem rather implausible."

"I'll tell you what." Brent yanked the plug out of the wall and picked up the sewing machine. "I'm going to get my money back. I'll buy you something else for Mother's Day. It won't be as nice as this, but at least it will work."

"I'm sure whatever you give me will be fine."

Brent studied her. "Mom? Is something wrong?"

"No. Of course not, honey. It's just . . ." She looked around her sewing table. "This morning I had some quilt block pieces right here by the sewing machine, but now they're gone."

"Oh." Brent thought hard. He had brushed some fabric out of the way— where? "Here," he said, indicating under her table with a foot. "There's some fabric back there. It must have slipped between the table and the wall."

His mother kneeled down to check, then reached out to gather up the scraps. "Yes. This is what I lost."

Her voice seemed strained. He wished he didn't have to take her sewing machine, but what choice did he have? "I'm really sorry, Mom."

"That's all right." She hesitated. "Brent?"

"What, Mom?"

She sat on the floor looking up at him. "Nothing. Never mind. Don't be gone too long."

"I'll be back before supper," he promised, hurrying out the door, the sewing machine in his arms.

❧

On the last day of March, Gwen turned off her computer, packed her satchel with a heavy heart, and left her office. She had an hour before her first class at Elm Creek Manor. Maybe she would get a cup of coffee and sit at the bus stop across the street from Grandma's Attic and stare at the red-and-gold sign for a while. All too soon some other sign would hang in its place. Bonnie had already promised to save the sign and display it in Elm Creek Manor. No one who saw it, camper or teacher, would ever forget Grandma's Attic.

Just the day before, Gwen had paused on her way home from work to gaze wistfully at the little shop, once such an important gathering place for Waterford's quilters. A woman leaving the shoe store next door saw her and said, "Did you hear it's closing? If I had known they were doing so poorly, I would have shopped there more often instead of driving all the way to the Fabric Warehouse."

Gwen tried unsuccessfully to suppress her anger. "You shouldn't be surprised when the things you fail to support are no longer there when you want them."

She turned and left the woman gaping at her.

Gwen couldn't help her outrage, her disgust. Granted, it was wonderful that Waterford's quilters had rallied to Bonnie's cause at the end, but where had they been in all the months and years before, when the shop balanced on the edge of bankruptcy? Greater support then might have made the difference.

Gwen still couldn't imagine a Main Street without Grandma's Attic.

She sighed and locked the office door behind her, then started as a young man in a Waterford High School varsity jacket hurried by, nearly crashing into her. "Scuse me," he mumbled.

"William?"

The young man halted. "Oh. Hi, Professor."

It was obvious he didn't remember her, but a department chair's son was savvy enough to recognize an occasion warranting good manners. "I haven't seen you since the department picnic last summer," said Gwen. "Are you looking forward to graduation?"

He glanced down the hall toward his father's office. "Um, yeah."

"I can see you're in a hurry, so I won't keep you." She held up a hand as he nodded and prepared to hurry off. "Just one question. Where did you get the shears and the rotary cutter you gave your dad?"

His eyes widened. "Uh, at the store."

"Oh. That's funny, because I heard you got them from school. Which store would that be, then? I'd like to get some myself, but the quilt shop downtown is closing and they don't sell them at Fabric Warehouse. I checked."

"I meant to say I got them at school." Will began to edge away. "*They* got them from a store."

Gwen fixed him with a fierce grin. "Yes, but which one? That's the real mystery, isn't it?"

"I don't know." He backed away. "I'll check and let you know."

He turned and broke into a run.

"Thanks," Gwen called after him. She watched as he disappeared into the department office.

"Professor Sullivan?" someone called out from behind her.

"Yes?" She turned to find one of the custodial staff approaching, a large cardboard carton in her arms.

"I'm so glad I caught you," the dark-haired woman said. "One of our crew just found this a few minutes ago in the boiler room. It was with the trash to be burned, but when some of the stuff fell out, we thought we ought to wait. And since everyone in the building calls you the Quilt Lady . . ." She grinned, and set the carton on the floor. "Well, we thought you could tell us if this is valuable or not."

"What's in the box?"

In reply, the woman opened the lid.

Inside were the missing blocks for Sylvia's bridal quilt.

CHAPTER TEN

Sylvia

S ylvia sat on the cornerstone patio sipping tea and enjoying the fragrance of lilacs blooming all around her. She looked up from her book to smile fondly at Andrew, who sat beside her tying flies. It was Sunday morning on the first week of Waterford College's summer break, and since the Elm Creek Quilt Camp faculty would be at full strength for the first time all season, that afternoon Sylvia and Andrew planned to embark on an overdue trip to visit Andrew's daughter and son-in-law in Connecticut.

Sylvia was grateful Andrew's children had come much closer to accepting the marriage they had once opposed strongly enough to avoid the wedding. Frequent visits, letters, and phone calls had given Sylvia occasion to show them how much she loved their father, and over the past few months, Amy and Bob seemed to have reconciled themselves to their father's choices. In fact, they had finally realized how fortunate their father was to have found a loving companion. Amy had even confided to Sylvia that she worried less about how her father spent his days so far from his children and grandchildren knowing that Sylvia was there to keep him company.

Andrew looked up and smiled; she reached over and patted his arm. What a comfort he had been throughout the turmoil of the past few months. Sylvia had tried to be that sort of reassuring confidante to her friends, but she wondered how helpful she had truly been. When she had challenged Summer to ask herself why she had not told her friends about her new domestic arrangement, she never imagined Summer would end up moving into Elm Creek Manor. Although she had helped Gwen find a new research topic, Gwen's status in her department and the chair's appreciation of her work seemed unchanged. Her suggestion that Diane tell Bonnie how she felt about her position at Grandma's Attic was moot now that the quilt shop was no more. Sylvia's only consolation was that her meddling had not made matters worse.

Of course, the proposal she intended to make to Bonnie might yet do some good.

"Have you seen Sarah yet this morning?" Sylvia asked Andrew. "I meant to discuss a business idea with her at breakfast, but she didn't come down."

"I saw Matt carrying a tray upstairs to their room."

"Again? That's the third morning in a row."

Andrew grinned. "I guess he's trying to be romantic."

"I suppose." Sylvia pondered this and shrugged. "Well, more power to him. I for one prefer to eat at the table. I don't want to tea-dye my quilts unintentionally."

Andrew chuckled, and both looked up at the sound of the door. "Good morning, all," said Diane, stepping outside onto the patio. "Sarah said you'd be out here."

"Oh? So she's emerged from her boudoir?"

Diane's brow furrowed. "What?"

"Never mind." Sylvia smiled as Agnes exited the manor behind Diane, a battered notebook in her hand. "Oh, hello, dear. So you're here, too?" She glanced at her watch to confirm that she had not lost track of time. "Why so early? We don't have to set up for camper registration for another two hours."

"We'll get to that." Diane rolled her eyes as Agnes returned Sylvia's greeting with an absent nod, seated herself on a wooden bench at the edge of the patio, and slowly paged through the notebook. "Don't expect to get another word out of her. She's had her nose in that old thing since I picked her up."

"Why didn't you wait and come with Bonnie?" asked Andrew.

"At the last minute Bonnie got a phone call from the detective in charge of her case. She's at home waiting for him to come over, but she'll get here as soon as she can."

Sylvia hardly thought that two hours early was at the last minute, but before she could press Diane for details, Andrew said, "The detective needs to see her on a Sunday morning?"

Satisfaction lit up Diane's pretty features. "Apparently there was a development in the case and he needed to speak with her urgently."

"Don't let Diane fool you," said Gwen as she closed the door behind her. "I suspect she had a little something to do with that development."

"So did you," said Diane. "I can't hog all the credit."

Sylvia looked from one to the other in amazement. "What on earth do you mean?"

"My key to Grandma's Attic disappeared right before the burglary," admitted Diane. "I didn't mention it earlier because—well, I had my reasons. One of my son's friends had spent the night, and I thought he might have taken the keys. I had no proof, so I went to his mother."

"Who, ironically enough, happens to be Diane's worst enemy," remarked Gwen.

"Ah," said Sylvia with a knowing smile. "Your notorious next-door neighbor."

Diane nodded emphatically. "Naturally she denied everything and gave Brent an alibi."

"You would have done the same for your sons," said Agnes, without looking up from her notebook.

Diane flushed, and Gwen jumped in. "We all would have. Anyway, while Diane was pondering the mystery of the missing keys, I noticed that my department chair's son had suddenly turned up with a pair of ergonomic shears and a rotary cutter. Since the Fabric Warehouse doesn't sell them, they must have come from Grandma's Attic."

Andrew looked dubious. "He could have ordered them through the mail."

"That's true, dear, but don't you think it's unlikely that a teenage boy would ever peruse a quilt supply catalog?" Sylvia turned to Diane and Gwen and urged, "Go on."

"His story was that he got them from school, which turned out to be an easily disproven lie, but I digress," said Gwen. "So Diane and I independently went to the police with our suspicions."

"Weeks ago," added Diane dryly.

"It wasn't until later that we compared notes. Diane checked with her son, who told us my department chair's son and Mary Beth's son are friends. We passed that along to the police, too, but we haven't heard anything since." Gwen glanced at Diane. "At least I haven't. How about you?"

Diane shook her head.

"Perhaps they needed time to put the pieces together," said Sylvia. She hoped for Bonnie's sake that the detective was not coming over to tell her the case had stalled again.

At that moment, Summer joined them. "Hi, guys." She glanced around the circle quickly. "So we're still waiting on Bonnie?"

As the others nodded, Sylvia impatiently said, "She has another two hours, for goodness' sake. Sarah isn't even here yet."

Summer smiled. "Oh, she'll be along."

Gwen put her arm around her daughter. "How was your date last night?"

Summer's smile deepened so that her dimple showed. "Fine."

"Apparently it was better than fine," said Andrew, a trifle sternly. "She didn't come home until after midnight."

The others laughed as Summer blushed. "We were just talking."

"Uh-huh," said Diane.

"No, really. We have a lot to talk about."

Sylvia was glad that Summer and her young man had reconciled, but she couldn't keep the regret out of her voice when she asked, "Does this mean you'll be leaving us?"

Summer started. "Actually—if you mean am I moving out to move back in with Jeremy, no."

From the corner of her eye, Sylvia saw Agnes heave a sigh of relief, her gaze still fixed on the notebook.

"But—" Summer hesitated, twisting her fingers together. "I think I will be leaving within a year."

"Leaving the manor?" asked Sylvia.

"Yes." Summer glanced at her mother. "And leaving Waterford."

A gasp went up from the gathering of friends. "Why?" asked Diane. It was almost a wail.

"I'd like to go back to school."

Gwen, who knew her best, looked the most shocked. "You're kidding."

"I'm not," said Summer. "I'll hate to leave Elm Creek Quilts, but I really think I need to follow my dream."

"You mean follow your heart," accused Diane. "You're just going to follow that boyfriend of yours."

"That's actually not true," said Summer. "This is something I'm doing for myself. But Jeremy and I are going to make sure we end up in the same city eventually."

Gwen embraced her daughter, tears in her eyes. Sylvia could not make out the words they exchanged, but when they released each other, both were smiling.

"Well." Sylvia cleared her throat. "I'm sure you've given this a lot of thought, and I wish you all the best, but I hope you won't be going soon. We will never be able to replace you."

"I'll finish out the season at least," Summer promised. "After that, it depends on when I can get into grad school."

"I can call my contacts at Penn," offered her mother, but Summer laughed and told her she wanted to do this on her own.

"I guess this is a good a time as any to make my own announcement," said Judy, who had arrived unnoticed in the excitement and lingered near the door looking at least twice as nervous as Summer had.

"Oh, Judy, not you, too," said Diane, dismayed.

Judy nodded, unable to keep the broad smile off her face. "I've accepted a position on the faculty at Penn. I can't imagine what I'll do without my best friends around me every day, but it's an opportunity I can't pass up."

"Yes, you can," said Diane. "You just haven't tried hard enough."

Sylvia's heart sank even as she joined in the laughter. As Judy shared the details of her new job, Sylvia thought ahead to the breaking of the circle of friends. Judy would leave them by autumn, and Summer would part soon after. Elm Creek Quilts would never be the same.

Just then Bonnie arrived, looking dazed. "You aren't going to believe this," she said.

After the bombshells Summer and Judy had dropped, Sylvia would believe just about anything, but she asked, "Do you have news from the police?"

Bonnie nodded and sat down as her friends peppered her with questions. The police had three suspects, she told them, including an additional friend of the two boys Diane and Gwen had named. The parents of all but one of the boys were cooperating with the police.

"Let me guess," said Diane. "Mary Beth."

Bonnie nodded. "Mary Beth still claims her son was home that night, but the police say the other boys refute that." She sighed. "What the police can't tell me is why. It's no secret that Mary Beth and Diane don't get along, but why destroy my store? They're all about to graduate from high school and head off to good colleges in the fall. Why jeopardize their futures for a grudge?"

No one had an answer for her. Sylvia marveled that after all those three boys had done to Bonnie, she still looked as if she felt sorry for them.

"At least now you'll be able to get the insurance settlement, right?" asked Summer.

"I suppose." Bonnie smiled, rueful. "Unfortunately, it's too little, too late."

"Not necessarily," remarked Sylvia. "I have a proposition for you. Why not reopen your quilt shop right here in Elm Creek Manor?"

Bonnie stared at her, and the others gasped in excitement. "That's a fabulous idea," exclaimed Judy. "We have plenty of unused space in the ballroom."

"I was actually thinking of knocking out some walls in the first floor of the west wing, starting with the formal parlor," said Sylvia. "We would have ample space, ideal lighting—"

"And all those captive shoppers when quilt camp is in season," added Diane.

"True enough," said Sylvia as the others laughed, although she hoped to draw most of their business from Waterford. If Waterford's quilters were shown how welcome they were at Elm Creek Manor, perhaps the pointless estrangement between the Elm Creek Quilters and the Waterford Quilting Guild would cease once and for all. "Let's not forget that if local quilters are willing to drive all the way to the Fabric Warehouse, they surely won't object to driving here."

Diane said, "Mary Beth won't like it."

"I think she has enough to worry about, don't you?" said Judy. "Besides, I've heard through the grapevine that she withdrew from the election for guild president. I don't know how much influence she'll have anymore."

"We haven't heard whether Bonnie even likes the idea," said Sylvia, watching her friend. "Perhaps she has other plans."

All eyes went to Bonnie, who shook her head. "This is too much to absorb, too fast," she said. "As much as I'd love to reopen, even in a different location, I have to worry about my basic living expenses first."

"Maybe not," sang out Agnes, holding up her notebook in triumph. "Your ex-husband-to-be isn't as broke as he claims."

She waved them over and held open the notebook so they could all view a curious drawing of an intertwined W, K, and M encircled by a wreath of ivy. "What's that supposed to be?" asked Diane.

"I know I've seen this before, but I can't place it," said Gwen. "It resembles an insignia such as a silversmith's mark, placed on the bottom of a piece to indicate who created it."

"That's very good, Gwen, although this particular craftsman worked in wood and iron and cloth." Agnes's blue eyes were bright with excitement behind her pink-tinted glasses. "You'll recall that a great many years ago I had the unfortunate chore of selling off items from the manor to help support Sylvia's sister, brother-in-law, and myself. I met my husband, Joe, when an antique dealer advised me to consult a history professor from the college about particular pieces." She laughed aloud. "My grandson insisted my notebooks were a valuable record, but I didn't believe him until now."

"What's significant about this insignia?" asked Summer.

"It's the mark of the famous designer Wolfgang Kauffmann Mueller," said Agnes.

"I've heard of him," said Gwen. "He had a unique style drawing from different elements of New England and Pennsylvania history—a little bit of Shaker, some Amish, some German. Scholars often credit him with initiating the Arts and Crafts movement fifty years before it really took off."

Bonnie gasped. "That old furniture in Craig's office."

"Exactly," said Agnes. "His assistant told me he refurbished the offices out of his own pocket, which was my first clue that something wasn't quite right. No offense, Bonnie, dear, but it's no secret Craig is a cheapskate."

Bonnie shrugged. "No offense taken. I've called him far worse."

"So that's where he's been hiding his assets," said Judy.

"Just out of curiosity, Agnes," said Andrew, "how much is this furniture worth?"

"Bonnie's lawyer will have to seek an appraisal, of course," replied Agnes. "But I can tell you I sold a Wolfgang Kauffmann Mueller loveseat for ten thousand dollars, and that was more than fifty years ago."

Gwen's eyebrows shot up. "Considering how much more his work is appreciated now, Bonnie could be looking at hundreds of thousands of dollars."

Bonnie put a hand to her heart and reached behind her for a chair. "He redecorated his office five years ago. That's how long he's been planning this. That . . . that . . ."

"Jerk," finished Agnes.

"That's not the word I had in mind, but it suits him."

The door to the manor swung open and Sarah poked her head outside. "What suits whom?" She scanned the circle of friends without waiting for an answer. "Good. Everyone's here."

Sylvia glanced at her watch. "And none too soon. You're only an hour and forty-five minutes early."

"We have a little business to take care of before the campers arrive." Sarah stepped onto the cornerstone patio carrying a large box that appeared to be wrapped in fabric rather than paper, her husband Matt close behind. "Sylvia and Andrew, this is for you."

Speechless, Sylvia turned to Andrew to see if he knew what on earth was going on, but he looked as surprised as Sylvia felt.

Diane grinned as Andrew accepted the box. "It's a belated wedding gift from the Elm Creek Quilters."

"And one hundred thirty-three of your dearest friends," added Gwen.

"My goodness." Sylvia reached over to help Andrew open it. "And you wrapped it in fabric. Wasn't that clever of you!"

"We thought you could use the fabric later in a quilt," said Summer. "That's much better than tossing more paper into a landfill."

"We should have tied it with fishing line so that Andrew would have a little something extra, too," remarked Judy.

"We'll keep that in mind for their anniversary," said Sarah.

Sylvia eagerly lifted the lid and dug through tissue paper until her hands touched fabric. "Oh, my word, I knew it. You ladies are wonderful."

Diane nudged Gwen. "She hasn't even seen it yet."

"She knows a quilt when she feels one," said Andrew, helping Sylvia unfold it.

Her friends came forward to take the edges of the quilt and hold it open between them. "Oh, my," said Sylvia, and then she could only clasp her hands to her heart in joy.

It was a sampler quilt top in blue, rose, and greens of every hue, all blending and contrasting harmoniously in a frame of split LeMoyne Stars. Sylvia took in the arrangement of rows of blocks and quickly calculated that there were one hundred forty blocks, in every pieced and appliquéd pattern imaginable. Some of her favorites caught her eye: LeMoyne Star, Snow Crystals, Carpenter's Wheel.

"It's very nice," said Andrew, "but you forgot to finish it."

The women burst into laughter.

"We intend for our quilt campers to help us with the quilting," explained Agnes. "We couldn't put it in the quilt frame without you noticing, so we decided to surprise you with the quilt top."

"Don't feel bad, Andrew," said Matt. "I said the same thing the first time I saw it."

"It is exquisite," breathed Sylvia, tracing the appliquéd flower petals in a Bridal Wreath block with a fingertip. "I've never seen anything so lovely. How did you manage to keep this a secret?"

"It wasn't easy," said Sarah, with a sidelong look for her husband. She went on to explain how the quilt had come to be: an invitation sent out to Sylvia's friends and quilting colleagues, the requirement that the blocks represent the maker's relationship to Sylvia, the theft and reappearance of dozens of blocks, and the mad scramble at the end to complete the top.

Sylvia insisted that each of her friends point out her block and explain why she chose it. Sarah eagerly offered to go first, and pointed to an unfamiliar block in the fifth row. "This pattern is called Sarah's Favorite," she said. "And it should be obvious why I chose it, since Sylvia is my favorite person."

As her friends chimed in with their approval, Matt said, "Hey. What about me?"

"Let me amend that," said Sarah, hugging him. "Sylvia is my favorite woman, but you're definitely my favorite husband."

Everyone laughed as Matt shrugged and kissed his wife.

"My turn," said Diane, proudly indicating a block made of triangles, narrow rectangles, and a checkerboard trim along the bottom edge.

"Lincoln's Platform?" asked Sylvia.

Sarah looked perplexed. "Maybe it's one of those patterns that has several names."

"No, just Lincoln's Platform," said Diane, beaming. "I found it in a book. Oh, come on. Don't you get it?"

No one wanted to disappoint her, but one by one they shook their heads.

"Because Sylvia's such a good speaker," said Diane, exasperated. "You know, like Abraham Lincoln. I admire that about Sylvia. Her way of speaking her mind with sensitivity to other people's feelings is an example I try to follow."

"She has a long way to go," remarked Gwen in an aside that was a trifle too loud to be an aside.

"At least no one else chose the same pattern," offered Judy. "It adds variety."

"Thank you, Judy," said Diane. "Someone had to break free of all those Steps to the Altar and Wedding Ring clichés."

"As someone who gave in to cliché and made a Bridal Wreath—" began Agnes.

"I wasn't talking about you," said Diane. "Honestly. I should have just ignored the rules, made a Nine-Patch, and spared myself this interrogation."

Everyone but Diane burst into laughter. "Well, this is my Bridal Wreath block, cliché or not," said Agnes, then she smiled slyly and pointed to a block in the top right corner. "I made this one, too. I imagine Sylvia knows why."

It was a Bachelor's Puzzle block. Shocked, Sylvia shot an accusing look at Sarah, the one person she told about the nickname she and Claudia had secretly given Agnes so long ago. Sarah shook her head, wide-eyed and clearly just as surprised as Sylvia.

"I'm sure I don't know," said Sylvia. "Perhaps because it's a puzzle why Andrew married me?"

"Not to me it isn't," said Andrew, taking her hand.

"That's not it," said Agnes. "Give it some more thought. I'm sure you'll figure it out."

"If not, maybe the answer is in one of Agnes's notebooks," said Diane.

Sylvia ignored the rising heat in her cheeks. Oh, the things Agnes could have written about her back in those days! "If you insist on making me guess, I suppose I'll have to try. Later. How about you, Summer?" she asked, ignoring Agnes's laughter. "What block did you make?"

Summer pointed out a Mariner's Compass block with sixteen points in the center of the quilt. "I thought this pattern suited you best," she said, "because you're beautiful, you're difficult, and you guide us along our way."

A murmur of approval went up from the circle of friends. "Oh, nonsense," Sylvia scoffed. "I'm none of those things, except, perhaps, difficult. On a bad day."

"You can hide behind modesty all you like, but that won't change what you mean to us," said Summer, so affectionately that Sylvia thought she might be forced to return the quilt top to its box rather than endure any more embarrassing praise.

Fortunately, Judy announced that her block was made with Andrew in mind. "Sometimes we focus so exclusively on the bride that the groom feels incidental to everything related to the wedding. I made a Handy Andy block so he would know this quilt is a gift to him, too."

Matt gave Andrew a quizzical look. "'Andy'?"

"Handy Andrew, if you prefer," said Judy with a laugh.

"This one is mine." Gwen pointed out a block near the center of the quilt. Sylvia did not recognize the pattern, which resembled a gold comet streaking across a sunset-violet sky. "I adapted it from a design in a quilt entered in the 1933 World's Fair quilt competition. I chose it because while Sylvia is definitely an original, her art and influences are deeply rooted in quilting's oldest and best traditions. Since I don't know the original name of the block, I call it Sylvia's Shooting Star."

"'Sylvia's Shooting Star.'" Sylvia smiled, amused. "I like it."

"It's high time someone named a block after you," remarked Andrew.

"Thank you all so very much." Sylvia rose and reached out to embrace her friends. "I can't imagine a lovelier wedding gift. The stories of how you chose your blocks make it even more special."

"We're not done," said Sarah, nodding to the box on Andrew's lap. "You missed something."

Andrew dug through the tissue paper and came up with a white binder trimmed in fabrics of the same hues as the quilt. "What's this?"

"Letters from everyone who contributed a block," said Summer. "We asked them to share the stories behind their block choices, too."

Sylvia and Andrew held the binder open between them and paged through the letters, pausing to read some of the names aloud. Sylvia's eyes grew misty as she took in the familiar names of friends and faraway colleagues, quilt camp veterans and students she had met only recently, so many generous friends sending prayers and warm wishes for the happiness of the bride and groom.

"This is truly overwhelming," Sylvia began, then broke off at the sight of a letter from a very dear friend.

March 12, 2002

Dear Sylvia and the Elm Creek Quilters,

My first reaction to your news was to wonder how Sylvia could even think of getting married without me there. I thought we were friends! I would have talked her through those premarital jitters. I would have held her hand or the train of her gown, or both. At the very least I would have brought a nice gift!

Once I got over that initial burst of self-absorption, my thoughts turned to an appropriate block for Sylvia's bridal quilt. I could do nothing less for the woman who restored my art to me.

Our friendship goes back nearly twenty years, founded upon a mutual love of quilts and quilting history. While Sylvia was launching her quilters' retreat, I was working as a quilt artist, lecturer, and museum curator—and struggling with a serious case of "quilter's block" brought on by a recent diagnosis of multiple sclerosis. Although I experienced virtually no symptoms between exacerbations of the disease, I could no longer quilt as I once had. My inability had less to do with my increasing physical limitations, however, than the psychological paralysis of knowing that my life as I had known it was over, and that all the things I loved to do might one day be lost to me.

Sylvia was the friend and mentor who helped me find my way. She encouraged me to create because of my MS, not in spite of it, to use my grief and anger to inspire my art rather than pretend nothing had changed. She taught me to acknowledge that I could no longer do the same work as I had before, but not to accept that I could no longer be an artist.

The work I have created since Sylvia illuminated the possibilities might not be as technically perfect as what had gone before, but it is infused with a passion, a spiritualism, and a deep gratitude and respect for the healing power of the creative process. My art and my faith in God have enabled me to deal with the progression of my disease, which thankfully has been slow, but continuous enough to tax even the strongest will. I almost had to resign my position as museum curator, but thanks to my new medications, I have been able to resume most of my old activities. I almost had to give up my loft, but my daughter and grandson moved in with me instead, so when my symptoms act up, I am not alone. Even on my worst days, I find some way to quilt, whether that means appliquéing quilt blocks or simply examining my fabric stash and imagining new projects. Without Sylvia to encourage me, I would not have even that.

As most of you know, I'm not one to stick to traditional pieced blocks, so I decided to design a new appliqué pattern in the folk art style Sylvia would expect from me. The building in the background is Elm Creek Manor, of course, and the two women joining hands in friendship in the foreground are meant to be me and Sylvia but could be any of the thousands of quilters who have found friendship, solace, and sisterhood at Elm Creek Quilt Camp.

Many, many congratulations, prayers, and good wishes for the happy couple. May their marriage be blessed with love, joy, peace, and the companionship of good friends.

With Love,
Grace Daniels

Sylvia blinked back tears, looked up at her friends, and said, "Thank you." They smiled, knowing all she meant to convey with those two words.

Her heart ached with joy and with sadness, thinking of the friends who loved her so dearly, of the friends who would leave them too soon, of the inevitable changes that would touch them then and in the years to come. As much as she might wish to capture time and hold it still in that moment, it was a futile wish, and she had lived long enough to know it. Summer and Judy would leave, other friends might follow, and one day, she, too, would part from the home she had loved and abandoned and learned to love again.

But as she gazed upon the block Grace Daniels had given for her quilt, the appliquéd portrait of two women holding hands like steadfast friends, she understood that Elm Creek Quilts was greater than any single woman or even group of women who laughed and cried and quilted within the manor's gray stone walls. Teachers and campers would come and go, and long after the last Bergstrom had passed from the earth, the spirit of Elm Creek Quilts would endure. As long as it stood, Elm Creek Manor would welcome all who gathered there with love and acceptance and the promise of friendships as beautiful and as comforting as the quilts they made.

She gazed upon the smiling faces of her beloved friends and said, "I know the first order of business after we welcome our new quilt campers."

Sarah, the young woman she loved like a daughter, said, "Layer this top in the frame so we can start quilting it?"

Sylvia laughed. "Yes, of course that must be first. The second order of business, then."

Somewhere, she knew, two quilters who were meant to be among them waited to learn that Elm Creek Quilt Camp sought new teachers.

❧